PENGUIN BOOKS

My Mother She Killed Me, My Father He Ate Me

KATE BERNHEIMER is the founder and editor of the literary journal *Fairy Tale Review*; the author of the story collection *Horse, Flower, Bird* as well as a children's book and the novels *The Complete Tales of Ketzia Gold* and *The Complete Tales of Merry Gold*; and the editor of two anthologies, *Mirror, Mirror on the Wall: Women Writers Explore Their Favorite Fairy Tales* and *Brothers and Beasts: An Anthology of Men on Fairy Tales*. She has published stories in such journals as *Tin House, Western Humanities Review*, and *The Massachusetts Review* and has spoken on fairy tales in lecture series sponsored by the Museum of Modern Art, Ball State University Museum of Art, and the 92nd Street Y.

CARMEN GIMÉNEZ SMITH is the author of the poetry collection *Odalisque in Pieces* and the memoir *Bring Down the Little Birds*. She is also the publisher of Noemi Press and the editor in chief of the journal *Puerto del Sol*.

GREGORY MAGUIRE is the bestselling author of *Wicked*, the basis for the Tony Award–winning Broadway musical of the same name. He lives in Boston, Massachusetts.

My Mother She Killed Me, My Father He Ate Me

FORTY NEW FAIRY TALES

Edited by
· KATE BERNHEIMER ·

with
CARMEN GIMÉNEZ SMITH

Foreword by
GREGORY MAGUIRE

PENGUIN BOOKS

PENGUIN BOOKS
Published by the Penguin Group
Penguin Group (USA) Inc.,
375 Hudson Street, New York, New York 10014, U.S.A.
Penguin Group (Canada), 90 Eglinton Avenue East, Suite 700, Toronto,
Ontario, Canada M4P 2Y3 (a division of Pearson Penguin Canada Inc.)
Penguin Books Ltd, 80 Strand, London WC2R 0RL, England
Penguin Ireland, 25 St Stephen's Green, Dublin 2, Ireland
(a division of Penguin Books Ltd)
Penguin Group (Australia), 250 Camberwell Road, Camberwell,
Victoria 3124, Australia (a division of Pearson Australia Group Pty Ltd)
Penguin Books India Pvt Ltd, 11 Community Centre,
Panchsheel Park, New Delhi - 110 017, India
Penguin Group (NZ), 67 Apollo Drive, Rosedale, North Shore 0632,
New Zealand (a division of Pearson New Zealand Ltd)
Penguin Books (South Africa) (Pty) Ltd, 24 Sturdee Avenue,
Rosebank, Johannesburg 2196, South Africa

Penguin Books Ltd, Registered Offices:
80 Strand, London WC2R 0RL, England

First published in Penguin Books 2010

3   5   7   9   10   8   6   4

Selection and introduction copyright © Kate Bernheimer, 2010
Foreword copyright © Gregory Maguire, 2010
All rights reserved

Page 543 constitutes an extension of this copyright page.

PUBLISHER'S NOTE
These selections are works of fiction. Names, characters, places, and incidents either are
the product of the authors' imagination or are used fictitiously, and any resemblance to actual
persons, living or dead, business establishments, events, or locales is entirely coincidental.

LIBRARY OF CONGRESS CATALOGING IN PUBLICATION DATA
My mother she killed me, my father he ate me : forty new fairy tales / edited by Kate Bernheimer ;
with Carmen Giménez Smith ; foreword by Gregory Maguire.
p.   cm.
ISBN: 978-0-14-311784-1
1. Short stories, American.   2. Short stories, English.   3. Fairy tales—United States.
4. Fairy tales—Great Britain.   I. Bernheimer, Kate.   II. Giménez Smith, Carmen, 1971–
PS645.M9   2010
823'.0108—dc22   2010031401

Printed in the United States of America
Set in Minion with Lettres Eclatees Display
Designed by Elke Sigal

For Angela Carter

CONTENTS

You are walking down a familiar street at dusk. Meat is cooking. In the shadows down the block, you see a cardboard box, flaps open. The street is deserted; you will either be the first to look inside the box, or it has already been plundered; either way, there's no reason to hurry, but you do.

Warm Mouth: Chinscraper, why are you lying there in the road with your jaw shoved back through your brain and your guts blown out as if you'd tried to swallow the highway?

I met the girls and instantly liked the girls. Of course I liked the girls. A girl is better than a feast.
    This was before the arrest, before the indictment and the media stories.

It is just as she hoped. The worn path, the bells tinkling on the gate. The huge fir trees dropping their needles one by one. A sweet mushroomy smell, gnomes stationed in the underbrush, the sound of a mandolin far up on the hill.

There came a time when I, the youngest of twelve sons, each of which had imposed himself upon me in turn, could bear it no longer and fled the house. I left one morning without awakening either my parents or brothers, carrying only the clothes on my back.

I'd just moved back to the city, having been away for a long time during which I'd accomplished quite a bit of work—I'm no judge of the quality—and was crashing at the apartment of a friend I'd run into at Borders bookstore after two weeks of hapless wandering.

A soldier came walking down the road, raw from encounters with the enemy, high on release, walking down the road with no money. The road was lined with trees, and every so often a hovel hunched right there at its edge, droopy and mean, with a dirt yard like a pale sack at its feet.

A slender girl and her mother lived in our town, good people but poor. They had nothing to eat, like everyone else in our town.

Once't, you could spit on the ground and grow water.
They said back then that the rain would follow the plow. They lied.

Cats went in and out of the witch's house all day long. The windows stayed open, and the doors, and there were other doors, cat-sized and private, in the walls and up in the attic.

Ours is a highly individualized culture, with a great faith in the work of art as a unique one-off, and the artist as an original, a godlike and inspired creator of unique one-offs. But fairy tales are not like that, nor are their makers. Who first invented meatballs? In what country? Is there a definitive recipe for potato soup? Think in terms of the domestic arts. "This is how *I* make potato soup."

—ANGELA CARTER

INTRODUCTION

Despite its heft, this collection is a tiny hall of mirrors in the world's giant house of fairy tales. Fairy tales comprise thousands of stories written by thousands of writers over hundreds of years. A volume published in the mid–twentieth century that purported to catalog every type of folktale in existence had more than twenty-five hundred entries; since then, countless new stories have joyously entered the world via new translations, folkloric research, and artists working in a multitude of forms.

Readers love fairy tales. Even the most virulent critics of fairy tales can't look away. With their false brides, severed limbs, and talking donkeys, they are hypnotic. "All great novels are great fairy tales," wrote Nabokov. I would argue that all great *narratives* are great fairy tales . . . whatever their shape (novel, novella, short story, poem).

About fifteen years ago, when I began to acquaint myself with the scholarship surrounding fairy tales in order to think about my own body of work within the tradition, I became aware of a fairy-tale resurgence. Soon after that I edited my first collection, *Mirror, Mirror on the Wall*—essays by women writers about the influence of fairy tales on their work. I also embarked on a trilogy of novels about the influence of fairy-tale books on three sisters. And now I am thrilled to see an even more widespread infatuation with wonder stories—in popular book series like J. K. Rowling's *Harry Potter*, Philip Pullman's *His Dark Materials*, and Gregory Maguire's Oz books; in stand-alone novels such as Donna Tartt's *The Little Friend* and A. S. Byatt's *The Children's Book*; on television, whether obviously, as in any number of vampire shows, or quietly, as in the shape and surreal motifs of *Six Feet Under*; and in film, where *Eternal Sunshine of the Spotless Mind* and *Alice in Wonderland* are but two examples. Magic is in the air.

I was weaned on fairy tales. My grandfather, who may or may not have worked for Disney (nobody is certain) and who may or may not have worked with a Bostonian piano thief (we think he did), screened fairy-tale films in his basement for me and my siblings when we were young. The flying beds, cackling witches, and warbling birds shaped my being. In combination with terrifying Holocaust footage screened at my temple—and stories of burning bushes, singing "spring turtles," and parting seas—the consolation of magical stories was directly imprinted on me. I was shy, happiest inside books; their open world beckoned and took me in.

Over the past seven years, as founder and editor of *Fairy Tale Review*, I have seen the passionate interest fairy tales hold for the thousands of writers who submit to every issue. I founded the journal out of a sense that literary works based on fairy tales, like the lonely heroes of fairy tales themselves, lacked homes. I was immediately flooded with very good manuscripts. Many hopeful correspondents are well-known authors whose magical works have been turned down by older literary publications; others are true believers and have devoted their lives to folklore in unusual ways—creating fairy-tale newspapers, selling homemade fairy-tale wares, producing freely distributed fairy-tale comics; still others are grandfathers, mothers, teachers, biologists, or students who as new writers feel comfortable trying on the fairy-tale form. I am touched by every submission; each shines with love for fairy tales.

When I lecture on fairy tales, whether at museums or grade schools, I am always moved by the audience's deep pleasure in learning about fairy-tale techniques. Fairy tales defy the status quo: a reader will easily recognize a version of "Little Red Riding Hood" that contains *no* cape, *no* woods, and *no* wolf. See Matthew Bright's amazing film *Freeway*—in which a young Reese Witherspoon plays an abused kid who runs away from home—and you'll understand; it's a direct homage to "The Story of Grandmother," interpreted in this collection by the inimitable Kellie Wells. Fairy tales have a fairy-tale likeness.

I've had the privilege of introducing many students to the fairy tale's strange history, so carefully studied by such scholars as Maria Tatar and Jack Zipes, who teach us that originally fairy tales were not directed toward children, though they were overheard by youngsters around the hearth, and that they function in an almost totemic way for both young and old. My love of fairy tales drives all of my writing, whether a novel, a short story, or a book for children. I have the honor of making my day-to-day work the celebration of fairy tales. All of this—the journal editorship, the teaching of craft, the casual conversations, the life of a writer—reflects back to me that fairy tales are simply essential, and I want to share that with you.

But odd things, too, led me to gather this volume.

I have a sense that a proliferation of magical stories, especially fairy tales, is correlated to a growing awareness of human separation from the wild and natural world. In fairy tales, the human and animal worlds are equal and mutually dependent. The violence, suffering, and beauty are shared. Those drawn to fairy tales, perhaps, wish for a world that might live "forever after." My work as a preservationist of fairy tales is entwined with all kinds of extinction.

I was also inspired to collect this volume based on my experience in the community of writers and readers. A few years ago I presented a short manifesto about fairy tales to a large audience of creative writing professors and students. I was on a panel dedicated to nonrealist literature. I made an argument that fairy tales were at risk—they had been misunderstood, appropriated without proper homage by the realists and fabulists alike. Only at a writers' conference could this sort of statement provoke a gasp. (Yes, say what you will.) I am always that person in the room telling everyone, genuinely, that I love it all—realism, high modernism, surrealism, minimalism. I like stories. But apparently my defense of fairy tales, which I consider so poignantly inclusive, marginalized, and vast, was seen as outlandish. (Note: there are a lot of realists and nonrealists in this collection. Some of my best friends are realists—and nonrealists, too.) My statement, intended to be inspiring, to gather support for this humble, inventive, and communal tradition, created vibration, metallic and sharp. I realized the full weight of the fact that celebrating fairy tales in the center of a talk about "serious literature" to a roomful of writers was controversial. This surprised me—but it also emboldened me to put together this volume.

Indeed it was at that meeting that this book was born. I realized how essential this volume was, for it would gather *all* kinds of literary writers in the service of fairy tales. I realized then that while people may know and love—or love to hate—these stories, they really are not aware of the many ways they pervade contemporary literature.

As merely one example, the National Book Foundation, which administers the National Book Awards, states that "retellings of folk-tales, myths, and fairy-tales are not eligible" for their awards. Imagine guidelines that state, "Retellings of slavery, incest, and genocide are not eligible." Fairy tales contain all of those themes, and yet the implication is that something about fairy tales is simply . . . not literary. Perhaps the snobbery has something to do with their association with children and women. Or it could be that, lacking any single author, they discomfit a culture enchanted with the myth of the heroic artist. Or perhaps their tropes are so familiar that they are easily misunderstood as cliché. Possibly their collapsed world of real and unreal unsettles those who rely on that binary to give life some semblance of order.

The fact that fairy tales remain a literary underdog—undervalued and undermined—even as they shape so many popular stories, redoubles my certainty that it is time for contemporary fairy tales to be celebrated in a popular, literary collection. Fairy tales hold the secret to reading. This book can help us move forward as readers in a moment of insecurity about the future of books.

My Mother She Killed Me, My Father He Ate Me is like a beloved, handmade, topsy-turvy, cool doll. I had one as a kid (perhaps you did, too): on one side was Red Riding Hood, and underneath, the grandmother and wolf; how it scared and delighted me! If you peek under this book's voluminous skirt, you'll find some wonderful creatures hiding here, lovers of fairy tales all: Angela Carter, Hans Christian Andersen, J. R. R. Tolkien, Italo Calvino, Emily Dickinson, Barbara Comyns, the Brothers Grimm. Next time you go to the library, please say hello to them, to their other fine fairy-tale companions, and to the scholars who have charted the history of the form: Maria Tatar, Jack Zipes, Marina Warner, Ruth Bottigheimer, Donald Haase, Cristina Bacchilega, and many others.

Once you start looking, it is easy to see the variety—the sheer fractal ferocity—and intelligence of fairy tales. This collection contains stories reflective of current trends (fragment, pastiche, story-in-chapters); it also contains stories told in more linear, straightforward ways. Some of the selections pay homage to midcentury and later styles; others come poetically through modes associated with the tradition of oral folklore. You will find stories that hew closely to their enchantment, and others that announce hardly any magic—until you encounter a tiny keyhole in the wall of their language. In each instance, you will easily enter these secret gardens.

The goal was to bring together a variety of writers—in true fairy-tale spirit, not only those widely known; I sought out writers whose work had suggested "fairy tales" to me, whether in obvious or subtle ways. Initiating the process, I asked merely that writers select a fairy tale as a starting point and to take it from there, to write a new fairy tale. When asked by some contributors what a fairy tale was, I would answer: You already know. A fairy tale is a story with a fairy-tale feel, I told them. And we'd continue from there.

In her book *Enchanted Hunters*, Maria Tatar describes how fairy tales are so beloved because reading them is like falling in love with reading—they're that mesmerizing. By reading this book, you become part of a welcoming, old, nonhierarchical, and new tradition. Of course, this book can represent only a tiny sliver of the tradition. I consulted many authors, scholars, translators, students, and readers about whom to invite, and I was introduced to many new voices along the way, and lamented that the book could not be endless. I hope this is just the beginning of a brand-new acceptance of fairy tales as omnipresent. The house of wonder is infinite.

The stories are organized loosely by country of origin—just one of the many ways they could be organized, merely one path through their intricate forest. The contents offers the name of just one origin tale for each story, even though many of the stories draw from multiple variants from all around the world. These are not offered as definitive versions; rather, I hope that you'll follow these little bread crumbs to fairy-tale books for additional excellent reading. I have also gathered author comments, which follow each story. In these, you will find fascinating, personal insights into how the cited tales provided the authors with inspiration. The contents also offers the opening lines of each story—each "Once upon a time," if you will. In this way you may find a favorite writer or tale type, or simply a sentence that attracts your attention. Take these as signposts into your own, private hundred-acre woods—if that helps you. You may, of course, read the book in order—or backward! All you need to know is that no special expertise is required to appreciate *any* story in here—only an interest in reading.

I hope this book comprises not only a fantastic reading experience for you—a reintroduction to these stories with vintage and thrilling appeal—but also a call to preserve fairy tales for future generations.

For in a fairy tale, you find the most wonderful world. Yes, it is violent; and yes, there is loss. There is murder, incest, famine, and rot—all of these haunt the stories, as they haunt us. The fairy-tale world is a real world. Fairy tales contain a spell that is not false: an invocation to protect those most endangered on this earth. The meek shall inherit . . . went one of the very first stories I heard as a child. I believed it then, and still do.

Fairy tales, fairy-tale readers: This book belongs to you.

KATE BERNHEIMER

DRAWING THE CURTAIN

WE'RE HERE. WE BRAVED THE CROWDS AND BUCKED THE TRENDS AND overcame the obstacles (we located correct change for the crosstown bus) and we made it on time.

No need to try to smuggle a split of champagne past the usher. We won't need it. We have in our hands only mezzanine-seat tickets to an everyday hullabaloo. No red carpet. This isn't going to be featured on *Entertainment Tonight*. It's not a once-in-a-lifetime event. The domestic fairy tale, never having indulged in a farewell tour, is in no need of a comeback.

Why, then, are our hearts racing?

The excited murmur from the foyer, the boxes, the stalls, the orchestra seats, is contagious. The fairy tale is about to break upon us, once and still and again. We know what we're in for and, of course, we also don't, for fairy tale has more than one method by which to cast a spell. Attending, we'll have to attend. Tolkien, that philologist turned bard and pantocrator of Middle-earth, called it faërie, that which "holds the seas, the sun, the moon, the sky, the earth, and all things that are in it: tree and bird, water and stone, wine and bread, and ourselves, mortal men, when we are enchanted."

Indeed, with Tolkien's press release promising so much, we might as well know this place as the Globe Theatre, the way Shakespeare did.

And that's why we've rushed to get here in time for the curtain. We're anticipating an apparition of faërie promised, herein, as a series of episodes, all alike, all different. Whether they seem archaic or postmodern, conventional or avant-garde, whether their enchantments are apparent or invisible, in some ways they will all cavort without drawing attention to the sleight of faërie itself, which is a conjuring act that relies at once upon theatrical smoke-and-mirrors and upon deep magic.

We hold, in these initial pages, something of a program, one that contains no advertisements, no hint of coming attractions. Makes no suggestion for where to dine afterward. We're on our own. But, riffling through, from back to front, with curiosity, impatience, perhaps a sense of entitlement—we're not children here—what might we have come to expect?

In traditional tales the dramatis personae hail from central casting. We've a few moments; let's steal backstage. Let's open the door to the green room and peek to see who is waiting. A bevy of beauties, each more fetching, more modest, more loyal, more lovely than the next (no matter from which point you begin scanning the room). A gossiping group of grand dames, as kindly as godmothers or as corrupt as witches, or both by turns. Hags and harridans, huntsmen and hunchbacks. Kings and kings and kings, a congress of kings. Also, a sample of simpletons.

That's not all. An evanescence of sprites and pixies and guardian angels, in shimmering gossamer threads. An abundance of adversaries (in ascending order) from dwarves to giants. A passel of princes, mostly charming, occasionally brave and clever besides. Some equally stout-hearted steeds nickering nearby; and cats watching with moon-phase eyes; and the bear who can speak and won't is curled up next to the bear who can't speak and will. The cock of the roost, the lark of the morn, the owl who issues the midnight summons, and the goose that lays the golden eggs. (This goose may be Mother Goose herself, fixing her eye on the proceedings, but she keeps her own counsel, delivering her elementary bounty but not her vital statistics.)

As for the setting, take a look at the interchangeable flats, the painted scrims, the wing-and-drop sets hoisted in darkness above. Most likely the settings are modest and indefinite—the garden, the kitchen; the castle, the hovel; the sea, the cave; the market, the meadow; the well, the woods; the prison tower, the island sanctuary. That's a lot of world to be stacked backstage. But "To make a Prairie it takes / One Clover and one Bee / One Clover, and a Bee / And Reverie. / The Reverie alone will do / If bees are few—" as Emily Dickinson reminds us. To recognize a fairy-tale castle, we need little more than a Styrofoam throne. A woods is conjured by a single branch suspended on transparent Mylar fishing line. A cottage is conjured up by anyone onstage who utters the word *cottage*. Almost every spell begins with the conjure: "Now listen . . ."

Props? Already on the ready. The slipper, the spindle, the seashell, the sword. The coach, the comb, the cauldron, the cape. The apple, the bread, and the porridge. And look, even simpler things in the dusty shadows, from earlier iterations of these tales. The feather, the stone, the bucket of water; the knife, the bone, the bucket of blood.

We've still time. Glance into the conservatory adjacent the backstage area where techies and roustabouts prepare for the special effects to make the young believe, for nothing is more magical than what is truly alive: potted roses, potted thorny brambles, potted beanstalks. A silver nutmeg and a golden pear, and a talking nightingale in a cage, and a coppery talking carp in a bowl like a bubble. Is that a real or a costumed dragon? In any case he gives no autographs.

We haven't time to visit the costumier. A dash past the open door: the crown, the broom, the magic wand, the fur tippets, the toga, the shield, the cloak of many colors, the cloak of invisibility, the cloak of respectability . . . a hundred thousand cloaks on hangers stretching back like a forest we can almost remember . . . but we haven't time; on we dash.

Now back to the hall, and not a moment too soon. Now listen! The orchestra pit is bustling, practicing the traditional clarion call of invocation (once upon a time!) and the flourish of finale, nearly always in a major key (happily ever after!). But if Northrop Frye has taught us to read literature as a seasonal progression—spring comedy, summer romance, autumnal tragedy, and winter satire or irony—once again the fairy tale eludes classification, for it can be all of these at once, and more besides. Midrash, parable, griot's begats; pourquoi, koan, and cautionary fable.

And between these time-honored flourishes of salve and farewell, we'll hear the many sounds of a story's spell. The royal procession: a trumpet voluntary. The afternoon of a faun: a flute masquerading as panpipes. The score may include a glockenspiel-and-sitar cacophony or a maddened piccolo tarantella. It may feature the clicking of bamboo rods and harp glissades to suggest transformations, recipes, revelations. The kettledrum for war. The rattle of aluminum sheeting for jeremiad and storm. The cello for lament.

The woodwinds cover everything else—the oboe for the duck, the clarinet for the cat, as we remember. And always *die Zauberflöte* for the sound of magic. The flute for the mechanical nightingale; the flute for a change in the winds; the flute for the riddle, the rhyme, and the moral.

What moral? What is all this for? The moral, about which we may argue long after we go home—we may argue for centuries—is sometimes a couplet, stapled upon the end like a gospel amen, and sometimes a secret, coiled and arbitrary and encoded within the syllables of the script, the syllables of what is said and left unsaid. Useful to remember what Erik Christian Haugaard, translator from the Danish of the tales of Hans Christian Andersen, suggested: "The fairy tale belongs to the poor. I know of no fairy tale which upholds the tyrant, or takes the part of the strong against the weak. A fascist fairy tale is an absurdity."

We'll have to take that on faith until we experience what follows, so hush, settle your coats under your seats. They are tuning up the magic. It's almost time.

But what time is this? What is the time of the tale? Our program is cunning and obscure on the matter. Jane Langton, writer of evanescent and everyday fantasies for children, holds that the tale takes place sometime between the fall of Constantinople and the invention of the internal combustion engine. Accurate enough, or perhaps I mean vague enough; but the tale itself is a trickster and doesn't hesitate to lie. It is anachronistic with a vengeance. It emerges always and everywhere, overt or disguised, pureblood or hybrid, and healthy as sin.

Indeed—I'm gabbling now, in a whisper, for the houselights are dimming—the time of the tale, nearly upon us, is perhaps its greatest mystery. For, if anything else about it is dubious or nonessential, faërie's agency stems from its capacity to be mysteriously non sequitur. It is equally at home when it struts as ancient myth as when it postures as Pre-Raphaelite faux medieval chanson or capers as nonsense nursery rhyme. We recognize faërie from a long time ago in a galaxy far away. We recognize faërie vitally alert on the island of Ariel and Caliban and the magician Prospero. We know faërie even when it goes viral, as we encounter it in Hollywood's Cindergirl of the hour, caught this very moment on today's blogs and tabloids. But put away that cell phone and stop Googling her. We're attending deeper mysteries than Hollywood generally knows how to handle.

For, in faërie, how far are we, really, from the darkness brooding over the water and from the spirit of the Almighty breathed into the clay? How far from mistletoe and blood sacrifice, from the ancient transactions of scapegoating and ransom? How far from the flame-winged angel in a hundred biblical dreams, how far from Marley in chains or the phantom on the ramparts of Elsinore? How far from the savanna where the leopard got his spots or from the night sky of the frozen north, east of the sun and west of the moon, featuring the spangled celestial figures of myth? Faërie is born of the oldest question of our individual lives and of our species: why?

In faërie, how far are we from the golem? the reindeer on the roof? the lilies on the altar? the incense rising to the oculus? How far from the salt thrown over the shoulder, the blessing that follows the sneeze? How far from the presentation of our newborn to the village of life, how far from the presentation of our corpse to the necropolis of the lost? We cannot stop wondering why, and so faërie is nearer than we know.

Faëirie is origin and eschatology, writ cunning and runic. It speaks to darknesses on both sides of the glare of life, that glare brighter than spotlights.

We recognize it still—as adults—because our capacity to appreciate it was honed not only in the childhood of the race but in our own early years.

The stage before us will be shallow, its width limited. But how far from the raison d'être of faërie lies that other infinity of magic, the unmoored tale for children? How many miles to Babylon? How far to the lamppost in the snowy wood, the hole in the ground in which there lived a hobbit, the academies for wizards and witches? How far to the nanny goddess with the parrot-head umbrella, to the white rabbit in its Wonderland, to the tin woodsman on its own yellow road, to the boy clad in oak leaves who won't grow up?

How far from faërie to the wild wood, the greenwood, the Hundred Acre Wood; to the riverbank perfect for messing about in boats and to the Flood with its floating menagerie; to Mary Lennox's secret garden and to the Kensington Gardens, to Primrose Hill echoing with the twilight barking, to the Parisian *ascenseur* at the old Samaritaine hoisting a green-suited elephant and an Old Lady, to the articulate and articulated spiderweb in the sunlit rural doorway? Every domesticated stuffed bear or bunny fallen beneath your child's bed is related not only to Piglet and the Velveteen Rabbit but to the animals coiled in marginalia in medieval psalters, and to the animals at the manger memorialized in colored glass and in song, and the animals painted in black and blood on the walls of the ancient caves of the Pyrenees.

Turn off your cell phones, now. Sit back. Sit up. Pay attention or pay none. What will happen happens whether you pay heed or not, but what happens is sometimes called eucatastrophe—Tolkien again—or consolation. "The consolation of the imaginary is not imaginary consolation," says Roger Scruton, the British philosopher with whom I disagree on many other matters, but not this—but enough of my quoting. The velvet curtains part, side to side, like a parent playing peekaboo.

Luminaires panning, tilting, candlepower intensifying. Color gels shifting: the red of riding hoods, the Turkish blue chalcedony of Ottoman beards, the Lincoln green of Sherwood Forest, the silver of that apple of the sun, the golden of that apple of the moon. Is that Hans Christian Andersen's face projected on the scrim, with a saying in Danish scribbled in his own hand below? "Life itself is the most Wonderful of Fairy Tales."

Maybe we should have brought that bubbly; but there's something being served here more deeply inebriating than champagne. Hush.

The scrim rises into the fly space. An ancient skeleton approaches in a cloak of evergreen. Lean forward to hear what it says. "Now listen . . ." What will we make of it this time? What will it make of us?

GREGORY MAGUIRE

Baba Iaga and the Pelican Child

BABA IAGA HAD A DAUGHTER, A PELICAN CHILD. THIS DID NOT PLEASE her particularly. The pelican child was stunningly strange and beautiful as well as being very very good, which pleased Baba Iaga even less. It was difficult to live as a pelican in the deep dark woods, but the pelican child never seemed to think she belonged to any place other than here with her bony, ill-tempered Baba and the cat and the dog. They all lived in a little hut on chicken legs and they were not uncomfortable. Baba Iaga did not care for visitors, so when anyone approached, the chicken legs would move in a circle, turning the house so that the visitor could not find the door. This, too, was acceptable to them all.

When Baba Iaga went away—which she did frequently though she always always returned—she would warn the dog and cat and her beautiful pelican child against allowing strangers into the house. Even if they do not appear as strangers, don't let them in, Baba Iaga said. And she would go off on her strange errands in her iron mortar, which she would row through the heavens with a pestle. Often she would return with little fishes which the pelican and the cat relished and the dog did not. The dog had his own cache of food which he consumed judiciously—never too much and never too fast—though he did not hoard it. He was generous and noble to a fault really, though he was shabby and ferocious-looking.

One afternoon when Baba Iaga was away, a tall, somewhat formally attired man approached the house. The chicken legs immediately went into rotation so that the door could not be found. (Really, the legs looked as if they weren't even awake, but in fact they never slept.)

I have heard there is a beautiful bird here, the man shouted out, and I would like to draw her. He waved a sketchbook in the air. I'll make her immortal, he called. The pelican child and the dog and the cat remained sitting quietly in a circle on the floor where they had been playing dominoes. The man remained outside until darkness fell, occasionally calling out to them that he was an artist and very highly regarded. Then he went away. The cat turned on the lamp and they waited for Baba Iaga to return. There were two lamps in the hut, one that illuminated only what they knew already and another one which Baba Iaga kept locked in a closet that illuminated what they did not know.

Baba Iaga returned and said, I smell something outside. It smells like cruel death. Who has been here? And they described the man and what he had said. If he returns, under no circumstances let him in, Baba Iaga said. The next day she went off once again in her mortar and pestle. On foggy days one could see the faintest trail of her passage through the sky, so she brought her broom along to sweep away any trace of herself. Baba Iaga was usually very careful, though sometimes she was not.

The pelican child and the dog and the cat sat in a circle on the floor with their coloring books. The pelican child's favorite color was blue, the cat's black, and the dog pretty much preferred them all, he said. They felt the little house moving and their crayons slid across the floor. Once again the man had appeared and the chicken legs had prevented him from finding the door. He shouted up to them as before, proclaiming his devotion to the pelican child's strangeness and beauty and promising to make her immortal. My name is synonymous with beautiful birds, he said, waving his portfolio at the windows.

What is *synonymous*, the dog whispered. He had no idea what it meant and he never would.

Just then the entire forest commenced to rattle, for Baba Iaga had returned and was rushing toward the distinguished gentleman on her bony legs, ready to thrash him with her pestle. Wait, wait, he cried. I only want to create your daughter's portrait. You cannot keep such a splendid creature locked up here. As a mother you should want her to be appreciated. Others should be allowed to marvel at her. Come, look at the drawings I have made of her avian brothers and sisters.

And Baba Iaga, allowing curiosity to get the better of her and also because she *did* feel somewhat guilty raising her beautiful daughter in the dark woods, agreed to look at the drawings.

They *were* beautiful.

Herons and ibis and egrets and roseate spoonbills and storks feeding or flying or resting in their nests with their young or gliding above water that sparkled, so great was the gentleman's skill, sunlight pouring through their perfect wings.

Let us retire to your home and lay these pictures on the floor inside so you can study them and they won't be blown about by the wind, he said.

Indeed, a violent wind had come up as though it were trying to tell Baba Iaga something but she ignored it.

So the chicken legs obediently swung the hut around and Baba Iaga and the gentleman, whose name was John James Audubon, entered.

Well, put out some tea and biscuits for our guest, Baba Iaga snapped at the cat, but the cat said, We have no tea or biscuits. The dog growled, but Baba Iaga said to Audubon, Oh, pay no attention to him. This deeply hurt the dog's feelings.

It's quite dim in here, Audubon remarked. Would you have another lamp so that we can see the drawings better? I so want you to approve of them so you will allow me to draw your beautiful daughter.

I do have another lamp, Baba Iaga said gladly.

And please, grandmother, he said, could you be so kind as to lock the dog and cat away? The dog does frighten me a bit and I'm allergic to cats.

Baba Iaga put the dog and the cat in the closet and followed them in, looking for the other lamp. Oh, wouldn't you know, she muttered, I put it on the highest, most-difficult-to-reach shelf. Audubon slammed the door shut and bolted it. Baba Iaga and the dog and the cat were so stunned that for a moment they were completely speechless. Then they heard their beautiful pelican child say, Oh please sir, do not take me from this bright world! and then a sharp crack as though from a pistol, then terrible sounds of pain and surprise, and then nothing. The dog began to howl and the cat to hiss. Baba Iaga beat on the door with her bony hands and feet, which were sharp as a horse's hooves but the door was old and strong, the wood practically petrified, and they could not break through it. But the dog flung himself against the door again and again and worried a sliver loose with his teeth and claws, and then another sliver. He did not know how long he tore at the door. He had no conception of time. It seemed only yesterday he was a puppy hanging onto Baba Iaga's sock as she limped across the room, or pouncing at moths, or grinning with joy when he was allowed (before he got too big) to accompany Baba Iaga on her flights across the sky. It seemed only yesterday that his fur was soft and black, his paws so pink and tender, his teeth so white, or it seemed as though it could be tomorrow.

Finally, he had made a hole in the door just large enough for him to crawl through. What met his eyes was a scene so horrific he could not understand it. He began to tremble and howl. The beautiful pelican child was pierced through with cruel rods and was arranged in a position of life, her great wings extended, her elegant neck arched. But her life had been taken away, and her eyes were fathomless and dark. A *specimen*, the cat screamed behind him. He has made of our sister a specimen! And then he felt the tears of Baba Iaga striking him like hail.

He left. Outside he ran and ran through the forest. He could see the man running, too, clutching his wretched papers and pens. Often the dog stumbled and twice he fell, for his hips had been bad for some time and his poor old heart now pounded with sorrow. At last he gave up the pursuit for the evil one had far outdistanced him. After he rested and caught his breath, he smelled the dreadful scent of cruel death. Audubon's abandoned campsite was nearby and a fire of green branches still smoldered. Many were the trees that had been cut down, and on their stumps were colorful woodland birds, thrushes and larks and woodpeckers and tiny iridescent and colorfully patterned ones whose names the dog did not know. Long nails thrust through their small bodies kept them erect and thread and wire held their heads up and kept their wings aloft. Even more horrifying was the sight of birds dismembered, their pinions and claws severed for study. Whimpering, the dog fled, and after he had gone a short distance or a long distance, after a long time or a short time, he came to the little hut on chicken legs. The legs were weeping and Baba Iaga and the cat were weeping. Baba Iaga had enfolded her daughter in her arms and her tears fell without ceasing on the pelican child's brown breast.

In the morning, the cat said, We must do something.

I will go out again and find him and tear him to pieces, the dog said wearily.

I don't give a rat's ass about Audubon, the cat said. We must bring our beautiful pelican sister back.

Perhaps we should call for Prince Ivan, the dog suggested.

Useless, Baba Iaga said. He has his princess and his castle. He never calls, he never writes, he is of no use to us.

We will put the beautiful pelican child in the oven, the cat announced.

I couldn't bear to put my daughter in the cold cold oven, Baba Iaga said.

Who said anything about cold, the cat said. We will preheat it to oh say, two hundred fifty degrees and we will put her in for only half an hour.

Half an hour? the dog said.

That stove hasn't been used in years, Baba Iaga said.

But they did what the cat suggested for what else could they do?

Carefully, they lay the pelican child in the oven which was no longer cold but not too warm either. Oh her beautiful face, Baba Iaga cried, her beautiful bill, take care with her bill.

Then they waited.

Has it been a half an hour yet? the dog asked.

Not yet, the cat said.

At last the cat announced that it had been half an hour and Baba Iaga opened the oven and the pelican child, as beautiful as she had ever been, tumbled out and tottered into their happy arms, alive.

After this, Baba Iaga continued to fly through the skies in her mortar, navigating with her pestle. But instead of a broom, she carried the lamp that illuminated the things people did not know or were reluctant or refused to understand. And she would lower the lamp over a person and they would see how extraordinary were the birds and beasts of the world, and that they should be valued for their bright and beautiful and mysterious selves and not willfully harmed for they were more precious than castles or the golden rocks dug out from the earth.

But she could reach only a few people each day with the lamp.

Once, seven experienced its light but usually it was far less. It would take thousands of years, tens of thousands of years perhaps, to reach all human beings with the light.

Baba Iaga came home one evening—so tired—and she gathered her little family around her, the pelican child and the dog and the cat and said, My dear ones, I still have magic and power unrealized. Do you wish to become human beings, for some think you are under a hellish spell. Do you want to become human? The cat and the dog spoke. The pelican child had not spoken since the day of her return.

No, the dog and the cat said.

When I was doing some research for a book on the Florida Keys some twenty years ago, I discovered that John James Audubon,

despite his revered status, was a great slaughterer of birds. (Perhaps everyone was aware of this.) He killed tirelessly for pleasurable sport and would wipe out entire mangrove islands of its inhabitants because . . . well, because I guess it was easy once he got started. I do hope the curse of history will catch up with him. Perhaps Baba Iaga will be the great facilitator in that regard.

Some linguists posit that the baba component of her name derives from pelican. And the pelican is one of the great birds of legend. Returning to her nest to find her infants dead, she pierces her own breast and revives them with her blood.

Baba Iaga is the most marvelous creature in all of Russian folklore and totally unpredictable in her behavior. In this story, she becomes kind and sorrowful, even, perhaps, tragic.

—JW

Ardour

YOU MEET FOLKS WHO REMEMBER WHEN THIS COUNTRY STILL HAD A
winter, and one year led into another unhindered. Come the first
snow, men would leave the fields for fallow, to chop firewood in the
forest. Then not more than a day would go by before you'd hear that
one of them had seen *her*.

She wasn't somebody any of them knew, at least not personally, by
way of an affair or a mutual acquaintance. But long before, they'd
made up a name to use when talking to one another, as men will,
about a girl. They called her *Ardour*.

The story was ever the same. Resting alone in a clearing, burning
a small flame for warmth, a peasant would sense at first just a breath
within the dead trees' shadows. Then he'd see the sky-gray of two eyes,
watching. That was what she was always doing, the girl they called
Ardour, and, calling out to her, they'd each compete to draw her closer
than any of the others had done. Yet there was a certain distance that
she'd always keep.

It was not, evidently, a matter of modesty: Over her bare skin she
wore at most a coat of snow, often only a gloss of frost. Nor could
she seriously be considered a flirt: Unlike young women in town who
hid their flaws by making potential suitors notice only each other's
faults, Ardour had no perceptible imperfection. From behind their

fire, they'd call to her, and it was as if she simply wasn't sure how to respond.

Could she have known their ulterior motives? Each year echoed the one before. As she woke into the first snow, she recalled not what had happened the previous winter, but remembered only an urge that had yet gone unfulfilled.

It had begun as something she'd seen, who knew when, deep in the woods where she'd lived all eternity: A girl like her—breasts as steep as snow peaks beneath a blizzard of hair—came hand-in-hand with a man into an open meadow, where they embraced, and, it seemed, drew into a single skin. Then there were his words, her tears. A rupture, a quiver. They cradled, as if each were the other's wound.

Had Ardour known the word, perhaps she'd have called it *love*. As likely, had she known *hate*, that term would have occurred to her as she watched the couple wrangle. She hadn't had language to guide her. So she'd clutched her own numb flesh, and dreamed what it would be to—

To *feel*? To *desire*? How? Who can be lonely, even, if never not alone? After that, each year, under cover of winter, she hovered on the verge of humanity. And men urged her over the threshold.

They beseeched her all season long until at last she came too close to fire. As the frost thawed from her, she melted with it, into clear water. Then the cold brace of winter would follow her, flowing downriver through closed forest into the unknown. Beneath the snow would emerge a new spring. Work would begin again, the cycle of sowing and reaping that consumed everybody most of the year. There was so much to be done, to bring bread to the table. The only able peasant permitted by the king to remain idle was the man who had tempted Ardour from her forest cover. That was the reward for ending winter.

Every year men worked harder to lure Ardour to her fate. They sang to her, played the fiddle or the flute. If once they'd been attracted to her, after a while you no longer heard them at the tavern talking lustily about her blizzard of hair, those breasts as steep as snow peaks. Each man thought only of himself.

Yet, the more trouble they took, the less their efforts worked to draw her near. The king watched as his subjects flattered and bribed Ardour, tended to her more unctuously than to his majesty. The winter, previously a period of rest, was more trying than a season of sowing, and what did it reap? For all but the man who ushered Ardour's departure, another nine months of labor.

The wintertime clamor became almost intolerable, each man playing whatever instrument he knew, dancing, tendering bread, mead, gold. Ardour could scarcely choose which way to look, let alone who to let tempt her. One year she was drawn to the peasant who had the loudest horn, which she mistook—simple soul—for the force of his desire. Another winter, she went for the one who danced most gracefully, which she misunderstood—foolish girl—as a measure of his sensitivity. And then came the season that she fell for the man with the greatest goods, which she misinterpreted—dumb broad—as a token of his generosity.

After that, she entirely forgot what she'd wished once to find amongst men. She came back with winter, her annual ritual, and stormed around in search of bigger, better—*what?* No longer was she shy. She smothered fires, buried farmers under her coats of snow. The people called her cruel—no more dumb fool simple soul—and wondered how she'd come to resemble them.

Winter that year stretched into April, May, June, July. By August they were burning the days of their calendars for warmth. The king ordained that whoever brought about her fall would never work again. But the men who'd once fought so hard to woo her now just begged her to be gone. Horns and flutes abandoned, their voices became one: *Curse Ardour! Go away! Leave! Scram!*

September, October, November. Winter led into winter. The king's hunters laid traps to catch her. They shot to kill, sunk their munitions into snow. December, January, February, March. Months lost their meanings, years their numbering. Words were moot. Time was marked only by the aching advance of starvation. Folk looked forward to dying.

At last the king had only his son to send from his castle for fire-wood to warm his gruel. The boy had been quite young when that interminable winter began, and had heard of Ardour only as a mon-ster, insatiable in her appetite for human life. He knew well to fear her, a beast as immense as his country, her body encompassing mountains and valleys, a woman said to freeze men with her breath. His father didn't have to tell him to take care.

He wore boots of cowhide lined in fur, laced up to his thighs, triple-tied. His hat and gloves had been crafted from the same, fit to him so tight that there wasn't even the space for a shiver. The coat, though, was a nobler matter: It had been willed to the king by his father, to whom it had been given by his father's father—a tradition, in short, that went back to a generation before there was gold to leaf the family tree. What the coat was made of, though, people no longer knew: the skin of an extinct animal—a dragon, perhaps—or even the earth's own crust? That day, the king laid it on his son.

With ax and saw, the boy made his way into the woods. And it might have been the first time in his sixteen years that he was alone, were there not, he wondered, another set of eyes fixed on his own. They were, at a glance, an overcast gray, but cleared, as he stared, to two open pupils. They belonged to a girl such as he'd never seen be-fore. The snow covered her small body completely, her hair wrapped in the fierce weather that ravaged every inch of bare flesh.

He was not, in truth, especially brave. But had he been moved to rescue the girl from winter, to bring her to shelter, presumably he would have met the same fate as if he had thought to drive the weather away by attacking her. Instead, he approached with no motive other than to come closer.

Colder, colder, and colder. He reached out to her. The coat of snow was soft as fur. He brushed it off, and as it fell, her bare hands met his shoulders, to lift away his own shell.

It is said that the last sensation felt by a body freezing is an all-encompassing heat. As the girl drew nearer—frost melting from her breasts and hips, the stretch of her neck, the pale of her belly—he also let go deeper layers of clothing. Ardour then, folk say, led him away.

Winter withdrew into spring, fell fast on summer. The king went in quest of his son. But all he found, in a clearing, was that greatcoat the boy had worn. It wasn't bloodied by the bite of any beast. There weren't even bones to bury. Life went on.

That year, the winter didn't come. None of the peasants met Ardour. They worked clear through December, barely even seeing one another, so relentlessly did the land produce. Prosperous, who had time to rest? Another year passed, two and three more, four. The weather never dropped off enough for the fields to sleep a season beneath a blanket of snow. And so it went that the workers never more were idle.

Till and sow and reap and till and sow and reap and till. Only rarely was the rhythm broken for an hour by the sounding of a distant storm. The king, shut up in his castle, believed that it was the gods above weeping with him over the loss of his son. But the peasants knew that the tantrum came from the forest floor: the noise of Ardour struggling with her lover, the boy who had fallen for her and who made her feel furiously—could it be true?—human.

I can't say when I first heard about the Russian snow maiden Snegurochka, or who told me her legend. Moreover, I've never since encountered anything like the version I remember hearing. Presumably my recollection is mistaken; the version I remember perhaps doesn't exist. I wrote "Ardour" to preserve the Snegurochka who has lingered with me, even as a figment of my imagination.

Folklore is layered. Each recounting is a revision suited to a particular time and place. I would like to believe that this process can go on, even in a society that has shifted from a tradition of spontaneous storytelling to one that privileges writing and recording. The past century and a half has seen a ballet, an opera, and two movies based on the Russian snow maiden legend, which would suggest that Snegurochka at least has survived the transition to recorded media. She is very much alive, and if she seems quite different in each of these appearances—including my own story—it is in keeping with her chimerical ways.

—JK

LUDMILLA PETRUSHEVSKAYA

I'm Here

HOW CAN YOU FORGET THAT FEELING, IT COMES LIKE A BLOW, WHEN life flees from you, and happiness, and love, thought a woman, Olga, watching as her husband plunked himself down and practically inserted himself next to, essentially, a child—everyone here a grown-up and suddenly out of nowhere this girl-child. And then he stood up with her and went over to dance, addressing Olga gleefully on the way, "Look at this little treasure! I knew her when she was in the sixth grade." And laughed happily. It was the hosts' daughter—of course. She lives here. How'd she forget that, Olga thought as they rode the subway home, her partly drunk husband, a hearing aid in his ear under cover of his eyeglasses, taking a folded-up newspaper, self-importantly, from his pocket, then squinting morosely under the harsh subway light. They rode, they came home. He settled down with that same paper on the toilet and then fell asleep, apparently, because Olga had to wake him up with a loud knock at the door, and everything was so petty, so embarrassing, though of course everything is always embarrassing in one's own home, thought Olga. Her husband snored in bed, as he always did when he'd been drinking. "My God," thought Olga to herself. "Life is over. I'm an old woman. I'm over forty and no one needs me. It's all over, my life is gone."

In the morning Olga fixed breakfast for her family. She needed to go somewhere. Anywhere—to the movies, to an exhibit, maybe even the theater. But who'd go with her? It's a little odd, going alone. Olga called all her friends: one was sitting with a warm wrap—she had a condition she called "a movable feast," her kidneys were bad. They chatted. Another friend didn't answer, maybe they'd shut off the phone, another was just about to go out, she was at the door practically, yet another one of her elderly relatives had fallen ill. That one was a lonely spinster but was always cheerful, energetic, a saint almost. Not like us.

She might try cleaning the house—her boss used to say: "When I hit bottom, like when they gave me the diagnosis, the same as my sister's and she'd just died—well, I came home and just started mopping the floor." This was always followed by the tale of the diagnosis—magically mistaken! And the lesson was, Don't give up! Keep the floor clean!

The laundry, the dishes—everything everywhere after last night's preparations for that idiotic birthday with her husband's college friends. So Olga should clean up and all the while think about how no one does anything to help her? Her husband will get up, hungover, won't look them in the face, will nag, yell, brood over the magic vision of the little girl from last night, the daughter, that's right. Then he won't be back until evening. No, she needs to get out, get away, hide somewhere. Let them take care of themselves for once in their lives. She's tired.

And then Olga realized: Why not visit the only place on earth where no one will turn her away, where they'll always be happy to see her, where they'll sit her down, make her tea, ask how she is and even invite her to stay over; why not visit their old landlady, from the dacha, where they lived so many years in a row when Nastya was still little, and she and Seryozha still hoped for a better life? She was an especially dear memory, this landlady, for Olga; with her complicated relations with her own mother, Olga had become attached to this stranger, this wise and touching old woman. She even seemed beautiful to Olga, and kind, and clever like a child. Meanwhile Baba Anya had been long divorced, if you can say that, from a daughter who never visited and was sleeping around on a grand scale, and who left the mother something to remember her by in the form of little Marina, a beaten-down creature in black hair who was afraid of everyone.

Yes! When you've been abandoned by everyone close to you, do a kindness for a stranger, and you'll feel the warmth of their gratitude on your heart, and it will give your life meaning. And most of all, you will find a quiet refuge, and that's all we want from our friends, isn't it.

Inspired, Olga chuckled to herself, quickly cleaned everything, trying not to wake her family, and then went to look for her stash of Nastya's old things that she'd been collecting over the years for Baba Anya, knowing that her little girl was being raised without any outside help.

She even found something for Anya, a warm shawl, and just two hours later was running across the square in front of the train station, having almost been hit by a car on the way (now, that would really be something, wouldn't it, if she died, it would certainly be a solution to all sorts of problems, the disappearance of a person no one needs or wants, it would free everyone, Olga thought, and even paused on this thought for a while, amazed by it)—and a moment later, as if by magic, she was descending from the commuter train at the little rural station that she knew so well, and, dragging her big backpack behind her, walking down the familiar dirt road from the station to the edge of the settlement, in the direction of the river.

It was a Sunday in October. The place was light, empty, the trees were bare already, the air smelled of smoke and Russian baths. The fallen leaves gave off the scent of young wine and other people's established lives, as well as a whiff of the graveyard, somehow, and the windows were already lit, though it wasn't yet dark. Nostalgia, wide-open spaces, the pearly white skies and the happiness of years gone by, when she and Seryozha were young, when their friends came out here, all of them so happy, drinking, barbecuing, etc. And they helped Baba Anya, because something was always leaking, or collapsing, or needing someone to hammer something in. In those years you could leave little Nastya with her for an evening, Nastya had befriended silent little Marina. Baba Anya would put them in bed while Olga and Seryozha went into town for someone's birthday party, drank and sang until sunrise, and maybe wouldn't even make it back until the next evening. The whole time their daughter was safe, and Baba Anya would even say, Go on, take a vacation, you think I can't handle these two? So they did, they went south for two weeks. And Baba Anya also enjoyed it, they left her money and groceries. True, when they got back Nastya was so excited she immediately got sick and stayed sick for exactly two weeks. Their whole vacation was forgotten, their tans erased, Olga didn't sleep for ten nights: the girl almost died. Everything in life seeks equilibrium, Olga said to herself, walking with her backpack, said it with such assurance she might even have said it out loud.

The path was soft, the soil here was mostly damp clay, and up ahead, where the road curves, we take a left past the doctors' fence. That was what they called their neighbors, and it was true, in a way, the husband worked for the local epidemics control office. On Saturdays they'd pump out the waste from under their outhouse and pour it all over their garden, supposedly in the interests of ecology (actually because they didn't want to hire a truck to take it away), and the smell of this organic fertilizer carried through the village. The same rotten wind was blowing now (which explained the graveyard smell, thought Olga).

Baba Anya used to laugh at this agricultural program. She'd been a crops specialist herself, had worked at an institute, even went on business trips, and it was only after retiring and moving out here that she returned to her peasant roots, to the language of her ancestors, calling strawberries "redberries" (alternately, "victoria"), wearing a kerchief on her head and remains of rubber boots on her feet, going to the bathroom behind the bushes (now *that* was fertilizing). Everything grew in her garden as if by magic, all by itself. She'd moved out here a long time ago, leaving her apartment in the city to her daughter, supposedly to give her space (actually it was only after a protracted civil war that had led to the destruction of both sides, as civil wars always do).

Olga successfully navigated the overgrown path, through the thinning black wild grass; it looked like no one had passed this way in a while. She took the rusted ring, which they used instead of a latch, off the gate, ran the damp gate away from the fence, and happily swung herself toward the house, seeing that a curtain behind the window had just shivered.

Baba Anya was home! She must have been so happy to see Olga; she'd always loved their family.

Knocking on the door, which didn't even have a lock, Olga passed by the cold front hall and banged on the canvas that Baba Anya used in place of wallpaper.

"I'm coming, I'm coming," came the hollow little voice of Baba Anya.

Olga entered the warm house, the smells of someone else's home, and immediately her spirits rose at the sweetness of it.

"Hello, Babushka!" she cried, almost in tears. Warmth, a night's rest, a quiet refuge, awaited her. Baba Anya had become even shorter, dried-out, but her eyes shone in the darkness.

"I'm not bothering you?" Olga said happily. "I brought your Marinochka some of Nastya's things—tights, warm pants, a little coat."

"Marina's not here anymore," Baba Anya answered quickly. "She's not here anymore."

Olga, the smile still on her face, grew terrified. A chill ran up her spine.

"Go on," Baba Anya said, quite clearly. "Get out of here, Olga. Go. I don't need it."

"I brought you some things, too. I got salami, some milk, a bit of cheese."

"Then, take it all with you. I don't need it. Take it and go, Olga."

Baba Anya spoke, as always, in a thin, quiet, pleasant voice—she wasn't insane—but her words were inconceivable.

"Baba Anya, what happened?"

"Nothing happened. Everything's fine. Now get out of here."

Baba Anya couldn't be saying these things! Olga stood there scared and insulted. She didn't believe her ears.

"Have I done anything wrong, Baba Anya? I know I didn't visit for a long time. But I always thought of you. Just, life, somehow—"

"Life is life," Baba Anya said vaguely. "And death is death."

"I just couldn't find the time, somehow . . ."

"And I've got more time than I know what to do with. So go on your way, Olga."

"I'll just leave these things with you, then," she said. "I'll put them out, so I won't have to lug them all the way back with me."

(God, what could have happened?)

"For what, what for?" Baba Anya asked in a clear, aggressive voice, almost as if to herself. "I don't need anything anymore. It's over. I'm dead and buried. What do I need? Just a cross for the grave, nothing else."

"But what happened? Can't you just tell me?" Olga persisted in desperation.

The house was warm, and the floor of the corridor in which they stood was covered, as always, with cardboard, so there'd be no dirt in the house. The door to Baba Anya's room stood wide open and inside you could hear the radio, buzzing like a mosquito, and through the windows you could see out into the trees in the yard. Everything had remained as it was—but Baba Anya, it seemed, had lost her mind. The worst thing that can happen to someone still alive had happened to her.

"I'm telling you what happened," she said now. "I died."

"When?" Olga asked automatically.

"Two weeks ago now."

Horrible, it was horrible! Poor Baba Anya.

"Baba Anya, where's your little girl, where's Marina?"

"I don't know. They didn't bring her to the funeral. I just hope Svetlana didn't take her. Svetlana was no good, oh she was no good, she must have sold the apartment and spent the money, she came dressed in rags to the funeral. She fell apart completely. She had sores on her feet, open sores, wrapped in newspapers. Dmitry buried me. She was useless there. Dmitry shooed her away."

"Dmitry?"

"The one she left Marina with when she was just a baby. She was a one-year-old. Dmitry, Dmitry. He put little Marina in an orphanage then, I picked her up. You don't remember, or maybe I didn't tell you?"

"I remember something like that, yes."

"Maybe I didn't tell you. There were plenty like you here. They come, they leave, not a letter, not a word. I died alone. I fell down here. Marina was in school."

"But I've come! Here I am!"

"Dmitry buried me, but he just had me cremated, and he still hasn't picked up the urn. I wasn't buried, so I came here. I'm just here for the time being. Svetlana has gone all bad, she's a bum, a real bum. She doesn't even realize she can live here. Dmitry scared her out of the crematorium when she sat down and started wrapping her feet in newspapers. Somehow she found her way to me in the hospital, then the morgue. She came off the bus, pus was leaking out of her sores. She found a newspaper in the wastebasket. Svetlana, I know, she was hoping to get a drink at the wake. Dmitry found her somehow, he didn't know she'd become like that. But I won't be here long, just until the fortieth day. After that, it's good-bye. And that's it, Olga, now go."

"Baba Anya! You're just tired, that's all. Lie down! Maybe you'd like it if I stayed here with you a while? I'll find little Marina. When did she disappear?"

"Marina disappear? No, no. When I fell down, I couldn't remember anything at first, but then afterward, when they were taking me away, the only one I saw was Dmitry. Where was Marina? And Dmitry was the one who took me from the morgue."

"Dmitry, what was his last name?"

"I don't know," Baba Anya mumbled to herself. "Fedosev, I guess. Like Marina. She's Fedoseva. God bless him. He brought a priest to the funeral. That was it, they were the only ones there—no one was told, he didn't know who to tell. He told Sveta and then chased her off forever. She'll be here soon, I'm waiting for her. She's about to die."

"No one told me," Olga said suddenly.

"And who are you, Olga? You rented the cottage a long time ago. You haven't been here in how long—five years? Marina's twelve already! I just hope she'll stay away from here, oh I hope she doesn't come!"

Five years. Nastya is fifteen already, a teenager. They haven't had a summer here in five years! Nastya's grandmother has a house in the town of Slavyansk in the Kuban. There's a river there with ice-cold water in it. The girl comes back from there a total stranger, wild, smoking cigarettes. Already a woman, for certain.

"Forgive me, Baba Anya!"

"God will forgive you, he forgives everyone. Now go. Don't stay here. And take your old rags with you. The thieves have been here already. I open the door for them all. I'm no one now."

"These aren't rags, these are nice things for a little girl. Wool tights, a little coat, some T-shirts."

Olga was trying to convince Baba Anya that everything was fine, that this horror was just a fantasy imagined by her aching heart, which was, like Olga's, abandoned and hurt.

"Baba Anya, I came out here thinking this might be the last refuge for me."

"There's no such refuge for anyone on earth," Baba Anya said. "Every soul is its own last refuge."

"I thought at least you wouldn't chase me away, you'd take me in. I thought I'd sleep over."

"No, Olga, what are you talking about. I'm telling you. You can't, I don't exist anymore."

"I brought some food, please try it."

"You'll try it yourself later. Now go, go."

"It's cold out there. Here, in the village, the sky and the air are just . . . Baba Anya! I so much wanted to come here, I was hoping—"

Baba Anya answered firmly: "I'm worried about Marina. I'm very worried about her."

"I know, I understand that," said Olga. "I'll find her."

"Svetlana's on her way, she's lost everything, but she's still alive. If she were dead, she'd be here. But I don't want to see anyone here, do you understand? Leave me alone, all of you! Where's Marina? I don't want to see her. I don't want to, you get it?"

Baba Anya was obviously talking nonsense. Want, not want. But she stood firm, blocking the hallway with her diminutive frame.

Olga imagined walking home with her heavy load, the bread, the groceries, the liter of milk.

"Baba Anya, do you mind if I just sit here a minute. My legs hurt. My legs really hurt all of a sudden."

"And I'm telling you one more time: Go in peace! Take your legs from here while you still have them!"

Olga went past her, as if Baba Anya wasn't even there, and sat down on a chair in the room.

The smell of an outhouse from the neighbors came in even more strongly through the open window.

The room looked abandoned. There was a wrapped-up mattress on the bed. That never happened at Baba Anya's, she was meticulously neat. She always made the bed very carefully, topping it with lace-covered pillows. And that awful smell!

"Baba Anya, can you put some water on for tea?"

"There's no teakettle, I'm telling you, bad people came and took everything," Baba Anya said from the hallway in that same crystal-clear voice.

"And the water, is there any water?"

"Water . . . There hasn't been water in a while, only in the well. But I don't go out."

"I'll run out and get some water?" Olga offered from the room. "You haven't had tea in a while, probably?"

"I died two weeks ago."

"You still have the bucket for the well?"

"They took the bucket, too."

Olga took a deep breath, walked into the kitchen, and found it completely ransacked. The small cabinet was wide open, the floor was covered in broken glass, a beat-up aluminum pot lay on its side on the floor (Baba Anya used to make kasha in it). In the middle of the floor stood an empty three-liter can from some beans. Seryozha had brought that can once for some dinner, but they didn't open it, they had baked potatoes instead, and they left it for Baba Anya when they went back to the city in the fall.

Olga took the can in her hands.

"And take all your luggage, too!" Baba Anya said.

"How am I going to drag all this to the well?"

"Take it, take it! Take your purse!"

Olga obediently slung her purse over her shoulder and went out the door with the can. Baba Anya dragged the backpack after her, but for some reason she didn't come into the outer hall.

The cold met Olga outside, along with a strong fresh breeze, and everywhere in the abandoned garden were tall blackened weeds, their hollow seeds swaying in the wind. Olga stumbled over to the ravine, where the nearest well was. They'd put in running water for everyone long ago, except they didn't quite reach here, to the impoverished Baba Anya, who couldn't raise the funds for it.

The ravine was covered with old trash, it was practically a dump, and there was no bucket at the well, just a piece of folded brown string. The bucket had been expropriated, as Baba Anya used to say.

Here Olga's head began to spin, and everything around her turned clearly, blindingly white—but only for an instant. Without losing consciousness, Olga found a big crooked nail, and pulled a chunk of brick from the ground. She broke a hole in the side of the can, though in doing so slashed the index finger on her left hand—she sucked the blood out with her lips—found a fresh ribwort leaf, placed it on the wound, then somehow managed to tie the rope to the can, and released the catch. Her improvised bucket dropped, picked up water, she brought it back up, now as cold as ice, untied the rope from it, and, holding it away from her body, carried the cold can, full to the brim, thinking only of poor Baba Anya, who didn't have a drop of water in the house. She went up from the filthy ravine, up the clay path, her legs weren't used to it and hurt, or rather they were numb. At the top of the path Olga put the can down and looked around.

Baba Anya's tattered fence was filled with gaps, and you could see the house clearly from here. Now there were no curtains in the windows! Olga felt an ice-like fear, the dark fear of a healthy person before insanity—the sort of insanity that can tear all the curtains from the four windows in seven or eight minutes.

Still, Baba Anya needed to be fed or at least given something to drink. She'd call the doctors, lock the house, find Marina somehow, or Svetlana, or Dmitry Fedosev. As for who should live here—the homeless Sveta, the heir, who'll drink away the house in the blink of an eye, or poor homeless Marina—wasn't for us to decide. Or she'd take Marina herself! That's what she'd do, now that she was involved in this business. You wanted to leave your life, well, now you've left it and ended up in someone else's. No place in the world is free of lonely souls in need of help. Seryozha and Nastya will be against it; Seryozha won't say anything; Nastya will say, That's interesting, Mom, as if we didn't know already you were koo-koo. And her mother will of course cause a terrific scandal over the phone.

Olga stood there thinking all this over, with difficulty, knowing that she should keep going, but her legs had filled with lead, they refused to take orders, didn't want to carry three liters of ice-cold water to the pillaged house of the crazy old woman, didn't want to experience more hardship in this life. The sharp wind howled up the hill where Olga stood, frozen, a mother and wife, standing there like a homeless woman, like a pauper, with her only worldly possession at her feet in the form of a three-liter tin can filled with water. The sharp wind blew, the black skeletons of the trees screeched, and the fresh watermelon smell of winter appeared. It was cold, bitter, it was getting dark quickly, and she immediately wanted to transport herself home, to her warm, slightly drunken Seryozha, her living Nastya, who must have woken up by now, must be lying there in her nightshirt and robe, watching television, eating chips, drinking Coca-Cola and calling up her friends. Seryozha will be going to visit his old school friend now. They'll have some drinks. It was the usual Sunday program, so let it be. In a clean, warm, ordinary house. Without any problems.

Olga took the can in both hands and carried it down to Baba Anya, but slipped and fell on the clay, spilling half the water on herself. Oh, God! Her legs were hurting now for real.

But Baba Anya's door was locked, and no one opened even though she kicked at the door with her sick legs and yelled like a woman possessed.

Someone above her noted, very clearly, very quickly: "She's yelling."

But Olga knew another way into the house, through the ladder into the attic, and there through the chute, along the steps in the wall, you could make your way down to the terrace—they'd climbed into the house that way more than once, she and Seryozha, late at night, when they couldn't find the keys.

Olga left the can at the door.

Baba Anya was sitting inside that house, insane, without water, and there's no way she'd be able to take the food out of the fastened backpack, not in the mindless state she was in. How quickly it can happen to you, when you lose everything, and the intelligent, kind, wonderful human turns into a wary silly little animal . . .

With some difficulty Olga got the ladder out from under the house, placed it against the wall, climbed up the rickety rungs, the third one gave way and she fell, hurting her legs again (were they broken?). Moaning, she kept climbing, got up on the roof after all, managed to injure her hands, too, and her side was now in pain, and her head, and once again, for a moment, this great white space opened before her, but that was nothing, it disappeared right away, and then she barely dragged herself along the dusty attic, made it down to the terrace—the tortuous unbearable journey. And then the door from the terrace turned out to be locked, too. Apparently Baba Anya had thought of this, and put it on a hook, for fear of thieves.

All right.

Olga broke into tears and began banging on the door with her fists, yelling: "Anna Sergeevna! Hello! It's me, Olga! Let me in!"

She stood and listened for a moment—there was nothing—just a distant sound like some earth trickling down in a little stream.

"All right," Olga said finally. "I'm leaving. The water is in a can next to the door. There is bread and cheese in the big pocket of the backpack, at the front. The salami is there, too."

The way back up the wall was even harder than the way down, her hands wouldn't listen to her at all as she took hold of the notches, and Olga descended the ladder already in a state of half-madness, somehow avoiding the broken third rung. The white light shone in places through the twilight, the white light of unconsciousness.

When she made it to the station, she sat down on an ice-cold bench. It was so cold, her legs were frozen and ached terribly as if they'd been crushed. The train was a long time in coming. Olga curled up on the icy bench. Trains kept passing by the station, she was the only one on the platform. Now it had gotten dark for real.

And then Olga woke up on some kind of bed. Once again there opened before her (there it is!) that endless white space, as if she were surrounded by snow. Olga moaned and turned her gaze to the horizon. There she saw a window, half obstructed by a blue curtain. Outside the window it was night, and lights shone far away. Olga lay in a vast dark room with white walls; her covers were weighing her down like rubble. She couldn't raise her right arm, it was pressed down by some kind of weight. She raised her left hand and began examining it; it was so pale as to be almost transparent. There was a large dark scratch on her pointing finger—from where she'd picked up the brick at Baba Anya's house. But the wound was almost healed.

"Where am I?" Olga asked loudly. "Hey! Hello! Baba Anya!"

She tried to raise herself up—without any success. Her legs hurt fiercely, that much was certain. And a pain was cutting into her lower abdomen.

There was no one around.

Finally she managed to raise herself up, leaning on her right arm, and look around.

She was lying on a bed; a semitransparent tube was protruding from this bed.

A catheter! They'd put a catheter into her! Like they'd put one into her dying grandmother long ago, in the hospital. And this was a hospital. Nearby there was another bed with an inert mass of white in it.

"Hello! Oy! Help!" Olga called out. "Help Baba Anya! And Marina Fedoseva! Help them!"

The mass of white in the next bed started moving.

A nurse who'd just woken up walked into the room in her white robe.

"What are you yelling for?" she said. "Quiet. You'll wake everyone."

"Where am I?" Olga cried. "Let me up! Marina Fedoseva, you need to find her. Let me up!"

"And you will be up and about, you will. Now that you've . . . returned." She left and came back with a big needle. While she received her shot, Olga was trying to remember, painfully.

"What's wrong with me, nurse? Tell me."

"What's wrong is that your legs are broken, and your arm, and your pelvic bone. Lie still. Your husband will come tomorrow, and your mother, they'll tell you everything. Also a concussion. It's good you woke up. They've been coming here, waiting, and nothing. Can you feel your legs?"

"They hurt."

"That's good."

"But where, where? What happened?"

"You got hit by a car, don't you remember? Sleep now, sleep. You were hit by a car."

Olga was amazed, she gasped, and once again she was knocking at Baba Anya's door, trying to bring her water. It was a dark October evening, the windows in the cottage rattled from the wind, her tired legs hurt and so did her broken arm, but Baba Anya didn't want to let her in, apparently. And then on the other side of the window she saw the worn-out faces of her loved ones, covered in tears—her mother, Seryozha, Nastya. And Olga kept trying to tell them to look for Marina Fedoseva, Marina Dmitrievna, Baba Anya's Marina, something like that. Look for her, Olga said, look for her. And don't cry. I'm here.

—Translated from the Russian
by Keith Gessen and Anna Summers

At the beginning of many Russian fairy tales, the hero or heroine sets out on a quest to recover a beloved person or a precious object that has been lost or stolen. The quest takes them to a bizarre distant land where they encounter the old witch who lives in a wooden hut. The witch, in exchange for help, demands in tribute a magical object, such as the Water of Life, which the traveler obtains at great risk.

In "I'm Here," the heroine is a middle-aged woman, overwhelmed by domestic drudgery. Her great loss is a wasted life. Her quest is a one-day trip to the country in search of advice and consolation; the witch in a hut is her former landlady who occupies a shabby summer cottage. The heroine's tribute to the witch is a can of plain water from a nearby well. The bizarre distant land is, in fact, the realm of the dead, to which the heroine travels in a moment of unconsciousness. Instead of lost treasure the heroine brings back information, true or not, that may save a child's life.

Petrushevskaya disguises conventional plot elements with realistic detail and personal portraits: the impoverished Russian countryside; a desolate autumnal landscape; an alcoholic single mother and her wretched child. Petrushevskaya leaves it to the reader to decide whether the heroine's entire quest was a hallucination—and which of the two worlds in the story is more real.

This story emerges from several traditional Slavic folktales— but especially the motifs of any tale with Ivan Tsarevich, or John the Prince, in it. The tsar's third and youngest son, he appears in many Russian tales brought back to life from the dead. As a specter in the story, of course, we also have the figure of Baba Iaga, the witch whose house stands on chicken feet at the edge of the forest, and who likes to eat little children though she is perpetually thin.

—AS

The Brother and the Bird

MARLENE'S MOTHER CLEANED CONSTANTLY, BLEARY-EYED IN MUL-tiple hairnets, on her vigilant search for the impure; as she walked she so often rolled an antiquated upright vacuum alongside her that it grew to seem like an exterior organ, an intravenous device that performed dialysis or another lifesaving function. Marlene had no memory of Mother's bare hands, for they were always beneath thick, yellow kitchen gloves and had begun, as the years passed, to seem prosthetic. Fearful that dust might see her coming and scatter, Mother crept from one chore to another, hunched over, skulking around on the tips of her toes and raising each knee skyward with every step. What horrible shadows this cast upon the wall! Young Marlene would often shiver in bed and watch a ghastly outline bend steadily larger as Mother advanced down the hallway, the rubber gloves taking on the shape of oversized claws. Marlene's fright and anticipation usually became so intense that she'd let out an audible gasp when Mother finally appeared in front of the bedroom door. Mother would stop, sniff. "Good girls are asleep by now," she'd whisper, quiet enough to make Marlene wonder whether Mother even meant for this to be heard.

Father was friendlier, bear-like and aloof. When Marlene and Brother were little, they had delighted in running their fingers through the thick black curls on Father's chest and back and riding him like an animal. He'd obligingly take to all fours and crawl around the yard, giving in to their wishes for a spirit of manufactured danger. "I'm going to eat you!" he'd eventually growl, and their cheeks would glow pink as pigs.

But Father had always stopped their play if they got too close to the juniper tree, their yard's curious landmark. Halfway up, its trunk divided into two distinct sections that grew away from each other toward separate futures. Being children, Marlene and her brother always tested the limit—what was the closest they could get to the tree before Father excused himself and cited fatigue, or claimed to be growing old?

"It's the cremated human remains," Brother explained. He referred to his birth mother, Father's deceased first wife, whose urn was buried in the yard under the tree. Marlene had occasionally spied Mother watering its roots with bleach and kicking the tree, stomping atop the first wife's grave in a peculiar dance. And sometimes Mother picked up the large ax in the basement and spoke kindly to it, as though it were a baby, cradling it in her gloved hands and staring back at her reflection in the blade's clean mirror.

But Mother hated her husband's son even more than she did the tree. She beat him often and cleverly, across the body but never the face, with her heavy Bible and household objects made of wood. "I will clean the sin right out of you," Mother remarked, sweating. "You are not of my loins, wicked thing." Her own fictive brand of religion had curious rules; she'd stopped attending Mass long ago, remarking that the purification of one's household was tantamount to prayer.

Marlene wished for a life away from Mother where she and Brother had the home all to themselves. And Father could float in and out as he pleased, a furry satellite.

As the years passed, Marlene fell deeply in love with Brother. By the time she was twelve and he sixteen, simply thinking about him made her feel as full and sleepy as eating a large meal.

Marlene often snuck into Brother's room after Mother was asleep, and they would lie on his bed and listen to records. During each song he'd pick out a single line to sing, and Marlene liked to predict which one he was going to choose—when she was right she felt very good at loving. She'd watch Brother's mouth and could almost see his voice spinning into the air like invisible string. *"Bird, moon, fly away soon."* To keep track of time she thought of the record as an hourglass and the needle as sand, and when she heard its empty scratch she'd rise gently from the bed, take up the needle, and sneak quietly back to her room.

But one night Marlene and Brother drifted off to sleep. They woke to Mother standing overtop them with her large Bible. A broken blood vessel had stained the white of her left eye a deep red.

Brother sleepily lifted his neck. "Mother," he said, startled. "You look very angry."

"A dirty thing," Mother insisted, pointing at the two of them with a shaking rubber finger. The spongy pink curlers beneath her hairnet looked like an inflated brain.

Marlene tried to curl her body against Brother's, but she was quickly flung from the bed as Mother's Bible thrashed down upon Brother. This beating went on longer than Marlene thought possible, and just when Mother seemed to be done, a new wave of fury overtook her like a spell; she lifted her great weight upon Brother's chest, placed a pillow overtop his face, and pushed the heavy Bible down atop it. "A dirty, dirty thing," she hissed. Brother's feet kicked in high convulsions that lifted the sheets, but Mother did not dismount until his legs went still. Then she eased up and turned her smile toward the window and the sun.

"Remove your socks," Mother said.

Mother herself was naked, wearing nothing but an apron. She ordered Marlene to fully undress, then fitted her nude daughter into a smock and a matching pair of yellow kitchen gloves. Marlene sobbed; Mother was gazing upon Brother's corpse with grateful eyes, as though he were a gift basket of fruit. "Grab his feet," Mother directed. Together they hauled his body down into the basement. Marlene's stomach lurched when they neared the furnace, but Mother led them on farther, over to the laundry sink in the basement's left corner.

As Marlene held open the garbage bag, her hands began to shake. "Hail Mary," Mother started. A rosary dangled from the ax's handle like a beaded tail.

The blade hit into the corpse with a great thwack and Marlene saw Mother's flat buttocks clench tightly. This image placed Marlene into a catatonic state; she stopped blinking and errant blood began to dot the whites of her eyes.

They divided Brother's pieces into twelve bags of different shapes and sizes, then scattered him throughout the basement's deep freeze. Mother told Marlene to go take a long shower, and as Marlene climbed the stairs she spied a piece of Brother's flesh still lying beside the sink. Twice she stopped and stared, thinking that she'd seen it move; she cried each time she realized she was mistaken.

Father came home to a large sauerbraten flavored with dried juniper berries and a sauce crisped with gingersnap and honey-cake crumbs. He ate heartily, large tufts of hair spilling from his collar and shirt cuffs, their ends curling up from the dinner's steam. It wasn't until his plate was almost empty that he asked where Brother had gone off to.

Marlene's eyes moved to the Bible sitting in the living room. Mother had hidden its bloodstains beneath a quilted cover that bore an appliqué of a stitched cat face. The feline's whiskers were long strokes of thread; lace bordered its edges. Due to its size, the Bible now resembled a pillow.

"He's visiting a friend for a bit," Mother said, smiling. Her grin was fixed and still; she looked like a wicked doll that should never have come to life.

"Did he say when he'd be back?" Father asked. Marlene began to weep as Mother shook her head and adjusted her hairnet. Her yellow gloved hand moved a spoonful of gravy very slowly toward her husband's mouth, teasing.

The weeks that followed were a parade of heavy soups, sweetbreads, and full stews. Disgusted, Marlene resolved to rescue what was left of Brother's remains at any cost. Only nine bags were left in the freezer. One of these had been torn open, and when she peeked inside she saw butcher-like excisions on a shank of Brother's torso.

"I'll bury you with your mother under the tree," Marlene promised, "and no more of you will ever be eaten!"

It took Marlene several trips to get all the bags outside; she could carry only a few at a time. On each return to the basement she carefully checked to see if Mother was hiding beneath the stairs, if the ax was still hanging on the wall.

Marlene dropped to her knees beneath the tree and opened the bags, reaching her arm inside to search their contents for Brother's head. He looked quite different now. His cheeks and mouth had been pushed up against the freezer's wall and had frozen at an upward angle. Brother's iced flesh was as white-blond as his hair, and its heavy cold burned at her skin. When Marlene kissed him her wet lips stuck painfully to his; she tasted a bit of blood after she pulled herself free.

For what seemed like hours, Marlene dutifully struggled with the hard earth and the shovel. She feared that when the sun came up the hole would still be no bigger than a shoe box and she'd have no place to hide Brother's thawed parts. When the fluttering sound began, she dismissed it at first; it was buzzing and internal, like an insect too close to her ears. Then all the berries fell from the juniper tree at once.

Marlene's breath left her lungs as she eyed the now-covered ground around her—a blanket of berries inches thick. "I'll be caught for sure." She panicked, and her panic only grew as the berries began to shake and toss on the ground like roasting coffee beans, then cleared to reveal a soft gray circle in their center. Curious, Marlene reached over the berries and placed her hand onto its surface. "Ash," she gasped, but wouldn't say aloud what she was thinking: *cremated human remains.*

The fluttering sound loudened and the berries began to organize themselves like ants. They surrounded the pile of garbage bags, lifting them onto their backs and rolling them into the ash like an assembly line, the bags sinking down into its powder with the ease of rocks into a lake. When all the bags were gone, the berries formed a single line. They drained down into the ash like marbles. Finally a bird dived down from the tree and soundlessly followed the last berry into the ash.

Marlene was very tempted to jump inside and escape as well. But as she approached the gray surface she cried out in disappointment; the ground had set like a thick pudding, hardened into soil before her very eyes.

The next morning Marlene awoke to the horrible sensation of being watched. A thin stream of urine began to warm under her bottom.

"No one would ever have found him in the basement, frozen and quiet in little pieces," Mother whispered. She was seated on the edge of Marlene's bed, inching closer to her daughter's face. "But where is he now?" The grayish-black pockets beneath her eyes seemed full of tiny dark stones.

Her hands gripped Marlene's cheeks, their fingernails digging into Marlene's skin even through the rubber of the gloves. For a moment Mother stared into her eyes, searching, then she gave a full smile and left. Marlene watched the indention Mother had left on the bed raise up and fill, but she did not move until she heard the faraway wail of the vacuum begin to heave in heavy sucks.

In tears, Marlene ran into Brother's room. When she looked at his shirts hanging up in the closet, she felt the same affection for their cloth as for his skin. She buried her face in them, ran to his bed and ruffled his sheets, begged him to appear, appear. She did notice his guitar was missing. Had Mother cut it up as well?

Winter came and Father seemed to retreat into his woolly skin. He never pressed for further answers about where Brother was staying, but he often wished aloud for his son's return.

After dinner, as Mother and Marlene sat by the fire, it became common for Father to excuse himself and take his pipe outdoors. All the while he would stare at the juniper tree, whose branches were growing new berries despite the cold.

Mother peeked out the curtains and watched his every move. "How I think I'll take the ax to that tree," she'd remark, "so that Father might stay with us by the fire." Whenever she passed a window that looked out upon the tree, Mother made an upside-down cross with her gloved fingers and extended it toward the glass.

One night, right before she fell asleep, Marlene rolled over to find a feather on her pillow. The moment she touched it a deep dream began.

At first she saw nothing, and when she was able to see she realized the eyes were not her own but the eyes of a bird. She looked through them like two holes of a mask, the bird's long beak jutting up into her line of vision.

Underground, in a hollow space made of earth, she and the bird were pecking Brother's parts back together. The beak came down in small strikes that were a form of stitching. Occasionally it would stop and grab berries from a stockpile, using them to fill in holes where Mother had taken away meat. Pieces of pecked-through garbage bags were scattered everywhere like tissue paper. When finished, the bird cried out until Brother's body started moving.

The bird jumped ahead, leading Brother through a tunnel up into the juniper tree. Marlene watched as its trunk cracked open like an egg filled with light.

She and the bird flew up while Brother crawled out, and the tree closed up behind them.

Marlene then saw the sky and the roof of their home, and occasionally caught glimpses of Brother, naked far below, his flesh white and cloudy like a ridge of ice. Even from the air, she could make out the violet grafts on his arms where berries had patched his skin. When Brother walked into the house, the bird flew to Brother's bedroom window and waited.

Brother appeared in his room minutes later, gaunt and confused. He dressed in the dark, lifted his guitar, and left.

The bird flew very high until Brother became a silver-blond dot on the road below. A truck stopped and he entered it; the bird flew for quite a distance to follow him. There was the familiar sound of fluttering, the sound Marlene heard on the night she buried him, and there were long stretches of darkness that told of passing time. When the bird's eyes went black, Marlene heard a flapping noise, like musical paper, as the sound of wings sped up into an echo.

Finally the bird perched above a small tavern. Marlene could hear music and see Brother inside, a blanched shape performing a song on his guitar. She saw flashes of him in many towns, on many stages, and could feel his confusion as he wandered; his memory had been reduced to a vague longing, and this came and went spontaneously like strange desire. Just before she woke she saw him standing at a sidewalk storefront, eyeing a pair of red shoes that resembled the ones she wore every day.

When Marlene woke again she was in her room; the feather was floating in the air just inches above her pillow. Her hand reached out, but at the slightest touch it turned to ash in her fingers.

The dream caused Marlene to feel weary and flu-like. Even the next night, she was still shaky when she sat down to dinner with Mother and Father. Light organ music played on the radio, and Father was cutting his meal into tinier and tinier bits. "Can't you make the sauerbraten again?" he asked Mother, looking down at his plate with distant eyes.

Just then, the music on the radio abruptly stopped. Marlene's hand froze around her fork; a fluttering noise poured through the speakers. After a brief minute of static, a very peculiar song came on. "*My mother, she killed me,*" the voice sang. "*My father, he ate me. My sister, she saved my bones, tweet, tweet . . .*"

Mother crept over and turned down the radio's knob with her rubber fingers.

"Some quiet," she snipped. She then scowled at the radio and began to examine it carefully, as if it might be something more than it seemed.

The very next night Mother did indeed make sauerbraten, but this time it was not to Father's liking. He excused himself to go outside and smoke, and Marlene turned on the radio as Mother made a fire. They sat and listened to an organ's cheery song as flames seared the logs a deep white.

Just as Father came back inside the house, the radio's song turned to static. This slowly gave way to the sound of wings, then music.

"*Mother killed her little son; what a beautiful bird am I. Father ate 'til meat was gone; what a beautiful bird am I. Sister saved my bones; now I sing and fly . . .*"

Mother's eyes stared straight forward, wide with terror. "Looking at this fire," she remarked in a flat and breathy voice, "I feel like I am burning up."

Marlene awoke the next morning to a loud and constant wailing. Neither Mother nor Father seemed able to hear it; Father went away to work as usual and Mother spent her day on the patio killing bugs. Marlene desperately searched for the source of the noise, but she couldn't tell where it stopped or started. Was it Brother's room? The juniper tree? The basement?

The sound grew so loud that Marlene began to see small gray dots; occasionally it seemed as if birds were flying just beyond the corners of her vision.

For most of the afternoon, she lay in Brother's room listening to records and getting sick into a bag.

When her parents insisted she come down for dinner that evening, Marlene did not think she'd be able to accept the smell of food. But as she sat down, the deafening static leaped from the inside of her head onto the radio. "*My mother forced me quick to die.*" Brother's voice rang out inside the kitchen. "*My father ate me in a pie.*"

Mother leaped up and started her bony fingers toward the dial. "Some quiet," she said, but Father interrupted.

"Some music might be nice tonight."

"Perhaps a different tune, then," Mother suggested. But as she flipped the knob, she found that the song was on every station. *"Only my sister began to cry."*

Father stood up and squinted his eyes toward the window.

"Is someone walking toward the house?" Grabbing his pipe, he excused himself from the table to have a better look.

Mother slowly backed away from the radio, her eyes fixed upon the fireplace, her hands twisting. "When I look at the fire," she stammered, "I feel as if I'm being burned alive." Her smile grew lopsided; she began to unbutton her dress.

"But there isn't any fire, Mother."

Mother's gloved hands grabbed the radio and threw it to the floor. It split into as many pieces as Brother, but the song kept playing. Her gloves started ripping at her clothes; she buried her head beneath the faucet of the sink and began to shriek.

Panicked, Marlene ran outside to Father. But when she saw the pale figure coming down the path, her heart leaped. "Is it Brother?" she cried aloud. Hopeful, Father began to wave a hairy hand, and Mother burst from the house topless with soaked hair. Marlene's eyes flew to the ax Mother clutched in one yellow, gloved hand and the large Bible she held in the other. "I'll chop them all down," Mother screamed, her torn dress blowing off her body. "The tree and our visitor as well!"

But as Mother arrived beneath the tree, all its new berries rained down upon her and she halted in shock. The berries shook and spun on the ground, and as they cleared a hole around Mother, she and her ax dropped down right through the earth. Father and Marlene ran over just in time to see the white line of Mother's scalp disappear into a thick powder of ash, to see the ash harden back to soil, to see Mother's Bible fall to the ground. Its pages flew open and fluttered, then turned into white birds that sailed away. The berries lifted from the ground like a swarm of bees.

Their mass moved toward Brother as if to attack him; they landed everywhere upon his body and face and guitar until he was fully covered. Then, as if giving him juice to use as blood, the berries deflated and fell from his skin one by one, like dried scabs, flatter than onionskin. Marlene ran to him, breathless. "Look Father," she cried, "Brother is pink and new!"

But Father loomed quiet beneath the tree. He was bent over, running his fingers along the ground, searching for some trace of either wife below.

As a child, what fascinated me most about Grimms' tale of "The Juniper Tree" was that the father could not detect that he was eating his son; it seemed that such a bond would somehow be— dare I say—tasteable. Perhaps this is why I was so impressed years later when I discovered Angela Carter's "The Bloody Chamber," a story where the young woman's life is saved through her mother's devoted attention and sharp instinct. I find the primary modern relevance of Grimms' "The Juniper Tree" as having a great deal to do not only with the perils of mentally or emotionally absent parents but also with ignorance in general and the various ways that being uninformed can open a space for danger: Where are the things we buy coming from? Who is making them? How are they making them? What are our tax dollars funding? Which companies control our food? Hyperbolized as it may be, the original version of "The Juniper Tree" makes a great case for Knowing, for being vigilantly present and aware.

In my rewriting of the tale, I wanted to retain not only the father's ignorance but also the original source of hope for the murdered brother: his sister, Marlene. "Hansel and Gretel," a similar story of child abandonment, movingly describes a brother and sister who rely on each other for survival after their father's wife has convinced him to abandon the children. Most versions of "Hansel and Gretel" describe the pair returning to live with their father after their stepmother has died in the same way that "The Juniper Tree" ends, with the trinity of a father and his daughter and son. I am not a fan of giving these fathers a second chance, although I accept that the children, in their goodness, would grant it. So I wanted my retelling to emphasize that although the children accept their father, his emotional distance has rendered him unnecessary in their lives: the children's devotion to each other is what allows for their ultimate safety, and their happiness is not dependent upon him.

Although I altered the lyrics of the song, the plot structure of my story and the original tale of "The Juniper Tree" both rely on the transcendental and sorcerous power of music. The line "Bird, moon, fly away soon" is inspired by Bob Dylan's song "Jokerman," which is, like so much of Dylan's music, a fairy tale in itself.

—AN

FRANCINE PROSE

Hansel and Gretel

TACKED TO THE WALL OF THE BARN THAT SERVED AS LUCIA DE Medici's studio were 144 photographs of the artist having sex with her cat. Some of the pictures showed the couple sweetly nuzzling and snuggling; in some Lucia and her black cat, Hecuba, appeared to be kissing passionately, while still others tracked Hecuba's leathery rosebud of a mouth down Lucia's neck to her breasts until the cat disappeared off the edge of the frame and Lucia's handsome head tilted back . . .

This was twenty years ago, but I can still recall the weariness that came over me as I looked at Lucia's photos. I didn't want to have to look at them, particularly not with Lucia watching. I was twenty-one years old. I had been married for exactly ten days to a man named Nelson. It had seemed like a good idea to drop out of college and marry Nelson, and a good idea (it was Nelson's idea) to spend the weekend in Vermont at his friend Lucia's farm. At that time, I often did things because they seemed like a good idea, and I often did very important things for lack of a reason not to.

Lucia de Medici was an Italian countess, a direct descendant of the Florentine ruling family, and a famous conceptual artist. She was also, I'd just discovered, the mother of a woman named Marianna, the love of Nelson's life, an old girlfriend who, until that afternoon, I'd somehow assumed was dead.

Striped by the sunlight filtering in through the gaps between the barn boards, Lucia and I regarded each other: two zebras from different planets. She was a small woman of about fifty, witchy and despotic, her whole being ingeniously wired to telegraph beauty and discontent. And what was Lucia seeing, if she saw me at all? A girl with the power that came unearned from simply being young and with every reason not to act like such a quivering blob of Jell-O.

She said, "Up here in the wilderness I am working so in isolation, some days I want to ask the cows what do they think of my art."

"It's . . . really something," I said.

"Meaning what?" Lucia said. I was pleased she cared what I thought, but hadn't she just explained: when it came to Lucia's art, the cows' opinion counted? She frowned. "*Prego.* Watch out, please, not to back up into the fish tank."

I turned, glad for fish to focus on after Lucia and her cat. An enormous goldfish patrolled the tank with efficient shark-like menace, while several guppies hovered in place, rocking oddly from side to side. "I am scared of that big fish," Lucia confided. "He push his sister out of that water, I find her gasping dead on the floor."

"Are you sure it wasn't the cat?" I asked.

"Of that I am sure," she said.

I sensed that Lucia had tired of me, and I thought that now we would leave her studio. Instead, she switched on the stereo and voices filled the barn. Suddenly my eyes watered; it was my favorite piece of music, the trio from *Così fan tutte* that the women sing when their lovers are leaving and they beg the wind and water to be good to them on their way. Their sadness is a painful joke because their lovers aren't leaving but disguising themselves as Albanians and seducing the women as a test, a test the women eventually fail, a painful joke on them all.

I listened to the delicate, mournful tones, the liquid rippling of the strings, cradling and oceanic. There was grief in the women's voices, pitiful because it was wasted, pitiful and humiliating because we know it and they don't.

"It's beautiful," I said.

"So you say now," Lucia said. "This, too, is one of my projects. I think everything gets boring sooner or later, no? The most fantastic Mozart becomes unbearable after a while. So I have put this trio on a loop that plays over and over until the audience cannot stand it and runs screaming out of the room."

Lucia's project depressed me. I felt personally implicated, though I knew: there was no way that she could have had me and Nelson in mind. In the ten days since we'd been married, Nelson had changed so profoundly that he might as well have gone off and come back disguised as an Albanian. You hear women say: Before the marriage my husband never drank or hit me or looked at another woman. But with Nelson there was nothing so violent or dramatic. Before the wedding he'd liked me; afterwards he didn't.

He had been my lab instructor in a college biology course. He was a graduate student in anthropological botany, writing his thesis on the medicinal plants commonly used by the rain-forest tribes he'd lived among for two years. It was rumored that most of his research was on Amazonian hallucinogens, so it made sense that he was often strange, mumbly and withdrawn—but a perfectly capable and popular lab instructor. He was blond and handsome and tall; he looked lovely in a lab coat. He came from an old Boston family and played jazz clarinet.

Right from the start, our love had been tainted with cruelty. My lab partner was a squeamish boy, a Mormon from Idaho, who refused to cut into, or even touch, anything slimy. I enjoyed humiliating him. I feel I have to confess this, so as not to make myself sound nicer or more innocent than I was. From the other side of the lab table Nelson watched me grab the etherized frog from my partner's shaky hands and our eyes locked in the candle-like glow of the Bunsen burners. Later, Nelson told me that what had caught his attention was that my lab partner was in love with me and I had no idea. I believe that Nelson imagined this, but even so I was flattered—flattered and guilty and proud, all at once, for having made the Mormon boy suffer.

Nelson was moody, given to brooding silences in which I knew he was grieving over Marianna. He didn't like to talk about her or about his time in the jungle. I'd never met a man with a past he didn't like to discuss, or for that matter a man with any past at all. Nothing had ever happened to the boys I knew in college, but they were so touchingly eager to tell you all about it. I was young enough to be enthralled by what a man wouldn't say, and I believed the glitter dust of romance and adventure would sprinkle on me like confetti if I stood close enough to Nelson.

Marianna had gone with Nelson to the Amazon, but she was demonically restless, she'd left and flown back every few months. Nelson said he always *knew* the night before she arrived. She used to hitchhike in with the bush pilots who invited her along because she was so beautiful—beautiful and doomed.

"If those pilots knew her," Nelson said, "they wouldn't have taken her up in an elevator. Every time a plane took off, she was praying it would crash. She had a death wish instead of a conscience, she was born suicidal, it was a miracle she lasted long enough to meet me. Her suicide attempts got more and more serious until I couldn't do anything to . . ." His voice trailed off and he took a deep breath that ended the conversation.

I don't know why I assumed from this that Marianna was dead. It helped, I suppose, that I was never able to ask the obvious questions: when and where Marianna died, and how exactly she did it. Instead, I went through Nelson's possessions. I found his journal from the Amazon, and nowhere—nowhere—in it was one word about Marianna. Stupidly, this cheered me; it made her seem less important. I thought I'd learned something new about her, not something new about Nelson.

He told me I made him happy. He said we should get married. He said we shouldn't tell anyone, not even our parents or friends. I agreed, though it bothered me, not being able to boast that I'd been chosen by a handsome older man, the most popular lab instructor. In City Hall, we ducked behind a door when Nelson saw a judge who knew his father; and that was the last time he touched me, yanking me out of the judge's way.

For a week after the wedding he paced our hot cramped Cambridge apartment, staying up all night, listening to music: Bill Evans, Otis Redding, Bach—only the slow second movements. I couldn't ask him what was wrong, if he thought we'd made a mistake. It didn't take a genius to draw the logical conclusion when someone seemed so much happier before getting married—to you. I was not supposed to notice that I was sleeping alone in the bed that had changed unrecognizably, grown colder and less welcoming since when we used to spend all day there.

One morning Nelson brought me coffee. He said he knew he'd been rotten and he was mightily sorry. He said he'd eaten some things in the jungle that he shouldn't have eaten, and now he had these episodes, he was gone for days at a time.

"Episodes?" I said. "Gone?" Why hadn't he ever had one in all the months we'd lived together?

Nelson said we needed to get away: an impromptu honeymoon in Vermont. That morning we threw our knapsacks into his VW Bug. We drove with the windows open, my long hair streaming back, and for a time I felt like we'd left our problems in Cambridge, along with my toothbrush and contact-lens fluid and everything else I needed. I kept wondering about Nelson's episodes. Did he have them when he was driving?

Early in the afternoon we turned into Lucia's long, tree-lined driveway, which, Nelson said, always reminded him of the stately avenues of lime trees leading to Tolstoy's estate.

"How do you know Lucia?" I asked.

"Mutual friends," he said.

Lucia ran out of the rambling spotless white farmhouse and kissed Nelson three times, alternating cheeks, then grabbed his shoulders and gave him a smacky kiss on the mouth. She eyed me coolly, then smiled flirtatiously at Nelson, as if he'd come to amuse her by showing off his very large new pet.

"What's this?" she said.

"Polly. My new wife," he said. "Polly, this is Lucia."

"Your new *what*?" Lucia asked, only slightly dimming my pleasure in his finally having told someone. "Welcome." She embraced me swiftly, kissing my sweaty forehead.

"Guess what?" she asked Nelson. "Just yesterday I got a postcard from Marianna. She is in India at an ashram, fucking hundreds of people a day. She writes she is finding enlightenment through nonstop tantric fucking."

Nelson touched the top of his car. His hand came away black with grime, and for a moment the three of us stood there staring at his hand. "I'm sorry," Lucia said. "But if I can't tell you, who can I tell? All alone I am going crazy."

"Marianna?" I said.

"My daughter," said Lucia. "Nelson's friend."

I couldn't stop myself from saying, "But I thought she was dead!"

"My daughter is very much alive, thank you. Nelson, what have you been telling this child? Anyway, it is perfect you come. Marianna sends me a phone number where I can call her in India this weekend, we can go into town where is the nearest phone."

"There's no phone here?" I said.

"Of course not," Lucia said. "Now come to my studio and see my new piece. I call it *Così fan tutte*, starring me and my cat."

Nelson said he'd see it later, he needed to walk, he'd been in the car all morning; Lucia tried not to look disappointed at being left with me. Nelson headed off toward a horse barn and Lucia led me across a field on a path tunneled between high grasses. I didn't know what to say. I felt I should praise everything I could—nice house, nice land, nice view, nice sky—without sounding truly psychotic. Finally I said, "What beautiful blue flowers!" The field was completely blue.

"Bachelor's buttons." Lucia sighed. "In Europe they are weeds. For years I never grow them. Then I learn they keep their color forever, Etruscan tombs are full of them, Etruscans bury them with their dead to stay blue in the afterlife."

For an instant the waves of heat shimmering over the field resolved into a miniature phantom funeral procession, Etruscans in white, bearing scythes and armloads of blue flowers; and in that instant I wondered if Nelson's episodes might be catching.

Then we went to Lucia's studio and looked at the photos of her and her cat, and she played the Mozart that we listened to over and over. I could have listened forever and never gotten tired and been grateful for every minute by which it shortened the weekend. But after four or five times I said, "Okay! Enough!" It seemed required, like my admiring the field of blue flowers.

Lucia switched off the stereo and said, "I am right, am I not? Now go find Nelson, and I will do another five minutes of work."

But it was five hours before Lucia emerged from her studio and found us on the lawn, bouncing grumpily in our metal armchairs. We had been arguing about Lucia, furiously but without speaking, so perhaps only I was arguing and Nelson was thinking about something else.

Finally—after a walk through the scratchy fields matted with treacherous berry canes, and a long nap that Nelson took and I wasn't invited to join—I'd mentioned the photos of Lucia and her cat. I suppose I expected some conspiratorial expression of normal distaste.

Instead, Nelson said, "I love her. She's absolutely bananas." I recalled the lab partner I'd nearly dissected for Nelson's benefit, and now I needed Nelson, and he was taking Lucia's side. But there was no comparison. Lucia wasn't some squeamish kid who made you do all his experiments for him. Lucia was Nelson's very good friend and former mother-in-law.

I had spent Nelson's nap time in the airless library with its motley collection of books, tattered and reeking of mildew. These were mostly in Italian, but there were also some volumes in English on folklore, magic, and witchcraft. It was no accident that I was drawn to a volume of *Grimm's Fairy Tales*, nor was it accidental that I turned to "Hansel and Gretel" and read it for survival tips as much as for entertainment. This was the version in which the witch is fattening up the children and feeling the chicken bones Gretel holds out to deceive the witch into thinking the children are still thin.

After I mentioned the cat photos and Nelson defended Lucia, I thought how different the story would be if Hansel were in collusion with the witch. So when at last Lucia appeared from her studio and said, "You children must be starving! I will make chicken with mushrooms," I must have paled. Lucia said, "Nelson, look, your friend is half dead already from hunger."

"No," I said. "I'm not. I'm fine, I'm not hungry at all."

Inside the house we found Hecuba licking a stick of butter on the dining-room table. Lucia buried her face in the cat's black fur and, with many tiny kisses, set it on the floor. She opened a bottle of wine and put two glasses on the kitchen table.

"From the state liquor store," she said. "Imagine such a thing! I think it is so that they can keep track of how much and what we are drinking. Now you two sit down. In the kitchen, I am a wild woman. A maniac. Watch out."

With that, she began to fly about, chopping, stirring, frying. "After dinner, we will phone Marianna," she said. "When it is seven here, I think, is nine in India."

Lucia reached up and took down one of several large apothecary jars full of what appeared to be dried lizards. "My mushrooms," she said. "My beauties. I could kiss each one. This has been a fabulous year. Tonight with the chicken I will put in maybe eight kinds of mushrooms I find in the woods this spring."

"Do you . . . know a lot about mushrooms?" I couldn't hide the tremor in my voice.

Lucia laughed. "Nelson has eaten my mushrooms for years, and he is alive to tell the tale. Don't worry, every mushroom I pick, I send a spore print to Washington for analysis. No one knows you can do this, but it is the only safe way. I have a good friend, he finds mushrooms all his life, last spring, he eats something he has been picking for years, he barely has time to call Poison Control before he loses all sensation in his—"

"I've got an idea," said Nelson. "We feed Polly first and then watch her for twenty-four hours to see if she makes it."

It was the sort of intimate teasing that married couples indulge in, and I might have been encouraged that Nelson was choosing to do it if I hadn't suspected that they were capable of sitting at the table, discussing Nelson's research, Lucia's art, and occasionally checking to see if I had survived the dinner. It crossed my mind that if I did die from mushroom poisoning, I would be at least spared going into town and phoning Marianna.

It was reassuring that we all started to eat at once, food that was so delicious, who cared if it was lethal? Behind Nelson was a window and all through dinner I'd been distracted by dark shapes swooping near the glass.

"What kind of birds are those?" I finally asked.

"Bats, darling," said Lucia. "But my bats are very strange bats. Most bats squeak, you know, like mice. But my bats cry like kitties. Isn't that right, Hecuba, my love? Tell our friends what the little bats say."

Lucia couldn't remember if she had gas in her car, so we took Nelson's VW, with our sleeping bags still in back. I offered Lucia the front seat. I was shocked when she accepted. Since then I have met others who take you up on what's only politeness; it's like some spiteful playground trick you fall for again and again. I scrunched up in the backseat: a relief, in a way.

Lucia slid in front and said, "I don't believe in seat belts. To me, is a fascist plot."

Then the whole grim scenario played out before my eyes. Nelson having an episode, Lucia not wearing her seat belt. Was it more or less scary that this was wishful thinking on my part? I felt like a child in the backseat, sullen and resentful. I thought mean thoughts about Lucia and Nelson, that they had more in common than just Marianna. By temperament, they were spoilers, they enjoyed ruining your pleasure, making you hate what you might otherwise love: Mozart, bachelor's buttons, mushrooms, food . . . in Nelson's case, my whole life.

For just the briefest moment, I was sorry for Marianna. And suddenly I felt frightened, alone, at Lucia and Nelson's mercy, like a heroine in a thriller. Ingrid Bergman in *Notorious*, held prisoner in South America by Claude Rains and his evil mother. But Lucia and Nelson weren't conspiring to kill me. It was fine with them, enough for them, to make me acutely unhappy. Though it wasn't—ever—clear to me if they even knew, or cared.

It was a soft July evening. We drove along a river, past a waterfall. Light and water splashed on us, beading up on the car. A valley opened before us, rolling fields studded with barns, silos, farmhouses, kitchen gardens: quiet facades behind which families and household pets must have been eating dinner, inside, out of the golden light.

"Look!" I said unnecessarily. Nelson and Lucia were already staring at a blazing wedge of sun streaming down from one high cloud.

"People say I am imagining," said Lucia. "But I know for a fact I am psychic. Yesterday morning I woke up and I knew I would hear from Marianna though it was, oh Jesus Christ, early spring since I hear from her last. That time she turned on the gas in your apartment, Nelson, I was at a party in Manhattan, and at the very moment my daughter was trying to kill herself, I suddenly faint and throw up all over the dinner table."

There was a silence. Nelson said, "Two hundred years ago, my ancestors would have burned women like you and Marianna at the stake."

Now I was glad that I was in the back, I could burrow down in the lumpy seat and try not to be hurt that Nelson's forebears wouldn't have wasted their time burning a woman like me.

"So would the people in this town," Lucia said. "They would boil me in oil on Main Street if they knew anything about me."

Only then did I realize that we *were* in town. On the way to Lucia's, Nelson and I had passed many pretty country villages crowded with tourist couples shopping for maple products. But Lucia's town wasn't one of those. Two grim rows of water-stained Greek Revival houses led up to the business section, a dusty crossroads—gas station, post office, grocery, hardware—uninterested in a stranger's patronage or in any hospitable cosseting frills, like, for example, a sidewalk. I tried to imagine a life for myself and Nelson in such a town, in one of the nicer houses, near somewhere he could teach . . . but it didn't seem like a good idea, thinking too far into the future.

"If they knew . . ." Lucia said darkly. "About me and Hecuba . . . and my work. It is very anarchist, very un-Puritan and subversive. But to them I am just a crazy Italian, her house always needs fixing, her checks clear at the bank. Meanwhile, they tell me the gossip, the carpenters and electricians and plumbers. This town is a pit of snakes."

What people was she talking about? There was no one in this town, no children wheeling on their bikes as their parents watered the shaggy lawns. It was as if a bomb had dropped while we were out at Lucia's, and we hadn't known about it, and we were the only ones left.

"Turn here," Lucia instructed Nelson. Nelson pulled up to the grocery, a one-story brick-red-cinder-block structure streaked with patches of oily black. Against the wall was a phone booth and a rickety picnic bench with an uninterrupted view of the gas pump.

"Oh God! Oh God! Oh God!" cried Lucia.

"What is it?" Nelson said, and from the backseat I echoed lamely, "What's wrong?"

"I forgot my money. We must go home. I will miss Marianna!"

"I have money," said Nelson. "Can you get change in the store?"

"I can try." Lucia rolled her head and flared her nostrils, breathing harshly. I felt as if I were in the car with a small pony starting to panic.

"Two women work here, sisters, one nice, one bitch, you never know who you are getting . . ."

Nelson handed her a bill. "It's a ten," he said.

"I know that," snapped Lucia, groping for the door handle.

Nelson leaned across her. Presumably he meant to open the door, but he was restraining her, too. He had to twist around slightly. I was shocked by the look on his face. I was afraid he was having an episode. Then something in his expression reminded me of my lab partner in the split second he had to decide whether to relinquish the frog or fetal pig I was grabbing out of his hands. Briefly I wondered if Nelson had been right about the Mormon boy's secret passion for me. Because suddenly I recognized the expression of a man who has just realized that he will—that he is helpless not to—humiliate himself for love. And that was *my* psychic moment: I knew what was going to happen. I knew what Nelson was going to say long before he was able to make himself sound even slightly casual.

Nelson said, "Say hello to Marianna. Tell her I'm up here visiting with my new wife."

"Yes, of course," Lucia said and jumped out of the car.

The summer evening was warm and pretty, but Nelson and I stayed in the car. I didn't move up front. We stared at the storefront, on which there was nothing to see, not even a beer or cigarette ad or a sign announcing a special. Eventually Lucia appeared, holding a small paper bag. She gave us the V-sign and dipped her hand into the bag. The last rays of dusky evening light shone on the silver quarters raining back into the sack. I thought of how "Hansel and Gretel" ends with a shower of pearls and jewels that the children steal from the witch and play with when they get home.

As if we were at a drive-in movie, we watched Lucia kneel and gather some coins she'd dropped, then stuff them in the phone, and dial and listen and slam the coin return and begin all over again . . .

"You know, it's the strangest thing," I said. "I thought Marianna was dead."

"Dead?" said Nelson. "Right on the edge, and the worst part is, she could live on that edge till she's ninety. What else do you think she's doing, fucking an entire ashram in Bombay? Just *being* in Bombay. She got sick as a dog every time she came down to see me in the jungle. Once she found this empty patch of jungle and was squatting there puking and shitting and she looked up and saw a viper coiled around a branch just over her head."

In theory Nelson was talking to me, but he was looking at Lucia. And now it seemed, unbelievably, Lucia had placed her call. She was talking rapidly, gesticulating . . . She turned her back to us and leaned into the wall and bent her head as she listened and shouted . . .

At last Lucia got back in the car. "Okay, we go home now," she said.

This silence lasted the longest. "What did she say?" Nelson asked.

"Nothing," replied Lucia. "I couldn't reach her. That was someone at the ashram, a man who speaks Italian. Yes, they know her very well there. She has just left for the Himalayas. She will stay in the mountains until fall . . ."

We drove back to Lucia's, and when we got out of the car, Lucia said, "I am tired now. You can sleep in my studio. There is a little mattress with sheets and also towels. The first light switch inside the door."

Nelson bent to kiss Lucia good night. Lucia turned away.

A full moon was shining on the fields. We didn't stop to admire it. I tried a timid werewolf howl, but Nelson didn't laugh. He was walking ahead of me; he knew the way to the barn, which had cooled off considerably since the afternoon.

The switch lit an old-fashioned bedside lamp on a table near a mattress that Lucia had made up with pillows, clean white sheets, and a thin red quilt. She must have done it sometime before she left the studio to cook dinner, just when I was assuming she'd forgotten us completely.

The lamp threw out a circle of light, thankfully too modest to include the photos of the artist and her cat, or the killer fish in his tank. I didn't want to see those pictures now, I didn't want to feel jealous because Lucia's passion for her cat was deeper and more tender than what Nelson felt for me.

I shucked off my clothes and slid under the quilt. Nelson waited a moment. Then he took off his jeans and got into bed in his T-shirt and shorts. He rolled over so his back was to me.

"Good night, Polly," he said.

"Good night," I said.

"I love you," he said.

"I love you too," I said.

I think he may have fallen asleep. I remember that he slept. I turned off the night-light; bars of moonlight took its place. I lay in the dark and listened to the cat, mewing like a newborn, a cry that seemed to get louder when I realized it might be a bat.

I wished I could have found the switch on Lucia's stereo that activated the endless loop of the Mozart trio. It didn't matter how often I'd heard it, I couldn't remember it now when I most needed its soothing distractions. I wished I could recall exactly how it sounded, the voices of the women with their misdirected grief, each mourning because she imagines her lover is facing the dangers of travel, when her misfortune is beyond what she can imagine: the cruelty of a lover who would want to test her like that.

Twenty years later I went with my second husband and our children to visit friends in Vermont. Over dinner our friend reminisced about the past, the years when the woods in every direction were teeming with crazy artists. He mentioned people we all knew, who had lived there for a while . . .

My attention had drifted, lulled by the pleasures of friends, food, and wine, the distant shouts of children on the lawn, the sweet light of that summer evening. Then once more I had a moment when I knew what was going to happen, that my friend was going to mention an

Italian woman artist who had lived just through the forest, essentially next door . . .

I had forgotten, I never exactly knew, where precisely Lucia lived. And I wasn't thinking about that long-ago night at her house until the moment—that is, the instant before—my friend mentioned Lucia de Medici's name.

I said, "I used to know her. I spent a weekend at her farm." And everybody stared at me, because my voice shook so.

There was a second coincidence, a shadow of the first. For dinner that night we were having chicken with wild mushrooms. For all I knew, our hostess had picked the mushrooms in the woods, but when I asked her where the mushrooms came from and she heard my concern, she made a point of saying how much they cost, dried, in the store, because she knew that the fact of a store would reassure someone like me. To my friends, my having spent a weekend with their former neighbor was no more remarkable than having chicken with mushrooms twice in twenty years.

And really, it wasn't surprising for adults to know someone in common; by then the threads of our lives had stretched long enough to have converged at various places. But what shocked me was that my friends had known someone who seemed to belong to a whole other existence. I felt as if I'd been reincarnated and just now recognized the entire cast from my previous life: shuffled, playing brand-new parts, living in different houses.

I said, "Whatever happened to her? To Lucia?"

My friend said, "She went back to Italy. I think I heard something like that."

"Did you ever meet her daughter?" I said.

"Her daughter?" My friend considered. "Oh, yes, she had a crazy daughter. Lucia was always worrying. She was always in some nutty place, Machu Picchu or Kathmandu . . ."

"Was the daughter beautiful?" I said.

"Beautiful?" my friend repeated. "Sort of pretty, I guess. Very nervous, overbred . . . like a big trembly Afghan hound."

Then my friend mentioned another friend, a mutual friend, a friend so close our families often spent holidays together. And it seemed that this friend had also been a neighbor of Lucia's. He had also lived on a farm, but on the other side, and had lived there that same summer, perhaps that very same weekend. Did I know that? our host asked.

But how could I have known that? How could I have understood that two messengers from my future were, even as I lay awake in that barn, just beyond the hedge? I wondered how often the future waits on the other side of the wall, knocking very quietly, too politely for us to hear, and I was filled with longing to reach back into my life and inform that unhappy girl: all around her was physical evidence proving her sorrows would end. I wanted to tell her that she would be saved, but not by an act of will: clever Gretel pretending she couldn't tell if the oven was hot and tricking the witch into showing her and shoving the witch in the oven. What would rescue her was time itself and, above all, its inexorability, the utter impossibility of anything ever staying the same.

But I—that is, the girl I was—couldn't have possibly heard. She was too busy listening for the mewing of cats, or bats. To have even tried to tell her would be like rising up out of the audience just when those angelic voices are praying for gentle winds, a calm ocean, like interrupting the opera to comfort or warn the singers: Don't worry, there is no journey, no one is going away, there is nothing to fear but your own true love, disguised as an Albanian.

I wrote "Hansel and Gretel" backward, so to speak. That is, the "true" part of the story was the dinner with friends, at which our host mentioned an artist who used to live in the forest bordering his land, and I had what I suppose could be called a recovered memory of a miserable weekend I'd spent at the woman's house twenty years before. The artist in real life was nothing like the one in the story,

nor was I like my fictional heroine, nor was my life like hers. But "Hansel and Gretel" was, and is, "Hansel and Gretel." That is, the minute I thought about the witch in the forest, and the hapless couple, the nature of the configuration occurred to me, and I knew which fairy tale I was dealing with—if not why. All I had to do was transpose the brother and sister into a recently and already unhappily married couple. I had been listening to the Mozart trio nonstop, and so it naturally became the soundtrack played in the witch's lair. And the next thing I knew, as so often happens, Albanians popped into the story.

—FP

KEVIN BROCKMEIER

A Day in the Life
of Half of Rumpelstiltskin

7:45 A.M. HE SHOWERS AND DRESSES.

Half of Rumpelstiltskin awakens from a dream in which his body is a filament of straw, coiled and twined about itself so as to mimic the presence of flesh and entrails, of hands and ribs and muscles and a knotty, throbbing heart. In his dream, Half of Rumpelstiltskin is seated at a spinning wheel, his foot pumping furiously at the treadle, his body winding into gold around the spindle. He unravels top down— from the crown of his head to the unclipped edge of his big toenail— loosing a fog of dust and a moist, vegetal drizzle. When the last of him whisks from the treadle and into the air, he is gold, through and through. He lies there perfect, glinting, and altogether gone. Half of Rumpelstiltskin is the whole of the picture and nowhere in it. He is beautiful, and remunerative, and he isn't even there to see it. Half of Rumpelstiltskin has spun himself empty. There is nothing of him left.

When Half of Rumpelstiltskin awakens, there is nothing of him right. He is like a pentagram folded across its center or a tree split by lightning. He is like the left half of a slumberous mannequin, yawning and shuddering, rising from within the netlike architecture of his dreams. He is like that *exactly*. Half of Rumpelstiltskin sleeps in a

59

child's trundle bed. He turns down his linens and his thick, abrasive woolen blanket and hops to the bathroom.

Half of Rumpelstiltskin moves from point to point—bed to bathroom, *a* to *b*—in one of two ways. Either he hops on one foot, his left, or he arches his body to walk from toe to palm and palm to toe. When he hops, Half of Rumpelstiltskin lands on the flat of his foot, leaning backward to counter his momentum, which for many years pitched him straight to the floor. When he walks, Half of Rumpelstiltskin looks as might a banana with feet at both ends. Through the years, he has learned to plod and pace and shuffle, to shamble and saunter and stride. Half of Rumpelstiltskin doesn't own a car, and there's never been anyone to carry him.

In the shower, Half of Rumpelstiltskin scours himself with a bar of marbled green soap, a washcloth, and—for the skin at his extremities, as stubborn and scabrous as bark—a horsehair scrub brush. He lathers. He rinses. He dries himself with a plush cotton towel, sousing the water from his pancreas and his ligaments and the spongy marrow in the cavity of his sternum. Half of Rumpelstiltskin is the only man he knows whose forearm is a hard-to-reach place.

Outside his window, the sky is a startled blue, from horizon to horizon interrupted only by a dissipating jet trail and a bespotment of soaring birds. The jet trail is of uniform thickness all along its length, and try as he might, Half of Rumpelstiltskin can spot a jet at neither end. He runs his forefinger along the window sash, then flattens his palm against the pane. Both are warm and dry. Although it's only the beginning of March, Half of Rumpelstiltskin decides to dress lightly—a skullcap and a tawny brown slacks leg, a button-up shirt and a red canvas sneaker.

Before leaving for work, Half of Rumpelstiltskin brews a pot of coffee. He drinks it with a lump of sugar and a dash of half-and-half. The coffee bores through him like a colony of chittering termites—gnawing down the trunk of him, devouring the wood of his dreams. As he drinks, Half of Rumpelstiltskin watches a children's variety show on public television. The monster puppets are his favorite, with their blue fur, their ravenous appetites, and their whirling eyes. The children laugh at the monsters' jokes and ask them about the alphabet, and the monsters hug the children with their two pendant arms.

9:05 A.M. He goes to work.

Half of Rumpelstiltskin works three hours every morning, until noon, standing in for missing or vandalized mannequins at a department store in a nearby strip mall. Until recently, he worked in the warehouse, processing orders, cataloging merchandise, and inspecting enormous cardboard boxes with rusted staples the size of his pinkie finger. Lately, however, a spate of mannequin thefts—the result, police suspect, of a gang initiation ritual—has left local shopping centers dispossessed of display models, and Half of Rumpelstiltskin has been transferred in to fill the void. He considers this ironic.

—You're five minutes late, his boss tells him when he arrives. Don't let it happen again.

Half of Rumpelstiltskin's boss smells of cigar smoke and seafood.

—And from now on, I expect to see you clean-shaven when you come in, he says gruffly. Nobody likes a hairy mannequin. Now get changed and get to work.

Half of Rumpelstiltskin nods in reply. Cod, he thinks.

Half of Rumpelstiltskin soon emerges from wardrobe wearing a junior-size vinyl jumpsuit with a zippered front and a designer label. Around his head is swathed a stocking cap several sizes too large for him. It rests heavy on his eyebrow and plunges to the small of his back in a series of broad, rambling folds. His jumpsuit, on its right side, is as flaccid as the inner tube of a flat tire. Half of Rumpelstiltskin takes his place between two cold, trendy mannequins—one slate gray with both arms halved at the elbow, its head severed as if by a huntsman's ax from right ear to left jawbone, and the other a metal figure composed of flat geometric shapes with a polished black sheen, jointed together with transparent rods to resemble the human form. Half of

Rumpelstiltskin feels himself a true and vital part of the society of mannequins. With them, he fits right in.

An adolescent with close-cropped hair, a pierced eyebrow, and a scar extending like a smile from the corner of his lip to the prominence of his cheek approaches Half of Rumpelstiltskin near the end of his shift. Half of Rumpelstiltskin stands as still as a tree in the hope that the boy will walk past, but instead he circles and draws closer, like a dog bound to him by chain. Upon reaching the platform where Half of Rumpelstiltskin stands, the boy threads his arm through the jumpsuit's empty leg and takes hold of Half of Rumpelstiltskin's spleen. He appears surprised. He removes his hand—spleenless—and sniffs it. Shrugging, he reaches again for the jumpsuit's empty cuff.

I wouldn't do that if I were you, says Half of Rumpelstiltskin, and the boy backs calmly away. He stops, crooks his neck, and looks quizzically into Half of Rumpelstiltskin's eye. Then he brushes his fingers along the underside of his jaw and flicks them past the nub of his chin. His eyes glare scornfully at Half of Rumpelstiltskin. He strides confidently away, as if nothing at all has happened. Half of Rumpelstiltskin watches him exit the building through a pair of sliding glass doors. His boss steps out from behind a carousel hung with heavy flannel shirts.

—What was that all about? he asks.

Nothing, responds Half of Rumpelstiltskin.

—No fraternization with the customers. You should know better than that.

Okay, says Half of Rumpelstiltskin.

His boss shakes his head disapprovingly and, turning to leave, mutters under his breath.

—Fool, he whispers. Meathead. Hayseed. Half-wit.

Half of Rumpelstiltskin checks his wristwatch. It's quitting time.

12:15 P.M. He eats lunch in the park.

Beside the wooden bench on which he sits is a tree stump, its hollow banked with wood pulp and a few faded soda cans. Half of Rumpelstiltskin can't help but wonder what has become of the tree itself. A year ago it rose within the park, housing the sky, a thousand tatters of blue, within its overspread branches. Now it is gone, and this bench is here in its place. Possibly the bench itself was once a part of the tree—hewn, perhaps, from its thickset trunk—but if so, what had become of the rest? The only certainty is that it fell, releasing from its branches a host of harried birds and vagrant squirrels, galaxies and planets and the sure and vaulting sky. With so much restless weight between its leaves, it could just as well have burst like a balloon. *When you're trying to hold the sky inside you*, thinks Half of Rumpelstiltskin, *something is bound to fail. The sky is inevitable. The sky is a foregone conclusion.* Overhead, the sun pulses behind swells of heat, wobbling like an egg yolk. The jet trail has dispersed, blown ragged by the winds of early March.

Half of Rumpelstiltskin watches as, in the distance, a kite mounts its way into the air. Beneath it, a man stands in a meadow of dry yellow grass, unspooling a length of string. He tugs at the kite and the kite tugs back, yanking the man in fits and starts through the field and toward a playground. Half of Rumpelstiltskin sees children loosed from the plate of a restless, wheeling merry-go-round, holding to its metal bars with both arms, their bodies like streamers in the air. He sees swings arcing up and down and supine parents reading newspapers and smoking cigarettes. Beside the playground, a sandwich stand sprouts from the ground like a toadstool. Half of Rumpelstiltskin's stomach churns at the sight of it, rumbling like sneakers caught in a spin cycle. He places his hand against its interior lining, finds it dry and clean and webbed like ceiling insulation. Half of Rumpelstiltskin is hungry.

At the sandwich stand, he asks for peanut butter and jelly on wheat. Eating and hopping, he unwittingly lights on an anthill. It goes scattering ahead of him in a fine particulate brume. Half of Rumpelstiltskin lowers himself to the ground and sits with his haunch on his heel. He watches as ants swarm from the razed hill: they broadcast themselves in all directions, like bursting fireworks or ink on water. Within a matter of minutes, the tiny, volatile creatures have built a protective ring of dirt around the bore above their home. Half of Rumpelstiltskin finds the sight of creatures working as a collective a strange and unfamiliar one. It's spooky and—for some reason—a little bit sad. Half of Rumpelstiltskin has trouble enough comprehending the nature of individuality without throwing intersubjectivity into the pot. Although he has unmade anthills on many, many occasions, Half of Rumpelstiltskin has never stayed to watch the ants rebuild. As a gesture of goodwill, he leaves them that portion of his sandwich he has not yet swallowed. If they can't eat it, he thinks, perhaps they can build with it.

An abundance of drugstores lines the walk between the park and Half of Rumpelstiltskin's home, and he stops at one along the way. There he purchases a chocolate bar, a bottle of apple-green mouthwash, and a newspaper from the metroplex across the river, the headlines of which affirm what he has long held to be true—that the world tumbles its way through political conventions, economic treaties, televised sporting events, and invasive military tactics in starving third-world nations with utter indifference to the inglorious fact of his half-existence. The stock market columns report that gold is down—straw way, way down.

Half of Rumpelstiltskin has poor depth perception. Hopping home, he trips over a concrete parking block.

1:25 P.M. He receives a Mad Libs letter from his other Half.

3 March _____
(year)

Half of Rumpelstiltskin:

Not much new here in _____.
(place where you are not)

The _____ Queen has decided once again to levy a whole
     (term of derision)

new batch of taxes—and guess who the _____
                                   (ironic adjective)

victims are this time around: homunculi. That's right. Miss

_____ has decided that the time is ripe to tax
(what's her name)

_____, _____, _____, and
(things)   *(other things)*

homunculi. And who's the only homunculus on this whole _____
                                                    (color)

_____? Me! Rumpel- _____-
(land mass)   *(crude participial adjective)*

stiltskin . . . Sorry. Just need to vent some of my _____ and
                                              (bodily organ)

frustration. I should learn to control my temper—if there's a moral to this

whole affair, that must be it—but you know how it gets.

_____, at least we're not as bad as
(tame interjection)

_____.

(fictional character renowned for losing his or her temper to no good end)

Life on the personal front is no _____
                                (word that rhymes with letter)

than on the political. I'm still out of work—the _____
                                      (occupation)

position fell through—and I'm on the outs with

_____.

(person you and I know who used to keep me from being lonely sometimes)

Sometimes I wonder when and how it all turned so

_____.

(adjective expressing disconsolation)

When you get the chance, _____ your half of this
                                   (direction)

_____ to me, so I can find out what I've
   (word that rhymes with better*)*

written. When the words won't come to me, I figure they must be

yours. I miss you and _____ _____
                          (subject)   *(verb)*

_____ _____ _____.
  (object)   *(sad word)*   *(sad, sad, sad, sad word)*

      All Right:
      Half of Rumpelstiltskin

2:30 P.M. He delivers a speech to a local women's auxiliary organization.

Half of Rumpelstiltskin stands at a lectern fashioned of fluted, burnished cherrywood and speaks on "The Birthrights of First-Born Children," a topic in which he claims no small degree of expertise. Half of Rumpelstiltskin has had his fair share of ill-favored dealings with first-born children, particularly those of millers' daughters. As he speaks, the cheery, preoccupied faces before him exchange knowing glances and subtle pointed smiles. Half of Rumpelstiltskin, when asked to address this meeting, was not informed as to whether the auxiliary was *for* or *against* first-born children and their concomitant birthrights—and so he has taken what he considers to be a nonpartisan slant on the topic. Listening to the raspy coughs of the women in the audience and regarding their nodding, oblate heads, he can't decide whether he is offending or boring them. Half of Rumpelstiltskin concludes his speech to a smattering of polite applause that sounds like the last few popping kernels in a bag of prebuttered popcorn. When he steps out from behind the lectern and joins the women in the audience for a question-and-answer session, nobody has a thing to say about first-born children, birthrights, red pottage, or the nation of Israel. Instead, as he might have suspected, it's all *straw-to-gold* this and *fairy tale* that.

—What, the women ask, happened to your other half?

I split myself in two, says Half of Rumpelstiltskin, *when the Queen guessed my name. However*, he says, *that's a story that demands a discussion of first-born children. So then—*

—But, the women ask, *how* did you split yourself in two?

In a fit of anger, says Half of Rumpelstiltskin. *When the Queen guessed my name, I stamped explosively, burying my right leg to the waist beneath the floorboards. In trying to unearth myself, I took hold of my left foot, wrenching it so hard that I split down the center. My other half lives overseas. I myself emigrated.*

—I thought, say the women, that upon stamping the ground you fell to the center of the earth. Or that you merely bruised your heel and wandered off in a fit of malaise.

No, says Half of Rumpelstiltskin, *those are just myths.*

—Is it true, ask the women, that you wish to huff and puff and blow our houses down?

No, says Half of Rumpelstiltskin. *You're thinking of the Big Bad Wolf.*

—Is it true what we hear about you and the girl with the grand-mother?

No. That, too, is the Big Bad Wolf.

—Is it true that you'd like to cook our children in your large, cast-iron stewpot?

Half of Rumpelstiltskin sighs. *No*, he says, *I am in fact a strict vegetarian.*

—Do you believe in the interdependence of name and identity? ask the women.

Yes, I do.

—Why don't you change your name?

Because I'm still Rumpelstiltskin, says Half of Rumpelstiltskin. *I'm just not all of him.*

—You're still Rumpelstiltskin? Even after having lived as Half, and only half, of Rumpelstiltskin for oh-so-many years?

Yes.

—Is there a moral to all of this?

No. Half of Rumpelstiltskin checks his watch. *No, there isn't. I have time for one more question.*

—If you were granted only one wish, ask the women, what would you wish for?

Half of Rumpelstiltskin doesn't miss a beat. *Bilateral symmetry,* he says.

4:10 P.M. He shops for dinner at the grocery store.

Half of Rumpelstiltskin is standing in line at the checkout counter of a supermarket, reading the cover of a tabloid newspaper upon which is pictured a pair of Siamese twins and an infant the size of a walnut—who is actually curled, in the cover photograph, next to a walnut. The infant looks like the protean, half-formed bird Half of Rumpelstiltskin once saw when he split open a nested egg, and through his gelate, translucent skin is visible the kernel of a heart. The caption above the child claims that he was born without a brain. Half of Rumpelstiltskin, inching forward in line, finds himself thinking about the responsibilities delegated to either hemisphere of the brain. If, as they say, the right half of the brain controls the left half of the body—and the left half the right—Half of Rumpelstiltskin moves and talks, yawns and dances, under the edicts of the other Half of Rumpelstiltskin's portion of Rumpelstiltskin's brain. Is it possible, Half of Rumpelstiltskin wonders, that he is somewhere across the ocean, sitting in front of a fireplace or reading a magazine, operating under the delusion that he is standing here in the supermarket, buying ingredients for his evening's meal and looking at the tabloids? That through half a world's measure of Rumpelstiltskin-lessness, he sends directives, receives impressions, down a sequence of nodes and fibers concealed within the dense, Gordian anatomy of the earth—and his other half the same? That he is never where he thinks he is or heading where he hopes to be?

Half of Rumpelstiltskin sometimes feels absolutely and undeniably alienated from everyone and everything around him.

Asleep in the shopping cart in front of him, her head resting upon the pocked rind of a firm green cantaloupe, a baby lies beside a bag of crinkle-cut potato wedges. She is breathing softly through her nose, and her dark, wavy hair frames the pudge of her face. As the Halves of Rumpelstiltskin told the Queen when she offered the treasures of the kingdom in exchange for her first-born child, something living is more important to him than all the treasures in the world. The baby gurgles, her legs poking through the bars of the shopping cart, and pulls to her stomach a round of Gouda cheese the size of her hand. He would never have imagined, not for a heartbeat, that children were so easily come by. Had he known you could buy them at the supermarket, his life might not have become the mess it is today.

He watches as the woman in front of him purchases her groceries— potatoes and cheese; leafy vegetables and globose, pulpous fruits; several green plastic bottles of soda; a wedge of ham garnished with pineapples; and the baby—and wheels them to the parking lot. As the woman at the register of the checkout lane scans his groceries above a brilliant red scattering of light, Half of Rumpelstiltskin leafs through his wallet looking for a form of photo identification and a major credit card. On his license, he is pictured before a screen of powder blue. His head is tilted by a slim margin to the left, and looking closely he can just begin to see the white edge of his upper incisor and a sliver of cortical sponge. Half of Rumpelstiltskin was pleased to find that he was not grinning in his license photo. People who grin, he has always thought, look squirrelly and eccentric, sometimes barking mad, and, on occasion, dangerous and inconsonant—as if they're trying to hide something from the world, something virulent and bitter on the surface of their tongues. People whose teeth show in license photos are most often just the eccentric sort—but never completely harmless.

Half of Rumpelstiltskin had half a mind to return his own when he found that he could spot the edge of his upper incisor.

Half of Rumpelstiltskin pays the checkout attendant. He grasps his grocery sacks by their cutting plastic grips, hefts them over his shoulder, and hops through a set of yawning, automatic doors.

5:50 P.M. He cooks supper and dances a jig.

In his kitchen sits an outsize black cauldron, like a bubble blown by the mouth of the scullery floor. It is a few heads taller than Half of Rumpelstiltskin himself, and to see over its lip he must climb to the top tread of a stepladder propped against its side. From the brim of the cauldron spumes a thick, pallid yeast, and across its pitchy interior are layers of burned and crusted food. Half of Rumpelstiltskin stands at the cutting board with a finely edged knife, dicing onions, potatoes, and peppers into small, palmate segments. He scrapes these into a tin basin, adds spices and a queer lumpish mass that he pulls from his freezer, and hops up the stepladder to dump them into the cauldron. The vegetables, pitched into the stew, churn beneath its surface, interrupting the reddish-brown paste that thickens there into a skin.

Half of Rumpelstiltskin climbs to the kitchen floor. He washes his hand in the sink, then dries it on his slacks. Half of Rumpelstiltskin is pleased by the prospect of supper. He considers himself a true gourmand.

As is his custom prior to eating, Half of Rumpelstiltskin crooks himself from toe to palm and reels around his cauldron. Sometimes he holds his ankle in his hand and hoops his way through the kitchen; sometimes he cambers at the waist, bucking from head to toe like a seesaw. Half of Rumpelstiltskin dances, and hungers, and sings his dancing and hungering song—his voice ululating like that of a hound crying for its master:

> *Dancing dances, brewing feasts,*
> *Won't restore me in the least.*

Brewing feasts and singing songs,
Nights are slow and days are long.
Lamentation! Drudgery!
Half of Rumpelstiltskin's me.

10:35 P.M. He falls asleep watching *The Dating Game.*

Half of Rumpelstiltskin grows listless after heavy meals. In the bathroom, he rasps his mossy teeth with a fibrillar plastic brush until they feel smooth against his tongue. He gargles with his apple-green mouthwash, tilting his head there-side down so as not to dribble into the cavity of his body. Half of Rumpelstiltskin urinates, watching as a pale yellow fluid courses the length of his urethra into the toilet. Afterward, he leaves the seat up.

On his way to the couch, Half of Rumpelstiltskin presses his palm against the pane of his window. It's growing chilly outside. He retrieves an eiderdown quilt from the linen closet and settles in beneath it.

A man with brown hair—hair that rises above his forehead like a wave collapsing toward his crown—grins on the television. He speaks in sunny, urgent tones to a woman who looks to be about a half-bubble off-level. The woman is charged with the task of choosing a date from among three dapper men who introduce themselves as if there's something inside them gone empty without her. She asks the men a question, and they answer to a swell of applause from the studio audience. Name one word that describes the sky, says the woman. It's big, says the one man. It's wide, says another. It's inevitable, says the third. Half of Rumpelstiltskin is rooting for the third.

The people on the television seem lost. Somewhere, at some point, they forgot who they were or how to be happy. They found themselves wandering around behind the haze of their fear and desire. They stumbled into his television. The lucky ones will walk off with each other, out of his television and onto some beach beneath a soft and falling sun, heady with the confidence that they've found somebody— another voice, a pair of arms—to be happy with. Half of Rumpelstiltskin wishes them the best, but he knows something they don't—which perhaps they never will—something that may not even be true for them. He knows that it happens in this world that you can change in such a way as to never again be complete, that you can lose parts of who you once were—and sometimes you'll get better, but sometimes you'll never be anything more than fractional: than who you once were, a few parts hollow. He knows that sometimes what's missing isn't somebody else.

Half of Rumpelstiltskin sinks into sleep like a leaf subsiding to the floor of the moon. When next he opens his eye, the television will whisper behind a face of lambent snow.

The truth of it is that I wanted to write a Mad Libs story, one that put the old fill-in-the-blank template I remembered so fondly from my childhood to a use that was just as peculiar, perhaps, but more emotionally complicated. At the time, I was reading the Iona and Peter Opie edition of The Classic Fairy Tales, *and I became intrigued by one of the variant endings of the Rumpelstiltskin story, when, after his name is discovered, he stamps his foot so hard that he wrenches himself in two.*

Half a person, I thought. Half a person and therefore half a letter.

Though Rumpelstiltskin is presented as something of a villain in the original story, what he wants more than anything is a child, and this was a desire that appealed to me.

Also there was the pleasure I believed I would take in describing a man who existed without the right half of his body.

And finally I was interested in a philosophical puzzle I had heard: You're crossing the ocean on a wooden ship. One of the boards rots, so you replace it with another that you've stored in your hold. Is it still the same ship? Most people would agree that it is. But what if, bit by bit, as you make your journey, your ship sustains more and more damage, so that by the time you reach your destination, you have substituted each piece with its counterpart, and not a single bit of it remains unreplaced? Now is it the same ship? Why or why not? How much of a thing is its pattern and how much its physical material? I was fascinated by the question of whether and for how long you could remain the same person after casting off part of your body—or, for that matter, after casting off part of your history, part of your personality, part of your life.

Thus was born "A Day in the Life of Half of Rumpelstiltskin." It's the earliest of my stories to have seen publication, written when I was twenty-two and a senior in college.

—KB

With Hair of Hand-Spun Gold

I'M BACK.

I am back and you knew I would be. You knew it. Didn't you? Yes, you did, don't give me that look, you knew exactly what was going to—doesn't matter. I'm here now so we should get started, get this thing all started and going. Go ahead, you can throw up, it's not going to stop me, make me feel bad, I promise you. It's not. You're getting exactly what you deserve here, you are, you deserve it and that's what is going to happen. Fate, or Karma or, or whatever they call it. Kismet? I know that was a play or something, a musical, but I think that word means the same sort of thing. Something happening that was supposed to happen and then it does. It comes true. Wham! Just like that. "Instant Karma," isn't that what Lennon called it? Not the dictator, but the Beatles guy. In his song. Right? He said "it's gonna get you" and that is just so goddamn true. It reaches out—figures out where you are, takes its time to find you—and bam! Before you can even move or anything, it's got you by the throat and you are fucked. It's true, my dear. You are motherfucked. And so that's you, today, at this very minute. Or second, or whatever you wanna call it. You are about to be motherfucked. By me.

I can see by the look on your face you're surprised, so don't pretend. Do not pretend that you were ready for this one because you weren't. You were not. I came out of the blue, as they like to say, out of the darkness like some avenging angel—I'm not sure that's the exact right analogy but you get what I mean—I appeared and it has thrown you for a loop. A big ol' loop and you don't know what to do, what to say even, sitting there on a park bench with your mouth hanging open and staring at me. Wow. I really caught you off guard, didn't I? You knew this could happen but you still were not ready for it. Not today. Well, I can't say that it doesn't make me happy because it does. It makes me smile right down into my soul and that's the truth so you might as well know it. I am happy to see you sweat. Really. Honestly I am. I mean, who knew? How would I ever know that it'd be this easy to make that happen, to bring your little world to a halt, for it to come crashing down around your ears? How could I be privy to a thing like that? You can't, that's the answer. You wouldn't until you just go ahead and do it and now I have and I'm aware, by looking at your face I'm aware of the magnitude of what's going on right now, at this moment, as we sit here quietly in the middle of this park and your kid is playing on the swings and life bounces merrily along. If you could scream or draw a gun or kill me even, stab me and cover me with dirt right here in those bushes behind us, I think you would. I know it, actually. I know that you would. And, to be fair, I might do the same damn thing if I was you, shoe on the other foot or whatever people say to mean what I'm talking about. I might also want to do you harm. Well, I do, actually, want that, me, I'm saying, shoe on my own foot and staring at you right now. I do want to bring a kind of harm to your life. And I'm about to. Yes, I am. Yes indeed.

Did you ever think, I mean, years ago, when you first saw me— picked me out of some gym class as the one you wanted—could you ever even imagine that it might come to this? I can't believe that you would've, right? No, never, not in a million years or you probably wouldn't have done it, that's what I think. That has to be the truth because, I mean, why would you otherwise? You know? Yeah. It's true. You wouldn't. No, I was supposed to be a good boy, do what you say, nod when you ask, and that was going to be that. Easy as pie, that's the phrase. My mom uses it—still, to this day—and it fits and so that's why we say it, why I just said it now. Because it's true. You planned on using and discarding me along the way without my ever knowing it. As easy as pie. And you did, to be fair, you got away with it for a really long time. True? I mean, a good long time. Right up until about seven months ago, and that, my dear, is a hell of a run. Nice long run. You shouldn't look so nervous because you gave it a real go so that's at least something. And look, it's not like I plan on telling anybody, I really don't, I mean, who could I tell? Hmm? Who? I mean, who would ever believe a story like this one?

I don't mind that you're black, I don't, I've always been attracted to black women. Well, not necessarily black but darker-skinned people. Girls with tans and that sort of thing. And you were definitely that, which stood out at our school, didn't it? You certainly did. Talk of the town, some might say, a real object of interest, and I'm sure a few of those men you worked with—teachers and coaches and administrators—they probably found you rather exotic and worth chatting up in the lounge. I'm sure it happened, I know it did, in fact, because I would see you often from where I sat in the office, waiting to get yelled at again by the vice principal. What was that jerk's name, I don't remember now. It doesn't matter, he died years ago from cancer—one of the bad ones, like bowel or brain or something—and I recall not feeling a thing when I heard that news. Maybe even said "good" under my breath or smiled or something. Not instant, but Karma. But you didn't talk to those men, did you, my dear, because you were already married, already wrapped up in a relationship, and so you made a choice, you picked me out of the crowd—maybe there in the office rather than in gym class, now that I think about it, maybe so—and said to yourself that I was the one. The worthwhile one, the one to play with and drive wild with desire. I know you helped me, too, I know that, gave me a belief in myself and pushed me to study and try and get into junior college even, you did all that and I appreciate it, I do, but all the while you made me feel like I was your boy. The guy you wanted in your life, if only your husband wasn't around, if only things were different. If only. And I believed you, oh how I gobbled up the shit you spewed, gobbled it up and swallowed it down and smiled at you in the hall and from the bleachers and as you drove off in your dirty yellow bug on your way home each night. I believed you and loved you and gave you my little teenage heart there at West Valley High and I've never done that again, no, not ever, I haven't. To anyone ever ever ever again because my trust is gone, disappeared like you did the next year to a new school with the whisper of "it could never work" and "this is a real opportunity for me" and it was like you never existed. An empty office was your vapor trail (cutbacks didn't bring another of your kind, a counselor, into school until my senior year). Your desk and chair, alone in the dark, was where I would eat my lunch most days unless they caught me and threw me out—that was all that was left of our love and time together. And there was love, wasn't there? Real, abiding love. I swear there was. Look at me right now and tell me there was and I will go away, leave you to watch your little girl as she runs about in the bright sunshine and I'll be gone. Say it, just once, say it to me now and mean it, while I sit here with you. I beg you. Go on.

You can't, can you? No, of course you can't because it's not true and you wouldn't want to lie about that, lead me on or anything, now, would you? Absolutely not. Part of the strange, strict principles by which you live your life, even though our entire union was absolutely that. A pure and utter lie, one that you lived so easily and without remorse for so long. That's hardly fair, though, is it, because how could I know your feelings about me at that time? That's a good point and I stand corrected, or sit corrected, actually, sit corrected here on this bench with you. I-sit-corrected. Perhaps you did love me once, a while ago, a long, long time ago when I was sixteen and just learning to drive and we would meet off in the woods or at your home on an unexpected morning and make love. Yes, love, I'm sure it was, only that, never just fucking, and you taught me everything I know about that undiscovered country. It was well beyond description and nothing I plan to embarrass you with right now, not in front of your daughter as she plays, but it was something lovely and I remember it like it was just yesterday even though a decade or so has slipped away. Lying there, inside of you and looking into your eyes, the quiet of a forest above us and your beautiful skin soaking up the sun, kissing that mouth of yours, those lips that sucked me in and devoured me, I had no words for what you were doing to my life. And nothing now, now that I know the truth. The real truth of what we were doing there and why you loved me or said you did and watched me fall deeper and deeper into the endless chasm that was you.

Did I ever tell you that I imagined killing him? Your husband? Oh yes, so many times. When it was at its deepest and worst, the sickness of love made me want to be rid of him for all time and eternity. I planned his death a dozen times, in various ways and done so successfully by me that even you believed that the car wreck or the mugging or hanging was a suicide or a mistake or a simple twist of fate. And life goes on and I was suddenly with you always, at your side, and we made a new life for ourselves in another state or country or on an island somewhere and the last that anyone ever saw of us was us running, hand in hand, down the beach and off into that sunset people are always talking about. Yes. Was I wrong to think that? At the time I didn't feel I was, it felt justified by what you said about him, about your life together. Just phrases, really, a little clue tossed off now and again over a meal at A&W, some little comment that made me believe he didn't appreciate you, that he didn't want children with you or to grow old with you or anything anymore, that you were trapped and alone and I was your savior, me, that only I could rescue you from the coal mine of a life that your marriage had become. Some white guy from home, a good family and a bad mistake is what you called it, and I took it to heart, believed that his inability to father a child was of his own making rather than biology, that he was withholding from you and cold and distant and had even laid a finger—or more than that, a hand one time—on your sweet face that I had come to adore and would protect with my life. Did you know that at the time, that I would've done even that, died for you? Of course you did. Sixteen-year-olds can hide nothing. I was like some puppy chasing after you, big paws and tongue and silly and sweet. But you didn't want those things, did you? No, not all of them. Just one. One thing from me and when you had it you left so quickly, with such a fluttering of your wings that I was dazed and dazzled and I believed your whispers. I watched you drive away, even helped you pack your garage, if you can remember that, helped your husband pack up things into a U-Haul and swept it out and washed it down before you left. You paid me twenty dollars there in front of him, smiled at me like we'd never met, and off I trotted, back home to wait for a call that never came and an address that was never, not ever, no never sent.

And now you have your child, that thing you always said would make your life complete. Your husband, too, he got swept up in your miracle and never asked for a blood test that would tell him the horrid truth about you and your deeds. Your missteps. Your tiny plots. Instead you are a happy family living here, where I have found you and have now come to ask for something in return. Of course I have, don't look so surprised, my dear, for there is always a price to pay for things like this, when you have done what you have done, and now the time has come.

All I want is nothing. That is, that nothing should change from this very moment on. I want you to know I know where you're at, who you are and what you've become. No, you didn't eventually divorce as you imagined to me you would, a life on your own in another city where I might join you one day, "when you're grown," you would say, and oh how I believed you and your words. Those intoxicating words that spewed from your beautiful lips into my ear as I held you and hoped for such a day. But that day never came as you well know, it never did and on you stayed with your man—why wouldn't you, for there were never any plans on your part to leave him, to be alone, but to add, add a child to the mix and live happily ever after. My child. A child you took from me and I never even knew it. How clever of you, how smart and wily and clever. And almost perfect, the plan, it was almost the most perfect of plans but who knew that my sister— my stupid younger sister who I never really liked and I always thought was a little bit retarded—who could imagine that she could pass a course and would end up working for your doctor in town? You left no trace or so you thought, but files are files and so they stay, and one nosy day she glanced inside to see that your husband, that man I was so ready to hate and kill and despise, she saw that he was empty and void and unable to provide and she thought this was interesting and said so to me and my family one evening out of the blue. They all recalled you fondly and thought it was a sad and strange tidbit about a lovely woman who had been so helpful to their son, but I knew better, didn't I, my dear? I now knew that you had used me to become pregnant and then off you ran to hide your secret from the world. And me. The one who wanted to be your world but was really only a pawn. A sorry little pawn in your grisly and gory game of love.

But children grow up, God bless them, they do and reach out and up and try things all on their own, things that even their own parents don't always know about. And so I met your daughter, your little princess, on the Internet and have become her friend. What a place for people like us, you and I, the liars and braggarts and ghosts of this world. Such a nice place to hide and pretend and so I do, I am a lovely little teenage girl named "Samantha" with hair like hand-spun gold, and I live in Texas with my family of five with our dog named "Bubbles" and a boyfriend named "Cory"—yes, I used your husband's name, I knew it would seal the deal when a squeal from your daughter was followed by "That's my dad's name, too! LOL!" Oh yes, she is mine for hours at a time now and we dream and talk and chatter on about a life together at college or beyond. It has been beautiful and filled with laughter and delight, not ugly like what you did to me, not wrong like how you used me. No. It has been so so beautiful and it needs to continue, must continue, and I know you have set restrictions on her recently because she gets online the second you leave the house and complains about you and so I know. But you will let her have this friend, won't you? Yes, or everything will be revealed. Do you understand me? All of it and to the end. I will ruin you and your perfect little fairy-tale life if you stop her from "seeing" me. Obviously I can never meet her or tell her the truth, one day she will drift away from me and that will be that, as they say, I know this and accept it as fate. Kismet. Karma, not instant but destined and acceptable. But it is not for you to decide so stay away and so will I. That is the deal. That is the cost, my dear. She is yours, to be sure, but she is also mine now and mine she will stay. For as long as I can hold her she will be mine as well. Mine, mine, mine.

She's beautiful out there, isn't she? Dancing on the grass and running with her friends. I've had to send her photos of myself very carefully—using my little niece as a stand-in—but what I've seen of her has been no lie. She is perfect and golden and the one good thing to come out of the filthy ways you used me and soiled a part of my life. Don't look away because you know it's true. I hate women and their wily selves; I know men can suck and often do but you are a more treacherous creature overall, surely you recognize that as a truth. You ruined me and left me for dead. You built this burnished little life and happy little world on the shit and bones of my carcass without looking back—and now all I ask is that you continue to look away. Look off some other way when you see her sitting at the computer, giggling and talking with her "friends" on Facebook and Twitter and all the crap I've been reduced to just to be near her. My daughter. Look away, go into another room and leave us alone, and by doing so your own rotten, deceitful life can exist for yet another day. Do you agree, my dear? Oh, how I hope so. Here in my broken heart of hearts.

If you want me, need me, long for me as I do for you, my hated, hateful dear, you know where to find me. Lost in space. Out there, somewhere. Rump.69@hotmail.com.

I see you not looking at me. Head turned. Tears in your eyes. I so wish I knew what you were thinking, but then again, I never really did, did I, so why would it matter now? And it doesn't. All that matters is you know the truth. Where we stand. And the truth of the matter is I'm here now. I am here and I'm not going away, no, I'm not. Not ever, my dear. Not for a very very very long time.

I've always had a soft spot for the Rumpelstiltskin story and its title character—he's a nasty piece of work, but, for some reason, I feel for the little guy. After all, he does exactly what he promises to do and asks for only one thing in return; he keeps his promise when those around him break theirs and is publicly humiliated and sent shrieking off into the night (I suppose the fact that he's asking for a baby as his prize does make some difference). Still, I love the "person who returns" in literature and "Rumpelstiltskin" is a perfect example of revenge as a motif in the fairy tale. It's also just a lot of fun, the whole damn story—I mean, he spins gold out of straw, for God's sake!

I always felt like the deck was so improbably stacked against Rumpelstiltskin and still he plunges forward with his offer of salvation—he's a bit of a Shylock in this sense and anti-Semitic sentiment has even been heaped on his head throughout the ages. This guy can't cut a break!

I've always worried that we're too easy on the beautiful people in this world and so it's little surprise that I find my overweight, average self drawn to this most romantic and fated of antiheroes.

So it goes with writers—we can't help but imagine new ways in and out of age-old troubles.

This is my attempt at giving the man his due, set in an updated world and filtered through a modern sensibility. I sincerely hope you enjoyed the ride.

—NL

SHELLEY JACKSON

The Swan Brothers

YOU ARE WALKING DOWN A FAMILIAR STREET AT DUSK. MEAT IS cooking. In the shadows down the block, you see a cardboard box, flaps open. The street is deserted; you will either be the first to look inside the box, or it has already been plundered; either way, there's no reason to hurry, but you do. There is a limited variety of things left in boxes in your neighborhood: shoes gone the shape of feet, dusty videos, mugs with ceramic frogs amusingly glued inside them. You are hoping for books, and that's what you find. Not many—others have preceded you—but you stoop anyway and poke through the pile, pushing aside *The Big Book of Birds* and *What to Expect When You're Expecting*.

You are drawn to the shape, the color, the design of the book before you have made out the title. It is a durable old Dover paperback, its thick cover leathery with use and still bright red, except for a pink band along the top where a shorter neighboring book allowed sunlight to hit it. It is a small, fat, leather-bound book with marbled edges, its morocco binding glove-soft and chipped at the spine. It is a vintage pocket paperback with a keyhole on the spine, a map on the back, and a still life on the front: a quill pen, a bottle of ink, and a spindle.

When you flip through the book, more to feel the thick pages ruffle smoothly across your thumb, like an old deck of cards, than to check the contents, you find, pressed between two pages, a feather. It is white, it is black with an iridescent sheen, it is pigeon-gray, in any case you pin it to the left-hand page with your thumb as you begin reading, walking on. You like to start books in the middle. Maybe you like the challenge of trying to figure out what's going on. Maybe you just like doing things differently. In any case, you are soon engrossed, though the page waxes and wanes as you pass under the streetlights, and it is sometimes hard to make out the words.

It's a good thing you read so much when you were a child, or you wouldn't know what to think—you read—when you turn the corner on the greasy little street—a pigeon startles up, leaving a lone feather stuck to the asphalt—and see the dusty storefront into which the woman, her hands, wrists, and forearms so swollen that she appears to be wearing down opera gloves, is dragging a stuffed, heavy-duty lawn-and-leaf bag with numerous rents out of which what must be nettles are protruding. But since you have read every single one of Andrew Lang's color-coded Fairy Books, even the ugly olive-green one, you recognize at once that she is a daughter and, more important, a sister, who is involved in the long, difficult, and not always rewarding work of saving her brothers from—you duck reflexively at a whirring vortex in the air: that pigeon again.

The woman, who has held the door open with her rump while she edged the bag inside, turns into the brightly lit interior and lets the door slam shut. It doesn't matter, you can watch through the big shop window, despite the posters pasted all over it. Because you've read a lot of stories, you're not surprised when she seats herself at a spinning wheel, behind which a row of brown, bristly little shirts hang from hooks screwed into the wall.

Because you've also lived—you've been living and reading for years, sometimes both at once—you are not surprised that people often repeat their most unpleasant experiences. It's probably for the same reason we tell the same stories over and over, with minor variations—"The Seven Ravens," "The Seven Doves," "The Twelve

Ducks," "The Six Swans." It is cozy to have one's expectations met, though there is also, always, the possibility—is this is a happy thought or a sad one?—that things will turn out differently, this time.

The Performance Artist Remembers

A young woman, who must be rather good at the domestic arts, to spin thread out of nettles, to weave cloth from that thread, to sew shirts from that cloth—or who will certainly, in six years, become good at them—is sitting in a room made of stone, her tongue a stone. She has been silent for two years, three months, four days. The sun is slanting through an unglazed hole in the thick wall, warming her knee, lighting up one leg of the spinning wheel and the rim of the basket of nettles. A bug buzzes up from them and whacks the rim of the basket, crawls along it, crawls all the way around it.

She has wicked thoughts. For instance:

Is self-sacrifice always a virtue?

If their positions were reversed, would her brothers do the same for her?

Would she want them to?

What is it *like* to fly?

Here's how she imagines it: in a room just like this one, a basket of nettles at her knee, she is spinning. The stool knocks on the uneven floor as she foots the treadle. The thread is passing through her fingers, burning. Her skin prickles, comes out in bumps, more blisters no doubt, but on her chest, her ass, her back, her shoulders—that at least is new. Then she goes hot all over with tiny bursting pains, as if the blisters have broken all at once. Every pore is the head of a needle through which a thread is passing, or cloth through which a needle is passing; she is like a sun in an old painting, sending zips of light in every direction. Only it's quills now crowding through her skin. They are pinkish gray, tightly curled and wet from her insides, but in the air they unfurl and dry to white until she is thatched all over with feathers, and at the same time her legs are tightening, hardening, shrinking.

She walks out of the neck of her suddenly gigantic gown. A great force is pulling on her fingers, stretching them; feathers as strong as fingers shoot out of her wrists and the backs of her hands. She presses her lips together to keep herself from crying out and her whole face pouts and tightens. And then she cries out after all and, amazed by the sound she makes, spreads her wings and hurls herself through the window into the rushing sky.

She spins faster, to punish herself for her thoughts. The wheel thumps. The spindle twirls. Nettles race through her fingers. The pain is extraordinary. Her hands are no longer hands, but flames, or stars, or voices singing.

The Performance Artist Dreams

The performance artist has two kinds of dreams about flying. In one, she is swimming in air, doing a strenuous frog kick just to stay a few feet out of reach of the murderer who is calmly waiting for her to tire. In the other, after a running start, she simply lifts her feet and swoops up and away. She rises effortlessly, the sky is hers; suddenly, though, she is frightened, it seems that she is not flying but falling upward, she has gone too far, she may never return to earth, or to the murderer far below, who is now the only one who remembers her, but who has already stopped looking up at the shrinking speck in the sky, and is trudging home with the spade over her shoulder, thinking about dinner.

The Performance Artist Works

In a storefront gallery in a big city, a performance artist sits at a spinning wheel, spinning nettles into thread, sits at a loom, weaving thread into cloth for little shirts. She has made five and a half shirts. This has taken her five and a half years. In the beginning she had a lot of visitors. You wouldn't believe how fabulous they looked or how loudly they commented on her spinning wheel, her loom, her nettles, her blisters, and her patience. But no matter what they said, she did not speak or smile. The visitors commented on that, too, saying, smiling, that it would be harder for them not to speak or smile for six years than to spin thread out of nettles, weave that thread into cloth, make that cloth into shirts. That was probably true, thought the performance artist, severing a thread with her teeth.

Attendance fell off. The gallery owners, who had interests in Buenos Aires, Barcelona, Hong Kong, St. Petersburg, Istanbul, went on a long business trip. Her dealer stopped calling. The windows grew streaked and dusty. A row of posters advertising a burlesque show was pasted up—a woman dancing, naked as a prawn, within a storm of her own extraordinarily long, blond hair. Then flyers, their fringes of phone numbers fluttering: LOST RING, LOST DOG, LOST CHILD.

Occasionally a woman with silver hands comes, bringing pears.

The performance artist watches the sun move across the dusty glass while her hands twist and pluck. Once in a while, a winged shadow intersects the light.

Her Youngest Brother's Lover

He was sitting on the edge of my bed. I was on my knees in front of him, face in his lap, and suddenly there was this . . . *wind*.

Later I found feathers in my sheets, in my shoes. A small one floating, curved and lovely, in my water glass.

He has a huge, bulging forehead, like Edgar Allan Poe, and thin lips. Little round eyes, one raised shoulder. So no, he isn't handsome. I had him down as a one-night stand, but I couldn't stop thinking about it. The wing, beating. Flying.

Yes, every time he comes.

Her Parents

"My sons were the flighty ones. My daughter was always super down-to-earth," says the father. "It was a surprise when she told us she wanted to be an artist. We tried to steer her toward something more practical. My wife suggested she take Home Ec. That's where she learned to sew, so we feel that we've contributed. Indirectly."

HER SILENCE
Words rise in her throat like gas. She swallows them back.

HER HANDS
look like gloves, or fake hands inside of which her real hands are hidden.

HER EXPERIENCE OF TIME
Read this sentence; repeat for six years.

THE OPENING
One day, someone turns up with a bucket of soapy water, a razor blade, and a squeegee, and scrapes the years off the window. A janitor climbs a ladder and replaces a bulb. The floor is washed, a folding table is covered with a paper cloth and plastic cups, and then the gallery owners sweep in with great tans and lots of friends and the gallery is full again. There are five nettle shirts hung on the wall, dry and spiky and brown. They look dangerous, though also a little sad. A sixth shirt, laid out on the table, is finished except for the left sleeve.

The performance artist, at the loom, where the material for the last sleeve is slowly growing, doesn't look up.

A reporter leans over her with his pen poised over a notebook. "*Tsk*. Not until eight o'clock!" says the dealer, drawing him away.

When the minute hand snaps to twelve, an uncertain cheer goes up. It's eight, but the performance artist hasn't quite finished the last sleeve. But she gets right up. Her smile looks a little odd, but then, she hasn't smiled for six years.

There's a man looking at an empty hook on the wall. She hangs the last shirt there. "I thought it was you."

"Of course it's me."

"I'm not going to ask where the others are." She prods with a fingernail at a blister pillowing the tip of her baby finger. It looks like a drop of clear water.

"At happy hour, probably. Stop picking." He puts his wing around her. "What do you expect? They have their happy ending."

AFTERWARD

Your brothers are billing and cooing around you, nibbling their arms and puffing up their chests. One wing shudders, is stilled by a jeweled hand. The smell of burning meat hangs in the air; it is the king's mother, your mother-in-law, cooked like a goose. No one is sorry, not even the king, so smile. Do you remember how to smile?

THE OPENING, CONTINUED

"Fabulous," said a member of the Stepsisters' Collective, beetles spilling from her mouth. "I love it!"

The performance artist catches sight of her reflection in the window. She should not have put on lipstick, she can never remember that she is wearing it. It looks as though she has been eating something bloody.

No, it is her dealer whose lipstick is smeared, and who is now weaving purposefully through the crowd, one hand clenched in the sleeve of the critic, her smile hard.

No, what happened is that her dealer kissed her; possibly she intended a European peck on the cheek, and it was the performance artist's clumsiness that caused their mouths to meet. Or possibly that was the dealer's intention in the first place, since her mouth clung longer than necessary. But was that because she actually desired the performance artist, or because she wanted others to think they were sleeping together? And if the latter, was that to raise herself up, or to lower the performance artist, or both, or to make the art critic jealous so that he attached himself more firmly to the performance artist—or perhaps to the dealer herself—or to drive him away, so that if the dealer could not have him, neither could the performance artist?

Maybe it is not lipstick at all but sweet-and-sour sauce from the six little drumsticks that she served herself from a waiter who looked like her father, the bones of which are still folded in her napkin; she was always an enthusiastic eater.

Or, she has been eating something bloody.

ALSO ON DISPLAY

A teacup full of sand.

Three poppies.

A ball of yarn.

MAGIC

The ball of yarn rolls by itself, leading the way. All you have to do is hold on to the end.

FACT

A story is sometimes called a "yarn."

THE OPENING, CONTINUED

She pushes through the crowd and closes herself in the bathroom, swiping at the light switch, and hissing as she catches, as well, the sharp tip of a nail. She pops her pinkie in her mouth, smearing blood on her lips.

The bathroom doubles as a storeroom; there are six small narrow wooden beds jumbled or stacked in the corner or spaced neatly along the wall. They are the perfect size for her brothers, who, coincidentally, have just flown through the window, dropped their feathers in six neat heaps, and now crowd around her, goose-pimpled but human, congratulating her on her big night. But they can't stay, her brothers tell her, they will only retain human form for fifteen minutes, an hour, a night, and then the robbers whose den this is will return, and she, too, should leave at once.

How convenient that there were precisely six robbers, she thought. And such small ones!

I'm going, I'm going, she says. But do you have a Band-Aid?

THE YOUNGEST BROTHER'S LOVER

Once I caught him plucking it. The tip was already bare—a sorry raw red-spotted naked prong sticking out of a nest of feathers. I went down on it, which I think confused him more than it excited him. Me, too, really. Afterward I said, "Don't you ever do that again. I want you exactly the way you are." Which surprised me, because all I've ever thought about my whole life was turning into something else. That's something we have in common.

THE PERFORMANCE ARTIST DREAMS

Nettles sprout from her shoulder blades, sheathing her arms.

She awakes, a strange taste in her mouth. Where are her brothers— that is, her children? Has she eaten them? Have they flown away? Did she ever even have children?

THE OPENING, CONTINUED

Looking for gauze, she opens the small supply cabinet beside the sink. Reek of pine disinfectant, and she is in the forest. She can make out the path only by the slight tug of the yarn running drily through her fingers, that and the dark shapes of the recycling bins pulled out to the curbs for the Friday night pick-up. A shadow heaves up before her; her shoulder dashes into someone else's and a hand squeezes her arm apologetically. The blackout has made everyone temporarily friend-lier, and she wonders whether she shouldn't just sit down on a stoop, or a stump, and wait for someone to sit next to her.

Now headlights slide over the ball of yarn, which is pausing, turn-ing, continuing on its way. The yarn tugs at her hand and she keeps going, or someone does. Maybe it is her father, coming to see her! But no, it is a woman, so she hangs back. Her hands clamped on the cold stone, wishing her brothers weren't so trusting. Her chest is pressed against the parapet, which is so high she can barely see over it, and so cold it stifles her breath. Her youngest brother bends to scoop up the traitorous ball of yarn and the visitor throws something over him—a little white changing shape like a ghost: a shirt—and something happens. Then it happens again, and again, and again, and again, and again. Six times, dear reader.

"The King has six sons," being what the servants must have said. Not thinking to mention that he also had a daughter.

Let's be generous, perhaps the servants loved her best, and sought to keep her secret.

Let's be reasonable, how could they have known that when her six brothers ran forward, she would stay back?

And why did she stay back?

Perhaps she is a reader too, and knows that women are dangerous, especially when they are stepmothers, especially when they are witches or the daughters of witches, especially when they are Queens.

Perhaps the servants did mention her, and the Queen did not choose to sew her a shirt. Wishing to give the boys a fair chance, perhaps. Knowing that daughters can do things that sons can't, like spin nettles into thread, and keep their mouths shut. Daughters do their duty.

Things You Learn from Reading

Women are trouble—if it isn't an evil wife, it's an evil stepmother. Or mother-in-law. Mothers are usually all right, unless they're witches—watch out for witches. And their daughters.

You might be all right with kings, princes, and fathers, unless, as is usually the case, they're under the influence of someone else, usually a woman. Men are weak. Sometimes they rescue you, but they always have help—from ants or birds or women. Sometimes you rescue them. This is kind of sweet.

You can trust animals. Sometimes they turn into people, but don't hold that against them.

Children had better watch out.

THE OPENING, CONTINUED

"I play it back over and over," said the woman with silver hands. "Every damn time it's the same. I just put my hands on a stump"—laying them with a clunk on the table—"and say, 'Yes, father.' That reminds me." She has been going out with a man with chicken feet. He crams them into motorcycle boots and looks normal until they take off their clothes.

"Is that a problem for your sex life?" the performance artist asks.

"No," says the woman with silver hands, "I like his feet. I mean, my hands seem to like them, I can feel it."

"I want to introduce you to my brother," said the performance artist. "I mean he's gay but you'd never know."

The woman with silver hands wasn't listening. "He sleeps with an axe beside the bed—the window to the fire escape doesn't lock, he says, but I think he's tempting me to cut his feet off. Want a pear?"

The performance artist likes the lips of the woman with silver hands—a woman who could eat a pear off a tree with her stumps tied behind her back. She imagines balancing on a bed in boxers and socks, holding a pear by the stem, with the woman with silver hands on her knees before her. Later the woman with silver hands could climb a tree and throw down first her earrings, then her belt, then her boots, then her underpants, until she was naked as a pear.

"Thanks," says the performance artist, and takes a sweet, juicy bite, and without thinking about it, wipes her mouth with the back of her hand. Now she will have to go fix her lipstick.

WEAVING

Reading, your gaze is moving from left to right, left to right, left to right, like a shuttle across a loom. The page is a figured cloth, swan black, swan white.

ETYMOLOGY

L. *texere*, to weave; from which we derive *textile*, and *text*.

CARELESSNESS

The performance artist has tea at a sidewalk café with the woman with silver hands. Her own healing hands are silvery with scar tissue. "Now I can ask," she says, but doesn't. She is watching a pigeon strut and bob, his neck fat with desire. The harried-looking female pecks at a pebble, then suddenly flaps away. The performance artist smiles, inexpertly, and turns back to her friend. "To lose one hand might be regarded as a misfortune," she says; "to lose both looks like carelessness. I'm quoting. Ish."

"I was trying to jump a freight train with some friends, a girl I met in the shelter, an older guy who said you could get all the way to Reno that way and that it was cool. They made it, I didn't." She stirred her tea with a silver finger.

"Really?"

"No, my father cut them off with an axe. Otherwise, he said, the devil would wrap his tail around his, my father's, neck and drag him away."

"Sucks for you."

"Yep. Though . . ." They look at her hands.

THE OPENING, CONTINUED

She looks in the mirror and says, Oh for fuck's sake, and starts wiping her mouth with mean strokes. She has smeared her lipstick again; she has even managed to get some on her chin.

Or, she has just had oral sex on a hot afternoon with the woman with silver hands, who has previously pulled out her ghastly tampon by the string and slung it whooping out the window (later they would peer out and see it lying on top of the neighbor's air conditioner, like a dead mouse, and burst out laughing), and has slid up for a kiss that tasted like iron and salt, and caught sight of herself in the shards of mirror glued to the wall, a red halo around her mouth.

Or, she has eaten her own children. The children she made with the art critic. But who disappeared over the course of the six years she spent making shirts out of nettles. Little shirts that would no doubt fit the children she also made. She had suspected her dealer, whose jealousy—of her own artists!—was well-known. But she could not voice her suspicions, since she was not speaking at the time.

Across the room, she sees her dealer speaking to the art critic. He is bent forward to hear her in the noisy room, his head almost touching her breasts, which are offered up in a fashion not so much sexual as maternal.

Someone is talking about a glass mountain that has sprung up in midtown, or maybe it's just a new building by that architect, the one who did that thing in Barcelona. For some reason she is suddenly sure that that is where her children, that is, her brothers, no, her children, have gone.

The art critic has some difficulty with one of the miniature pork chops that are circulating on platters, and the dealer wipes his mouth for him in a fashion not so much maternal as sexual, though he is certainly at least half her age.

The art critic has a big head and longish, floppy, wavy hair like a cellist. He catches her eye from across the room and raises his plastic cup to her, sloshing a little sparkling water over his wrist. The light shines in his brown hair as if something golden were nestled there.

The performance artist nods, distracted. The children: where can they be hiding this time? Under the paper skirts of the table with its ranks of plastic cups? She can feel her dealer watching her. There is a smell of burning meat in the air—the mini sausages, maybe.

"Oh, no, here he comes," said the woman with silver hands. "Don't do it. You'll just live happily ever after. Again."

THE YOUNGEST BROTHER'S LOVER

He turns his back to me in bed and I tuck my hand under his wing. I can feel him thinking, thinking, thinking; then he softens to sleep.

I know what he thinks about, I was someone else once, too. I hopped it when she kissed me, scared of such a pink and hearty love.

I whose blood had not yet warmed, between whose fingers translucent webs still stretched. Ugly with gravity, I lugged myself back to the pond—weak jump, volcanic splash. *Quelle surprise!* The water barely covered my head.

Now I'm thick and pink myself and sometimes pull a sweater on. I have hair on my balls. Hell, I have balls. But I still blush green, and I knew him when I met him. Saw, in my mind, red legs coming down from a feathered sky. Neck coming down, pearls of air in the feathers. Robber's mask over bulging, vulnerable eyes. We had shared that cold world. I did not hold it against him that he once might have nibbled me up with the duckweed. If anything it thrilled me. But.

Sliding down the long curve of his throat, or lying next to him on a double futon: both are, I guess, love, but I choose this.

MOTHERHOOD, BROTHERHOOD

Time goes by. The children don't turn up. Did she ever have children? The performance artist considers adoption. She reads from the information packet: "Fees may be significantly lower for foolish and lazy youngest sons, children thumb-sized and smaller, those with the heads of hedgehogs or the ears of donkeys. Many so-called special needs, given proper care, will not significantly impact the future health and happiness of your child." She schedules a home study. "So they can determine whether I am likely to eat my children, I guess. When it should be obvious that I am responsible to a fault. But I do have doubts. My brothers, for example: I lost them. Who was it who said, 'to lose one brother may be regarded as a misfortune; to lose six looks like carelessness'?"

"You were how old?" said the woman with silver hands. "What kind of father leaves seven children alone in the woods? For that matter, what kind of father marries a woman he can't trust with his children?"

What kind of father cuts off his daughter's hands, thinks the performance artist.

"Anyway, you got them back," said the woman with silver hands. "How's your brother?"

"He and his boyfriend have bought a house in the Berkshires. Well, a cabin, really. You'd like it, it stands on a giant chicken foot. Hops around the yard. In winter they're going to 'tool down to Florida' in it. They've asked me if I want to come along, but I don't know."

THE PERFORMANCE ARTIST DAYDREAMS

A group of swans—six cobs and one pen—shift their weight uneasily as a woman walks toward them, carrying six little shirts.

LIVE POULTRY

The performance artist goes to a live poultry store in south Brooklyn. There are hand-painted Arabic letters on the yellow sign, and a proud white cock with one red foot raised. Inside are a lot of Hasidic men and Mexicans, or maybe Guatemalans or Colombians, who knows, and cages stacked to the ceiling, with dirty feathers sticking out of them. She bends and peels up a feather from the sticky floor.

She buys six swans, no, geese, the live poultry store does not sell swans, and barricades them into the backseat with cardboard boxes. They honk out the windows as she drives over the bridge, possibly smelling water, and draw startled looks from passing drivers. In the gallery, they walk around importantly, looking like art critics and nibbling at electrical cords. The next morning, the gallery reports the theft of artworks valued at thirty thousand dollars.

NEWS

Six small robbers are spotted on a department store security video, pulling on identical shirts and turning this way and that in front of the mirror, then dropping the shirts on the floor.

Six small robbers are caught on video attempting to enter the glass building by that architect, the one who did that thing in Sidney. They are frightened away by a night watchman.

Six small robbers are found sleeping in children's beds in the Red Hook IKEA. Locked in a room to await the arrival of a law-enforcement officer, they apparently escape through a third-floor window. Goose dung is discovered on the windowsill.

About Time

"Isn't it about time you came out with something new?" said the art critic. "Not that it's any of—"

"No, it isn't."

When they met, she wasn't speaking. They went for walks in the dark; sometimes she climbed a tree, and when he, growing impatient of the game, begged her to come down to bed, she would throw down her shoes, her stockings, her dress, aiming at the red light of his cigarette (several of her favorite dresses still had tiny round holes in them); she would unhook her bra and pull it out through her sleeve and throw that down, until she stood barefoot on a branch in nothing but her slip, looking down at the darkness where he stood.

"Marry me," he would say, to the pale shape roosting in the tree.

"Of course he knew I couldn't answer," she told the woman with silver hands.

Now that she is speaking, their relationship has deteriorated.

"It's about time you came out with something new, don't you think?" said the art dealer. "If you're ready."

"I think the art critic is sleeping with my dealer," said the performance artist to her friend.

"Ew," said the woman with silver hands.

Feathers Needed

The performance artist puts an ad on Craigslist. Feathers needed, swans preferred.

Facts

The best quill pens were cut from swan feathers.

A female swan is called a "pen."

Right-handed writers favored feathers from the tip of the left wing, which curved outward, away from the line of sight.

THE PERFORMANCE ARTIST WORKS (AGAIN)

In a storefront gallery in a big city, a performance artist sits at a spinning wheel, spinning feathers into thread, sits at a loom, weaving thread into cloth for little shirts. Down drifts around her, collecting in loose, dusty rolls on the floor. Her nose is running; she has developed an allergy.

THE PERFORMANCE ARTIST DREAMS

The feathers, too, sting her fingers.

THE PERFORMANCE ARTIST'S REVIEWS

"Lacks the critical edge of her best work" . . . "Has the performance artist lost her sting?" . . . "The aspirational tone is a welcome shift from the claustrophobia and bitterness of her 'Nettled' show, but the feather shirts, while frankly gorgeous, resolve the vexed issue of female domestic servitude perhaps too easily in resorting to the hackneyed metaphor of flight" . . . "In repeating with variations her own earlier work, is the performance artist cannily engaging the current trend of reenactment, or has she just run out of ideas?" . . . "Though the memory of pain lingers in the form of the scars that silver the artist's hands, the element of physical suffering has been removed from this new, softer work, and there is a corresponding loss of intensity" . . . "The trick has grown old. One wonders whether, after yet another six years of silence, anyone will be left who cares."

THE OPENING, CONTINUED

The room is hot, the air is thick. It stings her throat like nettles. It tickles her throat like feathers. Either way she can't breathe. No, it's not the air, it's a length of yarn twining round her neck; the children have appeared, the children have been found, wandering in the forest, shut up in yet another castle, it's joyous news, and they're running around their mother, the performance artist, with a ball of yarn they've found somewhere, and they don't realize, nobody realizes, how tight the loops have become. Unless it's her brothers, who have come after all, who are grateful after all, all six of them, pulled away from their barbecues, their robbers' dens, their high-stakes online poker games, their castles, their princesses, led of course by the youngest, the one with the disability, and as her knees give way they are severing the yarn with their beaks, fanning her with huge wings, lifting her up with their red, red feet—they're weaving a net, they too know how to weave, a net of nettles, they've taken the sides in their beaks and they're lifting her on it, beating their great wings, already she is high above the city, she sees the glass mountain rising before her—

Or it is the man with chicken feet helping her up, he's kicked off his boots to free his feet, he's more agile like that, and the woman with silver hands is fanning her, with one of her own shirts. What has happened? She must have slipped on the glass mountain and fallen. But luckily she still has the chicken bones folded into her napkin, and now she plants one in a crack in the glass, tests to see if it will support her weight, and plants another a little higher. Up she goes! Higher and higher into the rushing sky, her gaze steady, her knees only trembling a little. She is nearing the top. One more step and she will be able to reach—but the napkin is empty. She cuts off—with what? Bites off—her little finger. Stepping on her finger, she reaches the top.

There is the great arched door. It is locked, of course, but she has been given a chicken bone to use as a key. She carefully unfolds the stained napkin. There is nothing inside!

Now six robbers enter the art gallery. You can tell they are robbers because they wear black masks and black capes. They are small robbers—children, or dwarves. Each is exactly the same as all the others, except the sixth. There's something bulky and white sticking out from under his cape where his left arm should be, almost sweeping the ground. Something soft and white.

They do not bother with the wallets, rings, watches, and cell phones that the guests have already thrown down in anticipation of their demands, but move straight to the wall and take down the little shirts, as calmly as people getting dressed in the morning. There is one shirt each. Naturally, the robber with the white thing under his cape—okay, it's a wing—chooses the shirt with no left sleeve. He goes to it straightaway, as if he knew it would be there. Probably he did, probably he had cased the joint. He frees the defective shirt from its fiddly hook and falls in behind the others, who are already filing out through the door. The performance artist jerks after them, is stayed by a hand on her arm, her dealer's. Something confusing is happening outside, a sweeping and whirling—capes and shirts and feathers. A honking call sounds. The performance artist rises to her toes. Her feather boa stirs in the breeze from the closing door.

VARIATIONS

The performance artist picks up a shirt and puts it on. She spreads her wings and falls into the sky.

The performance artist picks up a knife and cuts off her baby finger. She inserts it into the glass lock, which clicks smoothly open. Inside are her three children and her six brothers, waiting with open arms, with spread wings, with eleven arms and one wing.

The performance artist picks up a pen. (It bites her.)

The performance artist picks up a ball of yarn.

The performance artist picks up a phone and buys a ticket to Florida.

SLEEPING AND FLYING

A man sleeps, one arm flung over his lover's chest. In the dark air over the bed, his wing beats; he is dreaming, of course, of flying. But his other arm holds on tight.

Elsewhere, a woman's hands silvered with scar tissue flutter, too. She is also dreaming of flying. No, she is dreaming *and* flying, reclining in a window seat, her crooked, scarred, shining hands folded in her lap.

YET ANOTHER SHIRT

"I was never very craft-y," says the woman with silver hands. "For two obvious reasons. But does it have to be feathers or nettles, nettles or feathers? Couldn't you do something with the yarn?"

READING AND FLYING

A girl is sitting in a room. The sun is slanting in the window, warming her knee, lighting up the book she holds open.

You are reading while walking, she reads. You can't see your feet. The spread pages glide over the sidewalk, mottled by leaf-shadow, by moonlight and streetlight. Over continents of shadow, continents of light. The book is a bird with white wings. *You* are a bird. Reading, you can fly. You are flying now.

I read hundreds of fairy tales when I was a kid, studied them as if they contained information I would eventually need to use, so I ran into many different versions of the story the Grimms called "The Six Swans." My experience of the story thus included the confused sense—which my own version attempts to capture—of a compulsive repetition with variation. All the versions agreed, though, that the girl didn't quite finish the last sleeve of the last shirt, so that her youngest brother kept his wing on that side. That

wing marred the happy ending in a way that felt truthful to me—a lasting reminder of her ordeal, and his. It was also surely a suggestion that the desire to fly was only ever dressed up in human clothes. That was the part left out of her story, I always thought: how she must have envied her brothers' animal freedom even as she worked to save them from it.

—SJ

JOYELLE MCSWEENEY

The Warm Mouth

WARM MOUTH: CHINSCRAPER, WHY ARE YOU LYING THERE IN THE road with your jaw shoved back through your brain and your guts blown out as if you'd tried to swallow the highway?

CHINSCRAPER: Warm Mouth, I used to make my way along the median strips and trashy shoulders, my head in the vinyl noose of a six-pack, pop tabs gilding my teeth. I could steal the grease off a Taco John bag. Styrofoam was my bread. Oh, how far that good life seems from me now, laid out in this attitude of supplication, my head smashed in by a speeding Jeep!

WARM MOUTH: Truly I feel for you, Chinscraper, for I am also alone this night. Climb into my warm mouth and we will investigate the night together.

WARM MOUTH: Kneescraper, why do you sit so still on that swollen chair which seems to breathe and groan all around you as if to swallow your small self?

KNEESCRAPER: It's not a chair, it's my grandmother's body. Don't worry, she's not dead, just sleeping, and below her is the wheelchair, but you can't see it for her girth. Maybe you've seen us neck deep in traffic or working our way across intersections like a fucked-up beetle, an evolutionary no-go, me in her lap and the motor straining to scoot us through the exhaust fumes with our groceries swinging from the arms: two-liters, Sno Balls, turkey jerky. She told me not to leave her but the night is so interesting with train tracks crisscrossing it like a game board and gilt-bellied delivery trucks slithering up to the gas stations. It's so hard to keep my promise!

WARM MOUTH: Kneescraper, I too am curious about this night and so is my friend Chinscraper. Climb up in my warm mouth and we will investigate the night together.

WARM MOUTH: Bentneck, why are you lying between the bed and the wall, stuffed into a few inches narrower than a grave, when the whole night spreads out dazzlingly beyond the Wooden Indian?

BENTNECK: Do I look pretty? It's hard to speak twisted up like this. My mother brings me here to meet men. They like me in my princess nightie and sometimes I do a few ballet steps from my Barbie DVD. Afterward I get a treat—a Slurpee, and I can choose the color. I hardly ever drink it all before I fall asleep. Everything is not always very nice for me but eventually it is over. Tonight was different, though at first it was the same. And now I'm shoved down between the bed and the wall with all these carpet fibers up my nose and something wet on my head and my hair's not very clean.

WARM MOUTH: Bentneck, we are also dirty, smashed up, bored, curious, and thirsty. Get up from under that bed, bad girl. Climb up into my warm mouth and we will investigate the night together.

BENTNECK: From now on, I will be called Beauty, for I will narrate this tale. That night, the Warm Mouth conducted similar interviews with a shot-up dog, the suppurating shinbone of a horse, and a blue egg impaled on a stick. All climbed up into the Warm Mouth until its lower lip ballooned like a bullfrog's and it grew harder and harder to move around. The stinking troupe tried to make camp on the walkway outside the public library, but hinges and bolts, bottle glass, and the plastic remains of a cheap pair of sunglasses littered the ground, irritating the Warm Mouth's skin and threatening to pierce its distended lip.

WARM MOUTH: Ow!

CHINSCRAPER: Ow!

KNEESCRAPER: Owl!

BENTNECK: Wowl!

DOG: Bowel Wowel!

WOUND: Yowl!

EGG: Buy a vowel!

BENTNECK: Ach, nothing's free! Life's a peep show, not a look-see!

BENTNECK: So they continued on. They came upon a shipwrecked motel in which people were sleeping behind blinds pinched or rifled or skewed in a pointed, irregular semaphore.

KNEESCRAPER: What does it signal? What can it mean? This pattern in the blinds and shades. This blind pattern. And how a gunshot's made a sunburst of the cashier's booth.

WOUND: You can't make a pattern without shattering a few pasterns.

DOG: But not a very large gauge. And the cashier's long since gone away. No cash changing hands here. These people are on the squat.

EGG: You can't make a cat without swallowing a canary. You can't make a Gatsby without firing a few gats.

CHINSCRAPER: Tell you what. I'm as worn out as a lobby rug. I'm falling apart here. Laid out flat. You can't make a catcall without catching a few winks.

BENTNECK: Just then they detected a spray of light behind the right-most room. They pressed closer to the glass, nearly bursting their viscous vehicle, peered through a chink in the blinds, and found themselves looking over the shoulder of a young man who was smoking and playing a boxing game on the TV. The room was bare and worn, but the troupe still thought it would be very nice to be inside lounging on the couch playing a boxing game instead of hunched up against the wall of a motel that looked ready to sink right through the ground. That is, it would be better to sink with the motel than fall in after it.

ALL: Sink Hole
    Whack a mole
    Bitch and moan
    All roll home
    We need the sink
    We got the hole
    We got the rust
    We need the blood
    We got the broke
    We need the mold
    All roll home, all roll home
    A hole that will take
    What we pour down its throat
    At the end of the day
    When daddy's come home
    Listen honey it's been sweet
    But I got honey of my own
    I'm shunting it off
    From a hole in my gut
    I've got jars of the stuff
    I've got problems of my own
BENTNECK: But now you've got only me. Byoo-tee.

BENTNECK: They were lost in this harmony when the young man relit his pipe and then, in a single motion, jumped up and swung around. He yanked at the blinds and peered out into the street. Then he pulled the blinds down so hard that they gave way from the ceiling on the right, exposing half the room. He went out of view and came back, tugging at his lower lip and rubbing at his gum.

YOUNG MAN:
> Think and think
> Thunk and thunk
> Trunk and glove
> Land the punch
> Bury the pitch
> Meat on meat
> Whore on whore
> Slunk and strove
> Strunk and White
> Struck and struck out
> White light from light
> Flight from white flight
> Trove, trove
> Soul's trove
> What God through me Hove
> The bad night I was born
> & became a lug
> -Nut in this case
> Historee.
> Locked up with the screws and the bolts.

BENTNECK: But now you've got only me. Byootee.

BENTNECK: At that, finally, he looked down and saw them: some road-kill, a starving boy, a murdered girl, a shot-up dog, the suppurating shinbone, and the impaled egg, all tucked up inside the Warm Mouth, which was stretched so thin it was nearly transparent, a clear fluid traced with pus seeping from one corner. They all blinked at the young man through their wounds, and their shattered and cramped limbs shifted wetly. Then they all started talking at once, making a sound like an upended graveyard or a circular blade.

(All make a sound like an upended graveyard or a circular blade.)

BENTNECK: The young man clutched at his own rubbery face and then he screamed, though it sounded more like a croak. Then he crashed out through the thin door and past them into the night, which was starting to go a little gray at the seams as if it had been washed too much.

BENTNECK: Chinscraper, Kneescraper, Beauty, the shot-up dog, the shinbone, the impaled egg, and the Warm Mouth were startled to find before them the very sight they had fantasized: an open door. They dragged themselves inside and sat on the couch. They attempted to manipulate the controls of the boxing game. Then they closed the broken door and the broken blinds as best they could and dropped off into a noisome sleep.

(All make barnyard noises.)

BENTNECK: Meanwhile day was dawning. The young man had run for a few blocks but was quickly winded. He climbed up onto a porch he knew and curled up under the remains of a swing that was hanging by one chain and made a kind of canted roof. As the day grew hotter the heat roused him from his cramped slumber, and he got up and banged on the door. He told his friend about his vision:

YOUNG MAN: I saw into the heart of me, I saw, like, into the heart of me, I saw beneath my, skin. I saw back into the, back of time, I saw like, out through the back of me, back through a hole in the skull of me, shot through a mouth in my skin, my life, like it had happened to me, the life, like, under my skin. And everything that would happen to me and everything I'd done like it had happened to me.

BENTNECK: His friend gave him a bump on credit, but also laughed at him.

FRIEND: Yeah man, but where's the gun and where's the stash? Where's the gun and where's the stash? Is it nestled up inside the shinbone of a horse, or sleeping in a smashed egg, or is it stuffed up in a murdered eight-year-old's cunt? You better get your ass back over there if you love your life. Ash and stash, gash and snatch, love and life, cunt and gut, gun and gas. Run back. Run back.

BENTNECK: Did he love his life? The young man did not ask himself this question. He jumped up like a man in reverse and moved backward through the streets to the motel, all the way tilting away from it. He moved like rewound footage. He moved like across the moon. In this way he slowly slowly reached the door that he had fled. He could hear the video game cycling through its start-up screens. He could smell a morgue with broken air-conditioning, a rifled grave, roadkill, a suppurating wound, a stiffening body, a room full of sweat and sex, an unwashed child. He knew and recognized each of these smells. Perhaps he was not such a young young man. Plus an ooze was trickling all around his sneakers, green and foul, threaded with black. With held breath he tipped open the door.

BENTNECK: What he saw inside was a burst spectacle, a room filled with stinking pus, flaps of skin and tissue driven into the walls, a room that pulsed and seemed to be digesting a horrible gallimaufry, the fur, bones, and innards of an animal rotted beyond recognition, a boy so skinny his ribs, wrists, and leg bones had finally splintered through his flesh, a girl with bulging eyes and a wrung neck, a peltless dog whose every muscle was being slowly worked from the bone, a suppurating wound without a body left to speak of, bits of shell, tooth, hair, tongue, claw, and fat bobbing and resurfacing in the fuming fluid that bathed everything, bathed even his own eyes. Then he closed his eyes, opened his mouth, and he took it all into his mouth, the room and the world, the causes and their outcomes, the couch and the game, the gun and the stash, the fix and the flesh, the anger and the relief, the hope and the violence, the illusions of adulthood, chief among which is childhood, the growth and the decay, the decay and the rot, he took it into his mouth until his mouth was warm and leaked a little and bulged at the lip like a piteous frog's.

This is Beauty speaking, with my warm mouth.

"The Warm Mouth" is a rewrite of Grimms' "The Bremen Town Musicians" that combines the violent strangeness of the original with the violent strangeness of life in the postindustrial-slash-rural ruins of northern Indiana (an area known as Michiana for its closeness to the Michigan border). Both the Grimms' story and my play also take up the problem of shelter, including the body as a kind of failed shelter. I live just up the road from Bremen, Indiana (pronounced BREE-min). The figures in "The Warm Mouth" are thus figures I could run into any day, literally, on the Bremen Highway—or see from a passing car in South Bend. Central to both my experience of life here in Michiana and to "The Warm Mouth" is the Wooden Indian, a "residential" motel that seems entirely made up of catwalks, staircases, and storage sheds, a shelter-without-shelter, without an interior. This structure, and its infirm yet resourceful inhabitants, who are always visible, since their building has no interior, thus manage to evoke somehow Bosch, Dante, and Deleuze. It also recently got a second wooden Indian, both of which are chained up by the Coke machine, which is also chained up—outside, naturally. In contrast to its surroundings and fellow residents, the Coke machine seems flushed and absently cheerful, as if demented or heavily medicated. Thinking about embodiment and pharmaceuticals, I also wanted to collapse the Grimms' musicians from their separable, intact species (dog, donkey, etc.) into one grotesque, gooey, hybrid body, the Warm Mouth, which is then swallowed by Beauty, most terrible of all.

—JM

LYDIA MILLET

Snow White, Rose Red

I MET THE GIRLS AND INSTANTLY LIKED THE GIRLS. OF COURSE I LIKED the girls. A girl is better than a feast.

This was before the arrest, before the indictment and the media stories.

The girls were sisters, as you may know, and lived, during the summer, in one of those upstate mansions built by the robber barons who made their fortunes off railroads and steel and unfair business practices. It was in the Low Peaks of the Adirondacks—the southern part with glassy lakes and green slopes and white-spotted fawns. The girls, who were innocent in the glut of their wealth because they'd never known anything else, called their summer house "the cottage" to distinguish it from "the apartment," which was a ten-thousand-square-foot penthouse on Fifth Avenue near Washington Square Park.

Their father was in real estate, but no one ever saw him. Correction: from time to time we caught sight of him briefly, the girls and I, getting in or out of a long gleaming car. Once, from the woods, I spotted him walking down to the dock in a pale-gray suit, his phone held to his ear.

He looked like a groom doll on a wedding cake. I wanted to tear his legs off.

At twilight, on the grounds of the massive yet log-cabin-style robber baron mansion, dozens of deer stood around, their graceful necks lowered, eating the grass. There's an abundance of deer up there, due to the hunters who've killed off all the animals that were supposed to be preying on them. So the deer.

And the girls, equally graceful with their light, carrying laughter and long limbs, spun glow-in-the-dark hula hoops or played croquet with ancient peeling mallets as the purple dusk fell. The older one had honey-colored hair and blue eyes; the younger had brown hair and her eyes were a shade of amber. They hardly looked like sisters, but they were. The blonde was called Nieve, Spanish for *snow*, and the brunette was Rosa but she went by Rose. Their mother—a former ballerina from Madrid who was both anorexic and mentally slow—had named them but often she forgot their names.

We only met because I came out of the woods one night. I came out of the woods and walked right across the rolling lawn, scattering the Bambis. The sun was setting over the lake and a slight breeze rippled the water.

I admit the girls appeared frightened. What Rosa told me later was this: those first few seconds, they actually mistook me for a bear.

They'd never seen a homeless guy before—they were that sheltered, even though they lived in downtown Manhattan; trust me, it can be done—and though I wasn't technically homeless I had that same dirty, hirsute aspect. I'm not a small man but tall and barrel-chested, and that June evening I wore filthy clothes and a long beard and needed badly to bathe in the lake.

I had a home in the forest, or a temporary shelter, anyway; but to girls that pampered and young there's no perceptible difference between an aging hippie and a transient.

So they were frightened at first, but I held up my hands as I walked up to the porch. The cottage had a wide wraparound porch, stone-floored, with swings, chairs, rugs, and potted plants. The girls retreated partway up the stairs and stood there uncertainly on the steps in their simple cotton frocks, clutching a Frisbee and a skipping rope. I held up my hands like a man who was surrendering.

I was lucky the help wasn't around and the mother, as usual, had gone to bed early. If anyone else had been there—the cook, for one, who was a domineering type—they probably would have run me off.

I'd had too much to drink, of course. It was my pastime then—the summer before my divorce, a strange and isolated time. I was camped out in an old airplane hangar on one of the smaller lakes and now and then I hitchhiked into town, bought booze and groceries, and prayed not to run into my estranged wife. We'd had our own more modest summer place nearby.

What I'd done was, I'd disappeared. I didn't want my wife to know where I had gone. It was the only trick I had left: hiding and vanishing. I got some meager satisfaction from an idea I had of her not knowing whether I lived or died—her wondering if maybe, defying all her expectations, I'd left my dull old self behind and flown off to a distant and unknown country.

Those girls were good. Plenty of rich girls aren't, we all know that. But those two girls were innocent. I don't know how they turned out that way, with the mother who wasn't all there and the father who wasn't there at all. That goodness came from them like milk from a rock.

Snow, as I came to call her because I couldn't be bothered to pronounce her real name, mostly liked books, and sat in the shade of the porch on afternoons, reading. Her sister was more social and spent her time talking to everyone. She rode her bicycle to an old folks' home most days and helped the people there.

As I stood on the lawn looking up at them, I noticed something I hadn't seen from a distance: the girls' skin glowed. Both of them had this luminous kind of skin.

That clear, young skin is part of what makes girls look so edible.

I asked them not to be afraid. I told them my name, and after a few moments they seemed to relax and told me theirs. They had a dog, an old Irish setter who lay around and barely raised his tail even for flies. I sat down on the steps and petted the dog, after a while.

So we were friends. Of course, I wouldn't have had a chance if the girls hadn't been left on their own so much. Now and then a friend their own age came up from the city to visit and I didn't intrude upon them then.

But those visits were rare. Often at dawn or dusk, when the deer and the girls were out, I was the only company they had. I kept a low profile and did not throw the Frisbee back and forth with them, in case someone could see us from the house. Usually we stood together and we talked, a little out of sight. Once or twice they sat on the end of the dock and trailed their feet through the water, and I swam, only my head above the darkening surface.

From the high bedroom windows of the cottage's second floor, that wouldn't have looked like anything.

The girls were kind to me. They let me use the canoes in the boat-house, even encouraged me, and some mornings I would row out into a hidden bay and sit and drift, trying idly to fish in the shade of a red pine. There were some old rods in the boathouse, and since I had none of my own I used to borrow them.

Snow would leave me sandwiches or sometimes bring a bowl of ice cream onto the porch. Rose offered small hotel bottles of shampoo and told me to use them.

These girls were both honest. Once Snow said to me, "You smell not too good. Did you know?"

I told her that I washed my clothes whenever I could, in the coin laundry in town or the lake. I also tried to swim and use soap on myself, but now and then I lost track and missed a day or two.

"I wish you wouldn't," said Snow wistfully.

My back hurt from sleeping on the cement floor of the hangar and I ended up asking the sisters for aspirin. For several days my back and neck had been sore, and the pills took the worst edge off the pain but that was all. Then Rose said I should sleep in the cottage, which had more bedrooms than could easily be counted. There was a certain servants' part of the house, they said, which had its own entrance, and none of the help used it. I could sneak in at night and sleep in the comfortable bed, which had down pillows and high-thread-count sheets.

I protested at first; I had some fear I'd run into one of the other members of the household. But it was silent when I snuck in there at night, after the girls had gone to bed. It was so quiet that it almost seemed to me they lived there by themselves, and food and water were furnished to them by invisible hands.

The bed was a nice change from concrete floors, so nice I almost questioned my recent course in life—hunkering down in the hangar, unshaved and unwashed, hiding from my soon-to-be-ex-wife. But then I came full circle; the hiding couldn't be so wrong for it had brought me here, to this great mansion with its soft sheets and gentle girls.

After that I often slipped in by the servants' narrow stairs and slept in my private room, tucked up under the roof. I set my wristwatch alarm and crept out at the crack of dawn. The cottage doors were never locked during the summer months; the family was always there, the family or the staff. I watched them from the shadows whenever I could. The Mexican groundskeeper rode around on his lawn tractor uselessly, mowing nothing, happy to sit aloft. The live-in maid smoked cigarettes near the garden shed and sometimes slipped away to have sex with him in the bushes.

One day the mother had a brief flash of life and donned her sparkling tennis whites. She ran outside and hit a few balls feebly with Rose on the clay tennis court. Meanwhile Snow, on the sidelines, took snapshots for the family album.

It was a rare occasion, to see the mother outside in the sun, acting alive like that.

But only fifteen minutes passed before the mother went inside again, apparently angry or depressed. She threw her racket down and blurted something that I couldn't quite make out. I saw the girls' faces as they watched her go. Their faces were both sad and calm; the girls were resigned to this beautiful, semiretarded mother with her spidery limbs and odd tantrums.

Perhaps she was never a ballerina, I thought to myself. There aren't too many retarded ballerinas in this world, is my perception of the thing, although there certainly are a few who, like the mother, starve themselves.

That evening, around dusk, the girls came swimming with me in the lake; Rose lathered my hair up with shampoo. It was one of the only times I felt the sisters' touch. They weren't too prone to physical contact. They hadn't grown up with affection, and also, I was an older, often bad-smelling man, quite unattractive to them. No doubt they were afraid that any touching would be mistaken for an invitation.

But on this occasion, beyond the end of the dock, Rose ducked my head under, laughing, and when I came up spluttering and trying to catch my breath Snow pushed my head under again, and both of them were playfully drowning me.

We were happy.

Then Rose said, "What would he look like with no beard?"

Snow looked at me, too, considering, and then climbed up onto the dock, toweled off, and ran into the house. She came back in a minute with shaving equipment. She even had scissors—clearly no razor, by itself, would be up to the task—and an old hand mirror of heavy silver.

Snow cut off the part of the beard that hung. Then they watched while I sat in the shallows and, with Rose holding up the mirror, shaved off the stubble that was left.

"He's not that bad," she said, when I was done.

I dipped my face under and came up again, wiping the water away from my eyes, the flecks of girl-scented shaving foam floating.

"He looks like that actor," said Snow, cocking her head. "You know, that big French one with the crooked nose."

"You look like that actor," concurred Rose, nodding.

"He's sort of ugly," said Snow. "And you have to like him."

"Exactly," said Rose. "Ugly, like you."

"But also likable," said her older sister.

"Girls," I said ruefully, "you're going to have to find a way to tell the truth a little less often."

"Why?" asked Snow.

"Well, for one thing, it hurts people's feelings."

"We're sorry," said Rose. "We didn't mean to."

"I know," I said. "I know. And B, if you get in this habit of telling men the truth, you'll never find true love and get married."

"I won't get married anyway," said Rose.

"I won't either," said Snow.

"How do you know?" I asked.

"It seems really stupid," said Snow.

"Like cutting off your leg," said Rose.

"Every marriage is different," I said.

"Get out," said Snow.

"Well, you're supposed to be married," said Rose. "But now your wife likes someone else better."

"So soon you won't be, anymore."

"More or less accurate," I conceded.

"Then why are you defending it?" asked Snow.

"Once you were practically normal," added Rose. "But now you carry a roll of toilet paper around in a greasy disgusting backpack," and she shuddered visibly.

"We're just saying," said Snow, almost apologetic.

It was then that we heard a rare sound—at least, rare to us in the tranquillity of those summer evenings: car tires crunching on gravel in front of the house.

"No way," breathed Snow.

"Daddy," said Rose.

"It's the third time this whole summer," said Snow.

"The first time lasted for an hour," Rose told me.

"The second was on my birthday," said Snow.

"He stayed fifteen minutes."

"He brought me a gift certificate."

I tensed up, worried I'd get caught with them. My clothes were heaped on the bank, except for the boxer shorts I wore. There was a clean line of sight if he came around the corner. But I had other clothes in the hangar so all I had to do was swim away—swim across to the part of the shore that was hidden from the house by trees, and from there retreat to my hangar.

"I should go," I said.

"Don't worry. We'll totally distract him," said Rose.

They climbed up onto the dock, legs dripping. Towels swirled up around their shoulders, feet left wet prints on the dry wood before they slipped into flip-flops. Then the girls were headed up the grassy slope—not running, not eager. Just dutiful.

I felt a rush of thankfulness that I'd never had children to disappoint. Though I wished the girls were my own daughters; even I would have shone in comparison with the gray doll.

I didn't have his wealth. But still.

I sank down in the water and spied on them, the waterline beneath my nose. I kept my mouth clamped shut.

The suit was undertaker-black this time and I could just make out a silver-colored headset. He talked into the headset as the girls went up the hill to meet him. Rose stepped toward him awkwardly, as though she wanted to embrace, but he held up his hand and shook his head and kept talking, turning around as he paced.

She stepped back.

It occurred to me then that they would be better off if he died, but it was an academic, impersonal thought. It had nothing to do with me.

A second later, it also occurred to me that if someone tore the groom in half, the girls would still have his money but not his cold and persistent disregard.

It was painful, on the other hand, the loss of a father. Even a negligent father. And with the semiretarded mother on the brink of death surprisingly often—due to the repeated self-starving activities, which made her subject to sudden hospital visits—the poor girls might be farmed out to relatives. Separated.

So as quickly as I had it, I gave up the idea of murdering him. You know: murder goes through your head sometimes, and then goes out again. It's normal, in my opinion.

Anyway, the thought had no bearing on subsequent events.

After a while the father stopped talking into his headset mouthpiece. By that time the girls had already given up and drifted into the house without, as far as I could tell, even a smile of greeting from him. Some fragments of his one-sided conversation floated down to me—a few words in the twilight, "value-added," "deal structure," and possibly "red herring."

Then he, too, disappeared.

What happened later that night was simple, as I would testify.

Around one in the morning, as I lay trying to sleep on the hangar floor, my back started to hurt. It hurt a lot, mainly because there was nothing between me and the cracked cement but a threadbare sleeping bag I'd filched from a Goodwill bin in Albany. During the vanishing act I hadn't wanted to reveal myself by using my joint-account ATM card. And I had no painkillers left from the prescription stash the girls had given me. So finally, driven by discomfort, I crept out onto the dirt road, pain shooting through my back, grasping my heavy, antique flashlight.

There was a dim glow in the ground-floor windows of the mansion where lamps had been left on, but through those windows I could see no one was reading by their light. The family was sleeping. So I went around behind the house and up the servants' stairs, taking off my shoes and walking in my sock feet. I found my room as usual and went to sleep myself, so relieved by the comfort of the bed that I forgot my back.

But presently I was woken up. There was a loud, terrible noise.

Bleary, I didn't recognize it at first. I thought it was a cat, in pain or trying to mate. Then I understood it was human—human and female. I sat right up, jolted with fear for those sweet girls. I had to do something, so I grabbed my flashlight and ran out into the corridor.

I didn't know the house at all, only the route to my secret cubby. So I was stumbling down narrow halls like I was in a maze, basically running blind, this way and that, trying to follow the screaming. It stopped for a short time and I faltered—partly in confusion, partly out of a growing conviction that the sound wasn't coming from either of the girls. It was too feral and too hoarse. But then it started up again and I ran, tearing up and down halls in a panic, because I couldn't be sure.

Eventually I came out into a wider hall where lights were ablaze; a long carpet down the middle, and there was the mother. She wore nothing at all and was so emaciated that her jutting ribs resembled zebra stripes. I couldn't help but notice she was shaved completely bare beneath. And there was the father, in seersucker pajamas, who seemed to be choking or suffocating her. They were thrashing around, and she must have been the one screaming, though now his fingers were over her mouth. He had the upper hand, clearly, being a man and not mentally or physically impaired. A fear seized me—though behind that fear I was relieved that Snow and Rose were not the targets of this violent assault—and without thinking I threw myself into the fray.

The flashlight was the only weapon I had, and as I said, it was heavy.

Before I knew it the groom doll lay upon the ground, the left side of his head stove in.

Once we understood the gravity of the situation, we threw ourselves into reviving him. I knelt beside him and performed CPR, which I'd learned as a lifeguard in the seventies; Rose, in her frilly teddy-bear nightgown, ran to the telephone and called 911; Snow sat, her face solemn, and held one of her father's limp white hands, which I noticed was almost effeminate in the perfection of its manicure. Only the starving mother, still naked, hung back, sitting with her knobby knees raised to her chin against the far wall's wainscoting, beneath the pompous portrait of a wattled ancestor.

As you may already be aware, if you're the type to follow crime-beat or society news stories, the father did not die. In fact—and this is little known—he came out of the hospital substantially improved. It was as though he'd had a personality alteration, the sort that might follow a frontal lobotomy, for instance. He was more pleasant, after he recovered. He had more time for his wife and his children.

I even heard from my lawyer that he sought professional help for the mother. Not for the retardation, I don't think—there isn't much they do for that—but for the eating disorder.

And me, I never heard from the girls again. Not personally. But they must be better off now, too.

Because the father, who'd already made enough money to keep the family in fine linens and silverware for life, was no longer interested in business. That part of his character had simply been removed, either by the impact of the flashlight or the subsequent brain bleed. It wasn't that, as my lawyer assures me, his cognitive capacity was reduced, per se. He still performed adequately in standard aptitude tests.

No, it seemed to be more a matter of a changed disposition.

Myself, I didn't fare so well. It adds up against you when you're indigent at the time of felony commission, abusing alcohol, etc., even if the crime was committed in defense of a vulnerable party. And there was the trespass issue—although the girls, I have to say, did not desert me in my hour of need. They told the police I'd had their full permission to sleep in the house that night. Sadly, due to their ages—eleven and twelve—that testimony did not go far to clear me of the trespass charge.

I sometimes dwell on my last moments with those girls. It's true we sat upon an old carpet, discolored by the father's spreading blood, between dark-painted walls adorned with grim, even judgmental-looking paintings of the girls' dead relatives. It's true our clothing was splattered and gruesome, and the unconscious father was stretched out between us, casting a pall.

But I gazed up and around, when I'd done all the CPR I could—it was a kind of coma, I guess, though it wouldn't last long once they got him to the emergency room—and saw the semiretarded mother. Even a ballerina, I remember thinking, did not deserve to be asphyxiated, and I was still glad I'd come to her aid. Now she was staring at me with eyes as big as saucers, murmuring something in her native tongue. She spoke the dialect of Spanish where everyone has a lisp. I saw Snow, whose lovely face, lit from within, bore the light, drying tracks of tears, and the vibrant Rose, nervous and biting her nails beside a Tiffany table lamp effulgent with orange-pink roses.

And I was overcome with a curious feeling of belonging and satisfaction, as though I'd eaten a full meal and was preparing now for a long winter sleep. With the father lying inert between us in his blue-and-white seersucker, I felt we were all where we were meant to be, all posed in a tableau whose composition had been perfectly chosen a very long time ago. Whatever came afterward, I recall thinking, this was a warm cave full of soft, harmless things.

Lately I've been dreaming about forests. I grew up in a city and I used to be bored by large groups of trees, which I considered tedious. Then suddenly I discovered the world: the smell of ponderosa pine in the sun, ladybugs teeming on a downed log. Herds of elk and a wolf running across a dirt road. Recently, when we were both somewhat drunk, an old friend told me she thought landscapes were boring. I knew just what she meant; I remembered that restless so-what as you gaze out the car window at the sight of mountains. And yet, I don't feel that way anymore. I decided I wanted to write a tale set in a forest—not the wild forests you still find in the West, where I now live, but the quieter forests of the

*Adirondacks, not far from New York City, where I had once spent
time with this dear friend. Fairy tales are set in or near forests so
frequently, the threat of shadowy woods, the romance and thrill of
the unknown or deeply buried, Hansel and Gretel and Little Red
Riding Hood and Sleeping Beauty enclosed in her hedge of thorns.
The dreams called me back to the lower peaks and offered me a
gesture of living there again, for a moment. So I wrote a story
about a family in a wood-paneled house by a blue lake, its green
lawn dotted with deer, and something that came into that house
out of a dark forest.*

—LM

SARAH SHUN-LIEN BYNUM

The Erlking

It is just as she hoped. The worn path, the bells tinkling on the gate. The huge fir trees dropping their needles one by one. A sweet mushroomy smell, gnomes stationed in the underbrush, the sound of a mandolin far up on the hill. We're here, we're here, Kate repeats to her child, who isn't walking fast enough and needs to be pulled along by the hand. Through the gate they go, up the dappled path, beneath the giant firs, across the parking lot and past the kettle-corn stand, into the heart of the elves' faire.

Her child is named Ondine but answers only to Ruthie. Ruthie's hand rests damply in her own, and together they watch two scrappy fairies race by, the swifter one waving a long string of raffle tickets. Don't you want to wear your wings? Kate asked that morning, but Ruthie wasn't in the mood. Sometimes they are in cahoots, sometimes not. Now they circle the great shady lawn, studying the activities. There is candle making, beekeeping, the weaving of god's eyes. A sign in purple calligraphy says that King Arthur will be appearing at noon. There's a tea garden and a bluegrass band, a man with a thin sandy beard and a hundred acorns pinned with bright ribbons to the folds of his tunic, boys thumping one another with jousting sticks. The ground is scattered with pine needles and hay. The lemonade cups are compostable. Everything is exactly as it should be, every small elfish detail attended to, and as Kate's heart fills with the pleasure of this, the pleasure of a world complete unto itself, she is also struck by the uneasy feeling that she could have but did not secure this for her child, and therein lies a misjudgment, a possibly grave mistake.

They had not even applied to a Waldorf school! Kate's associations at the time were vague but nervous-making: devil sticks, recorder playing, occasional illiteracy. She thought she remembered hearing about a boy who could map the entire Mongol empire but at nine years old was still sucking his fingers. That couldn't be good, could it? Everybody has to go into a 7-Eleven at some point in their lives, operate in the ordinary universe. So she hadn't even signed up for a tour. But no one ever told her about the whole *fairy* component. And now look at what Ruthie is missing. Magic. Nature. Flower hair wreaths, floating playsilks, an unpolluted, media-free encountering of the world. The chance to spend her days binding books and acting out stories with wonderful wooden animals made in Germany.

Ruthie wants to take one home with her, a baby giraffe. Mysteriously they have ended up at the sole spot in the elves' faire where commerce occurs and credit cards are accepted. Ruthie is not even looking at the baby giraffe; with some nonchalance she has it tucked under her arm as she touches all the other animals on the table.

"A macaw!" she cries softly to herself, reaching.

Kate finds a second baby giraffe caught between a buffalo and a penguin. Despite representing a wide range of the animal kingdom, the creatures all appear to belong to the same dear, blunt-nosed family. The little giraffe is light in her hand, and when she turns it over to read the tiny price tag stuck to the bottom of its feet, she puts it back down immediately. Seventeen dollars! Enough to feed an entire fairy family for a month. The Noah's Ark looming in the middle of the table now looks somewhat sinister. Two by two, two by two. It adds up.

How do the Waldorf parents manage? How do any parents manage? Kate hands over her Visa.

She says to Ruthie, "This is a very special thing. Your one special thing from the elves' faire, okay?"

"Okay," Ruthie says, looking for the first time at the animal that is now hers. She knows her mother likes giraffes; at the zoo she stands for five or ten minutes at the edge of the giraffe area, talking about their beautiful large eyes and their long lovely eyelashes. She picked the baby giraffe for her mother because it is her favorite. Also because she knew her mother would say yes, and she does not always say yes, for instance when asked about My Little Pony. So Ruthie was being clever but also being kind. She was thinking of her mother while also thinking of herself. Besides, there are no My Little Ponys to be found at this faire; she's looked. And a baby giraffe will need a mother to go with it. There was a bigger giraffe on the table, and maybe in five minutes Ruthie will ask if she can put it on her birthday list.

"Mommy," Ruthie says, "is my birthday before Christmas or after?"

"Well, it depends what you mean by before," Kate says unhelpfully.

Holding hands, they leave the elves' marketplace and climb up the sloping lawn to the heavy old house at the top of the hill, with its low-pitched roof and stout columns and green-painted rafters sticking out from the eaves. Kate guesses that this whole place was once the fresh-air retreat of a tubercular rich person from long ago, but now it's a center of child-initiated learning.

Ruthie's own school is housed in a flat, prefab trailer-type structure tucked behind the large parking lot of a Korean church. It's lovely in its own way, with a mass of morning glory vines softening things up a little, and, in lieu of actual trees, a mural of woodland scenes painted along the outside wall. And parking is never a problem, which is a plus, since that can be a real issue at drop-off and pick-up. At Wishing Well the parents take turns wearing reflective vests and walkie-talkies, just to manage the morning traffic inching through the school driveway! Or else there's the grim Good-bye Door at the Jewish

Montessori, beyond the threshold of which the dropping-off parent is forbidden to pass. For philosophical reasons, of course, but anyone who's ever seen the line of cars double-parked outside the building on a weekday morning might suppose a more practical agenda. To think this was once the school Kate had set her heart on! She wouldn't have survived that awful departure, the sound of her own weeping as she turned off her emergency blinkers and made her slow way down the street.

But she had been enchanted by the Jewish Montessori, helplessly enchanted, not even minding (truth be told) ghastly tales of the Door. Instantly she had loved the vaulted ceiling and skylights, the Frida Kahlo prints hanging on the walls, the dainty Shabbat candlesticks, and everywhere a feeling of coolness and order. On the day of her visit, she sat on a little canvas folding stool and watched in wonder as the children silently unfurled their small rugs around the room and then settled down into their private, absorbing, and intricate tasks. The classroom brimmed with beautiful, busy quiet. She felt her heart begin to slow, felt the relief of finally pressing the mute button on a chortling TV. How clearly she saw that she needn't have been burdened for all these years with her own harried and inefficient self, that her thoughts could have been more elegant, her neural pathways less congested—if only her parents had chosen differently for her. If only they had given her this!

It came as a surprise, then, that the school did not make the least impression on Ondine. Every Saturday morning for ten weeks the two of them shuffled up the steps with more than twenty other potential applicants and underwent a lengthy, rigorous audition process disguised as a Mommy and Me class. Kate would break out into a soft sweat straightaway. Ondine would show only occasional interest in spooning lima beans from a small wooden bowl into a slightly larger one. "Remember, that's *his* job," Kate would whisper urgently as Ondine made a grab for some other kid's eyedropper. The parents were supposed to preserve the integrity of each child's work space, and all of these odd little projects—the beans, the soap shavings, the tongs, and the muffin tin—even the puzzles—were supposed to be referred to as jobs.

Ten weeks of curious labor, and then the rejection letter arrived on rainbow stationery. Kate was such an idiot, she sat right down and wrote a thank-you note to the school's intimidating and faintly glamorous director in the hope of improving their chances for the following year. She had never been so crushed. "You're not even Jewish," said her mother, not a little uncharitably. Her friend Hilary, a Montessori Mommy and Me dropout, confessed to feeling kind of relieved on her behalf. "Didn't it seem, you know, a little robotic? Or maybe Dickensian? Like children in a boot-blacking factory." She reminded Kate about the director's car, which they had seen parked one Saturday morning in its specially reserved spot. "Aren't you glad you won't be paying for the plum-colored Porsche?"

She wasn't glad. And she did take it personally, despite everybody's advice not to. Week after week, she and her child had submitted themselves to the director's appraising, professional eye, and for all their earnest effort, they were still found wanting. What flawed or missing thing did she see in them that they couldn't yet see in themselves? Even though she spoke about the experience in a jokey, self-mocking way, she could tell it made people uncomfortable to hear her ask this question, and she learned to do so silently, when she was driving around the city by herself or with Ondine asleep in the back of the car.

"Can I get the mommy giraffe for Christmas?" Ruthie asks at the end of what she estimates is five minutes. She stops at the bottom of the steps leading up to the big green house and waits for an answer. She wants an answer but she also wants to practice ballet dancing, so she takes many quick tiny steps back and forth, back and forth, like a *Nutcracker* snowflake in toe shoes.

"People are trying to come down the stairs," says her mother. "Do you have to go potty? Let's go find the potty."

"I'm just dancing!" Ruthie says. "You're hurting my feelings."

"You have to go potty," her mother says, "I can tell." But Ruthie sees that she is not really concentrating, she is looking at the big map of the elves' faire and finding something interesting, and Ruthie will hold the jiggly snowflake feeling inside her body for as long as she wants. This means she wins, because when she doesn't go potty regular things like walking or standing are more exciting. She's having an adventure.

"It says there's a doll room. Does that sound fun? A special room filled with fairy dolls." Her mother leans closer to the map and then looks around at the real place, trying to make them match. "I think it's down there." She points with the hand that is not holding Ruthie's.

Ruthie wants to see what her mother is pointing at, but instead she sees a man. He is standing at the bottom of the lawn and looking up at her. He is not the acorn man, and he does not have a golden crown like the kind a king wears, or the pointy hat of a wizard. She has seen Father Christmas, by the raffle booth, and this is not him. This is not a father or a teacher or a neighbor. He does not smile like the brown man who sells Popsicles from a cart. This man is tall, thin, with a cape around his neck that is not black, not blue, but a color in between, a middle-of-the-night color, and he pushes back the hood on his head and looks at her like he knows her.

"Do you see where I'm pointing?" Kate asks, and suddenly squats down and peers into Ruthie's face. Sometimes there's a bit of a lag, she's noticed, a disturbing and faraway look. It could be lack of sleep: the consistent early bedtime that Dr. Weissbluth strongly recommends just hasn't happened for them yet. A simple enough thing when you read about it, but the reality! Every evening the clock is ticking—throughout dinner, dessert, bath, books, the last unwilling whiz of the day—and with all of the various diversions and spills and skirmishes, Kate wonders if it would be that much easier to disarm a bomb in the time allotted. And so Ruthie is often tired. Which could very well explain the slowness to respond; the intractability; the scary, humiliating fits. Maybe even the intensified thumb sucking? It's equally possible that Kate is just fooling herself into thinking this, and something is actually wrong.

Tonight she'll do a little research on the Internet.

Slowly Kate stands up and tugs at Ruthie's hand. They are heading back down the hill in search of the doll room. They are having a special day, just the two of them. They both like the feeling of being attached by the hand but with their thoughts branching off in different directions. It is similar to the feeling of falling asleep side by side, which they do sometimes in defiance of Dr. Weissbluth's guidelines, their bodies touching and their dreams going someplace separate but connected. They both like the feeling of not knowing who is leading, whether it's the grown-up or the child.

But Ruthie knows that neither of them is the leader right now. The man wearing the cape is the leader, and he wants them to come to the bottom of the hill. She can tell by the way he's looking at her—kind, but also like he could get a little angry. They have to come quickly. Spit spot! No getting distracted. These are the rules. They walk down the big lawn, past the face-painting table and some jugglers and the honeybees dancing behind glass, and Ruthie sees that her mother doesn't really have to come at all. Just her.

She has a sneaky feeling that the man, under his cape, is holding a present. It's supposed to be a surprise. A surprise that is small and very delicate like a music box but when you open it keeps going down like a rabbit hole, and inside there is everything, *everything* she's wanted: stickers, jewels, books, dolls, high heels, pets, ribbons, purses, toe shoes, makeup. Part of the present is that you don't have to sort it out. So many special and beautiful things, and she wants all of them, she will *have* all of them, and gone is the crazy feeling she gets when she's in Target and needs the Barbie Island Princess Styling Head so badly she thinks she's going to throw up. That's the sort of surprise it is. The man is holding a present for her and when she opens it she will be the kindest, luckiest person in the world. Also the prettiest. Not for pretend, for real life. She's serious. The man is a friend of her parents, and he has brought a present for her the way her parents' friends from New York or Canada sometimes do. She wants him to be like that, she wants him to be someone who looks familiar. She asks, "Mommy, do we know that man or not?" and her mother says, "The man with the guitar on his back?" but she's wrong, she's ruined it: he doesn't even have a guitar.

Ruthie doesn't see who her mother is talking about, or why her voice has gotten very quiet. "Oh, wow," her mother whispers. "That's John C. Reilly. How funny. His kids must go here." Then she sighs and says, "I bet they do." She looks at Ruthie strangely. "You know who John C. Reilly is?"

"Who's John C. Reilly?" Ruthie asks, but only a small part of her is talking with her mother, the rest of her is thinking about the surprise. The man has turned his head away, and she can see only the nighttime color of his cape. She is worried that he might not give it to her anymore. She is sure that her mother has ruined it.

"Just a person who's in movies. Grown-up movies." Kate's favorite is the one where he plays the tall, sad policeman: he was so lovable in that. Talking to himself, driving around all day in the rain. You just wanted to hand him a towel and give him a hug. And though something about that movie was off—the black woman handcuffed, obese, and screaming, and how the boy had to offer up a solemn little rap—John C. Reilly was not himself at fault. He was just doing his job. Playing the part. Even those squirmy scenes were shot through with his goodness. His homely radiance! The bumpy overhang of his brow. His big head packed full of good thoughts and goofy jokes. Imagine sitting next to him on a parent committee, or at Back-to-School Night! She'd missed her chance. Now he and his guitar are disappearing into the fir trees beyond the parking lot.

Kate sighs. "Daddy and I respect him a lot. He makes really interesting choices."

"Mommy!" Ruthie cries. "Stop talking. Stop talking!" She pulls her hand away and crosses her arms over her chest. "I'm so mad at you right now."

Because another girl, not her, is going to get the surprise. The man isn't even looking at her anymore. Her mother didn't see him, she saw only who she wanted to see, and now everything is so damaged and ruined. It's not going to work. "You're making me really angry," Ruthie tells her. "You did it on purpose! I'm going to kick you." She shows her teeth.

"What did I do now?" her mother asks. "What just happened?" She is asking an imaginary friend who's a grown-up standing next to her, and not Ruthie. She has nothing to say to Ruthie: she grabs her wrist and marches fast down the rest of the hill, trying to get them away from something, from Ruthie's bad mood probably, and Ruthie is about to cry because she is not having a good day, her wrist is stinging very badly, nothing is going her way, but just as her mother is dragging her through the door of a small barn she sees again the man with the surprise, he has turned back to look at her, so much closer now, and when he reaches out to touch her she sees that he has long, yellowish fingernails and under his cape he's made out of straw. He nods at her slowly. It's going to be okay.

Inside the barn, Kate takes a breath. It actually worked. Nothing like a little force and velocity! Ruthie has been yanked out from under whatever dark cloud she conjured up. Kate will have to try that again. The doll room, strung with Christmas lights, twinkles around her merrily. Bits of tulle and fuzzy yarn hang mistily from the rafters. As her eyes get used to the dim barn and its glimmering light she sees that there are dolls everywhere, of all possible sizes, perched on nests of leaves and swinging from birch branches and asleep in polished walnut-shell cradles. Like the wooden animals, they seem to be descended from the same bland and adorable ancestor, a wide-eyed, thin-lipped soul with barely any nose and a mane of bouclé hair. Despite being nearly featureless, they are all darling, irresistible: she wants to squeeze every last one of them and stroke the neat felt shoes on their feet. Little cardboard tags dangle from their hands or ankles, bearing the names of their makers, the names of faithful and nimble-fingered Waldorf mothers who can also, it's rumored, spin wool! On real wooden spinning wheels. What a magical, soothing, practical skill. Could that be what she's missing—a spinning wheel? Kate is still searching for the proper tools in the hope that maybe they will make her more equipped. But no sooner has the idea alighted than with perfect, disheartening clarity she sees the lovely spinning wheel languishing alongside the white-noise machine and the child-sized yoga mat and the big expensive bag of organic compost intended for the theoretical vegetable garden, a collection of great hopes now gathering deadly spiders in the back of the garage. She glances down at Ruthie—is she charmed? Happy?—And then looks anxiously around the room at its sweet assortment of milky faces peeking out from under tiny elf caps or heaps of luxuriant hair. Please let there be some brown dolls! she thinks. And please let them be cute. Wearing gauzy, sparkly fairy outfits like the others, and not overalls or bonnets, or dresses made of calico. A brown mermaid would be nice for once. A brown Ondine. She squeezes her daughter's hand in helpless apology: for even at the elves' faire, where all is enchanting and mindful and biodegradable, she is exposing her again to something toxic.

But Ruthie isn't even looking at the dolls because now she has to go pee very badly. Also she can't find her giraffe. It isn't there under her arm where she left it. Her baby giraffe! It must have slipped out somewhere. But where? There are many, many places it could be. Ruthie looks down at the floor of the barn, covered in bits of straw. Not here. She feels her stomach begin to hurt. It was her one special thing from the elves' faire. A present from her mother. Maybe her last present from her mother, who might say, "If you can't take care of your special things, then I won't be able to get you special things anymore." But she won't need special things anymore! She is going to get a surprise, one that gets bigger and bigger the more she thinks about it, because she has a feeling the man is able to do things her mother is not able to do, like let her live in a castle that is also a farm, where she can live in a beautiful tower and have a little kitten and build it a house and give it toys. Also she's going to have five, no, she means ten, pet butterflies.

The man is standing outside the barn, waiting for her, and maybe if she doesn't come out soon enough he'll walk right in and get her. Ruthie wants to run and scream, she can't tell if she's just happy or the most scared she's ever been. Noooooooo! She shrieks when her father holds her upside down and tickles her, but as soon as he stops she cries, Again, again! She always wants more of this, and her father and mother, they always stop too soon.

The man in the cape won't stop. The dolls in this room are children, children he has turned into dolls. Ruthie can help him, she'll be on his team. She'll say, "I'm going to put you in jail. Lock, lock! You're in jail. And I have the key. You can never get out until I tell you." Her friends from school, her ballet teacher, Miss Sara, her best friends, Lark and Chloe, her gymnastics coach, Tanya, her mommy and daddy, her favorite, specialest people, all sitting with their legs straight out and their eyes wide open and no one else can see them but her. She will be on the stage copying Dorothy, and they will be watching, she will do the whole *Wizard of Oz* for them from the beginning, and the man will paint her skin so it's bright not brown and make her hair so it's smooth and in braids and she looks like the real Dorothy. It will be the big surprise of their life!

Kate knows there must be a brown doll somewhere in this barn, and that it's possibly perfect. If anyone can make the doll she's been looking for, these Waldorf mothers can: something touchable and dreamy, something she could give her child to cherish and that her child would love and prefer instead of settle for. Considering that she's been searching for this doll since the moment Ondine was born, $130 is not so much to spend. For every doll in this barn can be purchased, she's just discovered; on the back of each little cardboard tag is a penciled number, and it's become interesting to compare the numbers and wonder why this redheaded doll in a polka-dot dress is twenty-five dollars more than the one wearing a cherry-print apron. She wanders farther into the barn, glancing at the names and numbers, idly doing arithmetic in her head: how much this day has cost so far (seventeen for the giraffe, eight for the smoothies, two for raffle tickets) and how much it might end up costing in the future. Because if she does find the doll she's looking for, it'd be wonderful to get that white shelf she's been thinking about, a white shelf she could buy at IKEA for much less than the similar version at Pottery Barn Kids and nearly as nice, a shelf she could hang in a cheerful spot in Ondine's yellow room from which the doll would then gaze down at her daughter with its benign embroidered eyes and cast its spell of protection. All told, with the doll and the giraffe and the smoothies and the shelf, this day could come in at close to $200, but who would blink at that? You're thinking about your child.

Ladies and gentleman! Ruthie will say, Welcome to the show! And the man with the cape will pull back the curtains and everybody will be so surprised by what they see, they will put their hands over their mouths and scream. But Ruthie's own surprise is already turning into something else, not a beautiful secret anymore but just a thing that she knows will happen, whether she wants it to or not, just like she knows she will have an accident in the barn and her giraffe will be lost and her mother will keep looking at the tags hanging from the dolls' feet, looking closely like she's reading an important announcement, looking closely and not seeing the puddle getting bigger on the floor. When it happens her mother will be holding her hand, she is always holding and pulling and squeezing her hand, which is impossible actually because Ruthie, clever girl, kind girl, ballet dancer, thumb sucker, brave and bright Dorothy, is already gone.

I first encountered the Erlking in Angela Carter's "The Bloody Chamber," and then later in the Schubert lied "Der Erlkönig," set to the text of Goethe's poem. In both incarnations he is a seductive

and deadly figure—in Carter's story, a pipe-playing forest dweller who transforms young girls into caged songbirds, and in Goethe's poem a malevolent spirit king who pursues a boy traveling with his father through the woods late at night, and who promises the child untold delights. Apparently the Goethe poem is often memorized by German schoolchildren.

Anxiety about school is what inspired my version of the Erlking story: not a child's anxiety, but a parent's anxiety. I belong to a generation of parents who tend to feel rather anguished over the choices they are making for their children. Among the more charming and radical of these choices, I've always felt, is a Waldorf education. (And being a literal thinker I immediately returned, when asked to write a "contemporary fairy tale," to the last time I saw some contemporary fairies, which was at the annual fundraiser held by the local Waldorf school.) I liked the possibility that something quite menacing could occur in such a lovely, protected place. Only later did I learn that Rudolph Steiner, the founder of the Waldorf approach, was enormously influenced by Goethe's work.

—SSB

BRIAN EVENSON

Dapplegrim

THERE CAME A TIME WHEN I, THE YOUNGEST OF TWELVE SONS, EACH
of whom had imposed himself upon me in turn, could bear it no longer
and fled the house. I left one morning without awakening either my
parents or brothers, carrying only the clothes on my back. I traveled for
many days, begging food where I could, until I came to a spacious castle
of white stone lying in the lee of a mountain. It was the exact converse
of the house in which I had been raised, the fourteen of us crammed
into narrow rooms and someone's elbow always gouging someone else's
eye. Here, I thought, I would be able to breathe freely and fully.

"Who lives there?" I asked the old woman who had shared her
table with me.

"A king," she said. "But he is unfortunate and a little mad and has
lost his daughter to a troll upon a mountaintop. You would do better
to stay far from him."

"Mark my words," I said to her, "I will find a place for myself with
him," and though she laughed at me this is exactly what I managed to
do, entering into the service of the king.

The king was a dour man, nervous in his opinions and surrounded by
a dozen advisors and councillors deft at making their thoughts and

opinions his own. I could see this from the first, but what was it to me? I served him faithfully and strictly to the letter. As his servant, I occupied a position for him somewhere midway between a living, breathing human and a piece of furniture. I flatter myself to think I did my task well enough that he had no cause to take notice of me until the moment when, at the end of the year, I approached his throne on my knees and begged his leave to return home to visit my parents.

"What?" he said, confused and surprised. "And who are you?"

I told him my name, but though it was he himself who had accepted me into service, it seemed to mean nothing to him. I explained to him my duties and there came a flicker of recognition.

"Ah, yes," he said. "The candle holder. You have held it well, lad. Yes, by all means go."

And so go I did.

So often it is the case that Death chooses to take to the road before we do, and so it was that I returned to find my parents dead. Of what cause my brothers claimed not to know, but I saw enough in their furtive glances one to another to suspect that they had helped my parents on their way.

"And my inheritance?" I asked.

They admitted to having already divvied the inheritance, thinking, so they claimed, that they had no reason to think me alive. *So they wished me dead*, I thought, *and perhaps still do. I must proceed with care.*

I unsheathed my knife, using it to section an apple, and then afterward left it beside my hand on the table, blade winking in the light like a living thing.

"Shall I, then, receive nothing for my inheritance?" I asked.

They conferred and ended by offering me twelve mares living free upon the hills. This was, as they well knew, much less than my proper share, but with only one of me on my side of the table and eleven of them clustered on the other, I knew better than to protest. I accepted their offer, thanked them, and left.

———

When I arrived in the hills it was to find that I had doubled my wealth. Each mare had come to foal, so that where I had thought to see one dozen I now saw two. And among this second dozen was a big dapple-gray foal much bigger than the others and with a coat so sleek it shone bright as a shivering pane of glass. He was a fine fellow, and I could not help but tell him so.

And it was there that things began to go odd for me, that the world I thought I knew took a dark turn, and I began to see that all I had thought I knew I knew not at all. For that dappled horse, staring at me with its dark eyes, snatched me outside of my body. And when I returned to myself again, I found myself standing in the midst of the eleven other foals. I myself was awash in blood, and all of the foals were dead and by me slaughtered.

But that dapple-gray foal, still alive, moved now from mare to mare, suckling off each in turn. Both foal and mares acted as though nothing had happened, while I stood there bloody, the flies already beginning to swarm around me as if I were Death himself.

For a year I tried not to think on the events of that afternoon. For a year, I served my master the king faithfully and told myself I would not return to that hillside, that I would surrender my inheritance and simply get on with my life.

Yet what sort of life was it? I, a servant, a half-man, always at the beck and call of my liege. Was this who I chose to be? And what in the meantime had happened to the rest of me? Was this merely the resting place on the way to some other self?

And I could hear, too, somewhere deep within my head, the neighing of that dapple-gray horse, drawing me out, calling to me. So that by the time the year had completed its sidelong gait and returned to where it had begun, I knew that I did not want to return. But I knew also that despite myself I would.

The first thing I glimpsed in climbing the hill was the dapple-gray foal I had left behind. He was a yearling now, and larger than a full-grown horse, and his coat bright as a burnished shield. His eyes were like flecks of fire and each inch of skin rippled with strength. And there were twelve new foals, one for each of the mares, and I thought, *Well, now, I can lead this dapple-gray yearling away and sell him and have done with him forever.*

But when I bridled him and tried to lead him away, he pushed his hooves into the ground and would not move.

And so I came closer to him and whispered in his ear and tried to coax him to follow me, and yet he would not budge, only swung his head toward me and stared at me with his dark, smoky eyes.

And here again a dark turn was taken within me and I was lost to it, as if my soul had fled my body. And when at last I had returned, did I not find, as before, myself standing amid the slaughtered, the bloody business done? So I cursed that horse and with blood christened him Dapplegrim, for grim was his business, and grim he made my own. Yet he paid me no heed and simply moved from mare to mare, and from each of them took suck.

And so another year of faithful servitude to my king, all the while in me a growing dread as I tried not to think of what might happen once the year had passed. This time, I told myself, I would not return.

And yet, when the day came, I felt Dapplegrim's hot breath within the confines of my skull and approached my king for his leave to go. His leave was given and I set out, and so found myself there again upon the hillside. And there was Dapplegrim, grown so big that he had to kneel before I could even think to mount him. His coat shone and glistened now as if a looking glass. His eyes were full of smoke and flame now and terrible to behold. And I saw that he was alone on the hilltop, for either he had driven the mares who had suckled him away or he had killed and eaten each of them in turn.

He turned and stared at me and again I felt myself grow dizzy. Before I knew it I had ridden him bareback to my parents' old house, where my brothers still lived. They, when they saw him, smote their hands together and made the sign of the cross, for never had they seen such a horse as Dapplegrim. And right they were to be afraid, for as I rode upon his back, Dapplegrim smote them each with his hooves, and though they screamed and fled they could not escape. So that in the end there were eleven dead brothers and only me left alive.

More did happen then, but I am loath to speak of it. I still have nightmares of how this monstrous horse forced me, by pushing his way into my mind, to grind my dead brothers into his fodder. All the while I shivered and cried for him to release me, but he would not, for this horse was master of me and refused to free me.

My brothers gone and consumed, Dapplegrim was far from through with me. He forced me to melt all the pots and tools and bits of iron in my family house down and beat them into shoes for him. He showed me where my brothers had buried my parents' wealth, their gold and silver, and with these I fashioned him a gold saddle and bridle that glittered from afar. And then he knelt before me and compelled me to mount him, and off we rode.

He thundered straight to the same castle in which I had served the last few years of my life, following the road without hesitation as if he had ridden it all his life. His shoes spat stones high into the air as we rode, and his saddle and bridle and coat, too, glistened and glowed in the sunlight.

When we reached the castle the king was standing at the gate, his advisors huddled around him. They watched the approach of myself and Dapplegrim as we sped toward them like a ball of liquid fire.

Said the king once we had arrived, "Never in my life have I seen such a thing."

And then Dapplegrim turned his long neck and looked at me with one fierce eye, and I felt myself leaking away again. Before I knew it I had told the king I had returned to his service and asked him for his best stable and sweet hay and oats for my steed. The king, perhaps himself transfixed by Dapplegrim's other eye, bowed his head and agreed.

I returned to my duties. At the appointed hour I lit the king's candle and carried it after him. At the appointed hour I extinguished it. It was all just the same as it had ever been, and yet it was different, too. For whereas before the king had seemed to look right through me, to consider me as he might a knife or a chair, now he noticed me and even regarded me thoughtfully.

"Tell me," he said one day. "Where did you come by such a steed?"

"He is my inheritance, sire," I said.

"All of it?" he asked.

"He has become," I reluctantly admitted, "all of it."

"And what do you suppose such a horse might be capable of?" he asked.

What indeed? Knowing not what to respond, heart sinking, I shook my head. "I do not know," I said.

"My advisors tell me," he said, "that a steed such as yours and a rider such as you are just the sort to rescue my daughter," he said.

I stammered something out. To be honest, the princess had been absent before I arrived at the castle and I had all but forgotten about her.

"You have my leave to go, and you shall marry her if you succeed," he said, already turning away. "But if you do not return in three days with my daughter, you shall be put to death."

Dapplegrim! I thought. *Dapplegrim!* For I knew it was not the king's advisors who were to blame but my own accursed horse, my only inheritance, who in growing strong had left countless bodies in his wake. And would, by the end, I was sure, leave countless more, perhaps my own among them.

I drew my sword and went to the stables, prepared to kill the animal. But as I entered he looked up quick and stared me down with blood-flecked eyes, and I became as meek as a newborn lamb. I sheathed my sword and took up the currying brush and rubbed his mirror-like coat even sleeker than it had been before. And as I did so, he was there within my mind itself, his hooves leaving bloody tracks across my brain. And when I had finished brushing him, I had grown calm and determined and knew exactly what I must do.

And so Dapplegrim and I rode out of the king's palace, a cloud of dust rising dark behind us. I loosed the reins and let the animal direct himself, and he rode swiftly over hill and dale, skirting the edge of a thick forest, moving, ever moving.

There came to be, in the distance, veiled in haze, a large squat shape which in the end resolved into a strange, steep-sided mountain. It was toward this we rode, and at last we were there.

Dapplegrim looked the mountain up and down, and then, snorting and pawing the ground, he rushed it.

But the wall of rock was as steep as the side of a house and smooth as a sheet of glass. Dapplegrim rode best he could and made it a good way up, but then his forelegs slipped and he tumbled down, and I along with him. How it was that neither of us was killed I must ascribe to the same dark power that had led to the horse becoming the monster he now was.

And so, I thought, *Dapplegrim has failed, and for this I shall lose my head.*

But barely did I have time to catch my breath when Dapplegrim was snorting and pawing the ground, and made his second charge.

And this time he made it farther and might even have made it all the way to the top had not one foreleg slipped and sent us hurtling and tumbling down. *Failed again*, I thought, but Dapplegrim would not have it so. In a moment he was up and pawing the ground and snorting, and then he charged forward, his hooves spitting rocks high in the air. And this time he did not slip but gained the top. There he stove in the head of the troll with his hooves while I threw the princess over the pommel of the golden saddle, and down we rode again.

My story should have ended there. I had done as I had been instructed. I had rescued the king's daughter and should by rights have had her hand in marriage. Happily ever after, as they say. By rights it should have gone thus, were lords as honest and just as they expect their servants to be. But by the time, on the evening of the third day, Dapplegrim and I had returned with the king's daughter, Dapplegrim choosing to carry us all directly into the throne room, the king had had ample time to think. He had time to reconsider a promise rashly made to a mere servant and, with the help of his advisors, had begun to wriggle free of it.

For as I returned and laid before the king the promise he had made me of his daughter's hand, I found he had grown cunning and deceitful.

"You have misunderstood me," he claimed. "For how could I give my only daughter to a servant unless he were to prove himself more than a servant?"

But what is this? I wondered. *How is this not what Dapplegrim and I have just done by rescuing her where all others have failed?*

But the king, fed his lines by his advisors and set upon repeating them as he had learned them, paid little attention to the expression on my face.

There were, he told me, three tasks to accomplish. I must first make the sun shine in his darkened palace despite the mountain blocking the way. As if that were not enough, I must find his daughter a steed as good as Dapplegrim for our wedding day. Third—but I had already stopped listening by this time, and would be hard-pressed to repeat what the third task was to be.

Then, when he was finished, the king leaned back and looked up at me, a satisfied expression smeared upon his face.

I nodded and thanked him for his indulgence, and then began to turn away. And it was just then that Dapplegrim caught my eye, and I was transfixed.

In retrospect, I am not surprised how things turned out. Indeed, each and every one of our yearly reunions upon the hillside should have suggested to me how things would end. For there was Dapplegrim galloping through my skull and a strange red haze overwhelming my vision. And before I knew it, I had drawn my sword and lopped free the head of my king. And then, as, screaming and whinnying, they tried to flee, the heads of his twelve advisors. And finally, for good measure, that of his beloved daughter.

It was not long after this that I myself became king, for the people were afraid to do otherwise. I have done my best to serve justly and flatter myself to think that more often than not I have done so. When I have not, it is less my own fault than that of the dapple-gray horse, huge and monstrous, who, when he fixes his eyes upon me and calls for blood and pain, I find I still cannot refuse.

So why have I told you, you who would serve me, this? Why does the mad king at whose feet you throw yourself and beg for a place bare his soul to you thus? Is it, you worry, that he has no intention of giving you anything?

No, you shall have a place if, after having listened to me, you still do so desire. But you must know it is not me you shall serve. You, like me, shall serve Dapplegrim. And he is not an easy master.

I grew up reading a blue hardbound multivolume illustrated set of fairy tales and myths the name of which I no longer remember, even though many of the stories and some of the illustrations I still carry around in the suitcase that is my skull. From there, I

graduated to Andrew Lang's compilations, and then I forgot about fairy tales for a while. It was only when I started reading the Brothers Grimm to my children that it became clear to what degree fairy tales had structured my thinking as a human and as a writer.

One of the tales I've thought about most over the years is the Norwegian folktale "Dapplegrim," collected by Lang in his Red Fairy Book. *It has an obsessiveness to it that I think is astounding, and I love the matter-of-fact way that slaughter becomes a founding principle for the story itself. I've always felt the story had a remarkably modern thrust to it, in the same way that some of the Icelandic Sagas, despite being written hundreds of years ago, do. My own telling of the tale tries to bring out what I think is psychologically implicit in the story. There's a tone and a darkness to the original that I love, and I also love the notion of the horse itself as a kind of embodiment of the subconscious, an indication of a split within the psyche that both enables the narrator and that he feels enslaved to. The result is, I hope, something like Nick Cave's updating of murder ballads: something true to the original which, despite maintaining the original setting, feels contemporary in attitude, mood, and thrust.*

—BE

MICHAEL CUNNINGHAM

The Wild Swans

HERE IN THE CITY LIVES A PRINCE WHOSE LEFT ARM IS LIKE ANY other man's and whose right arm is a swan's wing. He's a survivor of an old story. His eleven formerly enchanted brothers were turned from swans back into fully formed, handsome men. They married, had children, joined organizations, gave parties that thrilled everyone right down to the mice in the walls.

The twelfth brother, though, got the last of the magic cloaks, and his was missing a sleeve. So—eleven princes restored to manly perfection and one with a little something extra going on. That was the end of that story. "Happily ever after" fell onto everyone like the blade of a guillotine.

Since then, it's been hard for the twelfth brother. The royal family didn't really want him around, reminding them of their brush with the darker elements, stirring up their guilt about that single defective cloak. They made jokes about him, and insisted they were only meant in fun. His young nieces and nephews, the children of his brothers, hid whenever he'd enter a room and giggled from behind the chaises and tapestries. He grew introverted, which led many to believe that swan-armedness was also a sign of mental deficiency.

So finally he packed a few things and went out into the world. The world, however, was no easier than the palace had been. He could land only the most menial of jobs. Every now and then a woman got interested, but it always turned out that she was briefly drawn to some Leda fantasy or, worse, hoped her love could break the old spell and bring him his arm back. Nothing ever lasted long. The wing was graceful but large—it was awkward on the subway, impossible in cabs. It had to be checked constantly for lice. And unless it was washed daily, feather by feather, it turned from the creamy white of a French tulip to a linty, dispiriting gray.

He's still around, though. He pays his rent one way or another. He takes his love where he can find it. In late middle age he's grown ironic, and cheerful in a toughened, world-weary way. He's become possessed of a wry, mordant wit. Most of his brothers back at the palace are on their second or third wives. Their children, having been cosseted and catered to all their lives, can be difficult. The princes spend their days knocking golden balls into silver cups or skewering moths with their swords. At night they watch the jesters and jugglers and acrobats perform.

The twelfth brother can be found most nights in one of the bars on the city's outer edges, the ones that cater to people who were only partly cured of their spells and hexes, or not at all. There's the three-hundred-year-old woman who got nervous when she spoke to the magic fish and found herself crying, No, wait, I meant *young* forever into a suddenly empty ocean. There's the crownletted frog who can't seem to truly love any of the women willing to kiss him. In those places, a man with a single swan wing is considered lucky.

If you're free one night, go out and find him. Buy him a drink. He'll be glad to meet you, and he's surprisingly good company. He tells a great joke. He has some amazing stories to tell.

When I was a kid in the suburbs of Chicago my family had a copy
of the stories of Hans Christian Andersen, with beautiful, rather

*grotesque illustrations by Arthur Rackham, which I found so
terrifying that I could not only not open the book but could not, on
some of my more delicate days, enter the living room in which the
book was shelved. This terror metamorphosed eventually, naturally,
into fascination, and one day when I was six I forced myself to take
down the book, open it, and gaze unflinchingly, unaccompanied, at
its pictures. I believed that that day, I became a man.*

*I was particularly enamored of "The Wild Swans." I'll spare us
all any meditations on the alluring power, to a rather odd
suburban child, of a story that involved one of twelve princes who
emerged at story's end redeemed and restored up to a point, but
destined to bear a swan's wing instead of his right arm, because his
beloved sister hadn't had quite enough time to make all twelve of
the required magic cloaks. What more could possibly be said about
that?*

—MC

KAREN JOY FOWLER

Halfway People

THUNDER, WIND, AND WAVES. YOU IN YOUR CRADLE. YOU'VE NEVER
heard these noises before and they are making you cry.

Here, child. Let me wrap you in a blanket and my arms, take you
to the big chair by the fire, and tell you a story. My father's too old and
deaf to hear and you too young to understand. If you were older or he
younger, I couldn't tell it, this story so dangerous that tomorrow I
must forget it entirely and make up another.

But a story never told is also a danger, particularly to the people in
it. So here, tonight, while I remember.

It starts with a girl named Maura, which is my name, too.

In the winter, Maura lives by the sea. In the summer, she doesn't. In
the summer, she and her father rent two shabby rooms inland and she
walks every morning to the coast, where she spends the day washing
and changing bedding, sweeping the sand off the floors, scouring, and
dusting. She does this for many summer visitors, including the ones
who live in her house. Her father works at a big hotel on the point. He
wears a blue uniform, opens the heavy front door for guests and closes
it behind them. At night, Maura and her father walk on tired feet back
to their rooms. Sometimes it's hard for Maura to remember that this
was ever different.

But when she was little, she lived by the sea in all seasons. It was a lonely coast then, a place of rocky cliffs, forests, wild winds, and beaches of coarse sand. Maura could play from morning to night and never see another person, only gulls and dolphins and seals. Her father was a fisherman.

Then a doctor who lived in the capital began to recommend the sea air to his wealthy patients. A businessman built the hotel and shipped in finer sand. Pleasure boats with colored sails filled the fishing berths. The coast became fashionable, though nothing could be done about the winds.

One day the landlord came to tell Maura's father that he'd rented out their home to a wealthy friend. It was just for two weeks and for so much money, he could only say yes. The landlord said it would happen this once, and they could move right back when the two weeks were over.

But the next year he took it for the entire summer and then for every summer after that. The winter rent was also raised.

Maura's mother was still alive then. Maura's mother loved their house by the ocean. The inland summers made her pale and thin. She sat for hours at the window watching the sky for the southward migrations, the turn of the season. Sometimes she cried and couldn't say why.

Even when winter came, she was unhappy. She felt the lingering presence of the summer guests, their sorrows and troubles as chilled spaces she passed through in the halls and doorways. When she sat in her chair, the back of her neck was always cold; her fingers fretted and she couldn't stay still.

But Maura liked the bits of clues the summer people left behind—a strange spoon in a drawer, a half-eaten jar of jam on a shelf, the ashes of papers in the fireplace. She made up stories from them of different lives in different places. Lives worthy of stories.

The summer people brought gossip from the court and tales from even farther away. A woman had grown a pumpkin as big as a carriage in her garden, hollowed it out, and slept there, which for some reason couldn't be allowed, so now there was a law against sleeping in pumpkins. A new country had been found where the people had hair all over their bodies and ran about on their hands and feet like dogs, but were very musical. A child had been born in the east who could look at anyone and know how they would die, which frightened his neighbors so much, they'd killed him, as he'd always known they would. A new island had risen in the south, made of something too solid to be water and too liquid to be earth. The king had a son.

The summer Maura turned nine years old, her mother was all bone and eyes and bloody coughing. One night, her mother came to her bed and kissed her. "Keep warm," she whispered, in a voice so soft Maura was never certain she hadn't dreamed it. Then Maura's mother walked from the boardinghouse in her nightgown and was never seen again. Now it was Maura's father who grew thin and pale.

One year later, he returned from the beach in great excitement. He'd heard her mother's voice in the surf. She'd said she was happy now, repeated it in every wave. He began to tell Maura bedtime stories in which her mother lived in underwater palaces and ate off golden clamshells. Sometimes in these stories her mother was a fish. Sometimes a seal. Sometimes a woman. He watched Maura closely for signs of her mother's afflictions. But Maura was her father's daughter, able to travel in her mind and stay put in her body.

Years passed. One summer day, a group of young men arrived while Maura was still cleaning the seaside house. They stepped into the kitchen, threw their bags onto the floor, and raced one another down to the water. Maura didn't know that one had stayed behind until he spoke. "Which is your room?" he asked her. He had hair the color of sand.

She took him to her bedroom with its whitewashed walls, feather-filled pillows, window of buckled glass. He put his arms around her, breath in her ear. "I'll be in your bed tonight," he said. And then he released her and she left, her blood passing through her veins so quickly, she was never sure which she had wanted more, to be held or let go.

More years. The capital became a place where books and heretics were burned. The king died and his son became king, but he was a young king and it was really the archbishop who ruled. The pleasure-loving summer people said little about this or anything else. Even on the coast, they feared the archbishop's spies.

A man Maura might have married wed a summer girl instead. Maura's father grew old and hard of hearing, though if you looked him straight in the face when you spoke, he understood you well enough. If Maura minded seeing her former suitor walking along the cliffs with his wife and children, if her father minded no longer being able to hear her mother's voice in the waves, they never said so to each other.

The hotel had let her father go at the end of the last summer. They were very sorry, they told Maura, since he'd worked there so long. But guests had been complaining that they had to shout to make him hear, and he seemed with age to have sunk into a general confusion. Addled, they said.

Without his earnings, Maura and her father wouldn't make the winter rent. They had this one more winter and then would never live by the sea again. It was another thing they didn't say to each other. Possibly her father didn't know.

One morning, Maura realized that she was older than her mother had been on the night she'd disappeared. She realized that it had been many years since anyone had wondered aloud in her presence why such a pretty young girl wasn't married.

To shake off the sadness of these thoughts, she went for a walk along the cliffs. The wind was bitter and whipped the ends of her hair against her cheeks so hard they stung. She was about to go back when she saw a man wrapped in a great black cape. He stood without moving, staring down at the water and the rocks. He was so close to the cliff edge, Maura was afraid he meant to jump.

There now, child. This is the wrong time to go to sleep. Maura is about to fall in love.

Maura walked toward the man, carefully so as not to startle him. She reached out to touch him, then took hold of his arm through the thick cape. He didn't respond. When she turned him from the cliff, his eyes were empty, his face like glass. He was younger than she'd thought. He was many years younger than she.

"Come away from the edge," she told him, and still he gave no sign of hearing, but allowed himself to be led, step by slow step, back to the house.

"Where did he come from?" her father asked. "How long will he stay? What is his name?" And then he turned to address those same questions to the man himself. There was no answer.

Maura took the man's cape from him. One of his arms was an arm. The other was a wing of white feathers.

Someday, little one, you'll come to me with a wounded bird. It can't fly, you'll say, because it's too little or someone threw a stone or a cat mauled it. We'll bring it inside and put it in a warm corner, make a nest of old towels. We'll feed it with our hands and protect it, if we can, if it lives, until it's strong enough to leave us. As we do this, you'll be thinking of the bird, but I'll be thinking of how Maura once did all those things for a wounded man with a single wing.

Her father went to his room. Soon Maura heard him snoring. She made the young man tea and a bed by the fire. That first night, he couldn't stop shaking. He shook so hard Maura could hear his upper teeth banging against his lower teeth. He shivered and sweated until she lay down beside him, put her arms about him, and calmed him with stories, some of them true, about her mother, her life, the people who'd stayed in this house and drowsed through summer mornings in this room.

She felt the tension leave his body. As he slept, he turned onto his side, curled against her. His wing spread across her shoulder, her breasts. She listened all night, sometimes awake and sometimes in dreams, to his breathing. No woman in the world could sleep a night under that wing and not wake up in love.

He recovered slowly from his fevers and sweats. When he was strong enough, he found ways to make himself useful, though he seemed to know nothing about those tasks that keep a house running. One of the panes in the kitchen window had slipped its channel. If the wind blew east off the ocean, the kitchen smelled of salt and sang like a bell. Maura's father couldn't hear it, so he hadn't fixed it. Maura showed the young man how to true it up, his one hand soft between her two.

Soon her father had forgotten how recently he'd arrived and began to call him *my son* and *your brother*. His name, he told Maura, was Sewell. "I wanted to call him Dillon," her father said. "But your mother insisted on Sewell."

Sewell remembered nothing of his life before, believing himself to be, as he'd been told, the old man's son. He had such beautiful manners. He made Maura feel cared for, attended to in a way she'd never been before. He treated her with all the tenderness a boy could give his sister. Maura told herself it was enough.

She worried about the summer that was coming. Sewell fit into their winter life. She saw no place for him in summer. She was outside, putting laundry on the line, when a shadow passed over her, a great flock of white birds headed toward the sea. She heard them calling, the low-pitched, sonorous sound of horns. Sewell ran from the house, his face turned up, his wing open and beating like a heart. He remained there until the birds had vanished over the water. Then he turned to Maura. She saw his eyes and knew that he'd come back into himself. She could see it was a sorrowful place to be.

But he said nothing and neither did she, until that night, after her father had gone to bed. "What's your name?" she asked.

He was silent awhile. "You've both been so kind to me," he said finally. "I never imagined such kindness at the hands of strangers. I'd like to keep the name you gave me."

"Can the spell be broken?" Maura asked then, and he looked at her in confusion. She gestured to his wing.

"This?" he said, raising it. "This *is* the spell broken."

A log in the fire collapsed with a sound like a hiss. "You've heard of the king's marriage? To the witch-queen?" he asked.

Maura knew only that the king had married.

"It happened this way," he said, and told her how his sister had woven shirts of nettles and how the archbishop had accused her of witchcraft, and the people sent her to the fire. How the king, her husband, said he loved her, but did nothing to save her, and it was her brothers, all of them swans, who encircled her until she broke the spell, and they were men again, all except for his single wing.

So now she was wife to a king who would have let her burn, and queen of those who'd sent her to the fire. These were her people, this her life. There was little in it that he'd call love. "My brothers don't mind the way I do," he said. "They're not as close to her. We were the youngest together, she and I."

He said that his brothers had settled easily enough into life at court. He was the only one whose heart remained divided. "A halfway heart, unhappy to stay, unhappy to go," he said. "A heart like your mother's." This took Maura by surprise. She'd thought he'd slept through her stories about her mother. Her breath grew thin and quick. He must also remember, then, how she'd slept beside him.

He said that in his dreams, he still flew. It hurt to wake in the morning, find himself with nothing but his clumsy feet. And at the change of seasons, the longing to be in the air, to be on the move, was so intense, it overtook him. Maybe that was because the curse had never been completely lifted. Maybe it was because of the wing.

"You won't be staying, then," Maura said. She said this carefully, no shaking in her voice. Staying in the house by the sea had long been the thing Maura most wanted. She would still have a mother if they'd only been able to stay in the house by the sea.

"There's a woman I've loved all my life," he answered. "We quarreled when I left; I can't leave it like that. We don't choose whom we love," he told Maura, so gently that she knew he knew. If she wasn't to be loved in return, she would have liked not to be pitied for it. She got neither of these wishes. "But people have this advantage over swans, to put their unwise loves aside and love another. Not me. I'm too much swan for that."

He left the next morning. "Good-bye, Father," he said, kissing the old man. "I'm off to find my fortune." He kissed Maura. "Thanks for your kindness and your stories. You've the gift of contentment," he said, and as soon as he named it, he took it from her.

We come now to the final act. Keep your eyes shut tight, little one. The fire inside is dying and the wind outside. As I rock you, monsters are moving in the deep.

Maura's heart froze in her chest. Summertime came and she said good-bye to the seaside house and felt nothing. The landlord had sold it. He went straight to the bars to drink to his good fortune. "For more than it's worth," he told everyone, a few cups in. "Triple its worth," a few cups later.

The new owners took possession in the night. They kept to themselves, which made the curious locals more curious. A family of men, the baker told Maura. He'd seen them down at the docks. They asked more questions than they'd answer. They were looking for sailors off a ship called *The Faucon Dieu*. No one knew why they'd come or how long they'd stay, but they had the seaside house guarded as if it were a fort. Or a prison. You couldn't take the road past without one or another of them stopping you.

Gossip arrived from the capital—the queen's youngest brother had been banished and the queen, who loved him, was sick from it. She'd been sent into seclusion until her health and spirits returned. Maura overheard this in a kitchen as she was cleaning. There was more, but the sound of the ocean had filled Maura's ears and she couldn't hear the rest. Her heart shivered and her hands shook.

That night she couldn't sleep. She got up and, like her mother before her, walked out the door in her nightgown. She walked the long distance to the sea, skirting the seaside house. The moonlight was a road on the water. She could imagine walking on it as, perhaps, her mother had done. Instead she climbed to the cliff where she'd first seen Sewell. And there he stood again, just as she remembered, wrapped in his cape. She called to him, her breath catching so his name was a stutter. The man in the cape turned and he resembled Sewell strongly, but he had two arms and all of Maura's years. "I'm sorry," she said. "I thought you were someone else."

"Is it Maura?" he asked, and the voice was very like Sewell's voice. He walked toward her. "I meant to call on you," he said, "to thank you for your kindness to my brother."

The night wasn't cold, but Maura's nightgown was thin. The man took off his cape, put it around her shoulders as if she were a princess. It had been a long time since a man had treated her with such care. Sewell had been the last. But Sewell had been wrong about one thing. She would never trade her unwise love for another, even if offered by someone with Sewell's same gentleness and sorrow. "Is he here?" Maura asked.

He'd been exiled, the man said, and the penalty for helping him was death. But they'd had warning. He'd run for the coast, with the archbishop's men hard behind him, to a foreign ship where his brothers had arranged passage only hours before it became illegal to do so. The ship was to take him across the sea to the country where they'd lived as children. He was to send a pigeon to let them know he'd arrived, but no pigeon had come. "My sister, the queen," the man said, "has suffered from the not-knowing. We all have."

Then, just yesterday, for the price of a whiskey, a middle brother had gotten a story from a sailor at the docks. It was a story the sailor had heard recently in another harbor, not a story he'd lived. There was no way to know how much of it was true.

In this story there was a ship whose name the sailor didn't remember, becalmed in a sea he couldn't name. The food ran out and the crew lost their wits. There was a passenger on this ship, a man with a deformity, a wing where his arm should be. The crew decided he was the cause of their misfortunes. They'd seized him from his bed, dragged him up on deck, taken bets on how long he'd stay afloat. "Fly away," they told him as they threw him overboard. "Fly away, little bird."

And he did.

As he fell, his arm had become a second wing. For just one moment he'd been an angel. And then, a moment later, a swan. He'd circled the ship three times and vanished into the horizon. "My brother had seen the face of the mob before," the man said, "and it made him regret being human. If he's a swan again, he's glad."

Maura closed her eyes. She pushed the picture of Sewell the angel, Sewell the swan, away, made him a tiny figure in the distant sky. "Why was he exiled?" she asked.

"An unnatural intimacy with the queen. No proof, mind you. The king is a good man, but the archbishop calls the tune. And he's always hated our poor sister. Eager to believe the most vile gossip," said the man. "Our poor sister. Queen of a people who would have burned her and warmed their hands at the fire. Married to a man who'd let them."

"He said you didn't mind that," Maura told him.

"He was wrong."

The man walked Maura back to her rooms, his cape still around her. He said he'd see her again, but summer ended and winter came with no word. The weather turned bitter. Maura was bitter, too. She could taste her bitterness in the food she ate, the air she breathed.

Her father couldn't understand why they were still in their rented rooms. "Do we go home today?" he asked every morning and often more than once. September became October. November became December. January became February.

Then late one night, Sewell's brother knocked at Maura's window.

It was iced shut; she heard a crack when she forced it open. "We leave in the morning," the man said. "I'm here to say good-bye. And to beg you and your father to go to the house as soon as you wake tomorrow, without speaking to anyone. We thank you for the use of it, but it was always yours."

He was gone before Maura could find the thing that she should say *thank you* or *good-bye* or *please don't go.*

In the morning, she and her father did as directed. The coast was wrapped in a fog that grew thicker the farther they walked. As they neared the house, they saw shadows, the shapes of men in the mist. Ten men, clustered together around a smaller, slighter figure. The eldest brother waved Maura past him toward the house. Her father went to speak to him. Maura went inside.

Sometimes summer guests left cups and sometimes hairpins. These guests had left a letter, a cradle, and a baby.

The letter said: "My brother told me you could be trusted with this child. I give him to you. My brother told me you would make up a story explaining how you've come to own this house and have this child, a story so good that people would believe it. This child's life depends on you doing so. No one must ever know he exists. The truth is a danger none of us would survive."

"Burn this letter," is how it ended. There was no signature. The writing was a woman's.

Maura lifted the baby. She loosened the blanket in which he was wrapped. A boy. Two arms. Ten fingers. She wrapped him up again, rested her cheek on the curve of his scalp. He smelled of soap. And very faintly, beneath that, Maura smelled the sea. "This child will stay put," Maura said aloud, as if she had the power to cast such a spell.

No child should have a mother with a frozen heart. Maura's cracked and opened. All the love that she would someday have for this child was already there, inside her heart, waiting for him. But she couldn't feel one thing and not another. She found herself weeping, half joyful, half undone with grief. Good-bye to her mother in her castle underwater. Good-bye to the summer life of drudgery and rented rooms. Good-bye to Sewell in his castle in the air.

Her father came into the house. "They gave me money," he said wonderingly. His arms were full. Ten leather pouches. "So much money."

When you've heard more of the old stories, little one, you'll see that the usual return on a kindness to a stranger is three wishes. The usual wishes are for a fine house, fortune, and love. Maura was where she'd never thought to be, at the very center of one of the old stories, with a prince in her arms.

"Oh!" Her father saw the baby. He reached out and the pouches of money spilled to the floor. He stepped on them without noticing. "Oh!" He took the swaddled child from her. He, too, was crying. "I dreamed that Sewell was a grown man and left us," he said. "But now I wake and he's a baby. How wonderful to be at the beginning of his life with us instead of the end. Maura! How wonderful life is."

My son was born with a hole in his heart, which had to be fixed when he was eighteen months old. The operation left him with a curved scar on his back, exactly the scar you'd expect if you'd had a single wing surgically removed. Because of this and because "The Wild Swans" was one of my own favorite fairy tales as a child, I often read it to him. I could see that, same as me, he would have liked to have a wing. Lucky youngest brother!

As an adult, it does bug me, though—those clear instructions to the princess: if you speak before the task is finished, your brothers will die. How could the task be considered finished when the final shirt was not? How did she know it was okay to speak with that wing still in evidence? Isn't there, at the heart of the story, kind of a cheat? Am I okay with that? (And can I get away with something similar in my own work?)

The image of the single wing creeps into my writing a lot. It's all over my first novel, Sarah Canary. I've written poems about it, seen it in dreams. It has a hold on me. If I haven't read the fairy tale in a while, there are things about it I forget. But, just as it does in the story, in my memory and imagination, that wing persists.

—KJF

RIKKI DUCORNET

Green Air

ONCE PRIZED, NOW SHE LANGUISHES IN THE DRAWER, ONE OF MANY contained within a cedar chest. It stands beneath a window, shut against the day. His little dog guards it from intruders.

Exactly twelve months ago they had measured his ballroom together: 666 paces one way, 666 the other. Thriving they were then: fucking and spending. His kisses tasted like sweet tobacco, and after he gave her pleasure, her sex tasted like tobacco, too.

She has a matchbox in her pocket, an artifact from when she was the only one, or so she believed, to light his cigar. But now the victim of his bitter policy, she sighs all day till evening and the long night through, attempting to decipher his robber's mind, the reasons for her ritual incubation. Sleepless, she has all the time in the world to recall the looks of doubt and evil that often come to crowd his eyes and for which she once made a thousand excuses.

"My love!" she recalls now with horror her persistent request, "look kindly upon me!"

Yet he remains aloof, seemingly displeased with the roasted fowl, her failed attempts at conversation, the tenacity of her affection.

In her company he boils over with impatience when he is not deadly weary. She considers that if some aspire to the realms above the

165

moon, her husband has chosen to dwell beneath it and so shoulder that planet's shadow. Surely it is this that has corrupted his mind and darkened his mood. Yet in the whore's booths he rallies, his laughter clattering into the streets like hail. Dressed to kill he takes his ease in unknown places as she staggers under the load of his many inexplicable absences. Still she persists in her folly.

"Smile upon me, my beloved," she begs, pressing peaches upon him, the ripest fig. His eyes bright with malice, his snorted amusement frustrates her virtue. With real longing she watches his beautiful hand stroke down his beard. When for the last time he kisses her, he viciously bites her tongue. As the blood spills down her chin, he expulses her from their bed and drags her thrashing to the cedar chest although she cries out, "No! No! For I am no crone! But in the heat of youth! Even the beetles!" she shrieks, "move freely about! The insignificant snails! The tent pitchers! The camel drivers! Even the serpents make their way beneath the sun, the cool of dawn!"

That first night locked away, she notices how outside in the streets the hubbub decreases before ceasing altogether. Sprinkled with blood, the others in the chest are silent. Silenced their sobs, their barking tongues. The winter is a bitter one; no one recalls such cold! Catching a whiff of smoke from the merchant's coffee fires she lights a match. For an instant the world is kinder.

There in the drawer she is taught the final lesson: her nature—humble, generous, and kind—does not assure interest or compassion. Her one hope: that her dreadful condition may turn out to be unforeseen luck of a kind. Something might come of it; the ways of the world are mysterious. Something . . . dare she imagine it! *Wondrous*. (This is what the little dog had said, his tail held high, his eyes like two saucers, each set with a black yolked egg. "Wait and see! Wait and see! Something wondrous will come!")

The drawer is the only place where it could have ended because that is where it all began. Or rather, to be more precise, where she came upon the artifacts that caused her to consider that something was going on and not only in her head, mind you! That the marriage, so new! Barely begun! The prior wife's body still warm!—was a figment. And the drawer—as are all things belonging to husbands—was strictly taboo. As were his pockets holding small silver and keys: taboo! But then one day, sweetly occupied by the innocence of her own wifely tasks, the house flooded with light, she found herself propelled toward the very drawer in which she now languishes.

It was the fault of the little dog, you see, until then always so uncannily quiet, who at once began to raise a ruckus with all its throat, calling and calling out to her: "Come look at this!" Insisting, "Come! Here! Look at this!" And then it happens.

She goes to the chest, her heart thrashing, not only because what she is about to do is forbidden but because what she is about to find will change everything.

A box of gold rings. His sharp pencils and pens. The small brass instruments with which he navigates the streets. A box of matches she pockets without thinking. And she finds some little sticks meant to keep his shirt collars stiff. (It is prodigious how in the morning he arises an old man suffering desolation of mind as though in the night he had seen firsthand, perhaps even participated in, all the horror of the world, only to step into the shower, his dressing room, and so transform himself into a prince. Glad-eyed, he leaves the break-fast nook with a lion's muscled ease, sweetening her mind with long-ing throughout the day as the sun lifts and lowers in the deepening sky.)

Ah? But what can this be? Deep in the drawer she finds two little books coming unglued and held together with string. "You've found us!" they chirrup so shrilly she is startled. "High time! High time!" Raising their covers they fly directly into her hands. And the little dog prancing on his hind legs, he, too, cries out: "High Time! High Time!" It is hard to remove the string, her hands are shaking so.

The first book, the one on top, is familiar to her. It contains the name of the ship they sailed together on their brief honeymoon, the cities they visited, Pisa, Pompeii . . . the names of hotels, a list of gardens, museums—and she recalls all those distant places where it had seemed they had been madly in love, although . . . Everything written with his thick-nibbed pen and ink as black as tar. But now the second book shudders with such eagerness beneath the first she must attend to it at once. This book contains her husband's dreams, and it thrusts and rages into her heart.

There are a number of dreams, any number of dreams, about E. E in the green dress is how the dream begins, E in the green dress laughing. E, the dress now pushed above her legs, above her ass and he, the dreamer, the one who is her husband, fucking E, fucking E's cunt, E's ass; E naked on a green couch in a green room—why is everything green? How can her own terrible jealousy color a dream about which she knew nothing? How can it be that this venomous air, this green air that she is forced to breathe because there is no other air, is the dream's primary color?

In the dream E says, "I'll fuck you till you weep." But it is she, the one who is betrayed, who is weeping.

Outside the snow is falling. She has only one match left to light and so decides to save it. Nearly dead with cold, his dreams scramble into her mind like ferrets; they will not let her be.

He fucks a woman briefly encountered, a pale woman with hazel eyes flecked with gold. Yes. How fascinating women are—she can appreciate this—in all their variety. Flecked with gold, her white forehead as smooth as the egg of an ostrich. Her breasts, too, heavy and white. A woman she recognizes as someone she had once offered a perfect cup of tea, once upon a time in those days not long ago when she lived full of grace and wandered freely in rooms now impossible to reach. This woman she vividly recalls he fucks in a brothel within a maze or catacomb that extends beneath the Tower of Pisa or maybe it is Pompeii because there are ashes falling all around them. He chokes upon them. She chokes upon them.

Her husband's dreams are all fucking dreams. He fucks his own sons: the one who is lame, the club-footed son, the halting son. *Have I hurt you?* he asks in the dream. *Have I hurt you?* he insists, dreaming. But his sons do not speak. Their place in the dream belongs to silence.

A year unfolds reduced to letters of the alphabet and the colors of things dreamed: black ashes, a white body, the green weather within a room. In the final entry he is fucked by someone terrifying; he has no idea who. Without color or letter she is a shadow as filthy as death, and collapses heavily upon him. *A shroud?* He wonders. Has he been fucking beneath the shadow of death all along? Could it be that simple?

The cold is too intense to bear and she is forced to light her last match. Its heat and clarity offer her a moment of hope at once snapped up and swallowed. Hugging her knees she falls into a dream of her own, a dream that like all her dreams these days comes to her like a malefic visitation from some lethal galaxy.

In her dream they are standing together by the side of a country road, one somehow familiar. A movie screen has been set up in a ditch and E, the E of the green dress, stands behind a projector showing a snuff film. The images smear the screen like a filthy water.

She wants to turn away, but he forces her to look, holding her wrists behind her back as when inexplicably his lovemaking had become cruel. Her head and eyes, too, are immobilized so that she cannot look away, will forever be forced to see what he could not help but see, all those things he saw night after night in those terrible dreams of his.

Outside in the winter streets people come and go on their way home with wheels of yellow cheese and fruit of all colors imported from distant places. She hears the sounds of the fruit vendors calling, and overwhelmed with longing imagines what it would be like to bite into a red fruit, freshly picked and brimming with juice.

It comes to her that if leprosy is rampant in the region, it is because the gods in their legions are unquenchable.

At the moment Kate Bernheimer asked me for a fairy tale, I was working on a piece that I realized only then was very much rooted in both "Bluebeard" and "The Little Match Girl," who, in fact, often appear in one form or another in my work. (For example, Tubbs in The Jade Cabinet *is Bluebeard, and in* The Stain, *Charlotte is the Little Match Girl.) When I was just entering into adolescence, a friend of my father's dropped off a large box of old leather-bound fairy-tale books with thick yellow pages that had never been cut, a fabulous selection of tales from all over the known universe! After seriously damaging the first book, I learned how to cut the pages, and as my hands were stained red by the leather (the bindings were very fragile) devoured the entire collection again and again. I had always loved fairy tales, but these books were especially haunting for their beauty and their unbridled ferocity, even eroticism. (As I recall, Ondine was especially sparked with heat, and Bluebeard with bloody ice.) It could be that "Green Air," the story here, is one attempt among many to shake off the ghosts of those marvelous books, some of them nefarious! Not many years later, my mother gave the books away without my knowledge, and I continue to search for them.*

—RD

TIMOTHY SCHAFFERT

The Mermaid in the Tree

DESIREE, THE CHILD BRIDE, AND HER SISTER MIRANDA HAD GONE grave robbing for a wedding gown. In the north end of the cemetery, among the palatial mausoleums with their broken windows of stained glass where the ivy crept in, was the resting place of a young woman who'd been murdered at the altar while reciting her marital vows. The decaying tombstone, among the cemetery's most envied, was a limestone bride in despair, shoulders as slumped as a mule's, a bouquet of lilies strewn at her feet. Though her murder, by her groom's jealous mother, had been long in the past, everyone knew that her father had had her buried in her gown of lace and silk.

"Can you believe we're the only ones to have ever thought of this?" Miranda said, her knuckles bloodied from shoveling dirt, as she undid the delicate whalebone buttons lining the back of the skeleton's dress.

Desiree, however, was less inclined to be enthused, and she climbed from the hole, distracted, to light a cigarette on the flame of the lantern. She uncorked a jug, gulped down a few fingers of whiskey, and squinted at the horizon of plains burned black by old prairie fires, the setting sun leaving behind a thin ribbon of violet. *His heart isn't mine,* she thought.

The two sisters snuck back to Rothgutt's Asylum for Misspent

Youth, where the girls had lived since infancy, having been arrested then for taking candy from a baby. Desiree was fifteen now, Miranda fourteen, and Desiree's impending wedding, to take place at midnight in the all-night chapel of a seaside amusement park, excited Miranda far more than it did Desiree. The engagement burdened Desiree terrifically. As Miranda cinched Desiree into the corpse's stiff flounces of taffeta, then teased her straw-like hair into a glam fright-wig of poof and aerosol lift, Desiree plotted out how she might best jilt her betrothed.

"It needs a heavier blast of spritz," Miranda said, leaning back with one eye closed, surveying Desiree's hairdo. "Cover your face with this pillow."

As she did so, and as Miranda gave her hair a heavy fogging with the DDT pump she'd filled with her own mixture of liquor and sap, Desiree could hear, in the muffling from the pillow, the thick rise and fall of the ocean, and she knew this was the mermaid ghost beckoning her to the tree. The mermaid ghost had something important to tell her.

Desiree stood and tossed the pillow aside, and lifted the bottom of her dress just above her bare feet so she could run from the room. "Flowers," she told Miranda, and she hurried through the halls and into the walled-in courtyard and to the unruly thicket of rosebushes that concealed loose bricks. She got her hair snagged up in thorns but managed to escape Rothgutt's unnoticed by the young nun who manned, up in the turret, night security with an archer's bow and a narcotizing-tipped arrow.

About a mile away, in an open pasture overrun with musk thistle and cocklebur, stood a tree perfect for lynchings—one thick branch extended, leafless and sturdy, at a height that allowed for the knots of a noose, and yet prevented anyone who dangled there from gaining purchase with their toes tippied. At the base of the tree were the bones of many accused and convicted men and women, but also the bones of the mermaid who'd hung herself there only months ago. Her body had decayed quickly, plucked apart by the carrion that found her exotic flesh a delicacy. Whenever Desiree pricked the tip of her finger on the sharp end of a rib bone of the mermaid's skeleton, and a drop of blood bubbled up, the mermaid's ghost would appear among the many nooses that still lined the branch.

"Speak to me," Desiree said as the mermaid appeared again, swinging and mute—a misty apparition. Desiree wrapped her arms around the tree, its black bark tearing at the rotted lace of her dress. She pressed her cheek against it. She looked closely at the ghost and noticed, for the first time, that the mermaid's lips moved and trembled with words.

Desiree climbed the tree and eased out onto the branch, dangling down from it, walking herself over with her hands until she was next to the mermaid. In life, the mermaid's tongue had been cut out, but in death she could speak in a hush that sounded like the froth of a breaking wave. It was while hanging there, in her stolen wedding gown, next to the ghost, that Desiree learned the story, the truth of what had happened between the mermaid and Axel, the boy Desiree was to marry at midnight.

Much of the story Desiree already knew, having been there the night Axel found the mermaid, a girl he called Z, shortened from Zel, which he'd shortened from Rapunzel, which he'd called her first because of the wavy hair that rippled long down her back, down past the bottom of her fin.

It had been the first night of the Mermaid Parade at Mudpuddle Beach, the resort town that jingled and rang with the rickety calliopes of slug-machine parlors and where kids could buy every flavor of the razor-blade candy that was illegal in forty-six states, and where peep-show tattooed ladies unlaced their bikinis behind glass and subjected themselves to electrical shocks, and where wobble-legged rickshaws with ratty parasols clackety-clacked across the slats of the boardwalk— all the festive alliteration immortalized in that number-one hit song that Gideon Godley sang about working as a gigolo in a sailor suit in the dime-a-dance hall of the dilapidated but historic Hotel Mudpuddle (in a room of which Gideon Godley would, ironically or not, eventually croak, overdosed on angel's tit, the deadliest of trendy drug concoctions).

Many mermaids washed up each year on the shore of Mudpuddle Beach, the ocean air too thick for most of them to breathe, slowly choking them as if they were swallowing, inch by inch, a magician's endless rope of handkerchiefs. It would feel, at first, like just a gentle catch at the back of their throats, one they'd barely notice, as they were often transfixed by the overstimulation—strings of Christmas lights strung along the eaves of the oxygen dens, and the racket of the bands that trumpeted old favorites off-key in the gardens where people got drunk on prohibited liquors and danced dirty all night. But often before they were even spotted by a fisherman or a yacht party, before they'd even reached the sand castles abandoned on the beach, they'd breathe their last, strangled by the very air that brought the elderly and infirm to the beach for its clean, restorative properties.

And the most beautiful of the dead mermaids were collected and prepared for the Mermaid Parade. The city museum's art restorer, in her laboratory, would delicately bleed the mermaids, hanging them from their fins above a porcelain basin. After, in a claw-foot tub, she'd pump into their collapsing veins a solution of wax and plastic. Art students would then bend the stiffening mermaids into provocative poses, manipulating the girls' faces into expressions of rapture, and they'd pinken the trout-colored skin with a dye concocted from boiled sugar beets, syringed just beneath the flesh. The mermaids were ultimately floated in formaldehyde, in fishbowls the size of paddy wagons, which were then positioned atop carts bedecked with roses and wreaths.

The girls of Rothgutt's were allowed to attend the Mermaid Parade on condition they peddle the bicycles that pulled the fishbowls along Seaweed Boulevard, their legs strapped together in fins of muslin and green sequins, their cheeks glittered, their false eyelashes as leggy as spiders. They wore coconut-shell bras and a magnetic bracelet that, when activated by the invisible security fence electrified around the beach, would shoot a medicated spike into the vein, temporarily paralyzing the attempted-escapee for forty-five days.

Desiree's mermaid had red hair and green eyes and, as with all the other mermaids, she'd been denied any article of clothing. The art students had bent her fingers around a plum, one tiny bite bitten through the plum's black skin. They'd made her look peaceful, at least, having rolled her eyes just slightly heavenward and having parted her lips as if she'd just pulled away from a kiss. Not all the dead mermaids had been so lucky—Miranda's, for example, had been fashioned into death throes, mid-thrash and wide-eyed, as if paused in the act of drowning.

Desiree breathed against the glass of the bowl then wiped away the fog with the lace shawl she wore across her naked shoulders, polishing away smears on the glass. She named her mermaid after herself.

A whistle blasted with a frenetic tweeting, the parade captains marching about, smacking the girls with their batons, calling for order. Desiree stabbed at Miranda's fin with a shiv of broken windowpane, tearing at the costume, allowing Miranda's legs release for better peddling. She did the same for the other girls and, their fins trailing them like the trains of gowns, they all took their places on the bicycles and set off for the beach, jostling the mermaids in their formaldehyde swim. Seaweed Boulevard was lined with spectators, including the Sisterhood of Poseidon's Daughters, a faction of nuns in aquamarine habits that protested the Mermaid Parade each year. The nuns pelted the girls of Rothgutt's with a bumper crop of tomatoes they allowed to rot on the vine every late summer for this very purpose.

Not every mermaid that ever entered the atmosphere perished. One became a famous bawdy-house chanteuse, carried out onstage in a cardboard half-shell by four muscular bald men in handlebar mustaches and tight, striped swimsuits. Another became an intellectual, palled around with expatriates, and wrote, well into her eighties, feminist utopian novels. But most mermaid survivors were relegated to the carnival circuit or, worse yet, prostitution, though it was illegal to have sex with a mermaid, even without the exchange of cash; legislators considered it bestiality.

And still other mermaids were taken in by the Sisterhood of Poseidon's Daughters, a convent so radical it was considered by some a cult. It never failed that at every Mermaid Parade at least one nun would come under arrest for disrupting the procession in some manner— taking a hatchet to a fishbowl, for example, or sticking a broomstick into the spokes of one of the Rothgutt's girls' bicycle tires. Some of the mermaids the nuns rescued took the vows themselves, and could often become the most combative among them. One mermaid nun once famously set fire to herself.

As Desiree peddled down the parade path, she eyeballed the crowd for her true love, Axel, for the peppermint-striped jacket and knee breeches of his school uniform, but her fake lashes were nearly too heavy for her lids to lift. Axel attended the Starkwhip Academy of Breathtakingly Exceptional Young Men, the verdant campus of which, with its miles of sports fields and agrarian experiments, its ivy-overrun cathedrals, and its lecture halls of imported stone, was just on the other side of the wall from Rothgutt's, but might as well have been across the ocean. Desiree had met Axel on the beach following the Mermaid Parade of the summer before, collecting shells as the boys of Starkwhip Academy skinny-dipped and frolicked under the overprotective eyes of the professors shading themselves with umbrellas and pretending to read relevant texts.

The boys' parents paid such exorbitant tuition to keep their sons away from girls that the boys often fell in love with each other. When Desiree first saw Axel that one summer, he had been napping naked in the scrawny arms of a schoolmate, the boys' skin burning red as if marked by God as devilish. Desiree, on the other side of the barbed-wire fence that separated the public beach from the private had whistled into her cupped fists to trill out a melodic birdcall. Immodestly he'd stepped to the fence still naked, running his fingers through his sweaty blond locks, and had accepted Desiree's offer of a puff on her cigarette of dried corn silk. They had compared scars then, Desiree dropping the strap of her bikini to show the burn of a janitor's cigar. She'd lowered her bikini bottom a fraction of an inch to show him the clawing from a feral tom, and she'd lifted her chin and stretched her neck to show the nick from the kitchen knife when Cookie, the Roth-gutt dietitian, punished her for spilling the milk. She'd kept the rest of her scars hidden from him, wanting to save some for her wedding night. Axel had had only two scars: one on his penis from his circumcision by his nervous doctor (his father), and one on his ankle from the exhaust pipe of a motor scooter he'd got as a gift one Christmas.

They had talked until after dark that first night they'd met, feeling woozy from love and from the smell of the pig sizzling on the spit, a tusked warthog the boys had speared in the thicket of wilderness behind the public beach. And in the months after, Desiree and Axel had slipped each other love letters through a crack in the wall, and when they'd been able, they'd snuck away for clandestine meetings at a fork in the creek in the pastureland behind the school, where they had lain in each other's arms in the ribs of a rowboat run ashore into the weeds. Some nights they'd whispered only "I love you" over and over, and each time they'd felt it as if they hadn't already said it seconds before, as if they were saying it for the first time, and each time, whether hearing it or uttering it, quickened their hearts and trembled their breaths.

Meet me on the broken Ferris wheel, Axel had written to Desiree only the week before the next Mermaid Parade, referencing the old part of the amusement park where the pier had collapsed one catastrophic summer day and dropped all the carnival rides into the water.

Throughout the entire parade, as she tugged the redheaded mermaid's tank down Seaweed Boulevard, Desiree nervously gnawed at a hangnail, tearing at it until her thin blood dripped down her hand. She thought Axel might ask her to marry him that night—in the candy-colored chapels of Mudpuddle Beach, anyone over the age of thirteen could be pronounced man and wife. She'd never wanted anything more, so the potential for disappointment had made her grind her teeth and chew on her fingernails and suck hard on the ends of her hair.

After the parade ended, Desiree waited until nightfall to head off to meet Axel at the pier. She changed from her costume into a cocktail dress Miranda had sewn for her from the slick, midnight-blue kimono she'd stolen from the wardrobe of the warden of Rothgutt's. A gold tassel hung from the end of each short sleeve, and the sateen fabric was patterned with open parasols and butterflies. Miranda had Desiree kiss the end of a lipstick so that her lips were only just barely touched with red, all of it lost on the paper of her cigarette as she smoked on her walk across the beach. The shadowed, haphazard edges of the wreckage of the pier ahead of her were black against the sky, the Ferris wheel like a slipped cog, it having rolled from its axis and partly into the sea.

Desiree feared stepping past the invisible magnetic fence that would set off the poisoned spines in her bracelet, so she proceeded carefully among the crashed bumper cars, with her wrist to her ear, listening for the first hint of a click of the bracelet's workings. She crawled along twisted and knotted roller-coaster track, and as she climbed onto a spoke of the Ferris wheel, she felt a tug at her ankle, lost her balance, and fell with a shriek into Axel's arms. He caught her, but the force of her fall nearly knocked them both from the wooden seat that rocked fiercely just above the waves below. Her left slipper dropped into the water with a *plip-plop*. They clung to each other then, tightly, clawing at each other's backs and laughing at their crying. When the seat stopped swinging on its creaky hinges, they kissed for a while.

"My sister made this dress for me," Desiree said as Axel undid the buttons up the back, as he kissed her neck. "She took apart a kimono." Though she'd seen Axel naked on the first day they'd met a year before, and though she'd shown him her scars, she didn't want him undressing her. She loved him too much to risk being the girl who gave it all up too soon. Boys set girls up for failure all the time, Desiree had heard from one of the teenagers at Rothgutt's—a girl named Pearl with a broken-heart tattoo on her cheek. "Boys are too stupid to know that's what they're doing," Pearl had said, "but that's what they're doing. The boys think they're just dumb, and they are, but they're putting things together in their brains by accident."

Ask me to marry you, Desiree thought, as she brought her hands to the front of her dress, to hold it against herself. She then put her hands to his cheeks to push his face away, to look into his eyes. She scrunched up her eyebrows into sinister caterpillars, indicating she meant serious business. But she said nothing.

Finally Axel said, "Let's get a good start on ruining our lives together, huh?"

"A girl likes to get a ring before she says yes," Desiree said, though she had every intention of saying *yes yes yes yes yes yes*, endless *yeses*, ring or no ring. "So she can have something to show the other girls back at the asylum."

With that, Axel brought from his pocket the ring he'd bought on the boardwalk from a man's open raincoat, watches dangling from safety pins up and down the coat's lining, rings and necklaces tucked into the many pockets. *Give it a bite*, the man had said, inviting Axel to test the diamond's authenticity, to prove that Axel was being charged far, far too little for such stubbornly authentic jewelry, and Axel had stuck the ring on his pinkie and given the diamond a good hard bite, chipping a back tooth, causing a sharp thunderbolt of ache he felt through his body—in his temples, behind his ears, tingling his bones and back behind his testicles, and curling his toes.

"Give it a bite," he told Desiree, but before he could put it on her finger, it bounced from his hands and, in classic slapstick, tumbled about them like a clumsy dragonfly, seeming just within fingertip's reach, even knocking against a finger or a knuckle, then springing away opposite. Finally it joined Desiree's slipper in the sea with a soft and undramatic *plink*. Axel jumped in after it, but the water was as murky as squid's ink. Desiree twisted her hair around and around her finger in an effort to console herself as Axel came up for air, then dived back down, then back up, then back down. She made no suggestion that he abandon his search.

But Axel did abandon it after a few more dunks and he swam from the Ferris wheel, with urgency, as if he'd spotted the ring spirited away on the frothy top of a wave. But no, he'd heard something, someone weeping and gasping. The carousel horses, that had been perpetually suspended midstampede in the carnival's merry-go-round, fell apart with a sudden sweep of stormy weather, and Desiree watched as a white stallion broke away from its team. Its ceramic teeth bared and clenched around a green apple, the pink locks of its mane curled like plumes of smoke, it raced off. A girl's arms were wrapped around its long neck. Not a girl's, a mermaid's, Desiree saw, correcting herself with some delight, a mermaid topless, with long hair, riding away like a bucked-off Lady Godiva.

"She's alive!" Desiree yelled into the storm that had yet to produce any rain, only wind and howl. And the mermaid was not just alive, but *clinging* for life, *willing* herself to live. "Save her, Axel," Desiree whispered. Her almost-husband would be the night's hero, the ring no longer just a ring regrettably lost, but the ring lost on the night Axel rescued a mermaid from drowning.

When Axel reached the carousel horse, the mermaid allowed herself to be taken into his arms, and she held tightly to him, collapsing against him as if her fin were crippled, as he swam toward shore in the hectic waters, the waves teasing the two of them forward, then tugging them back. Desiree climbed from the Ferris wheel and along the creaking boards of the fallen pier. She ran across the sand. By the time she reached where Axel and the mermaid had washed up, Axel had coughed and vomited the ocean from his lungs. He picked up the mermaid and carried her across the desolate beach, her long wet hair coiled around his leg like a vine.

Desiree ran to keep up, gnawing at the heel of her palm to get at a sliver that pained her, as Axel rushed the mermaid to the empty lot near the casinos. There, a nurse was stationed to attend to drunkards and other overindulgent parade revelers in a collapsible medical shed slapped together for the weekend and painted orange. But just before reaching the lot, her hand to her mouth, Desiree heard the first suggestion of her bracelet's tyranny—the tiny but piercing squeak of the tightening of a spring—and her heart pounded and her feet stopped. She stumbled backward and fell into the sand, pinching and scratching at her legs to assure she still had feeling. She did. She lay on her side to wait for Axel to come back for her, watching the lightning outline the black clouds.

"I'd eaten some peaches I found," the mermaid ghost told Desiree as they dangled there from the hanging branch. Though Desiree could hear her clearly, the mermaid spoke with a click and an awkward knocking in her mouth, as if she were only just learning her way around the stump of her tongue. "I'd been swimming for hours to reach Mudpuddle Beach, and I was so hungry I was half-sick." The mermaid told Desiree that she'd rested on some rocks beneath the boardwalk in the hours before Axel rescued her. Up above had been people dancing, paper lanterns strung about and casting tall and jittery shadows up and down the walls of the casinos of red sandstone. In among the trash littering the rocks were tins with the lids cut open and jagged but with peaches still inside. The mermaid hadn't known the story of the tins, of course, of the summer tradition of cocktails mixed from their nectar, so she'd eaten all she could find.

The tins, every parade, were hauled out from a warehouse where thousands had been stored ever since a national recall. But the botulism-tainted juice, if consumed only in tiny spoonfuls, would produce a slightly out-of-body euphoria without causing illness, so bartenders added the toxic syrup to the Bruised Peach, a summer drink that also called for gin, ginger beer, and a cough drop to give it a tint of purple-black. The mermaid, however, had devoured the peaches by the fistful and, woozy, she'd fallen from the rocks and back into the sea. It was as if the carousel horse had stretched out its neck just for her as she'd floated past, allowing her to grasp the brass ring in his nose.

The nurse in the medical shed could not legally treat a mermaid in an emergency situation without filling out a kit of forms, getting it all notarized, submitting it to a government panel, and receiving in the mail (within sixty to ninety days) a permit to be posted within public sight. Fortunately for the mermaid, the nurse on duty that night had been a sympathizer, having worked for years alongside Dr. Penelope Clapp, a great pioneer in mermaid medical research (the Penny Valve, a cellophane innovation that partially humanized the mermaid's esophagus, was invented by her and named in her honor). The nurse undid the pins that kept her paper cap to her hair, unbuttoned the top buttons of her blouse, rolled up her sleeves, and locked the shed's door. She put on a pair of magnifying spectacles and ran her fingers along the rims of them, clicking through the various lenses for the correct degree before peering down the mermaid's labyrinthine throat.

"Bring me the satchel that's in the bottom drawer of the corner cabinet," the nurse ordered Axel, but he stood still, too startled by all that was going on before him. The nurse reached out and grabbed his elbow, her fingers digging into his skin. "I need your help," she said, scolding.

The bag was heavy and awkward—bottles of elixirs jostling around inside—and he nearly dropped it before reaching the bed. The nurse took from it a mask and a pump, syringes and scopes, all equipment that had been jimmied to best fit a mermaid's insides. As she gently snaked a ribbed tube up the mermaid's nostril, she handed Axel a square green-glass bottle. "Heat this up on the burner," she said. "To exactly one hundred degrees. There's a thermometer in the drawer." Together they worked in lamplight that the nurse had dimmed away to practically nothing, becoming so quickly intimate that they hardly had to speak at all, relying on gestures and glances, grunts and sighs.

Finally the mermaid breathed easy, snoring with little puffs of breath at her lips, like blown kisses. Axel had never seen anything more beautiful. She must dream of handsome sailors, he thought. Exhausted, the nurse lit a cigarette and began to strip from her sweaty uniform, down to her bra and slip, her back to Axel. A few scars ran across the skin of her thin, pale back and you could see the segments of her vertebrae. "Get her out of here," she said. "I could lose my license." She handed Axel her blouse. "Cover her breasts with this. Do you have money for a rickshaw?"

Axel reached into his pockets, pulling the damp lining inside out, demonstrating that any money he'd had he'd lost in the ocean. The nurse gave him some dollar bills she'd had tucked in her bra strap. "There's a cab stand in front of the fried jellyfish parlor down the street," she said. "Tell him to take you to the nuns. He'll probably say it's not on his route, so you'll tell him you'll pay double."

"Don't I need something to disguise her fin?" Axel asked, as he buttoned the mermaid into the nurse's blouse.

The nurse took a drag off her cigarette and exhaled heavy. "It's the Mermaid Parade," she said. "The place is crawling with people dressed up like her." She gave Axel a corked vial of a green liquid. "The nuns will know how to administer it."

"Tell *me*," he said. "In case they don't know how."

"They'll know how," she said.

"In case they don't," he said.

The nurse sighed, shook her head, stuck her cigarette in the corner of her mouth, and squinted from the smoke that rose into her eye. She wiggled her finger toward the satchel. "Get the little red tea tin out of there," she said, through clenched teeth. He did, and she showed him the double-pronged syringe inside. The tip of the needle was slightly curved. She demonstrated, on a vein of the mermaid's arm, how to give the shot. "A shot in the morning, at noon, and at night." She gave him more money from her bra and advised him to check into the flophouse at the corner of Atlantic and Pacific, "where the landlady don't ask questions."

But the landlady did ask Axel a question: "Need a drink?" She stood at the door to the room she'd assigned him and his mermaid, leaning against the jamb with a slouch intended to seduce. She wore a fuzzy, pink housecoat, roses embroidered on the lapels. Her dentures somewhere in a cup, her mouth sucked in on itself with a rhythmic smacking, and the downturned corners of her frown seemed to sag off her face entirely.

"No thank you," he said.

"Well, you might as well start scratching now, you prissy little thing, because those bedbugs will itch like hell." She slammed the door behind her.

But Axel and the mermaid did not sleep in the room; there were no other boarders on the second floor those first few nights, so Axel drew the mermaid a bath down the hall, and he lay on the floor beside her, the cold tiles cushioned only by a threadbare beach towel promoting a brand of cigarettes called Sailor's Lung—*Like having your head in a stormy cloud*, the slogan promised.

Her hair spilled over the side of the tub and began to slowly spring with curl as it dried. He combed his fingers through her golden locks. "Rapunzel, Rapunzel," he whispered, "let down your sweet hair." He practically chanted it, in a soft monkish drone, easing his anxious stomach with its rhythms and repetition. He then turned the chant into a song, his sleepiness rendering it nonsensical and poetic, a song about spotted pears and senile dogs. He wrote many songs those few days at Rapunzel's side, songs he then sang on the boardwalk when she got better, a hat overturned at his feet for coins, as the tourist season crept to an end. He bought Rapunzel a wicker wheelchair and a crocheted quilt to hide her fin, and she jiggled a tambourine he'd made from grapevine and sand dollars. As people stumbled from the casinos feeling they'd struck it rich, they took pity on the pretty girl in the chair, and would empty their pockets of coins into the hat. His banjo he'd bought with money he'd made working for a few weeks as a nanny to the sideshow's monkey boy, who'd really been nothing more than just a hirsute infant with wild yellow eyes.

Though the boardwalk crawled with private gumshoes investigating infidelities and runaways, Axel was not recognized by any of the men his parents had hired. The ocean air and summer sun had quickly turned his face craggy and dry and his blond hair had gone as white as rice noodles. He'd never before even been able to grow peach fuzz on his chin or upper lip, but his concern for Rapunzel had led to a full snow-white beard in only a week or so, concealing a weak momma's-boy chin.

Rapunzel's first drawing was of Axel looking years younger, though it depicted him from only a few weeks before: Axel swimming against the raging sea, as beautiful as a young prince, to rescue her from the drifting carousel horse. Axel had known from the beginning that she'd been unable to speak due to the tongue cut from her mouth, the primitive stitches of which he could feel with his own tongue when he kissed her, but he had not initially noticed she'd been unable to see clearly—when he brought her glasses bought from the drugstore, it was as if it improved her mind's eye as well, her backward glance blossoming in color and clarity. Her drawings looked as if torn from the pages of a book of fairy tales, the characters with eyes so round they consumed their faces.

Her illustrations also depicted Rapunzel in the life she'd left undersea, where she'd lived, like royalty, in the wreckage of a luxury liner. She'd eaten her octopus salad off broken plates of fine china and had drunk her kelp tea from cups of rusted silver. At parties, she'd made her entrances by swimming down the grand staircase lined with candelabra lit by phosphorescent jellyfish and she'd waltzed across a ballroom floor of Moroccan tile that chipped away with the sweep of her fin.

The drawings that made Axel cry were of the pirates who'd captured her and her sisters in a net as they'd swum, rebellious, near the surface to glimpse the ship's figurehead, a carving believed to be based on the mermaids' mother. Their mother, a stunning beauty who'd loved, as a girl, to swim up above the surface to sing torch songs, had become quite a legend, blamed for little yachts and sailboats capsizing in the rocky waters as sailors were lured forward by her melodious throat.

As one pirate had held Rapunzel down on the floor of the ship and another had held open her mouth, the captain had wrapped his fingers around the handle of a small knife and had pushed the blade against the tongue he held with his thumb, like slicing off a strip of apple peel. Onshore, professional singers and pop stars paid obscene amounts for mermaid tongue, which was believed to have enhancing properties. If licked within a few days of being cut fresh from the mouth, a mermaid tongue could strengthen the voice and perfect the pitch.

As Axel played his banjo on the boardwalk one drizzly evening, Rapunzel sat beneath the battered silk parasol he'd roped to her wheelchair and she drew a portrait of an opera singer collapsed on a fainting sofa in her dressing room, her spectacular breasts spilling over the top of her corset with busted laces, her wig in her lap, the tip of her long tongue curling at the tip of the mermaid tongue in her open palm. Madame Ernestine Swarth, the mezzo-soprano whose farewell performance at the Mudpuddle Hall had been selling out nightly for three years, happened by that evening and lifted the black veil of her feathery sinamay hat to look over Rapunzel's shoulder as she sketched. Charmed, she offered Rapunzel a tidy sum for the drawing.

From that point on, Axel pinned Rapunzel's drawings to the back of her wicker wheelchair, and up along the bent stem of her parasol, and her most gruesome portraits sold the quickest, the ones of mermaids in peril. She piled her hair atop her head and kept it in place with a handful of drawing pencils stuck through. She wore an artist's smock with deep pockets where she kept her wads of gum erasers and her Q-tips for blending and shading the charcoal.

At night in their flophouse bed, Axel sat cross-legged, naked, strumming the banjo and composing new songs about his love for Rapunzel as she lay next to him, singing along in her head.

Desiree, meanwhile, left notes for Axel in the usual place—stuffed into a jaggy crack along the wall between Rothgutt's and Starkwhip Academy, the crack hidden by the Japanese honeysuckle vine that climbed the bricks. But the notes went unretrieved for more than a month. Was he angry at her, she wondered, for not following him to the nurse's station? Or maybe he was embarrassed that he'd dropped her ring in the sea? *Blame me for everything*, she wrote in one of her unread notes to him, *if that will make you love me again. I won't claim innocence.*

One autumn day, the leaves of the vine having fallen, Desiree went to the crack in the wall and found all the notes gone. But her relief lasted only seconds. She was grabbed by the elbow by Sister Bathsheba and hurried to the chapel, where two detectives in dry raincoats stood gnawing their toothpicks to splinters. Her notes were spread out on a pew in front of them. Her own handwriting, so bare in the gaze of the rumpled men, startled her; her penmanship looked so poor, the loops of her *o*'s and *l*'s so girlie, the fat dots of her *i*'s so obnoxious.

"You were the last one to see him," said the detective on the left, and that was all the prompting she needed. Her heart lifted so that she nearly cried with joy. She could forgive Axel now, after weeks of hating him for hurting her. He hadn't abandoned her after all, he hadn't intended to leave all her notes in the wall and all her words unsaid. She told the detectives about the Ferris wheel, the ring dropping into the sea, the mermaid on the horse, each confession met with a scolding yet comical-sounding thwack on the back of the head by Sister Bathsheba's spank-paddle, saved from her days as a vaudeville clown. It wasn't until after Desiree had said everything that the worry—which had been such a relief, such a reprieve from feelings of rejection—began to twist her stomach. What had become of Axel?

And what *had* become of him? At that particular moment, Axel pushed Rapunzel's wheelchair up the cobbled walk of a mansion overlooking Mudpuddle Beach, where lived the owner of the Waterloo Casino and his invalid wife. The marrow-colored mansion resembled the skeleton of a whale, with portals of stained glass embedded in the porous rib bones. The windows depicted classic scenes of havoc at sea—Jonah devoured, the *Titanic* half-sunk, Captain Nemo wrestling the tentacle of a monster squid. The casino owner watched them navigate the walk that wound among the overgrown toad-spotted foxgloves, a snifter of brandy the size of a basketball cupped in his bird-boned hand. He stood on the deck, located in what would have been the hinge of the jaw of the open mouth. He swirled the brandy around, unsmiling, undrinking.

Rapunzel, against her every ounce of common sense, had become addicted to the nurse's murky green elixir, despite all the veins in her arms having fallen from Axel's inexpert stabbings with the syringe. Axel lately shot the drug into her neck, at least ten times every day, to keep her from sobbing and clawing at the itchy scales of her fin, but the street junk was watered down and costly. To access the clinical strength required the bribing of the delinquent pharmacist of Anemone Lane, and to afford the bribing, Rapunzel agreed to sell some of the organs she had doubles and triples of.

The casino owner's wife was a mermaid who'd been on land for twenty years, and suddenly she was failing rapidly. The pharmacist had put Axel in touch with a surgeon known around the county as the Malignant Dr. Benign, the Organ Grinder. The doctor would remove Rapunzel's middle swim bladder ("You can get by just *swimmingly* with just the two," he'd joked) and her upper marginella ("As useless as a tonsil!" he'd said unconvincingly; if it were so useless, then why was it worth triple the price of the swim bladder?) right there in the upstairs kitchen of the mansion. Axel had pushed the wheelchair along that winding walk to the mansion so many times over the next several weeks that Rapunzel began to resemble an over-loved ragdoll with all her crooked stitches.

One night as she soaked, groggy, in the flophouse tub after an injection of the elixir, Rapunzel put her fingers to Axel's lips, which had always meant she wanted him to tell her about the night he'd saved her life. Axel tried to tell the story, but couldn't without sobbing hysterically. Rapunzel, in her drifting to and from reality, tried to convince herself he was laughing from happiness.

In the middle of that night, Axel stood at the mirror and sawed at his tough beard with rusted scissors. He shaved away the old man's gray hair that covered his head, to get at the raw baby-pink skin there. But still he looked nothing like the boy he'd been only weeks before. Nonetheless, in the morning, he put on his turtleneck and peacoat and rolled up one of Rapunzel's illustrations of him walking, sopping wet, across the night beach, Rapunzel a precious ruin in his arms. He tied the drawing closed with a polka-dot hair ribbon and took the bus to the town of his childhood home.

Axel's parents desperately wanted this wrecked child to heal their broken hearts, but try as they may, they couldn't recognize a thing about him. It wasn't that they didn't believe he was who he said he was, but he was so absent of the beautiful, craven, childish need he'd once possessed that they couldn't reconcile themselves to his corruption. Axel's mother and father held tight to each other's fists, leaning against each other on the sofa in the parlor, unspeakingly agreeing to accept this lost soul. Axel sat across the room from them, atop a footstool with a needlepoint cushion, its cross-stitches having been mostly plucked out by his mother in her mourning. She'd spent all the days of Axel's disappearance undoing every sampler and embroidered homily she'd ever sewn.

"We love you, son," his father said, but calling this hardened, broken-backed man "son" choked him, and he cried so hard his nose bled.

"And I have a wife," Axel finally said, though he and Rapunzel had been pronounced married only by the flophouse landlady, her slumlord husband Axel's best man. Axel gave his parents the gift he'd brought. "She drew that," he said. "She's a talented artist."

"A wife?" his mother said. She picked at the pink monogram embroidered at the corner of her silk hankie.

"That's why I've come home," he said. "She's very sick. We need to find a doctor to help her." Axel leaned forward to point toward the illustration and said, softly, "That's her. That's Zel. My wife. In my arms, there. I saved her life. I've saved her life again and again and again."

This was all Axel's father needed to stifle any flicker of impulse to accept this boy back into his home. His back stiffened and he cleared his throat. He deepened and steadied his voice as if he could fool Axel into thinking he'd not shed a tear at all. "I don't think so, Axel," he said. "This is not . . . We didn't raise you to . . ." He shook his head. "The nerve. Your nerve. Coming into this house. An insult to your mother. Obscenity." He stood up. "I won't stand for it."

Axel's mother stepped forward to protect her husband from his own crushing sympathies. She held out her hand to Axel and was satisfied by the strange weight of his swollen knuckles and by the clammy chill of his skin. She led him to the front door, where she wrapped around his neck a striped woolen muffler she'd only half unraveled in his absence. "This had been yours," she told him, as if he hadn't known. She put her arm in his and walked him out onto the porch. "You let us believe you were dead," she said. "So don't go thinking that *we're* the terrible ones."

His mother had always smelled so comfortingly of nutmeg and orange peel, though she rarely stepped foot into the kitchen, not even to advise the cook. "I was so scared," Axel said, his chin trembling. He'd hoped to never have to see his Rapunzel through their eyes.

"Please know that we wish you nothing but the best," she told him with a friendly pat of dismissal. She went back into the house, and as he walked toward the front gate, she returned to the porch. "Wait," she called, and she met him at the gate. From behind her long skirt she produced Rapunzel's illustration, rolled back up and tied back closed. She smiled with pity as he took it from her, as if she felt sorry for him for having a mother and a father who no longer loved him, and she turned to walk back to the house.

At the flophouse, Rapunzel puffed on a long pipe fashioned from a hollow reed, a whittled acorn lashed to the end of it, in which a flower petal burned. She put the pipe aside and ran her cool hands over Axel's cheeks, red and puffy from all his weeping on the train. She wiped his nose with the cuff of her sleeve. She undressed, then she undressed Axel, who was so despondent he could barely lift his arms for her to pull his sweater off. She brought his head to her breast and followed her fingers softly along the grooves of his ear. She tried to remember the words to the songs she used to sing undersea, and their melodies, but it was as if they'd all escaped her with the severing of her tongue. A mechanism of the mind, she supposed, that kept her from lamenting their exact loss.

Axel smoked from the pipe, too, and his dark mood lifted into melancholy. Around midnight he wheeled Rapunzel over to The Ink and Stab, where an elegant old Japanese woman in a man's red smoking jacket, her white hair pinned up in a nautilus swirl, tattooed Axel's back. "Give the mermaid that pretty girl's face," he said, gesturing toward Rapunzel in her chair, her long secondhand prom dress reaching down past her fin. The tattooist, who herself was covered throat to toe with sea dragons committing gory violence, pumped the machine's pedal with the tip of her peg leg, setting the needle to buzzing. The pain she inflicted as she painted the many glittering green scales was excruciating, and he squeezed Rapunzel's hand so hard for comfort that she bit through the flesh of her lip. The tattooist wrote *cruel destiny* in a fluttering banner beneath the mermaid, in lettering that reminded Axel of the Popeye comic strip he used to read every Sunday after church.

"How much for that on your back?" the casino boss asked as Axel waited in the living room of the mansion, popping wheelies in

Rapunzel's chair. The doctor had Rapunzel up in the kitchen, bleeding her for a transfusion.

"What do you mean?" Axel asked.

The casino boss licked his bony middle finger and ran it across his own forehead, straightening the line of his comb-over. His shoe-polished hair was as black as the shiny suit he wore. He stepped behind Axel in the chair and tenderly touched his fingers to the back of Axel's neck. Axel leaned forward, and the casino boss's fingers followed the curls in Rapunzel's hair shaped like sea waves. "I meeeeeeean," the casino boss purred, *"how . . . much?"*

Ever since the tattoo had healed, Axel had gone shirtless everywhere, despite the unlifting fog that kept Mudpuddle Beach cold and wet in the late autumn. People would gather behind him, enraptured by the tattooist's art, as he strummed his banjo on the boardwalk and sang the love songs he wrote for Rapunzel.

"It's not for sale," Axel said, leaning forward, allowing the casino boss's fingers to follow the lines of the mermaid's hips, and down to where the points of her fins ended just above his ass. The casino boss playfully snapped at the elastic of Axel's briefs, which stuck up from his baggy dungarees.

"Nothing's not for sale," the casino boss said cheerfully. He took the lid from a vase on the credenza, and reached in for a thick roll of bills held together with a rubber band. "Think of all the intoxication you could buy your little sweetie. And a boy so young as yourself would heal in a matter of weeks. Our good doctor has all the latest medical gadgets. And strawberry-scented anesthesia to boot! You won't feel a thing."

Not only did Axel then agree to be skinned, but he signed a far more sinister contract with the casino boss. He promised he would give him a child. "You young people," the casino boss said, "have unwanted infants all the time. It's no loss." He then offered Axel a much-consulted pornographic pamphlet disguised as a medical guide: *Properly Defiling the Mermaid*, by Dr. H. W. Easterman, with illustrations by the author, its pages taped together and falling loose from the staples.

In the flophouse bathroom that night, Axel thumbed through the pamphlet with horror—the text and illustrations were graphic, but the photographs were more so: full-on mermaid snuff, the girls vivisected, their flesh peeled back and their innards laid open atop a clinical bench. He slapped the book shut and examined his back in the mirror, staring at the tattoo, divorcing himself from it, gritting his teeth and furrowing his brow, as if willing himself to slough off the skin painlessly.

He took Rapunzel to the roof then and, within the fence of wrought-iron spikes of the widow's walk, made love to her sweetly and passionately, in a variation on diagram #142 from the pamphlet. After, as he watched the stars flicker in and out within a netting of smoke-colored clouds, and considered the chilling magnitude of his own smallness, he knew he would be defaulting on all contracts with the casino boss. But the refusal of their first-born would most certainly be the end of them; the casino boss's spiny network of thugs infected every district of the world. Where could they go but into the air?

Just before dawn broke, Axel took Rapunzel to the convent of the Sisterhood of Poseidon's Daughters, its massive doors crafted from the hulls of retired ships, barnacles still crusting the wood. The door knocker was an anchor dangling from a chain. At the noise of it, a tall nun with a paralyzed hand swung out her claw and captured Rapunzel by the hair. "We have no place for boys who violate helpless creatures," the nun said in a voice gravelly with sleep and the whiskey she nursed every midnight, as she snatched away Axel's lover. Rapunzel, so long voiceless, howled with the keening of a rabbit in a trap, and she didn't stop, and Axel didn't leave the front garden, not for two days and two nights, until the nuns, unable to worship peacefully even with cotton in their ears, evicted Rapunzel, a twenty-dollar bill safety-pinned to her smock. Back in her wheelchair, Axel kneeling next to her, she wrote in her sketch pad, in a shivery, old-lady cursive: *I am an animal.*

Axel lifted his fingers to her lips. He parted her lips with his thumb and slipped his pinkie in to touch at the powerful stump of her near-soundless tongue. "Thank God for your terrible noise," he told her. He made love to her again, right there, in that garden overrun with a trumpet vine that attracted only flightless birds, and he knew they watched, the nuns, he knew they gathered in the crow's nest because he could see the stem of it warping with their weight, could see the nest of it leaning forward like the head of a sunflower. The nuns watched, their neutered flesh tucked away in mortifying panties of thorns, growing slick, throbbing with afterlife. *Never to be yours,* he said in his mind to the nuns, about his love, *never to be anybody's but ours,* and he knew this was true, because he and Rapunzel were impossible, everyone said so. And to hold something impossible in your hands, not just in your heart, was a rarity God afforded almost no one.

"Maybe our baby would be happier with them," Rapunzel wrote on her sketch pad as they escaped Mudpuddle after dark, Axel pushing her wheelchair through the forest. Though the chair bounced and bumped along the pinecone-strewn path, Rapunzel drew a portrait of the child they'd have and give away, a baby with legs and wrapped in fox-fur bunting, resting in a pram so elegant it resembled a hearse with its silk curtains and its curlicues of chrome on a waxed black cab. "We'd have a rich child," she wrote.

What Axel didn't tell her was that the silver duct tape he'd wrapped around his knuckles concealed a missing finger. He'd left the nun's garden only once during Rapunzel's captivity, to go to the boardwalk for some pralines to sustain him in his vigilance, and was there nabbed by a goon who'd taken him to the lower guts of the Waterloo Casino. Luckily for Axel, the goon had been too giddy with sadism, determined to luxuriate in Axel's slow torture. As the goon had delighted in Axel's lost finger, using it to scratch his nose and chewing on its hangnail, Axel had escaped through a vent.

And it was the goon who'd revealed to Axel the casino boss's true intentions—the organs of the first-born would be harvested. The casino boss's wife was failing fast and needed fresh parts that were as like new as possible.

"When he finally told me about his finger," the mermaid ghost told Desiree, "I felt so sad for our first-born. I cried and cried as if our baby existed, as if I'd seen him and lost him. So I don't know whose idea it was, when we came up to the hanging tree, that we should put our necks through those nooses. Have you ever seen *Romeo and Juliet* by William Shakespeare?" Desiree hadn't, but she'd had a part in Rothgutt's all-girl production of *Titus Andronicus* last year. "Axel and I saw it at the Mudpuddle Beach amphitheater. Romeo had been played by a forty-year-old actor in a wig and with circles of rouge on his cheeks, but he was quite good, and you could very much forget that he was too old."

"Like *Romeo and Juliet*," Axel told Rapunzel as he lifted her from her chair and helped her to the noose that had lynched many men. In Axel's arms, she felt euphoric, her soul given over entirely to this notion of absence, and she slipped her neck through the noose and reached up to tighten the knots. Axel stepped back, but couldn't bear to have her die before he did, so he leaped up onto the seat of the wheelchair to reach for the next noose on the tree. The wheelchair rolled from beneath him and he fell to the ground, hitting his head on the skull of a long-dead convict, knocking himself unconscious. When he woke, Rapunzel swayed lifeless above him.

"It wasn't that he changed his mind, Desiree," the mermaid ghost insisted, "but that he thought he could somehow keep *my* soul alive if *he* lived."

Upon hearing this, Desiree, her wrists too weak to hold on any longer, let go of the branch and fell to the ground. The mermaid's ghost went instantly vaporous. When Desiree landed hard on both feet, she felt her Achilles tendon tear in her ankle, and, like a stretched rubber band snipped with scissors, the tendon snapped up inside her leg and balled behind her knee. She passed out from the pain but woke only minutes later, Miranda lifting her into Rapunzel's wheel-chair, which had sat wrecked beneath the tree ever since the half-orchestrated suicide pact. Miranda, with the screwdriver she kept tucked in her sock for protection against the pervy mashers who crept among the forest paths, repaired the chair's wobbly wheels and pushed Desiree toward the wintry gray haze of the sky above the ocean, far in the distance.

"It's past midnight already," Miranda said, "but if he truly loves you, he'll still be waiting."

"I need a doctor," Desiree said. Her leg felt like her elbow felt whenever she banged her funny bone, but one hundred times worse.

"Shhhh, there's no time to talk," Miranda said, though it was at least a half hour's walk to the beach. Desiree closed her eyes and longed for sleep so she could dream dreams of Axel, so handsome in those days before he saved the mermaid from drowning.

It must have been only a week or two after Rapunzel's death that Desiree had found a note from Axel in their crack in the wall, which she had still visited every morning before going to the hives to collect the honey. She would run her fingertips through the break in the brick, hoping to scratch her skin on the edge of paper.

Dear Desiree, Are you still on the other side of this wall? Love, Axel.
Dear Axel, Yes. Love, Desiree.

Axel had returned to Starkwhip Academy, but not as a student. He now worked for the boys he had so adored, and for the professors and the deans. No one recognized him, and certainly no one believed him when he told them he was Axel. He became known only as Nine Fingers due to his missing pinkie, and whenever anything was stolen, he was blamed. *You've been nine-fingered*, the boys would say to one another when even so much as a single tooth of an old plastic comb turned up gone.

Every day he crawled through their crawlspaces and pipes with a hard-wire bristle-brush, dusting their chimneys and ducts—polishing every ventricle of the black lungs of the ancient halls in which the boys studied listlessly. In the basement, he stirred their laundry around with an oar in a kettle of boiling water and lye, and sometimes, when he folded their clothes, he'd put on a boy's uniform, skivvies and all, and fantasize about the life he'd once led. He'd lie back in a pile of quilts, rubbing his genitals through this other boy's britches, smoking a damp cigarette that frequently fizzled out from the humidity of the laundry room. He'd press his fingers hard against his tender throat, and he'd swallow, approximating the strangled breaths Rapunzel must have struggled for in her final minutes of life. *I'm worse than that pirate*, he thought, thinking of her knifed-out tongue. *How can I live with myself?* He pressed harder on his throat and imagined it being hard enough to choke all life from him, and he pictured Axel dead, and Nine Fingers alive, Nine Fingers the criminal, the villain, and he proposed to Desiree among the clouds of angered bees, her face hidden by a heavy net draping down to her shoes from the broad brim of her hat of black velveteen. The ring was a ruby one he'd stolen the night before from the headmaster's wife as she'd bathed; she'd safely tucked it away in an antique jewelry box with a pop-up ballerina that didn't pop up anymore. He'd tried to fix the ballerina by monkeying with a cog, but then he'd heard the sexy rush of water as the headmaster's wife had stood from her tub squeaky clean. "Don't let the ring fall from your finger this time," he told Desiree, either remembering the circumstances wrong, or hoping Desiree had forgotten how he'd fumbled his proposal on the Ferris wheel. She forgave him the little lie, the first of thousands of forgivenesses she could feel waiting to be granted, stuck in her teeth like an ache.

Though Desiree and Miranda arrived at the chapel long past midnight, Axel waited. He sat on the bumper of a rusted Volvo parked in front, beneath the pink of neon lovebirds, his legs crossed, the flood-level trousers of his tux revealing mismatched socks. He'd rented the tux, a dandelion yellow, from the chapel, fake shirt-ruffle and all.

"He mustn't see me in this chair," Desiree said, and Miranda rushed ahead, waving her arms, shooing.

"Bad luck!" Miranda yelled. "You can't see the bride in her wedding dress! Go inside!"

And he did as he was told. He went to the pastor's office to keep from seeing, and the pastor's wife helped Desiree into the chapel as Miranda hid the chair in the peony bushes of the parking lot. The pastor's wife seated Desiree in the front pew. "We usually charge a nickel to rent a bouquet," the pastor's wife said, pausing to allow for Desiree to offer a nickel, then she continued with, "but that'll be my present to you." She brought Desiree lilacs made of felt, their stems wrapped in an embroidered hankie.

Desiree took a deep breath and closed her eyes when she heard the pastor's wife begin to play an almost-melodic song on the pump organ. She thought of all the weddings she'd ever devised growing up—she thought of her play-marriage to Ophelia Littlenought in the third grade, her nightgown knotted atop her head and training behind her like an antique veil, her bouquet nothing but morning glories. She and Ophelia had mock-kissed—their hands over their mouths—in a corner of the yard where the gardener had just drowned a toad in a bucket. She remembered how, when a little older, she had talked herself to sleep reciting the vows she would write for the pretty-faced prince who'd been in the news when his mother fell to her death from a balcony—*If I ever stopped loving you for even a second, may the devil himself knock me over with a feather.* She remembered all the flowers she'd ever considered holding at the altar—all the tall violet glads, the plain-faced daisies, the tiger lilies with their vulgar spots. She'd decided on yellow roses until reading in an old book of manners that yellow roses were symbolic of jealousy.

My groom will not ruin my wedding, she vowed as she sat in the pew of that dollar-a-service chapel, and indeed he didn't. He was so beautiful in his suit that didn't fit. His Adam's apple up-and-downed with his sweet, nervous gulping, wiggling his bow tie that was knotted all wrong to begin with. She thanked God that he let Rapunzel die alone, and then she felt sick with guilt for thinking of Rapunzel at all.

"I do," he said, and Desiree said it, too, when asked. And tucked into her palm, in her closed fist, was a bone as tiny as one you'd choke on in a restaurant. Within the skeleton of the mermaid, which had broken to pieces beneath the hanging branch of the tree, had been another skeleton, Rapunzel's little part-boy part-fish, the first-born that never was. Desiree would hold onto this bone, keep it secret, until one terrible day in the future. Whenever she felt her husband might be drifting away for good—when the time came that he was completely lost to her—she would simply hold out this bone so small and white you could barely see it, and she would ruin him and she would bring him back.

A mermaid suicide figures in the plot of a fictional children's book at the heart of my novel The Coffins of Little Hope. *This fictional book, also called* The Coffins of Little Hope, *tells the tale of two wrongly accused sisters locked up in an all-girl criminal-orphan asylum, where fantastical threat lurks around every sharp corner. (This children's book series within the novel inspires a slavish fandom and obsession among its readership that begins to reflect the dark and venal impulses of the series' more despicable characters.) In fleshing out the story of the mermaid, I found myself drawn to the bride in the original Andersen tale—the girl the prince marries instead of the little mermaid. She's innocent in the tale, yet we feel compelled to cast her as the story's villain, due to her beauty and perfection, and the fact that she's marrying the prince and the mermaid is not. I was also moved by Andersen's portrait of the mermaid's undersea luxury among lost treasures and its contrast to her mute servility on land. But the bride in my tale gets the prince only after his love for the mermaid has ruined him, leading to broken hearts for everyone.*

—TS

KATHERINE VAZ

What the Conch Shell Sings
When the Body Is Gone

IT TOOK A LONG TIME TO FILL THE ENORMOUS TANK IN THEIR LIVING room. Meredith dragged in the garden hose, and Ray adjusted the stepladder so that he could direct the water over the rim. Their rented Victorian on Divisadero featured cathedral ceilings. The tank was Plexiglas, fifteen feet tall and twelve feet wide, acquired through a phone call to his father's company, a supplier of containers, whether to circuses, institutes of marine biology, or furniture conglomerates. Men used a gigantic dolly to convey the tank through the back garden and past the open French doors.

Meredith and Ray were water people. In their years together, they'd shared a fascination with anything aquatic. But they no longer went swimming, as they used to; they did not visit the ocean often, though it was a short drive away. She was afraid of scuba diving, and they enjoyed the fanciful notion that if they mastered the holding of their breaths, they could go lower than the snorkeling tourists and get to the stunning blue-lipped triggerfish in Hawaii, which they'd talked about visiting. And wouldn't that be simply heaven.

But now they hardly talked at all.

She found a book by an underwater photographer, a gift from him: swimmers wearing little or nothing in pools, lakes, tanks. The pictures fleshed out her idea of happiness: eyes shut with rapture at the body being suspended, as if the people in the photos were dropped to safety from a height. Look how peaceful they were, their skin almost melting, ravishing beyond belief.

The business with the tank and timing themselves started as a joke that became a game that became a method of dealing with the silence in the house.

Their bathing suits were stale from disuse. Polite—courtly, almost— they took turns mounting the ladder. There was a five-foot clearance between the tank's lip and the ceiling. Immersed, Meredith bubbled the water with exhalations so that she appeared to be boiling. She was tall and pale, her shade of hair was apricot; her pageboy was unchanged through a decade of marriage. Ray timed her at 22.0 seconds. She whip-kicked to the surface and climbed out, her suit sagging. She took the stopwatch. He lasted 32.33 seconds. Though they lacked any interest in training to compete, they tracked their scores on a whiteboard. They shared quite a laugh: Tom Sietas's breath-holding world record for being in water without inhaling bottled oxygen beforehand was 10 minutes and 12 seconds. They'd never get close.

On Sundays she always cooked eggs Benedict from a recipe popular at Bridle, the restaurant near the Presidio, in Cow Hollow on Chestnut, where she was a sous chef. Ray also liked toast and marmalade, the vitreous orange of it marbled with what looked disturbingly like burst capillaries. Today a red dot marred her soft-poached egg. Ray played a recording of Handel's *Harp Concerto* so loudly that Meredith could swear the vibration entered their utensils, so that they ate breakfast with tuning forks. "Do you want more?" she said, because it was easier to ask than *"Are you having an affair?"* "No," he said, more sharply than necessary, not looking at her. They were childless.

Meredith blamed their hours over the years: She put in nights at Bridle; Ray worked days as the host of a cooking show filmed in the Culinary Channel's studio at Fort Mason. Endless periods of standing caused a continual knife-like pain to shoot into her legs. The hotshot Young Chef favored creating foam on the plates . . . foam this, foam that! It looked like spit. She abhorred it. When she cut her hands, he ordered her to squeeze lemons, to teach her to be careful. She was old enough to be his mother. At the kitchen's porthole window, she gazed into the dining room, where the clientele seemed like children— wait on me, feed me—in some eternal realm, while she dodged eddies of burning chaos. Lifting her fingers off the fogged-up window, she left behind the shape of a clamshell.

She struggled to find openings to speak to her husband. The agony of that; they'd been friends really for just about forever before they'd married, had moaned about their separate heartbreaks until he'd said, "Shall we save each other from this pointless waste of time?"

She was fascinated at how far people could go to defy the body's limits. Many variations of static apnea exist: In 1993, Alejandro Ravelo held his breath in a pool for 6 minutes and 41 seconds. In 2008, David Blaine lasted 17:4.4 in a vat on *The Oprah Winfrey Show* but inhaled plenty of bottled oxygen ahead of time. (He was an illusionist—some people asked if he could be trusted.) Tom Sietas broke this record on *Live with Regis and Kelly*, 17:19. There's free diving with and without fins, and with weights to plummet on one breath for distance. But Meredith's heroine was Annette Kellerman, the Australian called the Million-Dollar Mermaid because she'd perform ballet in tanks filled with tables, plates, chairs, and lamps, as if to say: *This is home, and I am a breathless dream inside it.* Annette was selected in 1908 by a Harvard professor as "the Perfect Woman" because her contours were a virtual match for Venus de Milo's.

Ray Locke was one year shy of forty, and Meredith Paganelli Locke was forty-five.

They'd married when he was twenty-nine and she was thirty-five. Both of them young, back then; now they'd slipped into new categories, Ray still young but Meredith middle-aged. He'd proposed at the Japanese Tea Garden, the stream gurgling below the lacquered bridge, when they were rising stars at a restaurant inspired by Alice Waters. He grew up in a wealthy clan on Russian Hill, but she was the only child of elderly Italian parents in the Sunset with a view of the cables for the N Judah streetcar, vacillating like tightropes. Different worlds, but she and Ray met at high school food competitions at the Moscone Center, and one day, in his mother's spotless kitchen, they concocted a sourdough starter that exploded, and who could say why that tickled them with such horror and delight that it led to walks to buy joss sticks in Chinatown and her showing him how to whisper into a corner at the Neptune Society Columbarium so that his words traveled past the ashes of many pioneers and entered her ear in a far corner, and every Halloween they climbed to the Twin Towers to drink wine stolen from his father's cellar and, gazing down at the city glittering like pearls blinking a message in a black sea, who can say why they did not think of kissing but felt instead a peace that held them fast.

At a dive in the Haight, over poisonous drinks with her girlfriends, Meredith wondered aloud about the affair. "Do you have proof?" asked Beth Ann. "It's gone to his head, having his own show," said Lindsay, on her third drink. Susan chimed in that groupie types do it with anybody on television and Meredith should ask her friend Eve, who was Ray's director. "I'd stab him in the heart," said Teresa, and during the gales of laughter, Meredith set down her martini in a panic, because the bar seemed to be filling with something that was rising and lapping at her chin. The sconces were tendrils electric with light. Beth Ann voted for it being Lola, a platinum-blond ex-girlfriend of Ray's. "Lola's trouble," Teresa said. Maybe, though, it was a *lot* of silly groupie chef-show girls, hanging about the studio. Susan asked if she'd made a mistake to buy these spiked heels that *by the way were killing her feet*—and she hoisted her foot with its stylish shoe onto the table. Teresa screamed with amusement, constructing a plot for them all to lie in wait, catch Ray red-handed. Their faces looked buttery, their mouths stretched, their hair sprouted into fright wigs. In the ladies' room, sloshed, Meredith splashed water on her brow. She couldn't find the words to say to them, *But he's my best friend, or at least he once was.*

He hugged to himself the knowledge, almost sexual in its intensity, that he could stop before any damage, while simultaneously knowing just as powerfully that there was no way to hold back; the exquisite pleasure of going past the verge, drowning in kisses and frantic stolen grasping.

Of course there came the inevitable tipping into lies. Meredith waited at the War Memorial Opera House, the cars sailing by on Van Ness. Tonight was *Tristan and Isolde.* Her cell phone rang; Ray said he'd be filming late. He taught audiences how to cook inexpensive, fast dinners. *Leave my ticket at the will-call window, and I'll join you after intermission, I hope.* Her teal gown was backless with a fishtail. She cinched the belt of her raincoat; a summertime mist was forcing the crowd inside. She gave away for free both tickets to a young couple, Wagner devotees who were ecstatic. While treating herself to a napoleon in a pastry shop, the fellow at the counter asked if she was married, and, wanting to be invisible, not thinking, she replied, "No." He drawled, "So what's that on your finger?" She recalled an old joke as she held up her diamond band. "This? This is to keep the flies off." His grin was savagely unwavering, until she squirmed, and rose up, and paid, and fled, transparent even to strangers.

Eve Robideaux invited Meredith to the Ferry Building for an afternoon of teas. She ordered hers iced, in a glass so cold it was weeping. She thanked Meredith for getting her into rehab years ago, right after they'd met as line cooks at Bridle. Meredith had urged Eve to get into television after Eve repeatedly harped about cooking being a bore, unending hard work and nothing permanent to show for it. Bloated whales came and ate up your handiwork. It had been Meredith who put Ray in her care when he voiced the same frustration with being a chef. "We're worried, Merry," said Eve, fiddling with her saucer. "You look down." Tea made Meredith slightly ill, but Eve loved how it announced her being past an obsession with scotch; her parents had paid for the stay at a rehab favored by celebrities. Her childhood was like Ray's, pony rides at birthday parties, winter intercessions in Gstaad (where the wealthy dispensed with a sensible placement of vowels); her parents shelled out the clams to get her into that culinary temple, Le Cordon Bleu in Paris, and their princess could throw away what she'd learned there. Eve was a seductive example of being worry-free, of moving on. She was compact, dazzling; at thirty-two she could pass for twenty. Meredith's shaking hand spilled some tea that painted a maple leaf onto the tablecloth. "Are you ill? Should I worry about you?" said Eve, her expression knitted in concern. "Oh, a touch of something. Flu. I'm fine," said Meredith, clattering down her cup.

Her sheltered childhood, gladdened by visits to the tomato frogs at the Steinhart Aquarium. Wearing a bouclé suit for an interview for a cooking post at the Sea Wolf restaurant; after not getting the job, she learned to wear clogs and bring her set of knives. Her vacations with her elderly parents consisted of trips down the highway to a cabin in Santa Cruz owned by her aunt and uncle, who dived for abalone and spent the afternoons in raucous arguments while pounding the meat to tenderize it. Pried loose, abalone is a muscle, little else. The aunt and uncle lined their fence with the shells, the opalescent pans like baptismal fonts hot and gleaming from the beating of the sun.

He relished the illusion—knowing it to be that—of control. Stroking Eve's flat stomach, her breasts riding her inhalations, he said, "That seemed . . . mean, somehow. To ask her out so you could study her." "I wanted to make sure she's fine." "Should we tell her?" He repeated this and Eve frowned, her fingertips with their neon polish kneading his thigh. A reply would involve guessing if she and Ray would go the distance. "Come here," she said. Eve had taught him the term "bed hair"; she twisted her dark-blond waves into a rope she tossed onto her back. Her skin was flawless, her eyes sapphire glass. She was porous, always ready to be entered. He kissed her deeply and she encircled his neck. The slats of shadow in her Market Street loft (her parents had paid for that, too, in full) plastered ripples over them as a tide refigures sand.

Meredith showed a novice pastry chef how strudel dough should be stretched: Under the sheet of it, slowly move the backs of your hands. Sudden motions will tear it; a sonorous composure is required. "Pretend you're playing a harp that's tipped onto its side," Meredith said, gently, her knuckles small pink bumps under the buttered veil. A kind of quiet patience, that was what she and Ray had, and while that was not wild abandon and desperate gripping of each other and never had been, it evoked St. John to the Corinthians, those tender lines about love that vaunts not itself, does not struggle.

Back when they were just friends, Meredith taught him ballroom dancing. She was expert at it, once. She'd crossed over into betterfondness while he was dating someone else. She spent so many hours one week helping him rehearse to impress his new love that blood filled her shoes. Her womb happened to be bleeding, her fingers were bandaged from her classes at the Culinary Academy. Shy to the point of muteness, she waited and grew herbs in planters that quaked with the passing streetcar. She and her friends practiced Italian from language tapes: They fed their fixation with Rome, that grandly crumbling city doused in liquid sun.

Meredith and Ray played their breath-holding game when their schedules allowed. Alone one day, she plunged in and felt as limpid as those see-through shrimp that are visible only because of the filament of food moving in their gut. The sea: God's bathtub, God's bath toys. He dawdles there, puzzling out, via fish, a physical model to fix His origi-

nal design of human love. Each male anglerfish bites an available
female and hangs on, fusing to her forever, feeding off her wherever
she goes. Bonds that made flesh seamless: Meredith's mother had died
in her sleep a few years back, and then her father followed, ten days
later almost to the same hour. While floating and mulling, a bolt hit
Meredith out of the lucid blue: *Eve. My God, my husband is sleeping
with my friend Eve. I sent him to her when he wanted more than hiding
in a kitchen.* Eve with that intoxicating mix of being sweet and com-
manding. Meredith trembled so much that night in bed that she and
Ray turned to each other at some point lying in the dark, not making
love, but she found his arms natural and warm and the curve of his
long body as comfortable as a hammock set on its side.

She clicked into his e-mail and found the erotic pleadings, the
breathless anticipation. Never would she have imagined violating his
privacy so furiously.

He quit wearing bathing trunks in the tank. What was he—ninety?
Hey, where's the shuffleboard? He and Meredith were never naked
anymore; they had not made love for two years. God forbid they talk
about it. Without his glasses, the room outside the tank seemed to
dissolve and suggest that the Impressionist painters were onto something: There's beauty in slicing through outlines, boundaries. Today
he'd bought radishes, eagerly showed the camera's eye how, with a few
easy, deep cuts, anyone could convert them into flowers.

The heady danger of pretending that all would work out, "all" being
deliberately vague and tragically inclusive. Eve directed him to smile
and fill the airspace by chatting about himself while washing his hands
to demonstrate proper hygiene after handling chicken breasts. At her
loft, he showed her how to score and cube a mango off its skin. *Like
this?* she giggled, getting it wrong on purpose. Like *this*, he said. *Oh*
(her kissing him), *like this?* Or how about *like this*, like this, love this,
their limbs a tangle, him behind her directing her hand with the knife.

Much later, he would replay that chicken episode on YouTube, because he'd invited her to join him on camera, but she'd gestured, *Oh, no, I couldn't!* But her hand had entered the filming of the scene, and he couldn't resist hitting PAUSE again and again to look at it, that five-pointed starfish scuttling over the shoreline separating the unseen from the seen.

At a low ebb, out with the girls, Meredith reported slaving over a wedding cake only to have a drunken guest punch his fist into it. Aghast, she'd asked why he'd done it. "Because I can," he'd barked, lurching away. Lindsay said, "Wait, *wait*, Merry! You spent days on it, and he ruined it in a second?" "I'd be crazed," said Beth Ann. Susan demanded to know if Meredith had quizzed her pal Eve at the TV studio about the girls Ray was bedding in the broom closet. Insert here much gaiety. "I'd be in orbit," said Teresa, and it was unclear if she meant over Ray or over the cake despoiler. Meredith sipped her club soda and drifted back to the days when she and Ray decided to gamble their friendship and become engaged, and how giddy they were at their daring, strolling along China Beach, the waves ribbed vertically with foam so that they looked like king-sized hair combs, churned loose from the tabletops of the vanities of whales.

It would, in the time still to come, strike him as unfathomably, mercilessly cruel to have watched Meredith sautéing onions for a nothing-fancy dinner—cod and boiled potatoes—while he yakked about Eve's idea for a brand-new show: *Grand Escapes.* She'd research menus from around the globe, and instead of risking the chopping block with his show's good but not great ratings about cooking on the cheap, he could help viewers travel far without leaving their homes—*patatas bravas, pain perdu,* tandoori. ("I'll do the research, you're the talent," Eve had practically shouted. "It'll be unbelievable.") For the love of God, his regaling Meredith with this reminded him of how he sounded when he burdened her with the plot of a movie she'd missed. Look at her holding a mask of placidity. He knew her well. How to justify that hidden pleasure of carving the line of decency so close, to speak Eve's name aloud over and over so casually, innocently, just to hear it, to wallow in the presumed safety and thrill of it right then?

They sat reading magazines in their living room. The cherrywood buffet had such ancient panes that they rattled at the softest step on the wooden floor, and so the glass chattered when Meredith decided to get a drink of sparkling water from the kitchen, and she stopped and asked if he'd like her to get one for him, too. He was overcome with such a storm of love and regret that he bit his lip, and his eyes pooled with tears that he told himself he had no right to spring. Her chest rose and fell where she stood, watching him. And then came a moment they would both remember for the rest of their lives, because who can hope for another instance of such a divine connection? "Jesus Christ," he blurted, "and I don't know why I'm saying this, Merry. But is Beethoven's Ninth running through your head?" He tapped his left temple. "Your mind gets so loud sometimes I think I can hear it, too." She was startled; her palms flew to her mouth. She walked to him and he laid his head on her chest so her arms could circle him lightly, and his glasses slipped off and they rocked like that for a short while before she whispered, "Yes. I was at the part when the chorus goes insane, chanting *joy joy joy*."

Annette Kellerman was born with a defect in her legs that required braces until she found that moving through water cured her. Her performances in a tank at the New York Hippodrome gave birth to synchronized swimming. Her one-piece skintight bathing suit got her arrested on a Boston beach, and though she didn't understand the fuss, the world soon adopted her invention. She stayed married to a man she adored. Rich and famous in her lifetime and recognized as an artist, Annette reigned in a floating kingdom. Her hunger for water expanded into religion. Meredith, in the tank, told herself: If you can hold your breath for one second, you can endure a second longer. Her personal best was now 1:25.2; Ray's was 52.7.

You wait with bated breath. You decline to accept that *bated* also means the violent anger and fury of a roused hawk.

She cornered Eve at the TV studio. Ray was in a corner, wearing a paper collar while a woman powdered the shine off his high forehead. Meredith lost her voice with Eve, then found it. "Is it true? What are you planning with Ray?" Eve hardly moved. That smooth veneer of the easeful childhood that alternated with a sheen of addiction. Eve showed Meredith the clipboard she was gripping and said, "We're planning to show how to grind your own spices, Merry. You can stay and watch." Meredith could scarcely control her limbs as she stormed out. Ray strode after her, and she broke into a run.

The lure of breath-holding is how it violates the laws of the gods. Fasting, meditation, and prior hyperbreathing can prolong submersion; uncanny how many souls risk blackout, bloody lungs, damaged tissue, burst veins. Death. Legend has it that the ama divers of Japan brought up pearls, but the truth is more workaday; mostly they brought up abalones to sell the nacre interiors.

She screamed at some apprentices at Bridle who thought it would be hilarious to use beef stock for the vegetarian special. In the middle of the night, with Ray sleeping, she drank a bottle of wine, seized his ID card, and swiped her way into the Culinary Channel's studio. He'd told her that the subject of the next day's filming would be lamb stew, and it took more than an hour for her to march the vats of it, and the pans filled with the breakdown of the stages of preparation, out to her car. She took the food to St. Vincent's shelter. Ha, look at tomorrow's neat little script, turned into nothing.

So much energy squandered on being foolish. Ray almost got fired for having no idea how to improvise. Eve saved the day by defrosting some trout, taking center stage, and showing how to fillet and grill fish, skinning and boning it with a surgical skill that won her applause. She did not have to ponder much to figure out who had sabotaged

Everyday Triumphs, and she phoned Bridle and told the Young Chef. Meredith's work had been suffering; she burned orders, she was a sleepwalker. While chiding Meredith, the Young Chef smirked and said, "If you're going to steal hundreds of dollars' worth of lamb, at least bring it here." At first she was desperate to be fired, anything but his jollity at her distress. But when he wondered out loud if the kitchen's fumes had steam-cooked her brain, she absorbed in an instant the truth that genuine adulthood comes when one does not run off because of shame, when one stays and demands a home.

She roamed among the cosmetics counters at Macy's, seeking potions, wrinkle creams, hydrating salves. Skeletal women in tight black dresses held atomizers and spritzed her with rose and lilac mists. Their tuberous fingers waved like polypi, motioning her closer to the pots of coral paste, the shallow pans of shadows.

A trickling sound issued from their walls; they suspected brocade patches of mold and split pipes too expensive to get to. Meredith wondered if a crack had sprung in the Plexiglas. In homage to Annette, she put items in the water, a battered teakettle, a dial telephone, a broken lock from her gym bag, the shipwrecked items of ordinary existence.

Midway through their ten-year marriage, Meredith had had a fling—the word evoked a stick thrown as far as possible—that Ray, so far as she knew, was ignorant of. Marcus was a principal dancer with the San Francisco Ballet, and she still winced to recall the final meeting, their twenty-seventh in the span of three months, the afternoon at the Fairmont segueing into a grindingly awful finish in the parking lot of Muir Woods, the breezes ripping tufts of furry bark off the redwoods and pelting Marcus's Cadillac. He was announcing he'd found someone new. When she asked what she'd done, he said, "Nothing. It's the end we expected." They'd gone to concerts, and Lord, to go dancing with him. He'd clutched her once and moaned how much he needed her. "I could fall in love with you, you know." He'd said that.

She'd said it back. *Could*. At the Cable Car Museum, over the ear-assaulting whine of the gears as the frayed cables were getting soldered to a safer thickness, he'd asked if she could see herself ever living in London. *His native city*. She started breaking down in his car at Muir Woods, stopped mercifully short of pleading, but when she said she was shocked and ready to cry, he shouted, "Shocked?" A straight ballet dancer could have his pick of women—why, it was a fucking parade. Air refused to enter her lungs; she pushed against the passenger's door but it was as if she were drowning in a car. The utter shame of her fantasies, the gentle but firm phrasing she'd rehearsed to tell Ray she was leaving him; her heady mirages of soaring in that stratosphere where Marcus traveled, in the ether of the talented and famous; her sharply outlined mental pictures of gadding about London; the girlish rush of seeing a star leaping onstage after he'd sidled up to her at a charity fund-raiser and invited her to spend the night. When Ray had asked her why she was so sad, she'd replied, "Because how can I feel so old without having grown up."

At an extremity of breath-holding, a little-talked-about occurrence is a buckling of the body, a triggering of the sexual nerves, an arousal; sexual asphyxiation beckons. At 2:01.1 exactly, this frightened Meredith almost to death, and Ray jumped in to rescue her. She lay heaving and sobbing on the floor, and they called an end to everything. What was the prize? They hadn't concocted one! What was the point? Why hadn't they thought clear to the eventual need to drain the tank? They formed a bucket brigade, dashing the water into the garden, and the task was so laborious and ridiculous that they laughed, and when the men arrived to cart the tank away, Meredith and Ray held hands—they had not touched like this in so long that it was like an electrical prod to the tails of their spines.

With her hair tied into the topknot that they referred to as her Pebbles Flintstone, while wearing her UC Santa Cruz T-shirt with its marinara stain near the banana-slug mascot, *because who cares if I look like hell*, she cooked an omelet that was the most perfect he'd ever seen or smelled or tasted. It was plain. He was about to reach across the table and say, "I do so love you, and—" but he had no idea how to complete his sentence, and during that pause, she said she knew that he was leaving her, even if he didn't. Yet. His rib cage ached. "She'll take your show from you, Ray," she said, her back to him, clearing the plates. "How do you know?" he managed. He should have said, *I'm drowning, forgive me, come here.* "It's what pushy women do!" she screamed. She shattered a plate against a wall, in the manner of wronged vixens in movies, which had always struck him as too theatrical and deranged to occur in actual life. "They want to direct you and then eat you alive!" When he grabbed her arm, she blazed. "Go on, men think they'll live forever," she spat out.

Beth Ann insisted that Meredith and Lindsay join her in toasting Ray's departure. "Good fucking riddance!" she cried. Lindsay hooted, "His show sucks anyhow. Cooking shows are porn, stuff we watch but don't get to eat." Meredith chomped wasabi peas so she didn't have to speak, and when she choked, they pounded her back. How happy her friends were now that she'd joined their club of the solitary furies. While packing to move to an apartment on Green Street, she decided to prick her anguish by watching *Everyday Triumphs*, and what do you know, Eve was on camera with him, teamed up. She shut off the set, but walking past the silent box she couldn't help but see her husband still bobbing behind the glass, as if in a flat aquarium, trapped in the everlasting digital dots that passed for immortality.

The tank had soaked through the floor. Her boxes of childhood things in the basement were rotted. Her Chatty Cathy doll's hair sprouted mange. Her school papers were a smear. A plastic mermaid from an old fish bowl was corroded, her arms arrested in uplift, like the priest during the Major Elevation when he declares, "This is My Body."

She would come to associate his new marriage with pumpkins, because his wedding was in the autumn following their divorce. Squash soup was on the menu at Bridle; a blade slipped and she needed stitches. Pumpkin lattes and candle smoke seeping out of the den-tiled smile of jack-o'-lanterns: She pretended she could inhale his wedding as an aroma of fall. *Meredith, what were you thinking?* scolded Beth Ann. *You snuck into his* reception? At the Palace of Fine Arts, the wind threatened to overturn the tables under the sand-colored dome. Meredith hid behind a colonnade, unnerved to be in a pose like the female statues at the top of the dome, looking mournfully down, grieving at the thought of a world without art. Guzzling champagne until she drooled froth, Meredith pitied a tipsy bridesmaid wading into the lagoon. Ray gave a speech about his new bride, thanked her for saving him from loneliness. Eve gazed straight into his eyes, in a way Meredith was pretty sure she herself had never managed. Even at a distance, anyone could see that the welded vision of Ray to Eve was carrying them already to their wedding bed. She could picture them entwined.

The bed is soaked, the rest of the world drops away.

Meredith staggered to the wharf, let the spray hit her. A sailor was dropping stones to send widening circles into the Bay. At the Ripley's Believe It or Not! museum, she stared at a grain of rice on which a miniaturist had written the Lord's Prayer, the placard stating that each stroke of a letter was made between breaths, and *fast fast light*, between heartbeats, which the artist had spent years training himself to feel.

The fate of the lobster is famous. Consider also the primitive practice of pouring boiling water on eels in boxes rough enough for their writhing to scale them into a delicacy. Behind the facade, behind the counter, within the tiled place, is the steady drip caused by the kosher butcher. Consider the common blow that strikes a cow in an abat-toir; for a fraction of a second, the cow stands with a shocked, full register, equally alive and dead, knowing itself to be both living and gone. People realizing their mortal limits drift about in a condition too profound to bellow, one foot in this world and one in another.

She looked for God in her work. Her palate craved vegetables, tonic water, and crème brûlée; she swam in Aquatic Cove with the Dolphin Club. She traveled and found new menus that she convinced Bridle to offer; a few pleasant men dated her until one or the other of them lost interest. Either the passion was extreme and quick to explode, or nothing scaled past friendship. Without giddiness or rancor, she designed a fine farewell party when the Young Chef moved on to Dallas and the owner promoted her to head chef. She copied out her favorite quote from Annette Kellerman, which extolled the powers nigh onto eternity for those who can swim their "solitary course night or day and forget a black earth full of people that push."

She was neither gleeful nor sad when the news reached her that Eve was hosting a popular program called *Grand Escapes* on her own, while Ray's show was canceled. She was neither gleeful nor sad to hear of their divorce. Whenever she picked up the phone to reach him, stuck in neutral, there was no completing the call.

He sent a single word, MARVELOUS, in block letters on a stiff card when, in her third year as head chef of Bridle, the *Chronicle* featured her for having won one Michelin star.

He buried his father. He inherited very little. He watched a TV program that surprised him by mentioning that the ama divers could walk around for years seeming to be fine, but suddenly, toward old age, their eyes might flare up bright red, their organs rupture.

Meredith at long last took her moldy Chatty Cathy to a doll hospital at Hyde and Pine. A man who looked like a tailor in a children's fairy tale set aside a bisque torso he'd been gluing together to greet Meredith, who blurted, "Why do girls love pulling the heads off Barbies?" The doll doctor laughed and said, "Wow, I've often wondered." They bantered suggestions: Because the necks are so skinny! Because it makes it easier to play hammer throw, twirling the head by the pony-tail! None of this was monumental; there was nothing vital or even cosmically comic, and therefore she treasured the episode as truer to life as it's lived.

God is everywhere, but more in the *center* of everywhere. God lies within a step altered out of the ordinary, but more within the *center* of that new radius of a step.

At the Museum of Modern Art, staring up below the glass bridge, she saw the outline of a child's feet stopped. It can be frightening to walk that suspension. Larger feet waited next to the child's. All motionless. Meredith had a distinct sensation of sprouting cuts that were like gills; she could breathe nearly forever at the bottom of this sea. *Go on, go on, it's fine, you'll see:* She sent that heavenward, toward the child. And then the feet crossed the glass bridge together. Meredith left the museum feeling rinsed and cooled.

At a conference in Chattanooga about new American cuisine, she went to the Living Art Gallery, where bedding was set up for people who wanted to sleep surrounded by jellyfish. Pulsating moon jellies, transparent pink tissue like parasols. Living water. Oh, Annette! Didn't you suggest that power is born from piloting through the sea? Didn't you write that despite being a mermaid in the movies, you still devoutly desired to see a real one perched on a rock, combing her long green hair?

She ran into him at the Palace of the Legion of Honor, near Rodin's *The Thinker.* His hairline had receded. He was back to cooking, he said, at a fusion place in the Mission District. Eve was a network star, living with a high-powered lawyer. "Ah," Meredith said. He didn't de-grade her by asking for forgiveness. His fists were jammed into the pockets of his jacket. She gripped his elbows. He looked at her eyes in a manner they had never fully managed. She did not know how to mention her own affair without sounding as if she were either evening the score or letting him off the hook. So they did not speak much. But their look conveyed an entirety, without any fairy-tale ending: She was dating someone at the time; he was, too. But now it could happen that from time to time he could call her up and speak, and she could talk to him gladly.

In her youth, her tastes ran Baroque. French tapestries. Layered tortes. Now she craved simplicity. Consommé. Distillations.

Meredith Locke passed from middle-aged to older-but-still-relatively-young. Her legs were marbled with varicose veins from a career on her feet, but she kept her Michelin star and her post as head chef until she turned fifty-eight; without anxiety, without bitterness, she accepted the news one day that despite her faithful screenings, she was discovered to have breast cancer that had spread. Her time had simply arrived; that was all.

Ray Locke moved to a new restaurant, a Latin spot with cobalt walls. It would be his fate to jump from place to place. But for now he was living with a schoolteacher who was friendly with Meredith and understood how life twists about, trying to grab its tail and form circles. She told Ray to go care for Meredith, and then she'd welcome him back.

And so they were together again, for a short while. Her pain by then was extreme.

He brought her a gift he'd bought in Springfield, Illinois, ages ago but never used: a cookbook from the Civil War. In her apartment on Green Street, he prepared a carrageen blancmange. "You're the only person currently on the planet who'd like this," he said. "I love you. I adore you, you know." Her smile, the dark circles framing her eyes, the turquoise head scarf. Once upon a time, seaweed could travel to a druggist's in the Midwest in the mid-nineteenth century and cost little. It was prized as salubrious for those of a delicate constitution. The carrageen had to be washed thoroughly and boiled, and he added the barest handful to the milk, bitter almonds, sugar, cinnamon, and mace. He fed it to her in spoonfuls. "My dearest," she said.

In the end, one dissolves into atoms. Her affair with the ballet dancer: How was that so different from Ray with Eve? That desire for grandeur, release, an upper world. God peering down might see it all as some balanced math equation. Finally, wasn't it the strangest thing that passion should ebb with long-knowing, and yet people are born to want to find The One? Wasn't that the great human dilemma? What if a person aimed to find God within physicality, to have bodily desire increase? What idiocy to separate God's love from tactile human love.

At the shoreline at Lands End, Ray and Meredith stood bundled up. Bless Annette Kellerman, who said that water taught modesty of the soul: She remarked cheerily that "after leaving the shore behind, I seemed to shrink and shrink till I was nothing but a flecky bubble and feared that the bubble would burst."

But they were beyond words now.

His arm was around her, and hers were around him. He leaned down to kiss her at the exact second that she lifted her face to meet his in a lingering kiss.

It is the kiss of their lives.

The salted air. The sea rushes in to cover their bare feet with a spume of lace. The hermit crabs rest below the wet sand, their breathing holes like straws to drink in the tide. The tide ceaseless in its approach and retreat, its coming toward and going away, its brimming with peril even as it fully possesses the kind of rhythm loved since the dawn of time for how it sings a body to sleep.

——————

I am madly in love with Annette Kellerman. I always have been. Known as the Million-Dollar Mermaid, she performed self-styled ballet inside water-filled tanks, which in turn played a role in the birth of synchronized swimming. Fame and riches (and longtime love—that, too) were by-products. Gorgeous, shocking, inventive, artistic—she's a dream, breathless and suspended, overjoyed with how her immersion arrests the purity of a single moment. The earth with people who push was what she yearned to escape. She was very much in this world and very much in another.

One day I went swimming after not getting into a pool in a painfully long time, and my happiness at being back in water helped "The Little Mermaid" leap to mind as a story I'd enjoy reinventing. I could spend many hours in the realm of Annette. My choice of a fairy tale was as simple as that, I think.

I reread the original by Hans Christian Andersen—and good God! The prince is either monumentally cruel or blitheringly dumb. I wanted, first, to invent a smart, caring male character, though he makes the disastrous mistake of confusing love with the pursuit of a beautiful idea. Some critics dislike what they perceive as Andersen's do-gooder ending and his excruciating portrayal of a mute woman sacrificing herself for a frivolous rich boy, but I was quite taken at how much his story embraces the form of a classic romantic triangle, one that avoids a conventionally happy (fairy tale) conclusion: A wretched, overly patient, tongue-tied woman is dying for love and cannot convey her heartbreak while watching a man (with whom she's enjoyed a binding friendship) replace her with a fresher, younger ideal.

That's a tale as old as time. That was my springboard. At the heart of Andersen's remarkably melancholy narrative is the struggle to square mortal craving with a search for immortality, eternity— whatever we care to call it. I have profound compassion, as we all do, for the essential dilemma of wanting desire, love, and friendship to increase with one person, not die away simply because time passes. There's a lot to be said, as well, for fighting the need to separate human love from what we think to call holy.

The details fell into place. I wrote quickly after going shopping in a department store, because the women spritzing perfumes and reaching for me with their fluttering fingers suggested the polypi when the Little Mermaid goes to the Sea Witch to admit she's desperate to find a new life. That was the small image that triggered everything else.

—KV

KAREN BRENNAN

The Snow Queen

I

I'D JUST MOVED BACK TO THE CITY, HAVING BEEN AWAY FOR A LONG time during which I'd accomplished quite a bit of work—I'm no judge of the quality—and was crashing at the apartment of a friend I'd run into at Borders bookstore after two weeks of hapless wandering. It had been snowing, but it always seemed to be snowing here those days; even when it wasn't snowing one had the impression of snow about to or having just, and I was therefore cold. I was wearing only a flimsy red windbreaker, which is the same as saying I might as well have been wearing my bathing suit. I suppose it was pity when my friend asked where I was living or if I had a place to stay for the night. My general look of forlornness must have prompted him to say, I happen to have a free sofa, and he winked at me, which I considered very kind, very warm-hearted, of this friend who, as I recall, did not have a reputation for either warmth or kindness.

We were browsing the psychology section, he holding a book on the borderline personality and I holding a similar volume concerning narcissism. The *maladies de jour*, quipped my friend, if you don't count drug addiction. Ah, yes, drug addiction, I said vaguely. I wasn't sure I wanted to discuss drug addiction with this friend. I had known many drug addicts and they all were unbearably sad and I found it hard to be irreverent about them. One such was my own son, a pathetic person who wandered the streets homeless, perpetually checking himself into and out of detox units and trying to scam me into purchasing phony prescriptions. I wanted to forget about my son, to excise him from my mind, but the more I tried to do this, the more his presence asserted itself and I could see him, as if a movie were being played in front of my eyes, as a serious, overalled toddler and then as a tender, pudgy preteen with straight brown hair that hung over one eye.

Judge not and ye shall not be judged, warns the Bible, and actually I myself was homeless at the time, having just returned from a kind of vacation, really, during which I'd produced mountains of material (god knows how good any of it was). Still, I did not want to discuss my son.

My friend and I then repaired to the fiction section and explored the *As*—Jane Austen, all the Andersons, Agee, Alcott, and others, the usual great variety under *A*—and we each perused according to our tastes, slipping a book from the shelf, riffling through the pages, and replacing it, but not before chuckling over a title or author photo, the way you do.

I hadn't slept for a week. I'd been away, and when I returned to this city I found everything changed. For example, a certain street I'd remembered as going one way toward the state capital now pointed in a different direction. Where this boulevard had been tree-lined, it was now flanked with tall soulless buildings. A store that used to sell small appliances had sprung up in the place of the junior college where I'd once taught freshman composition and all the cars had new-style garish license plates. I do not remember the state motto being _____, but it's possible I'd never really attended to the state motto. It was very cold, as I've said, snowing or about to—whereas before it had been temperate, tending toward sea breezes, balmy and blue. Now, no sea in sight (though I searched until I exhausted myself) and a strange odor permeated the air, a cold odor, not quite fresh, as of old snow, but so recent that it did not qualify as memory, but more like the fleeting space between nostalgia and dread, frozen into permanence.

My friend was blind in one eye, and though he assured me he'd always been blind in one eye—the result of a sleigh-riding accident when he was ten—I don't remember him being blind in one eye. You must have hidden it well, I remarked. At this he bristled. It's not something you can exactly hide, he retorted. He was holding a paperback edition of H. C. Andersen's fairy tales—as far away from his face as his arms could stretch, because in addition to being blind in one eye he needed new reading glasses—and he insisted on sharing with me an excerpt from "The Snow Queen," which is all about a terrifying being called the Snow Queen who kidnaps a boy called Kay. I didn't want to be rude, but I'm not especially interested in fairy tales, no matter how capable and esteemed the author. In fact, "The Snow Queen" had a particularly perilous association for me, as she—the cold and beautiful woman—put me in mind of my mother, who had once read me that story. Therefore, while my friend read—*it was a lady, tall and slender and brilliantly white . . .*—I let my mind wander.

II

For two weeks, I'd been looking for the sea, sleeping where I could under whatever canopy or ledge I could find—bridges, which had been abundant in the old days, had vanished without a trace, and so I was reduced to buttresses—the new gargoyles, snow-laden and hideous, the tiny balconies that used to be so fragrant and flower-laden, where people now smoked cigarettes, pitching the still-smoldering rockets below, almost burning me to death on several occasions.

I did not like to ask my friend—or anyone for that matter—about the sea because it is entirely possible that I am misremembering my old home. While he read Andersen's "Snow Queen" in that excited way people have when they desperately want you to share their enthusiasm, their voices ratcheting up dramatically, my mind wandered the streets in the same manner that my body, for the past month, had wandered the streets. Still no sea.

My friend did not have the reputation for warmth or kindness, nevertheless he invited me to his apartment where he said there was an empty sofa with my name on it. He must have known I was extremely tired, yawning constantly and twirling and untwirling a strand of my hair around a forefinger, a habit when fatigued.

My friend said: All I ask is that you remember to put the shower curtain inside the tub. Otherwise the water will drip into the downstairs apartment and that bitch will have a fit.

That's easy enough, I said. We hadn't even arrived at his apartment when he gave me this rule about the water and shower. I wondered if there were other rules that would be more difficult to follow because, like anyone, I worry about unconscious behaviors, those which I cannot control, and then I worry that I am too old to change.

I don't see well, said the friend apropos of nothing. We were walking down some avenue or other—I should say sliding down some avenue or other, because it had of course recently snowed and the road held the tracks of sleds and skis as well as snow tires and chains—but there was really nothing to see, I wanted to point out to my friend, everything was white, the sky, the street, and all the things that might have been visible on a day without snow were now covered with snow—rows of automobiles to the point that I wasn't sure they were automobiles. For all I knew, they might have been great hulking sea monsters who had lost the sea like the rest of us.

Nevertheless, I gave my friend my arm, and he clutched my red windbreaker, which probably did the opposite of keeping me warm, it was of such a weird, cold material, and in this manner we eventually arrived at his apartment.

III

I was perfectly comfortable in my new surroundings; they beat the hell out of wandering the icy streets homeless, running into bands of thieves and drug addicts, my son not among those I'd encountered, thank god. I don't know what I would have done if I'd seen my pathetic son. My heart no longer bleeds for him, though there was a time when my heart was smashed to smithereens. Enough said. Every time I try to banish him from memory here he comes again with his tilted gray eyes, even in the guise of who I did not see in the past month, as he who was conspicuously absent from my wanderings.

Being homeless is no picnic and, unlike my son, I did it drug-free, with only my thoughts for comfort, my belief (mistaken) that the sea lurked somewhere, waiting to restore me to my bearings.

My friend had a sofa, a TV, a lamp, a rug, a stove, a fridge, a double bed, a closet full of shoes, and a cat. I hadn't realized he was such an austere fellow. He didn't have a reputation for warmth or kindness, but inviting me to his apartment suggested that this reputation was not entirely warranted.

I slept on the sofa, as instructed. It was foamy, not lumpy, and its velvet material a cocoon of sorts. We all like to feel swathed, I think. Also, my friend gave me a blanket—a nice blue blanket which I wrapped around myself multiple times—and a pillow that used to belong to the cat. In fact, the cat shared the pillow with me at night, which I didn't mind, the paddling and purring of the cat next to my ear as I slept, though I believe it colored my dreams.

The cat was cream-colored with large irregular splotches on its back, giving it the appearance of a small cow.

As cats go, it was medium-sized.

I dreamed of cows, therefore, and human infants who were pitched into dark holes and drug addicts sleeping on sofas belonging to other drug addicts.

The last time I saw my son he informed me that he was living in a "squat." I told him that that fact struck me as kind of ignominious.

I remember the ocean as being a deep gray color laden, on good days, with streaks of white, which gave it its characteristic shimmer. The sky on such days was lit with what looked to be rags hanging from a celestial clothesline. Very beautiful, but spooky.

IV

My friend was christened Frederick von Schlegel, after the German philosopher of the same name, but everyone called him Hans. My name was G, just the initial deprived of the clothing, I liked to say. The cat's name was Fur and I won't tell you my son the drug addict's name.

I had been away for an indeterminate amount of time during which I completed a great deal of work. I kept residuals in a suitcase which, until I met Hans in Borders bookstore, I lugged around with me through the city. The bulk was housed elsewhere. I had no idea if any of it was successful. In more optimistic moments, I liked to think so; but eventually something would happen—the tiniest alteration in the atmosphere, such as the time when the crow who frequented the fire-escape railing growled at me through the window—and then I would be in despair over my accomplishments. At such times I felt I understood the impulses of those who scourged themselves with cat-o'-nine-tails and slept on beds of nails. I, too, craved punishment for the unworthiness of my effort, indeed the unworthiness of my being.

Other than the sofa, Hans's apartment was replete with artificial flowers of every denomination. In the mornings, he would tend to these thousands with a translucent spray bottle, which would take a full hour. I could not shake the feeling that these flowers were about to speak, that there was more to them than twists of colored plastic or, in some cases, starched fabric. The cluster of pink ranunculus that sat stiffly on the coffee table in front of the sofa on which I slept seemed always about to discourse about psychology. The narcissist, they always seemed about to say, is generally a happier person than the comparatively hysterical borderline personality. Here they seemed to nod pointedly toward the daffodils, and I of course was reminded of my encounter with my friend at Borders bookstore when we each held those books on personality disorders only to abandon them (thankfully) for fiction. The tulips, I thought, seemed about to agree with me that the idea of personality disorders was kind of creepy and attractive at the same time, the notion that something surprising lurks under the surface of a person always a thrill, but perhaps, at times, an unwelcome thrill. On and on, the flowers seemed about to yak, and I admired their stamina. The fact that they all persisted in a season of profound winter was, I suppose, cause for celebration of some sort—or perhaps they were merely stir crazy, as was I.

Even so, I rarely left the apartment, but settled myself by the window where I indulged in an on-and-off sprightly communication with the crow. The crow would bring me news of my son, not welcome news, and much as I tried to dissuade him (or her) from these reports, she seemed to insist upon delivering them. You never know about the sensibilities of other species that are possibly impervious to that which we hold dear as humans. In this case, I was holding dear the absence of my son from my life. I cherished this absence as some might cherish inhabiting the premises of one who collected artificial flowers of every denomination and harbored a spotted cat.

The cat was not a communicator and, aside from our sleep time, kept its distance. There were times when I felt it was "giving me a look," but many feel this way about cats on account of the shapes of their eyes and the fact that they rarely blink. Perhaps, though, they have the capacity to stare into the soul; if this one had been able to gaze into mine, I doubt it would have insisted on sleeping with me. It would have discovered a clotted mess of conflicting desires and repugnancies, all of which I hid behind my usual sangfroid.

Hans and I spoke rarely, and when we did our conversation tended to get caught up in snarls of misunderstanding. He was, as I've said, blind in one eye, and this was the central fact of his life, to hear him talk about it. Once I tried to tell him that being blind in one eye was not all that disabling and he nearly bit my head off. You have no idea, do you? he said incredulously, and we went on from there, back and forth, like a Ping-Pong tournament I remember participating in (and losing) as a ten-year-old. Nerve-wracking to see that little white ball—innocuous as it may have been—barreling toward you, as if it might cripple you for life, which is the spirit in which we fought, Hans and I. You are the most self-indulgent person I've ever met, he shouted, and I shouted, At least I'm not deluded, and he shouted, You could at least tidy up a little around here, and I shouted, I can't hear myself think around here!

This last was a mean-spirited reference to Hans's incessant theremin playing, the spooky sounds reminiscent of bad sci-fi or a copulating cat or, less frequently, a flock of warbling mourning doves. Hans had not yet mastered the instrument, which was a difficult instrument to master, though if you asked me, anyone with a decent soprano could mime the sounds pretty accurately by intoning *ooooo* and *eeeee* to the tune of something plaintive.

When he played *O mio bambino cara*, though, in spite of myself, I was moved. There he would stand, at the helm of his peculiar instrument, a lumpen figure of a man with a large square head, his mouth pressed in a grim line, his hands like big roast beefs paddling the air— and the tender spectacle of this sad, blind-in-one-eye man, along with the Puccini—all the more poignant for being a little off-key—would unfailingly bring tears to my eyes.

I was settling in like a cat settles in, surrendering myself to unfamiliar surroundings, marking my own tiny territory, as it were, which consisted of the sofa and a plastic chair I had moved to the window for the purpose of looking outside. It was always snowing or about to snow and it fascinated me to watch the snowflakes, which resembled swarms of large white bees.

I began to dread the crow's visits, however, the news of my son always discouraging—he was caught scoring heroin and the police had broken his nose; he was contemplating injecting bleach into his arm, so despondent was he; he had checked himself into detox units, rehab programs, hospital psych wards; he was cohabiting with a Mormon bishop, a blond meth freak, a black cat who subsequently died in an alley. I had to cover my ears.

V

There came the day, as I knew it would, when I neglected to tuck the shower curtain inside the bathtub while taking my shower. Hans had gone for the afternoon—god knows where he went for hours at a time (I used to speculate that he had a woman stashed somewhere, a person who tended to his physical needs and complimented him on his taste in reading, his formidable intellect, and his sense of humor)—and when I had finished with my ablutions, I heard the angry pounding on the apartment door. Wearing only a towel, I peered through the little eyehole and perceived a tiny, misshapen woman with a large nose looking back at me.

You have some nerve, she said when I opened the door. My entire apartment is flooded, thanks to you. She was not as tiny as I'd thought, nor as misshapen. She was actually quite attractive in a cheerleaderish way—a certain type of big girl with crisp incisors renowned for a lack of irony. Permit me to help you clean up the mess, I said. Which is how I came to know Rita and her various boyfriends, one of whom was perched on top of a ladder reading a book on that first visit, where, for the rest of this tale, we will leave him.

Rita was a hairdresser with her own business, which had been recently revamped by a TV personality who went around revamping hairdresser salons. She was immensely grateful to this personage, claiming that her sales went up exponentially and her employees were far more respectful than before. All this was divulged after I'd done a fair job of sopping up the small lake in Rita's bedroom with two bath towels. When I'd wrung the last of my shower effluent from the towel into a large bucket, Rita was frowning over me. Your hair needs attention, she said.

This is how I happened to become a regular patron of Rita's Hair Salon. I'd been cooped up in Hans's small rooms for so long, I'd forgotten the sheer gleam of the outside world—its rivets and whorls, its dizzying frontal assault when, on my first time out, the snow bees attacked me. Bigger and bigger they grew until they transformed to giant chickens in front of my eyes, squawking and revving up their wings like jet engines, but silent (paradoxically), perfectly silent, so that the squawks and the revving were only in imagination (nevertheless loud).

And this is a curiosity—how the mind creates its own disturbances and how there is almost a kind of synesthesia involved when it comes to the workings of the imagination, a kind of leakage among compartments. Indeed, in imagination everything connects and overlaps—a disturbing vision is capable of hurting the ear and vice versa, and what was past returns uncannily to infect our present moments. Not only memories but stories, even the stories we held most dear as children, and the thought of who we were as children reading those stories, or listening to them, our mothers' warm breath on our necks . . .

Which is why I tried to banish all thoughts of my son.

Thankfully, Rita's salon did not entail much of a trek. It was a pleasant enough place with purple walls and elderly women sitting under hair driers with pink curlers and Rita running around snapping her precision scissors, which she ultimately employed on my own coif, cutting, shaping, and spraying to such an extent that I did not recognize the severe and helmeted visage—like a Roman foot soldier!—that looked back at me from her mirror.

An old woman to whom Rita applied her energetic ministrations, from I believe Finland or Lapland, engaged me in conversation; she talked about her children and her abilities as a fortune-teller, a little diminished, she admitted, with her great age. Her children and her children's children and even their children were getting on, she said, and the whole business made her feel very ancient, which in fact she was, displaying the ropy veins on her old hands with pride. Fabulous, no? she said. I am lucky to have made it so far as the world is endlessly—here she searched for the right word, then shook her head. The world is endlessly, she repeated, then laughed. Rita was teasing her hair into two towers, then situating tiny plastic windows in each. I like to do my part, said the old woman.

Then she took my hand in both of hers and read my palm. Ah, but you, she said. You have just been away on a, shall we say, sojourn, during which you completed a great deal of work. It is difficult, almost impossible, to judge this work—I'm not sure why. Then you wandered, looking for that which no longer exists. Then you happened upon a friend, not noted for his warmth and kindness, who took you in. Listen to the crow, she said. Follow the snow bees. Your son awaits you. At this the old woman began to weep so profusely that Rita gently escorted her to the restroom and I made my departure.

VI

"The Snow Queen," written by an unattractive, socially inept Dane, said Hans, is a sort of coming-of-age story. There are two children, a boy and a girl, who through a twist of fate become separated. The twist of fate is the Snow Queen herself, an enigmatic personage, beautiful and dangerous—"slender and dazzling"—who entrances the boy, invites him to ride on her sled, wraps him in her fur—"creep into my fur," she entreats seductively—and takes him to her ice palace. We know she is dangerous because on the way to the ice palace, the Snow Queen says, "And now you will have no more kisses . . . or else I shall kiss you to death!"

But the best part of the story, said Hans, is that before any of the above occurred, the devils dropped a special mirror which smashed into millions of pieces and became lodged in people's eyes and hearts, causing distorted views of the world. For some reason, don't ask me why, I love the idea of that mirror. You love contradictions, I pointed out, and calamities. No, said Hans, I love the idea of lost souls.

The story is a ludicrously obvious tale of sexual seduction, piped up the iris. The beautiful queen, the "fur" that "envelopes" the boy, the sleigh ride to "another land," even the palace with its postlapsarian, postcoital chill . . . who among us wants to surrender his penchant for enchantment?

We are all lost souls, Hans went on mournfully, and then he went mournfully to his theremin to play a version of "Over the Rainbow," which sounded like a duck quacking. But I was still thinking about the Snow Queen, who had always reminded me of my mother, who also was given to furs and a cold house and, for years in my young life, inhabited a place of mystery. And this made me think of my son, which I did not want to do, so I changed the course of my thinking and instead thought of the power of the imagination . . .

So though we cannot exactly envision the matter of "beyond our wildest dreams" (I reflected) since it has not yet been revealed, we can nonetheless attach to this imaginary empty place an ecstatic feeling; it can occupy all our thoughts and direct our smallest actions . . .

As if reading my mind, a chorus of violets seemed about to chant *obsessive compulsive disorder* a few times until interrupted by a single rose who seemed about to discourse on that personality disorder, claiming that Gerda demonstrated all the signs of OCD in her persistent quest, her inability to banish little Kay (who was no longer little) from her mind. In a way, the roses seemed about to say, Gerda was obsessed with the irrecoverable past, with childhood in all its one-dimensionality. One could say, the roses seemed about to continue, that she was unable to deal with the complexities of adulthood, especially her own impending adulthood.

Just then the crow appeared at the window, surrounded by its customary band of snow bees, looking a little worn out, as if it had been through an even fiercer blizzard than usual. You are both wrong, said the crow, the SQ is a gothic story, if you will, wherein a girl has an adventure—becomes, for the moment, the agent of her fate—and in the end discovers the prize wasn't worth it. Ha, added the crow cynically, as if this were the case with pursuits of any kind.

Or, said the cat, who for the first time in our acquaintance seemed to have an opinion, it is the story of incest. That story reminds me of the film *Psycho*, only it has a different outcome. The boy escapes the suffocating clutches of the girl and the grandmother and returns to this vale of tears, inevitably resigned. The Freudian drama to a T.

Lost souls! interjected Hans, after which we all fell silent.

VII

It wasn't until much later that I realized that Hans's love of lost souls might have explained his kindness to me.

I was on my way to Rita's Hair Salon in an even worse blizzard than usual. I could not see one foot in front of me as I walked; I proceeded, therefore, in blind faith, hoping not to fall into an open manhole or walk in front of a truck. The wind howled and buffeted and finally tore my umbrella from my hands and tossed it god-knows-where. I was quite cold and I was enacting that trick where you allow the cold into your body in order to nullify it.

In desperation, I slipped into the premises of an antiquities dealer called Fiske. This was a small, sad establishment that reeked of bygone dust and spiderwebs. Fiske himself emerged from a back room with a fistful of white bread crusts in one hand, wearing a slight smile. How can I help you? he inquired politely. I explained that I was just taking temporary shelter, but I'd be happy to browse.

Indeed, Fiske's Antiquities was a browser's paradise and included stuffed owls and warthogs, troops of books with battered spines, an array of boxes—little ceramic boxes, cloisonné boxes, ivory boxes—perfume bottles with semiprecious jewels dotting their circumferences, a collection of ink pens, and nineteenth-century costumes, notably a chimney-sweep costume worn by a manneqin with no eyes.

Idly peering into a wooden box decorated with the burned-wood tool of mid-twentieth century—its lid contained an image of a buck-toothed beaver with the word TOOTHPICKS clumsily embossed beneath—I experienced a jolt of déjà vu so severe that I had to grab Fiske by the forearm in order to steady myself.

Even when I'd settled into the winged-back chair that Fiske was kind enough to provide, I still could not shake the déjà vu. There was an odd familiarity to everything in the shop—the boxes, the pens, the costume, and especially the books. I took in their battered spines absentmindedly as I sat, running my eyes over the titles of books I had never heard of. Even so, they were familiar to me in the way that a story is familiar when you enter in medias res and cannot shake the feeling that you've read it before . . .

It was hardly a surprise, therefore, when I spotted a copy of H. C.

Andersen's fairy tales, illustrated with the tortuous images of Kay Neilson. It was such a volume from which my mother read "The Snow Queen," a story that terrified me as much as did the perfume of my mother.

In the penultimate scene (I recalled), the Snow Queen tells little Kay that if he can spell the word *ETERNITY* out of icicles she will give him his freedom. This Kay failed to do. Instead, Gerda appeared and melted his heart with the heat of her love.

Fiske said, I can give you a good deal on that book. But I didn't know if I wanted to own it. I'd been away for a long time and I'd accomplished a great deal of work whose quality was difficult to determine. The bulk was housed miles from the city—only the residuals remained and at this point they no longer made sense to me. The memory of them, even now, locked in a suitcase, brought to mind a row of walls with vague, poorly executed scrawls.

Whereas the memory of my son brought to mind the sea . . .

When last seen, he was living in a black Camry, terribly thin, begging for food by sticking his hand out the window. His face, reported the crow, had hardened into a contemptuous mask, and when a passerby declined to drop a dollar into his outstretched palm, he spit at him. These depressing reports nullified all memories of the sea—though my son persisted at the back of my mind, despite my best efforts to banish him.

Oh beauty, oh sadness! I thought, apropos of nothing. Though perhaps it was the beautiful boy making sandcastles who flashed before my eyes. His knees scraped up.

It was still snowing. Possibly it would always snow. It is hard to know what to do under any circumstances, much less those circumstances that require us to fight against the prevailing weather. His knees were scraped because he had fallen from his bicycle.

I'd dabbed on peroxide and plastered a few Band-Aids. The world was shining and perfect, the sea left a mustache of white foam on the shore. In a while we'd go home, make sandwiches, tell stories. Did I read him the story of the Snow Queen? I think not. It would have frightened him.

Although my mother, who looked uncannily like the Snow Queen, read the story to me.

In those days I would have done anything to protect my son.

If I were to encounter him now—in an alley, say, covered with snow—I would not be able to melt his heart. My love, unlike Gerda's, has gone cold. It appears that we are doomed to go our separate ways, to continue in the darkness of our own making, half-blind, and no longer who we once were.

That's the way most stories end, I mused sadly. Not with roses blooming, not with the onset of summer, not hand-in-hand.

In moments, I would pay Fiske the required amount, tuck the book inside my jacket, and head into the fray.

What I've attempted in my version of "The Snow Queen" is to recycle some of the motifs in Hans Christian Andersen's famous tale—snow, talking birds, and flowers—as well as the concepts of disappearance and loss. My interest is not so much in retelling the tale (the sublime original needs no retelling!) but in creating an innovative fiction of my own.

Like Andersen, I've divided my story into seven sections, but there the literal similarity more or less ends. In my "Snow Queen," I wanted to capture some of what has always enchanted me about the original—the eerie combination of danger and nostalgia and a chilled atmosphere that is mysterious and terrifying. One notable absence in my version is the Snow Queen herself, an absence which I intend as a kind of provocative lacuna at the heart of the tale— suggestive of her presence elsewhere, figured not only as the drugs which have "seduced" the narrator's son but also as the more abstract seductions of nostalgia and love.

I've added motifs of my own that are subtly related to Andersen's story. Chief among these is the notion of reading and its multiple functions: as interpretation, as social activity, as conduit for memory and its suppression. My version is necessarily fragmentary, unresolved . . .

Thus I do not tack on the happily-ever-after of Andersen's tale—instead, as per our contemporary sensibilities, I've suggested that the narrator comes to accept her loss and sorrow as inevitable.

My story, finally, is an exploration, a rummaging around in another text, a diving into the inchoate, fragmentary nature of experience, a hybridish piecing of this and that.

—KB

LUCY CORIN

Eyes of Dogs

soldier came walking down the road, raw
from encounters with the enemy, high
on release, walking down the road with
no money. The road was lined with trees,
and every so often a hovel hunched right
there at its edge, droopy and mean, with
a dirt yard like a pale sack at its feet. The
soldier thought he was walking home,
but at the end of the road no one was
there anyway. He passed a hovel with a
little dog outside, barking on a rope. The
dog's dish was just beyond the reach of
the rope, and he watched the dog run,
barking, to reach it, catch itself by the
neck at the end of the rope, bounce back
yelping, and then do this repeatedly, his
white ruff following the jerk of his head.
The soldier could see that there was
nothing in the bowl.

As he walked along, the trees grew
broader, filling in space, the canopy
more complete and farther above. He

passed a little girl on the stoop in front of a
blackened hovel door, breaking branches
into pieces for tinder, wearing a fancy dress
gone ragged. He could see, through the
tattered ribbons and limp lace bows, that the
fabric of the dress had once been bright,
rainbow colored, and shiny. The girl's eyes
looked very big because of the circles under
them, but her skin, smudged as it was with
ash, seemed to pulse dimly, just as the shine
of the dress did.

At the next hovel, an old woman was
stirring a large iron pot set up on coals in the
dirt yard. For an instant, the soldier thought
that this was his mother, and he took his
hands from his coat pockets to wave to her,
but then he could see that it was not his
mother; it was a witch. The resemblance,
however, remained, and part of him thought
that with all he'd done and seen he might
have made his mother into this. Another part
of him, though he could see she was a witch,
still felt the kind of trust and longing you
can feel toward a mother, even if she has
become a witch after all these years.

The witch called out to him, her face
rusty and sweating or beaded with steam,
holding a crooked spoon in a hand
concealed by her cloak: "Soldier! I see you
looking at me with your weird eyes. I can
see right through you, and I know what
you want."

The soldier said: "What's in the pot?"

He thought, *I bet you think I want to be a
better man.*

The witch said: "I know what you want. It's money, and I know where you can get it, and there's nothing to it, you just go and get it, and I know where."

She was right. That's what he wanted. He even forgot to ask her how it could be that she lived in a hovel and knew where there was money, but then there she was, and she was right, he wanted it, so the soldier forgot to ask about that, and about why the witch's hovel sagged to the side and why she wore a witch's rags, and if she had any sons who'd gone off to war, and he forgot about the pot, about what might be stewing and steaming in it, something awful, something good to eat or know. His mind cleared of everything except the idea of money.

"Tie this rope around your waist," said the witch. "Hop down this black hole into this deep hollow tree. You'll be tethered to me. Don't be frightened of what you'll see. Ha! You've seen worse than this. You'll see some dogs. Wink at the first dog, blink at the next dog, and for the third, squeeze your eyes shut, and wait to see. You will find a little

A Tinderbox is a little box that sparks to make fire. Like for lighting things.

leather purse in the earth down there, and all I ask is you bring it to me. If you don't, I won't pull you up, and then you'll have something to be frightened of."

So he wound the rope around his waist and the witch took the loose end. Then he hopped down into the hollow tree and fell deep into it and also underground. Smack! his feet hit the earth, and everything around him was so dark that he couldn't see anything. In the dark, he thought of the little dog, so stupid for lurching at the end of his leash. He thought of the little girl, and recognized the terrible whirl of ideas that had surged across his mind when he saw her: to hack her to pieces, to feed her soup and rock her to sleep, to gobble her up for himself, to dress her properly. He put his hands to the rope around his waist because he was having trouble breathing and felt like it was choking him from the gut up, but soon his eyes adjusted to the light. He could see the twisty shadows of the inner wood of the tree, all tunneled with wormholes and mud wasps making convex mazes all around him in the walls, but he couldn't tell a groove from a bulge. It wasn't only his eyes adjusting, though; the light was changing, too, and he stepped toward where it pushed at him through the darkness. The light expanded its reach, the space expanded with it, and soon he could see a whole inner chamber lit with a hundred burning lights.

This reminded him of something, this chamber, with passages leading off. Then he remembered: he remembered tearing open a man's belly with his sword in battle, and then seeing himself as if within the man's stomach, looking from that chamber down the man's bright bowels, which simultaneously lay beating on the ground before them both. And as if brought on by this thought, an enormous blue dog appeared, guarding a golden chest filled with money.

The dog had eyes as big as snow globes, sparkling and swimming with watery light, but the witch was right, the soldier had been through a lot, and very little fazed him. He didn't even need to think about her instructions; it was as if she were there with him, as if he could feel her through the rope. *You need to cut those apron strings and find your way in the world!* That's what people had said to him when they passed him chopping wood for his mother's hovel, that was one thing he'd thought when he enlisted, and that was what was on his mind, not the witch, when he winked at the enormous dog, and the dog lay down and tilted his head to the side and let the snow settle, an Eiffel Tower reflected in one eye, a Golden Pyramid glowing from the depths of the other, and let the soldier open the chest and fill his pockets with promissory notes.

This was disappointing. Promissory notes. Would he have to impersonate people in order to collect? Would he spend his life journeying from one debtor to the next, shaking people down in a sharkskin suit? It sounded like a job, not magic, but at least this was a path with money at many branching ends of it. The soldier looked at the affable dog. "You got me," he said, but stuffed his pockets anyway. The dog shook his head and the snow globes snowed and then snow settled in heaps on the Statue of Liberty and the Great Wall of China seen from afar. Then the vast lids lowered, and the cavern darkened again.

The soldier felt disoriented, annoyed, betrayed. He felt a rise of panic in the dark. He moved his hand to tug the rope, ready to get up there and give the witch a piece of his mind, but the room began to brighten, this time from the bottom up in sharp fanning shafts as from beneath a rising airplane shade, and there before him loomed an even more enormous dog, and bluer, this one grouchily awakening from a nap, yawning and stretching, great shoulder blades shifting like mountains through time, with eyes as big as the capitol dome, magic beaming from beneath the lids as they rose, as the light rose. This dog was so enormous his head pressed the top of the chamber, which even so must have grown to accommodate him and his eyes, and the soldier shook minutely in his boots. His mind went blank, and by luck, or the divine, he blinked.

This dog guarded jewels the soldier knew he'd have to hock, but still, they were beautiful to look at, calling to the whole histories of the many cultures they came from, dangling golden icons, some inscribed with poetry and the names of families and families of ancestors in uncountable languages and symbologies. Bracelets and brooches, watches and cuff links, remnants of happy humans behind them, fine times, worth passed down, desire fulfilled. The things that people wanted and created or received.

He dumped the notes and heaped his neck and arms with jewelry. He piled it on, all these pieces so designed and discrete,

made for a person to shine through.
Something about the weight against his
naked neck, and gravity pulling his limbs to
the earth—he started to feel grand, to sense
what it might be like to have all this,
everyone's heirlooms. Each piece blotted out
another and they all felt the same, strands
from so many lives, and at least for the
moment the soldier felt that any one of the
lives could have been his.

What had he been hoping to find at the
end of the road? His mother's arms, his
mother dead?

Dog three. Eyes as big as planets, one
ringed with rings, and one with a great red
spot floating gaseously in it. Hallucinatory
expansive light, light filled with fire and
ghosts. Light so fragmented and strobing the
soldier squeezed his eyes shut and held his
breath too, in terror, mind spasming with
several horrors: a childhood memory (being
poked with sticks), a war memory
(being poked with swords), an image of that
little girl in her blackened rainbow frock and
what he was doing that he wanted to do, a
blue three-headed dog coming upon his
wickedness and tearing him to pieces,
stealing the girl to safety, the girl on the back
of the blue dog holding the white dog with
its ruff in her lap, both of them glancing over
their shoulders and receding, watching them
recede, spying his limbs strewn in the trees
of the forest around him, these ideas and
many more, until he was just as frightened of
the world behind his eyes as he was of the

monster before him, and only because of this equity did he open them to the dog who lay placid as an ocean seen from space, fierce but distant, and entirely content without him.

And this chest held cash, in large bills for saving, in small bills for handy spending, and what this suggested was endless possibility anchored in safety, and this time when the sun went behind the eyes of the greatest and most awesome blue dog of all, the soldier nestled in the arms of an economic system yet to collapse, sleepy and warm in the dark of the beating chamber. In the womby light he dumped the jewels and lined his boots and cap with bills, stuffed his pockets in a stupor. Then he tugged the cord.

The witch hollered down: "Get that purse!" and he swept his eyes about until he found, in the dog's afterglow, a limp black leather sack with a drawstring mouth, which he snatched as his feet left the ground. Up, up he went, waist-first, empty as a hollow tree. There he stood on the road in the forest, eye to eye with the witch, adjusting to the light, and nicely. There he stood feeling his money, gripping the wrinkled pouch in his fist. "This is what you want?" the soldier said.

"Yes, and give it to me. You have everything," said the witch.

"Do you know my mother?" the soldier asked the witch. He peered at her eyes, which were the eyes of a rat—who knows—perhaps they were really the eyes of squirming rats that the witch had carved out and taken for

He feels very full of himself because of the money, so he hacks the witch to pieces with his sword and takes the Tinderbox without really thinking anything of it.

Then he goes into town, where he gains respectability, spends lavishly, and eventually has nothing but the Tinderbox left, which he finally notices. He strikes it, to light a candle stub, thinking about a princess that the king and queen have locked away, a bit of light in the darkness of a box. He's heard rumors of her beauty: more glinting in the dark. With the first strike appears the first dog with his great eyes. What does the soldier want? He wants money. Money is fetched. If he strikes twice, there comes the second dog, with its greater eyes and its more frightening character. Three times and the third dog is raised. Very, very scary, largest-ever eyes. But the first is plenty. The first brings the money, and then, when the soldier asks, the dog fetches the lovely princess from her bed in the night and in the night the soldier does whatever he wishes with her, which we know,

her own. Who knew if she'd ever had her own eyes. Who knew what was behind them, if she'd lost them or had them taken from her by her own mother. "I was on my way to find her," said the soldier, holding the purse so she could see it, letting a threatening skepticism control his voice, "when, what do you know, I met *you*."

"How would I know? Give me that purse. I know some people. How do I know what they do with their loins? I'm just a witch. Give me that purse."

The soldier picked up the rope, which had dropped in a heap from around his waist. He pushed the witch up against the tree, so that she blocked the hole in it, and then he bound her there.

"Let me go and I'll tell you how to make the purse work," said the witch. "I know you're a bottomless pit and you know, too, you fool. You've known it your whole life. Now let me go."

"Tell me first, witch. Tell me or I'll tell everyone who you are, because I know who you are, and I know what you're keeping from me."

"You don't know anything," said the witch. But then she told him. She said: "When you need the purse, the purse will say: 'I am an old purse with a pursed mouth and squeezed-out skin. I am a purse like a pot you put things in. I am the thing from which all things come and go. I am empty, and I am full, and that is all you need to know.'"

we know what he wishes, and in the morning the girl tells her dreams to her mother, and the queen sends a fleet-footed maid to keep watch. In the night comes the good blue dog with the eyes and the maid runs after him and marks an X on the door to the soldier's apartment, which the dog sees, and marks Xs on all the doors in town, but is foiled the next night by a trail of flour from a bag with a hole in it stashed under the girl's skirt, and so the soldier is caught, and set to be hanged for his crimes. There on the scaffold, with the rope around his neck, he asks for his Tinderbox so he might have one last smoke, and it is brought to him. So he strikes once, and twice, and three times, and there come the dogs and tear the king and queen to pieces and also much of the town and its people. Those who remain make the soldier king, and he marries the princess, who

"That's what the purse will say?"

"That's what it will say. When you need it, that's what the purse will say. You don't need to know anything."

The soldier thought about that. He thought about what he knew about witches from rumors and from experience. "But I still won't know what to do," he said. The more he looked, the more the witch looked both more and less like his mother. He couldn't tell. It was like she kept shifting, being more like his mother in one way, but then less in another. He could hardly remember that he had any money at all. He tried to hold on to the thought of having money, because of what it meant for his future. But it was slippery.

"You put your mouth to its mouth," said the witch. "You don't call with your voice, but you call with your mind, and your tongue, into the darkness. You close your eyes and feel it there. You will know what to do. You will want what you want, and there it will be."

So he gave up making any sense of her, but he could tell she was making fun of him and making him feel lewd. He had been planning to leave her there to encounter some helpful woodland animal or else starve, but instead he took his hunting knife and stabbed her, once, in the stomach, and all the blood and air came rushing out of her until she was one empty black rag sack tied to the tree like something—well—a little like many things but still like nothing he could put a finger on.

is said to enjoy being queen very much, all plausible enough, except perhaps for the part with the flour.

He went into town. He went to a bar and challenged a man to darts, and he won beer after beer playing darts. There was a girl there he recognized from high school who did not recognize him back. They went to her place. She'd grown much older than he had. He tried to see the girl she might have become within the girl she was, but all he could see was her. They ate cheese and crackers from her cabinets and she was happy to do just about any sexual thing you can think of with him, which they did for several hours, although her skin was bad and she was drunk and so emotionally confusing he stopped paying attention. In the morning, light slid in enough to show all the dirt. Her place smelled like the inside of a body. "Aren't you going to take me to breakfast, even?" she asked. First he said: "Sure. I'll take you anywhere you want. I'll take you places you've never been," but then he reached into his pockets, just to lay his fingers on his cash, and there was nothing in there but a handful of ash, and same in his boots, and same in his hat. So he went into the hallway, his heart frantic, and stared at the purse, willing it to speak, but it said nothing. So he ripped at the mouth of the purse until it opened. He put his mouth to its mouth, though it disgusted him more than anything: more than the girl with her pustuled skin, or the witch before her, or any moment in any war he knew or heard of, or anything his mother could ever have done or said, no matter what she ever really did or said, or any

thought he'd ever had that he'd ever tried
not to think. There has never been a thing
so awful as being mouth-to-mouth and
there's nothing there. Oh god, and what
about the dogs, what about the dogs, saying
nothing, so blue and enormous, with their
eyes, with everything in the world, fierce
and dopey and incomprehensible. Never
coming to our rescue even when we don't
deserve it.

*I thought of the image I hold most clearly in my memory from my
childhood fairy-tale reading, and that was a blue dog, with "eyes as
big as saucers," that phrase combined with the illustration from
whatever edition of "The Tinder Box" my parents kept in our
collection. I didn't remember the story, so when I returned to it, I
was thrilled with how apt the content of the original remains to my
interests as an adult. Of course the dogs, because I love a big dog
and everything that comes with one: borrowed power and mystery;
amorality, or at least a morality that challenges and complicates
my own ideas about morality; (ironically) blind loyalty ripe for
abuse. But also I find the original Andersen tale astonishingly and
terrifyingly insightful about how people become powerful, and
what poverty does to people. My first novel is about "psychokiller"
narratives, where and how they function in mythologies and
political histories, not just in contemporary pop culture, and here
was another example. I chose to retell the story twice, once in a way
that simply highlighted what was astonishing to me about the
original, and once to treat it in a "contemporary" way—in this
case by consciously giving the main character psychological depth,
and by moving the story from a "magical" narrative space in the*

beginning to a mundane "realistic" one in the end, mirroring a trend in storytelling through time, but also (I hope) making the world of banal realism horrifying as such. The side-by-side presentation should both acknowledge and honor the story's history, and call attention to the way retelling over time is part of experiencing a story as a sort of live creature in the world.

—LC

Little Pot

A SLENDER GIRL AND HER MOTHER LIVED IN OUR TOWN, GOOD PEOPLE but poor. They had nothing to eat, like everyone else in our town. The girl was always wandering in the forest. She walked, snapping the branches, scaring the squirrels, looking for something to put in her mouth. Here the story turns: The slender girl meets an old crone. The crone's hand opens. In the open hand, a pot.

A little pot. From nothing, it appeared.

The crone said: When you are hungry, say *Cook, little pot, cook* and the pot will give you sweet porridge. And she said a few other words. A few words, the old crone smiled, and vanished from this tale. As for the girl, she did what the girls do, she ran to her mother. They whispered *Cook, little pot, cook* as they swallowed sweet porridge. And the pot cooked, and they kept whispering. And the porridge was good. But the story keeps turning: Here, they feed a neighbor's aged child. Here, they share their porridge with a pigeon. Here, the girl walks to school where she learns from schoolbooks about cookbooks and from cookbooks about constitutions.

She walks. Her mother whispers: *Cook, little pot, cook.*

The pot cooked as the mother ate, the pot cooked. The mother ate and became full and asked the pot to stop—

But she had no words to make it stop.

Her slender girl knew the words. But she was at school learning of theorems and tomatoes and generals who liked tomatoes. The pot kept cooking. The mother kept eating. And the porridge kept bubbling over the top. And it cooked into the next paragraph and the next. And the kitchen floor was soon covered with porridge and the tables covered with porridge and the chairs. Then the stove covered, and then the bedroom where lights were on but the porridge put out even the lights. The town darkened.

And the pot did what pots do.

The porridge began to drip on the cobbled sidewalks, on the splintering staircases. The next house was covered with sweet porridge, the nearby street covered: its barbershop and its tailor shop and its bakery. And the neighbors sat on the pavement, eating biscuits and breads and sweet pies covered in porridge. The baker said, *eat! eat!* While his money-till filled with porridge.

The porridge was sweet.

And it rose to the branches of birch, the branches of ice, and the birds landed, and swam, and washed themselves. And they ate. And dogs swam, and ate. And the chickens made tiny noises. And then they began to drown. Everyone prayed for the pot to stop cooking, and everyone ate.

No one could stop.

Only one house remained that was not covered with sweet porridge to its copper roof. One house. All the neighbors sat on its roof and ate, their feet dangling in porridge. It was heavy on their feet. It was hard to pull their feet out, but they pulled. At last. The girl returned from school. A little girl swimming in the porridge on two large books. She yelled: *Stop, little pot, stop!* The townspeople all looked at one another and shook their heads.

This is how I remember my childhood. First a fantasia of plenty, yes: but then; eating my way back through time.

———

The second tale begins: eighteen-year-old peasant girl Talia and her husband, a White Army officer, had a baby girl, six months old. They walked the streets of Odessa with a cradle and ate chocolate cakes at Deribasovskaya. He bought her an umbrella and she was learning French. In the seventh month the government changed. The White Army officer had to escape because the color of his uniform was politically incorrect. Or perhaps something else about him was incorrect. He escaped from this story. But Talia stayed, her baby girl was seven months old.

In the eighth month the government closed the borders. Talia began to sew blue dresses so she could buy milk. She sewed day and night for the opera singers, she walked behind the stage after the performance taking measurements, giving compliments, taking measurements. They loved her. Talia was sewing, the opera was singing, the soup was in the little pot, the baby was turning nine months old.

In the tenth month the government prevented the food from coming into our province. It was an easy month. The opera was still open, the audiences still arrived. But soon the audiences began to walk out of our streets. They thought they could find food in the neighboring villages. But there was no food in the neighboring villages. There was no food in the farthest villages, but they did not learn of that. They died midway. And the borders remained closed. And there was no food on the table, there was no table, and there was no food even in the little pot. And the bellies began to sing, and then the singing stopped.

And the baby began its eleventh month. The opera singers left. Talia did not leave. Talia ate the earth. She dug a hole in the earth, she put the body of her baby girl into the box from the sewing machine and dug the earth. She dug the hole herself. She did everything herself. She even survived on her own somehow. She even married somehow. She even managed not to have another child—holding out till she was forty-two years old. That she did herself, against her new husband's wishes. When she was forty, everything changed. Everything changed.

She adopted my father. Everything changed. She told my father the story of the little pot when she taught him how to cook, how to chop vegetables, how to pinch the spices into the little pot. Her finger would weave through the air as she spoke. It landed on my father's forehead. "You must remember this."

Here the page turns. There was once a man who lived in an empire preoccupied with food. It was said of him that he opened an underground business that sold soups so good that when government officials tasted them, their eyes lit up and they carried that light into the higher offices and courts but could no longer pretend to be loyal to the system that ruled us—and they all lost their offices. But the soup factory kept going, tomato soups and spinach soups and onion soups with fish. His name was Vitya. He was of middle height, and at the time of my birth, his second son, he was middle-aged.

Tomato soup was not merely of a physical world—not as far as my father was concerned. What we put in our mouths feeds not only our bodies, but also what lives inside our bodies. There was something strange about that illegal soup factory of Sovetskaya Militsiya Street, everybody said so, but nobody knew for sure.

I heard Hans Christian Andersen's "Little Pot" from my grandmother, who never finished grade school, but learned to read in her sixties so that she could read fairy tales aloud to my cousin and me. When she finished, her finger would land on my forehead: "You must remember this."

Years later, in the United States, I saw "Little Pot" in my wife's Andersen volume and was surprised by how different it was from the story I knew. [In most volumes, the tale is called "The Teapot." —ed.] Imagination is just some remembering, from the other side, of course.

—*IK*

MICHAEL MARTONE

A Bucket of Warm Spit

ONCE'T, YOU COULD SPIT ON THE GROUND AND GROW WATER.

They said back then that the rain would follow the plow. They lied.

Our plows were painted grass green, and they broke open the green grass prairie hereabouts. Where it split and opened up, I swear, you could hear it leak, spitting a little spit, spitting a hiss-like hiss.

Spit of steam here, spit of steam there, the ground a rolling boil, all that steam boiled up into a smoke of steam.

The water rained from the ground pouring into the sky sighing as it went. The water, it up and went.

After a while all that water emptied into a big ol' cloud wall that hanged down from the sky and hugged the ground that fed it.

That big ol' cloud wall, it was made up of all these little drops of steam-water and seeded inside each of all these drops of steam-water were itty-bitty grains of dust that got carried away, snug, that the water would stick to.

When that big ol' cloud begun to move with the big ol' wind a-pushing it over the land, the grains of dust inside, they sanded the dry ground beneath it into more dust.

More more dust.

More dust got swallowed up by the dust and soon it was just dust in the big ol' cloud. That and a little paste of mud.

The land was wore away.

The land was wore away. The land was turned into air. We breathed it in.

The land, it filled our lungs like food filled up a stomach, but those were empty, our stomachs, even as we got to eating the dirt. We were eating dirt all the time as it up and went.

Jack, he kept burying his daddy.

Jack kept to burying his daddy in the dirt as it up and went.

Nobody farmed anymore. Nobody farmed.

We'd plow and the furrows would flatten. We'd plant and the seeds, they'd be blowed away. No need to hoe since the dirt-wind and the dirt-cloud scoured the ground-up ground clean of every weed.

Jack, he kept burying his daddy.

In that dirt-wind, Jack, he kept to burying his daddy.

Jack, he'd dig him a hole and roll his daddy, in his winding, into it.

The tailings Jack tossed into the hole turned to smoke on his shovel as he tossed them, trying to fill the hole he dug.

A whole spade full of soil smoking off the blade as he aimed for the hole with his daddy, in his winding, in it.

Jack, he'd end up scooping the sandy sides of the hole over the sides of the hole to fill the hole up.

Jack, he dozed the dust with his feet, pushed the dust into the hole to get it out of the wind, get the ground below ground out of the dirt-wind even as dirt-dirt washed away in the dirt-wind.

He'd finally get a blanket of that dirt-dirt over the body of his daddy, wrapped in the rotting winding.

Jack, he'd sit on top the dust he'd swept into the hole, but not to rest so much as to see if he could hold the dust down, keep it from drifting away again.

But the dust, it drifted away again.

He watched coils of dirt-dirt snake away from right under where he sat on it.

And Jack, he'd sink into the hole he dug as the dirt-dirt washed away from right under where he sat on it, wash away in the dirt-wind.

'Fore you know it, Jack, he would be all the way in the hole, sinking into it, with his daddy in his winding cloth. 'Cept there was no hole no more.

Jack, he'd stand back up and start to digging another hole to bury his daddy, his daddy in his rotting winding, lying in a heap on the shifting ground at his feet.

This went on a spell.

About then, the brindle cow, she run dry.

The brindle cow, she up and dried up.

Jack, he was in no ways surprised by this.

Jack, he'd been feeding the brindle cow wood from the barn, the red clapboards stripped of paint and sanded smooth by the dirt-wind.

Jack, he'd be back there massaging the bag to get the brindle cow to let down. The brindle cow, she'd be chewing and chewing the old barn wood all the time Jack was there in the back trying to get her to let down.

Jack, he'd work up a spit to spit on his hands to rub the boss's bag to get her to let down.

Before she give out, she'd give just one-half tin cup of rheumy cream.

To get that, Jack'd use all four teats for that one-half tin cup of rheumy cream the brindle cow would give after Jack'd massage her shrinking bag to get her to let down.

The brindle cow, she'd graze the sticking-out tops of the buried bob-wire fences.

The fence pickets and the bob-wire, they would knock the dirt-dust out of the wind and all get buried in the drift.

The brindle cow she would graze the fence tops, work the staples loose.

The brindle cow, she'd lick rust right off the bob-wire. Her big ol' tongue licking the rust right off the wire.

Jack, he found himself one of them ol' magnets. He found one of them big ol' bar magnets and fed it to the brindle cow.

The ol' magnet, it done lodged up in the crop.

That ol' magnet up in the crop, it draws all the hardware the brindle cow grazed on.

That ol' magnet, it didn't do no good.

That ol' magnet, it didn't do no good at all 'cause the brindle cow went dry as a bone.

The brindle cow, she stopped altogether letting down.

The brindle cow, she stopped altogether letting down, stopped giving milk, not even giving up a stringy spit of milky milk.

Jack's momma, she says to Jack to fetch the brindle cow into town.

Jack, Jack's momma says, fetch that ol' stopped-up cow into town.

She'll fetch a price, Jack's momma says, for her stringy meat if nothing else.

Jack's momma says the brindle cow's hide's done been already tanned by the wind. Her coat, she says, done been wore away. Her horns and hoofs done been hollowed out by the same dirt-wind wore the coat clean away.

And she's full-up with all that scrap, Jack's mamma says.

Jack's momma, she tells him to sell the scrap after the slaughter of the ol' brindle cow.

Jack, he says he will.

And the bones, Jack's momma says to Jack, fetch home them inside bones for bread.

Jack, he says he will.

And the tongue, Jack, Jack's momma says, fetch that home too. We can ring it out, ring it dry of water, the water that got leeched from the rust she's been licking from the bob-wire.

Jack and the brindle cow, they up and go, gone behind the big ol' cloud wall hanging from the sky and sweeping up dirt-cloud of dust at its feet.

Right away, Jack, he sees nothing but the cloud of dirt all around him.

Jack, he can't even see the brindle cow on the other end of that there rope.

Jack, he nickers. Jack, he says, come, boss, he says.

Jack, he hears the brindle cow say moo. Jack, he can't see her inside the dirt-cloud all around.

This goes on for a spell.

Then Jack and the brindle cow come to the forest. Jack, the brindle cow, and the forest are all in the dirt-cloud all around.

The forest isn't made up of no trees. It is a forest of old windmills. Hundreds of windmills. Hundreds. The windmills' blades make an aching sound in the gloom when the snaggle-tooth blades turn in the gritty dirt-wind.

The snaggle-tooth blades turn over out of sight inside the gritty ground-up dirt-cloud there overhead Jack and the brindle cow moo-ing in the gloom.

The windmills, they are only milling wind.

The windmills' screw gears, they done been wore away, been stripped clean by the gritty wind.

The windmills can't lift no water. No water to lift.

The windmill in the windmill forest done sucked up all the water out of the ground hereabouts long ago. The windmill forest, it is sinking into the ground, into the hollow place where all the water used to be.

All them windmills, they can't lift no more water. No water to lift. The windmills, they pump sand.

Jack and the brindle cow, they walk through the forest of the criss-crossed windmill towers, the windmill blades making their aching sound overhead.

The brindle cow, she hold up, stops to take a bite from the wood on one of them criss-crossed windmill towers. The brindle cow, she can't be budged.

That's when a man, he's been there all the time, says to Jack, say, what you got there at the end of that rope.

Jack, he says back to the man that he has a brindle cow all dried up he's taking to slaughter somewhere over there on the other side of the dirt-cloud.

The man, he says I can take her off your hands, says he's got something here way better than a dried-up brindle cow to trade.

Jack, he considers this for a spell.

Jack, he considers all the digging he's been doing, trying to keep his daddy in the ground. Jack, he considers what his momma said about the scrap metal and the hide and the sopping tongue and such.

Jack, he considers the big bones inside the brindle cow and the bone bread his momma wants to make with them.

The man, he says, after a spell, says what's it going to be?

Jack, he says to the man to tell him what's he got.

The man, he takes out a glass vial, a vial stopped up with a rubber stopper. The man, he holds it up right up to Jack's eye so as Jack can see into it.

Jack, he looks and looks.

Jack, he sees inside there an ocean of silver in the vial. An ocean, it has itty-bitty waves breaking and everything. Silver spume and such.

Jack, he is fair amazed.

The man, he says that that there is beads of quicksilver eating each other up. That there is melted metal that don't need no fire to melt. That there is magic beads.

Jack, he can't take his eyes off of them beads of quicksilver swallowing each other up inside the glass vial.

The man, he says this here is the rarest of the rare. Metal made outa water, water made outa metal. You go and spread that there metal-water on any ol' ground and see what grows up.

Jack, he's done thinking.

Jack, he up and takes the glass vial with the beads of quicksilver from the man right there and then.

Jack, he hands over the rope to the man. Somewhere out there on the other end of the rope is the brindle cow.

The brindle cow, she moos in the gloom.

Jack, he hears the man and the brindle cow go off that-a-way.

Jack, he turns the other way for home. The quicksilver in the glass vial, it gives off its own kind of silver light in the gloom.

The windmill blades over Jack's head, they make that aching sound, turning in the dirt-wind up inside the dirt-cloud.

This goes on for a spell.

Jack's momma, she asks Jack what he's got to show for the brindle cow. Jack's momma, she's been waiting for Jack for a spell. Dirt-drifts, they have drifted around her skirts where she waited for Jack on the house stoop.

Jack, he shows her there then what he had to show for the brindle cow.

Jack, he shows his momma the glass vial glowing in the gloom, filled up with the itty-bitty ocean of water-metal and metal-water.

Jack's momma, she's angry.

Jack, says Jack's momma, what about all that scrap metal and the leather tanned by the dirt-wind and the waterlogged tongue of that ol' stopped-up brindle cow?

Jack's momma, she says what about the big bones I was going to grind down to bonemeal to make our bread?

Jack, he says to his momma that there is quicksilver inside the glass vial, the rarest of the rare. Metal that ain't hard like metal. Water that ain't wet like water.

Jack, he says there ain't no telling what it can do.

Jack's momma, she don't say nothing, takes the glass vial right out of Jack's hands. The quicksilver inside the glass vial, it's glowing a little in the gloom.

Jack's momma, she considers for a spell.

Then, sudden-like, Jack's momma, she up and unstops the stopper there and just like that pours the water-metal metal-water on the ground.

The quicksilver is quick, quicker than quick, glows in the gloom as it slides through the dirt-air to the ground.

Jack's momma, she says this here is not worth a bucket of warm spit.

The quicksilver, it splashes on the ground. Where it splashes it kicks up little clouds of dusty dust. The way the quicksilver splashes, it makes a wet pattern like a map of the world 'cept the wet parts is the land and the dry parts is the vast ocean tracts I have only heard about in stories.

Jack and Jack's momma, they look down on the ground where the quicksilver, it makes a map of the world in the dirt.

Both of them stare as the silver-wet of the quicksilver sinks into the dirt-dirt, making a patch of gray mud that, right there and then, begins to dry up on the spot. But it isn't so much drying up as it is drying down. The wet soaking into, seeping into, that ground-up ground.

Jack and Jack's momma, they both stand still for a spell. They watch what little wet there was in those quicksilver beads turn into a big ol' dry.

In no time, even the big ol' dry, it's all dried up or, more exact, all dried down.

Jack and Jack's momma, they stand stock-still for a spell. Still long enough that the drifts of dirt begin to cover Jack's feet. Still long enough for the drifts of dirt to begin to cover the hem of Jack's momma's dress.

Enough, Jack's momma says after a spell.

Not enough, Jack thinks after another spell of saying nothing.

And both of them fall asleep then and there.

This goes on for a spell.

Then in the dark-dark of the night, Jack, he wakes up to take a leak. Jack, he wakes up and gets up from where he fell asleep on the dirt. Jack, he makes water.

In the yard, Jack, he makes water. The yard, it is so dark, Jack, he can't see the leak he is taking.

Jack, he hears the water he is making hit the ground. The water, it sounds like it sizzles when it hits the ground-up ground, sizzles like it turns to steam the second it strikes the ground.

After Jack takes a leak, after he has made water, Jack he goes back inside to his pallet of hard-packed dirt.

That night is when the thing growed up out of the ground-up ground.

The thing didn't need no sun to grow since it growed up in the nighttime.

That nighttime while Jack and Jack's momma sleep on their pallets of hard-packed dirt, the thing commences to grow.

First, there is this wrenching sound followed by a thumping bunch of big ol' hollow booms followed by a slide-whistling, followed by a scale pings and plucks followed by a string breaking on an out-of-tune fiddle followed by the kinks being peened out of an ol' washboard followed by a mucus-y pneumatic sneezing followed by the crinkling up of a tinfoil ball the size of the moon followed by the lumbering howl of a two-handed whipsaw being doubled up and honed with a horsetail bow to within an inch of its life to play a kind of toothy crosscut lullaby of ripped-up half-notes cut in half. And all of this followed by the ears of Jack in the dark-dark, a dark darker than dark on account of the dirt-cloud doubling the dark of the night.

Then, in the dark, there commences the no-mistaking-it sound of water running, water banging in plumbing that hasn't been bled yet, water glugging through too narrow a gauge pipe, water over a rapid, water filled with air bubbles, water fizzing with seltzer. Water plumb out of its mind with wet.

In the dark-dark, Jack hears it all. Jack, he heard the metal sounds and the water sounds growing together in the dark-dark.

In the morning, when the dark of the dark turns less dark and the dark becomes more of the regular gloom, Jack, he gets up off his dirt pallet and sees what he can see.

Jack, he sees that it is no longer dark-dark like the night but he also sees it isn't the regular gloom. The thing that growed up through the night with sound of metal and sound of water is so big as to cast a shadow on all the shade.

Out of the ground-up ground all around the wind-stripped wood of the wore-out house of Jack and Jack's momma, Jack, he sees these big ol' struts made of metal.

Jack, he sees a grove of these big ol' struts all studded with rivets, all trussed up and down with guy wires and ratlines growing out of the ground-up ground.

The big ol' struts, they're all riveted up and rigged all around with guy wires and ratlines, the big ol' struts also got rungs.

The rungs, they're tack-welded to the big ol' struts.

Jack, he looks up into the depths of the gloom of the dirt-cloud. Jack, he looks deep into the cloud.

Jack, he can't see no end to the big ol' struts growing up together into the depths of the dirt cloud.

Jack, he grabs hold of one of them tack-welded rungs.

Jack, he commences to climb one of them trussed-up struts.

Jack, he has no idea where he's going.

Jack, he has no idea where he's going but he gets going, climbs up them tack-welded rungs, hand over hand, up into the depths of the dirt-cloud.

The climb, it takes a spell.

After a spell, Jack, he looks back down from the rung he is hanging on to, back down through the rigging of the guy wires and ratlines going every which way between the big ol' struts. Jack, he sees nothing down below but the dirt-cloud and nothing up above but more dirt-cloud.

Jack, he commences to climb again.

Jack, he climbs up those rungs so long and so far he sleeps in the rigging of the guy wire and the ratlines.

After a spell of more climbing up the rungs and more sleeping in the guy wires and ratlines, Jack comes to the top of the dirt-cloud.

Jack, he pokes his head up above the top of the top of the dark ground-hugging dirt-cloud. And Jack, he sees out over the vast plain of the top of the dirt-cloud, a desert of dirt-cloud, and floating above that desert are cloud-clouds, all white and lovely-like.

Jack, he pokes his head through the top of the dirt-cloud, sees the cloud-clouds stretching above the dirt of the dirt-clouds, and then and there he ends up on a catwalk.

Jack, he ends up on this here catwalk after all that climbing up the rungs of the big ol' strut.

This here catwalk, it rings around a big ol' cloud, but this big ol' cloud is different from the white and lovely-like clouds floating all around it in the clear-clear air above the dirt-cloud.

This big ol' cloud, Jack, he sees, it's all made out of metal, metal studded all around with rivets and such. The big ol' metal cloud is being held up by the big ol' struts with the guy wires and the ratlines right at the top of the dirt-cloud. The big ol' metal cloud, it looks like it is floating there, a big ol' bar of soap floating on top of a bathtub of dirty cloud water.

Jack, he walks for a spell on the catwalk.

Jack, he walks on the catwalk and on one side, Jack, he sees all the while the white lovely-like clouds hanging in the deep blue sky, and on the other side, Jack, he sees the sheet metal of the big ol' metal cloud with its rivets and seams and such.

Walking on the catwalk, Jack, he comes to a hatch cut into the metal of the big ol' metal cloud.

Jack, he climbs through the hatch, he climbs inside the big ol' metal cloud, and inside there, here is this here other catwalk that Jack climbs down onto.

It is dark inside that big ol' metal cloud. It is dark and Jack, he waits a spell until his eyes can see the light that's in the dark.

And in the light inside the dark, Jack, he sees nothing but water. Inside the metal cloud, Jack sees nothing but water in an ocean of water stretching away to forever and ever.

Inside the metal cloud, Jack, he sees this ocean as far as he can see. This here ocean, it looks like an ocean with ocean waves breaking over each and such right up to the catwalk where Jack, he's standing.

Inside the metal cloud, the breeze in there is freshening. The freshening breeze, it sails over the endless ocean, over the breaking waves and such, and lights on Jack's grimy sweaty face.

Jack, he just lets that breeze light on his face. Jack, his face, it is all grimy and sweaty. And the breeze sailing over the ocean lighting on his face washes all that away.

The breeze, it lights on Jack's face with all its grime and sweat from climbing up inside the dirt-cloud, from living on the ground-up ground for so long.

The freshening breeze, it lights there, it licks the grime and the sweat right off of Jack's face.

This goes on a spell.

And Jack, he commences to cry right then and there. Jack, he's crying on that there catwalk, looking out over that endless ocean he sees in the light of the dark.

Jack, he cries these big ol' tears. These big ol' tears, they roll down Jack's once't grimy and sweaty skin of his face. And the breeze lighting there freeze-dries them big ol' tears right then and there.

That's when a woman, she's been there all the time, says to Jack, say, what you got there?

Jack, he says back to the woman that he don't know what she means.

The woman, she says I can take them off your hands, off your cheeks. The woman, she says she's got something here way better than them there freeze-dried tears.

Jack, he considers this for a spell.

Jack, he considers all the walking he's been doing, all the climbing. Jack, he considers all the dirt and all the water. Jack, he considers not even knowing about them there freeze-dried tears on his once't grimy and sweaty face.

Jack, he considers the big ol' tears on his face, how the freshening breeze squeezed them right out of him and freeze-dried them on his face.

The woman, she says, after a spell, says what's it going to be?

Jack, he says to the woman to tell him what she's got.

The woman, she takes out a glass dish, covered all over with a glass lid. The woman, she holds it up right up to Jack's eye so as Jack can see into it.

Jack, he looks and looks.

Jack, he sees inside there a frozen ocean of silver stuck on the glass dish. A frozen ocean, it has itty-bitty frozen waves breaking and everything. Frozen silver spume and such.

Jack, he is fair amazed.

The woman, she says that that there is flakes of iodide frozen on the dish. That there is frozen metal that don't melt. That there is magic flakes.

Jack, he can't take his eyes off of them flakes of iodide frozen on the glass dish.

The woman, she says this here is the rarest of the rare. Metal made outa no water, air made outa metal that don't melt. You go and spread that there air-metal on any ol' cloud and see what grows down.

Jack, he's done thinking.

Jack, he up and takes the glass dish with the flakes of iodide from the woman right there and then.

Jack, he chips off the big ol' freeze-dried tears from his face, hands them over to the woman.

Jack, he sees the woman turn to a purple smoke in front of his eyes right then and there.

Jack, he smells the blood in the freshening breeze.

Jack, he watches the purple smoke turn and twist. The iodide frozen on the glass dish, it gives off its own kind of silver light in the dark light inside the big ol' metal cloud.

The ocean waves below Jack's feet on the catwalk, they make that breaking sound, grinding down the waves into water.

The smoke, it turns and twists going up and up.

The turning and twisting smoke, it done turns into a stairway of smoke. The smoke, it done turns to a stairway right in front of Jack's eyes.

Jack, he knows there is more climbing to be done, knows he will have to climb these smoke stairs, turning and twisting.

Jack, he commences to start climbing the smoke stairs with the dish of iodide flakes giving off that silver light inside the big ol' metal cloud filled up with an ocean that goes on forever and ever.

This goes on for a spell.

The smoke at the top of the smoke stairs, it done drilled a Jack-sized hole in the metal of the top of the metal cloud.

Jack, he sees up ahead the hole the smoke done drilled there.

Jack, he sees the sunlight pour in through the hole the smoke done drilled.

The sunlight, it pours through the hole.

The sunlight, it pours through the hole and goes right for them iodide flakes under the glass lid on the glass dish.

Up inside there, up inside there the iodide flakes begin to melt. But them flakes don't melt as much as they don't turn into no water. Them iodide flakes, they turn right into more smoke turning and twisting under the glass lid.

Jack, he climbs himself right through that Jack-sized hole the smoke stairs done drilled in the top of the metal cloud. Jack, he climbs right out of that there hole in the cloud.

Jack, he is standing on top of that there cloud.

Jack, he is standing on top of that there cloud holding in his hand the glass-covered glass dish holding the cloud of purple smoke that once't was the silver flakes of iodide.

Jack, he lifts up the glass lid right then and there. And the smoke, it commences to expand. The smoke it begins to break into a million grains of smoke carried by the wind up there in the blue-blue sky.

Jack, he blows with the breath from his dirt-filled lungs the last of the smoke from the dish.

Jack, he sees the million grains of smoke go looking for the million cloud-clouds all white and lovely-like.

Jack, he's done climbing.

Jack, he is on top of the big ol' metal cloud and he is done climbing.

Jack, from way up there, he watches in the blue-blue sky the grains of smoke go looking for the cloud-clouds all white and lovely-like.

Jack, he's done climbing, he's done climbed all he was going to climb.

Jack, up there in the air, works up a bit of spit in his dry-dry mouth. It ain't much but enough.

Jack, he works up some spit.

Jack, he leans over the edge of that big ol' metal cloud he done climbed. He looks down into the dirt-cloud hanging there down below.

Jack, he spits.

———————

Growing up on a vast flat plane, I lived my life two-dimensionally on the x and z axes. Width and depth. Anything that drew my eyes to the height of y, then, was magical. Television towers, radio beacons, windbreaks and copses of trees, grain elevators, silos capped with lightning rods, lightning itself, windmills, and water towers. The I drawn upward. There is a reason, I think, that Chicago—the city of the flat prairie, the flat lake—is the birthplace of the skyscraper. Growing up, I visited, first, one tallest building after another as the first was replaced by the next. I went to the observation deck of the Prudential Building and watched them build the Standard Oil Building even higher. The Standard Oil Building didn't have an observation deck but the Hancock Building did, and from there I watched them build the Sears Tower, and from the Sears Tower I could see, well almost, forever or, at least, Gary and Indiana off in the vast distance. Growing up, I grew up. And growing up, I grew up on a vast flat plain that once was made up of devil's food cake topsoil that seemed endlessly endless. Growing up, plain on the plain so vast all of us and everything, even skyscrapers, seemed reduced to minute points in an infinitely

plain plane geometry. Growing up, I sang without really knowing that the corn was as high as an elephant's eye. Growing up was the drama of stark dimensions—x to y to z—rearranging themselves in this medium, this medium of time. Time running short. Time running long. Time running out.

—MM

KELLY LINK

Catskin

CATS WENT IN AND OUT OF THE WITCH'S HOUSE ALL DAY LONG. THE windows stayed open, and the doors, and there were other doors, cat-sized and private, in the walls and up in the attic. The cats were large and sleek and silent. No one knew their names, or even if they had names, except for the witch.

Some of the cats were cream-colored and some were brindled. Some were black as beetles. They were about the witch's business. Some came into the witch's bedroom with live things in their mouths. When they came out again, their mouths were empty.

The cats trotted and slunk and leaped and crouched. They were busy. Their movements were catlike, or perhaps clockwork. Their tails twitched like hairy pendulums. They paid no attention to the witch's children.

The witch had three living children at this time, although at one time she had had dozens, maybe more. No one, certainly not the witch, had ever bothered to tally them up. But at one time the house had bulged with cats and babies.

Now, since witches cannot have children in the usual way—their wombs are full of straw or bricks or stones, and when they give birth, they give birth to rabbits, kittens, tadpoles, houses, silk dresses, and yet even witches must have heirs, even witches wish to be mothers—the witch had acquired her children by other means: she had stolen or bought them.

She'd had a passion for children with a certain color of red hair. Twins she had never been able to abide (they were the wrong kind of magic), although she'd sometimes attempted to match up sets of children, as though she had been putting together a chess set, and not a family. If you were to say a witch's chess set, instead of a witch's family, there would be some truth in that. Perhaps this is true of other families as well.

One girl she had grown like a cyst, upon her thigh. Other children she had made out of things in her garden, or bits of trash that the cats brought her: aluminum foil with strings of chicken fat still crusted to it, broken television sets, cardboard boxes that the neighbors had thrown out. She had always been a thrifty witch.

Some of these children had run away and others had died. Some of them she had simply misplaced, or accidentally left behind on buses. It is to be hoped that these children were later adopted into good homes, or reunited with their natural parents. If you are looking for a happy ending in this story, then perhaps you should stop reading here and picture these children, these parents, their reunions.

Are you still reading? The witch, up in her bedroom, was dying. She had been poisoned by an enemy, a witch, a man named Lack. The child Finn, who had been her food taster, was dead already and so were three cats who'd licked her dish clean. The witch knew who had killed her and she snatched pieces of time, here and there, from the business of dying, to make her revenge. Once the question of this revenge had been settled to her satisfaction, the shape of it like a black ball of twine in her head, she began to divide up her estate between her three remaining children.

Flecks of vomit stuck to the corners of her mouth, and there was a basin beside the foot of the bed, which was full of black liquid. The room smelled like cats' piss and wet matches. The witch panted as if she were giving birth to her own death.

"Flora shall have my automobile," she said, "and also my purse, which will never be empty, so long as you always leave a coin at the bottom, my darling, my spendthrift, my profligate, my drop of poison, my pretty, pretty Flora. And when I am dead, take the road outside the house and go west. There's one last piece of advice."

Flora, who was the oldest of the witch's living children, was red-headed and stylish. She had been waiting for the witch's death for a long time now, although she had been patient. She kissed the witch's cheek and said, "Thank you, Mother."

The witch looked up at her, panting. She could see Flora's life, already laid out, flat as a map. Perhaps all mothers can see as far.

"Jack, my love, my birdsnest, my bite, my scrap of porridge," the witch said, "you shall have my books. I won't have any need of books where I am going. And when you leave my house, strike out in an easterly direction and you won't be any sorrier than you are now."

Jack, who had once been a little bundle of feathers and twigs and eggshell all tied up with a tatty piece of string, was a sturdy lad, almost full grown. If he knew how to read, only the cats knew it. But he nodded and kissed his mother's gray lips.

"And what shall I leave to my boy Small?" the witch said, convulsing. She threw up again in the basin. Cats came running, leaning on the lip of the basin to inspect her vomitus. The witch's hand dug into Small's leg.

"Oh it is hard, hard, so very hard, for a mother to leave her children (though I have done harder things). Children need a mother, even such a mother as I have been." She wiped at her eyes, and yet it is a fact that witches cannot cry.

Small, who still slept in the witch's bed, was the youngest of the witch's children. (Perhaps not as young as you think.) He sat upon the bed, and although he didn't cry, it was only because witch's children have no one to teach them the use of crying. His heart was breaking.

Small could juggle and sing and every morning he brushed and plaited the witch's long, silky hair. Surely every mother must wish for a boy like Small, a curly-headed, sweet-breathed, tenderhearted boy like Small, who can cook a fine omelet, and who has a good strong singing voice as well as a gentle hand with a hairbrush.

"Mother," he said, "if you must die, then you must die. And if I can't come along with you, then I'll do my best to live and make you proud. Give me your hairbrush to remember you by, and I'll go make my own way in the world."

"You shall have my hairbrush, then," said the witch to Small, looking, and panting, panting. "And I love you best of all. You shall have my tinderbox and my matches, and also my revenge, and you will make me proud, or I don't know my own children."

"What shall we do with the house, Mother?" said Jack. He said it as if he didn't care.

"When I am dead," the witch said, "this house will be of no use to anyone. I gave birth to it—that was a very long time ago—and raised it from just a dollhouse. Oh, it was the most dear, most darling dollhouse ever. It had eight rooms and a tin roof, and a staircase that went nowhere at all. But I nursed it and rocked it to sleep in a cradle, and it grew up to be a real house, and see how it has taken care of me, its parent, how it knows a child's duty to its mother. And perhaps you can see how it is now, how it pines, how it grows sick to see me dying like this. Leave it to the cats. They'll know what to do with it."

All this time the cats have been running in and out of the room, bringing things and taking things away. It seems as if they will never slow down, never come to rest, never nap, never have the time to sleep, or to die, or even to mourn. They have a certain proprietary look about them, as if the house is already theirs.

The witch vomits up mud, fur, glass buttons, tin soldiers, trowels, hat pins, thumbtacks, love letters (mislabeled or sent without the appropriate amount of postage and never read), and a dozen regiments of red ants, each ant as long and wide as a kidney bean. The ants swim across the perilous stinking basin, clamber up the sides of the basin, and go marching across the floor in a shiny ribbon. They are carrying pieces of Time in their mandibles. Time is heavy, even in such small pieces, but the ants have strong jaws, strong legs. Across the floor they go, and up the wall, and out the window. The cats watch, but don't interfere. The witch gasps and coughs and then lies still. Her hands beat against the bed once and then are still. Still the children wait, to make sure that she is dead, and that she has nothing else to say.

In the witch's house, the dead are sometimes quite talkative.

But the witch has nothing else to say at this time.

The house groans and all the cats begin to mew piteously, trotting in and out of the room as if they have dropped something and must go and hunt for it—they will never find it—and the children, at last, find they know how to cry, but the witch is perfectly still and quiet. There is a tiny smile on her face, as if everything has happened exactly to her satisfaction. Or maybe she is looking forward to the next part of the story.

The children buried the witch in one of her half-grown dollhouses. They crammed her into the downstairs parlor, and knocked out the inner walls so that her head rested on the kitchen table in the breakfast nook, and her ankles threaded through a bedroom door. Small brushed out her hair, and, because he wasn't sure what she should wear now that she was dead, he put all her dresses on her, one over the other over the other, until he could hardly see her white limbs at all beneath the stack of petticoats and coats and dresses. It didn't matter: once they'd nailed the dollhouse shut again, all they could see was the red crown of her head in the kitchen window, and the worn-down heels of her dancing shoes knocking against the shutters of the bedroom window.

Jack, who was handy, rigged a set of wheels for the dollhouse, and a harness so that it could be pulled. They put the harness on Small, and Small pulled and Flora pushed, and Jack talked and coaxed the house along, over the hill, down to the cemetery, and the cats ran along beside them.

The cats are beginning to look a bit shabby, as if they are molting. Their mouths look very empty. The ants have marched away, through the woods, and down into town, and they have built a nest on your yard, out of the bits of Time. And if you hold a magnifying glass over their nest, to see the ants dance and burn, Time will catch fire and you will be sorry.

Outside the cemetery gates, the cats had been digging a grave for the witch. The children tipped the dollhouse into the grave, kitchen window first. But then they saw that the grave wasn't deep enough, and the house sat there on its end, looking uncomfortable. Small began to cry (now that he'd learned how, it seemed he would spend all his time practicing), thinking how horrible it would be to spend one's death, all of eternity, upside down and not even properly buried, not even able to feel the rain when it beat down on the exposed shingles of the house, and seeped down into the house and filled your mouth and drowned you, so that you had to die all over again, every time it rained.

The dollhouse chimney had broken off and fallen on the ground. One of the cats picked it up and carried it away, like a souvenir. That cat carried the chimney into the woods and ate it, a mouthful at a time, and passed out of this story and into another one. It's no concern of ours.

The other cats began to carry up mouthfuls of dirt, dropping it and mounding it around the house with their paws. The children helped, and when they'd finished, they'd managed to bury the witch properly, so that only the bedroom window was visible, a little pane of glass like an eye at the top of a small dirt hill.

On the way home, Flora began to flirt with Jack. Perhaps she liked the way he looked in his funeral black. They talked about what they planned to be, now that they were grown up. Flora wanted to find her parents. She was a pretty girl: someone would want to look after her. Jack said he would like to marry someone rich. They began to make plans.

Small walked a little behind, slippery cats twining around his ankles. He had the witch's hairbrush in his pocket, and his fingers slipped around the figured horn handle for comfort.

The house, when they reached it, had a dangerous, grief-stricken look to it, as if it was beginning to pull away from itself. Flora and Jack wouldn't go back inside. They squeezed Small lovingly, and asked if he wouldn't want to come along with them. He would have liked to, but who would have looked after the witch's cats, the witch's revenge? So he watched as they drove off together. They went north. What child has ever heeded a mother's advice?

Jack hasn't even bothered to bring along the witch's library: he says there isn't space in the trunk for everything. He'll rely on Flora and her magic purse.

Small sat in the garden, and ate stalks of grass when he was hungry, and pretended that the grass was bread and milk and chocolate cake. He drank out of the garden hose. When it began to grow dark, he was lonelier than he had ever been in his life. The witch's cats were not good company. He said nothing to them and they had nothing to tell him, about the house, or the future, or the witch's revenge, or about where he was supposed to sleep. He had never slept anywhere except in the witch's bed, so at last he went back over the hill and down to the cemetery.

Some of the cats were still going up and down the grave, covering the base of the mound with leaves and grass and feathers, their own loose fur. It was a soft sort of nest to lie down on. The cats were still busy when Small fell asleep—cats are always busy—cheek pressed against the cool glass of the bedroom window, hand curled in his pocket around the hairbrush, but in the middle of the night, when he woke up, he was swaddled, head to foot, in warm, grass-scented cat bodies.

A tail is curled around his chin like a rope, and all the bodies are soughing breath in and out, whiskers and paws twitching, silky bellies rising and falling. All the cats are sleeping a frantic, exhausted, busy sleep, except for one, a white cat who sits near his head, looking down at him. Small has never seen this cat before, and yet he knows her, the way that you know the people who visit you in dreams: she's white everywhere, except for reddish tufts and frills at her ears and tail and paws, as if someone has embroidered her with fire around the edges.

"What's your name?" Small says. He's never talked to the witch's cats before.

The cat lifts a leg and licks herself in a private place. Then she looks at him. "You may call me Mother," she says.

But Small shakes his head. He can't call the cat that. Down under the blanket of cats, under the windowpane, the witch's Spanish heel is drinking in moonlight.

"Very well, then, you may call me The Witch's Revenge," the cat says. Her mouth doesn't move, but he hears her speak inside his head. Her voice is furry and sharp, like a blanket made of needles. "And you may comb my fur."

Small sits up, displacing sleeping cats, and lifts the brush out of his pocket. The bristles have left rows of little holes indented in the pink palm of his hand, like some sort of code. If he could read the code, it would say: Comb my fur.

Small combs the fur of The Witch's Revenge. There's grave dirt in the cat's fur, and one or two red ants, who drop and scurry away. The Witch's Revenge bends her head down to the ground, snaps them up in her jaws. The heap of cats around them is yawning and stretching. There are things to do.

"You must burn her house down," The Witch's Revenge says. "That's the first thing."

Small's comb catches a knot, and The Witch's Revenge turns and nips him on the wrist. Then she licks him in the tender place between his thumb and his first finger. "That's enough," she says. "There's work to do."

So they all go back to the house, Small stumbling in the dark, moving farther and farther away from the witch's grave, the cats trotting along, their eyes lit like torches, twigs and branches in their mouths, as if they plan to build a nest, a canoe, a fence to keep the world out. The house, when they reach it, is full of lights, and more cats, and piles of tinder. The house is making a noise, like an instrument that someone is breathing into. Small realizes that all the cats are mewing, endlessly, as they run in and out the doors, looking for more kindling. The Witch's Revenge says, "First we must latch all the doors."

So Small shuts all the doors and windows on the first floor, leaving open only the kitchen door, and The Witch's Revenge shuts the catches on the secret doors, the cat doors, the doors in the attic, and up on the roof, and the cellar doors. Not a single secret door is left open. Now all the noise is on the inside, and Small and The Witch's Revenge are on the outside.

All the cats have slipped into the house through the kitchen door. There isn't a single cat in the garden. Small can see the witch's cats through the windows, arranging their piles of twigs. The Witch's Revenge sits beside him, watching. "Now light a match and throw it in," says The Witch's Revenge.

Small lights a match. He throws it in. What boy doesn't love to start a fire?

"Now shut the kitchen door," says The Witch's Revenge, but Small can't do that. All the cats are inside. The Witch's Revenge stands on her hindpaws and pushes the kitchen door shut. Inside, the lit match catches something on fire. Fire runs along the floor and up the kitchen walls. Cats catch fire, and run into the other rooms of the house. Small can see all this through the windows. He stands with his face against the glass, which is cold, and then warm, and then hot. Burning cats with burning twigs in their mouths press up against the kitchen door, and the other doors of the house, but all the doors are locked. Small and The Witch's Revenge stand in the garden and watch the witch's house and the witch's books and the witch's sofas and the witch's cooking pots and the witch's cats, her cats, too, all her cats burn.

You should never burn down a house. You should never set a cat on fire. You should never watch and do nothing while a house is burning. You should never listen to a cat who says to do any of these things. You should listen to your mother when she tells you to come away from watching, to go to bed, to go to sleep. You should listen to your mother's revenge.

You should never poison a witch.

In the morning, Small woke up in the garden. Soot covered him in a greasy blanket. The Witch's Revenge was curled up asleep on his chest. The witch's house was still standing, but the windows had melted and run down the walls.

The Witch's Revenge woke and stretched and licked Small clean with her small sharkskin tongue. She demanded to be combed. Then she went into the house and came out, carrying a little bundle. It dangled, boneless, from her mouth, like a kitten.

It is a catskin, Small sees, only there is no longer a cat inside it. The Witch's Revenge drops it in his lap.

He picked it up and something shiny fell out of the loose light skin. It was a piece of gold, sloppy, slippery with fat. The Witch's Revenge brought out dozens and dozens of catskins, and there was a gold piece in every skin. While Small counted his fortune, The Witch's Revenge bit off one of her own claws, and pulled one long witch hair out of the witch's comb. She sat up, like a tailor, cross-legged in the grass, and began to stitch up a bag, out of the many catskins.

Small shivered. There was nothing to eat for breakfast but grass, and the grass was black and cooked.

"Are you cold?" said The Witch's Revenge. She put the bag aside and picked up another catskin, a fine black one. She slit a sharp claw down the middle. "We'll make you a warm suit."

She used the coat of a black cat, and the coat of a calico cat, and she put a trim around the paws, of gray-and-white-striped fur.

While she did this, she said to Small, "Did you know that there was once a battle, fought on this very patch of ground?"

Small shook his head no.

"Wherever there's a garden," The Witch's Revenge said, scratching with one paw at the ground, "I promise you there are people buried somewhere beneath it. Look here." She plucked up a little brown clot, put it in her mouth, and cleaned it with her tongue.

When she spat the little circle out again, Small saw it was an ivory regimental button. The Witch's Revenge dug more buttons out of the ground—as if buttons of ivory grew in the ground—and sewed them onto the catskin. She fashioned a hood with two eyeholes and a set of fine whiskers, and sewed four fine cat tails to the back of the suit, as if the single tail that grew there wasn't good enough for Small. She threaded a bell on each one. "Put this on," she said to Small.

Small puts on the suit and the bells chime. The Witch's Revenge laughs. "You make a fine-looking cat," she says. "Any mother would be proud."

The inside of the cat suit is soft and a little sticky against Small's skin. When he puts the hood over his head, the world disappears. He can see only the vivid corners of it through the eyeholes—grass, gold, the cat who sits cross-legged, stitching up her sack of skins—and air seeps in, down at the loosely sewn seam, where the skin droops and sags over his chest and around the gaping buttons. Small holds his tails in his clumsy fingerless paw, like a handful of eels, and swings them back and forth to hear them ring. The sound of the bells and the sooty, cooked smell of the air, the warm stickiness of the suit, the feel of his new fur against the ground: he falls asleep and dreams that hundreds of ants come and lift him and gently carry him off to bed.

When Small tipped his hood back again, he saw that The Witch's Revenge had finished with her needle and thread. Small helped her fill the bag with gold. The Witch's Revenge stood up on her hind legs, took the bag, and swung it over her shoulders. The gold coins went sliding against one another, mewling and hissing. The bag dragged along the grass, picking up ash, leaving a trail of green behind it. The Witch's Revenge strutted along as if she were carrying a sack of air.

Small put the hood on again, and he got down on his hands and knees. And then he trotted after The Witch's Revenge. They left the garden gate wide open and went into the forest, toward the house where the witch Lack lived.

The forest is smaller than it used to be. Small is growing, but the forest is shrinking. Trees have been cut down. Houses have been built. Lawns rolled, roads laid. The Witch's Revenge and Small walked alongside one of the roads. A school bus rolled by: The children inside looked out their windows and laughed when they saw The Witch's Revenge walking on her hind legs, and at her heels, Small, in his cat suit. Small lifted his head and peered out of his eyeholes after the school bus.

"Who lives in these houses?" he asked The Witch's Revenge.

"That's the wrong question, Small," said The Witch's Revenge, looking down at him and striding along.

Miaow, the catskin bag said. *Clink.*

"What's the right question, then?" Small said.

"Ask me who lives under the houses," The Witch's Revenge said.

Obediently, Small said, "Who lives under the houses?"

"What a good question!" said The Witch's Revenge. "You see, not everyone can give birth to their own house. Most people give birth to children instead. And when you have children, you need houses to put them in. So children and houses: most people give birth to the first and have to build the second. The houses, that is. A long time ago, when men and women were going to build a house, they would dig a hole first. And they'd make a little room—a little, wooden, one-room house—in the hole. And they'd steal or buy a child to put in the house in the hole, to live there. And then they built their house over that first little house."

"Did they make a door in the lid of the little house?" Small said.

"They did not make a door," said The Witch's Revenge.

"But, then, how did the girl or the boy climb out?" Small said.

"The boy or the girl stayed in that little house," said The Witch's Revenge. "They lived there all their life, and they are living in those houses still, under the other houses where the people live, and the people who live in the houses above may come and go as they please, and they don't ever think about how there are little houses with little children, sitting in little rooms, under their feet."

"But what about the mothers and fathers?" Small asked. "Didn't they ever go looking for their boys and girls?"

"Ah," said The Witch's Revenge. "Sometimes they did and sometimes they didn't. And after all, who was living under their houses? But that was a long time ago. Now people mostly bury a cat when they build their house, instead of a child. That's why we call cats house-cats. Which is why we must walk along smartly. As you can see, there are houses under construction here."

And so there are. They walk by clearings where men are digging little holes. First Small puts his hood back and walks on two legs, and then he puts on his hood again, and goes on all fours: He makes himself as small and slinky as possible, just like a cat. But the bells on his tails jounce and the coins in the bag that The Witch's Revenge carries go *clink, miaow,* and the men stop their work and watch them go by.

How many witches are there in the world? Have you ever seen one? Would you know a witch if you saw one? And what would you do if you saw one? For that matter, do you know a cat when you see one? Are you sure?

Small followed The Witch's Revenge. Small grew calluses on his knees and the pads of his fingers. He would have liked to carry the bag sometimes, but it was too heavy. How heavy? You would not have been able to carry it, either.

They drank out of streams. At night they opened the catskin bag and climbed inside to sleep, and when they were hungry they licked the coins, which seemed to sweat golden fat, and always more fat. As they went, The Witch's Revenge sang a song:

> I had no mother
> and my mother had no mother
> and her mother had no mother
> and her mother had no mother
> and her mother had no mother
> and you have no mother
> to sing you
> this song

The coins in the bag sang too, *miaow, miaow,* and the bells on Small's tails kept the rhythm.

Every night Small combs The Witch's Revenge's fur. And every morning The Witch's Revenge licks him all over, not neglecting the places behind his ears, and at the backs of his knees. And then he puts the catsuit back on, and she grooms him all over again.

Sometimes they were in the forest, and sometimes the forest became a town, and then The Witch's Revenge would tell Small stories about the people who lived in the houses, and the children who lived in the houses under the houses. Once, in the forest, The Witch's Revenge showed Small where there had once been a house. Now there were only the stones of the foundation, upholstered in moss, and the chimney stack, propped up with fat ropes and coils of ivy.

The Witch's Revenge rapped on the grassy ground, moving clockwise around the foundation, until both she and Small could hear a hollow sound; The Witch's Revenge dropped to all fours and clawed at the ground, tearing it up with her paws and biting at it, until they could see a little wooden roof. The Witch's Revenge knocked on the roof, and Small lashed his tails.

"Well, Small," said The Witch's Revenge, "shall we take off the roof and let the poor child go?"

Small crept up close to the hole she had made. He put his ear to it and listened, but he heard nothing at all. "There's no one in there," he said.

"Maybe they're shy," said The Witch's Revenge. "Shall we let them out, or shall we leave them be?"

"Let them out!" said Small, but what he meant to say was, "Leave them alone!" Or maybe he said *Leave them be!* although he meant the opposite. The Witch's Revenge looked at him, and Small thought he heard something then—beneath him where he crouched, frozen—very faint: a scrabbling at the dirty, sunken roof.

Small sprang away. The Witch's Revenge picked up a stone and brought it down hard, caving the roof in. When they peered inside, there was nothing except blackness and a faint smell. They waited, sitting on the ground, to see what might come out, but nothing came out. After a while, The Witch's Revenge picked up her catskin bag, and they set off again.

For several nights after that, Small dreamed that someone, something, was following them. It was small and thin and bleached and cold and dirty and afraid. One night it crept away again, and Small never knew where it went. But if you come to that part of the forest, where they sat and waited by the stone foundation, perhaps you will meet the thing that they set free.

No one knew the reason for the quarrel between the witch Small's mother and the witch Lack, although the witch Small's mother had died for it. The witch Lack was a handsome man and he loved his children dearly. He had stolen them out of the cribs and beds of palaces and manors and harems. He dressed his children in silks, as befitted their station, and they wore gold crowns and ate off gold plates. They drank from cups of gold. Lack's children, it was said, lacked nothing.

Perhaps the witch Lack had made some remark about the way the witch Small's mother was raising her children, or perhaps the witch Small's mother had boasted of her children's red hair. But it might have been something else. Witches are proud and they like to quarrel.

When Small and The Witch's Revenge came at last to the house of the witch Lack, The Witch's Revenge said to Small, "Look at this monstrosity! I've produced finer turds and buried them under leaves. And the smell, like an open sewer! How can his neighbors stand the stink?"

Male witches have no wombs, and must come by their houses in other ways, or else buy them from female witches. But Small thought it was a very fine house. There was a prince or a princess at each window staring down at him, as he sat on his haunches in the driveway, beside The Witch's Revenge. He said nothing, but he missed his brothers and sisters.

"Come along," said The Witch's Revenge. "We'll go a little ways off and wait for the witch Lack to come home."

Small followed The Witch's Revenge back into the forest, and in a while, two of the witch Lack's children came out of the house, carrying baskets made of gold. They went into the forest as well and began to pick blackberries.

The Witch's Revenge and Small sat in the briar and watched.

There was a wind in the briar. Small was thinking of his brothers and sisters. He thought of the taste of blackberries, the feel of them in his mouth, which was not at all like the taste of fat.

The Witch's Revenge nestled against the small of Small's back. She was licking down a lump of knotted fur at the base of his spine. The princesses were singing.

Small decided that he would live in the briar with The Witch's Revenge. They would live on berries and spy on the children who came to pick them, and The Witch's Revenge would change her name. The word *Mother* was in his mouth, along with the sweet taste of the blackberries.

"Now you must go out," said The Witch's Revenge, "and be kittenish. Be playful. Chase your tail. Be shy, but don't be too shy. Don't talk too much. Let them pet you. Don't bite."

She pushed at Small's rump, and Small tumbled out of the briar and sprawled at the feet of the witch Lack's children.

The Princess Georgia said, "Look! It's a dear little cat!"

Her sister Margaret said doubtfully, "But it has five tails. I've never seen a cat that needed so many tails. And its skin is done up with buttons and it's almost as large as you are."

Small, however, began to caper and prance. He swung his tails back and forth so that the bells rang out and then he pretended to be alarmed by this. First he ran away from his tails and then he chased his tails. The two princesses put down their baskets, half-full of blackberries, and spoke to him, calling him a silly puss.

At first he wouldn't go near them. But, slowly, he pretended to be won over. He allowed himself to be petted and fed blackberries. He chased a hair ribbon and he stretched out to let them admire the buttons up and down his belly. Princess Margaret's fingers tugged at his skin; then she slid one hand in between the loose catskin and Small's boy skin. He batted her hand away with a paw, and Margaret's sister Georgia said knowingly that cats didn't like to be petted on their bellies.

They were all good friends by the time The Witch's Revenge came out of the briar, standing on her hind legs and singing

> *I have no children*
> *and my children have no children*
> *and their children*
> *have no children*

and their children
have no whiskers
and no tails

At this sight, the Princesses Margaret and Georgia began to laugh and point. They had never heard a cat sing, or seen a cat walk on its hind legs. Small lashed his five tails furiously, and all the fur of the catskin stood up on his arched back, and they laughed at that too.

When they came back from the forest, with their baskets piled with berries, Small was stalking close at their heels, and The Witch's Revenge came walking just behind. But she left the bag of gold hidden in the briar.

That night, when the witch Lack came home, his hands were full of gifts for his children. One of his sons ran to meet him at the door and said, "Come and see what followed Margaret and Georgia home from the forest! Can we keep them?"

And the table had not been set for dinner, and the children of the witch Lack had not sat down to do their homework, and in the witch Lack's throne room, there was a cat with five tails, spinning in circles, while a second cat sat impudently upon his throne, and sang

Yes!
your father's house
is the shiniest
brownest largest
the most expensive
the sweetest-smelling
house
that has ever
come out of
anyone's
ass!

The witch Lack's children began to laugh at this, until they saw the witch, their father, standing there. Then they fell silent. Small stopped spinning.

"You!" said the witch Lack.

"Me!" said The Witch's Revenge, and sprang from the throne. Before anyone knew what she was about, her jaws were fastened about the witch Lack's neck, and then she ripped out his throat. Lack opened his mouth to speak and his blood fell out, making The Witch's Revenge's fur more red now than white. The witch Lack fell down dead, and red ants went marching out of the hole in his neck and the hole of his mouth, and they held pieces of Time in their jaws as tightly as The Witch's Revenge had held Lack's throat in hers. But she let Lack go and left him lying in his blood on the floor, and she snatched up the ants and ate them, quickly, as if she had been hungry for a very long time.

While this was happening, the witch Lack's children stood and watched and did nothing. Small sat on the floor, his tails curled about his paws. Children, all of them, they did nothing. They were too surprised. The Witch's Revenge, her belly full of ants, her mouth stained with blood, stood up and surveyed them.

"Go and fetch me my catskin bag," she said to Small.

Small found that he could move. Around him, the princes and princesses stayed absolutely still. The Witch's Revenge was holding them in her gaze.

"I'll need help," Small said. "The bag is too heavy for me to carry."

The Witch's Revenge yawned. She licked a paw and began to pat at her mouth. Small stood still.

"Very well," she said. "Take those big strong girls the Princesses Margaret and Georgia with you. They know the way."

The Princesses Margaret and Georgia, finding that they could move again, began to tremble. They gathered their courage and they went with Small, the two girls holding each other's hands, out of the throne room, not looking down at the body of their father, the witch Lack, and back into the forest.

Georgia began to weep, but the Princess Margaret said to Small: "Let us go!"

"Where will you go?" said Small. "The world is a dangerous place. There are people in it who mean you no good." He threw back his hood, and the Princess Georgia began to weep harder.

"Let us go," said the Princess Margaret. "My parents are the King and Queen of a country not three days' walk from here. They will be glad to see us again."

Small said nothing. They came to the briar and he sent the Princess Georgia in to hunt for the catskin bag. She came out scratched and bleeding, the bag in her hand. It had caught on the briars and torn open. Gold coins rolled out, like glossy drops of fat, falling on the ground.

"Your father killed my mother," said Small.

"And that cat, your mother's devil, will kill us, or worse," said Princess Margaret. "Let us go!"

Small lifted the catskin bag. There were no coins in it now. The Princess Georgia was on her hands and knees, scooping up coins and putting them into her pockets.

"Was he a good father?" Small asked.

"He thought he was," Princess Margaret said. "But I'm not sorry he's dead. When I grow up, I will be Queen. I'll make a law to put all the witches in the kingdom to death, and all their cats as well."

Small became afraid. He took up the catskin bag and ran back to the house of the witch Lack, leaving the two princesses in the forest. And whether they made their way home to the Princess Margaret's parents, or whether they fell into the hands of thieves, or whether they lived in the briar, or whether the Princess Margaret grew up and kept her promise and rid her kingdom of witches and cats, Small never knew, and neither do I, and neither shall you.

When he came back into the witch Lack's house, The Witch's Revenge saw at once what had happened. "Never mind," she said.

There were no children, no princes and princesses, in the throne room. The witch Lack's body still lay on the floor, but The Witch's

Revenge had skinned it like a coney, and sewn up the skin into a bag. The bag wriggled and jerked, the sides heaving as if the witch Lack were still alive somewhere inside. The Witch's Revenge held the witchskin bag in one hand, and with the other, she was stuffing a cat into the neck of the skin. The cat wailed as it went into the bag. The bag was full of wailing. But the discarded flesh of the witch Lack lolled, slack.

There was a little pile of gold crowns on the floor beside the flayed corpse, and transparent, papery things that blew about the room on a current of air, surprised looks on the thin, shed faces.

Cats were hiding in the corners of the room, and under the throne. "Go catch them," said The Witch's Revenge. "But leave the three prettiest alone."

"Where are the witch Lack's children?" Small said.

The Witch's Revenge nodded around the room. "As you see," she said. "I've slipped off their skins, and they were all cats underneath. They're cats now, but if we were to wait a year or two, they would shed these skins as well and become something new. Children are always growing."

Small chased the cats around the room. They were fast, but he was faster. They were nimble, but he was nimbler. He had worn his cat suit longer. He drove the cats down the length of the room, and The Witch's Revenge caught them and dropped them into her bag. At the end there were only three cats left in the throne room and they were as pretty a trio of cats as anyone could ask for. All the other cats were inside the bag.

"Well done and quickly done, too," said The Witch's Revenge, and she took her needle and stitched shut the neck of the bag. The skin of the witch Lack smiled up at Small, and a cat put its head through Lack's stained mouth, wailing. But The Witch's Revenge sewed Lack's mouth shut too, and the hole on the other end, where a house had come out. She left only his ear holes and his eyeholes and his nostrils, which were full of fur, rolled open so that the cats could breathe.

The Witch's Revenge slung the skin full of cats over her shoulder and stood up.

"Where are you going?" Small said.

"These cats have mothers and fathers," The Witch's Revenge said. "They have mothers and fathers who miss them very much."

She gazed at Small. He decided not to ask again. So he waited in the house with the two princesses and the prince in their new cat suits, while The Witch's Revenge went down to the river. Or perhaps she took them down to the market and sold them. Or maybe she took each cat home, to its own mother and father, back to the kingdom where it had been born. Maybe she wasn't so careful to make sure that each child was returned to the right mother and father. After all, she was in a hurry, and cats look very much alike at night.

No one saw where she went—but the market is closer than the palaces of the Kings and Queens whose children had been stolen by the witch Lack, and the river is closer still.

When The Witch's Revenge came back to Lack's house, she looked around her. The house was beginning to stink very badly. Even Small could smell it now.

"I suppose the Princess Margaret let you fuck her," said The Witch's Revenge, as if she had been thinking about this while she ran her errands. "And that is why you let them go. I don't mind. She was a pretty puss. I might have let her go myself."

She looked at Small's face and saw that he was confused. "Never mind," she said.

She had a length of string in her paw, and a cork, which she greased with a piece of fat she had cut from the witch Lack. She threaded the cork on the string, calling it a good, quick, little mouse, and greased the string as well, and she fed the wriggling cork to the tabby who had been curled up in Small's lap. And when she had the cork back again, she greased it again and fed it to the little black cat, and then she fed it to the cat with two white forepaws, so that she had all three cats upon her string.

She sewed up the rip in the catskin bag, and Small put the gold

292 · KELLY LINK

crowns in the bag, and it was nearly as heavy as it had been before. The Witch's Revenge carried the bag, and Small took the greased string, holding it in his teeth, so the three cats were forced to run along behind him as they left the house of the witch Lack.

Small strikes a match, and he lights the house of the dead witch, Lack, on fire, as they leave. But shit burns slowly, if at all, and that house might be burning still, if someone hasn't gone and put it out. And maybe, someday, someone will go fishing in the river near that house, and hook their line on a bag full of princes and princesses, wet and sorry and wriggling in their catsuit skins—that's one way to catch a husband or a wife.

Small and The Witch's Revenge walked without stopping and the three cats came behind them. They walked until they reached a little village very near where the witch Small's mother had lived and there they settled down in a room The Witch's Revenge rented from a butcher. They cut the greased string, and bought a cage and hung it from a hook in the kitchen. They kept the three cats in it, but Small bought collars and leashes, and sometimes he put one of the cats on a leash and took it for a walk around the town.

Sometimes he wore his own catsuit and went out prowling, but The Witch's Revenge used to scold him if she caught him dressed like that. There are country manners and there are town manners and Small was a boy about town now.

The Witch's Revenge kept house. She cleaned and she cooked and she made Small's bed in the morning. Like all of the witch's cats, she was always busy. She melted down the gold crowns in a stewpot, and minted them into coins.

The Witch's Revenge wore a silk dress and gloves and a heavy veil, and ran her errands in a fine carriage, Small at her side. She opened an account in a bank, and she enrolled Small in a private academy. She bought a piece of land to build a house on, and she sent Small off to school every morning, no matter how he cried. But at night she took off her clothes and slept on his pillow and he combed her red and white fur.

Sometimes at night she twitched and moaned, and when he asked her what she was dreaming, she said, "There are ants! Can't you comb them out? Be quick and catch them, if you love me."

But there were never any ants.

One day when Small came home, the little cat with the white front paws was gone. When he asked The Witch's Revenge, she said that the little cat had fallen out of the cage and through the open window and into the garden and before The Witch's Revenge could think what to do, a crow had swooped down and carried the little cat off.

They moved into their new house a few months later, and Small was always very careful when he went in and out the doorway, imagining the little cat, down there in the dark, under the doorstep, under his foot.

Small got bigger. He didn't make any friends in the village, or at his school, but when you're big enough, you don't need friends.

One day while he and The Witch's Revenge were eating their dinner, there was a knock at the door. When Small opened the door, there stood Flora and Jack. Flora was wearing a drab, thrift-store coat, and Jack looked more than ever like a bundle of sticks.

"Small!" said Flora. "How tall you've become!" She burst into tears, and wrung her beautiful hands. Jack said, looking at The Witch's Revenge, "And who are you?"

The Witch's Revenge said to Jack, "Who am I? I'm your mother's cat, and you're a handful of dry sticks in a suit two sizes too large. But I won't tell anyone if you won't tell, either."

Jack snorted at this, and Flora stopped crying. She began to look around the house, which was sunny and large and well appointed.

"There's room enough for both of you," said The Witch's Revenge, "if Small doesn't mind."

Small thought his heart would burst with happiness to have his family back again. He showed Flora to one bedroom and Jack to another. Then they went downstairs and had a second dinner, and Small and The Witch's Revenge listened, and the cats in their hanging cage listened, while Flora and Jack recounted their adventures.

A pickpocket had taken Flora's purse, and they'd sold the witch's automobile, and lost the money in a game of cards. Flora found her parents, but they were a pair of old scoundrels who had no use for her. (She was too old to sell again. She would have realized what they were up to.) She'd gone to work in a department store, and Jack had sold tickets in a movie theater. They'd quarreled and made up, and then fallen in love with other people, and had many disappointments. At last they had decided to go home to the witch's house and see if it would do for a squat, or if there was anything left, to carry away and sell.

But the house, of course, had burned down. As they argued about what to do next, Jack had smelled Small, his brother, down in the village. So here they were.

"You'll live here, with us," Small said.

Jack and Flora said they could not do that. They had ambitions, they said. They had plans. They would stay for a week, or two weeks, and then they would be off again. The Witch's Revenge nodded and said that this was sensible.

Every day Small came home from school and went out again, with Flora, on a bicycle built for two. Or he stayed home and Jack taught him how to hold a coin between two fingers, and how to follow the egg, as it moved from cup to cup. The Witch's Revenge taught them to play bridge, although Flora and Jack couldn't be partners. They quarreled with each other as if they were husband and wife.

"What do you want?" Small asked Flora one day. He was leaning against her, wishing he were still a cat, and could sit in her lap. She smelled of secrets. "Why do you have to go away again?"

Flora patted Small on the head. She said, "What do I want? That's easy enough! To never have to worry about money. I want to marry a man and know that he'll never cheat on me, or leave me." She looked at Jack as she said this.

Jack said, "I want a rich wife who won't talk back, who doesn't lie in bed all day, with the covers pulled up over her head, weeping and calling me a bundle of twigs." And he looked at Flora when he said this.

The Witch's Revenge put down the sweater that she was knitting for Small. She looked at Flora and she looked at Jack and then she looked at Small.

Small went into the kitchen and opened the door of the hanging cage. He lifted out the two cats and brought them to Flora and Jack. "Here," he said. "A husband for you, Flora, and a wife for Jack. A prince and a princess, and both of them beautiful, and well brought up, and wealthy, no doubt."

Flora picked up the little tomcat and said, "Don't tease at me, Small! Who ever heard of marrying a cat!"

The Witch's Revenge said, "The trick is to keep their catskins in a safe hiding place. And if they sulk, or treat you badly, sew them back into their catskin and put them into a bag and throw them in the river."

Then she took her claw and slit the skin of the tabby-colored cat suit, and Flora was holding a naked man. Flora shrieked and dropped him on the ground. He was a handsome man, well made, and he had a princely manner. He was not a man that anyone would ever mistake for a cat. He stood up and made a bow, very elegant, for all that he was naked. Flora blushed, but she looked pleased.

"Go fetch some clothes for the Prince and the Princess," The Witch's Revenge said to Small. When he got back, there was a naked princess hiding behind the sofa, and Jack was leering at her.

A few weeks after that, there were two weddings, and then Flora left with her new husband, and Jack went off with his new princess. Perhaps they lived happily ever after.

The Witch's Revenge said to Small, "We have no wife for you."

Small shrugged. "I'm still too young," he said.

But try as hard as he can, Small is getting older now. The catskin barely fits across his shoulders. The buttons strain when he fastens them. His grown-up fur—his people fur—is coming in. At night he dreams.

The witch his mother's Spanish heel beats against the pane of glass. The princess hangs in the briar. She's holding up her dress, so he can see the cat fur down there. Now she's under the house. She wants to marry him, but the house will fall down if he kisses her. He and Flora are children again, in the witch's house. Flora lifts up her skirt and says, see my pussy? There's a cat down there, peeking out at him, but it doesn't look like any cat he's ever seen. He says to Flora, I have a pussy, too. But his isn't the same.

At last he knows what happened to the little, starving, naked thing in the forest, where it went. It crawled into his catskin, while he was asleep, and then it climbed right inside him, his Small skin, and now it is huddled in his chest, still cold and sad and hungry. It is eating him from the inside, and getting bigger, and one day there will be no Small left at all, only that nameless, hungry child, wearing a Small skin.

Small moans in his sleep.

There are ants in The Witch's Revenge's skin, leaking out of her seams, and they march down into the sheets and pinch at him, down under his arms, and between his legs where his fur is growing in, and it hurts, it aches and aches. He dreams that The Witch's Revenge wakes now, and comes and licks him all over, until the pain melts. The pane of glass melts. The ants march away again on their long, greased thread.

"What do you want?" says The Witch's Revenge.

Small is no longer dreaming. He says, "I want my mother!"

Light from the moon comes down through the window over their bed. The Witch's Revenge is very beautiful—she looks like a Queen, like a knife, like a burning house, a cat—in the moonlight. Her fur shines. Her whiskers stand out like pulled stitches, wax and thread. The Witch's Revenge says, "Your mother is dead."

"Take off your skin," Small says. He's crying and The Witch's Revenge licks his tears away. Small's skin pricks all over, and down under the house, something small wails and wails. "Give me back my mother," he says.

"Oh, my darling," says his mother, the witch, The Witch's Revenge, "I can't do that. I'm full of ants. Take off my skin, and all the ants will spill out, and there will be nothing left of me."

Small says, "Why have you left me all alone?"

His mother the witch says, "I've never left you alone, not even for a minute. I sewed up my death in a catskin so I could stay with you."

"Take it off! Let me see you!" Small says. He pulls at the sheet on the bed, as if it were his mother's catskin.

The Witch's Revenge shakes her head. She trembles and beats her tail back and forth. She says, "How can you ask me for such a thing, and how can I say no to you? Do you know what you're asking me for? Tomorrow night. Ask me again, tomorrow night."

And Small has to be satisfied with that. All night long, Small combs his mother's fur. His fingers are looking for the seams in her catskin. When The Witch's Revenge yawns, he peers inside her mouth, hoping to catch a glimpse of his mother's face. He can feel himself becoming smaller and smaller. In the morning he will be so small that when he tries to put his catskin on, he can barely do up the buttons. He'll be so small, so sharp, you might mistake him for an ant, and when The Witch's Revenge yawns, he'll creep inside her mouth, he'll go down into her belly, he'll go find his mother. If he can, he'll help his mother cut her catskin open so that she can get out again and come and live in the world with him, and if she won't come out, then he won't, either. He'll live there, the way that sailors learn to live, inside the belly of fish who have eaten them, and keep house for his mother inside the house of her skin.

This is the end of the story. The Princess Margaret grows up to kill witches and cats. If she doesn't, then someone else will have to do it. There is no such thing as witches, and there is no such thing as cats, either, only people dressed up in catskin suits. They have their reasons, and who is to say that they might not live that way, happily ever after, until the ants have carried away all of the Time that there is, to build something new and better out of it?

I was living in Brooklyn, about to publish my first collection and drive across country, on tour with the writer Shelley Jackson. We'd decided it would be a good idea—and fun!—to have something to give away at readings, and so I wrote "Catskin." Shelley came up with an illustration for the cover. As best I can remember, I wanted to tackle two or three things: I wanted to write my own fairy tale, rather than a reworking or a reversal/revision of a fairy tale. I wanted to write something that sounded like someone else, not like me—this seemed appropriate for a story about inhabiting a skin. I also wanted to write something quickly—that is, write a story, proofread it, print up, and staple it into a zine—in the three days or so before we went on tour. I still have a stack of the original edition, and there's something fairy-tale-ish about them: hand-sized, handmade, plain brown, and roughly cut, with Shelley's pen-and-ink cover. As for the story, the starting place was witches and children, and why witches might want children so badly. "Catskin" isn't a reworking of any single fairy tale, but it does owe a debt especially to "Catskin," "Donkeyskin," and "Rapunzel," but really to almost all of them, as well as to writers like Angela Carter and Eudora Welty.

—KL

CHRIS ADRIAN

Teague O'Kane and the Corpse

ONCE THERE WAS A YOUNG MAN NAMED TEAGUE O'KANE. HE WAS probably too handsome for his own good, and certainly too handsome for the good of others, since he was loved by every boy and girl that he met, and he broke hearts by the dozen. He lived in Orlando, and had successfully auditioned for a boy band, and made no secret of this. In fact, it was usually the second thing he told people, after his name.

One night he went out dancing with his many friends, and, as was the usual case, many people wanted to dance with him. People approached him on the dance floor, and he might dance with them or he might not; it all depended on how he was feeling, and upon the quality of their groove, which he could evaluate at a distance, and in the semi-dark, so sometimes they were still a long way off when he had decided that they hadn't made his cut, and he turned his back on them. On this night there was the usual crowd of aspirants, and some of them were quite pleasant-looking, and others were quite ordinary, and some of them were excellent dancers, and some of them were merely enthusiastic. It was a typical night, until something extraordinary happened.

Teague was minding his own business, sort of dancing with a handsome girl on his left, but also sort of dancing with a pretty boy on his right, when an absolutely hideous man came bopping up to him and audaciously invaded his space, bumping aside the boy and the girl and doing a nasty grinding dance with his hips and his groin. Teague turned his back to him, but the man only stepped around and presented himself again. He was really quite amazingly ugly; Teague placed him somewhere in his fifties, if not his sixties, and he had flabby arms, and two chins, and terribly ill-advised hair. "Dance with me, Teague O'Kane!" he cried, and tried to put his hands on Teague's handsome hips, but Teague shook him off, and said, "Get away from me you old troll!" But he grabbed at him again twice more, and twice more Teague called him a troll and told him to get away. The man went away after that, but no sooner had he gone but a hideous woman had taken his place, a woman so ugly she could have been the troll's sister, with her own flabby arms, and her own abundance of chins, and her own terribly ill-advised hair. "Get away from me you hag!" Teague shouted, not even giving her the chance to ask him to dance, and he turned and danced away hurriedly to another side of the floor.

But three more times the old hag came and found Teague, once in the hinterlands of the dance floor and once at the bar and finally in line for the men's bathroom. He was standing there minding his own business when he felt a tickle on the back of his neck. He turned around and saw the woman standing there.

"Hey, baby," she said. "You want to dance?"

"Did you just touch me?" Teague asked.

"Maybe I did and maybe I didn't," she said. "But that isn't the question. The question is, do you want to dance with me?"

"Leave me alone," Teague said. "Don't you speak English?"

"I won't ask you but one more time, Teague O'Kane," the woman said. "Won't you dance with me?"

"Not in a gajillion years," Teague said, and he gave her a little push, which he regretted almost immediately, even though she didn't exactly fall down, but only stumbled back a few paces.

"That's a long time, Teague O'Kane!" the old hag said, and laughed at him, and it occurred to Teague to wonder how she and the man might have known his name, because even though he had successfully auditioned for a boy band, he wasn't famous yet.

"My night is ruined," he said to the urinal, rather too loudly, because a voice came out of the stall next to him, saying, "Mine too! Mine too!" in between horking exclamations of vomit.

"Mine's ruined worse," Teague said, aware that he was being peevish, and that he should go right back out on the dance floor and pretend like he hadn't been nearly molested by a hag and a troll, and that he had not spent his whole night so far oppressed by other people's ugliness and audacity. He should just get back out there and dance, and so he tried, but his heart just wasn't in it; his groove was compromised, and his moves, even his signature moves, somehow felt not like his moves. It was like someone else was dancing in his body, somebody who was sad, and ugly, and lonely. He decided to go home alone, and texted seven of his friends to announce that to them, because they were always texting him to say they were going home alone, as if that were his responsibility, or as if he should feel bad because they were going home alone and he was not.

He lived with his father in a big house on a lake, or rather, he lived very close to his father, in a much smaller house next door to the big house. The little house was a present on his sixteenth birthday from his father, who maintained that a boy needed independence as well as supervision, and so he had made his son a gift of the little house, but outfitted it with cameras to keep watch over Teague and make sure that he never did anything to compromise their good name. There was a driver who would have gladly come to fetch him from the club, but because he was feeling agitated from his bad night he decided to walk home, though the way was far. But he liked to walk whenever something unpleasant happened to him, because he could pretend that he was walking away from whatever it was that was troubling him. And as he walked away from the club, down the brightly lit streets of the downtown, and then the half-lit sidewalks of the old city, and finally the darkened paths of his father's estate, the horrible man and woman, and the bad time they had engendered with their saggy asses and their grabby hands, seemed more and more remote. He had almost forgotten about them entirely by the time he was on the last stretch of his walk, when he had entered into the orange groves that surrounded the house, and could see the light in his father's room twinkling through the trees. Perhaps, he thought, Father has sensed that I had a bad night, and is waiting up to comfort me.

He heard voices on the path ahead then, and wondered briefly if his father had come out of the house to welcome him. He stopped and leaned against a tree, and a heavy wind stirred the branches all of a sudden, making the fruit swing gently, and pummel him softly on the shoulders and face. The wind carried the voices to him, and he heard now clearly that there were many people ahead, and that none of them was his father. *Burglars!* he thought, and then, *Admirers!* because it had already been the case that various persons had invaded their property before both to steal from his father and to plead a case of love to Teague. He bent down to take up a small thick branch at his feet. It was light and soft with rot, and wouldn't hurt anybody if he hit them with it, but he thought it would make a good tool for a threat.

The wind shifted, and for a moment the voices were silent, and Teague cocked his head and squinted his eyes. "I've got a stick," he said, but not very loudly. A bell sounded, tinny and high, and the night seemed to darken. The voices returned in a rush of laughter, and then Teague saw figures—all he could make out was the shape of them—capering through the trees, skipping and dancing and falling now and then to roll briefly on the ground before springing up again. He raised his stick up and said it again, much louder this time, as they rushed toward him: "I have a stick!" "And a pretty stick it is!" said a voice that was very familiar, though it took him a moment to place it. "As pretty as the hand that wields it, eh, Porcupine?" The lady from the club came walking out of the gloom, and though the night stayed just as dark, she seemed oddly lit somehow, as if the sun were shining only for her and only on her. She was just as ugly as she ever had been, and seemed even shorter and more bent, and yet somehow she seemed less pathetic than she had in the club.

"Oh, yes, Aardvark, my dear," said another familiar voice. The man from the club came up behind her and put his arms around her, placing his head just to the side of her neck. Of course they were friends, Teague thought. That made perfect sense, even if it made no sense that they had just popped out of the night within sight of his house.

"What are you doing here?" Teague asked them in a whisper-shout. "Get off my property!"

"Duly, duly," said the woman. "Duly and in time. But first, won't you dance with me?"

"No!" Teague said. "Stop asking me that. Are you deaf? What part of not in a million years do you not understand?" The lady was hopping back and forth on her feet and smiling at him, and the man behind her was doing the same thing, but exactly out of sync, so he hopped on his left foot just as she hopped on her right, and he moved his head to peek at Teague from above one and then the other of the woman's shoulders. Others were coming up behind them, figures whose faces were lit just like the old woman's with a curious, sourceless light, so Teague could tell from far away that they were just as ugly as she was, and indeed some were even uglier, lumpier and more misshapen, or too big or too small, and it was obvious that none of them had given the least bit of thought to their hair, or to what they were wearing. They shuffled and danced toward him, and surrounded the old woman and the old man in a hideous huddle.

"A million years? Will you dance with me in a million years?"

"No!" Teague shouted, not caring anymore if he woke his father up. In fact, he wanted his father to come out with a flashlight and a shotgun, and scare the hideous weirdos away. "I said not in a million years. Not even. Aren't you listening to me?" The whole crowd of them laughed at him then, an odd sort of chuckle that circulated among the ones on the sides and the back and then came to the old man, who chuckled in the ugly lady's ear, and she uttered a sharp little bark of mirth.

"Not with me? Not with any of us?"

"No!" Teague said, and he reached into his pocket to get his phone. "I'm calling the police now," he said. "But I'll dial slowly, so you have time to just go away."

"Not with my friend?" the lady said, and indicated a large lumpy bundle which, he suddenly noticed, they were passing back and forth among them, each of them, even the small ones, shouldering the burden and passing it on. He thought it was a sack, but he couldn't tell for sure because the light that fell on them seemed to miss the thing they carried.

"I'm *dialing*," Teague said. But he was very slow about it, because he wasn't very good at dialing with one hand, and also because he was getting increasingly nervous and afraid, because they were something else besides just ugly and annoying. There were a lot of them—it seemed like there were more of them every time he looked—and he was starting to appreciate that they might want to do something else besides dance with him.

"For the last time, Teague O'Kane," the woman said, "won't you dance with one of us, even out of pity, or fellow-feeling, to share just a little of your undeserved beauty with those who have lost their own?"

"Hello, police?" Teague said into his phone. He had dialed 911, but it wasn't ringing yet. "I am being attacked by *ugly people*."

"Attacked?" the woman said. "We only wanted to dance!" But just then the ugly old man picked up an orange and threw it at Teague. It missed, but another, thrown from farther back in the crowd, connected solidly with his head.

"Hey!" he said, and then he was hit again, on the ear he was using for the phone. A lady answered just as the phone flew away. He scrambled after it, stooping to pick it up, but before his fingers could reach it another orange struck and knocked it farther. "Stop that!" he said, and three more oranges came hurtling out of the darkness, two for his face and one for his stomach. Then a whole barrage of them started, and he stood there for a moment, trying to protect his face and his stomach and his groin, but when he covered up one part of himself they only hit him in another. He turned and ran.

He hadn't gone very far before it occurred to him that he should be trying to run toward home, not away from it, that if he could make it to his front door he could rush through and lock it against them. And he hadn't gone very much farther than that when they started to appear in front of him in ones and twos, strangely lucent in the darkness under the trees, smiling at him hideously as they lobbed oranges at him. He and his friends had been in the habit lately of driving along Orange Blossom Trail and throwing oranges at the prostitutes, just for the fun of it, and now he found himself regretting that, as fruit after fruit connected with his head. Looking back, he saw that he was being pursued by the wily crowd. They ran close together, one roiling beast, and in their light he could see the sack (it was definitely a sack) balanced on their shoulders, being passed among them as they ran. There was something terrible about their faces, in the glimpse he had of them before he turned his head around again, that was very different from mere ugliness.

He put his arms over his head, peeking out between his elbows to watch his way, and ran as hard as he could, not caring whether he was going toward the house or away from the house, only wanting to get away from them, and very shortly tripped, whether over a root or an outstretched foot, he didn't know, but he found, as he fell down, that he was somewhat grateful for the trip, and he was less panicked, as he rolled and skidded on the dirt and coarse grass, than he had been as he ran. *Well,* he thought, *I tried to get away, but there are too many of them, and they have too many oranges, and now they are going to get me.* He lay on his back, looking up through the leaves of the orange trees at the dim stars, and they clustered around him.

"Orange you sad you didn't dance with us now?" said the hag. She leaned over him with the man, and all around them the others were giving him orange-rind smiles, wedges of fruit stuck in their mouths, and juice dripping down their hairy chins.

"Go on and do it," Teague said. "Rob me. Take my wallet. Take my jeans. They're not going to fit you, and they won't look good on anyone you know. But go on. Just get it over with."

"Rob you?" said the hag.

"We aren't here to take anything away," the old troll said.

"We've come to give you a gift, Teague O'Kane," the hag said. "It would have been a merry gift, if you had chosen to dance with us. It would have been a gift of poodle breath and panty lace and eyes bright with joyful tears. But you have spurned those who only meant to bless you, and now you must take another kind of gift from us entirely, and do a deed for us, or else."

"Or else what?" he asked.

"Or else dark deadliness of poodle!" the old man said. "And suffering sobs!" said the woman. "And an acid bitter sadness in your soul that will last a million years."

"A million billion!" said the man.

Teague wanted to say that was stupid, that nothing lasted that long, not—he was pretty sure—even the universe itself, but instead he asked, "What do you want me to do?"

"Only this," the woman said. "Take our friend home, and put him to rest." There was a flurry of activity among the others. Within a few seconds they threw down the bundle in the sack and uncovered it. Teague could tell there was something unpleasant in there by the noise it made when it hit the ground. *It's full of steak*, he thought, and *Who carries around a big sack of beef in the middle of the night?* It seemed to attract the darkness as it lay on the ground, but when they uncovered it he could plainly tell what it was, and he shuddered because he had never seen a corpse before, nor ever seen a body in such an unnatural posture as it assumed when they rolled it toward him with their feet. It lay with its back to him, one arm stretched out underneath it and another up over its head. Its feet and its chest were bare, and the face was turned away, but he could tell by the breadth of its shoulders and back that it was a man, and he could tell that his jeans were of a very high quality, because he had a special sense for things like that, and could tell a good pair of jeans from across the street, or in the dark, or by the touch of his hand against somebody's bottom.

"Take him and bury him inside the Catholic church at Pine Hills, or, if you cannot bury him there, in behind the Salty Pig sausage factory in Windermere if there is no room for him at the church, and if all else fails then take him to the Green Swamp near Orlo Vista and lay him to rest in the bog."

"Oh, all right," Teague said, sitting and then standing up slowly. "Is that all you want me to do?"

"Nothing more and nothing less."

"Okay, then," Teague said. "But first there's something you should know."

"What's that, Teague O'Kane?" she asked, smiling at him in a very unfriendly way.

"Just . . . this!" Teague said, and cast the orange he had picked up at her face. He didn't wait to see if it hit her or not, but turned to run again, leaping nimbly over the corpse and sprinting for home. But he hadn't been running for ten seconds before he was tackled from behind, and all those ugly old people were swarming all over him, their terrible moth-ball breath in his face and their starchy sprayed-up hair brushing his cheek and neck. It felt like they were all sitting on him—for a moment he could hardly breathe—and then the pressure let up, but there was still a great weight on him. They jumped back and away from him.

"There now!" said the woman. "Now you are ready!" Teague lay on his belly, slowly understanding that they had put the corpse on his back, and that the dead man's arms were crossed over his shoulders.

"What did you do?" he said. "Get it off of me!"

"We certainly won't," said the lady. "You alone will do that. Now take him to be buried and be quick about it. If the sun rises on you before it is done, you will regret it!"

"Get it off of me!" Teague said again, and now he was crying, and struggling on the ground, flopping around to throw the thing off, but the dead man held him fast.

"You do it," said the woman. "And remember what I said to you. Dark tears of the great poodle of sadness! Acid in your heart! Burning forever! Get you gone, Teague O'Kane. You have chosen not to dance with us, and the night is running out!"

"Get it off," Teague said again, but no one answered. When he looked up they were all gone, and if not for the weight on his back, he would have thought he had imagined them. He got slowly to his knees, and then he stood, the corpse very heavy on his back. When he looked around there was no sign of the crowd of ugly people, but they had left him a message on the ground, words spelled from torn rinds of orange. "We will be watching you," it said.

"Help!" he shouted. "Help, somebody!" His voice sounded very loud in his ears, but he had the sense that it wasn't carrying very far, and among the trees he could see none of the lights of his home, and he wasn't sure which way he should go for help. "And I don't even know where Orlo Vista *is*," he said sadly. At that a hand rose up before him pointing, and it took him a moment to realize who it belonged to. With a shout he started to run again, trying to get away from the corpse on his back, but he only fell again, and he lay there weeping again for a moment.

"Crying won't get me buried," the corpse said behind him then. "Get up, idiot."

Teague cried out again, and tried to crawl away, saying, "You can't talk to me! It's bad enough as it is but you're not allowed to *talk*."

"The dead do as they please," the thing said, but then it was silent. Teague lay panting with his face in the ground, and then he did get up, and started to walk in the direction that the corpse had pointed. It was very slow going at first. The corpse was heavy, and the night was dark, and he didn't know where he was, for all that he could not have been very far from his own house. But the trees looked strange, even when he left them behind he walked for what felt like an hour without encountering a highway, only a narrow dirt road that looked more fit for horses than cars, but was easier to walk on than the soft ground. If he had seen a car, he would have flagged it down to ask for help, though he wondered if anyone would have stopped for him, a man with a corpse on his back, no matter how handsome and alluring he might be. It occurred to him, as he trudged slowly down that road, half-fearing that the corpse would speak again, but half-hoping that it would as well, because he was feeling very lonely and afraid, that the night would have been much easier if he had agreed to dance with either the man or the woman, that he must be dreaming, and the changeless quality of the road made it seem this must be so, and he started to feel like he had been going along on it forever. "I'll just keep walking," he said, "until I wake up, and if later tonight I see any ugly people on the dance floor, I'll run away from them right away." He closed his eyes a moment—the road was so unchanging he suddenly decided there was no need even to watch where he was going. Then he was jolted by a sharp pain—the corpse had reached into his shirt and pinched him on the nipple! "What was that for?" Teague demanded, though of course he knew what it was for. He stopped a moment on the road, feeling very frightened and very awake.

Not long after that he saw the church, sitting all alone at the top of a hill, lit up by a single street lamp. The road led right to the door, and passed through a parking lot that was full of cars. It was hard going up the hill: when he got to the top he just wanted to lie down on the hood of one of the cars and rest for a long time. He went to the door of the church and paused there. "Are you supposed to knock on the door of a church before you go in?" he wondered aloud. He had never been in a church before.

"Not necessary," said the corpse.

Teague pushed the door open and went inside. The church was lit with candles, and the gentle flickering light made the faces of the many statues seem particularly alert and alive. It wouldn't have surprised him at all if they all started talking to him, insulting him or asking him the time or scolding him for not dancing with them. But they stayed silent. As he stared at them, though, he thought he recognized the light that had fallen so strangely on all those ugly old people: their faces looked like the statues, as if the light that shone on them came from invisible candles.

"We're here for a reason," the corpse said.

"You don't have to remind me," Teague said. He started to walk around the church, up and down the aisles, and peeked down the lines of pews, looking for a place to bury someone. People belonged in graveyards; it made no sense at all to him that somebody should be buried inside a church, even one that was carpeted, like this one was, in tacky indoor/outdoor carpeting. That was typical of Florida, he thought, a place where extremes of bad taste flourished.

"Dig!" said the corpse, when Teague had been looking for a while here and there for a place.

"With what? My hands?"

"Until they bleed and your bones poke through the skin!" it said harshly. But then it pointed Teague toward a closet, where, among tall stacks of kitty litter and ammonia and paper towels, a shovel was waiting. Teague took it and picked a spot near the altar. "Do it!" the corpse told him when he hesitated. He raised up the shovel in both hands and stabbed it down, thinking he was going to have to break through cement underneath the carpet to get to the ground. He gave a yell as he brought the shovel down, the loudest noise he had ever made, the angriest noise and also the saddest noise. He was sure the shovel was just going to bounce off the concrete, and that the wooden handle would split, and that his hand would break from the shock of it. He didn't care if it did.

But it was just soft ground underneath the carpet. The blade sank in completely, and he had to put his whole weight on it to pull up the earth and carpet. A smell rose up—an odor of fresh loamy earth that made Teague think of rainy days and earthworms. The corpse took a deep breath of it behind him, but didn't let it out. "I am about to get rid of you," Teague told it, but it didn't respond. He got to work, driv-

ing the blade of the shovel into the carpet again and again, and marking out a rectangle long enough to fit the corpse. He said it again and
again, speaking a word every time he made a blow with the shovel:
"I . . . am . . . going . . . to . . . get . . . rid . . . of . . . *you!*"

The corpse didn't talk back, and he was just starting to convince
himself that he wouldn't hear from it again when a hideous shriek
sounded in the air. "What?" he shouted, dropping the shovel and
jumping back. "What did I do? Why are you screaming?"

"Wasn't me," said the corpse, and there was another cry, much
softer but still angry. Someone was obviously very upset. Teague walked
to the edge of the grave he was digging—it was only a couple of feet
deep—and looked in. There was movement in the dirt. Something
was trembling underneath the soil. A sinkhole opened up in the dirt,
just mouth-sized. The dirt fell in, and then was spat out again in another scream, and then suddenly, horribly, a dead woman sat up out
of the shallow grave that Teague had been uncovering.

"Oh, oh, oh!" she cried. "What are you doing to me?"

"Nothing!" said Teague, which was patently untrue, but the first
thing he thought of to say.

"Nothing? Nothing? Why have you disturbed my rest, horrible
boy? Rude boy! Terrible boy!"

"I didn't mean . . ." Teague began. "I mean . . . I just wanted to bury
my friend!"

"He's not my friend," said the corpse behind him. "And he is very
rude. Terribly rude."

"Cover me up!" the woman, cried. "Cover me up, boy, before I get
cold."

Teague did as she said, heaping the dirt back on her when she lay
back down, and throwing the carpet on top in a disorganized heap
that he made no attempt to neaten. He left the shovel leaning on the
altar and ran out. He stood outside panting and feeling ready to cry
again. The corpse heaved an enormous sigh against his neck, and then
did it twice more.

"Stop that," Teague said. "Stop sighing. You don't need to sigh. You don't even need to breathe."

"I am disappointed. When I am disappointed, I sigh." It sighed again, and then Teague did it, too.

"I forget where the other place was," Teague said after a moment. "The other place I was supposed to take you." The corpse was silent, and Teague thought it figured that it would talk when he wanted it to shut up, and be silent when he was asking it for help, but then it lifted its hand again and pointed the way.

The Salty Pig sausage factory was set in a dell instead of high on a hill, surrounded by a greasy, low-lying fog that smelled of bacon. Teague carried his burden down the road for an hour until he smelled it, and it was another half hour before he saw the smokestack spires poking up, tall shadows against the stars. Instead of cars, the factory was surrounded on all sides by a field of gravestones, which made no sense at all until Teague was close enough to read some of the names on the stones: Snorty, Fatty, Missy, Mr. Snorfle, Petunia, Wilbur, Otis; they were pig names. "Why would they bury the pigs from the factory?"

"Respect," said the corpse.

"Where is the shovel?" Teague asked.

"In your hands," said the corpse. Teague held up his hands in front of them both, and it clarified, "Your hands are the shovels."

"That's not fair," Teague said to the corpse, and then he lifted his head and said it again to the air and the fog and the strange piggy graveyard. "That's not fair! I'm doing what you told me to. I'm doing what you asked. The least you could do is give me a shovel!" But silence was his only answer, so he knelt down in a place between graves that looked likely to be empty and started to dig with his hands, tearing up the coarse grass and then scooping up great double handfuls of earth and tossing them to one side or the other (when he tossed them over his shoulder the corpse complained bitterly). And he hadn't dug far before he touched on a leathery bit of something that proved upon examination to be a pig's ear, and shortly after that he uncovered the rest of the pig, a dried-up husk of muscle and skin with a slit down its belly. "But there's no stone!" Teague said. "And why are they burying the muscle parts? What did they put in the sausage?"

"Not meat," said the corpse. The pig opened an eye at that—the socket was quite empty—and began to squeal wordlessly, but Teague got the sense of what it was saying: *Cover me up. Leave me alone. I'm getting cold.* He covered it up swiftly, then knelt on the grave with his face in his hands.

"Get up!" said the corpse. "Try again. The dawn is coming, and if I'm not buried by then you'll be sorry sorry *sorry!*" Teague was so tired from digging, and so dispirited from failure, that he didn't even argue, but moved a few hundred feet away and tried again. But he had not been digging ten minutes before his hand touched on leathery skin, and a muffled sound of squealing came up through the dirt. Teague jerked his hand back and cried out. "Again! Again!" said the corpse, but the next time the squealing started as soon as he started to dig, and then there was squealing even when he trod on a grave, so with every step he took there was another squeal, each one in a slightly different tone, so as he stepped and jumped, trying not to step on a grave, he made an odd sort of music, and the whole graveyard had become an instrument for him to play, and he was its exhausted, unwilling virtuoso. When he finally escaped it he sank again to his knees and started to weep freely.

"There, there," said the corpse after a while. "There, there. It's not so bad as that. There's still the Green Swamp, and dawn is still a little while off."

"Dark dread diarrhea of poodle!" Teague said. "Deadly sad acid bitterness! I can feel it starting already!"

"That is something else you feel," the corpse said. "You have not yet failed in your mission, and the kindly ones keep their word to the letter. Get up and take me to the swamp. I hear my grave singing to me and feel sure you'll find a place for me there." So Teague pushed himself up, and followed the pointing finger of the corpse one last time.

It wasn't very long before the ground started to become soft, and not much longer after that that he was walking in places through sucking mud, and he very shortly lost his shoes, and then his socks. The stars began to dim, and the sky to lighten. "Hurry!" the corpse whispered to him. "Hurry! The sun is coming, but we are close, close!" Teague felt sure he could hear other voices telling him to hurry along. He thought he heard the voices of the old man and woman coming at him from the trees, telling him he was almost there, and being more encouraging than scolding when they demanded haste of him. He thought a possum, hanging upside down by its naked tail, told him to hurry it up, and an alligator, just a dark shape at the edge of a pond, opened its mouth and told him to run. He tried to do that, but he was so tired all he did was speed up his shambling, weeping lurch through the swamp. "Ah!" said the corpse. "The sun . . . the sun! Don't let it touch me . . . we are so close!" And indeed they were. There weren't any corners in the swamp, but Teague had the impression of rounding one, and then there it was: a tidy grave set under the sweeping branches of a willow, as pretty a place to be buried as you could ask for, and nicely dry as well for all that it was in the middle of a bog. Teague lurched toward it just as the sun was rising, and the gray swamp suddenly became green all around him. He was sure he was going to fall in with the corpse and be buried with it, but he fell short, and rolled on his side just to the edge. The corpse let go its hands and fell in.

Teague rolled over and looked in. "Are you down there?" he asked, because the grave was full of shadows. "Yes," said the corpse. "Goodbye, Teague O'Kane. Think of me every time you dance." Then it was quiet, and Teague never heard its voice again except in dreams. He stared another moment into the darkness, even though something in him told him he should look away, and so when the sun rose up and cast a little light into the grave he saw very plainly that the corpse's face was his own.

☠

I encountered Teague O'Kane in one of William Butler Yeats's Fairy and Folk Tales of Ireland. It stood out for me as being a pretty creepy story in a book whose stories tended more toward charming than creepy. It also stood out as particularly weird, which is saying something given the character of the other stories Yeats collected. There was something arresting about the image of a man with a corpse on his back, and something deeply affecting about the depths of suffering into which this unlikable young man has journeyed by the time dawn comes. The original story is considerably more complicated than my retelling—in the original the corpse is less chatty, and more profound in its silences, and can be seen to stand for more than just the intrusion of mortality upon callow youth. And in the original the corpse is never named or recognized, but it seemed obvious to me that Teague would recognize it if he were allowed to see its face.

—CA

JIM SHEPARD

Pleasure Boating in Lituya Bay

TWO AND A HALF WEEKS AFTER I WAS BORN, ON JULY 9, 1958, THE
plates that make up the Fairweather Range in the Alaskan panhandle
apparently slipped twenty-one feet on either side of the Fairweather
Fault, the northern end of a major league instability that runs the
length of North America. The thinking now is that the southwest side
and bottom of the inlets at the head of Lituya Bay jolted upward and
to the northwest, and the northeast shore and head of the bay jolted
downward and to the southeast. One way or the other, the result registered 8.3 on the Richter scale.

The bay is T-shaped and seven miles long and two wide, and according to those who were there it went from a glassy smoothness to
a full churn, a giant's Jacuzzi. Mountains twelve to fifteen thousand
feet high next to it twisted into themselves and lurched in contrary
directions. In Juneau, 122 miles to the southeast, people who'd turned
in early were pitched from their beds. The shock waves wiped out
bottom-dwelling marine life throughout the panhandle. In Seattle, a
thousand miles away, the University of Washington's seismograph
needle was jarred completely off its graph. And meanwhile, back at the
head of the bay, a spur of mountain and glacier the size of a half-mile-
wide city park—40 million cubic yards in volume—broke off and
dropped three thousand feet down the northeast cliff into the water.

This is all by way of saying that it was one of the greatest spasms, when it came to the release of destructive energy, in recorded history. It happened around 10:16 P.M. At that latitude and time of year, it was still light out. There were three small boats, carrying six people, anchored in the south end of the bay.

The rumbling from the earthquake generated vibrations that the occupants of the boats could feel on their skin like electric shocks. The impact of the rockfall that followed made a sound like Canada exploding. There were two women, three men, and a seven-year-old boy in the three boats. They looked up to see a wave breaking *over* the 1,700-foot-high southwest edge of Gilbert Inlet and heading for the opposite slope. What they were looking at was the largest wave ever recorded by human beings. It scythed off three-hundred-year-old pines and cedars and spruce, some of them with trunks three or four feet thick, along a trim line of 1,720 feet. That's a wave crest 500 feet higher than the Empire State Building.

Fill your bathtub. Hold a football at shoulder height and drop it into the water. Scale the height of the initial splash up, appropriately. Imagine the height of the tub above the waterline to be 2,000 feet.

When I was two years old, my mother decided she'd had enough of my father and hunted down an old high school girlfriend who'd wandered so far west that she'd taken a job teaching in a grammar school in Hawaii. The school was in a little town called Pepeekeo. All of this was told to me later by my mother's older sister. My mother and I moved in with the friend, who lived in a little beach cottage on the north shore of the island near an old mill, Pepeekeo Mill. We were about twelve miles north of Hilo. This was in 1960.

The friend's name was Chuck. Her real name was Charlotte something, but everyone apparently called her Chuck. My aunt had a photo she showed me of me playing in the sand with some breakers in the background. I'm wearing something that looks like overalls put on backward. Chuck's drinking beer from a can.

And one morning Chuck woke my mother and me up and asked if we wanted to see a tidal wave. I don't remember any of this. I was in pajamas and my mother put a robe on me and we trotted down the beach and looked around the point to the north. I told my mother I was scared and she said we'd go back to the house if the water got too high. We saw the ocean suck itself out to sea smoothly and quietly, and the muck of the sand and some flipping and turning white-bellied fish that had been left behind. Then we saw it come back, without any surf or real noise, like the tide coming in in time-lapse photography. It came past the high-tide mark and just up to our toes. Then it receded again. "Some wave," my mother told me. She lifted me up so I could see the end of it. Some older boys who lived on Mamalahoa Highway sprinted past us, chasing the water. They got way out, the mud spraying up behind their heels. And the water came back again, this time even smaller. The boys, as far out as they were, were still only up to their waists. We could hear how happy they were. Chuck told us the show was over and we headed up the beach to the house. My mother wanted me to walk but I wanted her to carry me. We heard a noise and when we looked we saw the third wave. It was already the size of the lighthouse out at Wailea. They got me into the cottage and halfway up the stairs to the second floor when the walls blew in. My mother managed to slide me onto a corner of the roof that was spinning half a foot above the water. Chuck went under and didn't come up again. My mother was carried out to sea, still hanging on to me and the roof chunk. She'd broken her hip and bitten through her lower lip. We were picked up later that day by a little boat near Honohina.

She was never the same after that, my aunt told me. This was maybe by way of explaining why I'd been put up for adoption a few months later. My mother had gone to teach somewhere in Alaska. Somewhere away from the coast, my aunt added with a smile. She pretended she didn't know exactly where. I'd been left with the Franciscan Sisters at the Catholic orphanage in Kahili. On the day of my graduation from the orphanage school, one of the Sisters who'd taken an interest in me grabbed me by both shoulders and shook me and said, "What is it you *want*? What's the *matter* with you?" They weren't bad questions, as far as I was concerned.

I saw my aunt that once, the year before college. My fiancée, many years later, asked if we were going to invite her to the wedding, and then later that night said, "I guess you're not going to answer, huh?"

Who decides when the time's right to have kids? Who decides how many kids to have? Who decides how they're going to be brought up? Who decides when the parents are going to stop having sex, and stop listening to each other? Who decides when everyone's not just going to walk out on everyone else? These are all group decisions. Mutual decisions. Decisions that a couple makes *in consultation with each other*.

I'm stressing that because it doesn't always work that way.

My wife's goal-oriented. Sometimes I can see on her face her *To Do* list when she looks at me. It makes me think she doesn't want me anymore, and the idea is so paralyzing and maddening that I lose track of myself: I just step in place and forget where I am for a minute or two. "What're you doing?" she asked once, outside a restaurant.

And of course I can't tell her that. Because then what do I do with whatever follows?

We have one kid, Donald, named for the single greatest man my wife has ever known. That would be her father. Donald's seven. When he's in a good mood he finds me in the house and wraps his arms around me, his chin on my hip. When he's in a bad mood I have to turn off the TV to get him to answer. He has a good arm and good hand-eye coordination but he gets easily frustrated. "Who's *that* sound like?" my wife always says when I point it out.

He loses everything. He loses stuff even if you physically put it in his hands when he's on his way home. Gloves, hats, knapsacks, lunch money, a bicycle, homework, pencils, pens, his dog, his friends, his way. Sometimes he doesn't worry about it; sometimes he's distraught. If he starts out not worrying about it, sometimes I make him distraught. When I tell these stories, I'm Mr. Glass Half Empty. Which is all by way of getting around to what my wife calls the central subject, which is my ingratitude. Do I always have to start with the negatives? Don't I think he *knows* when I always talk about him that way?

"She says you're too harsh," is the way my father-in-law put it. At the time he was sitting on my front porch and sucking down my beer. He said he thought of it as a kind of mean-spiritedness.

I had no comeback for him at the time. "You weren't very nice to my parents," my wife mentioned when they left.

Friends commiserate with her on the phone.

My father-in-law's a circuit court judge. I run a seaplane charter out of Ketchikan. Wild Wings Aviation. My wife snorts when I answer the phone that way. My father-in-law tells her, who knows, maybe I'll make a go of it. And if the thing does go under, I can always fly geologists around for one of the energy companies.

Even knowing what I make, he says that.

Number one on her *To Do* list is another kid. She says Donald very much wants a little brother. I haven't really heard him address the subject. She wants to know what *I* want. She asks with her mouth set, like she's already figured the odds that I'm going to let her down. It makes me what she calls unresponsive.

She's been after me about it for a year now. And two months ago, after three straight days of our being polite to each other—Good morning; How'd you sleep?—and avoiding brushing even shoulders when passing through doorways, I made an appointment with a Dr. Calvin at Bartlett Regional about a vasectomy. "Normally, couples come in together," he told me at the initial consult.

"This whole thing's been pretty hard on her," I told him.

Apparently it's an outpatient thing, and if I opt for the simpler procedure I could be out of his office and home in forty-five minutes. He quoted me a thousand dollars, but not much out of pocket, because our health insurance should cover it. I was told to go off and give it some thought and get back in touch if and when I was ready to schedule it. I called back two days later and scheduled it for the day before Memorial Day. "That'll give you some time to rest up afterward," the girl who did the scheduling pointed out.

"He *had* a pretty big trauma when he was a baby," my wife reminded her mom a few weeks ago. They didn't realize I was at the kitchen window. "A couple of traumas, actually." She said it like she understood that it was going to be a perennial on her *To Do* list.

So for the last two months I've gone around the house like a demolition expert who's already wired the entire thing to blow and keeps rechecking the charges and connections.

It was actually flying some geologists around that got me going on Lituya Bay in the first place. I flew in a couple of guys from Exxon-Mobil who taught me more than I wanted to know about Tertiary rocks and why they always got people salivating when it came to what they called petroleum investigations. But one of the guys also told the story of what happened there in 1958. He was the one who didn't want to camp in the bay. His buddy made serious fun of him. The next time I flew them in I'd done my research, and we talked about what a crazy place it was. I was staying overnight with them, because they could pay for it, and they had to be out at like dawn the next morning.

However you measure things like that, it has to be one of the most dangerous bodies of water on earth. It feels freakish even when you first see it. It's a tidal inlet that's hugely deep—I think at its center it's seven hundred feet—but at its entrance there's barely enough draft for a small boat. So at high and low tides the water moves through the bottleneck like from a fire hose. That twilight we watched a piece of driftwood *keep up* with a tern that was gliding with the wind. The whole bay is huge but the entrance is only eighty yards wide and broken up by boulders. Stuff coming in on the high tide is like on the world's largest water slide. And when the tide's running the other way, when it hits the ocean swells, it's as if surf's up on the north shore of Hawaii from both directions at once. We were two hundred yards away and had to shout over the noise. The Frenchman who discovered the bay lost twenty-one men and three boats at the entrance. The Tlingits lost so many people over the course of their time there that they named it Channel of the Water-Eyes, *water-eyes* being their word for the drowned.

But the scared guy had me motor him up to the head of the bay and showed me the other problem, the problem I'd already read about: as he put it, stupefyingly large and highly fractured rocks standing at vertiginous angles over deep water in an active fault zone. On top of that, their having absorbed heavy rainfall and constant freezing and thawing. The earthquakes on this fault were as violent as anywhere else in the world, and they'd be shaking unstable cliffs over a deep and tightly enclosed body of water.

"Yeah yeah yeah," his buddy said, passing around beef jerky from the backseat. I was putt-putting the seaplane back and forth as our water taxi at the top of the T. Forested cliffs went straight up five to six thousand feet all around us. I don't even know how trees that size grew like that.

"You have any kids?" the scared guy asked, out of nowhere. I said yeah. He said he did, too, and started hunting up a photo.

"Well, what's a body to do when millions of tons avalanche into it?" his buddy in the back asked.

The scared guy couldn't find the photo. He made a face at his wallet, like what else was new. "Make waves," he said. "Gi-normous waves."

While we crossed from shore to shore they pointed out some of the trim lines I'd read about. The lines went back as far as the middle of the 1800s. The experts figure the dates by cutting down trees and looking at the growth rings. The lines look like rows of plantings in a field, except we're talking about fifty-degree slopes and trees 80 to 90 feet high. There are five lines, and their heights are the heights of the waves. One from 1854 at 395 feet. One twenty years later at 80 feet. One twenty-five years after that at 200 feet. One from 1936 at 490 feet. And one from 1958 at 1,720.

That's five events in the last hundred years, or one every twenty. It's not hard to do the math, in terms of whether or not the bay's currently overdue.

In fact, that night we did the math, after lights-out in our little three-man tent. The scared guy's buddy was skeptical. He was still eating, having moved on to something called Moose Munch. We could hear the rustling of the bag and the crunching in the dark. He said that given that the waves occurred every twenty years, the odds of one occurring on any single day in the bay were about eight thousand to one. There was a plunk down by the shore when something jumped. After we were quiet for a minute, he joked, "That's one of the first signs."

The odds were way smaller than that, the scared guy finally answered. He asked his buddy to think about how much unstable slope they'd already seen from the air. All of that had been exposed by the last wave. And it had now been exposed almost fifty years, he said. There were open fractures that were already visible.

So what did *he* think the odds were? his buddy wanted to know.

Double digits, the scared guy said. The low double digits.

"If I thought they were in the double digits, I wouldn't be here," his buddy said.

"Yeah, well," the scared guy said. "What about you?" he asked me. It took me a minute to realize it, since we were lying in the dark.

"What about me?" I said.

"You ever notice anything out here?" he asked. "Any evidence of recent rockfalls or slides? Changes in the gravel deltas at the feet of the glaciers?"

"I only get out here once a year, if that," I told him. "It's not a big destination for people." I started going over in my head what I remembered, which was nothing.

"That's 'cause they're smart," the scared guy said.

"That's 'cause there's nothing here," his buddy answered.

"Well, there's a reason for that," the scared guy said. He told us he'd come across two censuses of the Tlingit tribes living in the bay from when the Russians owned the area. The populations had been listed as 241 in 1853 and 0 a year later.

"Good night," his buddy told him.

"Good night," the scared guy said.

"What was that? You feel that?" his buddy asked him.

"Aw, shut up," the scared guy said.

What's this thing about putting people to *use*? What's that all about? What happened to just loving being *around* someone? Once I got Donald up off his butt and made him throw the baseball around with me, and asked that out loud. I only knew I'd done it when he said, "*I* don't know." Then he asked if we could quit now.

"Did you ever really think you'd find someone that you weren't in some ways cynical about?" my wife asked the night we'd decided we were in love. I was flying for somebody else and we were lying under the wing of the Piper that we'd run up onto a beach. I'd been God's lonely man for however many years—twelve in the orphanage, four in high school, four in college, a hundred after that—and she was someone that I wanted to pour myself down into. I was having trouble communicating how unusual that was.

That morning she'd watched me load a family I didn't like into a twin-engine and I'd done this shoulder shake I do before something unpleasant. And she'd caught me, and her expression had given me a lift that carried me through the afternoon. That night back in my room she made a list of other things I did or thought, any one of which was proof she paid more attention than anyone else ever had. She held parts of me like she had never seen anything so beautiful. At three or four in the morning she used her arms to tent herself up over me and asked, "Don't we have to sleep?" and then had answered her own question.

Around noon we woke up spooning, and when I held on when she tried to head to the bathroom, we slid down the sheets to the floor. She finally lost me by crawling on all fours to the bathroom door.

"Well, she's as happy as *I've* ever seen her," her father told me at the rehearsal dinner. Twenty-three people had been invited and twenty-one were her family and friends.

"It's *so nice* to see her like this," her mother told me at the same dinner.

When I toasted her, she teared up. When she toasted me, she said only, "I never thought I would feel like this," and then sat down.

We honeymooned in San Francisco. Here's what that was like for me: I still root for that city's teams.

I've always been interested in the unprecedented. I just never got to experience it that often.

Her family is Juneau society, to the extent that such a thing exists. One brother's the arts editor for the *Juneau Empire*; another works for Bauer & Gates Real Estate, selling half-million-dollar wilderness vacation homes to second-tier Hollywood stars. Another, go figure, is a lawyer. On holidays they give one another things like Arctic Cats. Happy Birthday: here's a new 650 four-by-four. The real estate brother was 11-and-1 as a starter and team MVP for JDHS the year they won the state finals. The parents serve on every board there is. Their daughter when she turned sixteen was named Queen of the Spring Salmon Derby. She still has the tiara with the leaping sockeye.

They didn't stand in the way of our romance. That's what her dad told anyone who asked. Our wedding announcement said that the bride-elect was the daughter of Donald and Nila Bell and that she'd graduated from the University of Alaska summa cum laude and was a first-year account executive for Sitka Communications Systems. It said that the groom-elect was a meat cutter for the Super Bear supermarket. I'd done that before I'd gotten my pilot's license, when I'd first gotten to town, and the guy doing the article had fucked up.

"You don't think he could have *checked* something like that?" my wife wanted to know after she saw the paper. She was so upset on my behalf that I couldn't really complain.

It's not like I never had any advantages. I got a full ride, or nearly a full ride, at St. Mary's in Moraga, near Oakland. I liked science and what math I took, though I never really, as one teacher put it, found myself while I was there. A friend offered me a summer job as one of his family's set-net fishermen my junior year, and I liked it enough to go back. The friend's family got me some supermarket work to tide me over in the winter, and it turned out that meat cutting paid more than boning fish. "What do you *want* to do?" a girl at the checkout asked me one day, like if she heard me bitch about it once more she was going to pull all her hair out, and that afternoon I signed up at Fly Alaska and Bigfoot Air, and I got my commercial and multiengine, and two years later had my float rating. I hooked on with a local outfit and the year after that bought the business, which meant a three-room hut with a stove, a van, the name, and the client list. Now I lease two 206s and two 172s on EDO 2130 floats, have two other pilots working under me, and get fourteen to fifteen hundred dollars a load for round-trip flights in the area. Want an Arctic Cat? I can buy one out of petty cash. At least in the high season.

"So are we not going to talk about this?" my wife asked last week after her parents had been over for dinner. We'd had crab and her dad had been in a funk for most of the night, who knew why. We'd said good night and handled the cleanup and now I was lunging around on my knees trying to cover my son in Nerf basketball. He always turned into Game Fanatic at bedtime. We'd hung a Nerf hoop over the inside of the back door to accommodate that need. He took advantage of my distraction to try and drive the baseline but I funneled him into the doorknob.

"I'm ready to talk," I told her. "Let's talk."

She sat on one of the kitchen chairs with her hands together on her knees, willing to wait. Her hair wasn't having the best day and it was bothering her. She kept slipping it back behind her ear.

"You can't just stay around the basket," Donald complained, trying to lure me out so he could blow by me. He was a little teary with frustration.

"I was going to talk to Daddy about having another baby," she told him. His mind was pretty intensively elsewhere.

"Do you *want* a baby brother?" she asked.

"Not right now," he said.

"If you're not having fun, you shouldn't play," she told him.

That night in bed she was lying on her back with her hands behind her head. "I love you a lot," she said, when I finally got under the covers next to her. "But sometimes you just make it so hard."

"What do I do?" I asked her. This was one of the many times I could have told her. I could have even just told her I'd been thinking about making the initial appointment. "What do I do?" I asked again. I sounded mad but I wanted to know.

"What do you do," she said, like I had just proven her point.

"I think about you all the time," I said. "I feel like *you're* losing interest in *me*." Even saying that much was humiliating. The appointment at times like that seemed like a small but hard thing that I could hold on to.

She cleared her throat and pulled a hand from behind her head and wiped her eyes with it.

"I hate making you sad," I told her.

"I hate being made sad," she said.

It was only when she said things like that and I had to deal with it that I realized how much I depended on having made her happy. And how much all of that shook when she whacked at it. *Tell her*, I thought, with enough intensity that I thought she might've heard me.

"I don't *want* another kid," Donald called from his room. The panel doors in our bedrooms weren't great, in terms of privacy.

"Go to sleep," his mother called back.

We lay there waiting for him to go back to sleep. *Tell her you changed your mind*, I thought. *Tell her you want to make a kid, right now. Show her.* I had a hand on her thigh and she had her palm cupped over my crotch, as if that, at least, was on her side. "Shh," she said, and reached her other hand to my forehead and smoothed away my hair.

Set-net fishermen mostly work for families that hold the fishing permits and leases, which are not easy to get. The families sell during the season to vendors who buy fish along the beach. The season runs from mid-June to late July. We fished at Coffee Point on Bristol Bay. Two people lived there: a three-hundred-pound white guy and his mail-order bride. The bride was from the Philippines and didn't seem to know what had hit her. Nobody could pronounce her name. The town nearest the Point had a phone book that was a single mimeographed sheet with thirty-two names and numbers on it. The road signs were hand-painted, but it had a liquor store and a grocery store and a superhardened airstrip that looked capable of landing 747s, because the bigger companies had started figuring out how much money there was in shipping mass quantities of flash-frozen salmon.

We strung fifty-foot nets perpendicular to the shore just south of the King Salmon River, cork floats on top, lead weights on the bottom, and pickers like me rubber-rafted our way along the cork floats, hauling in a little net, freeing the salmon's snagged gills, and filling the raft at our feet. When we had enough we paddled ashore and emptied the rafts and started all over again.

Everybody knew what they were doing but me. And in that water with that much protective gear, people drowned when things went wrong. Learning the ropes meant figuring out what the real fishermen wanted, and the real fishermen never said boo. It was like I was in the land of the deaf and dumb and a million messages were going by. Someone might squint at me, or give me a look, and I'd give him a look back, and finally someone else would say to me, "That's too *tight*." It was nice training on how you could get in the way even when your help was essential.

How could you *do* such a thing if you love her so much? I think to myself with some regularity, lying there in bed. Well, that's the question, isn't it? is usually my next thought. "What's the day before Memorial Day circled for?" my wife asked a week ago, standing near our kitchen calendar. Memorial Day at that point stood two weeks off. The whole extended family would be showing up at Don and Nila's for a cookout. I'd probably be a little hobbled when it came to the annual volleyball game.

"Should you even *have* kids? Should you even have a wife?" my wife asked, once, after our first real fight. I'd taken a charter all the way up to Dry Bay and had stayed a couple of extra nights and hadn't called. I hadn't even called in to the office. She'd been beside herself with worry and then with anger. I'd told her to call me back before I'd left, and then when she hadn't, I'd been like, Okay, if you don't want to talk, you don't want to talk. I'd left my cell phone off. *That* I'm not supposed to do. The office even thought about calling Air-Sea Rescue.

"Bad move, Chief," even Doris, our girl working the phones, told me when I got back.

"So I'm wondering if I should go back to work," my wife tells me today. We're eating something she whipped up in her new wok. It's an off day—nothing scheduled until tomorrow, except some maintenance paperwork—and I was slow getting out of the house and she invited me to lunch. She was distracted during the rinsing-the-greens part, and every bite reminds me of a trip to the beach. She must notice the grit. She hates stuff like that more than I do.

"They still need someone to help out with the online accounts," she says. She has an expression like every single thing today has gone wrong.

"Do you want to go back to work?" I ask her. "Do you miss it?"

"I don't know if I *miss* it," she says. She adds something in a lower voice that I can't hear because of the crunch of the grit. She seems bothered that I don't respond.

"I think it's more, you know, if we're not going to do the other thing," she says. "Have the baby." She keeps herself from looking away, as if she wants to make clear that I'm not the only one humiliated by talks like this.

I push some spinach around and she pushes some spinach around. "I feel like first we need to talk about us," I finally tell her. I put my fork down and she puts her fork down.

"All right," she says. She turns both her palms up and raises her eyebrows, like: *Here I am.*

One time she came and found me at two o'clock in the afternoon in one of the hangars and turned me around by the shoulders and pinned me to one of the workstations with her kiss. A plane two hangars down warmed up, taxied over, and took off while we kissed. She kissed me the way lost people must act when they find water in the desert.

"Do you think about me the way you used to think about me?" I ask her.

She gives me a look. "How did I used to think about you?" she wants to know.

There aren't any particular ways of describing it that occur to me. I imagine myself saying with a pitiful voice, "Remember that time in the hangar?"

She looks at me, waiting. Lately that look has had a quality to it. One time in Ketchikan one of my pilots and me saw a drunk who'd spilled his Seven and Seven on the bar lapping some of it up off the wood. *That* look: the look we gave each other.

This is ridiculous. I rub my eyes.

"Is this taxing for you?" she wants to know, and her impatience makes me madder, too.

"No, it isn't taxing for me," I tell her.

She gets up and dumps her dish in the sink and goes down to the cellar. I can hear her rooting around in our big meat freezer for a Popsicle for dessert.

The phone rings and I don't get up. The answering machine takes over and Dr. Calvin's office leaves a message reminding me about my Friday appointment. The machine switches off. I don't get to it before my wife comes back upstairs.

She unwraps her Popsicle and slides it into her mouth. It's grape.

"You want one?" she asks.

"No," I tell her. I put my hands on the table and off again. They're not staying still. It's like they're about to go off.

"I should've asked when I was down there," she tells me.

She slurps on it a little, quietly. I push my plate away.

"You going to the doctor?" she says.

Outside a big terrier that's new to me is taking a dump near our hibachi. He's moving forward in little steps while he's doing it. "God damn," I say to myself. I sound like someone who's come home from a twelve-hour shift and still has to shovel his driveway.

"What's wrong with Moser?" she wants to know. Moser's our regular doctor.

"That was Moser," I tell her. "That was his office."

"It was?" she says.

"Yes, it was," I tell her.

"Put your dish in the sink," she reminds me. I put the dish in the sink and head into the living room and drop onto the couch.

"Checkup?" she calls from the kitchen.

"Pilot physical," I tell her. All she has to do is play the message.

She wanders into the living room without the Popsicle. Her lips are darker from it. She waits a minute near the couch and then drops down next to me. She leans forward, looking at me, and then leans into me. Her lips touch mine, and press, and then lift off and stay so close it's hard to know if they're touching or not. Mine are still moist from hers.

"Come upstairs," she whispers. "Come upstairs and show me what you're worried about." She puts three fingers on my erection and rides them along it until she stops on my belly.

"I love you so much," I tell her. That much is true.

"Come upstairs and show me," she tells me back.

That night in 1958 undersea communications cables from Anchorage to Seattle went dead. Boats at sea recorded a shocking hammering on their hulls. In Ketchikan and Anchorage, people ran into the streets. In Juneau, streetlights toppled and breakfronts emptied their contents. The eastern shore of Disenchantment Bay lifted itself forty-two feet out of the sea, the dead barnacles still visible there, impossibly high up on the rock faces. And at Yakutat, a postmaster in a skiff happened to be watching a cannery operator and his wife pick strawberries on a sandy point near a harbor navigation light, and the entire point with the light pitched into the air and then flushed itself as though driven underwater. The postmaster barely stayed in his skiff, and paddling around the whirlpools and junk waves afterward, found only the woman's hat.

"You know, I made some sacrifices here," my wife mentions to me later that same day. We're naked and both on the floor on our backs but our feet are still up on the bed. One of hers is twisted in the sheets. The room seems darker and I don't know if that's a change in the weather or we've just been here forever. One of our kisses was such a submersion that when we finally stopped we needed to lie still for a minute, holding on to each other, to recover.

"You mean as in having married me?" I ask her. Our skin is air-drying but still mostly sticky.

"I mean as in having married you," she says. Then she pulls her foot free of the sheets and rolls over me.

She told me as she was first easing me down onto the bed that she'd gone off the pill but that it was going to take at least a few weeks before she'd be ready. "So you know why I'm doing this?" she asked. She slid both thighs across me, her mouth at my ear. "I'm doing this because it's *amazing*."

We're still sticky and she's looking down into my face with her most serious expression. "I mean, you're a meat cutter," she says, fitting me inside her again. The next time we do this, I'll have had the operation. And despite everything, it's still the most amazing feeling of closeness.

"Why are you *crying*?" she whispers. Then she whispers, lowering her mouth to mine, "Shhh. Shhh."

Howard Ulrich and his little boy Sonny entered Lituya Bay at eight the night of the wave, and anchored on the south shore near the entrance.

He wrote about it afterward. Their fishing boat had a high bow, a single mast, and a pilothouse the size of a Portosan. Before they turned in, two other boats had followed them in and anchored even nearer the entrance. It was totally quiet. The water was a pane of glass from shore to shore. Small icebergs seemed to just sit in place. The gulls and terns that they usually saw circling Cenotaph Island in the middle of the bay were hunkered down on the shore. Sonny said it looked like they were waiting for something. His dad tucked him in bed just about ten, around sunset. He'd just climbed in himself when the boat started pitching and jerking against its anchor chain. He ran up on deck in his underwear and saw the mountains heaving themselves around and avalanching. Clouds of snow and rocks shot up high into the air. He said it looked like they were being shelled. Sonny came up on deck in his pj's, which had alternating wagon wheels and square-knotted ropes. He rubbed his eyes. Ninety million tons of rock dropped into Gilbert Inlet as a unit. The sonic concussion of the rock hitting the water knocked them both onto their backs on the deck.

It took the wave about two and a half minutes to cover the seven miles to their boat. In that time Sonny's dad tried to weigh anchor and discovered that he couldn't, the anchor stuck fast, and let out the anchor chain as far as he could, anyway, got a life preserver onto Sonny, and managed to turn his bow into the wave. As it passed Cenotaph Island it was still more than a hundred feet high and, extending from shore to shore, a wave front two miles wide.

The front was unbelievably steep, and when it hit, the anchor chain snapped immediately, whipping around the pilothouse and smashing the windows. The boat arrowed seventy-five feet up into the curl like they were climbing in an elevator. Their backs impacted the pilothouse wall like they'd been tilted back in barber's chairs. The wave's face was a wall of green taking them up into the sky. They were carried high over the south shore. Sixty-foot trees down below disappeared. Then they were pitched up over the crest and down the back slope, and the backwash spun them off again into the center of the bay.

Another couple, the Swansons, had also turned into the wave and had had their boat surfboard a quarter mile out to sea, and when the wave crest broke, the boat pitchpoled and hit bottom. They managed to find and float their emergency skiff in the debris afterward. The third couple, the Wagners, tried to make a run for the harbor entrance and were never seen again.

Four-foot-wide trees were washed away, along with the topsoil and everything else. Slopes were washed down to bedrock. Bigger trunks were snapped off at ground level. Trees at the edge of the trim line had their bark removed by the water pressure.

Sonny's dad was still in his underwear, teeth chattering, and Sonny was washing around on his side in some icy bilge water, making noises like a jungle bird. The sun was down by this point. Backwash and wavelets twenty feet high were crisscrossing the bay, spinning house-sized chunks of glacier ice that collided against one another. Clean-peeled tree trunks like pickup sticks knitted and upended, pitching and rolling. Water was still pouring down the slopes on both sides of the bay. The smell was like they were facedown in the dirt under an upended tree. And Sonny's dad said that that time afterward—when they'd realized that they'd survived, but still had to navigate through everything pinballing around them in the dark to get out of the bay—was worse than riding the wave itself.

A day or two later the geologists started arriving. No one believed the height of the wave at first. People thought that the devastation that high on the slopes had to have been caused by landslides. But they came around.

My wife fell asleep beside me, wrapped over me to keep me warm. We're still on the floor and now it really is dark. We've got to be late in terms of picking up Donald from his play date, but if his friend's parents called, I didn't hear the phone.

One of my professors at St. Mary's had this habit of finishing each class with four or five questions, none of which anyone could answer. It was a class called The Philosophy of Life. I got a C. If I took it now,

I'd do even worse. I'd sit there hoping he wouldn't see me and try not to let my mouth hang open while he fired off the questions. What makes us threaten the things we want most? What makes us so devoted to the comfort of the inadvertent? What makes us unwilling to gamble on the noncataclysmic?

Sonny's dad was famous for a while, telling stories for magazines like *Alaska Sportsman* and *Reader's Digest* with titles like "My Night of Terror." I read one or two of them to Donald, which my wife didn't like. "Do *you* like these stories?" he asked me that night. In the stories, Sonny's mom never gets mentioned. Whether she was mad or dead or divorced or proud never comes up. In one he talks about having jammed a life preserver over Sonny's head and then having forgotten about him entirely. In another he says something like, in that minute before it all happened, he'd never felt so alone. I imagine Sonny reading that a year or two later and going, Thanks, Dad. I imagine him looking at his dad later on, at times when his dad doesn't know he's watching, and thinking of all that his dad gave him and of all that he didn't. I imagine him never really figuring out what came between them. I imagine years later people saying about him that that was the thing about Sonny: the kid was just like the old man.

I'm pretty sure I first encountered Italo Calvino's Italian Folktales *in graduate school. I'd been poleaxed right around then by his* Cosmicomics *and especially* Invisible Cities, *and I remember buying* Italian Folktales *the minute I saw it, which was eloquent, given that it was the kind of hefty hardcover I assumed that only people like teachers, and not their students, could afford.*

The last of the two hundred tales he'd compiled was "Jump into My Sack," and any number of its elements stuck with me over the years. But maybe its most arresting aspect had to do with its protagonist, who starts out hyperaware of his own limitations—

"And what will a cripple like me do to earn his bread?" he wails when his father, facing famine, turns him and his eleven healthy brothers out into the countryside to try to survive there—and then feels with an equal keenness a passionately felt gratitude for the magical good fortune bestowed upon him by a fairy who appears as "the most beautiful maiden imaginable." She not only cures his lameness but offers him two more wishes as well, which he converts to a sack that will draw in anything he names and a stick that will do whatever he wishes. He's then able for years to provide for himself and for others with his good fortune.

"Do you think he was happy, though?" the story continues. "Of course not!"

It turns out he's pining for his family members, whose loss his sack can't replace (it can only retrieve their bones), and for the beautiful fairy. Waiting for her as an old man back where he first encountered her, he discovers Death instead. And her magic is even good for that. Her sack works to envelop Death and she reappears and offers our protagonist health and youth once more. And he refuses both: he says that, having seen her again, he's content to die. He offers us, offhandedly and without explanation, that paradox: she means so much to him that he forgoes his chance to extend his time with her. She vanishes and Death reappears and takes him, "bearing his mortal remains."

"Pleasure Boating in Lituya Bay" hadn't by any means originated as an attempt to rewrite that narrative. But I wasn't very far into it before my protagonist's debt to that earlier protagonist made me reread the tale. And there it all was: the notion of one's self as already too hopelessly damaged to be fully saved by miraculous good fortune, and the sadness of all of that good fortune seized in gratitude, and yet at nearly the same moment inexplicably refused.

—JS

KATHRYN DAVIS

Body-without-Soul

IT WAS A SUBURBAN STREET, ONE BLOCK LONG, THE HOUSES MADE OF brick and built to last like the third little pig's. Sycamore trees had been planted at regular intervals along the curb and the curbs themselves sparkled; I think the concrete was mixed with mica in it. I think the street was so new it couldn't help but draw attention to itself.

The families living on the street came from all over, but the children had no trouble forming friendships, the boys' based on roughhousing and ball games, the girls' on a series of strategic moves, tireless linkings and unlinkings, the bonds double, triple, covalent like molecules. "Heads up!" the boys would yell when a car appeared, interrupting their play; the girls sat on the porch stoops, cigar boxes of trading cards and stickers in their laps, making deals. School was about to start. The darkness welled up so gradually the only way anyone could tell night had fallen was the fireflies, prickling like light on water. The parents were inside, presumably keeping an eye on their children but also drinking highballs. Fireflies like falling stars, the tree trunks narrow as the girls' waists.

Occasionally something different occurred. One girl pasted a diadem of gold star stickers to her forehead and wandered from her stoop to get closer to where one of the boys stood bent slightly forward, his hands on his knees, waiting for another boy to hit the ball. This waiting boy was Eddie, who lived at the opposite end of the street from Mary, the girl with the diadem; their bond was exquisite, meaning it would never let go, though they were too young, really, to understand the implications. Once she fell roller-skating and skinned her knee and he stood spellbound, staring at the place on the sidewalk where he could see her blood. "I shouldn't have let it happen," he told her, even though he'd been at the dentist having a cavity filled at the time. When he described how much the drill hurt she gave him one of her two best trading cards, Pinkie, who she thought of as herself despite the fact that she, Mary, would never dream of wearing a hat that had to be secured with pink ribbons, not to mention the fact that she needed glasses and had mouse-brown hair and wasn't especially pretty despite her nice brown eyes. Giving him Pinkie meant she had to break up the pair with Blue Boy, who she thought looked like him with his dark hair and soft lips and studiously downcast expression. But, then, she wasn't sentimental like he was, either.

Bedtime, the end of summer. In the brick houses the clocks kept ticking away the time, chipping off pieces of it, some big ones piling thick and heavy under the brass weights of the grandfather clock in Eddie's parents' hallway, others so small and fast even the round watchful eyeballs of the cat clock in Mary's parents' kitchen couldn't track their flight. The crickets were rubbing their hind legs together, unrolling that endless band of sound that when combined with the sound of the sycamore trees tossing their heads in the heat-thickened breeze could break even the least sentimental human heart.

Headlights appeared; the boys scattered. The car was expensive and silver-gray and belonged to the sorcerer Body-without-Soul, a tall thin bald man with a small gray mustache who lived somewhere on the next block over with a woman everyone knew as Miss Vicks, the elementary school teacher, who also may or may not have been his wife. One minute Mary was standing there in her plaid shorts and white T-shirt, balanced like a stork on one leg, the headlights turning the lenses of her spectacles to blazing spinning disks of molten gold so she could no longer see the street, the sycamore trees, the brick houses—anything at all, really, let alone Eddie—and the next minute she was gone.

"Has anyone seen Mary?" Eddie asked.

"She disappeared," Roy Duffy told him, but he was joking.

Everyone knew how Mary was—here one minute, gone the next. Besides, they were all disappearing into their houses—it was only the beginning. The game was over; the next day school started. When the crest of one wave of light met the trough of another the result was blackness.

Miss Vicks handed out sheets of colored construction paper. They were to fold the paper in half and in half again and then in half again—in this way after unfolding the paper they would end up with eight boxes in each of which they were to work a problem in long division. A feeling attached to the act of being given instructions involving paper and folding it, a feeling of intense apprehension verging on almost insane excitement. Eddie filled his boxes with drawings of Mary, some of them not so bad; it was his plan to be an artist when he grew up. From time to time he looked to his left where his subject sat folding her piece of orange paper, folding and folding and folding it, many more times than they'd been instructed, many more times than it's physically possible to fold a piece of paper, in this universe at least. He tried getting her attention but it was as if she weren't there, the light bouncing off the glazed schoolyard pavement and onto her glasses. It was like looking at a robot, Eddie thought, but also like looking at an old-fashioned girl toiling up a steep hillside in a faraway land, carrying a bucket of cream.

"Mary is sick," Miss Vicks told them the next day. "She won't be coming back to school. Wouldn't it be nice if we made her a present?" The teacher was pretty and seemed no older than most of the students' parents, but in fact she was very old, old as a breastplate of hammered bronze, a virus.

"We could make a card," suggested Betsy Abbott, a suggestion Miss Vicks met with disdain verging on rage.

"Oh, a card," said Miss Vicks. "What good would that do?"

Someone was going to have to go to the old Poole estate. There they would find a black egg hidden somewhere in the middle of the knot garden, the only thing that could make Mary better. As Miss Vicks talked she paused from time to time and cocked her head like she was listening to someone or taking dictation. She described the egg in detail—the dark shell dappled with pale white spots that shifted when you weren't looking at them, as if sunlight were falling onto it from above through the shifting crowns of the trees, but you'd be wrong, oh so wrong, for this egg could only be found where there was no light at all, the aroma it released when you cracked it open unpleasant but also sweet, like a mouse decomposing in the wall of an old house, all of which made perfect sense given the fact that the egg could only be found in the body of a dying animal.

"Let's see," Miss Vicks said, looking around the room, pretending to think. She put one manicured fingernail to the delicately upturned tip of her chin. No one was surprised when her gaze fell on Eddie—everyone knew it had been headed there all along, which was also why no one except Eddie found her description of the egg disturbing, since he was the only one who had been listening. Eddie and Mary were a pair; they had been formed that way—everyone knew that.

"Edward, wait!" Miss Vicks said, reaching into her desk drawer and removing a small curved knife with a gold handle. "You'll need this. The shell is hard as rock."

To get to the Poole estate you went to the far end of the street, up the three little green hills beyond the school, and over the trestle bridge above the railroad tracks. Old Mr. Poole had abandoned the estate years earlier for some reason no one was able to remember—the parents had all warned their children to stay away from the place. The mansion was dangerous, its floors and staircases rotten, the windowpanes smashed to glittering daggers of glass. In the spring you could still find lilacs and forsythia growing in what had once been the formal gardens, but by summer's end the stringweed and creeper covered everything, leaving behind only the general shapes of things, disquieting like the sheeted furniture in Victorian novels, and if you weren't careful you would pitch into a cistern and drown.

Of course Eddie had been there—all of the children who lived on the block had been there on their bicycles. It was the best place to play hide-and-seek or sardines. Eddie knew without being told that some egg wasn't going to cure Mary, assuming she was sick. From the sound of it, in all likelihood it would probably make her sicker, if not kill her. Even so he rode his bike to the Poole estate that same afternoon. The minute he had passed beyond the formal entryway's twin pillars, one surmounted by an armless Athena, the other by a noseless Aphrodite, the air suddenly grew ice-cold, as if a thin veil of pretense had been let fall, the illusion of light and heat withdrawn, the planets swimming closer and closer, drawing into their orbits the dark chill nothing of outer space. "Is this because the season's changing," Eddie wondered, "or is this the way the world really is, or is this my mood because of Mary?"

He left his bike leaning against a pillar and began to explore, eventually locating the knot garden, more or less unrecognizable as anything at all under its blanket of vines. There at the garden's heart, lying on its side, was the dead body of one of the big gray hares that had appeared in the neighborhood the previous spring—the cause of many a minor automobile accident—but it didn't have an egg like the one Miss Vicks had described to him hidden in it. Nothing was hidden in the hare's body.

While he sat hunkered there, looking at the hare, night fell, taking Eddie by surprise. He'd brought no flashlight, forgetting how quickly the days grew shorter once the equinox was past. As unsentimental as Mary was, Eddie was suggestible. The hare's dead body frightened him, the glazed surface of its upward-facing eye reminding him of Mary's the other day in the classroom when she couldn't stop folding the piece of paper. He returned to where he'd left his bike leaning against the pillar and removed the curved knife from the basket. Then he retraced his steps to the maze and cut the hare's body into pieces.

By now it had grown so dark he could barely see a thing; if there was a moon most of it seemed to have slid through a slot in the sky. It took Eddie a long time to once again track down his bike. When he did, he found a big yellow cat sitting there by the front wheel waiting for him. "Pssst," the cat said, licking the hare's blood from its paws and flicking its long yellow tail from side to side like the cat on the clock in Mary's parents' kitchen. Atop Athena's head perched a flea-bitten crow, a string of entrails dangling from its beak; a rake-thin dog sprawled under a lilac bush, worrying a foot bone. "Thank you, Eddie," he heard a tiny voice say, and when he tried to figure out where it had come from, it seemed to be from the ant he saw crawling up his ankle. "We were starving."

It wasn't until he got home that he found the gifts the animals had left for him in his bike basket: a cat's claw and a dog's whisker, the feather of a crow and the leg of an ant. These things might come in handy, he thought, and he stowed them away along with the curved knife in the shoe box where he kept Mary's trading card.

Mary returned to school the following day as if nothing had happened, and Miss Vicks acted as if Mary had never been gone, withholding the usual favors she granted students snatched from the jaws of death, such as clapping the erasers or feeding the fish. At some point Mary got contact lenses and stopped wearing glasses; for a while in high school she and Eddie were sweethearts, but even when they started having sex things never went back to being the way they'd been when they were young.

In spite of that, though, the look of Eddie, his obvious preoccupation with an inner life he kept hidden from everyone, excited Mary; she would grow so moist she'd have to leave class. There was a cot in the furnace room where she would lie waiting for him, her skirt hiked up around her waist and her underpants down around her ankles. The one time he asked her where she'd gone that summer night so many years ago, she looked at him in amazement. "I was kidnapped," she told him. "I thought everyone knew."

Eventually Mary moved on to other boyfriends, some of them the same boys who'd played baseball in the street with Eddie. She developed a reputation for being fast. Then she got engaged to a much older man who was said to have a lot of money. Sometimes Eddie saw her standing by the magazine rack in the corner drugstore, teetering a little in her stiletto heels, her mouse-brown hair now bleached blond and worn in a French twist. She would be paging through a fashion magazine, but because she had on sunglasses Eddie couldn't tell if she'd noticed him too and was choosing to ignore him, or if she hadn't seen him at all.

After graduation he went off to the city to study painting at the Academy. He moved into a large apartment building where he lived by himself until one day the big yellow cat showed up at his apartment door, wrapping itself around his ankles while he was struggling with his key, and then slipping through the open door so quickly and curling itself so comfortably in his one good chair that it was as if it had always been there. Often he would talk to the cat about the past and the cat would offer monosyllables in exchange; Eddie told himself this was the way things were meant to work out. Whatever he had felt for Mary—and, really, he wasn't certain what that had been, only that it had been everything for him—he chalked up to the fires of youth, which he told himself were behind him. I think he was encouraged to feel this way, to belittle everything that had happened between him and Mary; time healed all wounds, everyone knew that!

What Eddie didn't take into account was the fact that while time did, indeed, heal all wounds, it was also the source of them—a fact the sorcerer Body-without-Soul was only too well aware of. It was the sorcerer's ambition to get rid of time altogether, and in so doing to make everything in the world duplicate his own grotesque condition.

For what granted the body its relation to time but the soul, the ageless, deathless soul—without the soul the lump of flesh that was the body would just sit there forever like the lump it was, unable to understand or feel a thing.

Eddie turned out to be a portrait artist of uncommon skill, his ability to capture the essence of a subject so uncanny he earned commissions from some from the city's most prominent citizens. He painted the newly appointed bishop with his gold mitre and ivory teeth; he painted the mayor's bony wife with her chubby daughter. In each case he was able to convey an almost painfully accurate representation of the subject's external appearance while at the same time laying bare what would otherwise remain occult, the bishop's unrequited love for his own handsome face, the daughter's delight at being the cause of her mother's embarrassment.

It wasn't long before Eddie could afford a studio of his own in a fashionable neighborhood. Initially society's darling, as the years passed he also became the object of serious critical attention. There were shows at the major galleries, articles in the best journals, adulatory monographs, even a coffee-table-sized book. For a while he was married to one of his patronesses; he had his share of love affairs as well. Then one evening he got the call that changed everything. "I have a job for you," said the sorcerer Body-without-Soul, disguising his voice to sound human. "I think you'll be pleasantly surprised."

The next day when Eddie entered his studio he found that a woman had let herself in and was standing on the dais with her back to him. She was wearing an organdy gown of a pinkness so pale as to be practically white, tied at the waist with a deep pink sash. On her head she wore a bonnet, its long pink streamers hanging loose to her shoulders, which were bare. She was the image of Pinkie, the girl on Mary's trading card, though unlike the woman in his studio, Pinkie would never have been caught dead with a cigarette. The woman glanced to one side. "Eddie," she said, exhaling smoke. "Darling." He got the fleetest glimpse of a single eye, refracting light and silver like mirror backing.

But if this was Mary, why was the yellow cat hissing at her, its back arched in a parody of feline anger? The woman looked no older than Mary had the last time Eddie had seen her, whereas he, Eddie, was losing his hair and needed glasses to read the paper, and the yellow cat had long surpassed one hundred in human years. The studio was overheated, the water banging in the radiators, the smell of turpentine and cigarette smoke overpowering. There had been some scandal, Eddie remembered, following which Mary had moved to the city. As he watched, she began removing her clothes. Her skin was that shade of milky white that's almost blue, like skim rather than whole milk, her hair a tumble of curls. Before she had a chance to turn to face him, he had bolted from the room, together with the shoe box and the cat.

Now he could no longer stand the sight of living flesh. For a while he drew the cadavers the hospital supplied for the use of the medical students; he had been told there was money to be made illustrating anatomy textbooks and this proved to be true. Later he preferred to find his subjects at the city morgue, where he was befriended by the coroner, a heavyset man with the drooping jowls of a hound and a long gray ponytail. When Eddie asked him the difference between a cadaver and a corpse, the man pointed to a recent arrival by way of reply. The bodies that came into the morgue were not always in such good shape, corpses—as opposed to cadavers—often having met a violent end. But Eddie could draw anything. "You're so good you can draw blood," the coroner liked to say, and then he would howl with laughter.

I suppose it's not surprising that eventually someone Eddie knew would show up there. He was sitting alone eating a sandwich, his drawing pad open on his knees, and had just started sketching.

"Remember me?" asked the corpse.

It was Miss Vicks lying on the marble slab, flat and pale as a flounder. "Listen to me, Edward," said Miss Vicks. "You've always been good at following directions. Do you still have that knife I gave you?" She asked him to cut her up in pieces the way he'd cut up the hare. When Miss Vicks spoke her mouth opened and closed like a small live entity all its own.

"Why should I do that?" Eddie asked, and he began to grow dizzy thinking of where the time went and how there wasn't that much of it left. "Besides," he said, "the last time I followed your directions I don't remember things going particularly well." Over the years he had grown so used to talking to the yellow cat he didn't find it that strange to be talking to a corpse.

"What on earth do you mean, Edward?" Miss Vicks asked. "It was Mary who didn't fold the paper the way I said, not you. Hurry up, please!" she added, flecks of spit appearing on her lips. "What's taking you so long?"

At some point rain had started falling, long strings of it from a sky the color of tin, pieces of which kept breaking loose and landing on the morgue roof, piling up there like the pieces of time in the case of the grandfather clock in Eddie's parents' hallway.

Eddie felt so dizzy, he hardly knew what he was doing. He took the knife from where he kept it in the shoe box. He cut off Miss Vicks's hands and feet and cut out her entrails and was just cutting off her head when he heard a tiny voice coming from his sandwich.

"Eddie," the voice said. "Don't listen to her. It's a trap."

Eddie looked down and saw an ant emerging from between the two slices of bread, the very same ant he'd saved so many years ago from starving. What Eddie had to do, the ant told him, was to hold onto the leg it had given him back then—did he remember? Eddie had put it in his shoe box. By holding onto its leg, the ant told Eddie, he would become an ant so small no one could see him, even with a magnifying glass. And indeed the second Eddie picked the leg up he found himself standing on the sandwich, the other ant at his side, as enormous as an elephant, its magnificent abdomen gleaming like patent leather.

"What do we do now?" Eddie asked.

"We wait and watch and listen," the ant replied.

When the coroner arrived at the morgue to find parts of Miss Vicks strewn across the slab, he couldn't believe what he was seeing. "Oh, Eddie," the coroner sighed. "How could you do this to me?" Clearly it was a case for the police. In no time at all Body-without-Soul had sped to the scene in his silver-gray car. "Tell me you haven't touched anything," he said to the coroner. "We'll dust for prints," he added, snatching Eddie's drawing without first bothering to put on his latex gloves. "You might as well go home," he told the coroner. But the minute the man was gone Body-without-Soul tore the drawing to bits. "They'll never get me," he said. "Most human beings are too stupid and sentimental and the only one who isn't I took care of years ago." Of course Miss Vicks knew he meant Mary. Precious Mary, as Miss Vicks thought of her, sourly.

Human beings would never be able to kill him, the sorcerer went on to say, because to do that would require tracking down his soul, which was hidden somewhere on the Poole estate in a black egg. A black egg in a black craw in a black heart in a black stomach. Someone was going to need the right tools—a bunch of body parts, he added, a trifle sadistically thought Miss Vicks—without which they'd never be able to make all the transformations needed to slit open the belly of the cat that ate the dog that ate the crow and find the egg that his soul would fly out of when you cracked its shell open. "Blah blah blah," said Body-without-Soul. "The usual song and dance. It's not going to happen."

Miss Vicks moved her mouth as if to answer. Nothing came out at first but a trickle of sound like tap water and then her hands balled into fists and the sound grew louder, churning and grinding and clicking like stones borne on the flood.

I think it's harder to return to the place where you lived your life when you were a child than it is to change from a man to an ant and back again. Eddie couldn't stop looking at his human arms and legs, wondering what had become of those six graceful appendages he'd come to prefer to his own, each one as translucent as amber and delicately feathered.

The street where he used to play baseball was jammed on both sides with parked cars, making the idea of playing anything there, even if he'd still been able to, impossible, and the sycamore trees, having first grown so immense that huge holes had been cut in their crowns to make room for telephone lines and electric wire, in the end had gotten chopped down completely. Mary's parents' house and the houses to either side of it had been changed into condominiums so you couldn't tell where one stopped and the next began. Eddie's parents' house looked more or less the same, except that the sloping front lawn his father had worked so hard to maintain was turned to chaff, the grass dead or dying and overrun with dandelions, and instead of the lush ivy plant his mother had kept in the front bow window there was a hideous gold lamp shaped like a naked woman.

Eddie was an old man now. The hair he still had left was white and his teeth false, the youthful promise of his career all but forgotten, the portraits he had painted so many years ago possible to track down with some effort in private collections, but considered stylistically quaint. The big yellow cat was dead, also the coroner, the cat's ashes in a plastic bag in Eddie's shoe box, the coroner's in a cemetery Eddie sometimes visited before he moved away from the city. The Poole estate had been sold to a developer who built a retirement community there, Poole Village, which included the nursing home where Eddie's father lived the last years of his life. But Eddie's father was dead, too.

As he walked along the neat brick pathways of Poole Village, Eddie could barely remember what it was he was supposed to have come back to do. The day was mild, the air sweet but with a smell of autumn in it, of burning leaves, and in the blue sky he could see a small wavering V of geese making their way south, hear the plaintive far-off sound of their honking. Mary had always made fun of him, of the way the end of summer made him sad—her eyes would mock him, lovingly. He remembered how she would sit on the porch stoop with one of the other girls, the two of them apparently in deep negotiation for some card, a dog or a horse or what the girls all referred to as a "scene," meaning a painting from the Romantic period showing a world where beautiful places like the Poole estate had once existed. Mary's head would be bent over the cigar box, her shoulders hunched, but he could tell she was more focused on him than she was on nothing else. No one or nothing else in his life had given him that same degree of attention.

Now a young woman orderly approached on the path, pushing an old woman toward him in a wheelchair. The young woman reminded him a little of his old elementary school teacher, Miss Vicks—she had the same red lips and fingernails, the same birdlike way of tilting her head when she talked, and her name, amazingly enough, was Vicky. The old woman was just an old woman; she wore the kind of sunglasses with side shields a person needed after cataract surgery, and her silver hair had been put up in a bun. "Are you going to lunch?" the old woman asked Eddie. "Today is Friday," she added, clapping together the swollen joints of her hands. "Swordfish!"

Eddie was about to say no, that while Poole Village certainly seemed nice enough, he wasn't yet a resident. But then he was once again filled with a sense of having forgotten something important, something he was supposed to have come back there to accomplish. He seemed to remember something about a sorcerer, but that was in a fairy tale he'd heard in his childhood. Something about someone wearing a diadem of star stickers, about a girl wearing a diadem of star stickers on her forehead.

The three of them—Eddie and Vicky and the old woman—were making their slow way along an avenue of shade trees, the leaves casting moving shadows across their faces. Eddie felt cold; what the stickers signified, it suddenly came to him, was more than the fact that one girl had been set apart from the other girls. Something had happened to her, something bad.

He followed Vicky and the old woman into the building. "Whatever you do," the old woman told Vicky, laughing, "don't push me down there." She was pointing toward the blue hallway that led to the level-three nursing home; when you went down that hallway you never came out again except as a cadaver.

Eventually they arrived at the dining room. The room was full of old people sitting in groups of four or six around tables covered with white tablecloths. It was a pleasant room, almost like a restaurant, with artificial floral centerpieces and aproned waitstaff, except all the waitstaff could perform CPR. Eddie put the shoe box on the table beside him. There was a plate in front of him with a piece of fish on it and a pile of peas and a pile of rice but he had no appetite.

"What have you got there?" asked the attractive young man who came to wait on their table.

"You have to speak up," Vicky said. "Otherwise he can't hear you."

The old woman reached across the table and put her hand on his and held it and he could feel a tremor run through his whole body that either came from him or from her, he couldn't tell the difference.

He also couldn't tell where he was but he thought he could see a sky like gray padding with a handful of black specks swirling just beneath it, birds busy looking for things to use to build their nests. There was the smell of knotweed, a little like the smell of cat urine, and sure enough there was his yellow cat, big and sleek the way he used to be when Eddie first saw him, scratching in the dirt. Eddie's hands were shaking so hard he almost couldn't open the shoe box.

"See if he can manage this," the attractive young man said to Vicky. He set a bowl of broth on the table.

"Here, let me help you," she said, propping up Eddie, who had slid so far down in his chair he couldn't reach the table. "I'm going to break an egg into it to give it more body," she explained. Then she reached into the shoe box for the curved knife and gave the egg a whack, separating the two halves of the shell and dropping the contents into Eddie's broth.

The room grew very quiet. Shadows padded along the walls, poured over Eddie like rain.

The old woman leaned closer. "Uh-oh," she said. "It looks like he's wet himself."

She took off her sunglasses to get a better look.

She was wearing a long robe of a heavy lustrous fabric like the satin they stopped making years ago, and it set off her skin—she allowed just the right amount of animal fat in her diet to keep it thick and creamy, hydrated it just enough to keep it translucent. "I have something to tell you, Mister," she said to Eddie, looking up over her fork at him, lifting her eyes which weren't cloudy and dull but alive and dark and lit by the fire of her spirit, which, like the sun, couldn't be confronted directly but had to be filtered through the vitreous humor of her material self. Eddie remembered those eyes watching him, and as he did he heard the sound of the crickets, a sound he hadn't heard in a very long time, and with it the voice of his mother calling him in, and his father whistling as he adjusted the sprinkler, its lazy arc above the freshly mowed lawn, and there was Mary in her plaid shorts and white T-shirt, standing on one leg like a stork.

"You look like you just saw a ghost," the attractive young man said. It was the very last thing Eddie heard before his soul flew out of his body.

My story has two sources. The first is the Italian fairy tale "Body-without-Soul." I was attracted to its obsession with the physical body, as well as its elaborate and gruesome set of rules for tracking down the soul, and I took elements of its plot for my own. The second source is less specific but stems from the role time plays in the fairy tales of Hans Christian Andersen, where it overpowers

everything, including magic. In his fairy tales it's time above all else that is magical, elastic, strange—even with otherworldly help you can't escape it. I wanted to write a story reflecting this condition, and I thought "Body-without-Soul" would provide a good container.

—KD

KELLIE WELLS

The Girl, the Wolf, the Crone

MORE THAN ONCE THERE WAS A SOON-TO-BE-OLD WOMAN WHO HAD A loaf of bread, held it in her hands she did, and it was inconvenient to have a loaf of bread always sitting in her hands as she tried to sweep or sew or sneeze, so she said to her daughter, the one with cheeks the appalling color of let blood: "With a face like that, you haven't anything better to do, so here, take this bread off my hands!" The woman said she knew a sickly wolf who would like nothing better than to receive stale bread from a girl like her, "but be careful," said the girl's mother, "as the woods are full of primordial women with faces like the bottom of a river and who long to feel the weight of bread in their twisted mitts once more." The minute the woman handed the bread to the girl, her face grew dark as thunder, and she barked, "Git!"

The girl fled with the loaf under her arm, and at the fork where everyone chooses wrongly, she saw a crusty old woman with a face like a fallen cake, and the woman yowled, "You're headed the wrong way, dear heart!"

"But I haven't chosen yet!" said the girl with the objectionable cheeks.

"As if that mattered," muttered the woman, and for a moment her face looked like a weathered map leading nowhere good.

The girl examined the tines of the forking path and could see that in one direction the road was covered in spoons and in the other it was littered with blood sausages. The girl had always preferred spoon to sausage and so she confidently strode in that direction. The sunlight that needled its way through the branches of the forest struck the bowed bellies of the spoons, splintered in every direction, and pricked the girl's skin as she walked. She tried to brush away the light that beetled along her arms and up her throat with its sticky legs. The light, pragmatic and cowardly at heart, would not go near those cheeks red as a carbuncle.

The old woman, knowing what was expected of her, cackled. She swiftly slipped and wobbled atop the sausages and cursed herself for having forgotten to bring along a growler of beer. No matter, she'd be at the house of the ailing wolf soon enough, and then she'd have her fill, boy howdy.

When she reached the house of the wolf, the cunning beldam let herself in and shook her head at the sight of him: he looked half-dead already, more moth-eaten pelt than glamorous savage, not even fit to be a stole. She spit a bolus of sausage at the foot of his bed. The wolf weakly stirred at the sound.

"Well, I suppose I haven't any choice but to eat you," said the woman.

"I suppose not," said the wolf, who'd had a hunch the saving catholicon of the bread would not make it to him in time. There is no rescuing a wolf, not in this world or any other. He unzipped his coat and dragged his body dutifully into her mouth, and the woman, who found him a little gamey, spit the bones onto the bed.

From inside her belly, the wolf's muffled voice came, *Take, eat,* he said, *this is my body, which is broken for you.*

Such theatrics, heavens to betsy! thought the old woman, and she socked herself in the stomach and belched. If she ate before sundown, her meals always repeated on her.

The ancienne noblesse began to undress, lace-up peep toes, garters, support hose, daisied duster, crocheted shrug, ragged bonnet.

A yellow cat lying curled before the hearth unwound himself, sat up, and said, "Get a load of Granny's gams, ooh-wee hubba-hubba!" then whistled like a sailor newly on leave.

The ripe old dame, whose sister had a weakness for strays of every stripe, had had her fill of cheeky gibs and she booted him across the room. Then she stepped inside the wolf skin, which fit a skosh too snugly, and slipped beneath the covers. She struck a wan pose and conjured a pallor that announced she was on the verge of oblivion and should be the recipient of a steady supply of pity and bread and the affection of innocents, and just as she did, Little Miss Red Cheeks knocked at the door.

"Allow me," said the limping tom, who wanted to hotfoot it to a place free of irascible old grimalkins, notorious collectors of the likes of him, and he slid out the door sly as butter.

And there the girl was, laden with spoons she'd collected along the way, a crumbling loaf, eager to be cradled in the hands of a long-fallow hag, under her arm.

"Hello, sick wolf," said the poppy, and she set the spoons and the bread upon the floor.

My soul is exceeding sorrowful, lamented the wolf inside the woman, and she coughed hoarsely and slapped her chest, and the girl said, "What was that?" and the woman replied, "My cold is leaving my snout full," and she coughed again.

"I have bread," said the girl, who blushed brash as an open wound, "bread that has never left the hands of my mother until now, bread that can save you."

I will smite the shepherd and scatter the sheep, said the wolf, and the woman poked herself hard in the gut and her stomach emitted a feeble growl.

The little radish knew there was no love lost between wolf and sheep, but there wasn't a flock to be found for miles around, and she smiled at him pityingly, thinking some poor creatures are simply doomed by instinct, helpless to hallucinate more reachable goals, slave to implausible diets. She picked up two spoons and began to tap a melody on her knees, which made her legs involuntarily kick.

The woman threw back the covers and exposed more fully her lupine duds.

"My, what big breasts you have!" exclaimed the girl with cheeks like molten embers. She dropped the spoons, which landed with a timpanic plonk upon the pile.

So sad when a girl goes ruddy, thought the woman, tsk.

The old woman adjusted her dugs, which, raised in the wild away from the civilizing influence of brassieres, were a little claustrophobic and so tried to escape the suffocating skin of the wolf. She corralled them and they nickered. "The better to suckle you with, dear heart!" said the woman. Pitiful little strawberry, thought she, whom I might once have been able to save had your mother, grrrr, not pinched the loaf from my withered fingers. It is always advisable to bear in mind that the embezzlement of fertility necessarily exacts a stiff tariff.

"Oh, wolf, what blue hair you have!" said the girl. The old woman had only yesterday been to the beauty parlor and chosen a rinse the color of irises. Sprigs of hair escaped through the wolf's ears, and the woman tried to tuck them back inside.

Behold, he is at hand that doth betray me, croaked the woman's belly. She was having a little trouble restraining her feral anatomy, and she put a hand to her complicated crotch and her befurred breasts and gave everything a shake and an upward tug. *Oof*, went her stomach.

"What opposable thumbs you have, wolf!" bleated the girl, who began to fear that this blue and breasted creature was not all that he seemed, this womanly wolf that smelled vaguely medicinal, giving off an odor of vitamins, blood, and moldering roses. And thumbs, he smelled of thumbs!

"Oh, wolf!" cried the girl. "Your bones, your bones!" She pointed at the pile. "How can you heave your body from hill to dale without them? How can you properly terrorize woodland creatures with only raggedy fur and a pudding of flesh with which to spook them?" Bones were an essential ingredient of both locomotion and thuggery, the girl well knew.

The old woman now saw she'd left the bones in plain view on the bed, an osteological oversight, and she took up the wolf's femurs and drummed on the headboard behind her. "If I carry them with me," said the woman, "they don't poke me as much. And, well, they're, uh, erf, much more percussive when not swimming inside me!" The woman halted the racket and could see she was straining even this rosily jowled gull's willful naïveté, so necessary to the telling of stories and the entrapment of children.

The girl bent to fetch the loaf of bread that she hoped would help provoke the wolf's natural canine vitality, and when she did, she spied beneath the bed the old woman's clothes. She remembered what her mother had told her, and she was relieved at the thought that there was one less old woman in the woods to worry about. She put on the old woman's shift and the old woman's shawl and the old woman's bonnet and she clomped about in the old woman's shoes and she pretended to scold invisible children and to dab at imaginary dewlaps with an embroidered hankie that she kept tucked beneath her wristwatch, then she picked up the bread and crawled into bed with the wolf, who seemed to her to suffer from womanhood, the worst of all afflictions, a disease she would likely contract in time, and the wolf, quick as the flick of a lizard's tongue, quick as a badger's dander, swallowed her whole like the meat of an oyster. The old woman felt the satisfied satiety of having dined on bread and girl. The girl shimmied down the throat of the wolf clutching the loaf to her breast only to meet another throat on her way to the wolf's stomach and she could see this was not the shriveled throat of a bruised peach past her prime. Only then did she realize she'd been bamboozled and was now curled inside the true wolf's boneless belly as if waiting to be born, half wood-sprite battle-ax, half consumptive cur, nuts! She heard the old woman licking her fingers, and she stretched herself inside the flesh of the wolf and began to jab the old woman in the kidneys. "Say, stop that!" howled the old woman. "Nobody likes an impudent lunch!"

Just then, punctual as misery, fragrant as the coming of bungled valor, there appeared at the door a huntsman. The huntsman took one look at the bloated wolf, put two and two together (crack huntsman, he), and reckoned all parties worth saving were at this moment being digested. He'd been sent by the young tomato's mother to reclaim the loaf of bread, which she had decided she could not live without. The huntsman, to summon the requisite mettle, lifted to his mouth the wineskin slung over his shoulder and squeezed a stream of port into his gullet. *Drink ye all of it, for this is my blood,* came a gauzy voice as if from under a hidden pillow. "What's that?" asked the huntsman. A higher-pitched voice said, "My, oh, my, what a big spleen you have!" And another voice, clearer but sporting an incognito hoarseness, said, "The better to chide you with, lovey!" And the woman, wrapped in a swaddling of wolf, let rip a musical belch and the girl inside her immediately recognized the melody of those windy gripes and she added to them by gasping: Grandmother! She hadn't seen her maternal grandmother for many years, not since Nana and her mother angrily parted after an argument about how best to attend to the loaf. The girl remembered the delicious wolf soup her grandmother used to make her and felt a fond stirring in her own kishkas.

And the huntsman, so easily sidetracked when a quarry began to spill its guts, hastily reached a brawny fist into the wolf's maw and extracted . . . a frumpy girl! Whose cheeks were so frightfully abloom he thought she might be better off left to the vagaries of the wolf's intestines, but she held the bread in her hands, so he dropped her onto the ground. Next, with the skill and boredom of a surgeon performing his one-thousandth appendectomy, he carefully plucked a quivering aspic of flesh from the throat of the wolf and decided the old woman, with her long nose and big ears, was likely beyond saving and he dropped the slop of her onto the floor and wiped the residual goo onto his gambeson, but when thick-nailed, corn-tumored toes poked through the fur as though it were a footed sleeper a size too small, the huntsman reached in again with the resentful finesse of a down-on-his-luck magician who believes he's bound for a destiny far grander than the endless extraction of rabbits from hats, and he neatly skinned what turned out to be . . . a very old woman, ta-daa! Well, fancy that. The wolf's weathered exterior, heavily trafficked of late he could see, lay rumpled at the old woman's feet like a discarded cape too threadbare to repair. This nested zoology made the huntsman vertiginous, and he dropped himself onto a chair. Just then the jumble of flesh inched up the bed, enveloped the bones, then slid into the fur and got back under the covers, where he rattled a final breath and went limp with extinction. The girl, with a face like a rusted skillet, clutched the bread, and when she saw the huntsman, she went, stem to stern, red as the end of the world; the huntsman took one look at the girl and thought *Bolshevik* and decided no brazen-faced rose that rutilant was worth deflowering, bread or no bread, and he pumped the bladder beneath his arm and took another slug of wine; and the naked old crone? She smiled at the pair of them and bowed her head at the wolf, messianic with mange, who had just been alive then inside her. Then alive again, repatriated to the fatherland of his ailing skin. He'd be back, that one, sure as pokeweed.

The old-old woman, much older now than when she'd arrived, a coon's age older than when she'd grudgingly passed down that loaf of bread to her daughter, picked up a sausage between her fingers and pretended to smoke it, then looked at herself in the shiny dowager's hump of a soup spoon, and admired the salvaged eyesore she'd become.

This is what I started to think about at some point in the rewriting and corruption of "Little Red Riding Hood": I like the idea that a character can be flat and complex at once if one abandons

attachment to conventional notions of character psychology and allows characters to become a container for ideas. If you flatten a character, the reader doesn't have to feel anxious about sniffing out motivations and you make way for other kinds of interpretive or subtextual richness. As Kate Bernheimer says in "Fairy Tale Is Form, Form Is Fairy Tale," the essay that provoked these ideas and this story, this willful flatness of character "allows for depth of response in the reader," and if interpreting psychology is your exegetical wont, this allows you to put the whole story on the couch.

A statement of the obvious: if you're working with language, everything is representation, a letter symbolizing a sound, a word symbolizing an object or notion, and in writing "The Girl, the Wolf, the Crone," I liked the (not original, certainly) idea of acknowledging and exploiting the mediation in an effort to tell a story, and maybe to untell a story too in a way, but I'm fond of narrative and wanted things to happen and so didn't want the story to be merely a metafictional exposé; that is, I wasn't interested in calling attention to the artifice in order to dispel the dream that is fiction but rather to create a different kind of garishly lit, demi-lucid dream. I think the form of the fairy tale is liberating in allowing both writer and reader to be mindful of the fact that anything we refer to as "reality" in fiction is just a shared hallucination, however seductive, while at the same time casting come-hither glances of its own.

—KW

My Brother Gary Made a Movie and This Is What Happened

ALTHOUGH HE IS WEARING A PAPER BAG OVER HIS HEAD, I INSTANTLY recognize Gary. Gary is my brother, and he is making a movie. Don't get me wrong, the eyes were cut out. I mean, Gary could *see*. "What's the name of the movie, Gary?" "The name of the moobie," said Gary, "is *My Family*." "You said moobie, Gary." "No, I didn't. I said, moobie." "You did it again, Gary."

Gary's eyes moved very quickly back and forth. Gary was miffed. "I'm going to flip out!" shouted Gary. "I'm sorry, Gary." Gary had trouble with words. It was his sorest spot. Sometimes he was so tragically far off I wanted to gather him up in my arms, climb a tree, and leave him in the largest nest I could find. He'd mean to say "human" and it would come out "cantaloupe." He'd mean to say "dad" and it would come out "sock." Even my name he malapropped. He called me Mouse.

"Did you build that camera yourself, Gary?" The camera was an old tin can with a bunch of leaves pasted to it. Gary held the tin can up in the air. A few leaves fluttered off. "Action?" he whispered. And then, even softer, he whispered, "Cut?" "May I make a suggestion, Gary?" "What is it, Mouse?" "Maybe you want to point the camera at something." "Like what?" "Maybe like an actor, Gary. Like an actor who is saying words." "Like these actors?" asked Gary. I was proud of his pronunciation. He led me behind the couch.

The actors groaned in a heap. "Is that Grandpa, Gary?" It was unquestionably Grandpa. He was on the very, very tippy top. "Hi, Grandpa," I said. "Hello," said Grandpa. He was not excited to see me. I had married a black man, and he was still ticked off. "This is not about you," said Grandpa. "This is about Gary, and his burden of dreams."

"Look!" said Gary. "There's Sock." Gary meant our dad. "Hi, Dad." My father gave a little wave. He was about four actors from the bottom. My eleven other brothers also were there: Eugene, Jack, Sid, Benjamin, Daniel, Saul, Eli, Walter, Adam, Richard, and Gus. They groaned. Aunt Rosa was shoved between my mother and grandmother. A bunch of cousins were balled up at the bottom.

"Hand me that shovel," said Gary. "What shovel?" I asked. But Gary already was pointing his tin can straight at the heap. "Lights," said Gary. "Turn off the lights!" I turned off the lights. "Camera," said Gary. "Action," said Gary. "Cut," said Gary.

"May I ask a question, Gary?" "What is it, Mouse?" "Why are you shooting in the dark, Gary?"

"I've had it," yelled my mother. "We've been here for six goddamn years." Aunt Rosa made little clucking sounds. I turned on the lights. Gary went into the kitchen and returned with a large tray filled with tiny cups of water.

"I can't live in a heap this close to your father," yelled my mother.

I began to wonder about footage.

"I need a mani-pedi," yelled my mother. "I need a goddamn blowout." "You look beautiful," I said. "This is not about you," yelled my mother. "This is about Gary and his burden of dreams." I handed her a cup of water. "This water tastes fake," yelled my mother. "It is fake," said Gary.

My father's beeper went off. His patients were dying.

"Did you know," asked Grandma, "that the fear of being touched is called aphenphosmphobia?" My mother rolled her eyes.

"What's the movie about, Gary?" "The moobie's about the Holocaust," said Gary.

"Is there a script, Gary?" "Bring me that ladder," said Gary. I brought him the ladder. He leaned it against the heap, climbed all the way up, and stood on top of Grandpa. Grandpa smiled.

Gary pulled the paper bag off his head. His silver hair tumbled out. The actors oohed and aahed. Gary blushed. He turned the paper bag inside out, and off of it he read the script: *"Thou shalt have no other Gods; Thou shalt not make any graven images; Thou shalt not take the Lord's name in vain; Remember the Sabbath day; Honor thy father and mother; Thou shalt not kill; Thou shalt not commit adultery; Thou shalt not steal; Thou shalt not bear false witness against thy neighbor; Thou shalt not covet thy neighbor's house . . . nor anything that is his."*

"Such a good boy," said Aunt Rosa. "Such a good boy," said Grandpa. "Such a good boy," said my father. "Go to hell," said my mother. My eleven other brothers groaned.

"Did you know," said Grandma, "that the fear of the skins of animals is called doraphobia?" I began to wonder whose heart was a doomed spoon. Mine or Gary's.

The best I could do for Gary at this point was hold him, and ask him what he was going to do after.

"After what?" asked Gary. "After shooting," I said. "I'm going to Barcelona," said Gary. Now, that really ceiled me. I would've said "that really threw me off the heap," but I wasn't invited to be on the heap. Wasn't really sure I ever wanted to be on the heap. "There are these scrambled eggs in Barcelona," said Gary, "I really need to try." "Oh, come on, Gary. You know you'll scream the whole way." In the States Gary was just fussy. Overseas he screamed.

And then I remembered Gary's problem with malapropping. "Barcelona?" I asked. "Barcelona," said Gary. "Scrambled eggs?" I asked. "Scrambled eggs," said Gary. I looked over at the heap. My mother was halfway out of there. "Six more years," she yelled, "and then I quit." My father gave Gary an idealistic thumbs-up. "Did you know," said Grandma, "that the fear of puppets is called pupaphobia?" "Well," said Grandpa, "bye." "I'm not going yet," I said. I was still holding Gary. I held him as tightly as I hold my breath when I pass the cemetery. "Why do you do that?" asked Gary. "Do what?" "Hold your breath when you pass the cemetery?" I looked over at the heap. Aunt Rosa smacked her hand over her mouth to muffle her laughter, but she wasn't even laughing. She wasn't even smiling. "Because I don't," I whispered, "want to make the ghosts jealous." "This isn't about you," said Gary. "This is about me and my burden of dreams." "I know, Gary." "I know you know," said Gary. He picked a few leaves off the tin can and handed them to me. I put them in my mouth, chewed, and swallowed. A month later I was pregnant.

I stayed on the set until my husband, the black man, came to pick me up.

There once was a very old man with large gray eyes who collected all the fairy tales in the whole wide world. He put them in a large sack, and carried the sack from village to village. Some believed the sack to be filled with gold, others bones, but all were too afraid to ask. I know this because the very old man with large gray eyes is my great-great-grandfather. He left me this sack when he died. For many years I would not open it. I hung the sack from a tree in my yard. At first it swung drowsily, but the years turned the sack savage and soon it whipped around even when the air was still. Little yellow teeth began to poke through. It was not until my seventy-seventh birthday that I opened the sack. What was inside will not astonish you: glass coffins, the belly of the big bad wolf, ovens, forests, magic mirrors, men caught inside beasts, and frogs, and cats, hundreds of shoes, and a glittering sea. At the very bottom of the sack was a girl who had once, long, long ago in a land far away, become pregnant by swallowing a rose petal. I asked her who she was. "Before the sack?" she asked. "Yes," I said, "before the sack." She told me that before the sack she lived inside a fairy tale called "The Young Slave" by Giambattista Basile. I believed her because

she was pretty and sad. "Do you want to know," she asked, "what all the things inside the sack filled with fairy tales are like?" "Very much," I said. She brought my hand to her belly. "They are like home." "Home?" I asked. I felt confused. "Containers," she said. "Either we are inside or we are outside." "Who?" I asked. "Us," she said. "The figures"—she blushed—"of fairy tales. Either we are inside . . ." She climbed inside the sack. "Or we are outside." She climbed back out. "It is like in your story 'My Brother Gary Made a Movie and This Is What Happened,' how you are outside the heap." "It's not really me," I said. "Exactly," she said. "You are outside of you." I looked at my story. "Gary's head is inside the paper bag!" "Now you're catching on," she said. "Even the moobie is a container," explained the girl. "Because Gary is trying to capture the Holocaust?" I asked. "Exactly," said the girl, who was both pretty and sad. "Fairy tales are about questions of belonging, and Mouse does not belong." "Me?" I asked. "Yes, Mouse," said the girl, "you." "Because I married a black man?" I asked. "This is not about you," said the girl. "Oh, right," I said. The girl handed me a rose petal. I put it in my mouth, chewed, and swallowed. Nine months later I gave birth to a very old man with large gray eyes.

—SOM

AIMEE BENDER

The Color Master

OUR STORE WAS EXPENSIVE, I MEAN EX-PEN-SIVE, AS ANYTHING would be if all its requests were clothing in the colors of natural elements. The Duke's son wanted shoes the color of rock, so he could walk in the rock and not see his feet. He was vain that way, he did not like to see his feet. He wanted to appear, from a distance, as a floating pair of ankles. But rock, of course, is many colors. It's subtle, but it is not just one plain gray, that I can promise, and in order to truly blend in, it would not do to give the Duke a regular pair of lovely pure gray-dyed shoes. So, we had to trek over as a group to his dukedom, a three-day trip, and take bagfuls of the rocks back with us, the rocks he would be walking on, and then use those, at the studio, as guides. I spent five hours, one afternoon, just staring at a rock, trying to see into its color scheme. Gray, my head kept saying. I see gray.

At the shop, in general, we built clothing and shoes, soles and heels, shirts and coats; we treated the leather, shaped and wove the cloth, and even when an item wasn't ordered as a special request, one pair of shoes or one robe might cost as much as a pony or a month's food from the market stalls. Most villagers did not have this kind of money so the bulk of our customers were royalty, or the occasional traveler riding through town who had heard rumors of our skills. For this pair, for the Duke, all of us tailors and shoemakers, who numbered about twelve, were working round the clock. One man had the idea to grind bits of rock into particles, and then he added those particles to the dye washing bin. This helped, a little. We attended visualization seminars, where we tried to imagine what it was like to be a rock, and then, quietly, after an hour of deep thought and breathing, returned to our desks and tried to insert that imagery into our choices about how long to leave the shoes in the dye bath. We felt the power of the mountain, in the rock, and let that play a subtle subtextual role. And then, once the dye had reached ultimate power, and once the shoes were a beautiful pure gray, a rocky gray, but still gray, we summoned the Color Master.

She lived about a half mile away. In a cottage, behind the scrubby oak grove. We summoned her by sending off a goat down the lane, because she did not like to be disturbed by people, and the goat would trot down the road and butt on the door as her cue. She'd set up our studio and shop, in the first place, years ago; she does the final work. But the Color Master has been looking unwell these days. For our last project, the Duchess's handbag, which was supposed to look like a just-blooming rose, she wore herself out thinking about pink, and was in bed for weeks after, recovering, which had never happened before. Pink, she kept saying, as she tossed around, in her bed. Birth, sex, blushes, kisses. She had a very high fever, and lost too much weight. Dark circles ringed her eyes. Also her younger brother suffers from terrible back problems and cannot move or work and lives with her, on the sofa, all day long. Also she is growing older, and she is certainly the most talented in the kingdom and gets zero recognition. We, the tailors and shoemakers, we know of her gifts, but does the King? Do the townsfolk? She walks among them, like an ordinary being, shopping for tomatoes, and no one knows that the world she's seeing is about a thousand times more detailed than the world anyone else is looking at. When you see a tomato, like me, you probably see a very nice red orb with a green stem, smelling fresh and delectable, with a gentle give to the touch. When she sees a tomato, she sees blues and browns and yellows and curves, and the vine it came on, and she can probably even guess how many seeds are in a given tomato based on how heavy it feels in her hand.

So, we sent over the goat, and when she came into the studio, with the goat, we'd just finished the fourth dying of the rock shoes. They were drying on a mat, and they looked pretty good. I told Cheryl that her visualization of the mountain had definitely helped, because it was a deeper, stronger gray than I'd expected. Cheryl blushed. She's one of the nicer ones. I said, too, that Edwin's addition of the rocks to the dye had added a useful kind of rough texture. He kicked a stool leg, pleased. I hadn't done much; I'm not the most skilled, but I like to commend good work when I see it. But the thing is, even with all our hard work, with all our deepening, they still looked like really beautiful gray shoes. The kind any normal person would love, if they didn't have this curious vanity about vanishing feet.

The Color Master walked in, wearing a linen sheath woven with blue threadings. Her face hinting at gaunt. She greeted us all by nodding, and stood at the counter where the shoes were drip-drying.

Very nice work, she said. Esther, who had fronted the dying process, curtsied.

We sprinkled rocks into the dye, she said.

A fine choice, said the Color Master.

Edwin did a little dance in place, over at his table.

The goat settled on a pillow in the corner, and began to eat the stuffing.

The Color Master rolled her shoulders a few times, and when the shoes were dry, she laid her hands upon them. She lifted them up, to the sunlight. She picked up a rock, next to the shoe, and looked at the rock, in the light, next to the shoe. She circled both, inside different light rays. Then she went to the palette area and took out a handful of blue dust. We have about 150 metal bins of this dust, in a range of colors. The bins stand side by side, running the perimeter of the studio. They are narrow, so we can fit a whole lot of colors, and if someone brings in a new color, we hammer down a new bin and slide it into the spectrum, wherever it fits. One tailor found an amazing deep burgundy off in the driest part of the forest, on a series of leaves; I located, once, a type of dirt that was a deeper brown than sand but not like rich mud, over by the reddish iron deposits near the lake. Someone else found a new blue, in a dried-out pansy flower, and another in the feathers of a dead bird. We have instructions to hunt for color everywhere, at all times. The Color Master toured the room, and then took that handful of blue dust (and always, when I watch, I am thrilled— blue? How does she know, blue? It was a darkish blue, too, seemingly far too dark for shoes this light, unless he wanted wet rock shoes) and she rubbed the dust into the shoe. Back to the bins and then she got a black, a dusty black, and then some sage green. All rubbed into the gray shoe. While she worked everyone stood around, quiet. We dropped our usual drudgery and chit-chat.

The Color Master worked swiftly, but she added, usually, something on the level of forty colors, so the process, even quickly, took more than two hours. She added a color here, a color there, sometimes at the size of salt particles, and the gray in the shoe shifted and shaded under her hands. She would reach a level and ask for sealant and Esther would step forward and the CM would coat the shoe to seal in the colors and then return to the sunlight, holding a shoe up, with the rock in her other hand. This went on for about four rounds. I swear, I could start to feel the original mountain's presence, in the room, the great heavy lumbering voice of it.

When she was done, the pair was so gray, so rock-like, you could hardly believe they were made of leather at all. They looked as if they had been sheared straight from the craggy mountainside.

Done, she said.

We circled her, bowing our heads.

Beautiful, I said.

Another triumph, murmured Sandy, next to me, who cannot color-mix to save her life.

The Color Master swept her gaze around the room, and her eyes rested on each of us, searching, slowly, until they finally settled on me. Me?

Will you walk me home? she said, in a deep voice, while Esther tied an invoice to the foot of a pigeon and then threw it out the window in the direction of the dukedom.

I would be honored, I said. I took her arm. The goat, full of pillow, tripped along behind us.

I am a quiet sort, except for the paying of compliments, and I didn't know if I should ask her anything on the walk. As far as I knew, she didn't usually ask for an escort home at all. Mainly I just looked at all the stones and rocks on the path, and for the first time saw that blue hint, and the blackness, and the shades of green, and that faint edge of purple if the light hit just so. She seemed relieved that I wasn't asking questions, so much so that it occurred to me that that was probably why she'd asked me to walk her home in the first place.

At her door, she fixed her eyes on me: gray, steady, aging at the corners. She was almost twice my age, but had always had a sexiness I'd admired. A way of holding her body that let you know there was a body there, but that it was private, that stuff happened on it, in it, to it, but it was stuff I would never see. It made me sad, seeing that, while also knowing about her husband who had gone off to the war years ago, and had never returned, and how it was difficult for her to have people over because of her brother with the bad back, and how long ago she had fled her own town for a reason she never spoke of, plus she had a thick cough and her own money issues, which seemed so unfair when she should've been living in the palace, as far as I was concerned.

Listen, she said. She held me in her gaze.

Yes?

There's a big request coming in, she said. I've heard rumors. Big. Huge.

What is it? I said.

I don't know yet. But start preparing. You'll have to take over. I will die soon, she said.

Excuse me?

Soon, she said. I can feel it, brewing. Death. It's not dark, nor is it white. It's almost a blue-purple, she said. Her eyes went past me, to the sky.

I will do my best, she said. I will do a fair bit of prep. But start preparing your color skills, Missy.

She lowered her brow, and her look was stern.

My name is Patty, I said.

She laughed.

How do you know? I said. Do you mean it? Are you ill?

No, she said. Yes. I mean it. I'm asking for your help, she said. And when I die, it will be your job to finish.

But I'm not very good, I said. Like at all. You can't die. You should ask Esther, or Hans—

You, she said, and with a little curt nod, she went into her house, and shut the door.

The Duke's son loved his shoes so much he sent us a drawing, by the court illustrator, of him, in them, floating, it appeared, on a pile of rocks. I love them, he said, in swirly handwriting, I love them, I love them! And then he added a small cash bonus, including horse rides, and a feast at the dukedom. We all attended, in all our finery, and it was a great time. It was the last time I saw the Color Master dancing, in her pearl-gray gown, and I knew it was the last, even as I watched it, her hair swirling out as she glided through the group. The Duke kept tapping his toe on the side, holding the Duchess's hand, her free one grasping a handbag the perfect pink of a rose, so vivid and fresh it seemed to carry over a sweet scent, even across the ballroom.

Two weeks later, almost everyone was away when the King's courtier came riding over with the request: a dress the color of the moon.

The Color Master was not feeling well, and had asked not to be disturbed; Esther's father was ill, so she was off taking care of him; Hans's wife was giving birth to twins, so he was off with her; the two others ahead of me had caught whooping cough, and someone else was on a travel trip to find a new shade of orange. So the request, written on a scroll, went to me, the apprentice. Just as the Color Master had hoped.

I unrolled the scroll and read it quietly by the window.

A dress the color of the moon?

It was impossible.

First of all, the moon is not a color. It is a reflection of a color. Second, it is not even the reflection of a color. It is the reflection of what appears to be a color, but is really in fact a bunch of bursting hydrogen atoms, far far away. Third, the moon shines. A dress cannot shine like the moon, unless the dress is also reflecting something, and reflective materials are generally tacky-looking, or too industrial. Our only options were silk and cotton and leather. The moon? It is white, it is silver, it is silver-white, it is not an easy color to dye. A dress the color of the moon? The whole thing made me irritable.

But this was not a small order. This was, after all, the King's daughter. The Princess. And, since the Queen had died a few months before, of pneumonia, this was now a dress for the most important woman in the kingdom.

I paced several times around the studio, and I went against policy and tried knocking on the door of the Color Master's cabin, but she called out, in a strong voice, from a window, Just do it! Are you okay? I asked, and she said, Come back once you've started!

I walked back, kicking twigs and acorns.

I ate a few oranges off the tree out back, until I felt a little better.

Since I was in charge, due to the pecking-order issue, I gathered together everyone who was left in the studio, and asked for a seminar on reflection, to reflect upon reflection. In particular for Cheryl, who really used the seminars well. Those of us who were there gathered in a circle in the side room, and we talked about mirrors, and still water, and wells, and feeling understood, and opals, and then we did a creative writing exercise about our first memory of the moon, and how it affected us, and the moment when we realized it followed us (Sandy had a charming story about going on a walk as a child and trying to lose it but not being able to), and then we wrote haiku. Mine was this: Moon, you silver thing/Floating in the sky like that/Make me a dress. Please.

After a few tears over Edwin's story of realizing his father in the army was seeing the same moon he saw, from home, we drifted out of the seminar room and began dying the silk. It had to be silk, of course, and we selected a very very fine weave, a really elegant one from the loom studio that had a touch of shimmer in the fabric already. I let Cheryl start the dying with shades of white, on the silk, because I could see a kind of shining light in her eyes, from the seminar. She is so receptive that way. When we did our series on bugs, I could practically spot the fighting ants in her pupils. Today, reflective light, in the irises, and even a luminosity to her skin. While she began that first layer, I went to see the Color Master again. She was in bed. It was shocking, how quickly she was going downhill. No one usually went over there but I let myself in, got her brother a glass of water and an apple/cheese snack—Angel, he called me—and then I settled next to the bed where she lay resting, her hair spread over the pillows in rays of silver. She was not very old, the Color Master, but she had gone silver early. Wait, can we use your hair? I said.

Sure. She didn't seem bothered by my presence, and pulled out a few strands and handed them over. This'll help, I said, looking at the glint. If we try to make this into particles?

Good, she said. Good thinking.

How are you doing? I asked.

Moon today, sun soon, she said. I heard word.

What?

Sun soon. How goes moon?

It's hard, I said. I mean, hard. And, with your hair, that'll help, but to reflect?

Use blue, she said.

What kind?

Several kinds, she said. Her voice was weaker, but I could hear the steel behind it, as she walked through the bins in her mind.

The pale blue, but don't be afraid of the darker blue. Never be afraid of the darker colors.

I'm a terrible color mixer, I said. Are you in pain?

No, she said. Just weak. The moon is easier than you think, she said. Blue, and then black, to provide shading.

On the dress? Black?

A tiny bit, she said. She pulled out a few more strands of hair. Here, she said. And, she said, shavings of opal, do we have those?

Too expensive, I said.

Go to the mine, she said. There are always shavings there. Get opals, shave 'em, add to the mix, a new bin. An opalescent bin. Do you know the king wants to marry his daughter? Her eyes flashed, for a second, with anger.

What?

Put that in the dress, too, she said. She dropped her voice to a whisper, every word sharp and clear. Anger, she said. Put anger in the dress. The moon, as our guide. A daughter should not be ordered to marry her father, she said.

Put anger in the dress?

When you mix, she said. Got it? When you're putting the opal shavings in? The dress is supposed to be a dowry gift, but give the daughter the strength to leave instead. All right?

Her eyes were shining at me, so bright I wanted to put them in the dress, too. Okay, I said, faltering. I'm not sure—

You have it in you, she said. I see it. Truly. Or I would never have given you the job.

Then she fell back on her pillows and was asleep in seconds, exhausted.

On the walk back, through the scrubby oak grove, I felt as I usually felt, both moved and shitty. Because what she saw in me could just as easily have been the result of some kind of fever. Was she hallucinating? Didn't she realize I had gotten the job only because I'd complimented Esther on her scarf at the faire, plus I always took out the trash on time? Who's to say that there was anything to it? To me, really?

Anger in the dress?

I didn't feel angry, just defeated and bad about myself, but I didn't put that in the dress, it didn't seem fair to anyone. Instead I went to the mine and befriended the head miner, Manny, who I knew a little from my cousin who had worked there awhile back to make some extra cash, and Manny gave me a handful of opals that were too small for any jewelry and would work well as shavings. I spent the afternoon with the sharpest picks and awls I could find, breaking open opals and making a new bin for the dust. Cheryl had done wonders with the white, and the dress was like a gleaming pearl—almost moonlike but not enough, yet. I added the opals and we re-dyed, and then you could see a hint of rainbow, hovering below the surface. Not so moonlike, but still somehow good, like the sun was shimmering in there, too, and that was addressing the reflective issue. When it came time to color-mix I felt like I was going to throw up, but I did what she'd asked, and went for blue, then black, and I was incredibly slow, like incredibly slow, but for one moment, I felt something, as I hovered over the bins of blue. I just felt a tug of guidance from the white of the dress, and it led my hand to the middle blue. It felt, for a second, like harmonizing in a choir, the moment where the voice sinks into the chord structure and the sound becomes larger, more layered and full than it had been before. So that was the right choice. Wasn't so on the mark for the black, which was slightly too light, and seemed to make the moon more like the moon when it's just setting, when the light of day has already started to rise and encroach, which isn't the moon they wanted— they wanted black-of-night moon, of course. But when we held it up, in the middle of the room, there it was, moonlike—not as good as anything the CM had done, maybe one one-hundredth as good, but there was something in it that would pass the test of the assignment. Like, the King and Princess wouldn't collapse in awe, but they would be pleased, maybe even a little stirred. Color is nothing unless next to other colors, the Color Master told us, all the time. Color does not exist alone. And I got it, for a second, with that blue, I did.

Cheryl and I packed the dress carefully in a box, and sent off the pigeon with the invoice, and waited for the King's courtiers to come by, and they did, with a carriage for the dress only, and we laid it carefully on the velvet backseat, and they gave us a hunk of chocolate as a bonus, which Cheryl and I ate together in the side room, exhausted. Relieved. I went home and slept for twenty hours. I had put no anger in the dress; I remembered that when I woke up. Who can put anger in a dress when so focused on just making an acceptable moon feeling for the assignment? They didn't ask for anger, I said, showering, eating a few apples for breakfast. They asked for the moon, and I gave them something vaguely moonlike, I said, spitting toothpaste into the sink.

That afternoon, I went to see the Color Master to tell her all about it. I left out the absence of the anger, and she didn't ask. I told her I'd messed up on the black, and she laughed and laughed, from her bed. She liked hearing it. I told her about the moon being more of a morning moon. I told her what I'd felt at the blue, the feeling of the chord, and she picked up my hand. Squeezed it lightly, and smiled at me.

Death is glowing, she said. I can see it.

I felt a heaviness rustle in my chest. How long? I said.

A few weeks, I think, she said. The sun will come in soon. The Princess still has not left the castle.

But we need you, I said, and with effort, she squeezed my hand again. It is dark and glowing, she said, her eyes sliding over to lock onto mine. It is like loam, she said.

The sun? I said.

Tomorrow, she said. She closed her eyes.

At the studio, the absentees were returning, slowly, from their various tangents, but I'd received such good marks on the moon dress that I was assigned to the King's next order, because everyone felt a little jittery about the Color Master's absence and wanted to go with what/whoever seemed to work. And sure enough, when I got to work the next day, there was an elaborate thank-you note from the castle with a lot of praise for the moon dress, in this over-the-top fancy calligraphy, and a bonus bolt of fuchsia silk, and then the new assignment, for a dress the color of the sun. Esther told me congratulations. I did a few deep knee bends and got to work.

I liked that guy at the mine a little bit, the Manny guy, so I went back to ask about tourmaline, for the sun, even though it didn't really fit, color-wise, and I knew I wouldn't use any shavings. But we had a nice roast turkey lunch together in the sunspot outside the rocky opening of the cave, and I told him about the dress I was making for the Princess. Sun, he said, shaking his head. What color *is* the sun? Beats me, I said. We're not supposed to look at it, right? All kids make it yellow, I said, but I think that's not quite right.

Ivory? he said.

Sort of burned white, I said. But with a halo?

That's hard work, he said, folding up his sandwich paper. He had a nice face to him, something chunky in his nose that I could get behind; it made him into the kind of guy you'd want to call on in an emergency.

Yours, too, I said. His hands were rough from pulling at the walls for years.

Want to go to the faire sometime? he asked. The outdoor faire happened on the weekends, in the main square, where everything was sold.

Sure, I said.

Maybe there's some sun stuff there, he said.

I'd love to, I said.

We began the first round of dying at the end of the week, focusing initially on the pale yellows. Cheryl was very careful not to overly yellow the dye—yellow is always more powerful than it appears in the bin. It is a stealth dominator, and can take days and days to undo. She did that all Saturday, while I went to the faire. It was a clear warm afternoon, and the faire offered all sorts of goodies and a delicious meat pie. Nothing looked helpful for the dress, but Manny and I laughed about the latest tapestry unicorn craze and shared a nice kiss at the end, near the scrubby oaks. Everything was feeling a little more alive than usual. We held another seminar at the studio, and Cheryl did a session on warmth, and seasons, and how we all revolved around the sun. Central, she said. The theme of the sun is central. The center of us, she said. Core. Fire.

Careful with red, said the Color Master, when I went to visit. She was thinner and weaker, but her eyes were still coals. Her brother had gotten up to try to take care of her and had thrown out his back to the worst degree and was now in the medicine arena, strapped to a board. My sister is dying, he told the doctors, but he couldn't move, so all they did was shake their heads together. The Color Master had refused any help. I want to see Death as clearly as possible, she'd said. No drugs. I made her some toast but she ate only a few bites and then pushed it aside.

It's tempting, to think of red, for sun, she said. But it has to be just a dash of red, not much. More of a dark orange, and a hint of brown. And then white on yellow on white.

White, I said. No, really?

Not bright white, she said. The kind of white that makes you squint, but in a softer way.

Yeah, I said, sighing. And where does one find that kind of white?

Keep looking, she said.

Last time I used your hair, for silver, I said.

She smiled, feebly. Go look at fire for a while, she said. Go spend some time with fire.

I don't want you to die, I said.

Yes, well, she said. And?

Looking at fire was interesting, I have to admit. I sat with a candle for a couple hours. It has these stages of color, the white, the yellow, the red, the tiny spot of blue I'd heard mentioned but never experienced. So I decided it made sense to use all of those in the dress: the white, the yellow, the red, a little spot of blue. We hung the dress in the center of the room and we all revolved around it, spinning, imagining we were planets and what did we need. It needs to be hotter, said Hans, who was playing the part of Mercury, and then he put a blowtorch to some silk and made some dust materials out of that and we re-dipped the dress. Cheryl was off in the corner, cross-legged in a sunspot, her eyes closed, trying to soak it up. We need to soak it! she said, standing. So we left it in the dipping longer than usual. I walked by the bins, trying to feel that harmony feeling, what could call me, or not call me. I felt a tug to the dark brown so I brought a bit of it out and tossed it in the mix, and it was too dark but with a little yellow-white from dried lily flowers, and something started to pop a bit. Light, said Cheryl. It's also daylight—it's light. It's our only true light, she said again. Without it, we live in darkness and cold. The dress drip-dried in the middle of the room, and it was getting closer, and just needed that factor of squinting—a dress so bright it couldn't quite be looked at. How to get that?

Remember, the Color Master said. She sat up, in bed. I keep forgetting, she said, but the King wants to Marry his Daughter, she said. Her voice pointed to each word, hard. That is not right, she said, okay? Got it? Put anger in the dress. Righteous anger. Do you hear me?

I do not, I said, though I nodded. I didn't say "I do not," I just thought that part. I played with the wooden knob of her bed frame. I had tried to put some anger in the sun dress, but I was so consumed with trying to factor in the squint that all I really got in there was confusion. I think the confusion was what made an onlooker squint more than the brightness. Confusion does make people squint though, so I ended up fulfilling the request accidentally. We had sent it off in the carriage, after working all night on the light factor that Cheryl had mentioned by adding bits of diamond dust to the mix. Diamonds are light inside darkness! she'd announced, at three A.M., with a bialy in her hand, triumphant. On the whole, it was a weaker product than the moon dress, but not bad—the variance in subtlety is unnoticed by most, and our level of general artistry and craft is high, so we could get away with a lot without anyone running over and asking for his money back.

The sky, the Color Master told me, after I had filled her in on the latest. She had fallen back down into her pillows, and was so weak she spoke with eyes closed. When I held her hand she only rested hers in mine: not limp, not grasping.

Sky is last, she said.

And death?

Soon, she said. She didn't move, with her hand on mine, and she fell asleep, midway through our conversation. I stayed all night. I slept, too, sitting up, and sometimes I woke and just sat and watched her, sleeping. What a very precious person she was, really. I hadn't known her very well, but she had picked me, for some reason, and that picking was changing me, I could feel it, and it was like being warmed by the presence of the sun, a little. The way a ray of sun can seem to choose you, as you walk outside from the cold interior. I wanted to put her in that sun dress, to drape her in it, but it wasn't an option; we had sent it off to the princess and it wasn't even the right size and wasn't really her style, either. But I guess I just knew that the sun dress we sent was something of a facsimile, and this person here was the real sun, the real center for us all, and even through the dark night, I felt the light of her, burning, even in the rasping breathing of a dying woman.

In the morning, she woke up, saw I was still there, and smiled a little. I brought her tea. She sat up to drink it.

The anger! she said, as if she had just remembered. Which maybe she had. She raised up on her elbows, face blazing. Don't forget to put anger in this last dress, she said. Okay?

Drink your tea, I said.

Listen, she said. It's important, she said. The King wants to marry his own daughter. She shook her head. It was written, in pain, all over her forehead. It is wrong, she said. She sat up higher, on her elbows. She looked beyond me, through me, and I could feel meaning, thick, in her. She picked her words carefully.

You cannot bring it into the world, and then bring it back into you, she said. It is the wrong action, she said.

Her face was clear of emphasis, and she spoke plainly, as plainly as possible, as if there were no taboo about fathers marrying daughters, as if the sex factor were not a biological risk, as if it weren't just disturbing and upsetting as a given. She held herself steady, on her elbows. This is why she was the Color Master. There was no stigma, or judgment, no societal subscription, no trigger morality, but just a clean and pure anger, fresh, as if she were thinking the possibility over for the first time.

You birth someone, she said. Leaning in. You birth someone, she said. And then you release her. You do not marry her, which is a bringing back in. You let her go.

Put anger in the dress, she said. She gripped my hand, and suddenly all the weakness was gone, and she was right there, an electric pulse of a person, and I knew this was the last time we would talk, I knew it so clearly that everything sharpened into incredible focus.

I could see the threads of the weave of her nightgown, the microscopic bright cells in the whites of her eyes.

Her nails bit into my hand. I felt the tears rising up in me. The teacup wobbling on the nightstand.

Got it? she said.

Yes, I said.

I put the anger in the dress, the color of sky. I put it in there so much I could hardly stand it—that she was about to die, that she would die unrecognized, that none of us would ever live up to her and that we were the only witnesses. That we are all so small after all that. That everybody dies anyway. I put the anger in there so much that the blue of the sky was fiercely stark, an electric blue like the core of the fire, so much that it was hard to look at. It was much harder to look at than the sun dress; the sky dress was of a whole different order. Intensely, shockingly, bluely vivid. Let her go? This was the righteous anger she had asked for, yards of it, bolts of it, even though, paradoxically, it was anger I felt because soon she would be gone.

She died the following morning, in her sleep. Even at her funeral, all I could feel was the rage, pouring out of me, while we all stood around her coffin, crying, leaning on one another, sprinkling colors from the dye bins into her hands, the colors of heaven, we hoped, while the rest of the town went about its business. Her brother rolled in on a stretcher, weeping. I had gone over to see her that morning, and found her, dead, in her bed. So quiet. The morning sun, white and clear, through the windowpanes. I stroked her hair down for an hour, her silver hair, before I left to tell anyone. The dress request had already come in, the day before, as predicted.

At the studio, under deadline, Cheryl led a seminar on blue, and sky, and space, and atmosphere, and depth, and it was successful and mournful, especially during the week after the funeral. Blue. I attended but mostly I was nurturing the feeling in me, that rage. Tending to it like a little flame candle, cupped against the wind. I knew it was the right kind, I knew it. I didn't think I'd do much better than this dress, ever; I would go on to do good things in my life, have other meaningful moments, share in the experience of being a human being in the world, but I knew this was my big moment, and I had to be equal to it. So I sat at the seminar with half a focus, just cupping that candle flame of rage, and I half-participated in the dying of the fabric and the discussion of the various shades, and then, when they had done all they could do, and the dress was hanging in the middle, a clear and beautiful blue, I sent everyone home. Are you sure? Cheryl asked, buttoning up her coat. Go, I said. Yes. It was night, and the blue sky was unlit, and it was a new moon, so it was up to me to find the blue sky in here, only. It was draped over us all, but hidden. I went to the bins, and listened for the chords, and felt her in me. I felt the ghost of her, passing through me, as I mixed and dyed, and I felt the rage in me, that she had to be a ghost: the softness of the ghost, right up next to and surrounding the sharp and burning core of my anger. Both guided my hands. I picked the right colors to mix with blue, a little of so many other colors and then so many different kinds of blue and gray and more blue and more. And in it all, the sense of shaking my fists, at the sky, shaking my fists high up to the sky because that is what we do, when someone dies too early, too beautiful, too undervalued by the world, or sometimes just at all, we shake our fists at the sky, the vast sky, the big blue beautiful indifferent sky, and the anger is righteous and strong and helpless and huge. I shook and I shook, and I put all of it into the dress.

When the sun rose, it was a clear morning, the early sky pale and wide. I had worked all night. I wasn't tired yet but I could feel the pricklings of it, around me, peripheral. I made a pot of coffee and sat in the chill with a cup and the dress, which I had hung again from a hanger in the middle of the room. The rest of the tailors drifted over in the morning, one by one, and no one said anything. They entered the room and looked up, and then they surrounded it with me, and we held hands and they said I was the new Color Master, and I said okay, because it was obvious that that was true, even though I knew I would never reach her levels again, but at least, for this one dress, I did. They didn't even praise me, they just looked at it and cried. We all cried.

Esther sent off the invoice pigeon, and with care, we placed the dress into its package, and when the carriage came by, we laid it carefully over the backseat, as usual. Manny came by right before the carriage left, and he looked at an edge of fabric to see the color as we were packing it up, and he held me close. We ate our hunk of gift chocolate. We cleaned up the area around the bins, and swept the floor of dust, and talked to a builder, a friend of Manny's, about expanding one of the rooms into an official seminar studio. The carriage trotted off, with the dress in the backseat, led by two white horses.

From what I heard, soon after the Princess got the third dress, she left town. The rest I do not know.

The rest of the story—known, I'm told, as "Donkeyskin"—is hers.

I read "Donkeyskin" many times as a kid, and what I loved most were those dresses. Inside an unsettling, provocative story—the king marrying his daughter?—was the universe revealed in fabric. What would it look like, a dress the color of the moon? It seemed this princess, in having dresses that seemed to go way beyond anything one might wear to a regular ball, was dabbling in something bigger, or had a connection to something truly magical in the kingdom. Who were these tailors and seamstresses? I didn't think about any of this directly, but the pull to read and reread the story often had to do with the breathlessness I felt, imagining a dress the color of the sky. Which sky? Blue-sky day, or cloudy day? A cumulus cloud boa or a nimbus collar?

I feel the same when watching movies of deep-sea fish. Their unusual shapes and colors, which often do seem to resurface in fashion—ruffles that look like a kind of coral, or capes that seem to be taken straight from the black sweep of a manta ray. Clothing that reflects nature. It was great fun to spend time thinking about how those colors happened because it had to be difficult. No way that dress was just an ordinary blue.

—AB

MARJORIE SANDOR

The White Cat

IN THE STORIES YOU LIKED BEST AS A CHILD, MY LOVE, THERE WAS always a terrible repetition of tests. The hero, in order to win a wife and make his fortune, set out full of confidence to retrieve some object not even precious to himself. He was driven by the father-king who, facing the wobbling end of his reign, was in an unusually selfish, wheedling mood. And, let's face it, this father had never been a noble fellow: forever trying to steal a kingdom, or defend his own against imagined enemies.

Three times the hero plunges back into the unknown world he has by dream or accident discovered, where the treasure—coveted by the king, whose hungers are unconscious and therefore impossible to sate—lies surrounded by obstacle, tedium, dragon. Three times he plunges in, three times risks his life to get the prize: first it's the golden apple; second, the magical linen woven of thread so fine the whole cloth can pass through the smallest needle; and at last, the tiniest dog in the world, who can be heard barking inside a corn kernel, itself enclosed in a walnut shell.

The trouble is, in that other world, there appears someone more alluring than the object of the quest, for instance a beautiful white cat who begs the hero to stay—without words, of course. Please stay. Take the treasure back to the king, but come back. I need you here. I am forbidden to say why.

The mystery of the white cat's need, not to mention her startlingly human beauty and intelligence, is far more deep and fulfilling and morally necessary than the foolish king's demand for a golden some-thing-or-other. It in fact turns the quest trivial, wrong, and inconse-quential.

With each successive journey it gets harder and harder to cross the border back to the king, the real world. The reward—wife and land and future fortune—goes dim, the whole thing revealed for what it is, a repetitive, pointless exercise, an exchange of commodities: golden apple for king's kingdom, princess-bride, etc. The taste of ashes in his mouth, the hero travels into middle age. Meanwhile, deep in the woods of his awakened imagination, the cat-queen, who can offer no mate-rial reward or even a logical reason why he should give up the world for her, waits helplessly by the midnight gates of her kingdom, bound by an ancient curse of silence, forbidden to ask favors or tell her story. Who is she? You don't know, but the prince's third and final return to his father's castle, with apple, linen, dog at last acceptable to the king, and the earthly reward achieved, always left you feeling hollow, incomplete.

By now the lost domain, with its caverns and balustrades, its pointed gates and absolute danger, had gotten hold of you.

Meanwhile, back in the king's palace, the elusive world is dismissed with shocking ease by courtiers and peasants alike. The prince himself is now bound by silence, too, his story trapped behind walls and briars and the hills in the distance, until, like the blurry cluster of the Pleiades, it is only visible when you gaze to the side.

But it's too late: your heart's been surprised, its true domain awak-ened. A domain that will haunt you until you go looking for it once more, on your own and without assignment, without hope that it will bring you anything useful in this world. Certainly it won't make your fortune. It will, in fact, destroy you, as far as the king and his courtiers are concerned. Is this the world you lean toward, the one you cannot reenter a fourth time without dying, without abandoning the life lived reasonably, dutifully, under the king? Do you fear that if you put your sword to that life, everything, including the white cat, your silenced queen, might turn to ash along with everything else?

In the fairy tales of your childhood, my love, recall that the hero never came to this pass. He stayed home after the third journey, ever dutiful, and was rewarded by the last-minute appearance of a girl, strangely familiar, but from another kingdom entirely. And in that same moment, the father-king is released from the terrible grasp of his desires. Who can say which is the greater miracle? Never mind: the kingdom rejoices.

You rejoice, too, but even at the height of celebration you suspect the truth. I do, too: I watch you sleeping. I know that when you look across the border in your dreams, you see her plainly there, the white cat lost in her castle, her woods, her kingdom, she of fantastic, inhuman dignity, forever awaiting rescue. Observe her closely: she is your own kerneled heart, woven of miraculous thread and thrice-protected from human view, she whose life will open like a palm on the day—please, God, far from now—of your death.

White cat, I am revealed for what I am: his human wife. Be patient. Keep by the gate as you must. Silent sufferer, cruelly bound, wait as we wait, but on the other side.

In my effort to reconstruct the making of this little piece, I went looking for our picture-book of "The White Cat," the elegant French fairy tale that inspired my retelling in the first place. It was, for a long time, my daughter's favorite bedtime story, but she is packing for college this week, and her room, for the first time in eighteen years, is miraculously spare. A few days ago she delivered a stack of children's books to a local used bookshop, and it is

*possible that for all her early passion for it, she let "The White Cat"
go—though she is just as baffled by its disappearance as I am. With
any luck, it is, as I write this, finding its way into the lap of another
child in this town.*

*It seems right that I can't find it. The picture-book—and the
writing of my piece—belong to a moment ten years ago, a moment
both remote and always near, not unlike a fairy tale.*

*My daughter was eight at the time, and we had just joined
households with the man I would marry six months later. Within
days of our moving in together, he collapsed, and underwent
double bypass surgery. Like the hero of "The White Cat," he
traveled back and forth between two worlds with courage and quiet
patience, and in the midst of my terror of losing him, I clung to the
notion that he was on a solitary journey, making his way back to
me. I could do nothing but wait, so I did what we do at such times:
I started a little story that turned into a love letter, and from there
into a prayer, a plea, a stay against death.*

—MS

Blue-bearded Lover

I.

WHEN WE WALKED TOGETHER HE HELD MY HAND UNNATURALLY HIGH, at the level of his chest, as no man had done before. In this way he made his claim.

When we stood at night beneath the great winking sky he instructed me gently in its deceit. The stars you see above you, he said, have vanished thousands of millions of years ago; it is precisely the stars you cannot see that exist, and exert their influence upon you.

When we lay together in the tall cold grasses the grasses curled lightly over us as if to hide us.

II.

A man's passion is his triumph, I have learned. And to be the receptacle of a man's passion is a woman's triumph.

III.

He made me his bride and brought me to his great house which smelled of time and death. Passageways and doors and high-ceilinged rooms and tall windows opening out onto nothing. Have you ever loved another man as you now love me? my blue-bearded lover asked. Do you give your life to me?

What is a woman's life that cannot be thrown away!

He told me of the doors I may unlock and the rooms I may enter freely. He told me of the seventh door, the forbidden door, which I may not unlock: for behind it lies a forbidden room which I may not enter. Why may I not enter it? I asked, for I saw that he expected it of me, and he said, kissing my brow, Because I have forbidden it.

And he entrusted me with the key to the door, for he was going away on a long journey.

IV.

Here it is: a small golden key, weighing no more than a feather in the palm of my hand.

It is faintly stained as if with blood. It glistens when I hold it to the light.

Did I not know that my lover's previous brides had been brought to this house to die?—that they had failed him, one by one, and had deserved their fate?

I have slipped the golden key into my bosom, to wear against my heart, as a token of my lover's trust in me.

V.

When my blue-bearded lover returned from his long journey he was gratified to see that the door to the forbidden room remained locked; and when he examined the key, still warm from my bosom, he saw that the stain was an old, old stain, and not of my doing.

And he declared with great passion that I was now truly his wife; and that he loved me above all women.

VI.

Through the opened windows the invisible stars exert their power.

But if it is a power that is known, are the stars invisible?

When I sleep in our sumptuous bed I sleep deeply, and dream dreams that I cannot remember afterward, of extraordinary beauty, I think, and magic, and wonder. Sometimes in the morning my husband will recall them for me, for their marvels are such they invade even his dreams. How is it that you of all persons can dream such dreams, he says—such curious works of art!

And he kisses me, and seems to forgive me.

And I will be bearing his child soon. The first of his many children.

The legend of Bluebeard and his horrific castle is the oldest of cautionary fairy tales for women: here is the nobleman who marries young, beautiful girls, uses them up, and murders them to make way for the next young, beautiful, naive bride; to each bride he issues a warning—there is a room in his castle which she may not enter. But when Bluebeard leaves on a journey, entrusting her with a key, the overly curious young woman invariably unlocks the door, and discovers the corpses of her predecessors.

Because she has disobeyed her husband and master, the young woman is murdered by him.

In my variant of this fairy tale, the "young, beautiful, naive bride" is really not naive. She is calculating, canny. She will outwit Bluebeard by obeying his instructions—as he doesn't expect her to—as if she were refuting the biblical Eve, who gave in to temptation. In this way, by totally succumbing to the rapacious male, the young woman "conquers" him—she is the first of his brides to become pregnant, and will bear his child in a lineage that is a compromise with the age-old rapacity of man.

There is no love here, no romance—only a kind of cold, cynical sexual manipulation.

But out of this manipulation comes the possibility of female survival—and the bearing of children.

I did not mean my young-woman figure to be exemplary. She is not a "sister" to her predecessors—she knows that if she aligns herself with them, Bluebeard will murder her as he'd murdered them. "Blue-bearded Lover" is a cautionary tale of its own, a tragic little fable, from which the reader should recoil with a shudder— "Thank God I am not like that. I would never compromise with evil!"

—JCO

JOHN UPDIKE

Bluebeard in Ireland

"YES, THE PEOPLE ARE WONDERFUL," GEORGE ALLENSON HAD TO agree, there in Kenmare. His wife, Vivian, was twenty years younger than he, but almost as tall, with dark hair and decided, sharp features, and it placed the least strain on their marriage if he agreed with her assertions. Yet he harbored an inner doubt. If the Irish were so wonderful, why was Ireland such a sad and empty country? Vivian, a full generation removed from him, was an instinctive feminist, but to him any history of unrelieved victimization seemed suspect. Not that it wasn't astonishing to see the eighty-room palaces the British landlords had built for themselves, and touching to see the ruins—stone end walls still standing, thatched roofs collapsed—of the hovels where the Irish had lived, eaten their potatoes and drunk their whiskey, and died. Vivian loved the hovels, inexplicably; they all looked alike from the outside, and, when it was possible to enter a doorless doorway or peek through a sashless window-hole, the inside showed a muddy dirt floor, a clutter of rotting boards that might once have been furniture, and a few plastic or aluminum leavings of intruders like themselves.

Vivian could see he was unconvinced. "The way they use the language," she insisted, "and leave little children to run their shops for them."

"Wonderful," he agreed again. He was sitting with his, he hoped, not ridiculously much younger wife in the lounge of their hotel, before a flickering blue fire that was either a gas imitation of a peat fire or the real thing, Allenson wasn't sure. A glass of whiskey whose one ice cube had melted away added to his natural sleepiness. He had driven them around the Dingle Peninsula today in a foggy rain, and then south to Kenmare over a narrow mountain road from Killarney, Vivian screaming with anxiety all the way, and it had left him exhausted. After a vacation in Italy two years ago, he had vowed never to rent a foreign car with her again, but he had, in a place with narrower roads and left-handed drive. During the trickiest stretch today, over fabled Moll's Gap, with a Mercedes full of gesturing Germans pushing him from behind, Vivian had twisted in her seat and pressed her face against the headrest rather than look, and sobbed and called him a sadistic fiend.

Afterwards, safely delivered to the hotel parking lot, she complained that she had twisted so violently her lower back hurt. What he resented most about her attacks of hysteria was how, when she recovered from them, she expected him to have recovered, too. For all her feminism she still claimed the feminine right to meaningless storms of emotion, followed by the automatic sunshine of male forgiveness.

As if sensing the sulky residue of a grudge within him, and determined to erase it, she flashed there by the sluggish fire an impeccable smile. Her lips were long and mobile but thin and sharp, as if—it seemed to him in his drowsy condition, by the gassy flickering fire— her eyebrows had been duplicated and sewn together at the ends to make a mouth. "Remember," she said, offering to make a memory of what had occurred mere hours ago, "the lady shopkeeper out there beyond Dingle, where I begged you to stop?"

"You in*sis*ted I stop," he corrected. She had said that if he didn't admit he was lost she would jump out of the car and walk back. How could they be lost, he had argued, with the sea on their left and hills on their right? But the sea was obscured by fog and the stony hills vanished upward into rain clouds and she was not persuaded; at last he had slammed on the brakes. Both of them had flounced out of the car. The dim-lit store looked empty, and they had been about to turn away from the door when a shadow materialized within, beyond the lace curtains—the proprietress, emerging from a room where she lived, waiting, rocking perhaps, watching what meagre channels of television reached this remoteness. He had been surprised, in southwestern Ireland, by how little television there was to watch, and by the sound of Gaelic being spoken all about him, in shops and pubs, by the young as well as the old. It was part of his own provincialism to be surprised by the provincialism of others; he expected America, its language and all its channels, to be everywhere by now.

This was indeed a store; its shadowy shelves held goods in cans and polyethylene packets, and a cloudy case held candies and newspapers bearing today's date. But it was hard for the Allensons to see it as anything but a stage cleverly set for their entrance and exit. The village around them seemed deserted. The proprietress—her hair knotted straight back, her straight figure clad in a dress of nunnish gray—felt younger than she looked, like an actress tricked out in bifocals and a gray rat, and she described the local turnings as if in all her years on a cliff above the sea she had never before been asked to direct a pair of tourists. There was a grave ceremoniousness to the occasion that chastened the fractious couple. To pay her for her trouble, they bought a copy of the local newspaper and some bags of candy. In Ireland, they had reverted to candy, which they ate in the car—Licorice Allsorts for him, for her chocolate-covered malt balls called Maltezers.

They had got back into the car enhanced by the encounter, the irritating currents between them momentarily quelled. Yet, even so, for all those theatrically precise directions, Allenson must have taken a wrong turning, for they never passed the Gallarus Oratory, which he had wanted to see. It was the Chartres of beehive chapels. In Ireland, the sights were mostly stones. Allenson found himself driving endlessly upward on the north side of the Dingle Peninsula, and needing to traverse the Slieve Mish Mountains to avoid Tralee, and being tailgated by the Germans on Moll's Gap, while Vivian had hysterics and he reflected upon the gaps between people, even those consecrated to intimacy.

He had had three wives. He had meant Vivian to see him into the grave, but unexpected resistances in her were stimulating, rather than lulling, his will to live. In his simple and innocent manhood he had taken on a swarming host of sexist resentments—men were incompetent (his driving in foreign lands), men were ridiculous (his desire to see, *faute de mieux*, old Ireland's lichened gray beehive huts, dolmens, menhirs, and ruined abbeys), men were lethal. Two years ago, out of sheer political superstition, this youthful wife had become furious in Gabriele D'Annunzio's estate above Lake Garda, all because the world-renowned poet and adventurer had enshrined himself and his thirteen loyal followers in matching sarcophagi, lifted up to the sun on pillars. Men were Fascists, this had led Vivian to realize. She proved to be violently allergic to history, and her silver-haired husband loomed to her as history's bearer. So he had, for their next trip abroad, suggested Eire, a land whose history was muffled in legend and ignominy. Just its shape on the map next to Great Britain's spiky upstanding silhouette, suggested the huddled roundness of a docile spouse.

"You insisted," he repeated, "and then we got lost anyway, and saw none of the sights. I missed the Gallarus Oratory."

Vivian brushed his resentful memory away, there by the hotel fire. "The whole countryside is the sight," she said, "and the wonderful people. Everybody knows that. And all day, with you jerking that poor Japanese compact this way and that like a crazy teenaged hood, I couldn't enjoy looking out. If I take my eyes off the map for an instant, you get lost. You're not getting me back into that car tomorrow, I tell you that."

Itching to give the fire a poke, he gave it to her instead. "Darling, I thought we were going to drive south, to Bantry and Skibbereen. Bantry House in the morning, and Creagh Gardens in the afternoon, with a quick lunch at Ballydehob." Allenson smiled.

"You're a monster," Vivian said cheerfully. "You really would put me through a whole day of you at the wheel on these awful roads? We're going to *walk*."

"Walk?"

"George, I talked it over with the man in the office, the assistant manager, while you were putting on a shirt and tie. He couldn't have been sweeter, and said what the tourists do in Kenmare is they take walks. He gave me a map."

"A map?" Another whiskey would sink him to the bottom of the sea. But would that be so bad? This woman was a talking nightmare. She had produced a little map, printed by photocopy on green paper, showing a pattern of numbered lines surrounding the phallic thrust of the Kenmare estuary. "I've come all this way to take a walk?" But there was no arguing. Vivian was so irrational that, because her predecessor wife had been called Claire, she had refused, planning the trip, to include County Clare, where the good cliffs and primitive churches were, and off whose shore part of the Spanish Armada had wrecked.

Next morning, the devil in him, prompted by the guidebook, could not resist teasing her. "Today's the day," he announced, "to drive the Ring of Bera. We can see the Ogham Stone at Ballycrovane, and if there's time take the cable car to Dursey Island, the only such wonder in this green and wondrous land. The blessed roadway meanders, it says here, through mountainous coastal areas providing panoramic views of both Bantry and Kenmare bays. A famous stone circle there is, and just two miles further, the ruins of Puxley's mansion! A mere hundred and forty kilometers, the entire ring is claimed to be; that's eighty-eight miles of purest pleasure, not counting the cable car."

"You must be out of your gourd," Vivian said, using one of those youthful slang expressions that she knew he detested. "I'm not getting back into any car with you at the wheel until we head to Shannon Airport. If then."

Allenson shrugged to hide his hurt. "Well, we could walk down-town to the local circle again. I'm not sure I grasped all the nuances the first time."

It had been charming, in a way. They had driven up a little cul-de-sac at the shabbier end of Kenmare and a small girl in a school jumper had been pushed from a house, while her mother and siblings watched from the window, and shyly asked for the fifty-pence admission. Then through a swinging gate and up a muddy lane the couple had walked, past stacks of roof tiles and a ditch brimming with plastic trash, arriv-ing at a small mown plateau where fifteen mismatched stones in a rough circle held their mute pattern. He had paced among them, try-ing to unearth in his atavistic heart the meaning of these pre-Celtic stones. Sacrifice. This must have been, at certain moments of heavenly alignment, a place of sacrifice, he thought, turning to see Vivian stand-ing at the ring's center in too vividly blue a raincoat.

"We're walking," she agreed with him, "but not back to those awful rocks that got you so excited, I'll never know why. It's *stupid* to keep looking at rocks somebody could have arranged yesterday for all we know. There are more of these supposedly prehistoric beehive huts today than there were a hundred years ago, the nice young man in the office was telling me yesterday. He says what sensible people who come to Kenmare do is take long walks."

"Who is this guy, that he's become so fucking big in my life suddenly? Why doesn't *he* take you for the walk, if that's what's on his mind?"

Did she blush? "George, *really*—he's young enough to be my son." This was an awkward assertion, made in the sweep of the moment. She could be the mother of a twenty-one-year-old, if she had been pregnant at nineteen; but in truth she had never borne a child, and when they were first married, and she was in her mid-thirties, she had hoped to have a child by him. But he had ogerishly refused; he had had enough children—a daughter by Jeaneanne, two sons by Claire. Now the possibility had slipped away. He thought of his present wife as racily younger than himself but her fortieth birthday had come and gone, and since the days when they had surreptitiously courted, in the flattering shadows of Claire's unknowing, Vivian's face had grown angular and incised with lines of recurrent vexation.

The young man in the office—a kind of rabbit hole around the corner from the key rack, in which the Irish staff could be heard scuffling and guffawing—was at least twenty-five, and may have been thirty, with children of his own. He was slender, black-eyed, milky-skinned, and impeccably courteous. Yet his courtesy carried a charge, a lilt, of mischief. "Yes, and walking is the thing in these parts— we're not much for the organized sports that are the custom in the States."

"We passed some golf courses, driving here," Allenson said, not really wanting to argue.

"Would you call golf organized?" the assistant manager said quickly. "Not the way I play it, I fear. As we say, it's an ungrateful way to take a walk."

"Speaking of walks—" Vivian produced her little green map. "Which of these would you recommend for my husband and me?"

With his bright-black eyes he looked from one to the other and then settled on looking at her, with a cock to his neatly combed head. "And how hardy a man would he be?"

Wifely to a fault, Vivian took the question seriously. "Well, his driving is erratic, but other than that he manages pretty well."

Allenson resented this discussion. "The last time I saw my doctor," he announced, "he told me I had beautiful arteries."

"Ah, I would have guessed as much," said the young man, looking him benignly in the face.

"We don't want to start him out on anything too steep," Vivian said.

"Currabeg might be your best option, then. It's mostly on the level road, with fine views of the Roughty Valley and the bay. Take an umbrella against the mist, along with your fine blue coat, and if he happens to begin to look poorly in the face you might hail a passing motorcar to bring the body in."

"Are we going to be walking in traffic?" She sounded alarmed. For all her assertiveness, Vivian had irritating pockets of timidity. Claire, Allenson remembered, drove on a motor scooter all over Bermuda with him, clinging to his midriff trustfully, twenty years ago, and would race with the children on bicycles all over Nantucket. Jeaneanne and he had owned a Ford Thunderbird convertible when they lived in Texas, and would commonly hit a hundred miles an hour in the stretch between Lubbock and Abilene, the top down and the dips in Route 84 full of watery mirages. He remembered how her hair, bleached blond in Fifties-style streaks, would whip back from her sweaty temples, and how she would hike her skirt up to her waist to give her crotch air, there under the steering wheel. Jeancanne had been tough, but her exudations had been nectar, until her recklessness and love of speed had carried her right out of Allenson's life. The loss had hardened him.

The assistant manager appeared to give Vivian's anxiety his solemn consideration; there was, in his second of feigned thought, that ceremonious touch of parody with which the Irish bring music to the most factual transactions. "Oh, I judge this off-time of year there won't be enough to interfere with your easiness. These are high country roads. You park at the crossing, as the map shows clearly, and take the two rights to bring you back."

Still, Allenson felt, their adviser felt some politely unspoken reservation about their undertaking. In their rented car, with its mirrors where you didn't expect them and a balky jumble of gears on the floor, while Vivian transparently tried to hold her tongue from criticism, he drove them out of Kenmare, past a cemetery containing famous holy wells, over a one-lane hump of a stone bridge, up between occluding hedgerows into the bare hills whose silhouettes, in the view from the Allensons' hotel room, were doubled by the mirroring sheen of the lakelike estuary. They met no other cars, so Vivian had less need to tense up than on the ring roads.

The map in her lap, she announced at last, "This must be the cross-roads." A modest intersection, with barely enough parking space for one car on the dirt shoulder. They parked in the space and locked the car. It was the middle of a morning of watery wan sunshine. A bite in the breeze told them they were higher than in Kenmare.

On foot they followed a long straight road, not as long and shimmering as the straightaways in Texas, yet with something of the same potential for mirage. They crossed a stream hidden but for its gurgle in the greenery. A house being built, or rebuilt, stood back and up from the road, with no sign of life. Land and houses must be cheap. Ireland had been emptying out for ages. Cromwell had reduced the Irish to half a million, but they had stubbornly bred back, only to be decimated by the potato famine two centuries later.

At first, Vivian athletically strode ahead, hungry for hovels and unspoiled views. She had brought new running shoes on the trip— snow-white, red-chevroned, bulky with the newest wrinkles of pedal technology. They were not flattering, but, then, compared with Jeane-anne's, this wife's ankles were rather thick. Her feet looked silly, under the hem of her bright-blue raincoat, flickering along the road surface, striped like birds. Where were the real birds? Ireland didn't seem to have many. Perhaps they had migrated with the people. Famines are hard on birds, but that had been long ago.

The hedgerows thinned, and after the invisible stream the road had a steady upward trend. He found himself overtaking his young wife, and then slowing his pace to match hers. "You know," she told him, "I really *did* twist my back in the car yesterday, and these new sneakers aren't all they were advertised. They have so much structure inside, my feet feel bullied. It's as if they keep pushing my hips out of alignment."

"Well," he said, "you could go barefoot." Jeaneanne would have. Claire might have. "Or we could go back to the car. We've gone less than a mile."

"That's all? I wouldn't *dream* of telling them at the hotel that we couldn't do their walk. This must be the first right turn already, coming up."

The T-crossing was unmarked. He looked at the green map and wished it weren't quite so schematic. "This must be it," he agreed, uncertainly, and up the road they went.

A smaller road, it continued the upward trend, through emptier terrain. Irish emptiness had a quality different from that of Texas emptiness, or that of the Scots Highland, where he and Claire had once toured. The desolation here was intimate. Domes of stone-littered grass formed a high horizon, under roiling clouds with brackish centers. There was little color in anything; he had expected greener grass, bluer sky. The landscape wore the dull chastened colors of the people in the towns. It was a shy, unassuming sort of desolation. "I suppose," Allenson said, to break the silence of their laborious walking, "all this was once full of farms."

"I haven't seen a single hovel," Vivian said, with a querulousness he blamed on her back.

"Some of these heaps of stone—it's hard to tell if a man or God, so to speak, put them there." Jeananne had been a liberated Baptist, Claire a practicing Episcopalian. Vivian was from a determinedly unchurched family of ex-Catholic scientists whose treeless Christmases and thankless Thanksgivings Allenson found chilling. Strange, he thought as he walked along, he had never had a Jewish wife, though Jewish women had been his best lovers—the warmest, the cleverest.

"It said in the guidebook that even up in the hills you could see the green places left by the old potato patches but I haven't seen a single one," Vivian complained.

Time passed wordlessly, since he declined to answer. He hadn't written the guidebook. The soles of their feet slithered and scratched.

Allenson cleared his throat and said, "You can see why Beckett wrote the way he did." He had lost track of how long their forward-plodding silence had stretched; his voice felt rusty. "There's an amazing amount of nothingness in the Irish landscape." On cue, a gap in the clouds sent a silvery light scudding across the tops of the dull hills slowly drawing closer.

"I *know* this isn't the road," Vivian said. "We haven't seen a sign, a house, a car, *any*thing." She sounded near tears.

"But we've seen *sheep*," he said, with an enthusiasm that was becoming cruel. "Hundreds of them."

It was true. Paler than boulders but no less opaque, scattered sheep populated the wide fields that unrolled on both sides of the road. With their rectangular purple pupils the animals stared in profile at the couple. Sometimes an especially buoyant ram, his chest powdered a startling turquoise or magenta color, dashed back among the ewes at the approach of these human intruders. Single strands of barbed wire reinforced the stone walls and rotting fences of an older pastoralism. Only these wires, and the pine poles bearing wires overhead, testified that twentieth-century people had been here before them. The land dipped and crested; each new rise revealed more sheep, more road. A cloud with an especially large leaden center darkened this lunar landscape and rained a few drops; by the time Vivian had put up their umbrella, the sprinkle had passed. Allenson looked around for a rainbow, but it eluded his vision, like the leprechauns promised yesterday at Moll's Gap, in the droll roadside sign LEPRECHAUN CROSSING.

"Where *is* that second right turn?" Vivian asked. "Give me back the map."

"The map tells us nothing," he said. "The way it's drawn it looks like we're walking around a city block."

"I *knew* this was the wrong road, I don't know *why* I let you talk me into it. We've gone miles. My back is killing me, damn you. I *hate* these bossy, clunky running shoes."

"You picked them out," he reminded her. "And they were far from cheap." Trying to recover a little kindness, Allenson went on, "The total walk is four and a half miles. Americans have lost all sense of how long a mile is. They think it's a minute of sitting in a car." Or less, Jeaneanne were driving, her skirt tucked up to air her crotch.

"Don't be so pedantic," Vivian told him. "I hate men. They grab the map out of your hands and never ask directions and then refuse to admit they're lost."

"Whom, my dear, would we have asked directions of? We haven't seen a soul. The last soul we saw was your cow-eyed pal at the hotel. I can hear them now, talking to the police. 'Ah, the American couple,' he'll be saying. 'She a mere raven-haired colleen, and he a grizzly old fella. They were headin' for the McGillycuddy Reeks, wi' scarcely a cup of poteen or a pig's plump knuckle in their knapsacks.'"

"Not funny," she said, in a new, on-the-edge voice. Without his noticing it, she had become frantic. There was a silvery light in her dark eyes, tears. "I can't walk another step," she announced. "I can't and I won't."

"Here," he said, pointing out a convenient large stone in the wall at the side of the road. "Rest a bit."

She sat and repeated, as if proudly, "I will not go another step. I can't, George. I'm in agony." She flipped back her bandanna with a decisive gesture, but the effect was not the same as Jeaneanne's gold-streaked hair whipping back in the convertible. Vivian looked old, worn. Lamed.

"What do you want me to do? Walk back and bring the car?" He meant the offer to be absurd, but she didn't reject it, merely thinned her lips and stared at him angrily, defiantly.

"You've got us lost and won't admit it. I'm not walking another step."

He pictured it, her never moving. Her body would weaken and die within a week; her skin and bones would be washed by the weather and blend into the earth like the corpse of a stillborn lamb. Only the sheep would witness it. Only the sheep were watching them now, with the sides of their heads. Allenson turned his own head away, gazing up the road, so Vivian wouldn't see the calm mercilessness in his face.

———

"Darling, look," he said, after a moment. "Way up the road, see the way the line of telephone poles turns? I bet that's the second right turn. We're on the map!"

"I don't see anything turning," Vivian said, but in a voice that wanted to be persuaded.

"Just under the silhouette of the second little hill. Follow the road with your eyes, darling." Allenson was feeling abnormally tall, as if his vision of Vivian stuck in the Irish landscape forever had a centrifugal force, spilling him outward, into a fresh future, toward yet another wife. What would she be like, this fourth Mrs. Allenson? Jewish, with a rapid, humorous tongue and heavy hips and clattering bracelets on her sweetly hairy forearms? Black, a stately fashion model whom he would rescue from her cocaine habit? A little Japanese, silken and fiery within her kimono? Or perhaps one of his old mistresses, whom he couldn't marry at the time, but whose love had never lessened and who was miraculously unaged? Still, in a kind of social inertia, he kept pleading with Vivian. "If there's no right turn up there, then you can sit down on a rock and I'll walk back for the car."

"How can you walk back?" she despairingly asked. "It'll take forever."

"I won't walk, I'll run," he promised. "I'll trot."

"You'll have a heart attack."

"What do you care? One male killer less in the world. One less splash of testosterone." Death, the thought of either of their deaths, felt exalting, in this green-gray landscape emptied by famine and English savagery. British soldiers, he had read, would break the roof-beams of the starving natives' cottages and ignite the thatch.

"I care," Vivian said. She sounded subdued. Seated on her stone, she looked prim and hopeful, a wallflower waiting to be asked to dance.

He asked, "How's your back?"

"I'll stand and see," she said.

Her figure, he noticed when she stood, had broadened since he first knew her—thicker in the waist and ankles, chunky like her aggravating shoes. And developing a bad back besides. As if she were hurrying to catch up to him in the aging process. She took a few experimental steps, on the narrow macadam road built, it seemed, solely for the Allensons' pilgrimage.

"Let's go," she said combatively. She added, "I'm doing this just to prove you're wrong."

But he was right. The road branched; the thinner piece of it continued straight, over the little hill, and the thicker turned right, with the wooden power poles. Parallel to the rocky crests on the left, with a view of valley on the right, the road went up and down in an animated, diverting way, and took them past houses now and then, and small plowed areas to vary the stony pastures. "You think those are potato patches?" he asked. He felt sheepish, wondered how many of his murderous thoughts she had read. His vision of her sitting there, as good as a corpse, kept widening its rings in his mind, like a stone dropped in black water. The momentary ecstasy of a stone smartly applied to her skull, or a piece of flint sharp as a knife whipped across her throat—had these visions been his, back in that Biblical wilderness?

Now, on the higher, winding road, a car passed them, and then another. It was Sunday morning, and unsmiling country families were driving to mass. Their faces were less friendly than those of the shopkeepers in Kenmare; no waves were offered, or invitations to ride. Once, on a blind curve, the couple had to jump to the grassy shoulder to avoid being hit. Vivian seemed quite agile, in the pinch.

"How's your poor back holding up? he asked. "Your sneakers still pushing your hips around?"

"I'm better," she said, "when I don't think about it."

"Oh. I'm sorry."

He should have let her have a baby. Now it was too late. Still, he wasn't sorry. Life was complicated enough.

The road turned the third right on their map gradually, unmistakably, while several gravelled driveways led off into the hills. Though

Kenmare Bay gleamed ahead of them, a tongue of silver in the smoky distance, they were still being carried upward, dipping and turning, ever closer to the rocky crests, which were becoming dramatic. The sheep, now, seemed to be unfenced; a ram with a crimson chest skittered down a rock face and across the road, spilling scree with its hooves. In what could have been another nation, so far away it now appeared, a line of minuscule telephone poles marked the straight road where Vivian had announced she would not move another step. Overhead, faint whistling signalled a hawk—a pair of hawks, drifting motionless near the highest face of rock, hanging in a wind the Allensons could not feel. Their thin hesitant cry felt forgiving to Allenson, as did Vivian's voice announcing, "Now I have this killing need to pee."

"Go ahead."

"Suppose a car comes?"

"It won't. They're all in church now."

"There's no place to go behind anything," she complained.

"Just squat down beside the road. My goodness, what a little fussbudget."

"I'll loose my balance." He had noticed on other occasions, on ice or on heights, how precarious her sense of balance was.

"No you won't. Here. Give me your hand and prop yourself against my leg. Just don't pee on my shoe."

"Or on my own," she said, letting herself be lowered into a squatting position.

"It might soften them up," he said.

"Don't make me laugh. I'll get urinary impotence." It was a concept out of Nabokov's *Pale Fire* that they both had admired, in the days when their courtship had tentatively proceeded through the socially acceptable sharing of books. She managed. In Ireland's great silence of abandonment the tender splashing sound seemed loud. *Pssshshshhlipip.* Allenson looked up to see if the hawks were watching. Hawks could read a newspaper, he had once read, from the height of a mile. But what would they make of it? The headlines, the halftones? Who could know what a hawk saw? Or a sheep? They saw only what they needed to see. A tuft of edible grass, or the twitch of a vole scurrying for cover.

Vivian stood, pulling up over the quick-glimpsed thicket of her pubic hair her underpants and pantyhose. A powerful ammoniac scent followed her up, rising invisible from the roadside turf. *Oh, let's have a baby*, he thought, but left the inner cry unexpressed. Too late, too old. The couple moved on, numbed by the miles that had passed beneath their feet. They reached the road's highest point, and saw far below, as small as an orange star, their Eurodollar Toyota compact, parked at a tilt on the shoulder of their first crossroads. As they descended on to it, Vivian asked, "Would Jeaneanne have enjoyed Ireland?"

What an effort it now seemed, to cast his mind so far back! "Jeaneanne," he answered, "enjoyed everything, for the first seven minutes. Then she got bored. What made you think of Jeaneanne?"

"You. Your face when we started out had its Jeaneanne look. Which is different from its Claire look. Your Claire look is sort of woebegone. Your Jeaneanne look is fierce."

"Darling," he told her. "You're fantasizing."

"Jeaneanne and you were so young," she pursued. "At the age I was just entering graduate school, you and she were married, with a child."

"We had that Fifties greed. We thought we could have it all," he said, rather absently, trying to agree. His own feet in their much-used cordovans were beginning to protest; walking downhill, surprisingly, was the most difficult.

"You still do. You haven't asked me if *I* liked Ireland. The Becketty nothingness of it."

"Do you?" he asked.

"I do," she said.

They were back where they had started.

*Charles Perrault's "Bluebeard" is sometimes interpreted as a tale
intended to prepare young women for the brutality and shock of
marriage. This theme is well served by the tale's goriness: it must
have both titillated and horrified its readers. However, many of the
bloodless contemporary variations of the tale, particularly this
version by the late John Updike, are just as powerful. Despite being
contemporary, educated, and clearly fond of each other, this couple
is nonetheless burdened by a frail institution demanding
concessions and secrets that, while not involving rooms full of
bloodied limbs, are still that harrowing in their own right. George
and Vivian's problem isn't that they don't love each other, but
rather that love doesn't invalidate the quiet darkness of every
marriage. Even when we choose our lovers, we are still at the mercy
of their interior lives, the place where they do the most living.*

—CGS

RABIH ALAMEDDINE

A Kiss to Wake the Sleeper

MOTHER ISSUED DIRECTIONS AND HER ASSISTANTS CLEANED. ONE scrubbed the floor and mopped, covering it with lye, and the other suctioned dust out of the living room. Mother fanned her magazines out on the coffee table, making sure that each title could be discerned at a glance. I had nothing better to do than witness.

I reached for my brush, combed and combed my hair, a ritual of untangling. "I'm a mess," I announced.

Mother hesitated, stopped what she was doing for only an instant. "I dislike that word."

"I am a mess."

"All right," she said. "You may be a mess, but you're clean. You're a clean mess."

"I'm a fine mess."

"Well, you're my mess," Mother said, "and today we're going to fix you," and she began washing her hands. She had a smile on her face, or maybe a grimace. You cannot decipher nuance through plastic.

I was a mess. I had SCID (no dirty jokes about skid marks, not that kind of mess—ha, ha), Severe Combined Immunodeficiency. No B cells, no T cells, nothing to protect me from any organism wishing to penetrate my body. A walking, talking gossamer. It sucked.

Thirteen years—thirteen years of living inside an antiseptic bubble, making sure my environment was scoured clean, daily scrubbing of every inch of skin, keeping the world and its dangers at bay. It double sucked.

Mother was sure the nuns would be able to cure me—sure of it, emphatic about it, double emphatic, triple emphatic. She'd heard about them, talked to them, and believed in their miracles. But she couldn't convince them to come to us no matter how much she offered them. The healing chamber couldn't be moved. I had to leave my bubble for the first time in years and go there. We had to travel hundreds of miles to some suckhole castle in some podunk village in the middle of nowhere.

How would you pack for that?

The driver stopped the car in front of the pack of camels. Three nuns in full Halloween costume, white habits and all, waited for us. We'd driven through a forest on a gutted, gravelly road (Mercedes shock absorbers weren't as perfect as advertised). Lushness still surrounded the car on three sides, but before us lay emptiness—a desert where nothing grew, not one thing.

"Camels?" Mother fumed. "Stay here and let me deal with this."

I ignored her command. A camel ride might prove interesting, a change, if nothing else. Getting out of the car wearing the protective suit and lugging the oxygen tank was no mean feat. Mother argued with the nuns, until one of them interrupted to ask if she was ill as well.

"No," my mother replied, "just my child. I wear this so she doesn't feel odd." *In solidarity* was what she usually said. She had on the same protective suit, sans oxygen tank, except hers fit better, of course. "We can drive there," she said. "We don't need camels. You ladies should keep up with some of our modern conveniences."

"A car won't survive the drive," one nun said.

"The camels barely do," another said.

"Once you cross the line," the third said, "nothing survives, not for long. No human, no plant, no infection. Until she reaches the room."

"She will not need the suit."

"No one can accompany her. Only seekers live."

"The camels might return."

"If they're fortunate."

"If the princess smiles upon their fate."

While my mother interjected, "No, this won't do," "You must be completely mad," "This is insane," and, "Can she at least take the pâté de campagne with her," the nuns explained what I must do: how to reach the room, how not to disturb the sleeper, how to look for possible signs that I was cured, how to parcel out the three loaves of bread and three eggs, and, most important, how to make sure that I had enough energy for the perilous return trip.

Hungry. I was hungry. My belly twisted and spasmed, my stomach grumbled and growled, and at least once every hour, a mewl escaped my lips.

Yet dare I touch the last egg? I dared not.

On the cherry-colored night table, the last boiled egg and loaf of bread lay next to the clay water pitcher, the loaf as fresh as the day I walked into the chamber. As for the egg, as long as it rested next to the princess, rot it would not. The sleeping beauty exuded much power, much goodness. Peace and tranquillity seeped from her every pore, health and well-being resided in her domain. I'd never been more hale, or more hungry. I hadn't needed my suit or tank since I arrived. In the beginning I felt liberated and unshackled. Without the bubble, my breath was light. I was even able to pinch myself. But I definitely needed food.

My gaze returned to the egg, and my stomach whimpered.

Upon first discovering the sleeping princess, the nuns, wanting her curative powers close at hand, attempted to bring her to the convent, but were unable to lift her. Indeed, a cluster of cloistered virgins could not move a single pebble out of the room.

Frankly, I could understand her position.

Since the mountain would not come, the nuns chose to erect a cloister next to the castle, but building was halted mid-brick, plans dropped, once they understood that for three leagues around, nothing outside of the healing chamber survived. Life flourished within, death without—a reverse Disneyland. (Please! You know it's true.) In a small room in the tower the beauty slept and breathed, while everything else in the palace, everyone else, breathed no more. Carcasses of her family, skeletons of nobles and attendants, of servants and slaves, of pets and parasites littered the crumbling castle. I stepped over many a pile of bones when I ascended the stairs. Terribly unpleasant.

Wild forest turned to desert precisely three leagues from the room. The transformation was immediate and striking: before an invisible line, forest; desert after. No creature, no plant, crossed. I noticed not a single living thing after I passed the boundary, not till I reached the princess lying on her altar of a bed in the middle of the chamber. Inside the room, the princess wore the healing if slightly off-putting color forest green. Outside, what was once a lush garden had atrophied. Man-made lines delineated arid squares. Outsized trunks and gnarled roots, sculptures created by an insane or indifferent artist, were all that remained of the once-great oaks, the beeches, birches, and lindens. Desert dust invaded every nook in the castle, except for the sleeper's pristine chamber, where no mote dared enter.

And I was so hungry. The perfectly shaped egg called to me. The perfectly shaped egg knew my name. "Don't I look sumptuous and luscious?" it said. "Come eat me. Devour me as you did my sisters."

Devour her sisters I had. I was supposed to wait before eating the first egg and its accompanying loaf, then wait some more for the second. The third should be consumed toward the end because of the rigors of the return trip. I didn't wait. I was hungry. I was weak. Can you blame me? The minute I walked into the room, I was hungry as never before.

One egg left, one loaf, and an awful journey back. How was I going to withstand it? I would die, obscure and nameless, in a strange land far from home. Since it was unlikely that I would survive, should I eat the egg and sate my hunger sooner rather than later? A morsel? A tiny bite?

I needed distraction. A ritual of ennui, that was what this was, a rite of tedium. No magazines, no television, nothing. Through the window, I saw the same view I had seen every day, desiccated land to the thin horizon, overwhelming and barren—and boring, boring, boring. Even the plastic bubble was better than this.

I prayed for a flood, torrents and storms, but would have settled for a drop of rain, a drip of variance.

The sleeper's slow and steady breathing was the only sound to be heard, never varying, never ending. The whole chamber smelled of her. It was the first thing I noticed when I walked in, the scent of summer flowers, jasmine and lilac, of summer days, never varying, never ending. Before boredom set in, I endeavored to discover where the scent emanated from, what part of her body. My nose reconnoitered all of her: her clothes, her hair, her mouth, her arms, her feet. I even examined under her skirt—still smooth there. The puberty fairy hadn't yet struck her either. The scent was all of her. She never needed to be bathed, her hair never needed combing or untangling. She was pristine in slumber, perfection in human form. Before I grew so weak, I could not stop myself from touching her skin—its smoothness, its suppleness, seduced me.

I prayed for a blemish. If only to ameliorate the tedium.

And my prayer was answered.

I felt a little flutter on the back of my left wrist, slightly below the sleeve of my shirt. Instinctively, as if I'd been doing it all my life, my right hand smacked my wrist. The sound of the slap echoed and reverberated in the sacred room. I removed my hand to see what was underneath. On the back of my wrist, the remnants of a mosquito and our blood, a minuscule cave painting in brown and red.

Where had it come from? How could it have invaded her space? Nothing had ever disturbed this room. I forced myself to stand. I had to examine the princess's skin. Could she have been bitten too? Would

I be punished if the princess was harmed on my watch—harmed by a mosquito bite? Would that mosquito live for years or centuries instead of days?

I felt dizzy as I stood, queasy. A faint sour smell tortured my nostrils. It was a delicate and wispy odor, and yet stark. Led by my nose, I discovered that the princess was the source, but I couldn't pinpoint where precisely. I heard a feeble flicker of a sound on the windowpane. A butterfly, yellow spotted with red, fought the glass trying to break into the room. I walked over to let her in—a butterfly in the room, how remarkable! In an instant, a loud thump: a bird, probably a starling, had flown into the glass and fallen, disappearing from view. The frightened butterfly followed suit. I opened the window to see where the bird landed, if it was still alive. I couldn't differentiate anything on the desert floor so far below.

The breeze was fresh, no longer broiling and stifling. Spring in the desert inferno?

I allowed myself to enjoy the unsullied air tickling my face. This was so new to me. I leaned on the windowsill and remembered all the languorous hours I'd spend staring out the plastic window. I considered opening all four windows in the tower to ventilate the chamber.

Another butterfly, deeper yellow, redder spots, came in through the chamber window. The sky looked different, then not. Was it changing color? I looked to the horizon. Nothing. I stared, and distinctions began to materialize, as when shapes slowly reveal themselves after your eyes adjust to darkness. Clouds were forming in the distance—in the great distance, but moving rather rapidly. Everything was. In the great distance, I could just make out the shape of a human approaching, a female form leaning on a staff. An awkward gait, an aged walk, it was an older woman, probably as old as Mother, older even. She had wild hair, not a hat, not a habit—wild white hair like a halo about her head. The crazy crone moved gingerly, but not slowly at all.

My heart beat faster, thumped harder within my ribs, my mouth as dry as the desert outside.

But then, was it dry outside?

The air felt moist.

What was happening?

I drew in a sustained breath. The acidic smell was faint no longer. It invaded the room, coupling with the fresh air entering the chamber, but it was no longer so unappealing. My senses must have become inured. The red-spotted butterfly hovered over the sleeping princess, deciding where to land. I raised my arm to shoo her away and noted a thin film of moisture on my skin.

Had I broken out in sweat?

A drop of water landed on the windowsill.

What magic was this?

I ran my index finger through the wetness. Dark, pregnant clouds scudded below a heavy sky laden with clouds only slightly less dark. The mad crone appeared in the once-great garden, no longer moving. She was standing next to a beast; not just a beast, a hyena—a hyena? She was looking up at my window, her unkempt hair sparkling, rumpling in the wind. I wondered if she was looking at me or simply at the chamber. Neither, it seemed. Her eyes were trained on the castle wall below. Mine followed.

From my lips, which had emitted not a sound in days, came a scream. Slithering up the jagged wall, coming right at me, was a long and heavy desert snake. Its eyes bored into mine. In its mouth, the starling struggled still; around its mouth, streaks of live blood. I screamed and screamed and shut the window, trying to hold the snake, the world, at bay. The windows I had kept closed against the scorching wind outside I would now keep closed against more hideous threats.

Water was pelleting the windows. The mother storm had erupted. The crazy crone, arms raised to the sky in joy and in command, glared at me. The hyena at her side moved not. They both cackled, and I heard them through the panes. The snake writhed at the window, its gullet now engorged with bird. It, too, glared at me. Birds began flying into all four windows, all kinds of birds, starlings, finches, and cardinals, ducks, loons, and herons. Two pigeons landed on the ledge of the east window and pecked on the pane. Then they began to copulate before my eyes, in the rain, a slow and languid mating. A stork alit on the north ledge and glared. Snails inched across the pane, their viscous trails polluting the streaks of rain. The stork began feasting on them, cracking their shells with its long beak, which was soon covered with waxy muck. Insects on all the windows, flies, mosquitoes, crickets, ants. The old fairy gestured with her arm toward the tower. The hyena nodded its head. The fairy spoke, and her words echoed in the room as if she stood next to me.

"The time has come, goddaughter."

Was she a relative?

I panicked. It was so embarrassing when I did not recognize a family member. Yet even from a distance, she did not look like anyone I knew. She looked like a witch. I tried to concentrate on her facial features. Evidently she had not been speaking to me. My godmother was still young.

A plant of some kind sprouted and wound itself around the fairy godmother's calf. Plants everywhere, on all sides, shoots, roots, trees, grass, hemlock, all entwined with poison ivy, poison oak, poison sumac. All over, sprouting, shooting upward. Thistles, so many thistles, brambles, blackberry, and brier, sweetbrier, greenbrier. Within minutes, a tangled messy mass of impenetrable thorns encircled the tower, a deadly poisonous brier patch, a vast thorny wood.

The rain stopped. Rats invaded the brier patch first, then snakes, scorpions, spiders, mosquitoes, flies. What had been a dry, clear desert was now a moist, teaming thicket of menace.

How would I ever leave this castle?

But leave I must.

The air in the chamber had turned oppressive and smothering, unbearably humid, astringent. The princess reeked of sweat, of brine and yeast, of uncovered and uncooked meat, of rank humanity. Smells I most certainly was not used to. The red-spotted butterfly rested on the princess's groin, its spread wings seeming to have doubled in size.

What strange occurrence was this?

Stranger yet, men began to arrive.

Outside, a hunting party halted at the outskirts of the brier. Their leader, the prince, jumped off his horse and unsheathed his sword, using it to clear a path through the thorns. None could follow him, for the brier closed rank behind him. Another prince arrived by himself, not ten yards away from the first. He too unsheathed his sword and commenced his journey. To the south, more princes, yet more from the east and more from the west, a multitude of princes—desperate princes, all seeking entry.

Where had they all come from? What had called them?

Many were unable to enter the thicket of thorn. Princes struck and slashed and cut but could not come through—weak princes. Exhausted by their ineffective efforts, they laid their bodies on the ground to recuperate, and the brier extended itself and swallowed them dead. Stronger princes, those who entered, met no happier fate. Murderous plants killed some, poisonous snakes killed others. Princes bled to death, wounded by many a thorn. Princes grew tired and could not keep their swords raised. Their death was the most horrific of all. The brier attacked them, lifted their bodies for one last look at the tower, the desideratum, teased them with one last look at the sky, then devoured them whole. A few, too few, still struggled below, but so many died, a massacre, a princely genocide.

I watched in horror, forgetting everything around me. I retreated from the window, nauseated. I clutched my stomach, as if I had been punched, as if its lining were being carved by a knife. I doubled up in pain. I vomited, but nothing came up. I had not eaten, nothing had entered me, in so long.

Then I heard heavy footsteps rushing up the stairs: thump, thump, thump, thump. The thick wooden door swung open, flew off its hinges, and slammed into the wall. It shattered into pieces. The prince bolted into the room, stormed to the bed, and stopped before the sleeping beauty. He had eyes for nothing else, while mine were glued to him.

The hero had come through. He had lost his sword, his shirt, and his shoes to the brier. Streaked in blood, he had deep wounds on his forehead, on his side, on both palms. Blood ran down his virile, hairy, powerful, masculine calves. The front of his pantaloons exhibited no small excitement. Sweaty, perspiring, he too reeked, yet my stomach had no wish to rebel—surrender, yes. I cleared my throat, ahemmed, but he paid me no mind. Nothing but the princess was his world. He ran his hand along the softness of her bare arm. He seemed surprised at the lack of a response. I wanted to tell him that it was not his fault, that she had not wakened, had not moved, in a hundred years. I wanted only to save him time, to protect him from frustration. I wanted to tell him she was not the one for him, not at all. But he bent his golden torso and smelled her, inhaled deeply, and I almost fainted. He extended his tongue and licked the moistness of her cleavage. And then he kissed her.

He kissed her.

And he kissed her.

She remained asleep, her breathing slow and steady as ever. He licked her lips, then her neck. He lifted himself atop the bed and straddled her. The engorged groin within the pantaloons loomed larger. He bent and kissed the princess once more. He tore off her blouse and chemise, squeezed her milk-white breasts, pinched them, bit them with abandon.

I wanted to stop him. I wanted to warn him that she was an archetype. But if I could not keep a butterfly off her, I would never be able to fend off a prince. My knees felt weak, my breathing was shallow, my skin sensitive and sweaty. I had to sit down.

And he tore off her skirt and undergarments. Still she slept.

I opened my mouth to scream, but what left my lips was a deep, sensuous sigh.

Where once all was smooth and barren, now grew a follicle forest, and into that forest the prince's face disappeared.

I moaned and the princess echoed me. I was stunned.

She did not open her eyes, and I was unsure whether she had

wakened, but she moaned once more. He grunted, buried his face deeper, and she moved. She spread her naked legs wider. Her lips parted, taking in a deep breath. She moaned, he moaned, I moaned. A volcano erupted in my stomach, its heat flooding my body.

The princess's eyelids flew open. The sleeper had awakened. Her lashes fluttered, and I felt as if I were being whipped.

She sat up on her elbows, bent her knees. With one hand, she held the prince's head and bucked. He grunted, grunted, grunted, like a pig finding truffle.

She screamed in ecstasy. I screamed in ecstasy.

The room was stifling. My body was stifling.

The prince lifted himself off her. The princess growled. I mewled.

She tore off his pantaloons and his erection sprang up. I whimpered.

The prince entered the princess brutally. She pushed herself into him in return. I could no longer distinguish the sounds they were making. They attacked each other in an aggressive ancestral rhythm.

The lava reached my groin. The lava reached my eyes, and tears rolled. The heat rattled my soul. My body shook and spasmed.

The prince kissed the princess, and their tongues fought, intertwined, became one. Their lips coupled and melded. Their hips merged. His hands cleaved to her breasts, hers to his back. Their feet joined. Before my eyes, two humans disappeared into a monstrous, nebulous one. The prince and the princess rocked back and forth but only for a few moments. They finally settled into a solid amorphous shape on the bed, a weird conjoined entity.

It took time, slow time, to regain some semblance of control over my senses. I was sopping wet, exhausted, but no longer weak. I decided to depart from this room. I did not care whether harm had come to the princess. I did not know whether I was healed or not, but this certainly was a sign. I snatched the egg and the loaf, devoured the latter first. It was damp, not fresh, and I loved it. I bit into the egg, ate half of it in one swallow. It was rank, sour, almost rotten, and utterly delicious. I finished it and licked my hands and my fingers.

As soon as I exited the room, my first drop of blood appeared—a pellet of blood struck the sand dust of the tower's stairwell. More blood as I descended, as I stepped over the skeletons of the princess's family. Outside, the weather was pitch-perfect. As a light wind flirted with my face, I felt healthy and joyful. The brier had left the hero's slashed path for my egress. I walked on, corpses of failed princes to my right and left, above my head, offering a final farewell. Surrounded by brier I traveled, thorns pricked me everywhere, pulled at my hair, snagged and tangled it.

Bloodied and bleeding, refreshed and rejuvenated, upon my head a tiara of thorns, I returned to Mother.

The tale of the sleeping princess (commonly known as "Sleeping Beauty" but known as "The Sleeping Beauty in the Wood" in French) has had a hold on my imagination for as long as I can remember. I have tried in the last ten years to write stories informed by the fairy tale, variations around a leitmotif. This is the first attempt where the main protagonist is neither the sleeper nor the waker.

—RA

STACEY RICHTER

A Case Study of Emergency Room Procedure and Risk Management by Hospital Staff Members in the Urban Facility

I.

SUBJECT 525, A CAUCASIAN FEMALE IN HER EARLY TO MID-TWENTIES, entered an emergency medical facility at around 11 P.M. presenting symptoms of an acute psychotic episode. Paranoia, heightened sensitivity to physical contact, and high-volume vocal emanations were noted at triage by the medical staff. The subject complained of the hearing of voices, specifically "a chorus of amphibians" who were entreating the subject to "pretty please guard the product from the evil frog prince." The staff reported that the subject's bizarre behavior was augmented by an unusual sartorial style, commenting that she was "an ethereal young woman wearing a Renaissance-type dress, with huge knots in her long, otherwise flowing hair." She was accompanied by a strange odor, tentatively identified as "cat urine."

During the intake interview, the subject volunteered the information that she had nasally inhaled "crystal," estimating that she had nasally inhaled (snorted) between 50 and 250 mg of "crystal" in the twenty-four hours prior to hospital admission. "Crystal," it was determined, is a slang term for methamphetamine, a central nervous system stimulant similar to prescription amphetamines such as Benzedrine. Methamphetamine is a "street" drug-of-abuse that has become popular in recent years due to its easy manufacture possibilities (Osborne, 1988). It's sometimes referred to by the terms *crystal, speed, zooma-zoom,* and *go fast* (Durken, 1972). In a brief moment of lucidity, Subject 525 theorized that her psychotic state might be due to the large quantity of methamphetamine she had "snorted," and the staff agreed to put her in a "nice, quiet, white room" for a period of observation. The head resident thought it advisable to administer antipsychotic medication, but the subject, who by all accounts exhibited an uncanny amount of personal charm, prevailed upon the staff to give her a can of beer instead.

II.

After approximately sixty minutes of observation, a member of the nursing staff noted that the subject had begun to complain that "a beslimed prince" was causing certain problems for her, namely "using copper fittings" and "not ventilating right." This "prince" was, as the nurse understood it, acting "all mean and horrible" concerning the manufacture of methamphetamine, which the subject had cheerfully volunteered as her occupation during the intake interview. The nurse, who was formerly employed in a federal prison and had considerable experience treating denizens of the *demimonde,* theorized that "Prince" might be a moniker used by the subject's "old man"; this was particularly likely, the nurse indicated, since the manufacture of methamphetamine is the customary province of "gangs" of motorcycle riders, who often use colorful nicknames as a way of asserting their "outsider" status in society (Ethel Kreztchner, RN, 2002).

The nurse further asserted that this would explain why the subject had offered, at intake, only the name "Princess," and would indicate no surname. By then the hour had grown rather late, and as the emergency room was quiet, much of the staff gathered around the subject ("Princess"), who began to tell a lively tale of capture and imprisonment by a handsome but wicked "Prince" who was, in fact, "an evil enchanter." The tradition of shape-shifting sorcerers is a familiar one in old German folktales (Grimm, ca. 1812), though these tales have been widely regarded as fanciful narratives concocted to intimidate and control unruly juveniles (twelve and under) in diverse cultural contexts and are rarely considered historical evidence. Nevertheless, the Princess claimed that the Prince had captured her from an orphanage near Eloy, Arizona, where she had spent her days climbing trees in pursuit of nuts. Chasing butterflies, according to the subject, was another activity she enjoyed in her youth. But that all changed when a handsome young man approached the girl and offered her a pony made of candy. The pony was beautiful and delicious, and though the Princess wished to save it forever, she found she devoured it anyway. With every bite the pony grew smaller. And with every bite the handsome "young man" became more fearsome and wicked-looking.

The staff gathered close, listening with great interest. The Princess went on to indicate that the Prince/Sorcerer had bewitched her with the candy horse, and had since imprisoned her in a prefabricated "home" near a foul-smelling landfill, where she was kept locked up in a "tin can with carpet taped over the windows." There, the Prince had prevailed upon her to undertake the smelly and dangerous manufacture of methamphetamine by means of his sorcerer's power. All day long, the Princess said, she was forced to "boil down Mexican ephedrine in a triple-neck flask, bubble hydrogen through a stainless steel tank, or titrate ethyl ether out of lock defrosting fluid, dressed only in filthy rags," while the Prince rode his shiny "hog" through tall pines in the mountains to the north of town. Or the Prince would "relax and kick back with a can of brew" while the Princess "slaved over a hot chemistry set." The only positive aspect of the experience, the Princess noted, was that she "cooked the best damn product in Arizona," a substance that was uncommonly potent and white, she said, with a "real clean buzz."

The Princess explained, in a sweetly chiming voice, that these endeavors were dangerous, particularly under the conditions imposed by the Prince, who habitually smoked marijuana cigarettes in the vicinity of fumes. She had survived because she was protected by a special angel, one with "gills" who could exist underwater or possibly "inside a solution." She referred to this angel as "Gilbert" (possibly "Gillbert"), and noted that Gilbert appeared to her when she imbibed heavily of "the product." The manifestation of angels, seraphim, djinns, and Elvis Presley is common during episodes of psychosis (Hotchkiss, 1969), and much of the staff believed that the Princess was describing an aspect of methamphetamine-induced hallucination. Others on staff found themselves strangely moved by the Princess's story of forced enslavement and the high-risk game of organic chemistry, and wondered if there might be some sort of truth to it.

The head resident, in particular, took an interest in the subject's case, indicating to researchers that he was "bored that night, as usual" and that he found the Princess "interesting." The resident further indicated that his prodigious academic success was based on his above-average intelligence, which was also "a curse" because it led him to feel a feeling of "boredom" and intolerance with all of "the idiots around him," which, he made clear, also applied to the researchers gathering data on this case. Researchers in turn described the resident as rather "vain and haughty," or "arrogant," though most theorized that these traits covered up insecurity about his youth combined with a doomed romanticism undercut by a persistent tendency toward bitterness.

The Princess was exhibiting fewer symptoms of psychosis, and had become quite comfortable in her surroundings, curling up in a nest of pillows "like a cat" (Overhand, 2002). She said that she loved the medical staff and was grateful to them for helping to save her from the evilness of the Prince and the pungent squalidness of methamphetamine manufacture. The head resident shuffled his feet and pointed out that the Princess herself had actually contributed to her own care by wisely seeking medical treatment when she felt overwhelmed by drug-induced psychosis, whereas a lot of "tweaked-out idiots" just went ahead and did something stupid or violent. Then the two stared for a while into each other's eyes.

It was then that lateness of the hour was nervously remarked upon by all, and several staff members complained that they had been on duty for an excessive length of time. The Princess made a "general comment" that her product could "give a person a little pick-me-up" that theoretically might make the staff members feel like "they were operating at one hundred and fifty percent."

The staff was curious about the efficacy of the Princess's home-made methamphetamine, though their enthusiasm abated somewhat after a phlebotomist (a "pretty plump girl who never wore any makeup and never smiled or said hello to nobody beneath her," according to the environmental control officer) recited aloud in a high and quavering voice a list of the possible effects of nasally inhaling meth-amphetamine, including "nervousness, sweating, teeth-gnashing, ir-ritability, incessant talking, sleeplessness, and the obsessive assembling and disassembling of machinery" (PDR, 2002). Interest swelled once again when the Princess pointed out that the young phlebotomist had mumbled while mentioning one of the chief effects of the substance: euphoria.

After that, the staff cleared from the small room where the Princess was being kept sequestered by herself, though occasionally a lone member would disappear inside, to emerge a few moments later wip-ing their nose with eyes unusually wild. Such staff members were also observed tidying their work areas, peering into the mirror, smoking cigarettes, and talking to one another with great animation and enthu-siasm but little content (Overhand, 2002). The receptionist was ob-served taking apart a telephone, so that she could "clean it." The overall effect was that the staff was unusually energetic and "happy" (see below).

III.

Shortly before dawn, several nurses returned to the Princess's bedside, where they adjusted the lighting in the small room so a warm glow bathed the subject. They worked with combs to untangle the knots in the subject's hair. The head resident had entered the room as well, and kept his boyish face, so incongruous beneath his balding head, hunched toward his chest while he made notes in the subject's chart.

It was then that the subject began to speak softly about a set of ponies she had made out of old tires. The Princess explained how she had "freed" the ponies from the rubber with a cutting implement, and that a "herd" of such ponies hung from ropes in the trees around her prefabricated housing unit, where they blew back and forth in the breeze, bumping against one another with hollow thuds. They possessed the spirit of "running things," she explained, though they had no "legs to speak of"; she could look at them and feel the feeling of "something wild and running away." The subject further explained that nasally inhaling or "skin popping" (subcutaneous injection) of methamphetamine gave her relief from a feeling that "nothing important would ever happen to her" and replaced it with the sensation that she was, like the ponies fashioned from discarded tires, something "wild and running away."

She indicated that these feelings of flight accounted for the only times that she ever truly felt like a princess.

IV.

The notes in the subject's chart at this point become "tiny and very, very neat," according to researchers (Plank et al., 2002). The notes themselves indicate that the subject was "an exceptionally attractive woman," and that the medical staff found her "enchanting." She was "like them but different—more perfect—yet at the same time more glassine and fragile." The chart noted that the subject had become sleepy, perhaps due to the fatigue that often follows the ingestion of methamphetamine (Nintzel, 1982). It was indicated that some members of the staff wished to allow her to sleep, while others had an urgent need to "pester her; to poke her in the leg with a stick over and over," to keep her awake.

Verbal accounts indicate that not all the members of the night staff were equally smitten with the subject. Several members demurred, in particular the phlebotomist, who commented that the subject was "a disgusting drug addict" who was "manipulative." She added that she hated men "who fall for those poor lost creatures," even though such "creatures" were in the process of getting "exactly what they signed up for." The phlebotomist indicated that it was futile to try to help the subject, save medically, because the subject had freely chosen her own seedy destiny, despite her weird story of kidnapping, adding that "not everybody who suffers has a burning need to dramatize it with scarves and eyeliner."

V.

Videotapes from the security cameras in the waiting area provide a clear visual record of the intrusion that occurred at approximately 4:12 A.M. The tapes show a clean, tiled area violently rent by the shiny chrome form of a very large motorcycle (or "hog") piloted by the "Prince," who gained ingress by method of riding through the glass doors, where he continued to gun his motorcycle in circles through a reception area furnished with chairs which became smashed. The "Prince" was reported to be a large, muscular male of indeterminate race sporting "a pair of sideburns as big as teacups." He was reportedly clad in "enough black leather to denude several cows," though naturally it has not been determined how many cows would have been needed to provide the amount of leather the Prince was wearing. Much of the hospital staff on duty also reported that the intruder had a "tail, slimy and black, sort of like the tail of a tadpole." Careful scrutiny of security videotapes does reveal the presence of a whiplike appendage dangling from the back of the Prince's "hog," though the possibility that this might in fact be a literal "tail" has been discounted by researchers, who have chalked up this and several other aspects of the medical staff's report to group suggestibility (Johansen, 2002). (For example, the hospital staff also reported that the Prince had "eyes that glowed red like coals" and that "lizards and snakes slithered from his boots.")

It was reported that the Prince then parked his "hog" and proceeded past the reception area, stalking the warren-like halls of the emergency treatment facility in his heavy boots, scuffing the floor, screaming that someone had taken his "woman," and wondering aloud, in a yelling tone, where he could find his "kitten."

At this the Princess and hospital staff fled to a supply closet, where they cowered, leaving the issue of how to properly control the "Prince" open for resolution. It was agreed that the police, as well as the hospital security guards, should be alerted; it was lamented however that there was no available phone in the supply closet and such action would require someone to dash out into the hallway where the Prince was raging and overturning carts and smashing his hammer-like hands into walls while eating candy reserved for children who were unfortunate enough to wind up in the emergency room. The Princess, whose melodic voice was muffled due to the press of bodies in the supply closet, pointed out that the Prince possessed special evil magic powers and that anyone who challenged him must be good in heart and clever both, and carry with him or her a small silver bell which the Princess kept on a chain around her neck.

As the destructive noises of the Prince's rampage became louder, the head resident indicated that he felt he should be the one to make an effort to save himself, the staff, and the once psychotic but now quite sweet Princess. The staff was surprised to hear this, as they had never noticed any behavior related to bravery or even simple kindness on the part of the head resident. They continued to be surprised when they heard him say, in a quavering voice, that though it was true he might not be good-hearted, he certainly was *clever* enough, so why not give it a go? Everyone in the closet gave him a quiet but heartfelt round of applause. The Princess begged him to be careful and hung the bell around his neck with a trembling hand. She bestowed upon him a soft kiss as he slipped out the door.

The "rescue" of women by handsome, effeminate men is a staple of old folktales, engineered to reconcile a young woman's inclination toward feckless independence with the prevailing custom of marriage by casting the potential husband as really nice and sort of harmless and at the very least a whole lot better than the alternative of living with her fucked-up family (cf. *Cinderella*, Grimm, 1812). Despite the tradition of the effeminate male triumphing over the more sexual, "animal" challenger, it seemed uncertain to all present that the head resident could defeat the "Prince" using the tools at his disposal—a stethoscope, some pens, and a pager. It's difficult to determine, though, what kind of damage the resident may have been capable of inflicting with these devices, since, according to his own account, when confronted with the fierce and gruesome "Prince," who "smelled like burning rubber and had white stuff hanging off his beard," he froze, then mutely raised a traitorous arm to point to the supply closet where the Princess and the rest of the staff were hiding.

The Prince wrenched open the door with a huge paw, and out popped the Princess.

According to the staff, the Princess screamed with a high-pitched yelp when the Prince grabbed her, smearing her lovely Renaissance-style dress with grease. The records note that the Prince and the Princess together presented quite an odd picture, one that brought to mind "a nightmare creature clawing a plate of petit fours" (Petix, 2002). The Princess is reported to have said, "It's okay," and, "No, but I want to go with him, really," and, "He's my old man!" in a tone of tense brightness, but the staff plainly did not believe her and theorized that she was simply trying to "appease her oppressor" in order to minimize the likelihood of domestic violence. Before the staff was able to contact the authorities, the "Prince" settled himself astride his hog and pulled the Princess up behind him.

The Prince and Princess roared out of the building and vanished into the night in a cloud of exhaust.

CONCLUSION

After the Prince and Princess had departed, the staff grumbled that the head resident had behaved "most cowardly," and complained that the Princess had been "sacrificed," to be "whisked off to a prefabricated house where everything is always fast and tinged with madness, or else dark and sad and falling asleep." Much of the staff argued that *something* should have been done to help the girl, though some felt it was the curse of the phylum *Princess* to be always at the mercy of one prince-type or another, and that her best chance was to save herself, which seemed unlikely. The resident, for his part, quickly aligned himself with the phlebotomist, agreeing that the Princess was "just an addict" who had come in "exhibiting drug-seeking behavior anyway," and implying, in word and action, that drug addicts were by nature less than human and so deserved whatever nasty fate they got. Then he skulked off down a fluorescent-lit hallway with his hands shoved into his pockets.

Though he wore the silver bell around his neck to the end of his days.

At the same time that I wrote this story for my friend, the poet Richard Siken, I was doing a lot of research into the production of crystal meth (I wish I could say I was setting up a clandestine lab, but it was a writing project). This was back when the Internet was not the rich vein of drug information it is today, so I was forced to actually go to the library and browse the stacks. Deep within the university's compact shelving units, I found a pile of sociology journals that dealt with the subject of methamphetamine abusers. Now, I'm sure there are plenty of brilliant sociologists doing trenchant work on the mores of drug use, but what I found was a deposit of dry, heavily footnoted prose about tweakers. These papers were so good. I was so happy. It's probably always inadvertently funny when sex, drugs, and rock and roll are subjected to rigorous

academic study, but the articles I found were so funny, and so credulous, that it was sort of moving. Beneath the footnotes and citations, the naiveté of the researchers shone through with touching clarity.

Though this wasn't the information I needed, I was so fascinated that I took notes in the library all afternoon. I could see the researchers sitting at plastic tables, interviewing a series of addled, strung-out dirtbags who bounced their knees and fiddled their pencils while they answered questions. And as I read, I began to notice that some of the facts didn't ring true. It began to dawn on me that a lot of this information wasn't very accurate. And really, why would it be? I'd guess that meth heads are not a particularly truthful bunch. I was especially taken by the unlikely drug slang they'd concocted, presented in heartbreaking italics, probably verbatim—so stupid, so obvious and colorful. I wondered if the researchers were really so easily fleeced, or just so desperate to publish that they didn't care? (I was hoping fleeced.) I used some of these terms in the story and made up a few more of my own. Now I'm not sure which is which, an indication of how absurd the slang was.

I hadn't planned to write a story based on these academic articles, but when I began to write a fairy tale for Richard Siken, I found myself considering the natural intersection between fairy tales, drug-induced psychosis, and gullible scientists. After all, we may think we know the world as it is, but most of our human experiences suffer from a lack of empirical data. The truth is useful, but half-truths have the allure of the shadows on the edge of sleep, or the swirl of a chemical high. This is the only place where most of us get to meet mythical beings such as witches, fairies, monsters, princesses, and trustworthy drug addicts. Maybe we all only believe what we want to believe in the end.

—SR

NEIL GAIMAN

Orange

(Third Subject's Responses to Investigator's Written Questionnaire)

EYES ONLY

1. Jemima Glorfindel Petula Ramsey.

2. 17 on June the 9th.

3. The last 5 years. Before that we lived in Glasgow (Scotland). Before that, Cardiff (Wales).

4. I don't know. I think he's in magazine publishing now. He doesn't talk to us anymore. The divorce was pretty bad and Mum wound up paying him a lot of money. Which seems sort of wrong to me. But maybe it was worth it just to get shot of him.

5. An inventor and entrepreneur. She invented the Stuffed Muffin(™), and started the Stuffed Muffin chain. I used to like them when I was a kid, but you can get kind of sick of stuffed muffins for every meal, especially because Mum used us as guinea pigs. The Complete Turkey Dinner Christmas Stuffed Muffin was the worst. But she sold out her interest in the Stuffed Muffin chain about five years ago, to start work on My Mum's Colored Bubbles (not actually ™ yet).

6. Two. My sister Nerys, who was just 15, and my brother Pryderi, 12.

7. Several times a day.

8. No.

9. Through the Internet. Probably on eBay.

10. She's been buying colors and dyes from all over the world ever since she decided that the world was crying out for brightly colored Day-Glo bubbles. The kind you can blow, with bubble mixture.

11. It's not really a laboratory. I mean, she calls it that, but really it's just the garage. Only she took some of the Stuffed Muffins(TM) money and converted it, so it has sinks and bathtubs and Bunsen burners and things, and tiles on the walls and the floor to make it easier to clean.

12. I don't know. Nerys used to be pretty normal. When she turned 13 she started reading these magazines and putting pictures of these strange bimbo women up on her wall like Britney Spears and so on. Sorry if anyone reading this is a Britney fan ;) but I just don't get it. The whole orange thing didn't start until last year.

13. Artificial tanning creams. You couldn't go near her for hours after she put it on. And she'd never give it time to dry after she smeared it on her skin, so it would come off on her sheets and on the fridge door and in the shower leaving smears of orange everywhere. Her friends would wear it too, but they never put it on like she did. I mean, she'd slather on the cream, with no attempt to look even human-colored, and she thought she looked great. She did the tanning salon thing once, but I don't think she liked it, because she never went back.

14. Tangerine Girl. The Oompaloompa. Carrot-top. Go-Mango. Orangina.

15. Not very well. But she didn't seem to care, really. I mean, this is a girl who said that she couldn't see the point of science or maths because she was going to be a pole dancer as soon as she left school. I said, nobody's going to pay to see you in the altogether, and she said how do you know? and I told her that I saw the little quick-time films she'd made of herself dancing nuddy and left in the

camera and she screamed and said give me that, and I told her I'd wiped them. But honestly, I don't think she was ever going to be the next Bettie Page or whoever. She's a sort of squarish shape, for a start.

16. German measles, mumps and I think Pryderi had chicken pox when he was staying in Melbourne with the Grandparents.

17. In a small pot. It looked a bit like a jam jar, I suppose.

18. I don't think so. Nothing that looked like a warning label anyway. But there was a return address. It came from abroad, and the return address was in some kind of foreign lettering.

19. You have to understand that Mum had been buying colors and dyes from all over the world for five years. The thing with the Day-Glo bubbles is not that someone can blow glowing colored bubbles, it's that they don't pop and leave splashes of dye all over everything. Mum says that would be a lawsuit waiting to happen. So, no.

20. There was some kind of shouting match between Nerys and Mum to begin with, because Mum had come back from the shops and not bought anything from Nerys's shopping list except the shampoo. Mum said she couldn't find the tanning cream at the supermarket but I think she just forgot. So Nerys stormed off and slammed the door and went into her bedroom and played something that was probably Britney Spears really loudly. I was out the back, feeding the three cats, the chinchilla, and a guinea pig named Roland who looks like a hairy cushion, and I missed it all.

21. On the kitchen table.

22. When I found the empty jam jar in the back garden the next morning. It was underneath Nerys's window. It didn't take Sherlock Holmes to figure it out.

23. Honestly, I couldn't be bothered. I figured it would just be more yelling, you know? And Mum would work it out soon enough.

24. Yes, it was stupid. But it wasn't uniquely stupid, if you see what I mean. Which is to say, it was par-for-the-course-for-Nerys stupid.

25. That she was glowing.

26. A sort of pulsating orange.

27. When she started telling us that she was going to be worshipped like a god, as she was in the dawn times.

28. Pryderi said she was floating about an inch above the ground. But I didn't actually see this. I thought he was just playing along with her newfound weirdness.

29. She didn't answer to "Nerys" anymore. She described herself mostly as either My Immanence or The Vehicle. ("It is time to feed the Vehicle.")

30. Dark chocolate. Which was weird because in the old days I was the only one in the house who even sort-of liked it. But Pryderi had to go out and buy her bars and bars of it.

31. No. Mum and me just thought it was more Nerys. Just a bit more imaginatively weirdo Nerys than usual.

32. That night, when it started to get dark. You could see the orange pulsing under the door. Like a glow-worm or something. Or a light show. The weirdest thing was that I could still see it with my eyes closed.

33. The next morning. All of us.

34. It was pretty obvious by this point. She didn't really even look like Nerys any longer. She looked sort of *smudged*. Like an after-image. I thought about it, and it's . . . Okay. Suppose you were staring at something really bright, that was a blue color. Then you closed your eyes, and you'd see this glowing yellowy-orange after-image in your eyes? That was what she looked like.

35. They didn't work either.

36. She let Pryderi leave to get her more chocolate. Mum and I weren't allowed to leave the house anymore.

37. Mostly I just sat in the back garden and read a book. There wasn't very much else I really could do. I started wearing dark glasses, so did Mum, because the orange light hurt our eyes. Other than that, nothing.

38. Only when we tried to leave or call anybody. There was food in the house, though. And Stuffed Muffins$^{(TM)}$ in the freezer.

39. "If you'd just stopped her wearing that stupid tanning cream a year ago we wouldn't be in this mess!" But it was unfair, and I apologized afterward.

40. When Pryderi came back with the dark chocolate bars. He said he'd gone up to a traffic warden and told him that his sister had turned into a giant orange glow and was controlling our minds. He said the man was extremely rude to him.

41. I don't have a boyfriend. I did, but we broke up after he went to a Rolling Stones concert with the evil bottle-blond former friend whose name I do not mention. Also, I mean, the Rolling Stones? These little old goat-men hopping around the stage pretending to be all rock and roll? Please. So, no.

42. I'd quite like to be a vet. But then I think about having to put animals down, and I don't know. I want to travel for a bit before I make any decisions.

43. The garden hose. We turned it on full, while she was eating her chocolate bars, and distracted, and we sprayed it at her.

44. Just orange steam, really. Mum said that she had solvents and things in the laboratory, if we could get in there, but by now Her Immanence was hissing mad (literally), and she sort of fixed us to the floor. I can't explain it. I mean, I wasn't stuck, but I couldn't leave or move my legs. I was just where she left me.

45. About half a meter above the carpet. She'd sink down a bit to go through doors, so she didn't bump her head. And after the hose incident she didn't go back to her room, just stayed in the main room and floated about grumpily, the color of a luminous carrot.

46. Complete world domination.

47. I wrote it down on a piece of paper and gave it to Pryderi.

48. He had to carry it back. I don't think Her Immanence really understood money.

49. I don't know. It was Mum's idea more than mine. I think she hoped

that the solvent might remove the orange. And at that point, it couldn't hurt. Nothing could have made things worse.

50. It didn't even upset her, like the hose-water did. I'm pretty sure she liked it. I think I saw her dipping her chocolate bars into it, before she ate them, although I had to sort of squint up my eyes to see anything where she was. It was all a sort of great orange glow.

51. That we were all going to die. Mum told Pryderi that if the Great Oompaloompa let him out to buy chocolate again, he just shouldn't bother coming back. And I was getting really upset about the animals—I hadn't fed the chinchilla or Roland the guinea pig for two days, because I couldn't go into the back garden. I couldn't go anywhere. Except the loo, and then I had to ask.

52. I suppose because they thought the house was on fire. All the orange light. I mean, it was a natural mistake.

53. We were glad she hadn't done that to us. Mum said it proved that Nerys was still in there somewhere, because if she had the power to turn us into goo, like she did the fire-fighters, she would have done. I said that maybe she just wasn't powerful enough to turn us into goo at the beginning and now she couldn't be bothered.

54. You couldn't even see a person in there anymore. It was a bright orange pulsing light, and sometimes it talked straight into your head.

55. When the spaceship landed.

56. I don't know. I mean, it was bigger than the whole block, but it didn't crush anything. It sort of materialized around us, so that our whole house was inside it. And the whole street was inside it too.

57. No. But what else could it have been?

58. A sort of pale blue. They didn't pulse, either. They twinkled.

59. More than six, less than twenty. It's not that easy to tell if this is the same intelligent blue light you were just speaking to five minutes ago.

60. Three things. First of all, a promise that Nerys wouldn't be hurt or

harmed. Second, that if they were ever able to return her to the way she was, they'd let us know, and bring her back. Thirdly, a recipe for fluorescent bubble mixture. (I can only assume they were reading Mum's mind, because she didn't say anything. It's possible that Her Immanence told them, though. She definitely had access to some of "the Vehicle's" memories.) Also, they gave Pryderi a thing like a glass skateboard.

61. A sort of a liquid sound. Then everything became transparent. I was crying, and so was Mum. And Pryderi said "Cool beans," and I started to giggle while crying, and then it was just our house again.

62. We went out into the back garden and looked up. There was something blinking blue and orange, very high, getting smaller and smaller, and we watched it until it was out of sight.

63. Because I didn't want to.

64. I fed the remaining animals. Roland was in a state. The cats just seemed happy that someone was feeding them again. I don't know how the chinchilla got out.

65. Sometimes. I mean, you have to bear in mind that she was the single most irritating person on the planet, even before the whole Her Immanence thing. But yes, I guess so. If I'm honest.

66. Sitting outside at night, staring up at the sky, wondering what she's doing now.

67. He wants his glass skateboard back. He says that it's his, and the government has no right to keep it. (You are the government, aren't you?) Mum seems happy to share the patent for the Colored Bubble recipe with the government though. The man said that it might be the basis of a whole new branch of molecular something or other. Nobody gave me anything, so I don't have to worry.

68. Once, in the back garden, looking up at the night sky. I think it was only an orangeyish star, actually. It could have been Mars, I know they call it the red planet. Although once in a while I think that maybe she's back to herself again, and dancing, up there, wherever

she is, and all the aliens love her pole dancing because they just don't know any better, and they think it's a whole new art-form, and they don't even mind that she's sort of square.

69. I don't know. Sitting in the back garden talking to the cats, maybe. Or blowing silly-colored bubbles.

70. Until the day that I die.

I attest that this is a true statement of events.

Signed:

Date:

"Sun, come you in," sing the giants in R. A. Lafferty's retelling of the travels of Odysseus, Space Chantey, *and the tame sun comes in each morning, like a pet dog.*

Really, this is a very old, very simple story. It's a mistake story, a little-magic-shop story, a things-we-were-not-meant-to-know story. It's a two sisters story (the wise one, and the unwise) in which something that was never meant to be a tanning cream replaces the diamonds and the toads that tumble from our mouths.

Sir Sacheverell Sitwell was the first person, as far as I know, to point out that it is the mystery that lingers and not the explanation, the question and not the answer, that stays with us. But sometimes answers and explanations in their turn can build mysteries, or leave behind spaces and empty places, and sometimes it is only if we know what the questions were that we can understand what the answers mean.

The way the story is told defines the story. It tells us who we should be cheering for, who we hope will survive the story. "Editors," Roger Zelazny told me, "believe that they are buying the stories, but they are not. They are buying the way the story is told."

Sometimes it is best if the sun does not come in. This is a cautionary tale, after all, and I think they even predate How

Things Came To Be This Way stories (*"Don't go there. That was
how your uncle was eaten by a cave lion. Don't eat that. Let me tell
you what it did to my guts.") and it would not be a cautionary tale
if things began well and ended even better.*

*But there is a possibility of a happy ending, and we must take
them where we can find them. Sun, come you in.*

—NG

FRANCESCA LIA BLOCK

Psyche's Dark Night

PSYCHE MET CUPID ONLINE. THEY HAD ALREADY BEEN THROUGH A lot of failed relationships at this point so they were both wary. Psyche's last relationship was with a guy who said he was divorced but turned out to be separated from his wife, whom he was still in love with. When Psyche had told this man she loved him, before she knew about the wife, he had said, "I love you, too. I love everybody. We are all one." Cupid's last relationship involved a narcissistic, domineering actress who broke up with him suddenly while he was out of town visiting his narcissistic, domineering mother. "You're too subservient," she'd said, although she hadn't seemed to mind when he behaved that way around her. But in spite of these experiences, Cupid and Psyche were also both very attracted to each other's profile so they got over their fears and talked on the phone a few times. They got along so well on the phone that Psyche kept expecting Cupid to ask her to coffee or tea, which was customary after a few good phone calls, but he never did. One night she drunk-dialed him after a party she had been to where none of the men interested her in any way or ignored her entirely and she and Cupid stayed on the phone laughing and flirting for hours. Finally, Psyche invited Cupid over. It was two in the morning and he came.

Psyche told Cupid to come in through her back door—it would be unlocked. Psyche lived in a cottage apartment near the beach. She could smell the sea from her bedroom and there was a small courtyard garden with a jacaranda tree that tossed purple flowers into a small pond surrounded by a ring of mossy stones. Psyche liked to imagine that fairies lived in that garden.

She held her breath as she heard the back door open. Why was she doing this? she wondered, suddenly feeling a tender nostalgia for her cute fairy apartment that was in walking distance from the beach. Cupid could have been a serial killer and he could kill her and she would be dead and never be able to live in her adorable rent-controlled apartment again. But his voice had sounded so warm and natural; she was sure he wasn't a serial killer. What if he just wasn't cute? In his pictures he looked gorgeous but he could have used fake pictures.

Cupid was wondering these same things about Psyche. Were her pictures old? Had she gained a large amount of weight since they were taken? Were they her pictures at all? Was she an alcoholic (Cupid was sober)? Was she a psycho-girl who would decide she was in love with him right away and stalk him when he rejected her? These were the reasons why you were always supposed to meet in a public place first.

But neither Cupid nor Psyche had had sex in a long time and there was so much chemistry on the phone that they gave in to their loneliness and desire. It was dark in Psyche's room but as soon as their lips met and they felt each other's bodies, smelled each other, fell to the bed, they knew they had not made a mistake about their attraction. (He's not a serial killer! She's not psycho!) Cupid felt huge and strong in Psyche's arms and Psyche felt lithe and soft and her long, light brown curls wrapped around him and tickled his lips.

The attraction was so strong that Cupid came to Psyche's bed every Saturday night for a month and they made love ecstatically and then held each other and talked. Psyche was a kindergarten teacher who had had one unsuccessful relationship after another for the past eight years. Both her parents were dead. Her best friend had recently gotten married and was pregnant so they rarely saw each other anymore.

Psyche liked to read poetry and do yoga in her spare time. Cupid was an aspiring actor who had given up his dream and now worked a delivery job. He had a tumultuous relationship with his mother and hadn't seen his dad since he was a little boy. Cupid attended weekly AA meetings where he was currently the meeting secretary. Like Psyche he did yoga and he liked to read books on spirituality. Cupid and Psyche had similar taste in music and movies. They had both listed *Led Zeppelin IV* and *Wings of Desire* as two of their favorite classics, respectively. They both loved dogs but couldn't own one where they lived.

These were the facts—the things they had learned from reading each other's profiles and talking on the phone. There were other things they could not have learned, like how Cupid snorted in a soft, charming way when he laughed and how Psyche giggled like a little girl so that their laughter formed a perfect song; how Cupid's body temperature always ran a little high and Psyche's a little low so that they balanced each other out in exactly the right way; how they both knew how to kiss fiercely but tenderly and knew how to adjust their force or gentleness to work with what the other was doing; how the chemicals that each of their bodies produced blended together to make some kind of perfume that, especially mixed with the smell of the sea and the garden, would have taken a master chemist years to create. They could not have known that the other would know exactly what to say at exactly the right time, like how Psyche told Cupid gently that she thought he was probably a wonderful actor—she could tell by his comic timing, magnetic personality, and beautiful voice, and how Cupid told Psyche, as he was coming, that she had a beautiful, beautiful soul.

The sex was great. The pillow talk was great. But it only happened at night.

Psyche wanted more. After she and Cupid made love she wanted to have him sleep over and take her out for omelets. She wanted them to sit on her bed in the afternoon watching movies and eating pizza with mushrooms and caramelized onions or reading aloud to each other. Psyche wanted to do Cupid's laundry with him. She wanted them to go to the farmers' market together and buy baskets of strawberries. She wanted to give Cupid natural supplements for depression and fatigue. Someday she wanted to have a child with him, a baby girl named Joy. (Cupid had once wondered aloud to her, "If you know right away when you meet someone that you want a baby with them, is that because you are supposed to have babies with them or is it just hormones and projection?" She had been afraid to answer so she had shrugged in the dark and kissed him again.) Besides wanting to have his baby, Psyche wanted to buy Cupid shirts the color of his eyes, or at least the color she imagined his eyes were, because she could not see them—he always came in the dark, made love to her, and left before it was light.

In fact, she did buy him a shirt at a thrift store, a size large cream-colored French cotton shirt covered with blue irises (she hadn't been shopping for him; she'd been trying to find a vintage dress with roses on it but the shirt had caught her eye), but she knew she could not give it to him yet because it would scare him away even more (although less than the knowledge that she had already picked out the name of their unborn daughter), and so she put it in the back of her closet to save it for the day when he was no longer afraid. She imagined giving it to him then with a casual smile: "Oh, yeah, I just found this today. Hopefully it fits." (It would in fact fit; she had measured the breadth of his shoulders with her hands while they were making love).

Psyche was right; Cupid would not want the shirt even though it did in fact match his eyes and fit his shoulders. The shirt would have felt like a symbol of some kind of commitment and he was afraid of commitment; he knew he even had trouble committing to himself. His day job was draining him. Cupid was a gifted actor—he had been in a theater group in college and had gotten the attention of a number of agents—but he was afraid that if he fully devoted himself to his art he might fail. He had gone out for auditions after he graduated but he hadn't had any luck. He began to drink more heavily. Finally his agent fired him. Now he was sober but he didn't even do theater anymore; he told people he didn't have time for it, he was too drained from his job. He was fond of Psyche and loved being with her but she scared him a little. She sent him such passionate poems by her favorite poets like Pablo Neruda and Sappho, and she didn't even know him yet! It seemed as if she wanted to drag him into the daylight, dress him up like a doll and take him out with her to show him off to the world. He came to her in the dark for a reason. The reason was not, as she suspected, that he was ashamed of being seen with her in the world (after all the bad relationships Psyche was feeling a little insecure about her appearance) or that he didn't want to look at her in the sunlight or that he didn't care about her as a person, but only as someone to fuck. No, he knew that in the dark he could hold onto himself. Cupid did not want to lose himself in anyone. He knew what it was like to go on a date with someone, then see her the next night and the next. By the fourth or fifth time he knew what it was like to feel as if he were completely invisible. That was why he came to Psyche only at night. He would not get lost in her. He was already invisible in the darkness so he could not disappear. For this reason he insisted that Psyche never see him in the light.

Psyche was in therapy and knew that she was projecting a lot onto Cupid. The fact that he came to her only at night allowed her to project onto him even more. She felt blind with Cupid and panicky, the way she had felt when she was a child playing hide-and-seek and she was the blindfolded one. "It."

One night Cupid fell asleep after they had made love. Psyche was hoping that he would sleep through until morning so that she could see his face in the light and they could go out to breakfast. She lay awake for a long time watching the clock and waiting for the sun to rise. The room felt hot and stuffy. Finally Psyche could not wait anymore. She got up, lit a candle, and watched Cupid as he lay sleeping beside her. She saw that he was not a beast as she had sometimes suspected when she felt the fur on his chest and the prick of his horn (not that she would have cared if he were a beast; she would still have wanted to buy him groceries and supplements—maybe even more supplements!—and go out to breakfast with him) but a tall beautiful man with eyes like blue irises, as she had also suspected. He did look exactly like his online pictures. He took her breath away and tears came to her eyes suddenly like a pang in your chest. But then some candle wax fell on Cupid's chest, above his heart. He woke and saw Psyche watching him. There was so much love and need in her eyes and it scared him. He wanted to run away.

"You don't love me as much as I love you," Psyche cried when she saw the fear lit in his eyes. "I've been in relationships like this before. I can't do this again."

This made Cupid more afraid and he said, "I don't know how I feel about you. I am fond of you and I love being with you but that's all I know. I haven't seen anyone else."

"You've been seeing someone else?" Psyche shouted, all her senses distorted now with fear.

This made Cupid angry. He spoke slowly. "No. Psyche. I haven't seen anyone else." Then he added, coolly, "But I might have tea with somebody if it came up."

"Tea?" Psyche shouted. "What does tea with somebody mean? Is tea a euphemism for fucking? I can't do this." Psyche said I can't do this too often. She said it whenever she got scared in a relationship and then she regretted it because the man she said it to heard her and decided, in that moment, he couldn't do "this," either.

"I can't talk anymore," Cupid said.

"Wait," said Psyche, softening as the adrenaline drained from her body, as she realized how far she had gone, like the other times with the other men, and that it was probably too late. "I just want to tell you that I think you are wonderful and I don't want us to hurt each other anymore. No one is right or wrong. We just want different things."

Cupid, also softening with resignation and with compassion for

Psyche, replied, "You are beautiful and wonderful and I don't want this to get fucked up. It's no one's fault. We just want different things."

Then he blew out the candle, went out the back door, and left her shaking with regret in the darkness.

The darkness was not safety for Psyche. If she disappeared in it she felt she might never return.

But there were so many tasks to do there. It was where she had to be.

Psyche worked hard in the figurative darkness. She taught her kindergartners, marketed, did the laundry, cleaned her apartment, did yoga until she was soaked through with sweat, meditated in her fairy garden, ran on the beach, worked out with weights, paid all the bills. She also tried to keep up her appearance. She got haircuts, facials, manicures, pedicures, and went shopping for cheap cute clothes at thrift stores (she scrupulously avoided the men's section) so that she would not feel as if she had completely vanished into the dark. Even though her life looked light and bright and happy, and she was happy with her children at school and by herself in her sunny little apartment on weekends—the walls covered with the construction paper, tissue, crayon, and glitter art the kids had made for her—she felt so dark and empty when the sun went down, as if someone had stolen her organs and run off with them and she was left hollow as a scooped-out gourd, rotting in the night. She felt like an old pumpkin that you could smash with your fist, that would crumple in on itself if you even touched it. After Psyche got in bed and read a few chapters of a novel, she cried herself to sleep in the dark. She was always surprised, in the morning, when she was still there.

On Monday afternoons, Psyche saw her therapist Sophia. Luckily, Psyche had a really great therapist who kept the rates low so Psyche could see her every week. (If your name is Psyche you really better have a fucking great therapist like this one.) Sophia had been away for a month in Italy when Psyche confronted Cupid. If her therapist had not been away, Psyche would probably not have lit the candle at all.

She would not have attacked Cupid and they would still be making love in the dark. Psyche had a history of breaking up with men while her therapists were away. None of the other therapists had been as good, though. One of them had been an actual psycho and called Psyche a bitch when she told the therapist things weren't working out and that she wanted to move on. One of them got a rare disease and died soon after the vacation during which Psyche had broken up with her boyfriend at the time. Psyche did not have a good pattern around therapists on vacation and boyfriends. But Sophia, she was very wise. When she got back from her vacation in Italy, Sophia told Psyche a few very important things:

1. Love is pain. You cannot avoid pain. It is part of love. (Psyche hated this one.)
2. The pain can feel like it will kill you but it won't. (This one was better.)
3. When a baby and a mother are relating to each other, there are more incidents of misattunement, when they don't understand each other or connect, than attunement.
4. The key to a successful relationship is not how many times you have misattunement, which is inevitable, but how many times you are able to heal those breaks with kind communication.

"Why don't you call him?" Sophia asked Psyche.

"He doesn't like phone calls," Psyche said. "He acts weird on the phone if I call. He likes to be the one in control of the timing of things. Maybe I can send him an e-mail explaining that he made me think he really liked me and so I got carried away and started to like him and then I got scared because he wouldn't let me see him in the light and I was just curious and so I lit the candle and then I saw how scared he looked and I was more scared because he is so beautiful so I attacked him and then he told me he wanted to have tea with other women which scared me because he had never mentioned anything like that before and I didn't want to attack him anymore, any worse, so I just pushed him away and ended it for good."

"Don't be the lawyer," Sophia said.

"Oh," said Psyche. "You're right. He wouldn't like the lawyer."

"Just send him a single line asking if he would be willing to talk to you." And Sophia added, "In person. In the daytime. So you can really see what's what."

Sophia smiled. Sophia was so beautiful, Psyche thought. She had hair that softly framed her gentle face. She wore soft colors and a mix of beautiful jade and metals and saltwater pearls. Her office had a large stone Quan Yin statue, which watched Psyche lovingly from the corner, and a midnight-blue rug with pink peonies. Sophia was a painter before she became a therapist and had raised three children on her own. She never spoke about herself, unlike all the other therapists Psyche had had who always talked about themselves. Sophia was smarter and kinder than all of them combined. She had better boundaries and more love.

Psyche trusted Sophia and sent Cupid a one line e-mail asking if he would be willing to talk with her. In person. During the day.

Cupid had felt pressured by Psyche and then wounded when she suddenly rejected him. It had all happened so fast. One moment they were making love, then he was asleep in her arms, then he was awake and she was telling him he didn't love her enough. and then, that she didn't want to see him anymore. After Cupid left Psyche's bedroom he had become mildly depressed. Although he had had a series of unsatisfactory romantic relationships, he usually had a positive effect on people. He had been elected secretary of his AA meeting three times and everyone seemed to perk up when he walked into the room. He was always introducing people to each other and some of the people he had introduced had fallen in love and two couples had gotten married. Cupid was proud of this and liked to consider himself a pretty good guy who generally made people happy. So it disturbed him that he had hurt Psyche, that she had been harsh with him because of it, and he began to withdraw. His term as secretary ended and he didn't take on any new duties. He still went to meetings but he kept to himself. Women flirted with him—they always flirted with him—and he had gone to tea with a few of them. While he drank the tea he thought of Psyche, who he had never had tea with in the light, and then of all the other failed relationships in his life, and he became more depressed. His heart felt heavy and sore.

He wrote back to Psyche and said maybe, maybe he would meet her. Psyche waited a week and didn't hear from him. At last he wrote to her and asked what she wanted to talk with him about. Psyche said she wanted to apologize for being overreactive and she wanted to see his face.

Cupid was still hurt. He wrote, "I've moved on. But I'll think about it."

Psyche pretended she was not devastated by this response and kept doing her tasks. She forced herself to get up every morning, wash her hair, get dressed in something halfway cute, make breakfast, pack her lunch, go to work, go to the gym, go to the grocery store, eat dinner, do the dishes, get in bed with a book, and not give in to the black hole that wanted to swallow her up. She fell into it a little though, every time she checked her computer for a message from Cupid that didn't come.

He has moved on, she thought. But I can't.

But then Cupid e-mailed her. When she saw his name in her inbox—she had gotten out of bed in the middle of the night to check, and as it turned out he had just sent the e-mail five minutes before—her heart was pounding so hard she thought she might faint. The e-mail said, "I'm not ready to meet with you at this time."

Psyche could no longer pretend not to be devastated. She told Sophia what had happened with Cupid.

"I think we just need to dig in here," Sophia said. "And look at you, your past, your unconscious. Everything else will work itself out from there."

Psyche usually avoided talking about her childhood, her relationship with her parents, her fears. She spent most of her therapy time talking about the men she was dating. Sophia told her she thought she was distracting herself from the truth. So Psyche started keeping a journal of her dreams and bringing in childhood photos as Sophia had suggested so she could put the focus back on herself. She spent the next few months crying in Sophia's office, teaching her kids, and walking around in a daze most of the rest of the time. She let her online dating subscription expire so that she wouldn't compulsively check the site over and over, sometimes accidentally coming upon Cupid's smiling picture. She felt like she was sorting endless tiny seeds of grain or stealing something precious from a vicious creature or going down into the underworld again and again.

Even on bright days it felt like the middle of night when you lie awake in despair waiting for morning. Once Psyche had believed in love. She had believed, as a little girl, that you meet your twin flame quite easily, that you are naturally drawn to each other across time and space, and that you know right away and as soon as you meet you embark on a journey together until you die. If problems arise you work through them together. Even if the days are long and hard you have the comfort of knowing that the other person will be there beside you in the quiet and peace of the night to soothe you with their body and their voice as you are there to soothe them. She had learned this by watching her parents, who had such a relationship. But when Psyche's father had died, her mother had been so broken-hearted that she had died within a year. Psyche's mother had said, "I don't want to live without him," and Psyche had begged her to stay, but she had died anyway because nothing was more important than the pain of living without her husband, not even her daughter. From that time on, Psyche was dubious about true love because she knew that even if you find it, it will one day come to an end, leaving you devastated. Perhaps that is why she picked such inappropriate men over and over again, even though they did not necessarily appear that way on the surface. They were men who were easy to project a lot of fantasies onto. They were usually quiet men who didn't express their feelings a lot and who had experienced childhoods where it was necessary to adapt to dysfunctional situations by staying under the radar. More than one was an alcoholic. More than one was an actor. Psyche was a pretty, nice, well-educated young woman with a job she liked and a cute beach apartment. People who met her were surprised that she was still alone. But Psyche was beginning to understand.

One day at school one of her kinders was crying. Psyche knelt beside her and asked her why. The little girl said, "It's my birthday tomorrow and no one is going to come."

"How do you know?" Psyche asked. "Because I am going to come."

"I just do," said the little girl. "No one will come." And she began to cry again.

Psyche thought that the way she had pushed Cupid away was not unlike what the little girl was feeling. If you were sad about something that hadn't happened yet you couldn't be disappointed.

After a particularly disappointing tea with an online woman who looked nothing like her profile picture and had no real interest in the things she had mentioned in her profile (yoga, reading, foreign films, spirituality—she was an atheist and a personal trainer, who knew only what downward dog was; she had never heard of Wim Wenders or Eckhart Tolle), Cupid began to focus on his true work instead of on relationships. He remembered how Psyche had encouraged him to find an acting class during their late-night talks, and one day he did. He played Oberon from *A Midsummer Night's Dream* in one scene. His Oberon was charming and savage. When he was acting Cupid felt alive. His skin glowed, his eyes sparkled, and his stomach stopped churning. People began to flourish in his presence again. When Cupid made the students in his class laugh or cry, during a scene or an exercise, he felt like he was flying.

Nine months had passed since Psyche had seen Cupid. One day Psyche woke up from a dream of being kissed by an invisible man and sat down at her computer and e-mailed Cupid.

"Just thinking of you, hope you are well," she typed.

Cupid wrote back almost immediately. "I've been thinking about you, too. Have you been dancing under the moonlight in your garden with the fairies? I felt it."

"I would like to see you again sometime to talk," Psyche wrote back the next day. She made herself wait twenty-four hours, just to be cool.

"What is your schedule like on weekend days?" Cupid wrote.

He figured that she had already seen him in the light and that now that they weren't having sex it would be okay to hang out during daylight hours. He sensed that Psyche was the one lost in the darkness now and he wanted her to feel better so he chose to meet her at the Roman villa overlooking the sea.

Psyche drove up the road among the laurel and sycamore trees with the Pacific Ocean glittering mirthfully beneath her. It was a perfect day of blueness everywhere. She met Cupid in front of the villa and they hugged lightly and looked into each other's eyes for a moment. Psyche told herself, Don't fall into his eyes. You are a different person than he is. She understood, finally, why Cupid had wanted it to be dark when they were together.

Cupid thought how lovely Psyche looked in the daylight. With her long brown curls loose around her bare, pale shoulders and her cream-colored silk vintage dress with its red watercolor roses, she looked as beautiful as her soul had felt in his arms. He wondered why he had never gone out with her in the day before.

Psyche thought that Cupid looked tired but peaceful except for the deep crease between his eyebrows. She wanted to smooth it with her finger.

They walked up the wide steps and wandered through an herb garden, under a grape arbor, past a fountain with theatrical masks spouting water, and along a walkway with walls painted with trompe l'oeil architecture in pale, clear colors. They walked around a long reflecting pool where black bronze statues with eerie, pale, painted-on eyes lined the pool among the hedges and fruit trees.

The inlaid marble floors of the villa echoed with their footsteps. Black figures—nymphs and Satyrs with erections—caroused on terracotta urns. Unself-consciously nude marble gods and goddesses observed Cupid and Psyche coolly from pedestals.

There was a giant statue of Venus; Psyche stood below her. With her flawless marble skin and curves, Venus intimidated Psyche. As Psyche gazed up into Venus's blank eyes, she had to keep tears from filling her own. Haven't I done enough yet? she wondered. How long will it take?

Cupid looked up at Venus, winked and thought, pleasantly, Bitch.

Cupid and Psyche went to the museum café and sat and drank tea and shared a piece of carrot cake with a tiny orange carrot drawn on it in cream cheese frosting, and talked about what they had been doing. Psyche told Cupid about some of her tasks. She spoke breezily and laughed a lot, even though thinking of her life suddenly made her feel weary and close to tears again. (She had no real friends anymore, her job was low-paid and tiring, she had been through a series of bad relationships, therapy was hard.) Cupid told Psyche he had cut back the hours of his day job so he could take acting lessons again. He was auditioning for student films. He tried to sound positive for Psyche's sake and his own, but he was filled with self-doubt. (What if he couldn't even get a part in a student film?)

Psyche felt so happy for him when he said that he had returned to acting that she wanted to hug him again but she refrained.

Instead, as a way to convey warmth and affection, she said, "When I was leaving my apartment my neighbor was walking her dog, Pegasus. He wanted me to scratch his belly but I was running late so I told him, 'Pegasus, I'm sorry but I can't scratch you. I might have to get used to seeing big, beautiful boys and walking away from them.'"

Cupid smiled and blushed. Psyche was surprised that he blushed; she'd never seen him in the light before, remember. She hoped the story had conveyed what she meant it to—that he was a big, beautiful boy and that she might have to let him go but not that she wanted to let him go. She thought the blush indicated the story had been understood.

Since they were on the subject of dogs, Psyche told Cupid about a party one of her students had invited her to where the parents brought in a bunch of puppies to play with the children. (It was, significantly, the party that the little girl had been crying to Psyche about and everyone had come and had a great time.) Psyche had held a small dachshund named Wendy on her lap and it had immediately fallen asleep there. It had long eyelashes and delicate, feminine features. Psyche was in love and wished she could have kept it.

Cupid, who had spent his childhood feeling closer to his dogs than to his parents, told Psyche that he wished he could hire the puppy people to come to him so that he could just spend the afternoon petting puppies.

"Want to join me?" Cupid asked.

Psyche restrained herself from reaching out and touching his hand.

Cupid asked kindly, "What did you want to talk to me about?" and so Psyche began.

She apologized for overreacting when they had been together last. She said, "When you said you wanted to have tea with other women I heard you say you wanted to find someone prettier, someone you would be proud to be seen with in the day. But you didn't say that and it was my own fear that made me shut you off like that."

Cupid said, "Before I said that I felt like you were trying to get me to define my feelings for you and, for whatever reason that I should probably take a look at, when people do that to me I have trouble with it. But it's not about finding someone prettier or someone I'm proud to be seen with."

"I was pressuring you," Psyche said. "I got scared. I'm sorry."

"Part of relationships is communicating like this, talking about shadows in the light," Cupid said. "Not that I know that much about it but that's what I've heard." Since he had stopped seeing Psyche he had sought out advice from the few happily married couples he knew and this is one thing he had learned from them.

"When I'm with you I lose myself," Psyche said. "It's like I'm watching the Cupid show." (Here Cupid couldn't help but smile; he was, after all, a performer.) "I forgot I'm there. I think that's part of what happened."

"I understand," said Cupid. "I want to be with the person all the time and then after a certain amount of time I start feeling really bad and I have to go find myself again."

They talked for a while more and then Psyche had to go to the yoga class she had promised she would make herself attend that afternoon—she would rather have stayed with Cupid. Cupid walked her down the steps and into the parking lot to her car and kissed her on the lips. She kissed his neck with a succession of rapid kisses. She had done this at night, in the dark, while he came, praising the beauty of her soul, but never in the light.

"Just in case," she said. Which meant both *just in case I never see you again I want to remember what it feels like to kiss your neck* and *just in case we are going to be together again I am going to kiss your neck as a promise of things to come.*

Cupid did not say anything to let her know what he thought would happen because he really did not know, but he squeezed Psyche's small body in the watercolor rose dress to his broad chest and when he looked at her for the last time his eyes were gentle as blue irises and Psyche, even in her fear, thought she would probably see them again. Maybe she would even be able to give him his shirt. She had come to think of the man's shirt hanging in the back of her closet as his. But, of course, she wasn't sure if she would ever see him or give him the shirt.

Cupid walked away whistling to himself. He felt lighter, almost buoyant. He didn't mind this kind of uncertainty; in fact it comforted him. He would like this state of noncommitment, warmth, and hope to go on forever.

Psyche, on the other hand, wanted clarity and reassurance and plans for a second date, but for now she did not turn her head and longingly watch Cupid walk away. Instead, she checked her own eyes in the car mirror.

They looked big and bright. They belonged to her and they could see.

Both fairy tales and myths have guided my life and my work. I have always loved the story of Cupid and Psyche but considered it more of the latter than the former. However, I am starting to see the interconnectedness of all cultures and stories and so I decided to explore this favorite tale as the märchen that it was often considered to be.

I am particularly fascinated with the idea of the tasks the soul must accomplish, the journey it must take, in order to be prepared for the rigors of romantic love. The story has a contemporary setting (Cupid and Psyche meet online and go on a date to the Getty Villa in Malibu, California) and I have written it through a third-person point of view that shows the inner experience of both characters. As always, it layers my life experiences with the guiding force of ancient story.

As an addendum, I suddenly, dramatically, and permanently lost a great deal of the sight in one eye after this story was written. I find it interesting how our work often knows things before we do.

—FLB

LILY HOANG

The Story of the Mosquito

ONCE, IN A PLACE FAR AWAY FROM THIS PLACE, IN A TIME THAT WAS
before this time, a woman named Ngoc lived in a village. Although she
lived in a village, she wanted to live in a city. Cities, you see, offer riches
and rich men and rich husbands and rich suitors, and villages, you see,
offer none of these things.

Ngoc means "jade" or "treasure." It's a fitting name. Not only is she
a treasure in and of herself—a real gem of a gal!—but she also desires
treasure.

This is a story like all other magic stories. Don't be fooled. Just
because our characters have different names does not make them fun-
damentally any different from the archetypal characters you've come
to know and love. These names are just markers, a way to signal to you
that they are set in a place that is not this place. These names are just
markers to explain that their values and culture may be slightly variant
from yours, but you really don't need to be scared. We understand:
things that are different can be frightening, but this is not a ghost
story. This is a magic story, and although it ends with sadness, those
who are good will be rewarded and those who are bad will be punished. We are a just people, even though we look different and speak a
different language and our people have different names. We, too, believe in justice.

Now, Ngoc lived in a village, a very poor village, and although she was very beautiful—as all female characters in magic stories are—she was stuck. How beautiful was Ngoc? Well, we probably shouldn't indulge in encouraging her propensity for superficialities, but her hair was the deepest black, stained darker than shadow. This magnified her bright skin, which turned rosy in the sun. Her eyes were simple slits, more eyelash than eye. They were illusive smoke. And her body, well, let us suffice to say she was a dream. She was naturally what women today can achieve only through science and artificialities.

But all of this meant nothing because Ngoc and her family had no money, and so like all women—beautiful or not—who come to a certain age, her family married her to a man. Although she didn't eat much, her family was so poor that providing anything at all was providing too much.

The night before the marriage ceremony, Ngoc dreamed her husband would be old and ugly, with a gut sagging past his testicles. But she dreamed he was rich. He could buy her anything she wanted, and she wanted everything. He moved her to the city, and although she would have to satisfy him, he would allow her to take lovers as well, because her old husband understood that young, beautiful women have needs, too, needs that old men with sagging guts could not necessarily—let us say—rise to meet.

So Ngoc, when she awoke from the most glorious of dreams, prayed it would become truth. As she dressed in her red *ao dai* and pulled her hair away from her face, she imagined the moment her new husband would take his wrinkly, arthritic hand to pull back her veil to reveal her face, how excited he would be, how he would shower her not with affection but with money. This was what she desired most.

Instead, of course, her husband was a young man—exceedingly handsome and without a penny to his name.

But having never met her, he loved her immediately. He was a faithful mule, and he wanted to give her whatever she wanted, if only because she looked all the more beautiful when she was happy. He was the kind of husband all women dream of, except, of course, for Ngoc. To her, he was a nightmare.

His name was Hien, which means gentle. She would have preferred a man with a name that predicted wealth. Hien was educated, smart, with a love for literature and the arts. He could speak English, having gone to university in Saigon, but he wanted a traditional wife, and so he returned to his village to find her. His parents, being old friends with Ngoc's parents, knew they had a beautiful, eligible daughter. Of course, if his parents had known what a money-hungry woman she was, they never would have chosen her.

And it was not as though Ngoc did not get anything she wanted. Immediately after the marriage ceremony, she demanded they move to Saigon. Given he had a post at the university, he had planned that anyway, but he didn't tell her this. Instead, Hien hesitated only momentarily before saying, "If that's what you want."

But life in the city was not what she imagined. Hien had a modest apartment. He worked incessantly but did not bring home much money. She didn't have the jewels she wanted.

In truth, Hien wasn't nearly as poor as people thought he was. He wanted to live simply. He didn't believe in excess. He brought home only a small portion of his salary; the rest he gave to the poor, which were many in Saigon, or to his family. Hien understood that his wife wanted riches and jewels, and although he could have provided those to her, he didn't think it was fair that his small family should have so much when so many more were without.

Ngoc, however, believed her husband was a fool: a man with education, who worked as an educator, who ate rice and fish sauce for every meal, only occasionally indulging in meat. And of course, she was a fool to stay with a foolish man.

———

Because her husband was at his office for most of the day, Ngoc began to wander. She met rich men, men who desired her, and even though she was married, there was nothing wrong with accepting gifts.

Then, one day, Ngoc fell ill. She fell ill, and there were not enough doctors to cure her. All the money Hien had stashed away was depleted, taking her to the best doctors and hospitals in Saigon. She coughed blood and lost flesh. Her face changed color. Her teeth became weak.

Hien sat at her bedside, as in love as ever, and promised that if she would become well again, he would give her all the money and jewels she wanted. All she had to do was recover, but by then, it was too late.

Before Ngoc died, she had asked her husband to lift her body from the bed. Below, she had stashed her treasures: gold bracelets, jade pendants, excess, excess. Ngoc asked her husband to dress her in the finest silk *ao dai* and adorn her with all her jewelry, and although he was disgusted, he obliged his wife, because she was, after all, his wife, and he loved her.

She died within the hour, and Hien could not be consoled. He cried until his tears rose to the level of her deathbed. Then, he cried until his dead wife floated. Even then, his tears were not exhausted and he continued to cry.

After three days of crying, a fairy appeared. She said, "Hien, this isn't right. She was a bad wife, one who neither loved nor appreciated you. What are you doing, crying like this?"

Hien said, "What you say may be true, but she was my wife. How could I not be devastated?"

The fairy said, "But she was unworthy."

Hien said, "But I was unworthy."

The fairy, frustrated, said, "There is something. If you loved her, truly loved her, remove three drops of blood from your body to nourish her back to health, but be careful. You are giving your life for hers. What will you do if she doesn't love you in return?"

But he did not hear her warning. He put a knife to his wrist and made a small incision. He let three drops of his clean blood fall onto her lips, which were cracked and pale.

Ngoc opened her eyes. The fairy disappeared.

But she did not change her ways. Ngoc continued to wander, even though her husband gave her a healthy allowance. With the money Hien gave her, she could afford fine silks and the purest jewels, but it was not enough. She had nearly died. She had to live her life fully.

And Hien continued to work and love his wife. He sacrificed more and more, giving her money while denying himself any pleasure.

Until the day came when Ngoc found another man, an old man with a belly sagging down to his testicles, who wanted to marry her.

She said, "I'm leaving you."

Hien was confused. He couldn't understand, but she had packed all her possessions.

He said, "But I love you."

She said, "If you loved me, how could you deny me anything? Love is extravagance. If you loved me, you would show me by giving me everything I want!"

He said, "But I've given you everything. You don't lack food or shelter or even jewelry! And you have me. I've done nothing but adore you!"

She said, "But your adoration is empty. It means nothing."

Hien thought about this. His love meant nothing.

His love meant her life.

He demanded his three drops of blood back.

She laughed. "Who needs your three pathetic drops of blood? That's all you've ever given me, and what sacrifice was it to you?"

Just as quickly as she said it, she took a pin to her forefinger and spilled his three drops of blood. They fell from her finger and saturated the ground.

The mosquito was born that day, wandering here and there in search of those three drops of blood to bring her back to life.

As for Hien, after his wife vanished, which to him, she did simply vanish, the fairy knocked on his door. She appeared before him, a humble woman with kind eyes, and together, they lived happily ever after.

So here you see: this was in fact a magic story just like any other magic story. If only we'd taken the time to change the names, you would have never known the difference, because mosquitoes are everywhere, and everywhere, they are greedy and unforgiving.

When I was growing up, my parents spoke minimal English, but of course, being in the States, they wanted to encourage me to learn English while not forgetting my "roots." I had several books of fairy tales that were written in English on one side, Vietnamese on the other. I don't have a very clear memory of the contents of these books, except that they weren't traditional—by which I mean Western—fairy tales. The only story I remember with any certainty is "The Story of the Mosquito," which I have retold here.

My memory of these books is tainted though: a fairy tale set inside another fairy tale, one which I don't remember, but it's a story my parents have told me until the story itself has frayed, worn thin. Their fairy tale features me—a voracious reader, quick-witted, wise, and smart, though not particularly pretty—and by the time I was three, I could read, not only in English but also in Vietnamese. At parties, my parents would display me as some mixture of sideshow and genius. I would read these books to their friends: first in English, then in Vietnamese, my accent in both perfect. And here, here is the magic: of course, I couldn't read when I was three. I'd memorized these books, and though they weren't long, maybe thirty to fifty pages each, I'd managed to learn when pages should turn, where words stop and pick up, and so on.

I have looked and looked, and none of my research has turned up either this Vietnamese mosquito fairy tale or the volume in which I read it. [Part of the inspiration for this anthology is the hoped-for revival of older fairy tales, often at risk of disappearing. Perhaps this tale will be discovered one day. Ed.]

I wasn't supposed to be a writer. No one in my family has supported this decision. No, I was supposed to be a doctor, but in many ways, my pilfering of story began there, then, when I was three, with this very fairy tale.

—LH

NAOKO AWA

First Day of Snow

IT WAS A COLD DAY IN LATE AUTUMN. ON A PATH RUNNING STRAIGHT through the village, a young girl crouched down, looking at the ground. She tilted her head and breathed deeply. "Who was hopscotching here?" she wondered aloud.

Hopscotch rings, drawn in chalk, continued endlessly on the path—across the bridge and toward the mountains. The girl stood up. "What a long hopscotch!" she cried, widening her eyes. When she hopped into a ring, her body became as light as a bouncing ball.

One foot, one foot, two feet, one . . . With her hands in her pockets, the girl hopped forward. She hopped across the bridge and down a narrow path through cabbage fields, then past the only tobacco shop in the village.

"Oh, you have a lot of energy!" said an old woman who minded the shop. Panting for breath, the girl smiled proudly. In front of the candy shop, a large dog barked and bared its teeth.

"Who on earth drew a hopscotch this long?" the girl thought as she hopped. When she reached the bus stop, snow flurries began to blow. The hopscotch rings kept going. The girl kept hopping, her red face sweaty.

One foot, one foot, two feet, one . . . The sky had turned dark, and a cold wind blew. The snow started to fall heavily and left white spots on the girl's red sweater.

"It may turn into a blizzard," the girl thought. "Maybe I should go home now."

Then she heard a voice from behind her: "One foot, two feet, hop, hop, hop." Surprised, she turned around and saw a snow-white rabbit hopscotching after her.

"One foot, two feet, hop, hop, hop." When the girl looked closely, she saw another rabbit behind that one. As the snow kept falling, many more white rabbits began following her. She gaped in amazement.

This time she heard a voice from ahead. "White rabbits behind you, white rabbits in front. One foot, two feet, hop, hop, hop."

When she looked ahead, the girl saw a long line of white rabbits hopping. "Oh, I had no idea." She felt as if she were in a dream. "Where are you going?" she asked. "Where does this lead to?"

The rabbit in front of her answered, "To the end, to the end of the world. We're snow rabbits who make snow fall."

"What?" The girl was startled. She remembered a story her grandmother once told her. On the first day of snow, a herd of white rabbits came from north. They went from village to village, dropping the snow. They moved so fast humans saw only a white line.

"You have to be careful," her grandmother said. "If you're caught in the herd of white rabbits, you can never come home. You hop to the end of the world with the rabbits and turn into a chunk of snow."

When the girl first heard this story, a chill ran down her spine. Now she was about to be taken away by the rabbits.

"I'm in trouble!" the girl screamed inside her head. She tried to stop. She tried to stop her feet from stepping into the next ring.

Then the rabbit behind her said, "Don't stop! We're right behind you. One foot, two feet, hop, hop, hop." Her body bounced like a rubber ball, hopping along the hopscotch rings.

While hopping, the girl remembered her grandmother telling a story. Her grandmother had stopped sewing for a moment and said, "Once there was a girl who came home alive after being taken away by rabbits. She chanted with all her might: 'mugwort, mugwort, mugwort in spring.' Mugwort is a charm against evil."

"I'm going to do the same," the girl thought. As she hopped, she imagined a mugwort field. She thought about the warm sunlight, dandelions, honeybees, and butterflies. She took a deep breath. When she was about to say, "Mugwort, mugwort," she was interrupted by the rabbits' singing.

> *"We're snow rabbits white as snow*
> *And snow falls everywhere we go*
> *White as snow, we never stop*
> *One foot, two feet, hop, hop, hop."*

The girl covered her ears with her hands. But the rabbits' singing became louder and louder and spilled into her ears through the gaps between her fingers and kept her from chanting the mugwort charm.

The herd of rabbits and the girl went through a fir forest, crossed a frozen lake, and reached faraway places she had never seen. She saw villages lined with small grass-roofed houses, small towns strewn with sasanqua blossoms, and big cities crowded with factories. But no one noticed the rabbits and the girl. "Oh, it's the first snow of winter," people mumbled and hurried away.

As she hopped, the girl tried to chant the charm, but her voice was drowned out by the rabbits' song.

> *"We're the color of snow*
> *One foot, two feet, hop, hop, hop."*

The girl's limbs were numb with cold, as cold as ice. Her cheeks turned pale, and her lips quivered.

"Grandmother, help!" she thought. Then she hopped into a ring and found a leaf. She picked it up and saw it was a mugwort leaf, bright green. On the back, it had fluffy white hairs.

"Oh! Who dropped this for me?" the girl thought. She held the mugwort leaf to her chest. Then she felt someone cheering for her. She felt many small creatures rooting for her.

She could hear the voices of seeds under the snow, breathing, enduring the cold beneath the ground.

A wonderful riddle came into her mind. She closed her eyes, took a deep breath, and cried, "Why is the back of a mugwort leaf so white?"

Hearing this, the rabbit ahead of her tottered. He stopped singing and turned around. "The back of a mugwort leaf?" he said.

"I wonder why?" said the rabbit behind her, stumbling. The rabbits' singing broke off, and their pace slowed down.

Seizing the moment, the girl said, "That's easy. It's rabbit fur. Rabbits roll around in the field and shed their hair on mugwort leaves."

"Yes, you're right!" said the rabbits, delighted. They started singing a new song:

> "We're the color of spring
> of the hairs on a mugwort leaf
> One foot, two feet, hop, hop, hop."

Then the girl thought she smelled the fragrance of flowers in the air. She heard the chirping of small birds. She imagined herself hopscotching in a mugwort field, bathed in the spring sun. Her cheeks turned rosy. She closed her eyes, took a deep breath, and shouted, "Mugwort, mugwort, mugwort in spring!"

When she opened her eyes, she was hopping alone along a strange path in a strange town. She saw no rabbits ahead or behind. Snow flurried. The hopscotch rings were no longer on the path, and the mugwort leaf was gone from her hand.

"Ah, I'm safe," the girl thought. But she couldn't take another step.

A crowd of strangers gathered around her and asked for her name and address. When she told them the name of her village, they looked at each other, muttering, "I can't believe it." They didn't think a child could have walked from such a faraway place beyond many mountains. Then an old woman said, "She must have been led away by rabbits."

The townspeople fed the girl warm food and put her on a bus home before dark.

—*Translated from the Japanese by Toshiya Kamei*

"First Day of Snow" borrows elements from different folktales about disappearance. In Japanese tradition, the mysterious disappearance of a person is often attributed to an angry deity. This is called kamikakushi, *or "hidden by gods." There are many tales in which this motif appears. The girl in "First Day of Snow" is almost spirited away. You might recognize this motif from the anime film* Spirited Away, *directed by Hayao Miyazaki. Rabbits also play an important role in Japanese mythology. They live on the moon and make* mochi *(sticky rice cake). In "The White Rabbit of Inaba," a rabbit deity tells the fortune of Okuninushi, who is treated like a slave by his brothers. This is a lovely story, full of the delicacy and mystery of the fairy-tale tradition.*

—TK

I Am Anjuhimeko

THE LAUGHING BODY

I AM ANJUHIMEKO, THREE YEARS OLD.

In stories, it seems to me the person they refer to as father usually wasn't around or was absence itself, no matter what story I happened to hear, the person called father would be dead in the house or out somewhere traveling or listening to whatever the stepmother was telling him to do, but in my house, there is someone called father, and he is intent on killing me, he is always doing his best to do so, but I don't know what to do, I've had nothing but hardship since I was born.

My father said this baby's mouth is so monstrously big it seems to stretch all the way to her ears, her eyelids have folds in them, her face is flat, she's got moles and birthmarks all over, her ears are big, big, big, something is wrong with her, it's like she's the freakish baby of some old priest, no way she's mine, no way, I'll call her Anjuhimeko, after those Anju—those lowly priests living in little cells for hermits—that's what I'll call her, and I'll bury her in the sand, and if she can survive for three years then she can be my child.

Something's the matter with me, he says, look, I was born and here I am now, who cares if I've got one or two heads, who cares if I've got one or two hands, one too few or one too many? none of that really matters anyway, but that's not what father says, he says let's try burying her in the sand and waiting for three years, mother was willing to just go along with that, that was a big disappointment, but, well, here's the problem, I'm just a newborn who can't even see, and I can't even utter a word to talk back, so I was wrapped in my mother's silk underclothes and buried in a sandy spot near a river.

Speaking of which, the sandy place near the river is the place where everybody buries their babies.

To both the right and left of the place I was buried, there were so many buried babies that they jostled against one another, some were breathing, some weren't, some had struggled partway out of the sand and then dried up, some had managed to escape all the way out of the sand and crawl away.

Just crawl a little bit and there is a big bush, mosquitoes and flies sting any baby who tries to get there, but if they are able to escape from the fierce sun and take shelter from the rain and wind, they can pluck grass or leaves to eat, and if they manage to make it to the river, they can just go right in and live in the water, even though I was still buried in the sand, I watched the others around me, I watched the babies as they died, the ones who were already dead, and the ones who managed to survive and get away.

That's right, how could anyone possibly have karma as bad as mine?

In only three years I gave birth to three children, but my husband buried one of the babies I'd gone to all the trouble to bear, he buried her in the sand, and now my swollen breasts are too much to bear, the holes in my breast where the milk should come out are plugged up, feverish, and swollen, just a simple touch and my breasts hurt so badly I think they'll rip open, but between the pain in my breast and the sorrow at having my child buried, I spend every day weeping from dawn to dusk, and in the process of all this weeping, I have ruined my eyes, when that happened my husband said to me he didn't want me in the house any longer because I'd gone blind, you're the one who gave birth to the baby that wasn't fit for anything except burial, no doubt you've got something deep and dark in your karmic past that made you give birth to that child and made you go blind, if you stay here, your deep, dark karma will rub off on me, so before that happens, do me the favor of dying or at least getting the hell out of the house, shit, I wish I could have buried you in the sand, too, that's what he said.

Then, the next day, I check that the two children on my right and my left are still asleep, and I hold my breath as I quietly sneak out, I creep out of the house as quietly as I can, I'm going to dig a hole in the sand and hide myself in it, where was it that baby was buried? every day more and more people come to bury their babies so I don't have any idea where mine is, I have no idea, but I dig a hole in the sand and bury myself in it anyway, and as I do so, the cries of the children reach my ears, I feel the faint warmth of the bodies of the buried babies, as long as I stay buried here in the sun, I can't forget what has happened to me, if I'd known this was what fate had in store for me, I wouldn't have obeyed my husband and buried the baby, that wasn't a good idea, if things were all that bad, there must have been some other way, there must have been something I could've done, but no matter how much I regret it, no matter how much, no matter how much, no matter how much, it still isn't enough, and I weep hysterically.

When I look around, I see footprints in the sand, handprints in the sand, what are those? in them, I see the outlines of five toes and even the swirls of the prints of the individual toes, they're the size of an adult's feet—no, wait, here and there among the big prints are a couple of prints from a child's foot, but there are only one or two of them, maybe those prints are Anjuhimeko's, I see the patterns of fingers, several strands of hair, dried bloodstains, wet patches, many, many bodies of all different sorts, which of them belongs to her? I can't say, does that handprint belong to her? could that footprint be hers? what about that fingerprint? is that strand of hair one of hers? when she was buried, the last thing I saw was her ear, a big, big, big ear, I could see the sand pouring into it so I took the hollow stalk of a reed and stuck it in the hole in her ear, and that was the last I saw of her, the hole was all filled in.

Will my husband change his mind and come get me? what if he doesn't? I don't know, meanwhile, it seems as if I can hear the cries of the buried babies emerging here and there from the sandy patch of land, I don't know, I feel what seems like the weight of a baby or something on my shoulders and on my back, it's on my hands and arms, I feel as if I'm touching the children's corpses, will my husband come or not? the stench of the babies reaches me every time the wind blows, I feel like the stench is accusing me every time the wind blows, if I'd known how things would work out, I would've gotten rid of the baby a long time ago when I was pregnant, that's what I keep thinking to myself, but I didn't and so that's why these horrible things are happening to me, will my husband come or not? will he or won't he? maybe he will and maybe he won't, maybe he won't, as I think these things to myself, the children accuse me and I feel their reproaches sink deep into my skin.

And then I think that even if one was buried, two of my babies still remain, people keep telling me I should give up on her, I should give up on her, but even if I've given up on my buried baby, I still can't give up on the husband who threw me out, buried here in the sand, all I can think about is whether or not he'll suddenly change his mind and come take me away, that's the only thing on my mind, dead child, go ahead and die, die, don't look back, I want to live.

Then go ahead and get out of the sand, you can't really do anything, you should go and chase sparrows out of the millet fields for a living, that's what people tell me so that's what I do, I climb out of the sand, and here I am.

No matter where I go, the sun beats down on me, the rain has stopped so the sun beats down, I keep walking, and with each passing minute the burning sun roasts me a little more, I keep walking, just a look and you can see how burned I am, as I walk, the steam rises from my burned body yet I keep walking the country roads, this is the fate that has befallen me, I cry out, excuse me please, excuse me, and in response, a master of a nearby house emerges, without saying anything, I clasp my hands, begin weeping, and explain I can chase the sparrows from his millet fields, he asks me why I've come, I tell him my baby was buried alive in the sand by my husband, my breasts were swollen, I missed my buried baby, I wept so much I went blind, my husband threw me out when I went blind, I could feel the buried children reproaching me when I tried burying myself in the sand, and that was more than I could bear, but then someone came and told me to chase sparrows so I came here intending to do just that.

He says my story is a heart-wrenching one, and so he'll hire me, I can work for him chasing sparrows, perhaps then my spirits might lift a little, that's what he says to me, and so from that day forth, I have chased the sparrows from his millet fields Tsusōmaru, my son, how I miss you!—hoy! hoy!—Anjuhimeko, my daughter, how I miss you! As I chase the sparrows with my cries—hoy! hoy!—the little children surround me and stick their fingers in my face saying, Auntie! here's your Anjuhimeko! Auntie! I'm your Tsusōmaru, I'm blind so they tease me in unspeakable ways, I'm miserable, and still the children tease me in unspeakable ways.

Stories go fast in the telling, three years later, my father says, it's the third anniversary of the day I buried Anjuhimeko, why don't I try digging her up to see if she's dead or alive?

And when he digs me up, here I am, I'm not dead, I haven't dried up, I just warmed myself in the sand, a growing, a laughing, living body.

Mother stuck the hollow stalk of a reed in the hole in my ear to mark where I was, so morning and night, I would suck the dew through the tiny, tiny, tiny hole in the stalk, and so I grew, a laughing, living body.

That's right, they dig me up and here I am, I'm not dead, I haven't dried up, I just warmed myself in the sand, a growing, laughing, living body, mother stuck a stalk in the hole in my ear to mark me, morning and night I would suck the dew through the tiny, tiny, tiny hole, and here I am, a growing, laughing, living body, a growing, laughing living body, a growing, laughing, living body, that is what I am, that is who I am!

RESURRECTION

Father says, it is outrageous that this child was buried three years and didn't die, this won't do, let's send her into exile on another island, he gazes across the sea and sees a boat out where the water is deep, he says, I'm going to put you on that boat and send you away, but you're still my own child so I'll call out to Amida Buddha once before I send you away, and as he is calling out to Amida Buddha, the boat disappears off the far edge of the sea, he says, since the boat has disappeared, I'll put you on a boat of mud or planks and get rid of you, with this, he puts me on a nearby raft, and I'm sent into exile adrift on the water, thank goodness the wind and the tides send me in a good direction, I pray three times, oh raft, here I am, send me home, send me home, send me home just as I am! with me on it, just as I am, the raft smashes into my house, the raft smashes into my father, and as it smashes into him, he says, this is a strange raft, with the waves so high it should be all wet, with the wreck it should be damaged, but without getting wet or getting damaged the raft has come back all the way to the house, what a strange raft, she is probably on it somewhere, what a strange raft, he looks everywhere to see if I, Anjuhimeko, am on it somewhere, but I'm not there for him to see, I've climbed ashore already, after tearing off the silk undergarments in which my mother wrapped me, I make my way into the grassy fields and woods, I have no destination in mind, I just make my way deep into the forest, there the ivy is all tangled, and it is like dusk even in the middle of day, I have no destination, I have no home, I hear the faint, faint, faint sound of a drum and samisen, I wonder if these sounds are made by human beings, I hurry to the spot, and there I see a man who is pounding on a drum and plucking the strings of a samisen, he is in the middle of a performance of sacred music and dance, he asks why I'm here so I answer, when I explain to him all that has befallen me, the man tells me to come with him and he'll hire me, that's how I decide to get a job, he says he'll give me pleasant thoughts, he'll raise me well, that's how I decide to get a job even though I don't know the first thing about the man.

When I get a job from the man about whom I know nothing, for two or three days he pampers me with sweet talk, calling me his butterfly and his flower, but when ten days go by, he torments me, saying, Anjuhimeko, go pound the millet, go pound the rice, here I am, three years old, I can't possibly hold a pestle with this little body of mine, so he hangs me upside down over a pile of burning cattails and he begins roasting me, I'm helpless, I just keep roasting, there is nothing I can do but hang there and roast, do men always say such unreasonable things?

Just as I'm wondering what he's going to say next, he torments me, telling me there are pebbles scattered all over the field in front of me, he tells me to pick them all up before the sun sets, I hurry as much as I can to pick up the pebbles, but mine are the fingers of a three-year-old, the skin on all ten finger pads wears thin, and red blood begins to trickle out, there is no way I can finish so he ends up hanging me upside down and roasting me with the cattails, that's why even now the sight of a cattail makes me sick.

Just as I'm wondering what he's going to say next, the man saunters over nonchalantly and torments me, telling me I need to go break apart the stones on the mountain in the distance, he tells me to dig up the dirt and haul it here, he tells me to haul seven cauldrons' worth in seven days, here I am, three years old, if I try breaking apart the stones, digging the dirt and hauling it here, wouldn't I be crushed under all its weight? do men always say such unreasonable things? I hate this man who says such unreasonable things, but if after he says these unreasonable things he roasts me over the cattails and I lose my life, then

I don't know what the purpose of having survived all this time will have been, in the end, I don't go to sleep, instead I break apart the stones, dig up the dirt, and haul seven full cauldrons' worth in seven days, that's what I did, I showed them, and here I am.

Just as I'm wondering what he's going to say next, the man saunters over nonchalantly and torments me, telling me I need to scoop up some water, just as I'm wondering what he's going to give me to do it with, he hands me a bamboo basket, I look at it and see there are holes in it so big that fish, big and little ones, could slip right through, as I stare at it wondering how on earth to keep water in it, tears well up in my eyes, the tears well up as fast as I wipe them away, I go to the riverbank as I weep, and there the water flows steadily along, I don't know how deep it is, I look and see myself reflected once, twice upon the water, there I am, if I had a regular life I could live to be more than a hundred years old, but can I make it that far? what would my mother, who wrapped me in silk underclothes and stuck a stalk in the hole in my ear, think if she knew about this? but there's no way I can scoop up water in a bamboo basket with holes, maybe if I ask the spirit-child who lives in this abundant river that flows along so steadily, he might give me divine aid and help me scoop up the water, so here I am standing on the railing on the bridge and praying, oh, Spirit-Child of the River! I want to scoop up the water from this river but I can't, I want to but I can't, I want to but I can't, when I stand up straight and intone this three times with tears falling, an oil vendor comes from the far side of the bridge.

Is this child weeping because she can't scoop up water? look, I'll give you this oil paper, paste it on your basket then scoop up the water, with this the oil vendor takes a piece of oiled paper in his big hands and gives it to me, when I paste it on my basket, I scoop up the water and my task is complete.

Now, just as I'm wondering what he's going to say next, the man saunters nonchalantly over and torments me again, telling me to use my fingernails to cut down ten reeds and bring them to him, how can my fingernails possibly cut down reeds? my fingernails are the thin, thin nails of a three-year-old child, thinner than even the reeds, they are soft, soft, so very soft, but if I don't cut them I'll get roasted again in the cattails, do men always say such unreasonable things? tears well up at the question, but then a man in black comes toward me, he says, is this child weeping because she can't cut down reeds? with this, he takes out a knife, the knife the man in black has shines in the sun, the blade is big, and it cuts down ten reeds right before my very eyes, how terribly grateful I am!

Then the man saunters nonchalantly over and torments me, telling me, Anjuhimeko, suck on this, so I suck on it hating it the whole time, next he torments me, telling me to hold it in my mouth, I think how much I hate this, but I think how awful it is to be roasted by cattails so I hold it in my mouth hating it the whole time, next he torments me, telling me, Anjuhimeko, put this down there, here I am, a three-year-old child, if I put that thing down there my body will split wide open and that'll be the end of me, I beg him with tears, no, not that, anything but that, but the man makes scary faces at me, it'll be the cattails for me, the cattails for me, do men always say such unreasonable things? I don't want to be broiled over the cattails anymore, even if I die I'll be none the worse for it, so I stick that thing down there, to my surprise it isn't all that I thought it would be, but I do feel like my guts are being all stirred up and popping out, I pick up my guts one by one and put them back into my body, my guts and my flesh spring out and slide around so it is really hard to put them back in, however I am happy because my guts are such pretty colors, I'm happy because they are bright blue and bright red, colors that really wake you up.

Next he lights fires under the seven cauldrons, then torments me again, telling me, now Anjuhimeko, I've taken the water you scooped up and poured it over the cauldrons of soil you dug and lit fires underneath with the reeds you cut, now walk over here with no clothes and no shoes, the cauldrons are boiling hot and making bubbling noises, I stand on the edge, do men always keep saying such unreasonable things one after another? I cry out loudly, here I'm in tears when a sparrow comes flying by, the man is looking the other way when it chirps to me, now is the time to run, oh Anjuhimeko, three years old, now is the time to run, so with no clothes and no shoes, I escape following the sparrow, finally, I arrive at an unfamiliar house standing in the middle of a field.

Excuse me, excuse me, I call out, and a man comes from deep inside the house, he asks me, where've you come from with no clothes and no shoes? just looking at you, I can see you're still only a child of three years old, I want to give you shelter, but if that man chases you here then he'll torment me, too, he'll broil me with cattails and kill me too, please, get out of here quickly, when I go outside, the day is rapidly drawing to a close, a heavy rain is beginning to fall, what shall I do? the man is chasing after me, if he catches me this time I really will die, what shall I do? then I hear a voice saying, little girl, little girl, come back, there's no doubt the voice is calling me, it is a man's voice, I return along the path and dash into the unfamiliar house in the middle of the field.

Little girl, little girl, you've come back? here, quick, have some rice to eat, then get into this bag and I'll hang you from the rafters, you've come to me asking for help because of some karmic connection, I've decided to save you no matter how much he torments me or roasts me with cattails, here, quick, have some rice to eat, then get into the bag, once you're in the bag hanging from the rafters, you mustn't scratch your ears or even break wind, and with this he picks me up and the bag, too, he is so powerful, so stalwart, so strong, the man who was chasing me arrives at the house, he reproaches the man in the house, asking if Anjuhimeko hasn't come here, Anjuhimeko who is three years old, every time I tell her to do something, she plays tricks on me like a good-for-nothing and slips away, she's a cunning little brat, there's no place other than here for her to go, look, that bag hanging over there just swung a little, get it down and show me what's inside.

I'm resigned that once I'm down, I'm going to die, I'm resigned that both I and the man who has given me shelter will die, roasted over cattails, but the man who has given me shelter says to the man who was chasing me, I'll lower the bag if you repent for what you've done, then the man who was chasing me says, I'll cut it down with a saw, then the man who has given me shelter scoops some water into a basin and shoves it in front of the man who was chasing me, when he saw his reflection in the water, his mouth was ripped open so wide his lips extended to the back of his neck and his teeth jutted out in every direction, the man who'd given me shelter jeered at him, saying, so you're really a demon at heart? repent, repent, we don't need any demons here, repent, repent, no demons here, repent, repent, and finally, the man who was chasing me disappears, he is gone, nowhere to be seen.

THE TRAVELING CHILD

Here I am, clad in dyed-black clothes, indigo leggings, cotton *tabi* and belt of straw, ready to set out to see my mother, but nowhere do I see the woman called mother, I travel around these sixty-some provinces to find her, but nowhere do I see the woman whom I call mother, I sleep in both fields and mountains, I sleep upon my folding fan as a pillow, and I use my straw hat as a screen to stop the wind, the rain falls on me, the wind blows at me, dogs bark and bite at me, I'm afraid of the laughter of the crows and the loud rustling of the trees so I cover my ears and run past, but I don't see my mother anywhere, my mother was the one who gave birth to me so long ago, but she has disappeared, and I can't find her anywhere, still her child has grown up like this even without a mother, her child has grown even though she didn't suckle at her mother's breast, I wish my mother would just die prematurely, die and show me her body just as it is, that way I wouldn't have to go see her, but since that doesn't happen, she must be living somewhere, and so I have to go see her.

I'm seven years old, and it is spring, around the month of April, I walk on and on, the days grow dark and draw to a close, I make my way into mountains so deep that one can't tell forward from back-ward, I want to stay in an inn but there are no villages, finally, as the day is drawing to a close, I look and see a hut of grassy bamboo in the distance, there is a light, I try to go there in search of lodgings, but I can't get there, in front of the hut is a big river, I look both upstream and downstream, but there is no bridge, I've come this far but I can't cross, I can't cross, how sad I am! I try to pray to the spirit-child of this rapidly flowing river, thinking that perhaps his divine grace will help me cross, oh, Spirit-Child of the River! I want to cross this river but can't, I want to cross but can't, I want to cross but can't, I intone this request three times, and then a dead tree falls down all by itself, then a second dead tree falls down all by itself, and then a third dead tree falls down all by itself, forming a bridge over the river, how terribly grateful I am, this is all thanks to the divine child of the river!

Excuse me, excuse me, I call out, going into the bamboo hut, and there is a young woman, her voice makes her sound so young, she invites me in, and with this I'm let into the hut, finally, after something to eat, I heave a big sigh, thinking I'll try having a conversation about this and that with the young woman, and so I ask her, young lady, have you been blind since birth?

She says, oh child, you ask questions without any reserve, how could anyone possibly have karma as bad as mine? I've not been blind since birth, in only three years I gave birth to three children, but my husband buried in the sand one of the babies I'd gone to all the trouble to bear, the milk welled up in my breast, my breasts swelled, and be-cause I missed the child buried in the sand so much, I wept until my eyes went bad, when I went blind, my husband sent me away, I tried burying myself in the sand because I wanted to die, but as I was look-ing at the traces of the children buried there in the sand, I thought I would try living by chasing away sparrows so I crawled out of the sand, now here I am chasing away sparrows by crying out, Tsusōmaru, my beloved son, how I miss you!—hoy! hoy!—Anjuhimeko, my daughter, how I miss you!—hoy! hoy!

I am Anjuhimeko, mother! I am Anjuhimeko, and I'm alive, I'm here in this world!

Astonished, mother says, how could my Anjuhimeko have come here? the dead shouldn't come back, some kind of changeling must've come to me from some mysterious place this evening, no, my Anjuhimeko has a large mole on her right ankle and a red birthmark on her left shoulder, this year would have been her seventh year, every day I light my lantern and pray for her, there's no way she would appear here lost, mother says this through tears of astonishment.

Hearing this much, I know we are mother and child, but if she can't see, then she can't see I have a mole, she can't see I have a birthmark, the tears well up in my eyes as I think nothing could be more terrible than this, but then I hear her asking me to rub her right eye, so I do as she asks and rub her right eye, as her eye rubs against the palm of my hand, discharge and tears spill forth, and her eye suddenly pops open, mother! I am Anjuhimeko, and I'm alive, I'm here in this world!

Mother and I weep and laugh all night, our reunion lasts all night.

Ten days later, I ask mother for some time alone because I want to visit my father, Anjuhimeko! you say such foolish things, where is the man called father? what fatherly thing has he ever done for you? if your father was really your father, why would he put you in the sand, Anjuhimeko? why would he hate you so much he'd cast you out to sea, he bids you to complete unreasonable and difficult hardships, he has roasted you with cattails and made you suffer every kind of cruelty imaginable.

That isn't true, mother! I'm here in this world because I have my father, if I had no father I would never have been buried in the sand but I also never would have been able to emerge again, if I had no father, I never would have been cast to sea but I also never would have been able to return to land again, if I had no father, I never would have undergone such unreasonable and difficult hardships but I also never would have been able to scoop up water in a bamboo basket full of holes or cut down ten reeds, if I had no father, I wouldn't have been hung from the rafters but I never would have been here doing the things I'm doing now, that is why I have to go see father, I want to go see him, I want to go see him, I want to go see him, I say this like it was the greatest dream in my whole life.

I don't remember the man called father, there was a man out there who had the face of a demon and who ran off, he was definitely my father, but the only thing I remember about him is his demonic face, there was a man who chased off the father with the face of the demon for me, he was definitely my father, too, but the only thing I remember about him is that he had such strong arms when he hung me from the rafters, that's all, there was a man who took out a knife and cut down some reeds for me, he was definitely my father, too, but the only thing I remember about him is that his shiny knife was so sharp, that's all, there was a man who gave me a piece of oil paper when I was on the riverbank looking bewildered, I only remember how big his hands were but he was definitely my father, too, but that's all I remember.

Mother, what you say is right, my father buried me in sand, he dug me out and set me adrift on the sea, then he tormented me by telling me to pound the millet and pound the rice and dig up dirt and scoop up water, he turned me upside down and roasted me with cattails, there are many scars left on my body, there are many scars left on my body, my skin got burned when he roasted me, I got calluses when I picked up pebbles and the calluses split and broke and blood ran forth, my fingers got broken when I broke the stones apart, how many trembling fingers did I have that were held together by nothing but a single thin layer of skin? surely the man they call my father is nowhere to be found.

Getting roasted, getting beaten, getting killed, getting stuck through the genitals—these things are all the same to me, but the father who is really called father believed I was happy with him sticking himself through my genitals, that is a grave mistake, however, even though I understand that, I have to believe that my father did it because he loved me, because he loved me, because he loved me, I have to believe that even if I was roasted with cattails, even if I underwent such unreasonable and difficult hardships, even if I was chased around with him wearing his demonic face, even if he did stick himself through my genitals, I have to believe that all this happened because father loved me, if even terrible things and painful things befall me, I'll quickly forget them, I believe it's all because father loves me.

With a face stained by tears, mother says, this is what they are talking about when they say parting is like a live tree splitting apart, this is the child for whom my womb ached, the child to whom I gave birth, the child who fattened while suckling at my breast, the child whose dirty bottom I would lick clean, the child who flustered me so much as I held her trying to comfort her tears, the child whose sleeping face I would gaze at untiringly all day and all night, my mother said these things as she pulled out her shriveled breasts, this is what they are talking about when they say parting is like a live tree splitting apart, the live tree that split when you were buried in the sand is once again splitting, but blood will pour out instead of sap.

Not necessarily, mother! I'll cut off the little finger of my right hand and leave it for you, no matter how many years it takes me before I return, all you have to do is lick it and you won't go hungry, you'll be fine even without chasing the sparrows away, please live here in comfort as you grow old, please wait until I return, for the first time my mother gives me a smile, if you cut off your little finger, it'll hurt, but I say, look mother! it doesn't hurt, it's just a little blood coming out, just blood coming out, just blood trickling out, and blood that trickles will stop soon.

And so at last, here I am, clad in dyed-black clothes, indigo leggings, cotton *tabi*, ready to set out to see my father, I meet many different kinds of fathers during my search for my father, I meet fathers with whiskers and fathers without whiskers, the smell of fathers exudes from their pores, I meet fathers with stuffed-up noses and fathers without stuffed-up noses, I meet fathers with bald heads and fathers with full heads of hair, I meet fathers as skinny as bags of bones and fathers so big they jiggle with fat, fathers covered with freckles, fathers covered with body hair, fathers with small hands, fathers with big hands, fathers with bent fingers, fathers with straight fingers, I meet fathers with skin diseases and fathers without skin diseases, one father has eczema that has turned into wet and running sores, one father who is seated under the scattering cherry blossoms has a body colored brilliant hues of red and blue, one father in front of the chrysanthemums who has a body colored gold and silver, one father who is so short I could crush him underfoot, one father who has hair so long it hangs all the way to his hips and he has to untangle it constantly with a comb, one father who has strong underarm odor, I put my head under his arm and take a deep, deep, deep breath, where was it that I met that father?

I Am Anjuhimeko

I am Anjuhimeko, I am Anjuhimeko, the girl who was sexually molested by her father but who still grew up, I'm that wretched girl Anjuhimeko whose father tried to kill her, I am Anjuhimeko, the girl whose was sexually molested by, almost killed by, and now abandoned by her father, I'm that wretched, wretched, wretched girl Anjuhimeko who once died, that's who I am, I try to run away but my father appears to me in many different forms and tries to kill me, and it's such a hardship every time he does.

It's such a hardship every time he does, will I survive this time? no, I won't survive this time, will I? I've thought this so many, many, many times, when I think I won't survive, I hold my hand into the sky and I stare hard at it, I stare hard, so hard at it, with my hand in the air I can see right through it, each time I think this time I might not make it, I can see right through my hand, I feel like I can see the bones, the blood vessels, the flow of blood, and even the fate that will carry me to my death, it's such a hardship.

It's always such a hardship.

I am Anjuhimeko, I am Anjuhimeko who was unable to survive and who died as a result, I have to bring Anjuhimeko back to life again, I'm Anjuhimeko, the one who died thinking I must bring Anjuhimeko back to life and take her to Tennoji, or maybe if I can just take her to Tennoji then I, Anjuhimeko who is dead, will be able to come back to life, I'll take myself to Tennoji, that's a good idea, but I don't have any idea what Tennoji is or where I could possibly find it, that child will help me out, I should go see the child and ask, the child will surely know what Tennoji is and where I could find it, I'll know if I meet the child, I'll know all about Tennoji, that's all I can think of, the child is all that I can think of, is there any way other than asking the child? I don't know, asking the child is all that I can think of, maybe I'll never meet the child again, but that's all that I can think of.

One day I get word from the child.

He says to me, for some reason I've also been thinking of you often, I'm certain that's the name of a place and I'm certain I know the way there, I think it would be wonderful if I were able to take you to Tennoji, but I'm sick, you're sick, I'm no less sick than you, you're no less sick than I, it is strange, did we call to each other because we're both sick? ages ago you forgot me, I forgot you, and we both went to live among other people, but still I heard you, how many years has it been since we have talked? the last time we met, you were still a small, small, small child, yes and I was also a small, small, small child, didn't we often hide from adults, show each other our naked bodies and urinate together? didn't we also take fruits from the trees and eat them? didn't we pickle the fruits and bugs we caught in our own urine? I'm certain I know the way to Tennoji, but I'm sick, I no longer have the energy to walk all the way there.

He says, when I remember you, those memories come flooding back, in those days I was also a young child, almost a baby, never since have I ever thought about things so much as I did then, I used to think, I used to think about everything I could see, about the grass, the trees,

the wind, and the clouds, and you were always also there, one day I
took a cookie in one hand and I suddenly became aware of the concept of nothingness, I tried to tell mother about this, but she didn't
understand so I told you about it instead, you were a small, small,
small child back then, you used to wear red clothes, you used to always
be at my side, you used to wear red clothes, I told you about it, about
the concept of nothingness I'd grasped, one child little more than an
infant told another child little more than an infant about nothingness in the words of a child little more than an infant, I think you
understood, but now there is nothing I can do for you, I don't have the
strength to walk.

He says, you weren't able to pronounce more than a few sounds in
those days, the words you said sounded like mush in your mouth, back
in those days and back when you were a small, small, small child, did
you have a voice as lovely as yours is now? your voice now is so lovely,
I hear the child say these things, now his voice sounds like that of an
old, old, old man and I hear it across the distance, while I'm looking
lost, not knowing what to do next, a *yamanba*, one of those old trickster witches from the mountains, comes up to me, she says, this is my
dying wish, please carry me on your back to that place, that place in
the mountains, the *yamanba* says, this is my dying wish, I want to have
intercourse, I say to her, what is this? before today you've grabbed so
many people and gobbled them up, what, now you have a request?
come on! when I confront her like this, the *yamanba* laughs scornfully
at me and says, what? when I've eaten you, haven't you always come
back to life without any problem? I wanted to bring you back to life,
that's why I'm always eating, as long as I leave your navel or your
clitoris, you'll come back to life, even if I grind you to dust in my teeth,
even if I burn you black, even if I mash you to bits, or even if I pound
you to smithereens.

She says this is her dying wish, but this isn't a trifling thing she
asks, my heart feels heavy as I ask, if I carry you on my back into the
mountains, you'll probably start gnawing at me from where you sit on

my back, you'll grind me to dust in your teeth, you'll burn me black, you'll mash me to bits, you'll pound me up and swallow me, and after that you'll no doubt turn me into shit and squeeze me out, then if I come back to life, you'll once again pretend to be a praiseworthy person and come trick me again.

The *yamanba* laughs and says, and then you'll come back to life, it is precisely because I squeeze you from the hole in my backside that you come back to life.

The *yamanba* says, but I want to have intercourse, I want to have intercourse, I really want to, when you get to be my age you'll understand, at that time, who is going to carry you on their back into the mountains?

So with that, I carry her on my back into the mountains.

It was a hardship, she doesn't just allow herself to be carried quietly along, she undoes my hair, she pulls out my hair, she rubs her feces and urine into my back, she gouges out my moles with her fingernails and eats them, the *yamanba* does every bad thing she can possibly do while I'm carrying her, when I stop and give her a fierce look like I'm going to let her go and take off, I see the woman on my back is just a tiny, tiny, tiny, regular old woman, she says to me, please, please, please take pity on me, and she begins crying, she says in a heart-wrenching voice, because here are the breasts that once nursed you, the breasts she shows me are very, very, very shriveled.

I walk into the mountains, once there, the *yamanba* rediscovers a huge, huge, huge phallus she'd located in the past, and she has intercourse with it.

The *yamanba* says, just watch me! listen to what kind of voices I make! watch what kind of expressions I make! Anjuhimeko, your job is to bear witness! so I say I'll watch her, the *yamanba* shouts out in a loud voice, this is how you came out, too! as she speaks, she makes sure I can see her and gives her hips a strong shake, and with this, she gives birth to something I can't make heads or tails of, she says, Anjuhimeko! this is quite a godsend! I give it to you, here, take it, I listen to her and take it but I can't make heads or tails of it so I don't know what to name it, I ask, what should I call it? the *yamanba* answers, you should call it Hiruko, "the Leech-Child."

I put the leech-child on my back, and as I do so, I hear a voice telling me the way to Tennoji.

Without thinking I look at the *yamanba*, but she is so wrapped up in having intercourse that she doesn't even cast a single glance back at me, I watch her from a little ways away, and I see her give birth to slippery slimy things one after another, I can't make heads or tails of them but I know they are also leech-children, they are less well formed than the leech-child on my back, but the *yamanba* doesn't tell me to take them, she is just completely wrapped up in having intercourse.

Again I hear the voice tell me the way to Tennoji.

I say, oh, Leech-Child! Leech-Child! will you please tell me once more? in response to my question, the leech-child points in the direction of Tennoji, it points with something hardly worth calling a finger but that reminded me of a finger anyway.

The leech-child asks me why I'm going to Tennoji, what do I want to do there? do you even need to ask? I repeat, I am Anjuhimeko, the girl who was sexually molested by her father, I am Anjuhimeko, the girl who was sexually molested over and over by her father, Anjuhimeko, the girl who was sexually molested over and over by her father, is I, I'm that wretched, wretched, wretched girl Anjuhimeko, but each time I say these words, they seem to slide right off the slippery surface of the understanding between the leech-child and me, either that or they are absorbed right into its surface, but in any case, I suddenly realize the leech-child has no language.

A leech-child which has no language shouldn't be able to tell me the way to Tennoji, but there is no doubt it was the leech-child that told me the way to go, the leech-child was also the one who asked me what I'm going to do there, yes, it is the leech-child I'm carrying on my back, then the leech-child asks me all sorts of questions, I respond with all sorts of answers, but the leech-child has no language so the meanings of all the words I say just slide over the slippery surface of the intention of what I am trying to convey, or perhaps they are absorbed directly into the intention, I don't know what to say, but the leech-child's desire to know conveys itself to me, and I respond with language, I don't know if this is good or not, but all I have is language, the only way I have to respond is language, all I have is language, I respond with language, I respond, and as I respond, I sense the desire of the leech-child I carry on my back slowly being satisfied.

—*Translated from the Japanese by Jeffrey Angles*

In medieval Japan, there emerged a kind of popular entertainment known as sekkyō-bushi—*stories that itinerant storytellers would recite and sing to musical accompaniment. The most famous* sekkyō-bushi *is the tale of "Sanshō the Steward" (Sanshō dayū), which Western audiences might know through a modern retelling by the novelist Ōgai Mori or the 1954 film adaptation by the celebrated director Kenji Mizoguchi. The earliest known written versions of the story, recorded in the early seventeenth century, describe the tale of a brother and sister separated from their parents then sold into slavery by unscrupulous slave traders. With the divine aid of the deity bodhisattva Jizō, the son eventually escapes and travels across the country to find his mother, who has gone blind and has been reduced to poverty. Happily, his tears restore her sight. Meanwhile, however, things do not end so happily for the daughter who remains in slavery. She sacrifices herself by refusing to tell where her brother has gone, and as punishment, her owner tortures her in grisly ways until she is dead.*

In the process of exploring the world of sekkyō-bushi *and Japanese folklore, Hiromi Itō, the author of the version included in this anthology, came across an alternative version of this story recorded in northeastern Japan. In August 1931, the anthropologist Nagao Takeuchi recorded an account of spirit possession from a medium named Sue Sakuraba. She had learned the text from her predecessors, yet when she performed it, the text appeared to be the spontaneously generated speech of a spirit possessing her. Interestingly, this alternative version recorded from the shamanesses focuses exclusively on the daughter, who does not die but instead escapes and struggles toward freedom. In fact, it is she who is the centerpiece of this version.*

In Itō's retelling of this seemingly more "feminist" version, she adds a subplot that describes the sexual subjugation that a young girl separated from her parents might likely have undergone. (The original versions of the story do not involve any explicit reference to sexual subjugation.) Moreover, Itō adds the sections about the character Anjuhimeko's attempt to locate Tennōji, a temple in Osaka that was known for being a refuge for the poor and sick.

Perhaps the most important original addition, however, comes in the ending scene with the yamanba *mountain witch. Throughout much folklore, the* yamanba *has represented a nonconformist who rejects home, work, and family to live in the wilds and follow her own will. In Itō's poem, the* yamanba *represents the voice of a powerful, liberated sexual desire ordinarily constrained by patriarchal society. In the scenes when she copulates with the stone pillar, Itō is refashioning the creation myth told in the eighth-century semimythological history of Japan called the Kojiki (Record of Ancient Matters). According to the Kojiki, the male deity Izanagi and his female partner Izanami descend to earth from the heavens and erect a great pillar. After walking around it, the two have conjugal intercourse for the first time, but this intercourse fails because the female deity Izanami speaks before her male counterpart, thus failing to cede to the "proper" order of things. The result of their union is a malformed "Leech-Child" that they set adrift on the sea. In Itō's reworking, the* yamanba *takes her own sexual desire firmly in hand and copulates wildly with the stone pillar. Rather than subjugating her desire to the "proper order of things," she celebrates it in a way that brings her ecstatic, orgiastic pleasure.*

—JA

MICHAEL MEJIA

Coyote Takes Us Home

THE TWINS STOWED BENEATH THE SPARE TIRE TELL US A STORY ABOUT
a small, square jardín in deep Jalisco with neatly trimmed laurel
trees and a cast-iron bandstand where Porfirio Díaz once stood and
scratched his balls. Where Pancho Villa farted. Where Lázaro Cárdenas
spat. Where Vicente Fox picked his teeth. This was the exact spot
where Subcomandante Marcos, Tía Chila's big-balled, black Chihua-
hua, peed and peed and peed and then mounted little diaperless Na-
tividad. People came running. Nobody had seen a hybrid baby since
before the war, since Juan el Oso, whose mother was taken to Acapulco
by a circus bear from León.

The twins were waiting on the curb, they say, watching the procession of the bloody martyr, when Coyote finally came out of the cantina. The silver scorpion on his belt buckle clacked its claws and made
seven blind sisters dance.

"Will you take us?" the twins asked.

Coyote sniffed the air and measured the moon between his thumb
and his forefinger. It was more than half full and the twins had had a
strange delivery. But Coyote wasn't concerned. He led them across
the bridge and down through the park to the dry creek bed where we
were all asleep in the Nova among the stained herons, busted appli-

ances, tires, maricóns, and used condoms. A woman was weeping on a television.

"Move over, little ones," Coyote whispered. "Make room, periquitos."

A few leaves fall for no reason in this story. And even now we hear the band playing, just as the twins say it is: the trumpets and clarinets spiraling like crazy rockets, exploding into pink sparks above the crowd. This all happened at a time of balloons and marionettes, they say. Is that the engine or the tuba? The transmission or the snare drum? Dust and stones become asphalt. A desert appears at blue sunrise. Some rocks, a red-flowering nopal, a thin horse, a goat.

It's fine, we say. That sounds like a beginning. We can believe in that. Éste era and we're gone.

In the morning we see some kids throwing rocks at a woman's head by the side of the road. They ride off on their bikes when we pull over.

"I met a man at a disco," the head tells us. The head of this woman tells us this man was a rich mestizo's son, and how she danced a polka with him and lost one of her shabby little huaraches. How he tracked her down and mashed her toes into a plastic slipper he found somewhere and declared he'd marry her. How he shot twins up inside her that night, and how when they were born her stepsisters sold them to some blue-eyed gringos from New Haven. The husband took his revenge by burying her up to her neck.

"Those bitches are drinking champagne up in Polanco now! But they'll be back for me," she says. "They'll be back, my little ones, my little white children." One of those rocks must've knocked something loose. We throw a few more while Coyote trots up the road to hike his leg on a spot where a woman buried the devil caught in a bottle.

"Mis gringitas!" the head cries. "Bring money!"

Pow!

We hear our parents are dragging long sacks through fields of broadleafed bitter greens that we don't recognize. They are working in an orchard of small gnarled trees, where children are cultivated with the help of bees. Our parents pluck them heavy from the branches, pinch them off their slender green stems, and redeem bushels of those kids for chits that mean food and cable television. The tractors start up and carry them to Chicago. Our parents work in a factory assembling little pink babies covered in feathers. They're waiting for us, our parents, stone-faced. They're laying out our shorts and T-shirts on a firm bunk bed, our parents. Our work clothes.

Coyote says: They found some devils in Arizona, in the desert, mingled in with the bloated corpses of those mojados from Guatemala and Nicaragua and Mexico. They were looking for work, too. It's not so easy for them either these days, you know.

Coyote says: Those boys, Corrín Corrán, Tirín Tirán, Oyín Oyán, Pedín Pedán, Comín Comán, they got themselves locked inside a grain car in Matamoros. Then they sat trapped in a rail yard in Iowa for four months. When they were found, there wasn't much left.

It's like Coyote is trying to trap us with his stories. It's like listening to him read the dictionary. "You can't trust just nobody," he says. We hate the frown of his jade driving mask, the deep stare of its shell eyes. If you look too long, you feel heavy. You feel old. So we let him talk, but we don't listen and we definitely don't keep still. We watch his words tumble out the open windows, turn to vultures on the road picking over something's small carcass. "What did you say, Coyote?" we ask. "What was that? What?" until he gets pissed off and stomps harder on the gas, making the Nova buck and fishtail. Anyway, he has hair in his ears.

The boy in the headrest has a sister carved from coral, and the iron girl beneath the backseat was a present to an old man from three blond sissies, lottery winners from Juárez.

Coyote told us to wait in the Nova, but we were hungry. Through the window of her house we could see the Witch of Guamúchil, her tits pounding together like two wet cheeses, Coyote's teeth clamped to the loose flesh of her withers, his pink skinny prick pumping in and out of her hairy rump. Once we threw some water on two dogs fucking. The girl from Tizapán killed a family pig by shoving a lit candle in its ass. As we crossed the highway, Pilar, Carlos, and Miguel were turned to paper by the touch of a southbound RV. They blew into the Sierra Madres. Adiós, muchachitos!

We were in a graveyard, watching our step. When the dead speak, it's like walking through a spider's web.

"Who's there?" they kept asking, but we couldn't remember our names. There was a lot of dog shit around.

"Don't marry a woman who can't keep a secret," one of them said.

"Don't keep idle sticks in the house," said another.

"Don't shelter orphan children," called out a third. We wrote it all down with a stick and some sand, like nothing we'd need on the other side.

We found the elotero sitting under a tree, eating the last of his ears of corn. "But we're hungry," we said.

"Don't whine," he said, and threatened us with an umbrella. Everybody got one kernel, except Julio, who got none. That's when we noticed that the elotero was a corpse.

"Someone stabbed me." He sounded apologetic.

"No, I didn't!" a voice objected.

He had a kind face, the elotero, and he led us over a hill to a pile of old silver coins topped by a turd. A sad-looking devil was sitting on a stone, trying to straighten three hairs.

"Diablito, is that yours?" we asked, pointing to the turd or the silver, depending on how you looked at it. He gave us three guesses.

Coyote craps at the PEMEX, and we find an empty peanut shell and the body of a princess beside a dry riverbed. Embedded in the soil are immense architectural forms carved with images of jaguars and frogs, lizards and fire. There are rotted clubs and sharp stones like little warriors. There are feathered masks with thick lips and empty eyes watching the sun, and there are images of fanged creatures that we don't know. That we don't want to know. The scene reminds us of the RV we saw outside of Tecuala, turned over in a ditch and on fire, all those bloody Chichimecs dancing around it, and the debris trail of DVDs and underwear and swimsuits stretching like a ragged quetzal plume for a half mile up the road.

"I'm frightened, Coyote," we say. He flicks us with his tail.

The dead princess is like paper. She is curling at the edges and brown. Someone has drawn pictures all over her, like a map, like a journey home. We cannot read them. "Help me, Coyote," we say, pointing, but he leads us back to the Nova and doesn't say a word for one hour.

Still, we are not certain where or when this idea of our parents originated. People you have never seen waiting to feed and clothe you? The perro taught us what was edible. The gato how to hunt small things. The ardilla to conserve. The vaca to digest. The burro to take blows. We learned to construct our shelters from the arañas, and the mono taught us to stay light, just out of reach. The tecolote taught us to stay alert all night long.

But then one day we woke up all wet thinking of San Diego, Tucson, Denver, Chicago, San Antonio, Atlanta. We woke up waiting on Coyote without knowing we were waiting, watching for the dust of his Nova that would be coming down the dirt track from the cuota. We felt a little sick. A burning in our stomach. Our sinuses, too. Our eyes were itchy. The man we call Tío gave us a black pill, but it didn't help.

"You'll be gone soon," he said. We had never seen him smile like that.

And then the animals wouldn't speak to us anymore. They looked away. They stood dumb in filthy boots and their unpainted wooden masks. They sulked at the edge of the field of stones. They turned the corner when we waved. We cursed their sorry asses. We finally found them at the edge of town, by the dry well, sitting together in a closed circle, drinking tequila and telling dirty jokes. In the mercado, their pale organs had been washed and laid out on a table.

Later, touching the little white feet of the plaster Virgin, we had a vision of the small wet opening between her legs. There was blood and hair and something else. A kind of worm. Who was going to tell us?

The phone rang and the woman we call Tía said: "Es tu Mamá. Es tu América."

A green bird circles the speeding Nova three times screeching warnings about our stepsisters. There's poison in the pipián! There's arsenic in the tamales! There's mercury in the crab soup! There's DDT in the huitlacoche! Then it snatches Adelita out of the glove box for its trouble.

At the edge of Hermosillo, everybody's looking for a ride north. Before the door of the cantina shuts, we peek in at a nude woman in the highest red heels holding a board painted with the number 8 above her head. Two pretty, cumin-scented boys are standing around by the broken car wash with their shirts off, showing their thin, hairless chests to truck drivers who spit, pat their macho hair, tug their belts, pretend not to look. The boys' stiff penises are like industrial tools straining against their loose-fitting jeans. Their oiled cockscombs shine silver in the moonlight.

"What is it, Coyote?" we ask, but he guides us away.

Twins. Like twin cities. Sister cities. And when they turn, their identical tattoos read: Queremos Engañarte. What does it mean, we want to know.

Back in the Nova, we are hot and uncomfortable, feeling just too big for our nests, our bodies like chopped pork sweating in the saucepan. We feel coated in a thick fluid.

"Touch me," someone says, before Coyote guns the motor. Then we all shudder and then we are asleep.

The girl in the headlamp tastes roses. Seeds in her mouth. She drools out a trail of hornless flowers and pearls that fly off into the desert. She is incomprehensible and stupid and will marry well to a bastard. That's what Coyote says.

"Shut up!" shouts her stepsister in the other headlamp, black snakes slipping soundlessly from the tips of her syllables, encircling her snugly, sucking and shucking.

We stop for the night at an abandoned hacienda, the engine of the Nova ticking and tocking in the dark. Thorny vines reach over the walls, pick the shadow's pocket. The blue agaves are suffering. The avocado tree wants a word with her brother in the carburetor.

"I gave my fruits to la madre, La Morenita," she says. "What else could I do?"

We can't sleep in the haunted dormitory. "Stay out of the cellar," Coyote says, but then he's snoring, so where else? We find a goat in a closet with the centuries-old reposados. A devil on a three-legged stool insists the goat's a princess, his ransom, his goddaughter, his bride-to-be.

"Pre-ci-o-so!" the devil says, showing his little gold teeth and their ivory fillings.

In the ballroom, scarred films flicker on the wall: plum-suited charros singing from horseback to the grazing herds and a hunchback burning the corpses of emaciated campesinos. The projectionist curled over his womanly machine sings along as he fondles its knobs. In matters of love, one never gets what one wants.

Out on the patio, beside a shattered staircase, a blackbird lies pierced by long shards of the broken glass. One wing's almost off and his breast is sheared open.

The delicate bones! The Pedro Infante face! The fluttering little heart!

This is the film version of our parents' romance.

His amante has a madwoman's hair, dirty little virgin feet. The lap of her nightgown holds a heart-shaped bloodstain. Her three stepsisters hang by their necks from the porch beams. One redhead, one blonde, and one brunette. So peaceful, like beloved sleepers. Now we can forgive them.

"I heard them whispering," our mother says, grabbing a pigeon and cutting its throat, draining the blood into a little clay pitcher. There are hundreds more gathering to gossip, perching on the hanging girls, in the trees, on the roof, waddling and pecking around the dry fountain. The empty halls echo with their coos and scratching nails. The sound effect is amplified to emphasize her dementia.

"It's the only cure for his curse," she says, cutting open another bird, spattering the fractured tiles with black constellations. Pure cinema! "What they said, yes, that's what they said, what they said." Our mother looks at us. No fool after all. She is an international star. "The only way you can ever be born," she says as the camera slowly zooms in. She looks away, a defiant tear in her eye. We are in love.

"Mamá," we sing, "your cantarito is only one-quarter full, so we'll join in your slaughter just until we get bored." But we work fast. Maybe carelessly. Is it our fault some of the slower kids get in the way?

We wander into the kitchen where beans are bubbling on the stove. A steaming pozole and the moon making fresh tortillas. It has a big ass and smells like canela. "Ay, niños," it sighs, wiping its hands on its apron. "You're so late! You need to eat. But where is Yolanda? Where is Areli? What's happened to Pancho and Enrique?" The truth is not pretty. We are so hungry, but then the sun bursts in wearing stained underpants and throws a brick at us. A watermelon. A mango. A boot.

We swear: that was for nothing. Ask the blackbird in the avocado tree, the mad amante hanging herself from the Milky Way.

That pack of dogs snuck up on us. They came up out of a culvert in the dark, quiet and with no eyes in their heads to reflect the moonlight. Before we could roll up the windows they'd carried off Cruz, Rosario, and Virgilio, torn open their bellies and plucked out their eyes.

"Ojos! Hijos! Huesos! Lobos!" they bark. They come at us with bloody jaws and those stolen eyes resting like pearls on their tongues. "How many of us have been blinded because of you? To prove that the order to kill you has been carried out! Mocosos! You live while we're left to be kicked and to struggle for scraps, run off and run over! Jau! Jau! Jau!"

Coyote has the Nova in gear now and he's swerving through the grove trying to get us back to the road.

They're snapping at the kids in the rear bumper, barking their names like some wild Chichimec gang: Brokerib! Pinchback! Swellfoot! Droptooth!

Little Cuauhtémoc huddles himself around the radio, comforted by the sizzling static and the stone in his mouth shaped like a human heart.

Oh, now it's rush hour, golden hour, and all the Cadillacs chauffeuring our mothers to the suburban Seven Cities Mall are backed up for a glittering mile, and we are here in the Nova making time with some fine-ass white boys and girls on the service road, passing more public storage units and strip malls, legal services and sandwich shops and blood-testing agencies and nail salons, like a never-ending, ever-repeating commercial for what we call El Norte. Ice cream, Coyote! Starbucks! Party rentals! Outback! Two for one tattoos and piercings! He must not hear us.

You don't believe us?

Okay, so suppose it's just more underdeveloped Sonora sand and cactus out there, squalid shelters rigged out of cinder blocks, sticks, and plastic, and we're tired of playing I Spy and License Plate Lotería. And the sun hurts our eyes because we lost our hats, and Coyote says there's no extra money to buy us any. So there's a young man on horseback, a tejano prince in a tall white hat, Coyote. And he doesn't squint, Coyote. So he's handsome. He's got a million MySpace friends—mostly gay men and twelve-year-old girls—and a great big contract with Televisa. He will be our president. Si se puede! And there's a woman in a maid's uniform who loves him, and who doesn't know yet that she's pregnant, and she's crossing the highway to dust the furniture and vacuum the floors and wash the sheets and towels and sex toys at the Yanqui-owned time-shares overlooking El Mar Vermijo. Each air-conditioned unit has tinted windows, according to the brochure, so you have no idea what those sunburned gringos are up to, do you? And the maid lady, Coyote: she's wearing cheap sunglasses and a thong that she borrowed from her nasty prima who's home doing her nails and getting fucked like a goat by the maid lady's infected boyfriend who's trying to watch the Toluca match and keeps asking: "Are we there yet? Are we there yet? Are we there yet?"

So, hey, Coyote: we're getting a little cranky. Are we there yet?

Gol! Gol! Gol! Gol! Gooooool!

Francisco, the Goat-Boy of Ameca, rides round and round in our hubcap stroking the bloody left ear he sliced off Bofo's bald head, a trophy of that championship season in Guadalajara. Cisco's parents clean the lab where he'll be studied in Portland. That's what Coyote says. "CHI-VAS," Cisco shouts every time we hit a hole. "CHI-VAS! CAM-PE-ÓN!"

And the girl we call La Sirena. She won't say where she's from. She swims so many laps around the radiator she grows flippers and a tail. She's going to boil and turn red. When the cap blows she'll be riding those flaming plumes of gas, oil, brake fluid, and transmission fluid right into downtown Nogales. La Princesa! La Reina! La Gloria! Wouldn't you like to see? She will have her own apocalyptic cult. Nuestra Señora de la Nova. She is carrying the furious daughter of God.

Coyote's friend Conejo is waiting outside the bus station: all las Flechas Amarillas cocked and aimed south at Celaya, Palenque, Pachuco, Querétaro, Mérida, Pátzcuaro, Potosí, Tollan, Veracruz, Aztlán.

We're going to Gringolandia! Adiós! Adiós, pendejos, adiós! Vaya bien!

Coyote whistles and Conejo gets in, his jeans and work boots crusted with plaster from building walls on the Heights for los ricos.

God damn it's hot.

Conejo strums his guitar. Conejo says, "Let's get the kids some ice cream."

Coyote drives the car.

"Let's get the kids some ice cream," Conejo says and Coyote says okay.

"Ay, qué rica!" Sometimes Conejo will lose his head.

They have a thousand flavors. Las viejitas hand out cups of elote, aguacate, mango, mole, cerveza, sensemilla, cacahuate, nopal, chicharrón, chorizo, lengua, frijol, and there're tents all around selling sopes and tacos—al pastor, bistec, flor de calabaza, gusano, hormiga, chapulín—Cantinflas masks, huaraches, guayaberas, Chiapas amber, Chivas wallets, bikinis, Zapata marionettes, popguns, tops, Jaguares keychains, piggy banks, balloons, Oaxacan silver, chickens, roosters, goats. We don't keep our hands to ourselves until they get chopped off and tossed into the cazuela.

Borrachos!

A procession of staggering Yaquis circles the square with a pig wearing a crown of cactus thorns and a Patriots "Undefeated!" T-shirt.

Father Pelotas, waving a feather and a valve from the uncorrupted heart of San Caloca, conjures a bloody little Jesús to scourge them. "Infiels!" Jesús shouts. "Nihilistas! Apóstatas!" He snaps his whip against those bent Indian backs. He hopped out of a perfect little cloud. Every good dog barks fanatically.

And then one thing leads to another. The thirteenth apostle slips out of a mural and sneaks off to a motel with Concepción. Osvaldo and Elvira get sucked into an infernal sphincter. Jaime is forced to enlist with the garrison.

The concheros' rattling chalchihuites start the ritual lucha between La Morenita and La Malinche. Our Lady clobbers the other with a chair. She's bloody. She breaks a nail. She cracks a rib. She gets her ass beat with a cornstalk. That one's got some cojones. Juan Diego and Cortés tag in, slapping, pulling hair, gouging eyes. The loser will be shaved.

Later, we're cruising the Heights with Morenita cuddling her bloody little Jesús in the Nova's backseat, tickling his beard, teasing him with his whip, the tip of it just beyond his delicate grasping fingers with their trimmed nails. He squeals and she nurses him, nurses us all with her Extremaduran rompope until we're laid out—all except Coyote, whose shell eyes are glowing at us in the rearview mirror—drunk and happy on her magnificent jiggling lap, the map light of her countenance guiding our dreams toward board games and bunk beds. Let there be bicycles. Golden, slick banana seats and temperate, green summer.

"You won't come to my house?" Morenita asks. Her breath stinks. We see one black curling hair on her chin.

These bright, vacant streets, lamplit and sober. Conejo sings a narco-corrido that gives everyone the creeps. A private security guard in a bulletproof vest raises his atlatl. He says, "Get the fuck out."

"No tocar," Conejo sings. "No tocar, no tocar, no tocar. Ay, que barbaro."

Something smells like Fabuloso. Walls of bougainvillea that protect the beautiful sleeping families.

Conejo says: There was this kid who loved the Dodgers, see. Chávez Ravine, Fernandomania, all that shit. He had this friend who worked in them new fortress-condos in Tijuana, you know? High-rise! And they snuck past security and got up on the roof and ran him up the flagpole and he was up there. Way up. Up above the clouds! Just so he could see all the way to Los Angeles.

"José!" they started calling at him. "José! José! José!"

They got so worried. Someone's going to kill them.

Si, le oigo! José calls down. Like a little angel, eh, kids? Fucking Angel José, huh?

And, you know, these kids call back:

"José, José . . . José can you see?"

. . . a la lu-u-u-uz de la aurora? José is singing.

Lo que tanto aclamamos la noche al caer?

Ay ja ja! And Coyote punches Conejo right in the mouth.

That broke his last good tooth. Conejo sucks a lime.

She's emerging through the static: big-titted Fronterista in chaps and mirrored sunglasses. You've got mother's milk on your breath, chica. You've got a juicy pera, death's-head thighs, semiautomatic eyes. You're a shock to our guts, our inflamed rectum. We do a Mixtec boogaloo, an Otomi polka, a Yanqui tango. Now we're setting the Nova bouncing like a madrefucking lowrider.

At our last stop to pee before the border, we find an empty peanut shell and a naked girl in a maguey plant. A shotgun shell and a naked girl. Sea shells. Some spent shells. Coyote has to hold Conejo back, bind his filthy mouth shut with his belt.

She looks crazy as a Huichol, the moon in her eye, the sun in her head. We shudder in the heat.

She says: "Gemelos," and nods. As if it has never been said before. As if she is naming us. There is a busted-up Nahua keyboard in the dust, a blown-out VGA monitor, a snake or two. We walk around the saguaros, listening to the snap of Wal-Mart bags like little flags flying from the fingertips of the chollas. There is a bullet-riddled phone book. An empty zapato. There is the tall fence. And the Franciscan shelter where they hold the kids who don't make it over. They reach out through the barred, oval windows, grasping for birds and bugs, and the hooded monks pluck them out with giant tongs. Then they send them back around again to the rear, limping misshapen forms.

"Where are the others?" we ask.

Coyote touches our ears. "What others, periquitos? There's always only been you. You two. The two of you." He looks around. He smiles. "They paid for two."

We suckle the girl's dark, fat nipples, her milk picante, ashy, thick as the sludge of Tía's latrine. We bite. We tug. We tear. We have to try so hard, the girl's coaxing fingers in our hair. She digs in her nails until our scalps bleed. Coyote gets it all on video. She sighs as we sniff her almeja. We crawl up into the uterus and have never slept so well. We sprout feathers and short hair. There is something else curled up in one corner.

The stars are out when we return covered in blood. We have the taste of flesh in our mouths. We just want to dance beside the flaming maguey, let our arms and legs rotate free like the severed, spouting limbs of holy martyrs. We stomp the earth. One bare foot touches a rock. All our blood and sugar runs from our ears, mouths, eyes, assholes. The shit, chocolate, tears, and salt. Watch your fingers! We bite! It's been a long day. Pretty soon, we're over it. It passes.

It's dark.

Coyote licks us clean and puts us to bed while Conejo and a devil play cards for all the diablitos in Hell. As he wins, Conejo eats the diablitos, crushes their strong little bones between his rotten molars, throws the shells on the ground. But the devil keeps gambling. He plays two deer, a frog, and death. Conejo plays a rooster. Coyote packs beeswax in our ears and covers our aching eyes with dried pasillas.

"It works," we hear the devil say. "I've tried it. My wife, too."

We've been in line for hours and hours, the Nova crawling through the last chance tianguis. Conejo is buying gifts in American dollars: blankets and T-shirts, stinking herbal remedies, shot glasses, ashtrays, and Aztec sun stones carved from Tehuacán coprolites. We huddle, maize seeds in a matchbox. We pray they don't search us, or ask if Coyote's our daddy, or what school we go to. We are suffocating and sick, double-wrapped in plastic bubble wrap. Coyote is practicing calm responses, but that chingada Conejo can't stop giggling.

"We were visiting," Coyote will say.

"Our tiny little mothers," Conejo will say. "Pobrecitas!"

"Please step out of the car," the armed agent will say.

It's the Padres ahead one nothing in the bottom of the fifth.

We take a chance for a glance. Through the line of cars we can see to the other side. We see the yellow welcome sign beside América's freeway: Our Papá stumbling drunk on his way home, our Mamá running from La Migra dragging our Américan-born sister Conejita behind by one hand, her feet just leaving the ground.

It's all true, querida! All true!

She is flying! They can fly! Niños fly in Gringolandia!

And now we are too too too, out of the Nova, over Coyote and Conejo spread-eagled on hot concrete, we are flying as if through a windshield, through glass, through steel, through the smoke and haze, the choke and maize, the toke and craze, the Coke and phrasebook, we're flying. It's the way the chicken flies to the pot. Which came first: the fire or the flame? We are flying: feathered and boned to you, querida Mamá, naked and new, Papá, sin entrails y contrails, la raza limpia, raza pirata. Oscuro? How do you say? Deportesation? No. It's the way ESPN flies to Fox. Satellite eyes. You're beautiful. Something small on a wind crossing over. But before we forget.

Adipose. Otiose. Adidas. A radio. Game over.

"Coyote Takes Us Home" began with the image of a beat-up 1970 Chevy Nova packed with contraband children heading north toward the U.S.-Mexico border. I had heard, or thought I had, about U.S. Customs and Border Patrol stopping a car with immigrant kids hidden in the side panels. I can't find that story now, but there are plenty of others like it: Andres's parents leave him behind with relatives when they head north to find work in America. Lupe's parents will send for her sometime later, when they can afford it. Gabriel and his twin brother stow away on a train, or a relative hands Carlos off to a professional smuggler, a Coyote. Their parents are waiting in Phoenix. Maybe they're forced to pay an additional two thousand dollars to get Carla to Pennsylvania from Arizona. Maybe the operation gets busted in Las Vegas and Julia is deported to a shelter back in Mexico. They've got to start over. These kids are from Honduras. Those are from El Salvador. Jorge shows up. Or maybe he disappears somewhere between San Diego and Chicago. "The history of Mexico," Octavio Paz writes, "is the history of a man seeking his parentage, his origins."

That search gets a bit more complicated once you move next door. "Coyote" explores the confusion of personal and cultural history inherent to sub rosa immigration. What do these kids carry with them on the ride? What should matter to them if they're leaving anyway? What is the true name of the place where they're going? The story is obsessed with trash. Much of this detritus comes from folktales told to Howard True Wheeler and published in 1943 by The American Folklore Society as Tales from Jalisco, Mexico. *I*

*like the collection's subtle correspondences to Mexican history.
Some tales featuring coyotes and rabbits seem to have pre-
Colombian roots, while the variants on stories familiar from
Perrault and the Brothers Grimm may have drifted over in the long
wake of Cortés. A third group of stories, like the Virgin of
Guadalupe, reveals mixed parentage. Their dark sense of humor
and travesties of religious authority seem familiar to me, the most
Mexican. The laughing peasants have my father's sense of humor,
and his mother's. She came to America from Tequila, Jalisco, in
1924. He was born in Texas. I grew up in Sacramento, California.
So, for me, "Coyote" is also a sort of ticket home.*

—MM

KIM ADDONIZIO

Ever After

THE LOFT WHERE THE DWARVES LIVED HAD A VIEW OF THE CITY AND hardwood floors and skylights, but it was overpriced, and too small now that there were seven of them. It was a fifth-floor walkup, one soaring, track-lighted room. At the far end was the platform where Doc, Sneezy, Sleepy, and Bashful slept side by side on futons. Beneath them, Happy and Dopey shared a double bed. Grumpy, who pretty much stayed to himself, kept his nylon sleeping bag in a corner during the day and unrolled it at night on the floor between the couch and the coffee table. The kitchen was two facing zinc counters, a built-in range and microwave, and a steel refrigerator, all hidden behind a long bamboo partition that Doc had bought and Sneezy had painted a color called Cherry Jubilee. The kitchen and bathroom were the only places any sort of privacy was possible. To make the rent they all pooled their money from their jobs at the restaurant, except for Dopey, who didn't have a job unless you counted selling drugs when he wasn't running them up his arm; and Grumpy, who panhandled every day for spare change and never came up with more than a few wrinkled dollar bills when the first of the month rolled around. Sometimes the rest of them talked about kicking out Dopey and Grumpy, but no one quite had the heart. Besides, the Book said there were seven when she arrived, seven disciples of the goddess who would come with the

sacred apple and transform them. How, exactly, they would be transformed was a mystery that would be revealed when she got there. In
the meantime, it was their job to wait.

"When she comes, she'll make us big," said Sneezy. He had the
comics section of the Sunday paper, and an egg of Silly Putty, and was
flattening a doughy oval onto a panel of Calvin and Hobbes.

"Oh, bullshit," said Grumpy. "It's about *inner* transformation, man.
That's the whole point. Materialism is a trap. Identifying with your
body is a trap. All this shit"—Grumpy swept his arm to indicate not
just their loft but the tall downtown buildings beyond the windows,
and maybe more—"is an illusion. Maya. Samsara." He shook out the
last Marlboro from a pack, crumpled the pack, and tried a hook shot
into a wicker wastebasket by the window, but missed. He looked
around. "Matches? Lighter? Who's going for more cigs?"

"She will," insisted Sneezy. "She'll make us six feet if we want
to be."

"She can't change genetics, you dope," Grumpy said.

At the word *dope,* Dopey's head jerked up for an instant. He was
nodding on the couch at the opposite end from Grumpy, a lit cigarette
ready to fall from his hand. The couch had a few burn holes already.
One of these days, Doc thought, he's going to set the fucking place
on fire, and then where will we be? How will she ever find us? He got
up from the floor, where he'd been doing yoga stretches, and slid the
cigarette from Dopey's stained fingers. He ground it out in an ashtray
on the table, in the blue ceramic water of a moat that circled a ceramic castle. From the castle's tiny windows, a little incense smoke—
sandalwood—drifted out.

"She's not an alien from outer space who's going to perform weird
experiments," Doc said. He hunted through the newspaper for the
Food section.

"Where is she from, then?" Sneezy said. Sneezy was a sixteen-year-
old runaway, the youngest of them. From the sweet credulousness of
his expression, you'd never know what terrible things he had endured.

He'd been beaten, scarred between his shoulder blades with boiling water, forced into sex with his mother by his own father. Sneezy liked to ask the obvious questions for the sake of receiving the familiar, predictable answers.

"She's from the castle," Doc said. "She's the fairest in the land. She will come with the sacred apple and all will be changed." This much the Book said. *Once upon a time,* it said. But when was that, exactly? Doc wondered. They'd been here for more than six years already. Or he had, anyway. Ever since he'd found the Book in a Dumpster—the covers ripped away, most of its pages stained and torn—where he'd been looking for food a nearby restaurant always threw out. He'd been on the streets, addicted to cheap wine, not giving a shit about anything or anyone. He'd slept on cardboard in doorways, with a Buck knife under the rolled poncho he used for a pillow, had stolen children's shoes from outside the Moon Bounce at the park. He had humiliated himself performing drunken jigs in the bank plaza for change tossed into a baseball cap. The Book had changed all that. It had shown him there was a purpose to his life. To gather the others, to come to this place and make it ready. He had quit drinking and found a job, at the very restaurant whose Dumpster he used to scrounge through. He had gathered his brethren, one by one, as they drifted into the city from other places, broke and down on their luck, headed for the streets and shelters. They had become his staff—two dishwashers, a busboy, and a fry cook. The restaurant's name was Oz, and the owner had been willing to hire dwarf after dwarf and present them as ersatz munchkins. There had been a feature article in the *Weekly*, and write-ups in some food magazines, which had drawn a lot of business. The dwarves were mentioned in the guidebooks, so there were often tourists from Canada and Denmark and Japan, who brought their cameras to record the enchanting moment the dwarves trooped from the kitchen with a candle-lit torte to stand around a table and sing happy birthday. They used fake high voices, as though they'd been sucking on helium.

"Why is the apple sacred?" Sneezy said dreamily. He had abandoned the comics and now had a few Magic cards spread out on the floor and was picking them up one by one, studying them.

"Because she will die of the apple and be resurrected," Doc said. He glanced at one of Sneezy's cards: *Capashen Unicorn*. An armored unicorn raced through a glittery field, a white-robed rider on its back. Underneath, Doc read, *Capashen riders were stern and humorless even before their ancestral home was reduced to rubble.*

"Why do you collect that crap?" Doc said. "And those comic books you've always got your nose buried in. Read the Book again. Every time I read it, I discover something new. The Book is all you need. You have to focus on the Book."

"Check her out." Sneezy held up another card, of an anorectic-looking woman with green skin in a gold ballerina outfit. One long-nailed thumb and forefinger were raised in the air in some kind of salute. In her other hand she held aloft a green and white flag. A couple of men in armor rode behind her, and behind them rose broccoli-like trees, being erased by mist rising out of the ground. Doc read: *Llanowar Vanguard. Creature—Dryad. Llanowar rallied around Eladamri's banner and united in his name.*

"Will *she* look like that?" Sneezy asked.

"Give it a rest," Grumpy said, and nudged Dopey with his foot. "Hey, man," he said. "We're out of cigs."

Sneezy will outgrow it, Doc thought. Dryads and unicorns. Made-up creatures and clans and battles. "I don't know what she'll look like, exactly," he sighed. He stood up and began tidying the coffee table. Empty semicrushed cans of Bud Light that Grumpy and Dopey had drunk the night before. A half-eaten bag of tortilla chips. A plastic tub of salsa had spilled on the naked body of a Penthouse Pet. The magazine lay open to her spread legs, her long, slender fingers teasingly positioned above her pink slit; it glistened, as though it had been basted. What would *she* look like? Maybe she would look like this, would come and drag her fingers through the graying hair on his chest and position her sweet eager hips above him. Maybe she would whisper to Doc that he was the one she came for, the only one; they could leave all the others behind, now that she was there. They would leave the city and move to an Airstream in the woods, overlooking a little river, where he could catch bass and bluegills. She would stand in front of their stove in cutoffs and a white blouse, sliding a spatula under a fish sputtering in a pan. When the moon rose, the two of them would go down to the river and float together, naked. Their heads would be the same height above the water. Doc closed the magazine. He gathered up the beer cans, carried them into the kitchen, and threw them on top of the pile of trash overflowing from the can.

The next afternoon he left a note on the refrigerator, securing it with a magnet Bashful had bought, of the Virgin Mary's stroller with the baby Jesus riding in it. The magnet set included Mary in a nightgown, her hands raised in prayer, with several changes of clothes and accessories including a skateboard, a waitress uniform, flowered pants and a hippie shirt, a plaid skirt, and roller skates. Right now Mary had on just the nightgown, and was riding the skateboard. Another magnet, of a small Magic 8 Ball, had been stuck over her face. HOUSE MEETING 7 P.M., Doc had written. IMPORTANT!!! PLEASE EVERYONE. I'LL BUY THE BEER. He knew that would ensure that Grumpy and Dopey showed.

Dopey didn't arrive until 7:30, strolling in with a bag of peanut M&M's. But at least they were all there, with a couple of six-packs and cigarettes and Nacho Cheese Doritos in a bowl on the table. Doc was drinking his usual, caffeine-free Diet Coke. Bashful passed around a large order of McDonald's fries and unwrapped a Big Mac. Crap, Doc thought, watching him eat, but it smelled pretty good, and he couldn't resist a couple of the fries.

"Why do we need a house meeting?" Grumpy said. "I got things to do." He hadn't shaved in a while, and his black beard stubble went halfway down his neck. Not so long ago, Doc remembered, Grumpy used to shave every day, no matter what.

"Oh, I love house meetings," Happy said. Happy loved nearly everything. He loved communal living, and being a bus boy at Oz. He loved being one of the Chosen who had been selected to wait. He loved the Book and would defend it when anyone criticized it, which seemed to be more and more often lately. Just a couple of days ago, Sleepy, who was taking a community college class, had come home talking nonsense. "It's like the Bible," he said. "It's, like, a metaphor or something. You know the cross? Jesus on the cross? The professor said the cross is really like a pagan fertility symbol." Sleepy had no idea what a metaphor was, though. When pressed, he couldn't define *symbol*, either. "You don't know what you're saying," Happy had concluded, and Doc explained to Sleepy that the Book was nothing like the Bible. The Bible was meant for normals, Doc said, but the Book was for dwarves.

"I called the meeting," Doc said, "because I'm sick of picking up after all of you. Sleepy cleaned the bathroom and left soap streaks all over the mirror. I can barely see myself in it. And you, Grumpy, you and Dopey—all you do is strew beer cans and cigarette butts and fast-food trash from one end of this place to the other. And this morning Bashful put the dishes from the dishwasher back in the cupboards when they hadn't even been washed yet."

"Sorry," Bashful muttered.

"I have to do everything around here," Doc said.

"Don't be such a goddamned martyr," Grumpy said, popping his second bottle of Red Hook.

"You should try pulling your own weight for once," Doc said. "Don't think we're going to carry you forever."

"Oh, but we love you, Grumpy," Happy said. He put his hand on Grumpy's shoulder. "You're the bomb," Happy said, using an expression he'd picked up from Sneezy.

"Get your paw off me," Grumpy said. "Freak."

"Look who's talking." Happy had an edge in his voice now. The one thing Happy didn't love was being a dwarf. At four foot ten, Happy was the closest to normal-sized, and Doc often wondered if Happy stayed not only because of his dedication to the Book but because this was the only place he got to be bigger than everyone else.

"I don't need you freaks," Grumpy said, giving Happy a shove. They were sitting on the floor, and the shove sent Happy into the coffee table. He banged his head on the corner.

"Look what you did," Happy said, holding his temple. "I'm bleeding."

"He's bleeding," everyone concurred, in unison. All except Grumpy, who glared defiantly at the circle of dwarves, his arms crossed in front of him.

"Violence can't be tolerated," Doc said sternly.

"Oh, yeah? What are you gonna do about it?" Grumpy said. "You and your stupid Book. Nobody believes in that shit but you. They're all just humoring you, man."

"You're lying," Doc said. He looked around at the others. "He's lying, right?"

"Yeah, right," Sneezy said. "We believe."

"We believe," the others said. But it sounded wrong. Doc could hear the doubt in their voices, could see it in the way they shifted their eyes to the floor, hunching their shoulders. Bashful picked up his Big Mac in both hands and chewed, his head down.

"I absolutely, positively, believe," Sneezy said.

But Sneezy was a kid, Doc thought, who believed in dryads and unicorns, wizards and fairies, in Spiderman and Wolverine and other bullshit superheroes. Sneezy sat rapt in front of the Saturday morning cartoons, saying "Rad" and "Awesome." Sneezy's belief was not hard-won.

"Whatever gets you through," Dopey said, surprising everyone. Dopey never talked at house meetings. "It's cool," Dopey said. "She'll come, dudes." He lay back against the armrest of the couch and closed his eyes.

" It's just—" Bashful said.

"Just what," Doc said, his voice flat.

"We're kind of in a rut, I think. Maybe. Or something." Bashful stared at the hamburger in his hands. A little dribble of pink sauce was falling right onto the table Doc had cleaned.

"You have doubts," Doc said. "That's okay, that's perfectly natural."

But didn't Doc have his doubts, too? Didn't he lie awake at night, listening to the snores of the others, wondering if maybe she wasn't coming after all; didn't he try to bury those thoughts, to tell himself to be patient, to withstand the test of these long years? Some nights, when he couldn't sleep, he would get up and take the Book from the wooden lectern Bashful had built for it, and he would go into the bathroom and sit on the toilet lid and read it again. *Once upon a time. She ate the apple, she fell.* The dwarves were there, in the story—they took care of her. The Book was a mess of half-pages, missing pages, the story erratic, interrupted. But some things were clear. A few powerful words shone forth, in large letters. There were faded illustrations that had once been bright: a man with an ax. A hand holding a huge, shining red apple. The stepmother and her mirror. But the page that might reveal *her*, that page was only a scrap, and all it showed was a short puffy white sleeve, and an inch of a pale arm, against which lay a heartbreaking curl of long, blue-black hair. So many mysteries, so many things they might never know. But in the end, on the very last page of the Book, the promise, the words that had given him such hope the first time he read them: *They lived happily ever after.* She and the dwarves, Doc thought, all of them together. She would come, and see that he had made things ready. She would take the pain that had always been with him, the great ache of loneliness at the center of his life, into her hands, like a trembling bird; she would sing to it, and caress it, and then with one gesture fling it into the sky. A flutter of wings and it would rise away from him forever.

"They don't buy any of your religious mumbo-jumbo," Grumpy said. "They're just too chickenshit to tell you. Well, I'm done, buddy boy. *Basta.*" He lifted his chin and scratched his stubble, glaring at Doc.

"Grumpy," Sleepy said. "Don't go."

"And my name isn't Grumpy," Grumpy said. "It' s Carlos. I'm a Puerto Rican—" he paused "—*little person*," he said. "I'm sick of all of you with your fake names and voodoo loser fantasies about some chick who ain't coming. She ain't coming, man. Get it through your fat heads."

No one looked at him. Grumpy stood up.

"All right then," he said. He went to the corner where he kept his sleeping bag, and picked it up. "Adios, you chumps. See you around."

Doc listened to his boots on the stairs. It doesn't matter, he told himself. It doesn't matter. She'll still come.

"A dwarf by any other name—" Happy said.

"Would still be an asshole," Sleepy said.

"My name used to be Steven," Sneezy said, and Sleepy told him to shut his fucking piehole.

It was a Friday afternoon in November, full of wind and rain, and everyone who came into Oz shook out their umbrellas and dripped water onto the yellow brick tiles in the foyer, and asked for one of the tables close to the big stone fireplace.

Doc was short-staffed. A waiter was out with the flu, and Bashful had left town on Tuesday to attend an aunt's funeral. On Thursday, he had called to say he might not be coming back, except to pick up a few of his things.

"Of course you're coming back," Doc had said.

"She left me some money," Bashful said. "Nobody thought she had any, she lived in this crummy little studio apartment and never bought a thing. Turns out she had stocks from my grandfather, and she left it all to me and her cat. I'm the trustee for the cat."

"You can't just take off."

"I want to live here for a while. See how things go. I'm sorry, Doc. This just seems like the right thing for me now."

A couple of men came into the restaurant, dressed in matching red parkas, their arms around each other. The first man's hair was blond and combed back off a perfectly proportioned face; the other man had a square jaw, outlined by a thin black beard, and when he shucked his parka Doc saw his chest and biceps outlined in a tight thermal shirt.

"Nasty weather out there," Doc said. He stepped down from his stool behind the podium to lead them to a table near the fireplace. He heard one man whisper something to the other, and the second's "Shh, he'll hear you." He was used to comments. On the street, teenagers yelled to him from passing cars. People stared, or else tried not to, averting their eyes and then casting furtive glances in his direction. Children walked right up to him, fascinated that he was their size, but different. He'd learned to block it out. But when the men were seated he walked away from them, feeling a sudden, overwhelming rage.

Things were falling apart at home. At night he would sit on the couch, the Book on his lap, and read a few sentences aloud. In the old days, everyone would gather around, relaxing with cigarettes and beers, and maybe some dessert they'd brought back from the restaurant. But now they drifted away. To the kitchen, or up to the loft to turn on the TV and watch some inane show he could hear as he tried to focus on the words in the Book, the all-important words that were going to change their lives. That had changed Doc's life, given him hope. But now that hope was being drained away. One by one they were going to leave him. And she would never come, not to a lone dwarf. An old, balding dwarf whose feet and back hurt him every night so that he had to soak in a hot bath for some relief. She wouldn't take his gnarled, aching feet in her hands and massage them. In the black nights when he lay awake and empty, she wouldn't lay her long white body, smelling of apples, on top of his.

As the evening went on he forced himself to greet customers pleasantly, not to yell at Sleepy when he dropped a bus tray, or at Happy when he mixed up orders—Happy was usually a dishwasher, but he was filling in tonight for the absent waiter. Doc focused on keeping everything running smoothly, not letting it get chaotic. He let a German woman pull him onto her lap so her friends could take a picture with their cell phone, beaming the image to other friends in Stuttgart. He sang "Happy Birthday" with the other dwarves and handed a giant lollipop to a girl with a magenta buzz-cut and several facial piercings while her parents sat there with strained smiles on their faces, obviously uncomfortable that they found themselves with such a weird-looking daughter and were now confronted with several pseudo-munchkins in striped tights. By closing time he wanted to hit something. He took his time totaling up the evening's receipts, to give everyone time to finish up in the kitchen and leave him alone. Finally Sleepy, Happy, and Sneezy were finished and hovering around the office door.

"Just go," Doc said.

"What's the matter?" Happy said. "Is it me? I did my best. It's hard being a waiter. I never realized it was so hard, keeping everything straight."

"You did fine," Doc said.

"Do you really think so?" Happy looked thrilled.

"We'll wait for you," Sleepy said. "We can all share a cab."

"You guys go," Doc said.

"Cool, a cab," Sneezy said. "Here's something weird," he said. "Whenever I get in somebody's car, I make sure to buckle up. But in a cab, I never put on a seat belt. Isn't that weird?"

"You should," Doc said. He wanted to slap them. "Go," he said. "Just get the fuck out of here and leave me alone."

Sneezy and Happy stared. Sleepy pulled them each by a jacket sleeve. "Sure, man," Sleepy said. "No problem. You want to be alone, we'll leave you alone."

Finally they were gone. "Over the Rainbow" was playing softly on the stereo. Judy Garland's voice usually soothed him, but now Doc felt mocked by the promise in the song, the sappy land where dreams came true, the bluebirds and the bright colors everywhere, troubles melting away.

He locked the zippered bag of credit card slips and money into the safe. He switched off the stereo and straightened the stack of CDs beside it, then turned off the last of the lights. The alarm code had to be set by punching numbers into a keypad by the door that led from the kitchen to the alley; he was about to set it, but stopped. He walked back through the dark kitchen, out the swinging doors into the restaurant, and behind the bar, and took a bottle of Johnny Walker and a rocks glass.

At four A.M. the streets in this part of the city looked like a movie set about to be struck. The storefront businesses had mostly failed. Lights shone in the tall office buildings, where janitors were emptying wastebaskets and running vacuum cleaners. Doc knew what that was like; he'd done it, years ago, a flask in his back pocket that he'd drink from through the night, working under the fluorescent glare while everyone else slept. At dawn he'd be ready to pass out, and would reel off to find a hospitable bench or doorway. He'd forgotten the feeling of drunkenness, the happy, buzzy glow, how the world shifted pleasantly out of focus and retreated to a manageable distance. He staggered in the direction of the loft, clutching the bottle to his coat, hardly feeling the rain that was still falling, though not with its earlier force. Now it was soft, almost a mist, cold kisses on the top of his bare head, a damp chill coming up through his shoes.

He sang "Brown Eyed Girl" and "Swanee River." He stopped in the middle of the street and looked around to see if anyone had heard him, but there was no one. A cat slid away, around the corner of a building, pale against the dark bricks. He was breathing kind of hard, he realized. He stopped to rest in a small park, a square of grass with a single wrought-iron bench, a narrow border of dirt—mud, now— where there were white flowers in spring. He remembered the flowers, and looked sadly at the wet soil. No flowers. There would never be flowers again. It was never going to stop raining. The rain would wash away the soil, and the park, and himself; he would float down the river of rain, endlessly, until he sank beneath the surface of the water, down to the bottom like a rock, dead and inert, and finally at peace. He looked for his glass, to pour himself more liquor, but he had lost it somewhere. He had a vague memory of seeing it smash against bricks, the pieces, glittering like the rain, lying under a streetlight. He took a pull from the bottle and slumped against the freezing iron of the bench.

His dreams were confused: having his picture taken with tourists at the restaurant, only the restaurant was really an office building and their meals were being served on desks, and water was seeping through the carpet and he was down on his knees trying to find where it was coming from. When he woke he was lying on the wet grass, under a dripping tree. The rain had let up. It was getting light; the air was slate-colored. He was still slightly drunk, and could feel underneath the cushion of alcohol the hard, unyielding bedrock of a massive hangover. He got up and walked over to the bench, where the bottle was lying tucked under a newspaper like a tiny version of a homeless man. He picked up both and laid them gently in the wire trash receptacle next to the bench.

On the way home he passed a few actual homeless people, still asleep in doorways. He peered at each of them, but none of them was Grumpy. It had been nearly a month since he'd left, and no one had seen him. There was one dog, black and scrawny, that raised its head as Doc passed and then settled, sighing, next to its master.

He let himself into the building and trudged upstairs, stopping on each landing to catch his breath and stop the grinding in his head. He opened the door to the loft quietly, in case anyone was up. But it was too early. He could hear the steady snores of Happy and Sleepy, and Sneezy's asthmatic breathing. Dopey slept alone in the double bed, angled across it, one arm dangling out from the covers. Beside the bed were an overflowing ashtray, a box of wooden matches, and a litter of pistachio shells. Doc knelt down and scooped up the shells and threw them away in the kitchen. He went back and got the ashtray and matches, emptied the ashtray, put the box of matches on the shelf where they belonged. He rinsed a few dishes that were in the sink and set them in the dishwasher, then tidied up the counter—someone had apparently consumed a late-night snack of cereal and pretzels.

Someone had also brought home flowers. There were irises in a vase—a vase stolen from the restaurant, Doc noted—set on a cleared section of the counter. Around the main room were stalks of star lilies in quart beer bottles. On the coffee table, which had been cleaned off, was a Pyrex bowl of fruit—oranges and grapefruits and apples and a bunch of bananas—flanked by two candles that had burned down to stumps. Also on the table was a homemade card, featuring a drawing that looked like Sneezy's work. It was a pretty good likeness of Doc, and on the inside, in Happy's loopy script, *We Love You Doc* was written in blue across the yellow construction paper.

Doc took an apple and went to the row of windows. A few cars crawled by below, the first trickle of morning commuters, their headlights still on. Clouds hung over the city, gray and pearl smudges above gray buildings. There wasn't any glorious shaft of sunlight breaking through to set the thousands of windows glittering, or any rainbow arcing over the dense trees of the park at the far end of the city. There was no black-haired goddess, eyes dark and full of love, floating toward him. He polished the apple on his shirt. His was a small life. His head was barely higher than the windowsill, but he could see that out there, in the big world, there was nothing anymore to wish for.

I don't remember the genesis of this particular story. At the time I was interested in tales with some sort of fantastic or surreal premise: a pack of savage dogs in the room of a suburban home, an infant creature born from an egg found in a Dumpster, a half-vampire college student, etc. I think the trigger for "Ever After" had something to do with the idea of partial knowledge, with how easily a piece of something could be misinterpreted if you didn't

have the whole—or else used to create a whole. I'm interested in how communities form and then fracture, and in what kind of beliefs structure our lives and give them meaning. I don't see any difference between worshipping Snow White or the Virgin Mary or Allah, since they're all fantasies.

—KA

KATE BERNHEIMER

Whitework

THE COTTAGE INTO WHICH MY COMPANION HAD BROKEN, RATHER
than allow me, in my desperately wounded condition, to pass a night
in the thick-wooded forest, was one of those miniaturized and hand-
carved curiosities from the old German folktales that make people roll
their eyes in scorn. This, despite the great popularity of a collection of
German stories published the very same year of my birth! As to the
justifiability of this scornful reaction: I cannot abide it, nor can I avoid
it by altering the facts. This is where I found myself: in a fairy-tale cottage deep in the woods. And I had no use of my legs.

When we came upon the cottage we were certain, by its forlorn
appearance, that it had long ago been abandoned to the wind and the
night, and that we would be perfectly safe. Or rather, my dear companion was certain of this. As for me, I was certain of nothing—not
even of my own name, which still eludes me.

There were but few details for my enfeebled mind to record, as if
the cottage had been merely scribbled into existence by a dreamer's
hand. Tiny pot holders hung from the wall in the kitchen, beside tiny
dish towels embroidered with the days of the week. In each corner of
each room was tucked an empty mousetrap—open and ready but
lacking bait. At the entryway, on a rusted nail, hung a minuscule
locket, along with a golden key. As to whether the locket ever was

opened, and what it contained, I have conveniently misplaced any knowledge. About the key I will not presently speak.

My companion placed me onto a bed, though I would not know it was a trundle bed until morning. I had only vague notions as to how we had arrived at the cunningly thatched cottage, but I believe we had walked through the forest in search of safety. Perhaps we sought some gentle corner where we would not perish at the hands of those who pursued us. Or had we been banished, from a kingdom I no longer recall?

The room in which my companion put me to bed was the smallest and least furnished of all. It lay, strangely enough, down a long hallway and up a stairway—I say "strangely" because the house was so diminutive from outside. I realized, upon waking in morning, that I lay in a turret. Yet from outside, no curved wall was visible. With its thatched roof the house had resembled a square Christmas package, a gift for a favorite stuffed rabbit—a perfect dollhouse of a cottage, the sort I had painstakingly, as a child, decorated with wallpaper, curtains, and beds.

Though there was scarcely any furniture in this turret room, the sparse pieces were exactly correct—nothing more, nothing less: the trundle bed, empty and open; and the walls bedecked with no other ornamentation or decoration save whitework, the same sampler embroidered with the same message over and over. It was embroidered in French, which I do not speak: *Hommage à Ma Marraine.* In the center of each piece of linen was sewn an image of a priest holding two blackbirds, one on each hand. The edges of all the whitework were tattered, and some even had holes. To these white-on-white sewings, my foggy mind immediately fastened, with an idiot's interest—so intently that when my dear companion came up to the turret with a hard roll and coffee for breakfast, I became very angry with him for interrupting my studies.

What I was able to discern, looking about me, while nibbling the roll after my companion had left, was that some of the whitework contained a single gold thread as the accent over the *a*. Why the gold thread was used, I had no idea, and in considering this detail, along with the remarkable fact that blackbirds had been so expertly depicted in white, I finally asked my companion to return to the room. I called him and called him before he returned—disconcertingly, for it seemed he had returned only by accident, to fetch my empty teacup—and when he took the cup from my hand he gazed into it for a very long time without speaking a word.

At last, he closed the shutters of the windows tight, which was my wish, as it allowed me to see the whitework more clearly: I find I see better in the dark. A candle in the shape of a bluebird sat on the floor beside the bed, and I lit it, and turned it just-so, toward the wall. Luminous! I felt I had not, in many years, experienced such nocturnal bliss—even though the broad daylight shone outside the curtained windows, at least a day as broad as a day may shine in a deep and thickly wooded forest where real and grave danger does lurk.

This activity transfixed me for hours upon hours and days upon days.

In time, my companion and I so well established ourselves in the cottage that soon we felt that we had lived there our entire lives. I presume we had *not* lived there our entire lives; yet of the event that drove us into the forest to the cottage I cannot speak, and not only because I cannot recall it. But I can tell you that we had so well established ourselves in this cottage that I was shocked one morning to discover, under my feather pillow, a miniature book that had not been there before. It proposed to criticize and describe the whitework on the walls.

Bound in black velvet, with a pink ribbon as a placeholder, the volume fit precisely in the palm of my hand, just as if it had been bound for me to hold there. Long—long I read, and devoutly, devotedly I gazed. Rapidly and gloriously the hours flew by and then the deep midnight came. (Not that I knew the day from night with the curtains so tightly drawn.) The bluebird was guttering—just a puddle of blue now, with yellow claws fashioned from pipe cleaners protruding from the edges of the blue puddle. I reached my hand out to try to build the wax once more into the form of a bird, but I achieved merely a shapeless mass of color. Regardless, the candlelight flamed up and shone more brightly than ever upon the black velvet book with onion-skin pages.

In my zeal to illumine the onionskin, the better to learn about *Ma Marraine* and so on, I had, with the candle's light, also illumined the corners of the room, where sat the mousetraps. Yes, this turret had corners—quite a remarkable thing, as the room was a circle. If I failed to perceive the corners before, I cannot explain . . . truly this architectural marvel of corners was a marvel inside a marvel, since even the turret itself was not visible from outside.

With the corners of the room thus illumined, I now saw very clearly in one corner, behind a mousetrap, a very small portrait of a young girl just ripening into womanhood. I don't know how that phrase comes to me—"ripening into womanhood"—for I would pre-fer simply to describe the portrait as a very small portrait of a young lady. But, to continue, I could not look at the painting for long. I found I had to close my eyes as soon as I saw the portrait—why, I have no idea, but it seems to be that my injury, rather than being limited to my crippled legs, had crept inward to my mind, which had become more . . . impulsive or secretive, perhaps. I forced my eyes back on the portrait again.

It was nothing remarkable, more a vignette than an exposition. The girl was depicted from top to bottom, smudged here and there, fading into the background, reminiscent somehow of the *Kinder- und Hausmärchen* yes, you could describe her portrait as an illustration. She was a plain girl, not unlike me. Her eyes were sullen, her hair lank and unwashed, and even in the face and shoulders you could see she was undernourished—also not unlike me. (It is not my intention to plead my case to you or to anyone else, now or in the future; I merely *note* the resemblance.)

Something about the girl's portrait startled me back to life. I had not even realized what a stupor I'd lain in, there in the turret, but looking into her sullen eyes, I awoke. My awakening had nothing to do with the girl herself, I believe, but rather with the bizarre execution of this portrait, this tiny portrait—no bigger than that of a mouse, yet life-size. And it was painted entirely white upon white, just like the embroidery on the walls.

Though I felt more awake and alive than ever before, I found that I was also suddenly overcome with sadness. I don't know why, but I do know that when my companion brought me my nightly black coffee, I sent him away for a pitcher of blueberry wine. I asked for him also to bring me a pink-flowered teacup. My needs felt at once more urgent and delicate, and thankfully he was able to find articles in the cupboards that satisfied them.

For quite some time, drinking the wine, I gazed at the portrait of the sullen girl staring out of miniature eyes. At length, wholly unsatisfied with my inability to decipher the true secret of the portrait's effect (and apparently unaware that I very nearly was standing), I fell into the trundle. I turned my frustrated attentions back to the small book I had found under the pillow. Greedily, I turned its onionskin pages to the girl's portrait. "Flat, unadorned," the page read. The rest of the description was missing—everything except a peculiar exclamation for an encyclopedia to contain:

SHE WAS DEAD!

"And I died." Those are the words that came to my head. But I did not die then, nor did I many days and nights later, there in the forest, where I lived with my companion quite happily—not as husband and wife, yet neither as siblings: I cannot quite place the relation.

Soon, of course, I thought of nothing else but the girl in the painting. Nightly my companion brought me a teacup of blueberry wine, and nightly I drank it, asked for another, and wondered: *Who was she? Who am I?* I expected no answer—nay, nay, I did not wish for one either. For in my *wonder* I possessed complete satisfaction.

It was of no surprise to me, so accustomed to confusions, that one morning I awoke to find the painting vanished—and not only the painting but all the little priests with the little birds from the walls. No whitework, no turret, no companion. No blueberry wine. I found myself in a different small and dark room, again on a bed (not a trundle). An old woman and a doctor sat by my side.

"Poor dear," the old woman murmured. She added that I would do well to take courage. As you may imagine, the old woman and doctor were at once subjected to the greatest of my suspicions; and as I subjected them privately, I also protested publicly, for I knew I had done nothing to lose all I had learned to love there in that mysterious prison or home. No: I should have been very happy to be lame and blurred, to have my companion bring me teacups of wine at night, and in the morning my coffee and rolls. I never minded that the rolls were so tough to the bite that my teeth had become quite loose in their sockets, as loose as my brain or the bluebirds in the forest when their nests are looted by ravens.

Cheerfully, the doctor spoke over my protests. He said that my prognosis relied on one thing, and one thing alone: to eliminate every gloomy idea. He pointed toward a room I had not noticed before. "You have the key to the Library," he said. "Only be careful what you read."

I wrote this story in the public library in a small town in Massachusetts, in the summertime. It was fishing season at the time. Outside, children in yellow slickers slung lines over the bridge as I drove to the library, buckets of still-living fish by their feet. But it was always fishing season in the library, with its dioramas of schooners and nets with starfish on the knotty pine walls. I sat at a table across from an old man doing crossword puzzles. He really looked like he belonged in The Old Man and the Sea. *I had been reading Poe, and some scholarship on these instances in*

seventeenth-century novels of fairy-tale scenes. Somehow, the proximity of all that saltwater, combined with the Poe and the seventeenth-century German, transported me into this story. It is for me a most architectural story, a Joseph Cornell box or diorama, and by writing it I got, for a brief time, to live in the impossible cottage of my dreams. Certainly, it could be said to be a story about the anxiety of influence, or, perhaps more aptly, the influence of anxiety—it contains the code to my work with fairy tales as a writer, I think. But the code is submerged, just as secrets should be.

—KB

Sources

Edgar Allan Poe, "The Oval Portrait" (1848 version).

Karoline von Wolgozen, *Agnes von Lilien* (1798), as translated in Jeannine Blackwell's essay "German Fairy Tales: A User's Manual. Translation of Six Frames and Fragments by Romantic Women." In Haase, Donald, ed. *Fairy Tales and Feminism: New Approaches*. Detroit, MI: Wayne State University Press, 2004.

The End

ACKNOWLEDGMENTS

THIS BOOK HAS BEEN MANY YEARS IN THE MAKING. CONVERSATIONS with Maria Tatar about the perils and beauty of fairy-tale editorship provided inspiration and godmotherly guidance, as has her entire body of work. I would not have found John Siciliano at Penguin had Jack Zipes, a kind and most generous thinker, not pointed me toward him, and he is simply a national treasure. When invited to write a foreword to this collection, Gregory Maguire didn't hesitate for a moment: what a gem! Kristen Scharold at Penguin was a dream to work with throughout the entire editorial process: meticulous, enthusiastic, and kind, she deserves all gratitude. And the book would not exist had Carmen Giménez Smith and I not met after a fairy-tale reading at AWP and discussed our shared vision that a book like this would someday exist. In compiling this volume, odd research needs were fulfilled, often at the very last minute: so thank you, Amanda Phillips, Morgan Fahey, and Hanne Winarsky and Christopher Chung at Princeton University Press. To all the contributors to this volume—you must know that our correspondence over the years of this book's evolution has been illuminating, moving, and deeply satisfying to me. This book also owes so much to many writers, known and anonymous, past and present, who are the spirit of the tradition, and it belongs, too, to the children who are hearing fairy tales for the first time. From my graduate and undergraduate fairy-tale workshop students at the University of Alabama, I had the privilege of talking to a new generation of avid fairy-tale readers and future authors. To my parents, siblings, in-laws, and their children, your support is invaluable. The University of Nebraska Press, current publisher of *Fairy Tale Review*, and The University of Alabama Press, its former publisher, are rare and wonderful havens for fairy tales. I would also like to extend my deepest gratitude and admiration to Maria Massie and John Siciliano, who have honored my fairy-tale habit with care. Finally, Brent and Xia, you are my fairy-tale family, full of bliss.

—KB

Thank you to Kate Bernheimer. Kate's exquisite vision of the book's possibility and her ability to orchestrate such an ambitious endeavor is awe-inspiring. I'd also like to thank Evan Lavender-Smith, who helped me a great deal on this project, and Sofia and Jackson for giving their mother space when she needed to work. I'd like to thank Dylan Retzinger for his eleventh-hour help, and, finally, the writers, past and present, who bring us such joy in their work.

—CGS

ABOUT THE CONTRIBUTORS

Kim Addonizio is the author of several collections of poetry, including *Lucifer at the Starlite*, as well as the novels *Little Beauties* and *My Dreams Out in the Street* and the story collection *In the Box Called Pleasure*.

Chris Adrian is the author of the novels *Gob's Grief* and *The Children's Hospital* and a collection of stories, *A Better Angel*. He is a pediatrician in San Francisco.

Rabih Alameddine is the author of the novels *The Hakawati*, *Koolaids*, and *I, the Divine*, and the story collection *The Perv*. He lives in San Francisco and Beirut.

Naoko Awa (1943–1993) was an award-winning writer of modern fairy tales. As a child, she read fairy tales by Grimm, Andersen, and Hauff, as well as *The Arabian Nights*. She earned a bachelor's degree in Japanese literature from Japan Women's University.

Aimee Bender is the author of the story collections *The Girl in the Flammable Skirt* and *Willful Creatures* and the novels *An Invisible Sign of My Own* and *The Particular Sadness of Lemon Cake*. She teaches at the University of Southern California.

Francesca Lia Block is the author of many books, including *Dangerous Angels*, the *Weetzie Bat* books, *Wood Nymph Meets Centaur: A Mythological Dating Guide*, *Pretty Dead*, *Blood Roses*, and *The Rose and the Beast*.

Karen Brennan is the author of the poetry collection *The Real Enough World*, the story collection *The Garden in Which I Walk*, and the memoir *Being with Rachel*.

Kevin Brockmeier is the author of the novels *The Brief History of the Dead* and *The Truth About Celia*, the children's novels *City of Names* and *Grooves: A Kind of Mystery*, and the story collections *Things That Fall from the Sky* and *The View from the Seventh Layer*. He has received a PEN USA Award, a Guggenheim Fellowship, and an NEA grant.

Sarah Shun-lien Bynum is the author of two novels, *Ms. Hempel Chronicles*, a finalist for the 2009 PEN/Faulkner Award, and *Madeleine Is Sleeping*, a finalist for the 2004 National Book Award and winner of the Kafka Prize. She has been a recipient of a Whiting Writers' Award and an NEA fellowship, and her fiction has appeared in *The New Yorker*, *Tin House*, *The Georgia Review*, and *The Best American Short Stories*.

Lucy Corin is the author of the story collection *The Entire Predicament* and the novel *Everyday Psychokillers: A History for Girls*.

Michael Cunningham is the author of the novel *The Hours*, which won the Pulitzer Prize and the PEN/Faulkner Award and was adapted into the Academy Award–winning film of the same name, as well as the novels *A Home at the End of the World*, also adapted for the screen, *Specimen Days*, and *Flesh and Blood*.

Kathryn Davis lives in Vermont and spends part of the year as senior fiction writer in residence at Washington University in St. Louis. She is the author of the novels *Labrador*, *The Girl Who Trod on a Loaf*, *Hell*, *The Walking Tour*, *Versailles*, and *The Thin Place*, and is the recipient of the Kafka Prize, the Morton Dauwen Zabel Award from the American Academy of Arts and Letters, a Guggenheim fellowship, and the Lannan Literary Award.

Rikki Ducornet is the author of the novels *The Jade Cabinet*, a finalist for the National Book Critics' Circle Award, *The Fan Maker's Inquisition*, a *Los Angeles Times* Book of the Year, and *Netsuke*, among others. She has received a Lannan fellowship, a Lannan Literary Award, and an Academy Award in Literature from the American Academy of Arts and Letters.

Brian Evenson is the author *The Open Curtain*, a finalist for an Edgar Award, as well as *Last Days*, *Fugue State*, *The Wavering Knife*, *Dark Property*, and *The Brotherhood of Mutilation*. He has translated work by Christian Gailly, Jean Frémon, Claro, Jacques Jouet, and others.

Karen Joy Fowler is the author of several novels, including *Sister Noon* and *Wit's End*, as well as a number of short stories. She has won the Nebula Award, the World Fantasy Award, and the Commonwealth Medal, and has been a finalist for the PEN/Faulkner Award. Her novel *The Jane Austen Book Club* was a *New York Times* bestseller.

Neil Gaiman is the author of many books for adults and children, including *Coraline*, *American Gods*, *Anansi Boys*, and the Newbery Medal–winning *The Graveyard Book*.

Lily Hoang's books include *Parabola*, *Changing* (winner of the PEN/Beyond Margins Award), *The Evolutionary Revolution*, and *Invisible Women*.

Hiromi Itō has published more than a dozen critically acclaimed collections of poetry, several novels, and numerous books of essays. She has won many important Japanese literary prizes, including the Takami Jun Prize, the Hagiwara Sakutarō Prize, and the Izumi Shikibu Prize. For a selection of her work, see *Killing Kanoko: Selected Poetry of Hiromi Itō*.

Shelley Jackson is the author of the novel *Half-Life*, the story collection *The Melancholy of Anatomy*, the hypertext novel *Patchwork Girl*, several children's books, and "Skin," a story published in tattoos on the skin of more than two thousand volunteers.

Ilya Kaminsky was born in Odessa in the former USSR and came to the United States in 1993 when his family was granted asylum by the American government. He is the author of *Dancing in Odessa*, for which he won the Whiting Writers Award, the American Academy of Arts and Letters's Metcalf Award, the Dorset Prize, and the Lannan fellowship. He teaches at San Diego State University.

Jonathon Keats is a writer and artist. He is the author of the story collection *The Book of the Unknown* as well as two novels, *The Pathology of Lies* and *Lighter Than Vanity*. He is the art critic for *San Francisco Magazine*.

Neil LaBute is a writer, director, and playwright. His first film, *In the Company of Men*, debuted at the 1997 Sundance Film Festival and was followed by *Your Friends and Neighbors, Nurse Betty,* and *Possession,* among others. For the stage, LaBute has written plays that have been performed around the world, including *The Shape of Things, Fat Pig, Some Girls,* and the Tony Award–nominated *reasons to be pretty.* He is also the author of the story collection *Seconds of Pleasure.*

Kelly Link is the author of the story collections *Pretty Monsters, Magic for Beginners,* and *Stranger Things Happen.* Her stories have won Nebula awards, a Hugo Award, a Locus Award, and a World Fantasy Award. Link is cofounder and coeditor of Small Beer Press and of the zine *Lady Churchill Rosebud's Wristlet.*

Joyelle McSweeney is the author of the novels *Nylund, The Sarcographer,* and *Flet,* as well as the poetry books *The Red Bird* and *The Commandrine and Other Poems.* She is a cofounder and coeditor of Action Books and the online quarterly *Action, Yes.*

Sabrina Orah Mark is the author of the poetry collections *The Babies* and *Tsim Tsum* and of the chapbook *Walter B.'s Extraordinary Cousin Arrives for a Visit & Other Tales.* She has received fellowships from the Provincetown Fine Arts Work Center, the Glenn Schaeffer Foundation, and the National Endowment for the Arts.

Michael Martone is the author of many books of fiction and nonfiction, including *Michael Martone, The Flatness and Other Landscapes, The Blue Guide to Indiana, Pensées: The Thoughts of Dan Quayle,* and *Double Wide: Collected Fiction of Michael Martone.*

Michael Mejia is the author of the novel *Forgetfulness.* He has been the recipient of a Literature fellowship from the National Endowment for the Arts and a grant from the Ludwig Vogelstein Foundation.

Lydia Millet is the author of many works of fiction, including *Oh Pure and Radiant Heart* (shortlisted for the Arthur C. Clarke Prize), *How the Dead Dream, My Happy Life* (winner of the PEN USA Award for Fiction), *George Bush: Dark Prince of Love,* and *Love in Infant Monkeys.*

Alissa Nutting is the author of *Unclean Jobs for Women and Girls*, a collection of stories.

Joyce Carol Oates has won the National Book Award and the PEN/Malamud Award for Excellence in Short Fiction. She is the author of the national bestsellers *We Were the Mulvaneys* and *Blonde* (a finalist for the National Book Award and the Pulitzer Prize), among many other books.

Ludmilla Petrushevskaya is the award-winning author of more than fifteen collections of prose, including *There Once Lived a Woman Who Tried to Kill Her Neighbor's Baby: Scary Fairy Tales*. The progenitor of the women's fiction movement in modern Russian letters, she is also a playwright whose work has been staged by leading theater companies all over the world. She lives in Moscow.

Francine Prose is the author of more than twenty books. Her nonfiction includes *Anne Frank: The Book, the Life, the Afterlife*; *Sicilian Odyssey*; *The Lives of the Muses: Nine Women & the Artists They Inspired*; *Gluttony*; and *Caravaggio: Painter of Miracles*. Her novels include *Blue Angel*, which was a finalist for the National Book Award, *Goldengrove*, and *A Changed Man*.

Stacey Richter is the author of the story collections *My Date with Satan* and *Twin Study*.

Marjorie Sandor is the author of three books, including *Portrait of My Mother, Who Posed Nude in Wartime*, winner of the National Jewish Book Award in Fiction, and *The Night Gardener: A Search for Home*, which won the Oregon Book Award for Literary Nonfiction.

Timothy Schaffert is the author of the novels *The Phantom Limbs of the Rollow Sisters*, *The Singing and Dancing Daughters of God*, *Devils in the Sugar Shop*, and *The Coffins of Little Hope*. He is the online editor of *Prairie Schooner*, a contributing editor to *Fairy Tale Review*, and the director of the (downtown) Omaha lit fest and the Nebraska Summer Writers' Conference.

Jim Shepard's books include the novels *Project X* and *Nosferatu* and the story collection *Like You'd Understand, Anyway*, which won The Story Prize and was a finalist for the National Book Award.

John Updike (1932–2009) wrote more than fifty books, including collections of stories, poems, essays, and criticism. His novels have won the Pulitzer Prize, the National Book Award, the American Book Award, the National Book Critics Circle Award, the Rosenthal Award, and the Howells Medal.

Katherine Vaz is the author of the novels *Saudade* and *Mariana* and the story collections *Fado & Other Stories*, which won the Drue Heinz Literature Prize, and *Our Lady of the Artichokes*, which won the Prairie Schooner Book Prize.

Kellie Wells is the author of the story collection *Compression Scars*, which won the Flannery O'Connor Prize, and the novel *Skin*.

Joy Williams is the author of many books, including *The Quick and The Dead*, a finalist for the Pulitzer Prize, *The Changeling*, a finalist for the National Book Award, *Honored Guest*, and *Taking Care*.

Copyright Extension

"Ever After" by Kim Addonizio. First appeared in *Fairy Tale Review: The Blue Issue, 2006*. Copyright © Kim Addonizio, 2006. Reprinted by permission of the author.

"First Day of Snow" from *The Fox's Window and Other Stories* by Naoko Awa, translated by Toshiya Kamei (University of New Orleans Publishing, 2010). Translation copyright © Toshiya Kamei, 2010. Reprinted by permission of Akira Minegishi and Toshiya Kamei.

"Whitework" by Kate Bernheimer. First appeared in *Tin House*. Reprinted by permission of the author.

"A Day in the Life of Half of Rumpelstiltskin" from *Things That Fall from the Sky* by Kevin Brockmeier. Copyright © 2002 by Kevin Brockmeier. Used by permission of Pantheon Books, a division of Random House, Inc.

"Eyes of Dogs" by Lucy Corin. First appeared in *Conjunctions: The Web Forum of Innovative Writing*, 2008. Reprinted by permission of the author.

"Orange" by Neil Gaiman. Copyright © 2008 by Neil Gaiman. Originally published in *The Starry Rift*, edited by Jonathan Strahan (Viking, 2008). Reprinted by permission of the author.

"Little Pot" by Ilya Kaminsky. First appeared in *Brothers & Beasts*, edited by Kate Bernheimer (Wayne State University Press, 2007). Copyright © Ilya Kaminsky, 2007. Reprinted by permission of the author.

"Catskin" by Kelly Link. Copyright © 2003 by Kelly Link. First appeared in *McSweeney's Mammoth Treasury of Thrilling Tales* (Vintage, 2003). Reprinted by permission of the author.

"Coyote Takes Us Home" by Michael Mejia. Copyright © 2008 by Michael Mejia. First published in *Notre Dame Review*, Summer/Fall 2008. Reprinted by permission of the author.

"Blue-bearded Lover" from *The Assignation* by Joyce Carol Oates. Copyright © 1988 by Joyce Carol Oates. Reprinted by permission of HarperCollins Publishers and the author.

"I'm Here" by Ludmilla Petrushevskaya, translated by Keith Gessen and Anna Summers. Copyright © Ludmilla Petrushevskaya, 2001. Translation copyright © Keith Gessen and Anna Summers, 2010. By arrangement with the author and translators.

"Hansel and Gretel" from *The Peaceable Kingdom* by Francine Prose. Copyright © 1993 by Francine Prose. All rights reserved. Reprinted by permission of Farrar, Straus and Giroux, LLC and Denise Shannon Literary Agency, Inc.

"Case Study in Emergency Room Procedure in an Urban Facility" by Marjorie Sandor. Originally appeared in *Fairy Tale Review: The Blue Issue, 2006*. Reprinted by permission of the author.

"The White Cat" by Marjorie Sandor. Originally appeared in *The Fairy Tale Review, The Blue Issue, 2006*. Reprinted by permission of the author.

"Pleasure Boating in Lituya Bay" from *Like You'd Understand, Anyway: Stories* by Jim Shepard. Copyright © 2007 by Jim Shepard. Used by permission of Alfred A. Knopf, a division of Random House, Inc. and SLL/Sterling Lord Literistic, Inc.

"Bluebeard in Ireland" from *The Afterlife and Other Stories* by John Updike. Copyright © 1994 by John Updike. Used by permission of Alfred A. Knopf, a division of Random House, Inc. and Penguin Books Ltd.